First Lights

offplanet, book one

Regan Wolfrom

ACKNOWLEDGEMENTS

I'd like to acknowledge so many people... but I'm so tired. Seriously. There are a lot of words in this thing.

00

IT WAS mid-April, so la plage des Hattes hadn't gotten busy just yet; it wouldn't start filling with visitors until the rains started coming. There were a few hikers with tattered packs heading toward the western horizon, but other than that just a three mile strip of unlittered sand fringed by palms and low lush greenery. To the north was the Atlantic, over five hundred miles east of the Caribbean. To the west, across the muddy Maroni River, was the gentrified Eco-Republic of Suriname, where you could see some of the same sights as in French Guiana, but for three times the cash.

Riley Crouch was surprised that they even still had any ecological sights to see across the river, that the well-heeled tourists hadn't scared the animals away and repurposed half the forest for ultraluxe treehouses.

It wouldn't take much for the Dutch-speaking turtles to switch over to the next beach to the left, would it?

He waited as the sun started to set; nighttime was best.

Riley had promised himself that he'd never fail to savor the purple and orange of the sunsets. When he'd overwintered in Rothera as part of the sovereignty project—a bunch of uni students manning the evergreen dome—there were months where at most you'd get some dark purple around lunchtime, from a sun that was giving you a small speck of daylight from its place below the horizon. British Antarctica had been bad; French Guiana was paradise.

It wasn't long before he saw the first one, a leatherback turtle that was almost two meters long. She slowly moved along the sand, up from the water's edge.

Riley felt like he was watching something ageless; sea turtles like her had been coming to beaches like la plage des Hattes for over a hundred million years. There would have been soft-shelled ancestors of that mother turtle laying eggs in the age of the dinosaurs. That made the Westbury White Horse look like it had been scraped out last week.

He sat quietly and watched with his infrared glasses as the turtle crafted her nest in the sand, swiping and digging with her front flippers.

He'd set his glasses to record; he wanted not just to have the video, but to share it with everyone he knew. Sometimes it felt like his coworkers at the Guiana Space Centre never actually took any time away from work to see the beauty of the area. Maybe this would get them out. Maybe it would get Suzanne to join him sometime in July or August, when the eggs finally start to hatch.

He felt at peace, like everything he'd ever done was what should have been, since it had brought him there, to that beach, to that perfect moment.

He felt a hand grab him by the shoulder, pulling him back and down. His head hit the sand behind him.

His glasses were torn off his face.

More hands, at least four—maybe six—pulling at his clothing, removing his shirt, his shoes and socks. And finally his pants. Everything except his black boxer briefs.

They started dragging him along the sand, toward the water. He tried to fight back, but they held him by his elbows and two hands grasping his head.

He was in the water now, his legs wet up to his knees.

They pushed his head under the waves.

And held him under.

He held his breath, but eventually he couldn't hold it any more, and he sucked in the salt water. He couldn't get back up to the surface; he couldn't stop what was coming.

Riley Crouch eventually stopped fighting.

01

NICOLAS CLOUATRE had always preferred coffee to wine, which was only the most obvious indication of many that he wasn't a proper Frenchman. He also liked to eat dinner at his desk, while he cleared out any leftover paperwork from the day, and he sometimes wished that he could work right through the weekends without getting so much judgment from superiors and subtle disgust from the people under him.

He also felt that Jeanne-d'Arc was completely overrated, since the English wouldn't have held onto half of France forever.

That was probably why he'd made far more friends among the non-French working around the spaceport in Guyane than he'd ever had back home in Montpellier.

He was late—and without his morning coffee—because of some of those new friends, a couple from Catalunya who both worked on the environmentals, who'd made sure he had too much to drink from their strategic cava reserves. If he wasn't ten years older with the wrinkles and gut to show for it, he would've thought they were trying to seduce him. To be honest, he wasn't sure that wasn't their long term plan.

He wasn't sure how he felt about that.

Not as opposed to the idea as he would have expected. That surprised him.

His drive out of Korou was taking longer than usual, for a Tuesday or any other day, probably because he was running behind. It was more frustrating than usual because it wasn't even raining, which in May, was a rare occurrence.

"How can there be so much traffic?" he muttered. "It's not like these people have jobs to go to."

He was glad no one had heard him; it was not the kind of thing he wanted to be caught saying.

But he was in a bad mood. And hungover.

And late.

And Nicolas wasn't used to being late; another thing that didn't make him feel particularly French.

He reached the CSG Technical Centre with negative forty minutes to spare. His lateness was big news, almost a cause of celebration; if even Monsieur Clouatre could be late once in a century, it wasn't such a career killer, right?

Nicolas took it in stride. He liked to pretend he was a friendly manager; he was sure most managers liked to play pretend.

Simon was waiting outside Nicolas' office, cradling his tablet like it was a newborn.

"The transfer," Simon said.

"And good morning to you, too."

"My wife was asking."

"I can't imagine not wanting to see this project all the way through. We're making history. I just... and you'll miss us, Simon."

"I'll miss the creole food more. And I'll miss being seven thousand kilometers away from my wife." He laughed.

Nicolas didn't join in. He remembered making the same stupid jokes when he was married, when he and Madeleine had worked together. He regretted those little jabs more than anything else.

Simon handed him the tablet.

Nicolas took it. "What is this for?"

"The transfer. Your approval."

"They supply us all with tablets," Nicolas said.

"But I have it loaded up right here. Just need a thumb press, and—"

"I have my own tablet, Simon." He thrust the tablet back out at Simon, who took it and gave an unattractive little pout. "And after my coffee."

"*D'accord.*"

Nicolas walked into his office, shutting the door behind him. It was glass, just like his walls, but it would still send the right message. Specifically to Simon.

You don't hassle Nicolas Clouatre first thing in the morning.

You don't push Nicolas Clouatre to follow your little whims and transfer you off the most important project you'll ever be involved with.

That's not how you get ahead.

Nicolas had barely started his coffee when a message came in from Madame Bignard.

He straightened up in his chair.

Bignard doesn't send messages. Not unless the delirium was about to reach its climax and/or the shit was about to hit the fan.

And she'd even flagged it red.

Parliamentary committee to be created. More oversight for us.
Are we ready for it?

Nicolas sighed.

They'd lost an important team member two weeks before, a brilliant environmental engineer found drowned just off a beach by the border with Suriname. And that was the second death that year. That pattern had spooked someone back in Paris, it seemed.

And to add to that, more of the standard operating procedure for Lucille Bignard. Ask about something once it's way too late to actually be proactive.

The committee would be meeting once in June; he'd already heard that from a contact in Brussels. There would be members from both sides of the Eurospat, the socialists and the nationalists, with only the slightest majority given to the left.

And CSG would be ready for the poking and prodding, despite Bignard's best attempts to mess things up.

They'd had twenty-three launches already in the calendar year, all successful. And sixteen of those launches had been for *Nisi*, for "Island", if you included the two launches it had taken to slice off and tow a chunk of *4183 Cuno* to STeLa-4, raw material for any in situ construction required. Eight hundred kilometers above sea level, their bots had strung together a torus made up of the modules that were built on Earth, including the labs, initial habs, and the thrusters. Soon it would be more than a barebones donut-shaped skeleton, once the assemblers being launched on Friday get to the quarry in TeLuLa3, a lagrange-orbiting mass of nickel and iron ore his team had already managed to shave off from *Cuno*, an S-type Apollo that was just driving by on its transit past Venus and *putain* Mars!

They had paid handsomely for the license to manufacture the so-called "liquid metal" that would bounce back most of the cosmic rays and solar rads, while the two-ringed magnetoshield would work to limit what comes through in the first place.

They had taken years of research from every space agency on the planet and spacetested the solutions. Nicolas and his team had done that. No one else.

They were the ones who were creating the first true extraterran environment. The first manned spacecraft that didn't depend on luck and delayed cancer diagnoses to claim that it's safe. Once they transferred the finished product out past Earth's magnetopause, they'd have a design people can use to travel anywhere within the solar system, maybe even past the heliosphere with a few tweaks.

And so the waste-of-time committee would probably spend most of its time poking around the astronauts in Cologne, shaking hands and asking stupid questions about gardening in microgravity.

And Nicolas would make sure that his team was getting the damn thing finished. A self-sustaining space habitat. The most important project since Notre-Dame de Reims.

And unlike that floating beanstalk platform the Japanese were playing around with just offshore, *his* project would actually work, a beaded torus that already had six beads and their three spokes. Soon they would move up their life support beads, to make it *livable*.

And then, the politicians and bureaucrats would pat themselves on the back, while the engineers would move on to the next world-changing challenge.

Nicolas was still one of them, wasn't he? He was still an engineer.

Even if he spent most of his time with transfer requests from idiots, umbrella emails from higher-ups wanting to cover their ass, and writing a weekly report on how much energy's been saved over the week before.

They'd build *Nisi* in spite of the European Space Agency.

After responding to Bignard with reassurance and approving Simon's transfer, Nicolas spent his morning looking for any reason for the latest launch to go wrong.

Finding nothing, he ate his bag lunch at his desk, then spent his afternoon on the floor with his team, hoping to help out with any issues but mostly just trying to stay out of the way.

They were the best engineers in Europe—better than the guys at the Operations Centre in Darmstadt—and at least on level with the best in the US and China. He knew it sounded a little pompous and maybe a little pathetic, but his team was the best thing Nicolas had ever done.

And no one would ever know about them.

Once *Nisi* was completed, Darmstadt would take over and take all of the glory. Nicolas had fought to keep a team in Guyane, on the ground for the launches, and he knew it had paid off.

But he was still disgusted with Simon, for jumping at the first opportunity to transfer to Darmstadt. Crossing the Atlantic just for some worthless laurels, when the work hasn't even been completed.

It disgusted him.

Guyane was at least as important as anywhere else. No, more important. The most important piece of the puzzle, of making human settlement outside of Earth a reality.

Nicolas left the Technical Centre just after 18:00, driving toward the coast as the sun was setting behind him in a bank of rainclouds.

He knew that *Nisi* would be passing over Guyane at any time, and this was the clearest night they'd had in weeks. He never grew tired of seeing the light in the sky, larger than anything else humans had thrown up there; you could even make out the double wheels if you had eyes a little younger than his.

He wondered if he'd ever get a chance to go there, even while knowing full well that he wouldn't.

Seeing the light would have to be enough.

He'd received a message from the Catalonians about dinner, but he'd politely declined. Things were moving too fast with whatever that was.

He'd almost reached the edge of Korou when his tablet started buzzing. His console flashed the message from Simon.

Nisi's in trouble. Fire detected in multiple battery compartments. Possibly in all compartments.

He pulled onto the shoulder and got out of his car.

He could barely see it, to the northwest, just over the forested hills. The familiar reflecting sunlight of *Nisi* in LEO.

They'd designed the station to withstand a battery fire or two, to lose a couple of compartments to thermal runaway. But not all of them.

He watched as the light in the northern sky started breaking up. He knew if he saw any flame or smoke at all, it would only come as shards of *Nisi* eventually tumbled low enough to burn against the atmosphere.

02

THERE'S A little section of quiet in Battery Park, where, like every few blocks in Manhattan south of Washington Heights, there's a patch of ground at the bottom of a canyon of concrete and steel and oblivious New Yorkers looking down from great heights.

A metropol of thirty two million sets of eyes, but no one seems to notice you most of the time. Not that every piece of green in the city isn't carpeted with your neighbors.

But somehow, that one section a few blocks off Ground Zero and the Hudson River ferries is still mostly a secret.

Anita Singhal sat in Teardrop Park as a sunny but not too hot Tuesday lunchtime turned into a cloudy Tuesday afternoon, sitting with a Hipster Mug of home-brewed Starbuck's Dark Roast and the beat up fisherman's creel she'd bought on goodwill at that market in Tribeca. She'd left her clutch and its tablet on the ferry again, and she figured based on past and well-worn experience that it could take until about eight or nine pm before she got it back.

She knew she should have brought along the goddamn wristwatch. Because she wouldn't be caught dead wearing glasses.

No one would be able to get a hold of her now, at least not until she got back home.

Or to that *other* girl's home.

Anita liked to pretend she lived in Manhattan, wordlessly, to the people she met or just walked by and ignored, but mostly to herself. That other girl, that puffy-eyed brown girl with the frizzy hair, she was the one who lived on Staten Island, and even that girl only lived there from the hours of as-late-in-the-evenings-as-possible   to   as-early-as-she-could-climb-out-of-bed.

That girl lives where they used to send all the garbage, where they now send those people—basics—the ones who are described as not much more than trash under most people's breaths.

That girl isn't Anita.

Anita Singhal is a Manhattan girl. She comes to life at Whitehall, stepping off the Staten Island Ferry in that crush of commuting beef cattle.

A Manhattan girl who refuses to accept that she's turning fifty in less than a year. A forty-nine year old woman who'd left her tablet on the ferry for the millionth time.

13

Not really. She hadn't done that.

It was that disheveled girl from Staten Island who'd lost it.

Anita had an appointment with Danny Pyke at 2:30 to talk about his inner system communication project, at some officey faux-hovel in Alphabet City. A pretentious moron would have said that Anita had agreed to take a meeting, agreed to part with a little of her valuable time for an up-and-comer. But it that was true, wouldn't up-and-coming Danny have hustled his twenty-something ass over to see her?

Not that Anita had an office. Nothing aside from what work she'd stored in her red and gold tablet clutch, the one that was probably still cruising back and forth past Liberty Island with the European tourists.

Avenue C. She'd be late.

And she had no way of letting him know.

She laughed as she started picking up speed along Warren Street.

Heh.

Of course Danny would know.

Anyone who'd spent more than three minutes with Anita Singhal would know that *she is always late.*

Danny was dressed in a green three-button suit and trendy brown shoes, shoes that may or may not have been real leather. Anita wasn't sure. At a certain age you lose track of whether or not animal rights have become trendy again.

His office at the upstart Turnpike Exploration Tech had that look of budget chic, where cool meets eclectic, you know, because of the financial implications.

Not that Danny wasn't making money.

Just that he wasn't about to waste it on first impressions.

He'd met her at the elevator.

"You're early," he said with a grin.

He led Anita inside.

"Early because I got here before you left for the day?"

"Left for the day? Heh. I basically live here."

"That's not a virtue."

"I know."

She sat down on one of the three chairs that were collected around a metal and glass table in the middle of the oversized—oversized if we're talking the city—office, away from the antique drafting desk in the corner that Danny used as his workspace.

Danny sat down beside her.

He still looked at her like she was one of them.

How ridiculous, she thought.

"I got your notes," Danny said.

"You mean my thirty seconds of frothy naysaying?"

He nodded. "You're right about it, though. A lot of moving parts."

"A lot of moving parts," Anita said. "And a lot of solar interference."

"Hence the moving part… uh, of those parts…" He laughed.

Anita smiled, because that was the thing you did. Even when someone was starting to sound like an idiot.

Back when she was young, and trying not to think about getting old, she'd expected that when she was fifty, she'd look at kids like Danny and think they're just… kids. Precious little snowflakes, bundles of naive arrogance, with a notion that clearly the older generation had just never bothered to think things through. So much cringe…

But she couldn't help but feel inadequate. They were kids, sure. Naive and arrogant, of course. But Anita wasn't a kid, hadn't been for a very long time, and she missed being one. Missed not being slow. Not being forgetful…

"But it's possible," Danny said. "You didn't say it wasn't."

"I'm not god. I don't decide what's possible."

"You're as close as we've got, Ms. Singhal."

She gritted her teeth.

"You know it's true," he said.

"I've walked out of meetings for less than that," she said. "Don't try to flatter me, Danny."

"Yeah, alright. But it's possible."

"Of course it's possible. Anything is possible. Dyson spheres are possible. Build a giant lampshade around the sun. It's all about the cost."

She nodded toward the wall, the one side of the office that was painted white, opposite the window view of the Con Ed substation and the East River.

Danny held out a dry erase marker. "I hide these from most people. Don't like that whole sketch things out mentality. But you're not most people. You're on another level."

"I will walk out of here," she said, only half joking.

She took the blue marker and swirled a sun in the middle of the whiteboard. She then started drawing out the inner system, at what she liked to call the bird's eye angle, about thirty degrees above the invariable plane. She added Mercury, Venus, and Earth, the last one for reference. She added in a few Vulcanoids, Ekhi and Shapash, swooping them in orbits slightly off-kilter of the rest but well within ten degrees of the ecliptic, before pausing.

"I need another color," she said.

"I don't have another color."

"So I guess I'll bring my own office supplies next time."

She chose to go with dashed lines for the proposed constellation, running it around the Sun inside of Mercury, echoing the planes of the planets.

"That's the beauty of the solar system," she said, motioning to the egg-shaped ring of Mercury's orbit. "Everything that matters is where it ought to be."

"So that's why you should like this plan."

"You should move the Rebote Ring farther out from the sun. Putting anything inside of Mercury is asking for trouble."

"Trouble… so solar flares…"

"No… solar everything. Gravity, heat…"

"We know all that, Anita." He left his mouth open, like he figured he'd said something he shouldn't. For one thing, he'd never called her by her first name.

"Why am I here, then?" she asked. "Why are you wasting time with me if you have all the answers? I mean, your electric toothbrush could calculate orbits better than my old apps ever could."

"I'm sorry, Ms. Singhal. I forgot who I was talking to… I'm used to just… just being casual with people."

"You can be casual with me, Danny. Just don't waste our time. You know it's too hot for most of the homebrewed probes, but you want to wrap a garrote wire around the sun and see what happens."

"A garrote wire?"

"Yeah." She held her hands up to her neck like she was strangling herself.

"Never heard that one before."

"Put it near Venus," Anita said. "Don't make it more difficult than it has to be."

"That's double the distance from the Sun. That's an extra large pie instead of a small."

"The delay would be minimal; it's not like your fancy lasers will be traveling in Hohmann transfer orbit."

"Minimal? Our calculations say it adds as much as three minutes round trip on the Earth Mars Rebote."

"Boo hoo," she said. "So add three minutes to your forty five and save a serious load of heartache. And you'd probably need more redundancy to keep it inside Mercury, unless you want your fancy new communications grid to drop calls like a third-rate mobile provider. Hell, you might end up having to launch twice as many when half of them end up nosediving into the Sun."

"No one launches anymore," Danny said, sounding like a total asshole. "Everything's in situ."

And she remembered.

Why the young kids aren't so hot, why she and Bridget and Carter hadn't been so hot back when they were young, back when dinosaurs ruled The Bowery. Kids always think they're so effing smart. So much smarter than everyone who came before. Danny Pyke and friends weren't so much standing on the shoulders of giants as taking a giant stinking dump all over them.

She missed those days. Maybe just not everyone she'd spent them with.

"So?" he asked.

"So you're building it all in space?" she asked. "With pixie dust?"

"We've got a line on some assembly probes playing around in STeLa-4."

"Playing around? What's that supposed to mean?"

"Experiments. Hobbyists. Makers. Just casuals."

"When I was a kid, casuals was a four letter word."

"That's six letters," Danny said. She couldn't tell if he was serious. "Seven for the plural, obviously."

"So how many assemblers?"

"Eighteen… maybe a few more if we're lucky. Lots of projects out there."

"So hobby probes that were sent out to the easiest NEOs you can find, and you want to take those monstrosities and somehow toss them at the Sun?"

"And stop them from falling in," he said. He was grinning, like she remembered Carter always doing in their *goodish* old days, whenever he'd tell someone new about the sunshield. Grinning. Like a madman, really. Like the exact opposite facial expression you ought to have when you're explaining something that already starts off as crazy plus a thousand.

"Start from scratch," she said. "Don't try to do it on the cheap. Spend the time you need to spend, on the design, on putting together your crowd, the bylaws and everything."

"That's the old way."

"What was that?"

"We don't do things like that anymore," he said. "We don't want any crowds on this. We want to keep it in-house."

"Doing it for the love, right? While keeping a firm grip on something that was meant to be open to everyone."

"We want to make it our life's work. We don't want to lose control. We don't want it to be like your project."

Danny's gaping mouth made another appearance. He knew what he'd done.

"This is where I storm out," she said.

"Hey… sorry."

Anita put the marker down on the glass table. Gently enough.

"I don't advise people who are looking to make a quick buck," she said. "If you're looking to make money, you're looking at it wrong."

"We can work something out," Danny said. "Equity for your contributions."

"I don't need equity," she said.

And she stormed out, before Danny Pyke would get a chance to point out that she probably needed that equity more than anyone else.

Anita took an earlier ferry than she would have liked. But she couldn't think of anything else she'd wanted to do in the city, especially since most places downtown won't even consider goodwill. She was hungry and she'd run out of reasons to stay away.

Her clutch was waiting on her doorstep when she arrived home.

5:30 pm. Earlier than expected.

Maybe there's an NYC Loss and Recovery drone dedicated to flying over her place every few hours, since she was apparently their best customer these days.

She sighed. You don't want to waste money getting your shit back all the friggin time. Especially when you're basic.

She went inside and sat down on the pull-out bed that she can't recall having ever pushed back in.

She checked her messages.

Nothing that mattered.

She hadn't gotten a message from either of them, not for over a month. She knew it was partly because she'd never bothered to reply to the last few they'd sent.

That didn't mean that Bridget and Carter would stop trying to be her friends. Just that they'd give her some space. She appreciated all of it.

Even if she sometimes wanted to just close her eyes and hate their guts.

A message came in from Danny Pyke.

Knowing him, he'd timed it that way. It's pretty creepy when you think about it.

I'm sorry for the miscommunication, Ms. Singhal. I shouldn't be so focused on the business side. I should take the time to reflect on the real goal. Please consider working with us.

And at the bottom, a big fuck you:

We would still be offering the previously discussed equity, the proceeds of which you could then donate to a charity of your choosing.

He knew she was basic. Everyone knew. The journos had made sure of that. Not that the court transcripts weren't out there.

And not only that; Anita Singhal wouldn't be taking meetings with jerks like Danny Pyke if she wasn't washed up.

If she hadn't walked away from her life's work. And even then, gotten sued by her two best friends as an extra treat.

She took the bottle of white wine out of her fridge, a bottle large enough to sink any ship it was launching. But at least it wasn't a box.

She thought about what Bridget had joked with her about, that the best thing about being old and forgotten is that none of your wine sits in the fridge long enough to start tasting like vinegar.

She wanted to vent to *someone.*

But her little one-room apartment didn't include anyone else.

"I wish I had a cat," she said.

She wrapped herself in blankets and pretended she wasn't about to cry.

Carter Elgin was the most awkward guy at Cornell Tech.

That's saying a great deal about him.

Anita had known from the moment she'd met him that she'd fall for him, not just because of the awkwardness, which she'd always assumed was endearing to all girls who preferred books to eyeliner, but because of his punctuated intelligence; Carter Elgin was always the smartest person in any conversation.

But somehow, he didn't seem to know it.

Or he was really good at hiding it.

Bridget had provided a different theory, not long after they'd first bumped into Carter, at a meetup about private spaceflight.

"He's like a sponge," Bridget had said. "He soaks up everything around him, and then he can recall it in microseconds."

"That doesn't sound like a sponge," Anita replied. "Sounds more like a supercomputer."

"The analogy doesn't matter, dillweed. He's not as smart as we think he is."

"No," Anita said. "He's smarter."

Bridget stuck out her tongue like they were still in high school, not that Anita had ever seen what Bridget would have been like in high school.

Probably infuriating.

Anita had invited Carter to join them for a coffee afterward, and he'd awkwardly accepted, as she'd hoped he would. She'd especially enjoyed the awkwardness of it.

But he'd then spent the next two hours talking to Bridget instead of her, starting the pattern that had continued for over twenty five years.

Anita heard noises from outside. Not the standard Staten Island noises, but noises like people were more excited than scared.

She went out to her front porch, looking out at the crowd that was gathering on Grant Street and slowly moving around the basics highrises, toward Bay Street and the tracks.

They were staring up.

She followed the gaze.

A bright streak in the sky, to the southwest. One big one and many smaller ones, smaller but brighter.

Some like meteorites or falling satellites, a few pieces starting to burn against the atmosphere. She tracked the larger piece as it crossed the sky, toward the south. She recognized the curve of that orbit, from what she'd seen before.

It didn't take her long to realize what she was looking at.

03

THERE'S A remoteness to the town of Churchill, Manitoba, that you come to appreciate. It's a patch of land with short, crooked trees and more grass than you'd expect for the "barren" tundra. Or there would be grass, once the snow had melted.

It was only May.

In a month or so there'd even be carpets of white and purple flowers poking up through the grass, leaving only the occasional outcrops of rugged gray rock to remind you that you aren't in some field in central Illinois.

People talk about places like northern Nevada or the middle of Montana—or every square inch of Iowa—as being the middle of nowhere, but Churchill, on the southwest corner of Hudson Bay, is actually set squat in the center of nothing.

That's what Jared Koskela would call it. Not the middle of nowhere, since that's too cliched and overdone.

It's the center of nothing.

And the center of something very important, if you're into the idea of cutting-edge tech and saving the planet.

That's what Jared Koskela wants to do.

And he wants to look good doing it.

So he'd gone into the town of Churchill for a haircut. He had a few hours to kill before the next test. "Next test" sounded good, better than "*The* Test", which would make it feel that much worse when it fails.

It wasn't the first launch, but it was the first launch of the final design, the rocket equivalent of the molotov cocktail, something that could be put together and thrown from anywhere at anytime.

At a brigade level. By engineers or even by specially-trained infantry. Preparation for something Jared didn't even want to understand.

Churchill is a funny mix of tourist trap and subarctic favela, a town that wouldn't exist at all if it hadn't been for half-thought-out dreams of shorter shipping routes through the Canadian arctic; when the thaw started to slow, Churchill's upgrades got frozen instead, and if it wasn't for the natural gas operation in Hudson Bay, the town itself might have been completely forgotten.

Which wasn't the worst thing he could imagine; as much as he wanted to like the place, it didn't have much going for it. Jared had the distinct feeling that if it wasn't for the resurgence of polar bears—now that the temperatures were back to mean—the entire vicinity would be coated in stray dogs.

But May isn't polar bear season, and it isn't beluga season, either. May in Churchill is known locally as the "why the hell is it still winter" season, and Jared had still been wearing his winter parka wherever he went.

He knew that his thick blue jacket shouted American way more than his Chicago accent. If it had been any later in the year, people would have mistaken him for a tourist. And charged him accordingly.

But Jared managed to get the unwritten local rate at the salon in the boutique hotel, despite being in the gray area between local and walking money tree.

And the hairdresser was pretty cute, too, despite her goofy look with the half-shaved head on one side and the long blonde comb-over the flopped down on top of the stubble.

All in a perfectly good Tuesday, until he ran into Rachael on the way out, through the lobby.

She was looking done up, her dark hair styled down and straight, her eyelashes plumped with mascara. She looked for once like she wasn't working, like she had somewhere fun to be.

Jared was tempted to ask her about it.

"No time for your bullshit," she said as she walked by.

"What?"

She stopped and turned back to look at him. "Was that too harsh?"

He smiled.

She didn't.

"You working tomorrow?" he asked her.

She rolled her eyes at him.

"So I'm just headed out to do the big test," he said.

She glared at him. It was like she was telling him he should have led with something more interesting, while also letting him know he shouldn't have wasted her time to begin with.

"The rocket," he told her. "Final design."

She'd been into all of that before. Or at least she'd told him she was. The thing was one step below a state secret, complete with some cover story about tracking climate health, and he'd wanted to impress her...

Before he'd known that she'd been keeping tabs on all of it already...

"Good to know," she said. And started walking again.

He wasn't about to chase after her. Assuming that's what she wanted.

He didn't understand her. Not in the least.

He had a feeling she knew that. That she'd cultivated that.

Jared's older sister had always promised him that he'd understand girls well enough to drive them up the wall. That he'd know exactly what to do to get a rise out of them, good or bad.

And she'd been right. Right up until Rachael Duck.

Jared got back to the Fort Churchill launch site with thirty minutes to spare.

According to both Mohammed and Chloe, that wasn't enough time. They each decided to show their displeasure with the appropriate glares as he arrived at the small concrete launch pad.

Those two had spent too much time watching old videos of launches at Canaveral and Baikonur, where there was a countdown that lasted for days. You don't need a hundred days of prep for a tiny LOX/Kero rocket. You don't even need to register the launch of something that small with anyone other than the local air traffic control.

They weren't launching heavy lifters.

They were just trying to send a few tiny robots up to LEO, using the flimsiest of rockets. The babiest of baby steps, sold to the locals as a plan to cut costs on their climate monitoring satellites. So a little weird to be coming from the US Air Force, but no one seemed to have been too concerned.

Jared himself didn't understand why the US Air Force was conducting research for something they expected the Army to deploy.

And it was nothing that complicated, really. People were printing up heart valves and crotch rockets in their garages. Was this really any more difficult?

Yet Jared had a sinking feeling that he'd end up flat on his face.

"You look good," Chloe said, unconsciously tussling her own hair. "Nice haircut."

"The smiling face of failure," Jared said.

"It won't be bad," Mohammed said. "You gotta crack some eggs to make a space omelette."

"Probably won't explode or anything," Chloe said. "Or at least not until it's up high."

"Fireworks," Mohammed said. "Just in time for Victoria Day."

"I don't know what that is," Jared said.

"So…" Chloe said. "We just wait, I guess?"

Jared nodded. "Four o'clock is four o'clock."

"Be funny if we sent it up fifteen minutes early," Mohammed said. "Test our military preparedness."

"Yes, Mohammed," Chloe said, "I so want to get blown up today." She'd started to fidget with her pendant again. A sterling silver Celtic Cross, the best way to know when Chloe Nielson-Brown happened to be anxious about something.

They stood awkwardly around the pad, three civilian contractors staring at the little 3D-printed rocket that represented the latest and greatest of the United States Air Force. It felt weird to Jared, repeating a test that had been done over twenty years before, which consisted of nothing more than sending a rocket and some robots into space.

Of course, their little rocket was special, because it was 100% printed. No metal fab, no welds. Just a single print from a single multi-material machine that straddled the lab like a colossal metal and plastic monster with sixteen tentacles—its designers at Wright-Patterson had called it Cthulhu—running back and forth on tracks like a *futureporn* tank.

Elgin and Singhal hadn't been stupid enough to try and print the whole damn thing.

Those two—or three, if you gave Bridget Hawn some credit—started it as a weekend project, something mildly interesting to do when they weren't studying and doing whatever else engineering students do. They'd done it on basically no budget at all, and they hadn't even had the time or money to run the battery of tests Jared had run through with his strange little rocket, which Chloe had called Turaco and which no one had bothered so far to rename.

Designing the launchers, finding a way to scrape resources off an S-type asteroid with a robotic scoop, then sifting those resources to get what was needed and feeding the individual metals through the printers to build the shield bots. Elgin and Singhal had done it all.

And they'd started a revolution in crowdsourced space flight, and really, a revolution in almost everything else, too. Jared had heard academics, politicians, and folk singers talk about how the sunshield led to the crowdOrg movement, to a rebirth of delegative democracy, to universal basic income.

All of it over twenty years ago.

And now Jared was being paid by the United States Air Force to do what Elgin and Singhal had pretty much already done.

With a few other differences, aside from the big print.

Elgin and Singhal had open sourced the process, sharing their designs and—more importantly—their design flaws with the entire world. They'd asked people from anywhere and everywhere to bend, weld and print together their own rockets, and to design their own printer bots and miner bots and shield bots, and to test out those bots in whatever extreme conditions they could create on Earth. They'd taken donations for a lift on the Falcon Heavy, once both the US and China had started to push the rest of the world to stop those upstart "hobby launches" they'd inspired.

In the end, Elgin and Singhal had managed to send twenty thousand little printer—and as many miner bots, both types shipped in from all over the planet—out into space, on course to rendezvous with a tiny NEO, one that had been almost impossible to image and even less easy to analyze. And those bots had worked in tandem to assemble the crudest bits of solar shielding, making carbon steel and silicon cells, a process powered and heated solely by exothermic reactions on the side, the miner bots launching the waste matter out and driving the little rock and its anchored stowaways toward Earth-Sun Lagrangian Point 1—STeLa-1—where the next phase had begun.

That's where the little shield bots had jumped ship, using electric engines stolen from the now-anchored printer bots to boost themselves into place.

The whole thing had been so ridiculously ambitious. Elgin and Singhal had been so astoundingly naive.

So it had worked.

Jared had been two years old when it happened, when astronomers had taken the readings and determined that the thirty five hundred shield bots that had actually been assembled in space and were functioning—less than twenty percent of the total, but still utterly amazing—had actually reduced the amount of solar radiation reaching the planet by a barely traceable amount.

That had been enough to prove the concept.

By the time Jared was old enough to read about it in Second Grade, there were enough solar-shielding bots—over six million, he'd learned—to have lowered the earth's mean temperature by over one degree celsius. The bots had also weathered some of the worst bursts of cosmic rays and solar flares, with maybe twice the level of attrition that you'd find in geosynchronous satellites.

By the time Jared was in middle school, there were more bots than needed to keep the temperature steady with the current carbon load, and the biggest discussions in Carter Elgin's SolRescue NGO were around who would decide any changes to the formation, shifting position and density as needed to let more sunlight through, to keep the balance.

The "standby" bots, still receiving plenty of radiation and able to convert and transmit the energy to the collectors on Earth, were more lucrative—based on their positioning, away from the main cloud—than the bots that actually maintained the shield.

Every time a unit would go dark, whether from radiation damage and spacecraft charging, or from just the usual combination of poor construction and bad luck, the surviving units would be readjusted, and standbys brought in, often reducing the standby bot owners' cut of the royalties paid by the utility companies. It was never get-rich money, but it had proven to be riches enough to bicker about, with the members of the crowdsourced NGO that was meant to save humanity fighting over who would have to sacrifice their spending money to keep on saving the planet.

Jared figured that part of the reason Elgin and Singhal never followed up with their next big plan—to capture an asteroid into Earth's orbit—was because of the incredible hassle of dealing with those three hundred and fifty thousand members, some of whom had been lobbying for years to rotate their bots out of the shield area, so they could sit a little off the path to Earth, collecting a bigger share of solar energy without other bots crowding them and blocking out the sunlight.

But the bickering didn't matter so much in the big picture. Elgin and Singhal had stopped the melt of the Antarctic Ice Sheets, and by bringing ice back to the southern reaches of Hudson Bay, had saved the town of Churchill from the suffocating and once inevitable blanket of stray dogs.

The big difference between Elgin and Sindhal versus Jared and his little team was that the young idealists at Cornell Tech hadn't bothered to consider how easily their little bots could be destroyed.

Maybe they'd thought that not even the most unbalanced of terrorists would have wanted to turn the planet back into a heat lamp; and maybe they were right about that.

But, as well, they hadn't thought about the political realities of what they'd created, of what would happen—how the rest of the world would feel, on the outside, looking in—as a nebulous crowd of crowdOrg members kept control over the survival of global civilization.

They hadn't thought about what the US and China would think of having to give up so much power to a group of young idealists based on Roosevelt Island.

Or about how many corporations and shareholders and paid-off politicians were spurned by the sudden change in their future returns, when all of the money-making opportunities of runaway climate change were cut short.

It was amazing how many enemies you could make by saving the planet. Or buying the planet a little bit of time.

And while Jared didn't think of himself as a man of overt conviction, not that he was an asshole or anything, but sometimes he wavered on the work they were doing at Fort Churchill.

Sometimes he wondered if he was working toward a worse arrangement, where the United States Executive had sole control over the climate of the planet, if those silly delegate meetings that SolRescue held every month were better for everyone in the long run.

And sometimes he wondered if he just looked like a complete idiot, methodically retracing the design of the shieldbots just so he would know the systems and their weaknesses even better than Elgin and Sindhal had, and be able to rework it as much as he could, to something stronger, more indestructible, and something the Chinese military government wouldn't be able to sabotage or reverse engineer... at least, not right away.

Assuming that the Chinese government would even bother.

But the US government had bothered.

They'd told his team to replace the SolRescue bots, and replacing meant someone would need to be destroying what was in place right now. Who and how was need-to-know, and not something anyone had felt the need to share with Jared Koskela.

But honestly, he prefered it that way; as curious as he was, he knew he wouldn't really want to know how the US government planned on destroying Carter and Singhal's great work.

He knew the Chinese would one day try to do the same thing.

Maybe they were already working on it.

The little Turaco rocket lifted off successfully at 4:00:14 pm, dropping its reusable first stage after 160 seconds, as designed. The second stage reached LEO without difficulty, reaching an orbit of 320.56 km in altitude.

Jared was surprised; he'd so fully convinced himself that the first launch of the so-called final design would fail. He hadn't been cocky enough to assume it wouldn't.

Chloe let out a whoop, then wrapped her arms around Jared.

He hugged her back, if not as tightly.

She moved on to Mohammed, hesitating for a moment before giving him his hug.

It was clear from the awkward that neither of them were enjoying it.

"Maybe we don't need to hug every time something happens," Chloe said.

Mohammed smiled, warmly enough. "Now we get to the good part."

Chloe smirked. "Where it explodes?"

"You should be good to go," Jared said. He passed the hardened and oversized tablet over to Mohammed.

Mohammed nodded, then started getting to work.

It was just the preliminaries, Jared knew. Mohammed would need to go back to his desk in the lab for more than just getting some vital stats from his little robots.

But that wasn't Jared's concern. He wasn't in charge of the robots. He wasn't even supposed to know anything about them.

He walked over to the camera pod and quickly checked to make sure the recording hadn't failed. As great as it is to have automated tracking cameras, it meant that there was no one actively looking to see that the damn thing was actually filming something.

But it was all good.

He'd go back to his desk soon, too, to review the footage. It didn't *feel* particularly rational, but he knew that sometimes you could see something in the footage that the sensors couldn't tell you, something about how the rocket moved…

Okay.

He knew it wasn't rational, but he'd do it anyway.

Because it was up to him to make sure the next launch worked.

But before that, it was up to him to collect the first stage.

A current-gen commercial rocket usually has a reusable first stage that can find its own way back, with almost the same accuracy you'd get from a UAV. But when you're printing rockets in your lab in the center of nothing, you can't always waste time on the little things, so Jared had used an RFID tag instead. That didn't break the "rules" of his in situ mandate, since the rockets for the plan were always to be built and launched from Earth. There was no reason to add some weird endemic tracking component to the print. It wasn't like you needed to launch and track rockets on the surface of an asteroid. The rockets were considered one-use, since you wouldn't expect your launching brigade to be worried about core recovery.

Jared took his jeep out to check on the signal. Chloe asked to go with him, and he didn't know of a reason to not have her along. If nothing else, she was always the first person to spot the polar bears; just because there aren't many tourists in late May doesn't mean the bears aren't still out there, somewhere.

"Feels like we've finally got something to report," she said as he drove them past the white- and blue-cladded Northern Studies research centre, which Jared had learned is probably an even nicer place to stay then any of the hotels in town.

Jared nodded.

"We've spent three months with no news, you know?"

"I know," Jared said. "I've been the one submitting those empty progress reports to you."

"Well, you've done something now."

"Yeah… I copied something that was done thirty years ago."

"You're making it better, aren't you?"

Jared laughed.

"What?" she said. "What's so funny?"

"I'm making it different, Chloe. Not really better."

"I get the nuances, Jared. Don't worry. But it's still better. I know it is."

"And how do you know that?"

"Because they pay me to know."

"They pay you to manage projects," Jared said. "Not sure that's the same thing."

"It's 99% babysitting a team of jackasses," she said, "I'll give you that. But I do have a little knowledge on this stuff. Enough to know that you're going to start pushing for a GEO launch while Mohammed will want to keep doing LEO tests for a while."

"Those sound like made up acronyms," Jared said with a smirk.

She smirked back. "They're initializations."

"So who's side are you on?"

"What?"

"Me or Mohammed?"

"Come on."

"I'll bet you're on his side."

She nodded. "Fort Churchill is for LEO testing. Keeping this a secret from certain powers that be for as long as we can. You know that."

"I didn't agree to that. We're only launching eight tons. We should take the hit and accept that it'll cost a little more fuel to get to that rock in GEO for the mining tests."

"You're trying to put one over on me," she said.

"Huh?"

"It's more than a little fuel. People wouldn't have built launch platforms at the equator if the Arctic was almost as good. Especially for GEO."

He felt stupid for underestimating her.

"I'm sorry," he said. "I just don't want to give this up."

"You don't need to give anything up, Jared. This is your project. There's nothing stopping you from transferring to the Marshalls for the mining tests."

"And how long will that take? We had to wait six months before we even got up here. For all we know, they'll cancel the whole thing before we can move all our shit to the South Pacific."

"The Marshall Islands aren't in the South Pacific."

"Yeah, okay."

"Well, they're not."

She was grinning at him. Flirting, really. Not a standard component of the project management toolkit. But it worked for her, even if he wasn't interested. Well, not overly interested. But not uninterested, despite the dangers related to overeager pens and company ink.

"They'll want you to come to the Marshalls," she said. "I need you to come. Mohammed doesn't do rockets."

"We're not going anywhere yet," Jared said. "We should do at least one higher-than-LEO launch before we pack up. At least one."

She shook her head, but she was smiling.

It felt like he was wearing her down.

That kind of needling persistence was a huge part of his toolkit.

From the trajectory of the rocket, Jared had expected the first stage to land just shy of the water at Bird Cove, near the old wreck of the *Ithaka*, still rusting out on a gravel bank.

Just shy would be good. Landing in the water would not be… optimal. Just because you *can* print up another first stage doesn't mean you want to. For one thing, it would take around eighteen hours, and he'd have to sit and watch the entire process, one of the drawbacks of the single-printer design. Even if your hypothetical army brigade can get one of those giant Cthulhus into the field, someone has to keep an eye on the print while everyone else does the fighting.

And Jared didn't want to sit and wait for eighteen hours.

He's rather see if he could find a way to get things moving again with Rachael Duck.

Jared thanked Sagan when he saw the metallic booster, landed upright on its legs a good hundred meters from the beach, which had already started to refill with shorebirds who were apparently no longer startled by the flame and smoke of the descending rocket. He hadn't given his baby the skill to find its way home, but at least he'd added in enough for a slow descent, even if it was a straight drop down from wherever it happened to decouple.

"You're a genius, Jared," Chloe said, smiling at him.

"Tell me something the world doesn't know."

But Chloe wasn't looking at him anymore.

She was looking up.

At a collection of streaks just above the horizon, in the southeastern sky.

04

YOU KNOW you've been in Utah a long time when things like purity balls and temple garments and the eternal continuation of the Osmond dynasty seem normal. None of that was normal to Benj McPherson yet, but he had a feeling that it wouldn't take much longer.

But Utah was where the job was, and where he was now a proud home-owner with his own little garden of weeds, and where there was skiing for people who liked things warm and a little slushy. And where Benj was usually the only black guy on the chairlift, leading to the occasional assumption from whites and Japanese tourists alike that he must be there to provide security.

Still a little racist, but better than what his Mom had been used to getting back home in Missouri, forced by an asshole ex-husband into playing the part of the black single mother with the precocious kid.

Benj's father. The self-absorbed asshole.

Who only drifted back around when he wanted something.

That alone was the biggest fucking stereotype.

Benj had tasted a little of racial friction himself, mostly in college, when he realized that him and the only other African-American student in all of Westminster College's Computer Science department were friends by default, even if his new pal had smelled like tuna most of the time.

It's not that the white students had some kind of "issue" with him, it was just that they all seemed to assume he wasn't *really* interested in talking to them, even when he would walk right up to them and start a conversation.

It was a little like that still, in his new life on the southern fringe of Salt Lake City, at the NSA's Utah Data Center. There were more black people there, and quite a few Asians, but it seemed like there was still a sharp divide for who was friends with who. He'd had friendly chats with quite a few people, especially the women *for some reason*, but nothing had really worked to break him out of his default group.

And considering that just beyond the fence was the whitest state in the nation, Benj's group from work was pretty much the only group he had outside of the online conspiracy buffs he chatted with on nights he had trouble sleeping, i.e., most of them.

So even though he was in the middle of loading patches in the IT room, once his eyepiece notified him that 10:20 hit, he was on his way to the corridor for the morning break. A seven minute trip to the cafeteria and seven minutes back would leave a whole sixty seconds for coffee if he included his travel time, but it wasn't Benj's fault they no longer allowed beverages in the data halls. So his break would start the moment he sat down with his coffee, and he'd run out that fifteen minutes at the table. It would actually be eighteen minutes, actually, assuming no delays on getting there.

Samantha Yoon provided a delay in the corridor, stopping Benj to ask some inane question about her home setup. Benj's eyepiece notified him that her behavior was off, higher pulse, dilated pupils... nervous to talk to him.

But he didn't trust the signs; he'd been burned by that before. He just assumed she was nervous about something else.

He smiled and answered the question as best he could, gently letting her know that she was probably screwed if she kept on with her cheap hardware.

The whole exchange seemed odd to him; Sam had plenty of friends she could have asked. Assuming that she didn't already know the answers. She did work at one of the world's largest data centres, even if she was in QA.

There wasn't even a real reason for her to be in the corridor. In fact, there was probably a good reason for her to not be in there, since Benj wasn't even sure she had clearance.

It was flattering if a little unsettling for Benj to realize she'd come all the way down just to see him, even if the eyepiece wasn't right about her intent. Sure, they'd had some good little chats, and Benj had brought out his best material to get her to laugh. But he felt like it should take a little more primping to seal the deal.

But yet, there she was.

And the signs were there, fed onto the left lens of his black-framed retro eyewear. She wanted to make that deal.

"So my whole setup is crap?" she asked.

"I never said that. It's true, but you're the one who said it."

She laughed.

"Maybe you could give me some advice, you know?" she said, giving a little shrug with her shoulders. "Come by and check it out?"

"Beer or pizza?"

"Can't it be both?"

"I can handle that."

"Maybe tonight?" she asked.

"What?"

"Tonight. I know it's short notice, but I don't like unnecessary delay."

"Unnecessary delay?"

"Yeah."

"Uh... alright then."

"Sweetness," she said.

She gave his shoulder a tap, which felt more like a friendly gesture than a flirt. She didn't seem very practiced.

But Benj and his eyepiece still got the right vibe from her, that pizza and beer meant getting to know each other. And it was the perfect shorthand in Utah for telling someone that you aren't part of the Mormon mainstream, or, if you are, that you don't mind taking that signed photo of Joseph Smith on your nightstand and flipping it around, you know, if things get a little intimate.

Benj made it to coffee at 10:35 AM, but the missing five minutes didn't bother him in the least.

He sat down with a hazelnut coffee and his group, three guys and two girls in total, the Afro-American Contingent, as he'd called them a couple of times, to great aplomb.

He wasn't about to say anything about his corridor encounter, but Malik asked him about how the morning was going so he felt that door was open.

"Sam's been following me around," he said, nodding his head as he spoke.

"Sam?" Malik asked. "Is that one of the janitors?"

"Samantha Yoon. That Korean girl with the pretty eyes."

"Pretty eyes? You gonna write her a poem, too?"

"I think it's sweet," Cam said as he poured half the sweetener jar into his coffee. "Someone to make Benj forget about the last girl."

"How can I forget?" Benj asked, exaggerating an eye-roll. "You bring her up every time I see you."

"That's because I'm sitting right across the table from you two idiots," Taylor said, sounding like she was getting a little sick of the joke.

"Oh, hi, Taylor," Benj said with a grin. "Didn't see you there."

"I've never heard Samantha mention you," Laila said. "Funny."

Benj wasn't sure if she sounded a little jealous. He liked the concept.

"It's not like you and Samantha are best friends," Malik said. "You talk to her maybe twice a month."

"I thought you didn't know who she is?" Cam asked.

"Of course he knows her," Taylor said. "He probably has all the girls ranked and graded in his dirty little mind."

"I can sort by several attributes," Malik said. "Age, hair color, girth…"

"Girth?" Laila said. "Is that a joke?"

"Girth's not a bad thing," Benj said.

Laila glared at him.

Taylor laughed.

"He means he likes your backside," Malik said, grinning. "Probably why he's always recording it with the camera on his glasses."

"I'll thank you to keep your eyes and your devices off my backside," Laila said, still staring Benj down.

He felt like apologizing, but he had a feeling it wouldn't help. Clearly she was trying to burn a hole through his forehead, to drain out whatever idiocy she found inside.

Benj was well aware that there was a lot of it.

Taylor laughed again.

Laila burst out with her own laugh.

"Fuck," Benj said.

"You were a little worried there," Taylor said. "So funny."

"You taking her somewhere?" Cam asked. "Don't say a movie."

"What's wrong with a movie?" Malik said.

"You can't talk at a movie."

Malik grinned. "*I* talk at the movies."

"And that's why you're an asshole," Taylor said.

"I'm going over to her place," Benj said.

"You're insane," Malik said.

"What?"

"It's an ambush or something."

"Seriously, what?"

"Is she Mormon?" Malik asked.

"She's Korean."

"Koreans can be Mormons."

"I don't think she's Mormon," Benj said. "Does it matter?"

"She's going to try and proselytize you."

"Proselytize me?"

"Convert you."

"I know what it means. I just think you're crazy."

"I think she just wants the BBC," Taylor said.

Everyone looked over to her.

Benj's eyepiece threw the most likely translation for 'BBC' on his lens, unprompted. And unnecessary.

"You know," Taylor said. "Big black cock."

"We all know," Laila said. "You say that every time any girl comes around here. It's a little sad."

"It's not sad. It's called watching out for my boys."

"Your boys?" Malik said.

"They're fetishizing you," Taylor said. "These little white or Chinese girls—"

"Korean," Benj said.

"Whatever. These little girls grow up hearing that the black boys are so bad, but man are they hung like stallions."

"We're not all hung like stallions," Malik said. "Some of us are burdened with brachiosaurus-sized cocks."

"No one's fetishizing me," Benj said.

"Every girl in Utah has a little fantasy about you guys," Taylor said. "Some fantasy about the stablehand, the escaped fugitive, the ball player."

Benj laughed. "How about the network administrator? Because that sounds more like me."

"Yessum, Miss Samantha. I can stroke your thighs. Yessum, Miss Samantha, you sure are a pretty Chinese flower."

"Korean," Benj said.

"That sounds kinda hot," Laila said.

Benj realized she was looking right at him.

And that was when the buzzing started.

A broadcast message sent to their tablets. And to Benj's eyepiece, since the only reason he was allowed to bring it through the doors was because it had gone through the regular inspection process; the brass didn't mind extra devices for sending messaging. And it had been Malik who'd been given the task of ensuring that Benj's glasses could be trusted.

It was rather unusual to send a broadcast to everyone, in the world of the top secret.

"Lockdown," Benj said, reading the single word that had flashed on his lens."

No start date or end date. No further details.

He had to believe it had nothing to do with him and any of his not-so-approved activities. He'd been careful. He'd covered his tracks. It wasn't his first kick at the cat.

But still, Benj had a sense of deep foreboding, that even if he was in the clear, that there was a good chance he wouldn't find out just what a Korean girl's bedroom looks like.

Samantha Yoon walked into the IT room just as Benj was connecting to the last server on the patch list. She didn't seem lost, or nervous.

She walked right over to him.

"We need to talk," she said.

"I don't understand."

"This is important."

"Okay…"

"We need to go outside," she said.

"What?"

"Out of the building."

"We're under lockdown."

She sighed. "I know that. Come with me."

"Where?"

"Outside. You're usually a lot smarter than this."

He followed her out of the IT room, and over to the corridor. From there, she led him to a fire exit on the left, marked with the usual "Alarm will sound" signage.

She swiped her hand over the sensor. She pushed open the door.

No alarm, assuming it wasn't silent. His eyepiece wasn't 100% on detecting something like that.

"You seem to have too much clearance," Benj said as they stepped outside, facing the back perimeter of the complex. "You're supposed to be a software chick."

"Software chick? Sounds diminishing."

"It's endearing, really."

He couldn't help but wonder if she knew what he'd been up to. But how could she have found out?

And why wouldn't she have just told someone?

She led him across the road to the first security fence.

"We can talk here," she said.

"We're not even supposed to be out here," Benj said. "That door isn't even supposed to unlock unless the fire alarm goes off."

"You programmed it to unlock."

"What?"

"You coded a cute little hole so I could open the door for us. So we could be alone out here."

Benj took a step back from Samantha and the security fence. "I don't know what's happening right now," he said. "I don't think pranks should involve breaches of national security."

"You're getting fired tomorrow, Benjamin."

"What?"

"You'll have cracked the system just so you could flirt with one of the software chicks. We hang around out here, laugh and flirt and kiss a little. Then we head back in through the loading area and go our separate ways."

"You're losing me here, Samantha."

"Tonight you come to my house. We don't need to do anything, because no one's watching that close. You just need to stay overnight. Then tomorrow, we go back to work and we flirt a little more. Then we try to go out for another walk, and we get busted."

"We get busted? So you're getting fired, too?"

"Yup. And a few more people, too."

"What? Who?"

"The people you would have needed to pull this off. Malik and Laila, at the very least."

"You're fucking insane, Samantha."

"No, Benj, I'm not. I'm Q Group."

"Q Group. Not funny."

"Funny would be if I'd said I just want the BBC. Or if I'd made an off-handed comment about Laila's girth."

"Shit, Samantha. You listen in on every conversation we have?"

"This is the NSA, Benj. Don't be ridiculous. We listen in on fucking everything."

She smiled; Benj didn't get the point of that.

"We need your help," she said.

"Funny way of asking."

"There's been some chatter."

"There's always chatter. This is the NSA."

"Look up at the sky." She threw up her hands, toward the east.

A little overdramatic.

Benj looked up.

"Dammit," she said, "can't see it from here. Too many mountains in the way. And maybe the curvature of the Earth or something…"

"See what?"

"It's really something, Benj. It really is. A sight to see. Someone just killed the European space habitat."

"Someone," Benj said. "…not us, right?"

Samantha Yoon shrugged.

"What does that mean?"

"It means we don't know."

"Don't know?"

"That's right," she said. "We don't know who's responsible."

"Or if it was just an accident."

"Not an accident. Remember that chatter?"

"What was the chatter about?"

"It's pretty weird, really. Someone sent a warning to an engineer in French Guiana, about someone trying to remotely trigger thermal run-away."

"Who?" he asked.

"We don't know who. Just where."

"And where is *where*?"

"Northern Canada," she said. "A place called Churchill."

He almost flinched at the mention. "How northern?"

"Tundra and polar bears."

"And how I am supposed to help you narrow this down? I'm not a signal officer. I patch servers."

"You should kiss me," she said. "We've been chatting for too long."

"What?"

She went in for the kiss, pressing her lips against his.

He did his best to act the part, and soon it felt like he was back home, where he used to do things like that all the time. With girls who hadn't been trying to kill his career.

"So you don't need to feel me up or anything," she said. "But you do need to come to my house tonight and pretend like you're gonna. I've already texted you the address."

She gave him a final peck before walking toward the door.

"I need to swipe you into the loading bay," she said. "You thought of everything with this illegal breach of yours."

Benj couldn't think of another option. He felt like maybe he was in shock or something.

And a little unsure of just how much trouble he was in.

So he followed Samantha Yoon around to the loading area.

It took a while for Benj to catch his supervisor in her office. Lockdown usually puts all the higher-ups into headless chicken mode, running from meeting room to ops station, without any real progress being made.

He gave a quick knock at the open door before stepping in.

"Amelia," he said, "I need a minute."

"I have maybe half of one," she replied, still staring at her screen.

"This is a bigger problem than that."

"We're on lockdown, Benjamin. Do you remember what that is?"

"Someone is trying to get me fired."

Amelia let out a sigh. A big one.

Benj closed the door behind.

"They've been messing with the system," he said.

"You found something?"

"Well, no."

"Lockdown, Benjamin. Important stuff that requires people to do their jobs."

"It's someone from Q Group."

Amelia looked up from her screen. But she hadn't said anything else. She was simply staring at him, not staring him down like Laila would... just... staring.

"I don't know what to do," Benj said.

"Two possibilities here, Mr. McPherson. Either someone's playing a prank on you, or you need to forget you said anything to me."

"What?"

"Is it a prank?"

"Not really a prank."

"Then that's that," she said. She looked back at her screen. Then glanced back up at him. "That's that, Mr. McPherson."

"What the hell is going on, Amelia?"

"I'm not getting involved. I'm not a part of this."

"Are you kidding me? I mention Q Group and you just freeze up?"

"We're done here, Mr. McPherson. I'm busy."

"Come on, Amelia."

"Please," she said. "Get back to work, Benj. *Please.*"

She was looking at him differently now. She looked frightened. He'd never seen her frightened before. It was probably the most unsettling thing he'd seen in a long time.

What is there to be scared of behind a desk?

"Alright," Benj said. "I guess this never happened."

She nodded. Then she went back to her screen.

Lockdown had ended at seven in the evening, with no explanation given for what had caused it or why it was over. That was pretty standard, and he had no reason to believe it had anything to do with him and anything he'd done.

And the whole thing had left little time for Benj to figure out a Plan B.

So he drove his hatchback to the address Samantha had sent him. On top of the eyepiece he rarely took off, he'd brought his tablet, his passport, and a backpack with a change of clothes. He knew that it was something paranoid idiots tended to do, but he also knew the whole process of preparation had made him less tense, and less tense was always a good thing.

It was a strange apartment complex on University Blvd, one that looked like it couldn't decide if it was a home or a hotel.

She answered the door right after the first knock, dressed in a University of Wyoming sweatshirt and jeans.

"I was worried you weren't coming," she said with a slight smile.

"You don't have cameras in my house?"

"That's hilarious." She didn't laugh.

She waved him inside, then led him to a overly soft couch that stood out in a minimalist living room.

His eyepiece had no insights for him.

He sat down on the couch, and she followed, leaving about six inches of space between their thighs.

"Is this some kind of prank?" he asked her. "That thing with the doors? Running around outside during a lockdown?"

"Neither of us should have been able to open that door," she said. "You know that."

"So a stupid prank that will get us both fired?"

"Just you," she said. "Sorry. I'll be suspended with pay, officially. I guess Malik and Laila will get fired, too, though."

"What do you want from me, anyway?"

"You went to your boss. That was not the best idea."

"If you're so fucking smart, you should have predicted that."

She frowned. "I had hoped for a better outcome. That's all."

"So now you gotta kill me, right? Two in the head and dump me out in the back range."

"I can't tell you anything else just yet, Benj. Not until after tomorrow."

"Until after you get my ass fired."

"Yeah. And again… Malik and Laila, too."

"And what happens to them?"

"I'm sorry, Benj. I don't know."

"That's not acceptable. Not at all. They didn't do anything wrong. I didn't do anything wrong."

That anyone knew about.

"I know. You're a good guy. That's why we picked you. Well, part of the reason we singled you out."

She bit her bottom lip.

She'd known exactly how he'd take it.

"Fuck," he said. He got up from the couch.

"Like father, like son," she said.

"Is that supposed to help?" He was starting to pace a little, making a couple half laps around the room.

"Do you talk to your Dad at all?"

"I talk to my father, yeah. Do I call him Dad? Nope."

"I'm not your therapist, Benj. Now come lie down on my couch."

He stopped pacing. "This isn't funny."

"Your father works with Carter Elgin. You've met Elgin, haven't you?"

"Oh, good. Witchhunt time. Exactly why my father left the country. And I guess it's why Carter Elgin did, too."

"Your father took off and you took a job with the NSA. How Oedipal."

He honestly couldn't tell if she was trying to get a rise out of him, or if this was some new kind of flirting. Or if she knew everything, and was just toying with him before she dropped it all in his lap. His father had gotten him the job with the NSA, ostensibly to clean up his act, make his less of an embarrassment. Same way Benj had gotten that scholarship to Westminster.

Same way Benj had gotten that extra consideration when he came close to flunking out in the first four months.

He had a feeling she knew all of that.

"You know all about SolRescue and the sunshield," she said. "And I'm sure you know all about the covert plan to replace it."

"I don't know anything about that."

"Deniability gets a lot easier if you don't google all the hot topics," she said with a grin. "You've spent more than enough time looking at maps of the launch site. You know, in Churchill, that place you pretended you knew nothing about."

"So you got me dead to rights. I'm a traitor, apparently. For looking at a map that's available to anyone."

"Sit down, okay?"

He let her have that.

"I know you don't know me very well," she said.

"Or at all, apparently."

"Or at all... but trust me, Benj. This is a big deal."

"I didn't break any laws. I'm allowed to express my opinions online. And nothing my father has ever told me—"

"That's not what I mean," she said.

"Then what do you mean? Just come out and say it, then."

"Please, Benj. I can't give you anything else right now. Just in case."

"In case I go back to my boss about this."

"In case tomorrow doesn't go as planned."

He looked her over. Not the way he had before whenever she'd walk by, the way that guys do, when they know they're not hiding it at all. He wanted to trust her, because he was already half past fucked. NSA contractors can't be spouting conspiracy theories online. NSA contractors can't be sharing data on secret projects with their practically estranged fathers.

Either she was crazy, or she was Q Group and truly needed his help, or she was Q Group and he was going to federal prison. Or to that secret detention camp in backwoods Virginia. Or to one of those black sites in some faraway country that had never even come close to getting shut down, no matter what the government had promised.

He looked around her sparse living room. She had a single piece of decor art on the wall, Paris in the rain. Her couch had a single throw pillow; his eyepiece recognized it as still being available at the local Walmart. Same with the art.

And everything else his eyewear had bothered to scan.

She wanted to look so normal; no quirks, just a bunch of bland.

It gave her away. That she wasn't just a software chick. That this wasn't her real life, her real home.

And she wasn't crazy.

This was real.

And she had him dead to rights. If he wasn't lucky, she already had him for more than she'd said.

"So, bedroom off the kitchen or something?" he asked her.

"This is the bedroom. I sleep on the couch."

"Does it fold out?"

"Not really, no."

"So where do I sleep?"

She shrugged.

"And you're a top notch intelligence officer?"

"One of the best. I guess I can sleep in the bathtub. Or there might be enough room to spoon on this thing." She smiled. "Big or little spoon?"

"I can sleep on the floor," he said. "Assuming you have some extra sheets."

"That I have." She got up and walked over to what turned out to be a closet. "Still in its original packaging."

His eyepiece gave him the data.

She'd picked that up from Walmart, too.

Benj laughed.

Because once you're more than half past fucked, there's not much else you can do.

05

THEY DO not have pizza in Churchill. At least, not real pizza. No Chicago Deep Dish. No Brooklyn Style Pies.

So when Chloe had suggested the notion of splitting a large pepperoni, Jared tried not to laugh.

But he agreed to it, so she met him at his hotel room dressed in a low cut blouse and tight black capris. Her hair was down and she had more makeup than he'd remember seeing before.

He commented on how good she looked, and she seemed satisfied with his delivery.

She led him across the still-iced-over street, to the other major hotel in town.

"Wait," he said as they walked into what seemed to be an empty dining room. "That sign says Pizza Fridays. It's not Friday, Chloe. I'm pretty sure Tuesday night is reserved for something else."

"I know people," she said. "Don't worry."

An older woman came out through a back door and greeted them—she seemed to know Chloe, which wasn't surprising considering the size of the town and how long the two of them had been there—and sat them down at a dimly lit table against the back wall.

It felt like a date. Jared wondered if he should have gotten some clarification.

The woman filled up a couple of water glasses, then left without saying a word.

"No menus?" Jared said, as more of a judgment than a comment.

"You're such a sophisticate," Chloe said with a grin. "I'll bet you expect silverware, too."

"Just a feed bag."

"Yeah."

There was an awkward silence. It didn't usually feel awkward with her.

She started fiddling with her cross pendant.

"So Mohammed isn't joining us tonight?" Jared asked. He knew the answer, obviously, but he was just looking for something from her. Maybe that clarification?

"This isn't a date," she said. "Don't worry."

He laughed.

She leaned in over the table a little. "I know you're seeing someone. And

I know we work together."

"And I know you can do better."

"Slim pickings 'til bear season."

He still felt awkward. He wasn't sure why.

"So tell me what that was," she said. "The space station."

"It's the ESA habitat. *Nisi.*"

"I know that. Come on. I mean, *what was that?*"

"You think I know something you don't?"

"I think someone did that."

"That's what everyone says," Jared said. "Every time something bad happens. Someone needs to get blamed."

"So it was an accident? They just accidentally build a space station that just caught fire?"

He chuckled. He was always underestimating her. Not that he thought she wasn't smart, because she obviously was, but because he didn't think she would have paid that much attention.

Unless she'd just been watching the right news reports…

"Tell me, Jared. Tell me what kind of cascade of bad luck and hardcore fuck-ups it would take to make that happen."

"You're right. It couldn't be by accident. All those batteries burning up at the same time?"

"So someone in the ESA planned it," she said.

"What do you mean?"

The older woman came back out through the kitchen door, clutching a wine bottle and two glasses.

She poured a little bit into a glass and handed it to Jared.

"Uh, thanks?" he said.

"You're supposed to taste it," Chloe said. "Let her know it's good."

"And how would I know that?"

Chloe smiled and reached out for the glass.

He handed it to her.

"It's excellent," she said, once she'd taken a sip. "Thanks, Karen."

The woman nodded and disappeared again.

They were alone again. In an empty restaurant.

Not a date.

"You know wine tasting is pretty much woo, right?" he said.

She nodded. "It was an inside job."

"You sound a little paranoid, Chloe."

"I'm just making conversation."

"Yeah, okay."

"Someone wanted this project to fail."

"Could be the Chinese military government," Jared said. "The junta."

"I said someone inside the ESA."

"So maybe some Euroskeptic bureaucrat with a little too much house-hold debt. Maybe some weird French guy with one too many mistresses. It's not like anyone got hurt. It's industrial sabotage, just on a very large scale."

"So you don't think it was us," she said.

"What?"

"Why would it be China and not the US Government? We have just as much reason to slow the Europeans down."

"It's not a race," he said with a smirk.

"You're right. We lost the race. And there's some NGO holding the keys to the planet instead of us."

"I never would have expected you to buy into that anti-crowdOrg stuff."

"What's that supposed to mean, exactly?"

"I won't lie, Chloe. I trust people way more than I trust the govern-ment."

"You work in government, jackass."

"Well I don't have a problem with the sunshield. Or with SolRescue or Carter Elgin—"

"Then why are you here, Jared?"

"The frozen nothingness, mostly."

"God, Jared. Be serious with me, okay?"

"Carter Elgin is pretty much my personal hero. I just want to do what he did, make a difference. And maybe save the world from the hardline Chinese government, as necessary."

"This project is supposed to replace what Elgin did. Do you think your personal hero will be happy about that?"

"He'll be less happy if the Chinese generals take it over. But, to be honest, I never thought it would get this far. I thought we'd print up some rockets, maybe run a test or two, not really getting close to a final draft. I figured someone would cut the whole project."

"And then what? What would be the point of all this? How would that stop the Chinese?"

"I don't know. Some things are outside our control, you know? But either way, I'm learning a shit ton about this stuff. Real world experience."

"Just the right experience to take a job with Carter Elgin," she said.

Jared nodded. "I guess I kind of assumed you were in the same boat. Sure, it's great to serve your country, but we're mostly just building up our resumes."

She jutted her chin out, like she was trying to stab him with it. "No," she stammered. "I actually do care about the work I'm doing. Not just lip service."

Jared tried to hold in the laugh. She was so adorably ridiculous.

"I can't even tell you what I've gone through," she said. "What I've risked, not just on this project, but before, in Vietnam, in Ghana…"

He didn't know what to say. He certainly didn't feel like laughing anymore.

"I'm sorry," she said. It seemed to come out of nowhere.

"What? You don't need to apologize."

"You don't owe me anything. You don't need to prove anything, either."

"I like what we do," he said. "I like working with you, Chloe. I just want us to be happy with that, no matter what happens."

"Yeah. I get that."

He reached across the table for her hand. Instinct. A bad one. But it was too late to pull it back.

She laughed. "Not a date, remember?"

Jared went back with Chloe to her hotel room.

They'd both had wine, but just the one bottle, so it wasn't like they didn't know what was about to take place.

He started kissing her the moment they were through the door.

"Not yet," she said. "My room's a mess."

"You should have thought of that before you bought me that awful pizza."

She laughed, and he kissed her again.

He grabbed her hand and led her toward the unmade bed.

"No maid service?" he asked.

"I never let them in. National Security reasons, naturally."

He patted the mattress. "Hop on, buttercup."

"Buttercup?"

He kissed her for a third time. He'd never have considered himself a kisser.

She sat down on the bed.

He took off his shirt, feeling only slightly insecure about it.

She placed both her hands on his chest, one on each peck. She rubbed and gripped them. She let out a heavy sigh.

Hopefully a good one.

She looked him in the eye.

Like she was waiting for something.

He grabbed her by the shoulders and pushed her down onto the bed.

"Yeah," she said.

He started pulling her blouse up.

"No," she said. "Not the top."

He nodded. He moved one of his hands up and swept her hair off her forehead.

He kissed her neck.

She reached up for his hands. He clasped both her palms and pushed them down against the mattress.

She moaned.

"You're beautiful," he said.

"I know."

He reached down and grabbed her pants. He started pulling them off.

She didn't tell him not to.

So he brought his head down.

And she moaned a little more.

Once he'd finished, as well, he reached over for her.

"No," she said.

"What's wrong?"

"Nothing's wrong. Just don't hold me."

He pulled away.

"I just don't want us to act like this is something it isn't," she said.

"I actually don't know what this is."

"It's what we just did. That's all."

"Yeah, okay," he said.

It sounded like a good deal. But he couldn't help but feel a little rejected.

He got out of bed and started getting dressed.

"I'm guessing you don't want me to stay over," he said.

"You don't need to."

He knew what that meant. He knew when he wasn't wanted.

So Jared went back to his own hotel room and watched TV. He didn't know what he was supposed to do with himself. He just knew that didn't feel satisfied with how things had ended.

He checked the reports on *Nisi*, seeing what else had come out about what was still officially being called an accident. The ESA was hushed, and most of the media sources were babbling about nothing. The only real story was coming out of Russia, from the same outlet that had done an "exposé" the week before on an unsubstantiated secret deal between the US and China. They had anonymous sources, no real evidence… so business as usual.

But still, he knew China couldn't be trusted. They spent half their time launching cyberattacks at anyone and everyone. They still held sway over

Tibet and East Turkestan, they still rattled sabres about Taiwan and gazed longingly at the Russian Far East. They'd built up a navy that smelled suspiciously like the one the Germans had built up in the race to World War I.

China wanted to take on the United States, to push the teetering superpower over the cliff. There was no way the US would partner with them on taking over the sunshield.

It seemed like a laughably bad conspiracy theory.

But it wasn't China being blamed in that latest story; the Russians were calling out the United States as the prime suspect in the sabotage. Mentions of intercepted chatter that details the conspiracy, and of the repositioning of the Japanese elevator platform off French Guiana in case of debris.

There'd be no debris falling there from an exploding space station. That wasn't how reentry worked. Not to mention that the US probably wouldn't share its super secret plans with some public-private conglomerate that's pipe-dreaming a space elevator in the Atlantic.

That was almost as ridiculous as a secret pact with China.

There was one line, however, in the cluster of crap, that stood out to Jared:

The US Secretary of Defense had sparred earlier with EU President Géza Nikiš over the exploitation of 4183 Cuno.

He remembered Mohammed had mentioned *Cuno*, that it had been his first choice for the raw materials for their second gen sunshield, but that he'd been turned down due to some kind of nebulous political considerations. Their current option was a smaller and rockier object that stayed a little closer to Earth.

But that little rock was plenty good enough.

Any S-type rock was good enough.

There was no reason to associate US friction with Europe to the attack, but then again, there'd been no reason for that friction in the first place. Why did the Secretary of Defense care about the ESA's use of a chunk off Cuno?

Jared had a cramp in his stomach, not from bad pizza and commitment-free sex...

The project was going ahead. He was building the shield bots that would replace Elgin and Singhal's creation.

Once their creation was removed.

No, not removed.

Destroyed.

Did it really make sense to take over so the Chinese junta didn't get there first? Couldn't the US government sit down with Carter Elgin and work something out? If they'd stop pretending for a few hours that what

Elgin had done is criminal?

Jared knew that no one had even bothered to work it out with Sol-Rescue, that the US government had never been interested in compromise.

And that race against the Chinese, the reason Jared had even agreed to do it in the first place... that didn't make up for the wilful destruction of other people's property, in space or otherwise, not that destroying the sunshield was any less immoral than bombing the crap out of the Middle East for the millionth time.

He was reminded of that old Mitchell and Webb skit his older sister used to play for him—her favorite from back in her British Comedy phase—which had started with silly Monty Python skits about parrots and/or coconuts and had ended with some very dark jokes from the Brass Eye, about pedophiles.

There were two German soldiers, the SS, he thought, with skulls on their uniforms. And one of them took the other aside and asked a rather pertinent question.

"Are we the baddies?" Jared asked himself, out loud.

He chuckled.

But he couldn't help thinking it.

That what he was doing wasn't okay, or, even worse, that he didn't actually know what he was doing, or what the final goal would be. That he didn't know the whole story, least of all how it would end.

He was like a poor man's Oppenheimer.

If he and Carter Elgin ever met face to face, Elgin would probably knee him in the balls.

06

NICOLAS WAS surprised by how quickly eurocrats can work when the world is actually paying attention.

After a frenzied voice call with a panicked Madame Bignard, Nicolas decided to stay up all night working on his defense. By 3:00 he received the message from his boss' boss: the hearing would be at 9:00. He would be expected to provide any and all details of the events leading up to the incident.

And from what he'd found so far, the details made him look like a fool.

Someone had taken control over the sensors on the station. They'd tricked the environmentals on the station to think the temperature was dropping, so the venting was closed and heat increased to compensate. And the batteries started heating up.

Meanwhile, the sensors sent Status OK to the monitoring software at the CSG, which meant that no temperature alert was sent to his team.

So the temperature kept rising and no one knew what was happening. By the time the fire had been detected, it was too late to stop the cascade of failures. And the damned thing blew up.

Even without the temperature sensors, there was a log of autonomous actions that they should have been monitoring, in hindsight.

They likely monitored that properly on ISS/2 and OPSEK and Tiangong, but somehow Nicolas had been too busy with his wine-soaked evenings with the Catalonians to do a proper job.

The ESA wouldn't need to invent a sacrificial lamb. He'd served himself up with a big bowl of mint jelly.

He'd let his life's work fall apart.

And it got worse.

The logs all spat back one user account for every suspicious operation he could find that led to the takeover: Nicolas.Clouatre.

He was more than *Nic le Lampiste*, resident fall guy who might not even receive his severance pay. He was well on his way to prison.

And *Nisi* was dead and gone; Europe would lose its best chance at greatness.

His thoroughly French grandfather—who'd probably never been to temple—used to tell him about the suitcase under the bed, how every smart Jew would keep his travel documents, some clothes, and a wad of cash packed up, for when he had to be on the next train out of whatever country he lived in. The Hebrew Bug-Out Bag, Nicolas had always joked.

He felt stupid about that now. Alfred Dreyfus himself was held at Devil's Island, just off the coast.

Nicolas didn't have his bag packed, but he was tempted to get started on it.

He had enough savings to get a plane ticket, and to disappear for a while. He could find an out-of-the-way place, rent some tiny apartment or backwoods cabin…

He couldn't live like that. Sitting and waiting to die. Watching the rest of the world innovate and invent, and not being able to join in.

And they'd find him. He knew a great deal about just one thing, and he knew nothing about covering his tracks. He didn't know how to get a fake ID or switch all his money over to whatever cyber-currency is in vogue.

He came close to googling "going on the lam".

There was no point.

He'd either turn himself in after a week, or he'd end up bouncing around in homeless shelters.

You definitely don't want to get into any threesomes in the homeless shelter.

He compiled all of the data as best he could. At 13:00 he was at his desk; he hadn't gone down to the floor until sometime around 13:30. And that in itself made him look guilty, like he'd gone down to check if anyone had noticed his handiwork.

There was no way to make himself look better; he was guilty at worst and negligent at best. All he could do was tell the truth and take his punishment.

He'd be tried in France, most likely. Maybe Brussels.

He wouldn't have to worry about ending up in some eastern prison; maybe they'd even have work passes.

Maybe he'd end up at that place on Île-d'Aix, where hard time felt more like a summer vacation. His career would be over, his reputation destroyed and his reason for living snuffed out like a space station on unscheduled re-entry, but at least he'd be able to maintain his tan.

Nicolas heard his apartment door open. It was 5:30, too late for a drunk getting the wrong suite and—hopefully—too early for an escort from the gendarmes to some holding cell in the capital.

He was on the toilet at the time, which felt very *Pulp Fiction* to him. He couldn't help but think of himself shot up on the kitchen floor.

"Nicolas," a woman's voice called out. *"Où es-tu?"*

She was speaking French, but he recognized her voice and the accent. Mireia. The flawless female half of the Catalonians.

Had she expected to find him hanging from the doorknob, his eyes bulging and his neck stretched out?

Not much better than what Vincent Vega got.

"Nicolas, I'm worried."

"One instant, Mireia," he shouted from the bathroom.

He heard her chuckle nervously.

He washed and came out.

Mireia was standing in his living room, dressed in a leather jacket, her black hair pulled back in a way he'd never seen from her before.

She had a look of determination, despite the fact that she was shaking.

"What are you doing here?" he asked.

"We need to go," she said. "No packing."

"I'm not running." He wasn't sure if he sounded proud or stupid. Or both.

"We need to go. You cannot get arrested."

"You can find another old French dude," he said.

"This isn't a joke, Nicolas. Your life is in danger. And so is mine."

"That makes no sense."

"Let's go."

He didn't trust her. It hadn't all come together, but he knew that he couldn't just chalk her arrival up to a concerned friend. She was involved. She'd dragged him into it.

And she'd worked on the environmental systems.

"*Casse-toi,* Mireia," he said. "I don't know what you've done, but I'm not going to go along with it. That was my life's work. How could you?"

She grabbed him, hands on both shoulders. "Calm down," she said. "Trust me."

He shoved her forward.

She seemed unfazed. "We need to go."

"I'm not going anywhere. I'm going to tell them what I know."

"You don't know a goddamn thing."

He shook his head. "All I know is that you've fucked me over. And that there's no way I'm going anywhere with you."

"Don't make this hard, Nicolas."

He laughed.

She reached into her jacket.

He realized what it was she pulled out just as the electrodes struck him in the stomach.

He crumpled to the living room carpet. He'd never felt so much pain outside of last year's colonoscopy.

His door opened again. Alex—the husband—rushed in.

Mireia grabbed his ankles, and Alex his elbows.

As they carried him out of his apartment, it was clear that they'd never done anything like it before. At one point, Mireia dropped his feet as they were descending the stairwell.

He cursed at her.

She picked him back up and they kept going.

Soon he was in the backseat of their Toyota SUV, already soaked by a few seconds of heavy rain, and Alex was behind the wheel, driving them somewhere at a reasonably fast speed.

He slowly sat up, surprised at how sluggish he still felt.

They were heading south, not north; away from the CSG.

"I really thought he'd go with you," Alex said.

"We have a pack for you, Nicolas," Mireia said. "Three days of rations, but you won't need that much."

"Do I need to dig my own grave?" he asked.

"We're going hiking," Alex said.

"All three of us?"

"We're really starting to forge a bond," Mireia said.

"You realize that I'm here against my will?" Nicolas asked. "Do you realize that you're kidnapping me?"

Mireia chuckled. "Do you think your ex-wife will pay the ransom?"

"You sound unbalanced, my treasure," Alex said.

"Sorry," she said. "We're all worried, Nicolas. We're all out of our element."

"You own a stun gun," Nicolas said. "Obviously you're less out of your element than I am." He watched out the window as they left Korou on RN1. The clear skies were long gone, and they were back to the rainy season. Apparently god had seen fit to open up the skies just so Nicolas could see his dreams break up in the exosphere. "Are we going to Cayenne?"

"We're going to Brazil," Alex said.

"I don't have my passport."

"We're not driving to Brazil," Mireia said. "They already have a checkpoint right before Régina and the bridge over the Approuague, because of the incident. They won't be letting any suspicious ESA refugees through. So that's what the hiking is all about."

"You want to hike through the Amazon into Brazil," Nicolas said. "This is a joke."

"There's a couple rivers in the way," Alex said. "But we need to get to that first river at least, as a start. Then we'll see what we can arrange. Assuming the roads are passable."

"They won't be passable," Mireia said. "Not on any tracks past Coralie."

"You've been out there before?" Nicolas asked.

"We've done the trip a handful of times," Alex said. "But never during the rains."

"Why are you doing this?"

"To get to Brazil."

"I mean all of it, Alex. Why did you destroy *Nisi?* My *putain* life's work?"

"We didn't destroy *Nisi*," Mireia said. "We're not the bad guys."

"And I'm supposed to believe that?" Nicolas asked. "Without any proof? And after you dragged me out of my home?"

"We carried you out," Alex said.

"You guys haven't kept it secret," Mireia said. "The real reason for building that space station."

"There's no secret reason," Nicolas said. "It's a habitat in space. We want sustainable habitats in space. Ipso facto."

"The European Cabinet is cozy with Carter Elgin," Alex said.

Nicolas sighed. "That's not a secret. The man moved to Sweden for a reason."

"We work for Carter," Mireia said. "For SolRescue."

"No, you work for the European Space Agency. Were you needing some part time spending money?"

"He doesn't know," Alex said, looking at Nicolas like he was an errant schoolchild. Summarily dismissing him as any kind of player.

"Do you know where *Nisi* is supposed to go?" Mireia asked him. "Once it's mostly self-sustaining?"

"I'd made the recommendation," Nicolas said. "To set it at STeLa-4. Outside the magnetosphere, to prove what can be done."

"It's not going to STeLa-4," Alex said.

"What?"

"It's not."

He sounded smug. Too fucking smug.

"It was considered need-to-know," Mireia said. "And I'm guessing Madame Bignard didn't think you had to be told."

"Told what, exactly?" Nicolas asked.

"They're sending it to STeLa-1," Alex said. "To protect the sunshield. An agreement between Carter and the EU."

"Protect? It has no weapons." He didn't think it did; Nicolas would have never admitted how easy it would have been to hide some lethal payload from him as well.

"You don't understand," Mireia said, though she said it gently enough that it didn't piss him off. "By placing a human habitat there, they are creating an Exclusive Economic Zone for the European Union, just like that artificial island we built in the Indian Ocean, and like we're trying to carve out in British Antarctica with those big domes."

"Those concrete piles off Mauritius don't count for anything," Nicolas said.

Mireia nodded. "Not yet. But they'll be recognized eventually. Can't be ignored forever."

"Of course," Alex said, "in space, that zone is proposed at a thousand kilometers instead of two hundred nautical miles or whatever."

"Proposed," Nicolas said. "As in, not really agreed upon. Just like with the Mesh Skirt Project."

"It'll be good enough," Mireia said. "Once people live near the sunshield, it takes destroying the existing bots off the table. Gives us sovereignty and hopefully the defensive capabilities it requires."

"Destroy the bots?"

"The sunshield."

"Who would destroy the sunshield? That's insane."

"There's two sides to every story," Alex said. "The shield isn't just something that keeps the heat down and killed the melting arctic investments of several dozen of the largest resource companies. It's also a very powerful weapon, one that other governments can't get their hands on."

"The European Union wants to turn the sunshield into some kind of superweapon?" Nicolas said. "Like a James Bond villain? That is beyond ridiculous."

"It is ridiculous," Mireia said. "And we're not the ones who believe it."

"Just like we're not the ones who destroyed your space station," Alex said.

"There's no way the US or China sabotaged a European project," Nicolas said. "That's like an act of war."

Alex groaned. "China attacks us all the time, Nicolas. Come on. They melted half a German data centre last year."

"That was a cyber attack. That's totally different."

"How do you know this wasn't the same thing?" Mireia asked. "Or are you telling me that you really did fire those boosters?"

"The Chinese have over two hundred thousand people engaged in cyber warfare," Alex said. "The Americans have at least half as many. And what do we have to fight back? A few dozen guys in Munich? Not to mention the attacks on SolRescue."

"We don't know for sure who's responsible," Mireia said. "It could be someone at the CSG. It could even be Lucille Bignard, for all we know."

"She wouldn't even know how," Nicolas said.

"We're saying we don't know," Alex said. "What we do know is that they have your number, Nic. They want you to take the fall, and for all we know, they want to suicide you in a holding cell."

"That's a little paranoid, don't you think?"

"We're not going to risk it," Mireia said. "Other people on this project have had mysterious deaths. And you're too important, Nicolas."

"Once we cross into Brazil we're handing you off to some friends," Alex said. "They'll get you where you need to go."

"And where exactly do I need to go?" Nicolas asked.

"They didn't tell us," Mireia said. "Need-to-know."

"And how will we get there?"

"We already covered that," Alex said. "Into the jungle and across the river. Well, the two rivers."

"And if the roads are washed out?"

"Don't worry," Mireia said. "The trail isn't that bad. Some bugs, some much, a few *clandestins* with itchy machetes."

"Illegal miners," Alex said. "Gold panners, mostly. They might take us for claim jumpers."

"Are you trying to be funny?" Nicolas asked.

"It's *craignos*," Mireai said. "But not like *craignos craignos*. Just a little dangerous."

"And safer than staying here," Alex said.

"You haven't convinced me of that," Nicolas said.

"We're done having this debate," Mireia said. She sounded more worn down than angry. "Alex and I are crossing into Brazil. Whether or not you come with us... I don't care."

"So you'd let me out right here?"

Alex laughed. "Out in the forest in the middle of a downpour. We're coming up on Tonate. You decide if we should head straight into Cayenne to drop you off, or if we should go with the plan that doesn't get you killed."

"Drop me off in Cayenne," Nicolas said. "I can't run away from everything."

"Okay," Mireia said. "It's your choice."

"I know it is."

They passed through the village of Tonate in silence. Alex kept to the main highway, and they passed several marginal farms before reaching the long and low Pont du Larivot over the Cayenne River.

The driving rain had slowed traffic over the bridge to a crawl.

"Slowest getaway ever," Mireia said.

"You're really going to drop me off in Cayenne?" Nicolas asked.

"That's what we said," Alex said. "We're all still friends, Nic. Even if you don't trust us. And we really do need your help."

"How can I possibly help?" Nicolas asked. "You need another project ruined?"

"You'll have a chance to try again," Mireia said. "That's why we need you. This isn't the end of your story, you know?"

"Okay."

"Okay? Okay what?"

"I'll come with you."

She turned all the way around to look at him. "Too late," she said. "You're dead to us."

"What?"

She smiled.

Alex started laughing.

Somehow it still felt like they were flirting with him.

They turned off the main highway to Brazil, onto Piste de Belizon, a mud road that did still look like more of a road than a track, even if the May rains were doing their best to wash it away. It looked wide enough for cars to pass, though maybe not wide enough for anything bigger than a car. But unlike the forests in Brazil, there wasn't much logging in Guyane, so there probably wouldn't be much by way of logging trucks.

The forest was set off the road, which was better than Nicolas had expected; for some reason he'd had a vision in his head where they'd have to stop the SUV every five hundred meters to slash through the overgrowth.

But he realized that was silly, that the road was obviously there for a reason, that people used it to get places, whether that mean all the way into the rainforest to Saul, or just to wherever their illicit goldpanning spot happened to be.

They drove by two rusted cars sitting just off the road, one flipping on its side at the edge of the bush.

"Those have been here since I was a kid," Mireia said.

"You were here when you were a kid?" Nicolas asked.

"My father worked at CSG for a few years. I'm a rocket rat."

"These roads aren't that great," Alex said. "You know that when they don't even bother towing these wrecks out of here."

"I knew this place was underdeveloped," Nicolas said. "But this is…"

"It's beautiful," Mireia said.

"Someone's coming," Alex said.

Nicolas saw it, too, a 4x4 heading toward them, moving fast enough that they looked like they knew the road well.

Alex slowed down.

The 4x4 raced by, the two white men inside glaring at them in an unfriendly way.

"I don't feel welcome," Nicolas said.

"Don't worry," Mireia said, "you're definitely not welcome here. You're not just paranoid."

They'd passed by several forks, Alex giving the impression that he was well aware of which way to go, but at the fourth or fifth junction he stopped the Toyota.

"Left here," Mireia said, "then left again."

"You're sure?" he asked her.

"Ninety percent."

Alex took the left. The road was narrower, the forest creeping closer to the edge.

"We should be able to get right up to the river," Alex said.

"And then what?" Nicolas asked.

"You'll love this part," Mireia said. "We've got an inflatable raft in the back. We'll take turns blowing it up."

"No air pump? You don't sound very prepared."

"I needed room for the stun gun," she said with a smirk.

"Two cars," Alex said. His voice sounded uneven.

"Two?" Mireia said.

"I know how to count, Mireia."

"What's going on?" Nicolas asked.

Mireia shushed him.

Two 4x4s, similar models to the one that they'd passed before. But these two were stopped on the road, side by side, blocking the way.

Alex started slowing down.

"Don't slow down," Mireia said.

"They're blocking the track," he said.

"You'll make us look weak."

"We *are* weak."

"There's no one in those vehicles," Nicolas said. "They're just parked."

"What does that mean?" Alex asked. "What the hell does that mean?"

"Calm down," Mireia said. "We turn around. There's a longer loop that'll get us there."

"Okay…"

Nicolas was starting to become well aware that he hadn't had a chance to take his morning pee.

Alex carefully turned the SUV around, working to avoid the wettest patches of muck.

"Another one," Mireia said. "The same one."

"No," Alex said. "God."

"What the hell is going on?" Nicolas asked.

Alex took a deep breath. "We're about to get fucked."

"Take it easy," Mireia said. "We don't know that."

"So what do you suggest I do, Mireia?"

"Gun it. Get past that guy and we'll try for the other way in."

"And if we get stuck?"

"Then we ask them to help pull us out?"

Alex stopped the Toyota.

"That's not at all what I told you to do," Mireia said.

"You need to listen to her," Nicolas said. "Get us out of here."

Alex turned off the engine.

"What the hell are you doing?" Nicolas asked. "Are you crazy?"

Alex opened the door and stepped out into the rain.

Nicolas and Mireia didn't move from their seats.

The oncoming 4x4 stopped several car lengths in front.

The two men stepped out.

The passenger was holding a double barrel shotgun, pointed at the ground.

"They're going to kill us," Nicolas said.

"Don't panic," Mireia said. "There's no threat yet."

The passenger lifted his gun, aiming it at Alex.

"Oh my god," Mireia said.

Alex raised his hands.

"On your head," the man with the shotgun yelled, in accented English. Possibly a Brazilian. Definitely not French.

Nicolas wasn't an expert on Guyane, but he knew that a random batch of armed Brazilian men was probably not made up of welcome guests of La République.

They were most likely *garimpeiros,* illegal miners. The same men who'd been known to engage in gun battles with the French Foreign Legion.

Across the line in Amazon, some illegal miners had even taken to building their own ground drones, unmanned tanks to kill anyone along their path.

Some men had felt that what they were doing was worth killing over.

Men like the one with the gun.

The two men slowly walked closer to Alex, who'd put his hands on his head as ordered.

Nicolas leaned forward in his seat. "I think we'll be lucky if they don't kill us," he whispered to Mireia.

"Don't panic… please…"

"I'm not panicking. I'm doing the math."

"No civilians been murdered out here in over five years. Worst case they rob us, take our car."

"That's not worst case," Nicolas said. "You can't be sure of that."

"So what is it you want to do here, Nic? You want to lunge at that guy with my stun gun?"

"We need to give them a good reason not to kill us."

"Well, let me know when you think of one."

The driver shoved Alex away from the Toyota.

The man with the shotgun stood behind the SUV, pointing his gun toward the back window.

Nicolas realized the gun was pointed directly at him.

He saw two more men leaving the edge of the forest.

One grabbed Alex, pulling his arms down and pinning his elbows behind his back. The other man from the woods reached into his pocket and pulled something out, possibly a ziptie.

He bound Alex's wrists behind his back.

"He's okay," Mireia said, "they're just restraining him. They just want to rob us."

Nicolas' mind flashed to what might have been every image he'd ever seen of dead bodies left on the side of the road. From Mexico, Pakistan, but particularly from northern Brazil.

They tie your hands before they shoot you.

"Out of the car," the man with the shotgun said. "The man first."

"I need the stun gun," Nicolas said. "Where is it?"

"That's a stupid idea," she said. "Forget it. And they'd see me give it to you."

He'd only seen one gun so far. One gun and four men.

They probably had more. More guns, and possibly more men.

And machetes…

Nicolas slowly climbed out of the back seat, putting his hands on his head the moment he was standing in the mud.

The driver was making his way over, while the man with the shotgun kept his weapon aimed.

If Mireia was right, they were just getting robbed. They could hike back up the road, or make their way to the river. And if she was right, the only way they'd end up dead is if Nicolas did something stupid.

But if he was right… he had no way to be sure, and the moment they tied his wrists he'd lose his chance to do anything other than make a mad dash for the trees.

That would get him killed, most likely.

The driver pulled a plastic tie from his pocket.

Nicolas needed to make a goddamn decision…

"You have a right to be here," Nicolas said, in English. He didn't know any Portuguese. "The land should belong to all of the people."

The driver grabbed Nicolas' hands, pulling them down and behind his back then binding them with the ziptie.

"My name is Nicolas Clouatre. These are my colleagues, Alex Vives and Mireia Lona. We are from the Party of the European Left. We are here to learn about your work here."

"Be quiet," the man with the shotgun said. He'd had the barrels trained on Nicolas, but he started to move them back toward the Toyota. "Now, the woman. Out of the vehicle."

Mireia slowly got out of the Toyota. She put her hands on her head. She gave Nicolas a look, to let him know that she thought he was going to get them killed.

The driver bound her wrists as well.

They led Nicolas and Mireia over to where Alex had been placed, near the edge of the forest.

One of the men started emptying Nicolas' pockets.

"Nicolas Clouatre," the man said, reading off the driver's license.

"We'll be submitting a bill in the European Parliament," Nicolas said. "To allow for mining permits for Brazilian miners."

"Shut up," the man with the shotgun said.

Nicolas didn't fail to notice the gun was pointed back at him again.

"*Tu es un idiot*," Mireia told him, in French. And then she started speaking to the miners, in what he assumed was Portuguese.

He could make out some of it, *capitalismo, igualdade...* she was making a play for his idiotic idea. She sounded passionate, convincing... at least to someone who didn't speak the language.

One of the men responded in Portuguese. Not the man with the gun, one of the men who'd been concealing themselves in the woods.

He was the man in charge.

He was asking her questions, and she was answering them, without hesitation.

The man shook his head. "You are risking your lives out here," the man said. "It was stupid for you to come."

"We needed to come," Nicolas said.

Mireia shushed him again. Then she threw out a few more impassioned lines of Portuguese.

"Lie down on the ground," the man said. "All of you."

Alex was first to comply. He was obviously hoping against all odds that this wasn't going to end with three conveniently-located shotgun blasts.

Nicolas pissed his pants.

Then he lied down in the wet muck.

Mireia kept trying, speaking to the man, becoming more and more desperate.

The man grabbed her shoulders and pushed her down, slamming her face into the mud.

Nicolas waited for the gun to fire.

It was taking so long. He didn't want to keep waiting.

He just wanted it over and done.

He heard a chirp.

Then nothing else. Just the sounds of the rain.

He knew he was crying.

"*Olha a lista*," one of the other men said.

There was a pause.

He didn't hear any movement.

"*Deixá-los*," another man said.

He thought he heard footsteps.

Walking away.

He didn't dare move.

He listened as four engines were started, and as four vehicles drove away.

Then he slowly rolled onto his side.

The men were gone.

The cars were gone.

Including the Toyota.

"They said something about a list," Mireia said.

"Fuck," Alex said, "what list?"

"I don't know."

"They have a list," Nicolas said, "and I guess we're not on it. So possibly a list of people who should be shot in the back of the head."

"You sound so goddamn calm," Alex said.

"Sure… calm. You know that I peed myself, right?"

"We should get moving," Mireia said. "We have no supplies and we're in the middle of nowhere."

"We need to figure out where we're moving to," Nicolas said. "How are we supposed to cross the river without that raft?"

"We were going to take the raft to a camp downriver. They were going to let us know what came next."

"What came next? So you don't actually know?"

"The plan is evolving," Alex said. "It's not like we knew this was coming."

"Then why were you practicing the route?"

"It doesn't matter now," Mireia said. "We just need to get to that camp before nightfall."

"It's only midday," Nicolas said.

She sighed. "We don't have a raft anymore. We're going to have to get to that camp on foot. That means eventually leaving the road and hiking in the rainforest."

"There's no way that's safe."

Mireia shrugged. "It's all we've got."

They'd followed a side track for a little while until it curved away. From there, they'd moved into the trees. The heat was oppressive and the terrain was slippery and hard. After two hours of hiking through the bush, Mireia in the lead and trying to keep as straight of a line as they could, they reached a creek.

"Does this take us somewhere?" Nicolas asked.

"I have no idea," Mireia said. "We weren't planning on taking the scenic route."

"Downstream should take us to the river," Alex said.

Mireia shook her head. "But we don't know the river, so even if we get there, we won't know which way to follow it to reach the camp."

"Same thing with tromping blindly through the forest."

"I'm pointing us a little upriver from the camp. Or trying to. We hit the river and head down with the current. Hopefully we won't miss it."

"Fine," Alex said, "we keep going straight." He pushed in front and started leading the way.

Nicolas looked over to Mireia.

She rolled her eyes and smiled.

Then they both followed behind Alex.

It felt like they should be near the river. They'd stayed hydrated, thanks to the constant rain, but the wet had made each step heavy, as their feet sank into the moist groundcover. Nicolas was at a definite disadvantage, since he had only running shoes, while both Mireia and Alex had hiking boots that seemed designed for the wet.

The canvas shoes also made Nicolas paranoid about where he stepped; he'd heard stories of people who unwittingly landed on some poisonous creature and ended up dead.

"We need to stop for a minute," Mireia said.

"You don't look tired," Alex said.

She glanced back at Nicolas, making it obvious that she wanted to give the old guy some time to rest.

"I'm okay," Nicolas said. "We need to keep going."

"See?" Alex said. "He's fine. And he's right. We need to keep going."

Alex tripped.

He didn't make a noise as he went down.

Mireia rushed up to him as he pulled himself up with the help of a branch.

"We should take a break," Mireia said.

"I'm fine," Alex said. He took a heavy breath. Almost a heave.

"What's wrong?"

"I don't... I don't know."

Mireia knelt down to look him over. "Oh my god," she said.

"That bad, huh?"

"You're bleeding."

"Shit."

Nicolas moved up closer.

"Can you feel it, Alex?" Mireia asked.

"I don't feel anything," he said. "What is it?"

She looked over at Nicolas.

She was terrified.

As terrified as Nicolas had been when he'd pissed himself in the muck.

He took a closer look.

It wasn't a bite from a coral snake or some lost limb; it was a small puncture through his left thigh. But there was a great deal of blood, more than Nicolas would have expected.

Alex was bleeding out.

Nicolas started grabbing at his own shirt, trying to pull it off. He was having trouble getting his hands and arms to cooperate. He took a quick breath and tried again.

He pulled off his shirt and started tearing off a strip.

"We need to wrap it," he said. "We need to stop the bleeding."

"Fuck," Mireia said. "Wrap it."

Nicolas tied the strip of fabric around the leg, pulling it tight; he remembered his first aid training well enough.

"It won't work," Mireia said.

"*Estic acabandome*," Alex said. "*Gateta…*"

"No… Queda't amb mi…"

"*Gateta…*"

"How far is it?" Nicolas asked. "To the camp?"

"I don't know," she said. "Too far."

"We can help him out. We can carry him."

"We need to keep him here. I'll stay with him. You get to the camp."

"They have a doctor?"

"How the hell should I know? They'll have something. Just get there, alright?"

"We're going to lose him," Nicolas said.

"Shut up!" She turned back to Alex. "*Carinyo…*"

Alex was unconscious. The t-shirt tourniquet was soaked in blood. Nicolas was watching a man die. Something he'd never seen before, which at that moment seemed strange in itself.

"We need to go," he said, softly.

Mireia didn't respond.

"Mireia… we need to go. We can tell them what happened. At the camp…"

"I'm not going," she said.

"You can't stay here."

"Send someone back for us. I won't leave him out here on his own."

"Come on, Mireia. We've lost him. We need to go."

She glared at him. "Shut up, Nicolas. This is your fault. This is your doing."

"Please, Mireia. Come with me."

"I'd rather die out here."

Nicolas wondered what he'd do if he'd had her stun gun. If it hadn't been left in the Toyota to be stolen by a band of *garimpeiros*. Even if he had a way of pulling her away from Alex's body, it's not like he could carry her all the way to that camp, assuming he'd ever be able to find it.

He could leave her, and head back the way they came. Even in the rain and the dense forest, he was confident he could find his way back to the road.

But what would happen to Mireia? Eventually she'd come out of the shock of losing her husband, and then she'd be alone out there, possibly as night fell.

Would she make it to the camp on her own?

Nicolas honestly couldn't decide it that was his concern.

For all he knew, she and Alex had been the ones to sabotage his project. Even if they hadn't, they seemed to had some insight and yet they'd done nothing to stop it. They'd been watching him, studying him or distracting him, and they'd just let it happen.

And then they'd shot him with a stun gun and dragged him out of his home. Kidnapped him, and they came close to getting him killed.

It was almost some kind of defense for Nicolas; maybe not enough to clear his name, and definitely not enough to save his career.

And he would be a burden to his family back home, a national disgrace.

If there was any chance of redeeming himself, it wasn't something he'd find by heading back.

"I'm going to that camp," he said. "And you're coming with me, Mireia."

"Just shut up and leave me alone," she said.

"Blame me and hate me all you want. Or need to, I suppose. But you say I can help, that there is something we can do. So let's do it."

She didn't respond.

So he just stood in the downpour and waited.

After three or four minutes, she gave her husband a kiss and stood up.

She started walking, back to carving her straight line.

Nicolas didn't say another word as he followed in behind.

❧

They reached the river less than an hour later, and from there Mireia led Nicolas down to the camp. It was larger than he'd expected, with seven wood cabins, a large gazebo, and wooden walkways joining them all together.

Mireia walked directly to what appeared to be a bar.

The man behind the counter took one look at her and started pouring her a drink. He placed a small slip of paper on the bar, then placed the glass overtop.

She sat down on a stool.

Nicolas wasn't sure what to say to her.

Alex was still out there.

"I know," she said, without looking to him.

She picked up the glass of liquor and gave it a quick sip.

Nicolas took the stool beside her.

Mireia picked up the paper. She took another sip.

She nodded to the bartender, then stood up from the stool.

Nicolas wondered if he should have asked for a drink.

He followed her out of the bar.

"They have a pirogue waiting for us," she said. "You know what that is, right?"

"Don't tell me we have to paddle," Nicolas said.

She walked down a trail through the trees, to the river's edge. There was a dock with four long and flat boats; Nicolas had never actually sat in one.

"There's a helicopter landing pad upriver," she said. "About ten minutes away. They should be waiting there for us."

"A helicopter?"

"So I would assume."

"What about Alex?" he asked, trying to be gentle.

She took a deep breath, looking down at her feet.

He'd yet to see her cry.

"Alex is dead," she said.

07

BRIDGET HAWN had long been known to steal things from her older sister. Not just clothing and jewelry, but on one occasion a real live boyfriend.

But Anita had never judged her best friend for being a raging klepto, in particular because Bridget's big sister had purchased herself a Costco membership. And back when Briget and Anita were broke college students trying to eke by in New York City, a stolen member card from Costco was worth its weight in bulk pregnancy tests.

There was only the one Costco in all of Manhattan, and luckily for the students of Cornell Tech, it was only half an hour away if you could afford the $2.50 for the subway.

And since your lunch would be made up of free Costco samples, that $2.50 made you a pretty cheap date.

While the 1% hipstered it out in Brooklyn's Smorgasburg on the weekends, Anita and Bridget would spend Saturday or Sunday (once a week, so as not to arouse suspicion) perusing the aisles of Costco.

Then on one muggy Sunday afternoon in August, Carter Elgin decided to tag along.

"It's a bullshit idea from a career bullshitter," Bridget said as she and Carter tried the microwaved rib sandwiches.

Anita stood back and tried not to smell the samples, not that she didn't like the barbecue sauce part of it.

"You haven't known me long enough to know I'm making this into a career," Carter said.

Bridget smirked. "Only an idiot or a con artist would try to build robots in space. And I know you're not an idiot."

"So I'm an idiot," Anita said. "Message received, bitch."

Bridget laughed and gave her a wink.

Carter didn't join in for the laugh track. There was a chance he didn't know Anita was kidding around.

"We should do that ocean acidification project," Bridget said. "The one we talked to Julian about."

"Julian isn't on that anymore," Anita said.

"That's for the best," Carter said. "Julian's an idiot."

"You know what's great about working with the ocean?" Bridget said.

No one took the bait.

"There's a freaking ocean right across FDR Drive."

"Saving the ocean won't cut it," Anita said. "We need to cool the planet. So unless you want to spend several hundred trillion dollars trying to pull carbon dioxide out of the atmosphere, we should focus on blocking the sunlight. We should do whatever we can, before it's too late."

"I'm not interested in science fiction," Bridget said. "I want science fact, alright?" She chortled a little at herself.

They walked over to the next aisle; Anita spotted what looked like a table with pineapple slices.

"Geoengineering the ocean is a dead end," Carter said. "We don't have the tech right now."

"And we have *the tech* for robots in space?"

Anita laughed. "Have you heard of the Mars rovers, dumbass? Or maybe the Europa probe?"

"The Europa probe that didn't manage to drill through enough ice?"

They reached the pineapple station, discovering surprise mangoes as well. Anita had a feeling the sample lady knew their awful secret. College students tend to give off an air of entitled desperation.

"Listen," Carter said, "I know robotics. Anita, you know mechanical engineering, right?"

"Well, obviously," Anita said. "That's why I'm invited to all the best parties."

"Uh, I'm an engineering student, too," Bridget said. "Or did you forget about me?"

"You two handle the takeoffs and landings," Carter said. "I'll handle the resource extraction and assembly."

Bridget shook her head. "It will never work. When a plan needs five thousand things to go right, you better believe one of those five thousand things will go wrong. Not to mention how hostile things get once you leave the magnetosphere."

Carter gave that Carter smile. "I know," he said.

"What?"

"I know it probably won't work."

"It can work," Anita said. "It has to work."

"Could you be any more earnest?" Carter said with a chuckle.

"Don't be a douche," Bridget said.

"I'm just joking around."

Anita started for the next aisle.

"Hey," Carter said, "Anita. Hold up. I'm sorry, alright? I'm just being... well, a douche. Like she said."

"Don't waste my time," Anita said. "I do this because I actually want to make a difference. Because I believe I can."

"I know. And I really respect that."

"You think I'm just some naive idiot."

"You're an idealist," Bridget said. "And you have really soft hair that smells like lilac."

"We'll do our best," Carter said. "We'll try to raise some money, to do what we can. Even if we don't succeed, we'll get people talking. Maybe people will learn from that and keep going."

"I'm going to keep going," Anita said. "This isn't some cynical cash grab for me."

"It doesn't have to be." He turned to Bridget. "Look, I think we can all agree that sending robots into space is way cooler than dumping weird concoctions into the East River."

"I don't agree," Bridget said.

He laughed. "Yes you do. I'm wearing ya down."

"I want you to take this stuff seriously," Anita said. "I don't want this to feel like some engineering student version of a garage band."

"We had a garage band," Bridget said. "First year, remember? Or dorm band... I had that bass guitar and you had a flute."

"Piccolo."

"Too bad we never found a singer. Or you know, musical ability."

They continued on to another sample table, of crackers and somewhat questionable cheese spread, Bridget recounting more of her and Anita's attempt at fame, and Anita eventually giving in to the reminiscing.

After another ten minutes of browsing for free grub, they reached the far side of the store.

"Do we loop back and try it all again?" Carter asked.

"That's how noobs get caught," Bridget said with a laugh.

"Get caught and then what?"

"A brisk spanking. If you're lucky."

Anita felt the urge to try her hand at being... saucy, maybe? But she knew better than to try and compete with Bridget on that.

She couldn't say for sure that Carter was leaning toward Bridget, at least not 100%, but she had a pretty good idea of how things were moving.

Particularly when Carter followed Bridget's comment up with a slap on the ass.

Bridget giggled, and Anita started looking for a fire exit.

"But seriously," Carter said, "we need to do this. Three extra-good-looking Cornell students out to save the world. We'll be rich as Nazis."

"Anita really does want to save the world," Bridget said. "And that's okay."

"It's not funny," Anita said. "My deep-seated beliefs are not some stupid joke."

"Don't take life so seriously," Carter said. "It'll wear you out."

"I'm not worried about getting worn out."

"So we're really going to do this?" Bridget said. "The stupid space robot thing?"

"Yeah," Carter said. "The space robot thing. We'll shoot a video, throw it up on Kickstarter."

"And how do we get anyone on the planet to actually notice?" Anita asked.

Carter shrugged. "Wet t-shirt contest?"

"I have some ideas about that," Bridget said. "Just let me chew on it a little while."

When Anita reached the residence later that afternoon, after Bridget and Carter had veered off as what seemed to be evolving into a couple, she sat down at her laptop and started trying to collect her thoughts.

That was the first set of notes she'd written on the sunshield, and even after more than twenty years, Anita still had those notes saved.

She read them as she waited on the bench at the St. George ferry terminal. Sometimes she winced at the idealistic idiot she used to be. But she missed that girl, too.

She missed being someone who still believed in something good.

She missed the days before the world and Carter Elgin had chewed her up and spit her out.

As much as it had bothered her to have to give in, Anita had messaged Danny Pyke to accept his offer with Turnpike. She'd take his 0.5% stake and the small retainer, and in return she'd spit on his terrible ideas.

He'd replied enthusiastically, and had mentioned that he would like her to accompany him, on a trip out to their test range at Wallops Island.

That meant two hours by train and just over an hour on Interstate 101, assuming Danny would have arranged for a driverfree for the express lane. And that seemed very much like something Danny Pyke would have arranged.

They reached the launch pad just after lunchtime, and Anita wondered if she should warn Danny about just how cranky she can get when she doesn't eat. But then she realized that he was probably paying her specifically because of that crank.

She recognized the rocket on the pad: a Falcon Heavy; an oldie but a goody, and probably overkill for the stage Danny's project had reached.

Rocketry isn't like most things; you don't use the most expensive hammer for the easiest bunch of nails, because that very expensive hammer might blow up on the pad. And then you've spent three times as much as you needed to on your test rocket.

You start with something cheap to get your tests into orbit.

A Tsiolkovsky Vosmoy, for instance. Or one of those Chinese lifters. Even just a smaller Falcon, if you really love the gold-plated stuff.

"I know," Danny said. "Wrong rocket."

She smiled. Somehow.

"It's American-built and it looks really impressive to investors. And that matters."

"I'm sure it does. Money talks louder than common sense."

"That covers a good five thousand years of human history, yeah."

"So this really is what you're using?"

"It's not, actually," he said. "Haven't chosen our launchers yet. But I can almost rationalize using these guys. Use a well-known lifter for the big dance. Less unknowns to worry about."

"Sure. If you were worried about the lift, and not everything but."

"So you must be wondering why you're here."

"Certainly not to show me off to your fancy investors," she said.

"Actually—"

"Fuck you, Danny."

"You look great, Ms. Singhal."

"That's not the point," she said. But she knew he could tell she was pleased by the sentiment. Particularly how it even seemed sincere. "I'd like to know when I'm just another stupid prop."

"You're way more than that, Anita."

She sighed. She did want to punch him. "So what is it you're gonna do? Shoot some video?"

"Good guess."

"Forget it."

"But it's part of your contract. It's what you agreed to."

What she hadn't bothered to read before signing. Not that she hadn't known it would be in there. Not just other duties as assigned, but probably an entire clause on publicity. She just hadn't expected it to happen on Day One.

Which she realized was pretty goddamn stupid of her.

"You have some stupid script for me to read from?" she asked.

"No need. Whole thing will be a voiceover, just some shots of us speaking intently in front of this beautiful and borrowed piece of engineering."

"Fuck you, Danny."

He laughed.

Obviously she wasn't as intimidating now that he owned her.

After the stupid video shoot, Danny took her on a tour of the facility, including the NASA pieces that had little to do with his project.

But anyone who'd spent anytime looking her up would know that Anita Singhal still loves all that space shit, even if it up and ruined her life.

It was nearly 4 pm when they'd finished sightseeing, and Anita was surprised that her empty stomach hadn't led her to kill and eat her tour guide.

But Danny suggested an early dinner before heading back on the 101, and Anita agreed, and he then spent fifteen minutes apologizing about the restaurant he'd chosen.

As if he couldn't have chosen some place else, especially since it took over an hour to get to the oyster house, which stood vigil over the ocean next to an old wooden watchtower.

Anita's mother had always told her that only a monster would eat meat; this hadn't meshed well with her father's policy that he deserved mutton at least once a week, whether or not anyone ate it.

Anita had fallen somewhere in between when she was younger, but it had been over five years since the last time she'd eaten an animal.

And she certainly wasn't about to eat oysters.

But she watched as Danny went whole hog, eating like he hadn't eaten all day. Which, she realized, it was possible he hadn't.

Anita found it amusing, that he was stuffing his face on fresh seafood, that he'd brought a vegetarian there in the first place, and that after she'd ordered her Bahama Mama he'd asked for a lemon water. But the kicker was that the menu had only one vegetarian option, something with humus and garlic and pita bread that was definitely treated as an afterthought.

But the cocktail was good. Princess of the Hive, with enough wine in it to make it Anita-friendly.

Danny had a bottle of beer.

"Are you still friends with Carter?" he asked her.

No one ever asks her about Bridget.

"That's a pretty personal question, boss."

"Then give me a vague answer or something."

"I still talk to him," she said. "And to Bridget. Not that my lawyer thinks it's a good idea."

"Everyone knows you were the brains of the operation."

"That's not even true. Co-brains, maybe."

He spilled some oyster sauce on his shirt.

She snickered a little.

"Now the car will smell like clam," he said. "Sorry."

"I don't think you're sorry at all. I think you like causing these types of little annoyances. To see what kind of response you get."

He grinned. "You really are the brains."

"Don't tell me the contract says I have to listen to this crap."

That didn't seem to bother him. He went back to eating.

"So will this be every day at work?" she asked. "Surprise video shoots and watching you slop seafood all over yourself?"

"Tomorrow the real fun starts. We'll have a meeting, connect with the entire team. Early morning, if that's okay. We got folks in India who will be dialing in."

"Just provide me some kind of schedule," she said. "That's all I ask."

"Once I have it, I'll send it."

"Is that supposed to be a joke?"

"Don't worry, Anita. We'll figure all this out. How to work together and everything else."

"This isn't how you do it," she said.

"What?"

"This flightiness. The off-the-cuff scheduling. The disorganization. Adopting Carter Elgin's bad habits won't make you the next Carter Elgin. You can't fake genius and expect to make genius."

"Are you serious?"

"I know you aren't used to this," she said, "to people talking to you like this."

"Not a lot of people treat the boss like pig shit, no."

"It's part of my charm, I guess."

"I do like it a little, but please… not in front of the team tomorrow."

"I can't promise anything," she said. "I'll just say what I'm thinking."

"You don't say *everything* you're thinking."

"No, I pretty much do."

"Then tell me, Ms. Singhal," he said. "Tell me why you think this project is going to fail."

"I told you yesterday. Trying to build both laser transmitters and receivers completely in situ, without any real idea how you'll pull it off, putting your Rebote Constellation way too close to the sun—"

"No. Even if I do everything you tell me to do, you still think I'm going to fail."

She didn't know what to say to that.

How do you tell someone they're right when you know it makes you look like a complete ass?

"Just be honest," he said. "Like you want to believe you are."

"Because you're doing it for the wrong reasons."

"My *profit motive*."

"You don't care about open communications to Mars or anywhere else."

"There are easier ways to build a business."

"If the US government offered you a billion dollars to build it for them, you'd take it."

"The US government already has a system they use. It isn't good enough, what with the weeks of blackout time, but they do get to control it."

"And if yours is better, they might just make an offer, right?"

He didn't deny it.

"Doesn't even need to be the US, right?" she said. "If China wanted to get in on the ground floor, you'd let them."

"I don't see how any of this speculation means the whole project is going to fail. You're the only person on the team who seems bothered by the business plan."

"I haven't seen the business plan, Danny. But that's not the point."

"Then what is the point, Ms. Singhal?" He kept switching his tone just as often as how he addressed her.

"The point is that you're not passionate about it. You just want to build cool stuff in space. You want to build something cooler than what's out there already."

"That's why everyone does it."

"No," she said. "That isn't why. It's never been about that. Not for anyone who's actually made it work."

"You're serious…"

"We wanted to save the world. At least I did."

"And what about Carter?"

"I sold him on it," she said. "He was like you. And that's not a compliment."

"Then sell me on it."

"On what? An open, crowd-controlled communication system for the entire inner system?"

"Yeah… but everything else, too. Saving the world." He smiled. "I guess that sounds pretty cheesy."

"It doesn't work like that. That's not what I mean. It's not a goddamn sales pitch."

"It doesn't have to be, Anita. I just want you to help me. I can't do this if you don't think I can. You're too smart for me to dismiss all of this." He pulled out his tablet, sliding the keyboard out from the fold. "If we can meet at 7 am, at my office. Tell me what you think we need to do. Tell me how we can make this work."

"What if we can't make it work?"

"Please, Anita. Whatever it takes. We'll try it."

She nodded.

He thanked her quietly, then went back to work on his oysters.

Bridget had gone home for Thanksgiving, as had most of the non-New Yorkers at Cornell Tech.

Carter Elgin didn't bother with holidays, and Anita's family had never bothered with Thanksgiving in particular, not to mention that Wisconsin was pretty far away. So they spent the break on the project, doing whatever they didn't need Bridget for. Which, as they'd both suspected, was pretty much everything.

They were eating pizza in Anita and Bridget's suite, pizza that Carter had paid for, since Anita had made it clear she wasn't about to spend money on food when there was ramen, a bowl, and a microwave.

He'd ordered one extra large pie, with pineapple and sundried tomato, exactly what Anita liked; he'd said he didn't need meat on his half, and she hadn't fought him on it.

They worked through their meal, which was spaced over several hours, neither of them saying much to the other.

Anita knew she'd have to buckle down soon enough, and figure out the shield itself, but for the moment she felt like she needed to get into the flow of the project by starting with something a little more... she couldn't really call any of it *basic*.

Anita had three different vehicles to design, a rocket to take off from somewhere on Long Island, a lander that would be expelled from that rocket in geostationary transfer orbit and would make its way out to one of the three NEOs they'd identified as possibles, and the little guys who would be sent from that flying rock out to block a little piece of the sun.

If she'd only had to design the first one, she'd have had a manageable project. Even if she'd wanted to do it from scratch, which she didn't need to do with all the stuff that's already been done. That first rocket was the easy part. It was everything else that seemed near impossible.

She knew Carter's tasks weren't any better; he had to take what had come before in robotic spaceflight—which wasn't all that much—and blend it together with the latest in 3D printing. Multi-material printing had only been around for eight or nine years, partly because it was long and hard enough to print something from one simple ingredient.

So to extract those ingredients from a goddamn asteroid and then somehow assemble them into a reflective solar shield, autonomously and *in space*... if her stuff was impossible, his stuff was at least twice as bad.

And all he was trying to do for step one was determine what building materials he could extract from an S-type object, and how he would actually pull it off with his custom designed *outer space robots*.

There was a reason no one had done it, why no one had even talked about it outside of science fiction. Maybe Bridget was right, and they should have done something with the carbon stores in the ocean. Or maybe the answer really was in sequestration, like one her profs had said.

Anita knew why she was doing it; she was a naive idiot. But why was Carter doing it? Did he really believe that Bridget would be able to raise the money? That they could really sell this crazy idea to people?

"You stick your tongue out when you're concentrating," he said.

"Sorry."

"I like it. A real tic of genius."

"Tic of genius?"

"Yeah. Like a sign that you're running a little hotter than most people."

"So panting like a dog?"

He laughed. "I like to be around smart people, Anita. Smart girls are so hot right now."

"Tell that to my quiet Saturday nights."

"I'm pretty sure you'll be spending Saturday night with me," he said. "Saving the world."

"Heh."

"What?"

"Nothing," she said. "I'm just not sure what we're doing here."

"Eating pizza that is no longer hot."

"You don't really believe in this, do you?"

"Not yet."

"Oh." She'd expected more, somehow.

"But I believe that you believe in it."

"That might just be some circular reasoning."

"Not circular at all. *Do you even science?*"

She laughed.

"I love that laugh," he said. "Like a rapid-fire machine gun."

"My mother says it's more like a hyena, actually."

"She should know. She's your mom. I bet she's a scientist, too. You seem like the family business kind of scientist."

"Oh, so not passionate on my own?"

"No, no," he said, "just that you seem so comfortable with it."

"My mother's an admissions officer for the University of Wisconsin. But she loves astronomy. She bought me my first telescope, set it up for me, helped me with the first light."

"Let me guess," he said. "Crab nebula. Girls love the crab."

"The moon," Anita said, laughing. "I was six."

"Well, I'm glad she did all that. There's something special going on with you. Something in that big brain of yours. You know, you ought to have a much more pronounced case of *fivehead*..."

"That's not something you ever say to a woman."

"I can tell that we've got something here. Seriously. Like some kind of lightning that we just need to... to harness."

"That was way less articulate than I would have expected."

He smiled. And he was looking at her differently. The way she'd wanted him to, before she'd known he was more a fan of Bridget.

He looked away.

She felt embarrassed, but she didn't know why.

"I think we can get something from this," he said. "I don't think anyone could pull it all off, not from nothing. But I think we're clearing a path."

"Clearing a path. How wonderful. Like lawnmowers."

"Like *Sputnik*."

She almost laughed. It sounded so corny. So ridiculous.

Even to someone as ridiculously naive as Anita.

08

THE END of Benjamin McPherson's career went about as well as could be expected. And much better than it could have gone, all things considered. His supervisor asked him to come to her office, and both her boss and four security personnel were on hand for the big talk.

Amelia acted like he'd never come to her the day before, and Benj went along, since ranting about Q Group didn't seem like a magic wand to get him his job back.

Amelia's boss took a moment to let Benj know what a huge disappointment he was, how his recklessness had destroyed not only his career but those of two of his coworkers, and how he'd be lucky if charges do not result.

Benj just nodded.

He felt like he was a kid getting suspended from grade school.

All four of the security officers escorted him out, two driving him to the outer gate while the other two—having taken his keys while searching him—retrieved his car. He asked about his stuff, and one of the men bluntly told him that it would be shipped to his house.

Benj got in his car and drove up toward Redwood Road. He noticed that a security patrol car was following him.

He continued off base and north into Bluffdale.

Once he saw the patrol car turn back, he pulled into a fuel station parking lot. He didn't need a full charge, but he charged up anyway.

Once that was done he sat down in the front seat and waited, looking at funny animal pictures on his left lens.

He got the message from Malik around ten minutes later.

Benj was not surprised by the hate.

He told Malik where he was, that they should talk in person.

He didn't get a reply back.

He continued to wait.

He saw Laila's jeep first, pulling into the parking lot.

She parked a couple spaces away from him, which meant as far as she could, since there were only five spaces in total and he was smack in the middle.

She didn't look at him. She just stayed in her jeep.

Benj followed her lead and didn't get out.

Malik pulled in a few seconds later on his bike.

He parked beside Laila.

She got out just as Malik climbed off his motorcycle.

They walked toward Benj's car. He got out, expecting the worst.

"This is fucked up," Malik said, his voice shaking. "This is so fucked up."

"It's not true," Benj said. "Whatever they told you."

Malik shook his head. "It's the NSA. Of course it isn't true. But you must have done something, asshole."

"It's that conspiracy BS," Laila said. "They caught you on some stupid group, and now they're cleaning house."

"Haven't heard from Taylor or Cam," Malik said.

"It's just the three of us," Benj said. "That's all they needed."

"I'm pretty sure Laila's right about you," Malik said to him. "I know it wasn't me that caused this."

Benj took a deep breath. "Look, I can't really tell you all of it. All I can say is that it isn't what you think."

"Don't do this," Laila said. "Don't treat us like a couple of idiots, Benj. Just take responsibility."

"It is my fault. Or it's because of me, at least."

"I should knock you out," Malik said. "Right here in this parking lot. You ruined our careers. All of our careers. Not just yours."

"Do you think anyone will even touch us?" Laila asked. "Who wants to hire us now? They said it's going on our record. That we were somehow responsible for wiping several quads of data. This is like being blackballed."

"I'm sorry," Benj said. "I wish I could explain this all."

"Fuck you, Benj," Malik said. He turned to Laila. "We'll figure something out. Without this piece of garbage."

He walked back to his bike.

He was waiting for Laila.

But she was still standing by Benj's car.

"I need to know," she said. "I deserve to know."

"Don't bother," Malik called out. "He'll just make some shit up."

Laila didn't leave.

Malik drove off.

"I don't want to believe it," she said. "I want it to be something else. But you can't lie to me."

"I can't…"

She shook her head at him. "You really ruined things here, Benj. You really messed it all up." She started to cry.

She turned and started walking away.

He wanted to stop her.

But he didn't.

She got into her jeep and gave him another glance.

He looked down at his feet.

And didn't look up until she'd driven away.

Benj went home and didn't drink.

He didn't do anything.

He just sat at his kitchen table, his glasses off and set down beside him.

He knew something else would happen, but he wasn't sure it would be actually Samantha Yoon and some secret mission. It might be the FBI with an arrest warrant. Or some other group of Feds, maybe someone from Q Group who would tersely inform him that there was no special plan for him, that he was just a terminated employee ripe for interrogation.

He felt like he'd lost control of everything, and that he'd never even had a chance to be the one who fucked it up. It wasn't what he'd done, not at all. His apparent ruining of his life—and those of his friends—had happened completely outside of him, but he would be the one to wear it.

He wondered how many other people had gone through the same thing. Those stories you'd hear when people just get fucked by the universe. That guy who accidentally run over that mob boss' kid. That woman who was eaten by coyotes. That guy who was killed by a flying fire hydrant.

And that hapless moron at the Utah Data Center who hung himself after getting completely fucked over by some cute software chick who claimed to be from Q Group.

Nah, he wouldn't give her that.

If she really was fucking him over, he'd find a way to fuck her right back. There was something dark and violent in that thought, something he let seep in a little longer than he knew he ought to. Then he tried not to think about it, about that mix of attraction and anger, that urge to hurt her, the power he'd feel.

But he was thinking about it.

It started to make him sick.

That wasn't who he was. He'd decided that, long ago.

He went to his fridge and pulled out his special tupperware container. His most recent import from Colorado, since they'd somehow managed to still keep it illegal in both Utah and Wyoming.

He rolled a joint and lit it.

And laughed.

What would the great Derrick McPherson think of his son, unemployed and smoking up in his crappy little apartment? Back to square fucking one. When life gives you lemons, get baked. That's the lesson you take to heart when your father doesn't bother sticking around. It's really the same thing, isn't it? A lesson he'd learned from the best? Things get tough and you take off, whether that means running off to Europe without your kid or smoking a joint in your tastefully-squalid living room.

The result is pretty much the same.

Nothing gets fixed.

You just pretend you don't give a shit.

There was a knock at the door at eleven in the morning.

Better than a SWAT team coming in through the front entrance as well as the balcony.

Benj walked over, expecting Samantha, and preparing to lose his shit.

It was Laila.

"Hi," he said. He wasn't about to tell her that she shouldn't be there. No one had told him he had to keep people away.

"I want you to show me what you did," she said.

"What?"

"Whatever you got yourself into… this conspiracy stuff."

"It's not—"

"Just show me, Benj."

He stepped to the side to let her in.

"Where's your tablet?" she asked.

"It's not on my tablet. Or my eyepiece."

"Why can't you just own up to this?"

Benj pulled out his tablet and handed it to her.

She unfolded it and started pinching the screen with her left hand.

"You should be using an anonymizer for this stuff," she said. "Hardware's better. Do you have that set up?"

"I'm pretty sure I understand networking, Laila."

She shot him a glare. "No. Apparently you don't understand it nearly well enough."

"I use a hardwired BlackBrick router running three different anonymizers. That's three whole onions, not one onion with three layers."

"That doesn't make sense," she said. "How does stacking software routers do anything?"

"It doesn't stack, it rotates. And spits some less critical stuff in the clear. Makes it that much harder to put together any kind of profile on me. And harder to eavesdrop. And harder for bad apples—"

"So you're saying they didn't find anything? That you've been looking at stuff you shouldn't, but they have no way of knowing?"

"I'm not looking at anything, Laila. Nothing incriminating."

"No weird clown porn?"

"That's perfectly legal and not at all weird, thank you."

She sighed. "So why the heck am I out of a job, Benj? You say it's because of you."

"It's Q Group," he said.

"I can't believe that. Why would any of us matter to Q Group?"

"Because of my father."

"Your father."

"Derrick McPherson."

She rolled her eyes. "I know who your father is, Benj. I just don't see why it matters. Unless you've been talking to him about something—"

"No, it's not that."

But he could see from her face that she knew, that she could tell he wasn't being completely honest.

She could tell.

She knew him better than he would have thought. Or maybe she just knew people in general.

He had to tell her something. Whatever she came up with on her own would be worse. Would probably be more likely to get him in trouble. The truth wasn't really that bad.

"My father asked me to look into something," he said. "I honestly don't know if *they* know."

"Well obviously they know, since you got your stupid butt fired."

"They want me to do something for them. For Q Group."

"So they fired you? That's not usually how department transfers go."

"I don't know what they want me to do, but it's something the bosses can't know about."

"And so you told me. Sure, Benj. Totally believable. This is so stupid. So incredibly stupid. You can't even tell me the truth."

"Samantha Yoon is from Q Group. She's the one who told me. I expect her to show up here sometime between now and right after her normal shift. Depends on if she was suspended or not."

"So that's one person who didn't end up getting fired because of you. Congratulations."

"Look, I can't expect you to believe me," he said. "So wait here with me, if you want, and you can ask Samantha yourself when she shows up."

She stared blankly at him.

He didn't know what that meant.

She walked over to his couch and sat down. And glared some more.

Benj regretted the offer. Was he going to have her there all day?

"Or I could just call you later," he said.

"Or you could just tell me what the heck is going on."

He paced a little in front of the couch.

"Well?" she said.

"It has to do with that European space station. Not sure what. And I'm not sure if my father's involved somehow, or if Samantha came to me because she assumed I'd want to help. That they can trust me because of it."

"And what value do you bring to this cabal?"

"Cabal?"

"Need a dictionary?"

"I don't know why they want me. Or what I'd even do. I don't know anything, Laila."

"Clearly."

"So I'll call you?"

"I got nowhere to be."

"I've got to step out for a few minutes, actually, so—"

"You said she would be coming here. You're waiting on her. So I'll wait, too. Maybe I'll be able to find out why she's messing with us."

"I don't think that's such a great plan."

"Because you made it up. Because you screwed us over and decided to make up some crazy story that only an idiot would believe."

"Fine. Wait here. I'm sure she'll love seeing you here."

"I honestly don't care what she wants to see."

"Yeah, I know."

After an hour and a half of the most awkward wait in human history, Benj received a message on his tablet, since his eyepiece was still on the kitchen table.

From Samantha Yoon.

I can't wait to come by tonight and see you, honey. I hope you're okay. We just need some alone time together, you know?

A motherfucking code. He wasn't stupid.

She knew Laila was there and she wanted her to not be there when she arrived.

And all the while pretending she and Benj were a couple.

Fuck.

He decided to message her back.

Can't wait.

Not entirely dishonest, if he were to ignore the dread and then focus on wanting to get Laila out of his apartment.

He handed his tablet over to her.

"She won't be here until later," he said.

Laila took it and started checking it over.

"This is the second message she's ever sent you," she said.

"I thought you'd already checked on that kind of thing."

"I had. I'm just pointing it out."

"Yeah... alright, then."

"She's not very good at this."

"What?"

"It doesn't feel natural," she said.

"Oh, I see. You have NSA disease. You think you can decipher everyone's secret plans just from a couple of text messages."

"That's not the least bit funny."

"Then tell me your theory," Benj said. He tried not to sound like an ass.

"I don't have a theory. Not yet. I just know that there's something really wrong with that woman."

"Because she called me 'honey'?"

"That's a definite red flag," she said. She had a little bit of a smile. "But I'm starting to get that you're being messed with."

"And I'm sorry I dragged you and Malik into it."

"I'll just wait and see. See if I have a good reason to hate you."

Benj nodded.

And put his glasses back on.

And then they both waited.

Samantha Yoon arrived at 5:15 pm.

She took one look at Laila, still sitting on the couch, and shook her head. "You don't realize what this means," she told him.

"She needs to know the truth," Benj said. "You got her fired, Sam."

"Oh, okay, then. I'll just hand her a secret dossier and get her up to date on everything."

She just let that statement hang in the air.

Laila had switched her gaze and disdain over to Samantha.

Samantha walked over to the couch.

"I had to call this in," she said. "You shouldn't have talked to her about it, Benj."

"Call this in?" Laila said. "What's that supposed to mean? You already got me fired… bitch."

Samantha frowned. "It's going to get a lot worse."

Laila got up from the couch.

Benj started moving in between them.

"You will need to be detained," Samantha said. "From what I've been told they've already sent a car for Malik."

"I'm not afraid of you," Laila said.

"They won't come here. You need to go home and pack a bag. Don't try to run."

"Or what, they'll kill me?"

"Unless you have a wad of cash and a fake moustache, they'll track you down before midnight. Especially if you don't toss your tablet into a storm drain."

"This has gone too far, Samantha," Benj said. "This is not okay."

"I'm sorry I didn't explain how this works," Samantha told him. "I guess I figured you would have a little more common sense. You told your friend Laila about me and Q Group, so now she can't stick around to tell everyone else."

"But she could pull out her tablet right now and text someone."

"That's a bad idea."

"Sounds like pretty good insurance," Laila said. "I should broadcast to everyone in my contacts."

"Okay," Samantha said. "Go ahead. I'll wait."

Laila took out her tablet. She took a quick look and put it back in her pocket.

Benj took a look at his.

"I guess the network's down," Samantha said. "What an unfortunate coincidence. Must be some kind of late-season snowstorm."

Laila looked angry enough to start swinging, but she sat back down on the couch.

"So what happens now?" Benj asked.

"Laila leaves so we can get moving on this," Samantha said.

"No. To Laila."

"I already covered that. She goes home, she packs a bag, and someone will be around to pick her up. Actually, drive her out in her car. Extended vacation."

"You can't do that."

"You know they can," Laila said. "If she really is from Q Group. They can make me disappear forever."

"It's not forever," Samantha said. "And I really wish it wasn't happening at all. But you need to be moved out of here for a while. A few weeks, at least."

"And what if I just smash something big and heavy over your head," Laila said, "and Benj and I lock you in a closet and we take off?"

"Take off where? And with how many fake moustaches? You can kill me and it wouldn't help. It'll just make your detention a little more permanent."

"This is stupid," Benj said. "Laila isn't going to tell anyone anything. Right, Laila?"

"Oh," Samantha said, "so like a pinky promise? That's different."

"Come on."

"Laila needs to go home and pack a bag. That's the smart choice right now."

Samantha Yoon was maybe five foot five. Definitely not much more than a hundred and thirty pounds. And Benj saw no indication that she was armed.

She'd given him no concrete evidence that she really was from Q Group, or that there was a reason to trust her at all. Why didn't his boss know what was going on? Or his boss's boss?

For all he knew, she was the bad guy. Some crazy from the EFF looking to sabotage data collection. Or a spy from the new Chinese government. Even just an untreated schizophrenic.

What would happen if he and Laila just left? Would there really be unmarked sedans and black helicopters trailing them?

Did she bring the network done with nothing more powerful than some signal jammer sitting in her car?

What would his father have done?

"I don't know why I'm supposed to trust you," he said to Samantha. "So far you've done a great job of ruining our lives."

"I have something for that," she said. "Once Laila leaves."

"I'm not leaving," Laila said.

Samantha was looking to Benj. "She needs to leave."

"I can't make her leave," Benj said. "It's not like I'm going to call the cops on her."

"The more I show her the bigger a risk she becomes."

"I'll take that risk," Laila said.

Samantha rolled her eyes. "That's not what I mean at all."

"Just give me a reason to trust you," Benj said. "And give Laila a reason to believe any of what you're saying."

Samantha reached into her pocket.

Benj stepped back, mostly on instinct.

She pulled out a small tablet. Small and with what looked like a very hardened case. Not something that unfolds for movie time.

She swiped the screen, then input a passcode. Then she swiped once more, then entered a code again.

She handed him the tablet.

A photo on screen. An aerial photo, satellite probably.

Of what looked like a launch site.

"Wenchang Launch Centre," she said. "Hainan Island."

"I've heard of it," Benj said. "The public face of the Chinese space program."

"And this is the rocket." She pointed to one of four launch pads. "A Long March 7, until they rename them for something less *Mao-y*. This is from three weeks ago."

"That means little to nothing to me."

"Went up to Tiangong Station. Resupply run. Two new crew members for the rotation."

"Still nothing."

She swiped the screen. The next photo was a radar image. "They dropped something out of the crew capsule."

"What?"

"They dropped something. Two somethings, actually."

"Like space junk?"

"You can see them if you look closely." She pointed to two bright but tiny dots, one much smaller than the other. "This big one's the decoy. They're hoping we don't notice the little guy."

"And what's the little guy for?"

"To see if we spot it," she said. "It's a test."

"A test for what?"

She swiped again. Another radar image. "It's moving out from LEO."

"Moving out... moving higher."

"Yeah. Maybe even moving out of Earth's orbit. Small thrusts, taking its sweet time, and looking a little like that space junk you were talking about."

"And you think it's just a test."

"We know the NSA has been infiltrated, among other federal entities. By the Chinese, by the Russians, and probably even by SolRescue and the Europeans."

"Quid pro quo," Laila said.

"So that's where the secret starts," Benj said. "The cover up."

"There has been some concern among certain legislators," Samantha said, "that the US Executive knows about this Chinese project, and that they may actually be working *with* them."

"And you're talking all the way to the President."

"Yeah. And so we need to make sure the Chinese and the Executive Branch think that we didn't see that little guy."

"But what does this have to do with any of us?" Laila asked.

"Two birds with one stone," Samantha said. "We take Benj out and put him to work, and we get an incident that covers up some convenient data loss."

"All the initial chatter about the Chinese satellites," Laila said.

"That's mostly right. It won't make it to the analysts. And what will end up being reconstructed from the lost data won't mention that smaller guy."

"But why do you need me?" Benj asked. "Can't you just pack me up and lock me away with Laila and Malik?"

"No one's getting locked away. It's more of an outpatient type of thing. A heavily-monitored sabbatical."

"That sounds farfetched," Laila said.

"Well, none of that's my fault."

Laila let out a low-pitched growl. "It's completely your fault."

Benj looked over to her. She sighed and looked away.

"We got you a new job, Benj," Samantha said. "It's a great fit. IT manager for an aerospace company that's just coming on line."

"What?" Benj asked. "What company? What are you talking about?"

"It's called Turnpike Exploration Tech. Out of Manhattan, but they have a launch site at Wallops Island, in Virginia."

"You want me to move to the East Coast? Without seeing any formal offer?"

"I have all that stuff. Don't worry so much. But it's more of a travelling position ATM."

"ATM?"

"At the moment."

"Travel to where?"

"I think you can make an educated guess. I'll give you a hint: holy fuck it's cold."

"And what about me?" Laila asked. "You can't just get me a job there, too? I'm just as qualified as he is. I'm more qualified, actually."

"She already knows what's going on," Benj said. "I think she could be an asset."

Samantha chuckled. "You guys are so new at this," she said.

"What's that supposed to mean?" Laila asked.

"This isn't some exciting new adventure for our fearless hero. We aren't in the market for a plucky sidekick with some serious junk in the trunk—"

"You're a real bitch," Laila said.

"This is a national security issue and not something we're running off the cuff. Benjamin is an asset, because of his father and because of his profile. Laila is a liability, because we know enough about her to have made a reasoned judgement."

"So you ruin my life and that's that."

"It's temporary," Samantha said. "That's all you need to keep in mind."

"You're a real piece of work."

"Is that different than being a bitch? Did something change? Either way, you need to get home to pack that bag."

"That's not happening," Laila said.

"Well, it needs to start happening. This shit doesn't involve you, Laila. You're just collateral damage."

Laila stood up again. "Are you trying to get me to hit you?"

"I'm being honest," Samantha said. "That's what you need right now."

"You can shut up about what I need."

"Laila," Benj said, "please. Just go home. There's no reason for you to be here."

"So you're okay with this," she asked him. "You're okay with me being treated like garbage?"

He shrugged. "I can't fix this. I'm sorry."

First the glare.

And then the moment came when Laila up and spit in his face.

"I really expected more from you, Benj," she said.

She walked away as he wiped the mess away with his arm.

She left without saying anything else.

"I need to know..." he said. "That she's gonna be okay."

"I hope so," Samantha said. "I really can't make this all better, Benj."

"You still haven't convinced me. These images. They don't really mean anything."

"They mean enough to most people. But I'm not sure that really matters."

"What? Why?"

"Because you're unemployed and I just got you a job offer and a plane ticket."

"And whoever's keeping tabs on all of this... they won't notice me taking a business trip right after getting fired?"

She chuckled. "That's exactly how this stuff works. A go-getter like you, guy with enough initiative to fuck over the NSA? Of course you'd have something lined up."

"That sounds insane."

"Maybe let me handle the optics, okay? I think you've made enough mistakes since we started this."

"I guess I'm just not used to being some witless pawn," he said.

She shook her head. "I doubt it. You are a child of divorce, aren't you?"

He stood there for a few seconds with his mouth open. Like a fool.

"Last I checked, we elected the President," Benj said. "I don't remember casting a vote for Q Group. So even if this is all really true, why am I supposed to take your side?"

"Because we think the President of the United States is colluding with the Chinese military government to take control of the sunshield, by any means necessary. That's why they've stepped up attacks on the SolRescue network. That's why the Chinese are testing out stealth satellites. And that's why the US has reactivated that launch site in Churchill, the one you've been looking up in your spare time and pretending to know nothing about."

"Yeah, okay…"

"And that's why your father got you to provide him with comm logs between two ESA workers in French Guiana."

"What?"

"Yeah, you didn't cover your tracks, Benj. We've covered them for you, though, so you're welcome. So now it's not just that *we know* that someone caused that space station mishap, but we know that SolRescue knows it now, too."

"I'm pretty sure you got that all wrong," Benj said. "I didn't do anything like that."

"Don't waste my time, alright?"

He nodded.

"So you take the job and you take the flight to Churchill and you do what we ask of you," she said. "And then when it's all done you take your newly padded resume and you find some place else to work. Pretty simple, really."

"And that's it. I lose my friends and my home—"

"And avoid federal prison. You know, for espionage and maybe treason. Do you understand what kind of level you're playing on, now? This isn't slap-on-the-wrist land anymore." She sighed. "God, I'd really wanted to have this conversation someplace more… inspired. Such an important time in your life, Benj. Important for both of us."

What the hell was she talking about?

He wanted to slap her. So much.

He gave another nod. That was all he could do.

09

AN OLDER black man in a straw hat was waiting at the dock along the Approuague river.

Mireia pulled the pirogue into position. She waved an arm at the dock, and Nicolas, after a moment of uncertainty, hopped out, holding on to the mooring rope.

Mireia tied the hitch, then the two of them walked up to the man in the hat.

"Monsieur Clouatre," the man said. "I'm glad to meet you." He held out his hand and Nicolas shook it.

The man turned to Mireia.

He wrapped his arms around her. "I'm so sorry, Mireia."

She started to cry.

Nicolas held back on interrupting.

After ten seconds or so, the man turned back to him.

"I'm Derrick McPherson," he said. "I work with Carter Elgin at Sol-Rescue. Alex and Mireia are good friends of mine. And of Carter's."

"I have no idea what I'm supposed to be doing," Nicolas said. "I really don't know what's happening."

"We need to get moving," the man said. "We wouldn't want the Foreign Legion to spot us."

He walked them up a short trail to a helipad, where a small white and red helicopter was waiting.

"Where are we going?" Nicolas asked.

"Into Brazil," the man said.

"What's in Brazil?"

"It's what's not in Brazil that matters right now."

The four-storey and 20th century contemporary Hotel Manaós wasn't as fancy as what you'd find in the cores of most European cities, but it was a welcome change from the muck and murderous *garimpeiros* you'd find a few hundred kilometers to the north.

And the room—with only one bed—that Derrick McPherson had arranged for Nicolas and Mireia had a view of the Teatro Amazonas, the historic Manaus opera house with Italian marble columns and a dome of painted tiles in the green, yellow and blue of Brazil.

And there was coffee, which tasted fresh despite the packaging, and a clean and dry bathrobe to wear while his only set of clothes was laundered.

But it was uncomfortable being there with Mireia, not just because she'd just lost her husband in the rainforest, but because Nicolas felt like an interloper, like he didn't belong in the same room with someone who seemed so much stronger and self-assured despite the pain she was feeling.

She'd cried only once that he'd seen, when Derrick had held her; after that she'd dried her eyes and kept on.

And now she was sitting on a couch in her own white terrycloth robe, browsing on a small tablet that Derrick had provided. He'd given one to Nicolas, too, but he hadn't done anything with it. He knew that as bad as he expected the news to be, that it would likely be worse than he could have imagined.

There's a savagery to being the most hated man of the day that he knew he'd never be able to handle. The concept that so many people he'd never met would hate him more than anyone else they could name, his only fame being those lies about him.

"It's not that bad," Mireia said, without looking up. "Not that it's good."

"How bad is not that bad?"

"That we were saboteurs, that you and Alex and I were in a sexual relationship."

"All three of us?"

"That's what Simon Montet is saying."

"*Putain*," Nicolas stammered.

"He never liked you. Jealousy."

"I didn't like him, either. But I definitely wasn't jealous."

"I know."

Nicolas sighed. "I'm the most reviled man in Europe," he said.

"Don't bother with the self-pity, Nicolas. That's not what we're about."

"And what are we about?"

"You said it yourself. When Alex passed on. There's something we can do. So we do it."

"And what do we do?"

"I know what I'm supposed to do. But you'll need to wait for Derrick."

Derrick McPherson came to the room just after 17:00, carrying a hard-shell briefcase. He gave Nicolas a nod as he walked to the queen bed. He put the case down and opened it.

He pulled out an envelope and handed it to Nicolas.

"Your middle name is David," Derrick said, a statement and not a question.

Nicolas nodded.

"That's your new first name."

Nicolas opened the envelope and looked inside. He could see the navy blue passport and knew it wasn't French. He took it out.

"David Tarbion," Nicolas said. "Canadian Citizen."

Derrick nodded. "Much easier to use, since Canada was forced to dismantle their identity net. Imagine if you guys were both American citizens. That's the hardest to fix. Swapping out ID photos."

"Because our faces would already be in the system?"

"Exactly."

Derrick took out a second envelope and passed it to Mireia.

"And your lovely Portuguese-Canadian bride, Natália," he said. "Your mother tongues should work out okay. And the names are one-of-a-kind, yet sure to be unnoticed."

"You have my photo," Nicolas said. "But not the same as my real passport."

"They say that's the hardest part when the subject isn't available for a photo session."

"Why am I connected with him?" Mireia asked. "We don't need to be married. This wasn't part of the plan."

"You'll be travelling to the United States," Derrick said. "Married couples do better getting in."

"I can't go to the US," Nicolas said. "I might as well just head back to France if I'm just looking to go on trial."

"I'm not going," Mireia said.

"The project is located in the US. And we need both of you on that project."

"What project?" Nicolas asked.

"Another island," Derrick said. "Not as big or as fancy, but hopefully good enough to do the job."

"To do the job…"

"To protect the sunshield," Mireia said. "That's what you're doing."

"That's exactly right," Derrick said. "*Nisi* was too big a deal, too big of a target. We couldn't risk betting everything on it."

"Who's we?" Nicolas asked. "Europe or Carter Elgin?"

"Carter Elgin. SolRescue."

"That's not possible," Mireia said. "I'm a member, Derrick, just like you. And I haven't heard anything about this."

"It's not something we've announced."

"That's against the bylaws."

"I know."

"So wait," Nicolas said, "so Carter Elgin is building another space station in the US, a country that's always hated that he controls the sunshield?"

"Carter doesn't control the sunshield," Derrick said. "SolRescue—the crowdOrg—controls the sunshield."

"I don't think the US cares about that distinction."

"It's not really true, either," Mireia said. "Not with secret projects and no accountability."

"Now is not the time for a debate."

"That would have been some time before you guys started closing the door on the other org members."

"Look, Mireia, I know you're upset right now... about Alex..."

"Shut your fucking mouth, Derrick. I'm upset about the level of bullshit I've been getting from you and Carter. We bust our ass to get on the ESA project, we risk our lives—and Alex fucking loses his life—to slip out when an attack happens. An attack that you seem to have known about, since you had so much of this arranged in advance."

"We couldn't stop the attack—"

"You didn't even warn us. All we got was the world's shortest message to get our shit and get out, and take Nicolas with us. Do you understand that Alex is gone? That we're lucky that any us got out alive? You left us there to get fucked. And you could have stopped that, at least. At least you could have stopped that."

"It's not my job to protect you," Derrick said. "I'm sorry, but it isn't. It's my job to protect those bots up there. Warning you ahead of time would have tipped off the people who took that station out. You think they weren't monitoring every single communication coming in and out of French Guiana? Do you think they didn't see the message from Riley Crouch that likely got him killed?"

"What are you talking about?" Nicolas said. "About Riley?"

"I doubt you and Alex and Nicolas would have had much of a chance to get out at all."

"Being arrested is better than being dead," Mireia said.

Derrick shook his head. "No one's talking about getting arrested. We're talking about people getting killed. About the three of you dying in a house fire or from a catamaran flipping over off the beach."

"What are you talking about?" Nicolas said. "What about Riley?"

"There were two suspicious deaths already on your project," Derrick said. "Not just your engineer Riley Crouch, but the IT Director, Eduard Hubrak. Those men died for a reason. They'd had suspicions, that someone was accessing the network from outside. They'd been messaging each other about it, probably thought it was safe if it wasn't through the CSG network."

"But you don't know they were murdered, do you?"

"Well, Nicolas, even without those messages... two deaths from a team of a hundred and fifty is a definite anomaly."

Nicolas sighed. "So assuming you're right about all this, you want me and Mireia to take on fake identities and sneak into the US to work on a secret project that would be just as likely to be targeted?"

"You don't have a choice, Monsieur Clouatre."

"I do have a choice, thanks."

"These documents don't come free," Derrick said. "Either you work with us or you're on your own. With your regular passport and the warrant for your arrest and one change of clothes. And no cash."

"So now you're threatening me?"

"I'm not making threats. I'm just not sugarcoating the situation. I'm not going to continue sheltering you from the world if you're not going to help me. Why would I risk everything for no reason?"

"I don't want anything to do with this," Mireia said. "And I'm sorry, Nicolas, but I don't want to be here anymore. I just want to forget this." She handed the envelope back to Derrick. "We were supposed to go home. Alex and I. Together." She shook her head. "I'll take my chances on my own."

"They are looking for you, too, Mireia," Derrick said. "Did you think you could flee the country and they wouldn't become suspicious? Did Alex really think that, too?"

"I don't know what Alex thought. We didn't have much time to think, you know?"

"Well, you can't go home, Mireia. Not right now, at least."

"Then I won't go home. I know enough Portuguese. I know what I'm doing. I can disappear."

"But that won't do anything for Alex," Nicolas said.

"Don't you dare," she said. "Don't use Alex's death like a club."

Nicolas shook his head. "You can't just give up, Mireia. I know you can't."

"It's not my fault what happened to my husband. I don't need to redeem myself. And I'm too smart to believe that trying to get some kind of revenge will make anything better."

"But you're too stubborn to quit halfway. You need to see this through, just like I need to. It's not like you can just walk away from it."

"I can try," she said.

"You fly to Miami tonight," Derrick said. "10:30 PM. Either you both go or this whole thing starts falling apart. Fugitives are caught when patterns are broken. Two tickets and one passenger breaks the pattern. The FBI will be waiting on the tarmac if that happens."

"I doubt that," Nicolas said.

"You're now a terrorist, Nicolas, according to almost every government on Earth. And you, too, Mireia. And there's only one way to change that. And it doesn't involve going to trial and hoping you get cleared of the charges."

"I can't believe this is happening," Mireia said. "It's nowhere close to being fair."

"It is what it is," Derrick said. "And I'm sorry I can't fix that."

"I don't think you truly give a shit."

"I care about the work, Mireia. Above anything else. That doesn't make me a bad person."

She looked over to Nicolas.

She hadn't really looked at him since it had happened.

He knew that any normal person would hate him for all of it, would want him to have been the one left behind in the rain forest.

But she looked at him a different way. Like she pitied him.

He felt like that errant schoolchild again.

"I think we need to do this," Nicolas told her.

She nodded.

"Okay," Derrick said. "But understand this: any messages you send, voice calls you make... they will be overheard. People are listening and people are watching." He gave them each a nod goodbye and then he left the room.

Nicolas sat down on the bed, on the corner nearest the padded chair where Mireia was sitting, still holding her loaner tablet.

She looked at him and gave him half a smile.

"I think I'm just as out of my element as you are," she said. "This is way beyond what I signed up for."

"I know."

"Now I know why I can't sign in to anything on this thing. He didn't want us sending out any messages."

"Because we're not really here."

"Yeah," she said. "Just David and Natália are. The rest of us are gone."

He reached over and took her hand.

She gave him a smile, but he could tell it was the last thing she felt like doing.

10

THE FORT Churchill lab was nothing more than an inflatable quonset with a solar plant and backup geni, sited far enough away from town to be ignored by most people. It also meant a bit of a drive out each morning, and a feeling that once you were there you might as well stay late, rather than venture out into the cold of a northern Canadian May.

That isolation led to burnout every few days, which then led to midday visits to town for things that were not at all work-related. Any excuse to be anywhere else.

But Jared didn't want to be anywhere else at the moment. He just wanted to put his head down and get to work.

Mohammed asked Jared for help first thing, and Jared happily obliged. That was something he really respected about his coworker; he was not afraid to admit that Jared had more experience in additive manufacturing.

When they'd first started working together, and the haughty Arab-American had asked Jared for help he'd expected a ruse, like at some point there'd be some punchline about how ridiculous it was to have some printer jockey helping out the famous "Alchemist of Ann Arbor", who even had a pretty popular site devoted to his side projects.

But Mohammed had been sincere, and he'd always been the same since, more than willing to share the work and the cred with Jared.

Just not so much with Chloe, not that Jared could tell if that was from some weird sexism or just the standard engineer's notion that project managers are basically flotsam that couldn't contribute anything on their own merit. Jared found himself thinking the same way sometimes, when it felt like all Chloe did was get in the way.

She hadn't shown up so far that morning; considering both her job and what she and Jared had done together the night before, he wasn't too bothered by her absence.

And it gave him and Mohammed a big block of time to get shit done.

The issue was with the magnetic shielding; unlike SolRescue's bots, each American-as-apple-pie bot would have its own magnetic shield. While SolRescue often got bogged down in its succession planning, members fighting over the carcass—or the sunlight that carcass was now letting through—the US government wanted hardening on each bot to prevent that eventuality.

That was the wrong way to handle it, and both Jared and Mohammed had tried to make that clear, but the requirement was in the specs—magnetic shielding *not optional*—so they did what they were told.

And slipped in a casual mention every so often that it would have been cheaper to simply budget for the attrition that will happen no matter what.

Why were they printing rockets on the fly if they weren't expecting to launch replacements?

Mohammed had lab-tested the printerbots for every step, but the magnetic shield was faltering due to attempting to inflate it with plasma. There was no way to guarantee that the plasma would not escape confinement; if they had a way to do that, Jared had often joked, they might've gone and started building their own fusion reactor as a lucrative side business.

But building a shield without inflating meant not providing enough coverage with the magnetic shielding alone, which meant that they needed material shielding as well, more than just the rad-hardening that Jared had already included within the electronic circuits themselves.

And the only material that was light enough was considered off-limits by the US government, since the original American company had been purchased by a German firm. Jared understood the reason; the European Parliament tracked licensing of radiation shielding, and would be likely to notice any new agreements with the US Air Force.

If they could get the secret recipe… but Mohammed hadn't been able to get it. Neither had Jared.

A piece of the puzzle that was out of reach.

So Jared had a simple solution.

"We just have to misrepresent what we've built," he said, as they both sat staring at the results of the predictor model.

"There is no way we can do that," Mohammed told him. "It'll become clear soon enough."

"After they get there, you mean. If they get there."

Mohammed sighed. "You still believe this project won't get finished."

"That it'll get cancelled," Jared said. "Not that we'll fail."

"But we are failing this part, aren't we?"

"It's the specs that are failing. Here, guys, build a bridge over the Grand Canyon with toothpicks and scotch tape."

"It needs to withstand a high energy event."

"Yeah, but how high? Are we really going to try and build something that will survive a five-hundred-year event?"

"It's a false descriptor," Mohammed said. "We haven't been tracking these for five hundred years. But yes. That's what the specifications require."

"We take the risk, Mohammed. We roll the dice."

"We can't do that."

"Why not?" Jared asked.

"Because it needs to withstand that level of radiation."

"A level that's only hypothetical, some perfect storm of energy and spread, solar or gamma burst, to take out the entire shield."

"It might happen," Mohammed said.

"That's very unlikely. Like winning the lottery. A really sucky lottery."

He shook his head. "Trust me, Jared. It will happen, and we need to prepare for it."

"What do you mean?"

There was something more to it. Something Mohammed knew.

Mohammed looked up at the ceiling.

"Tell me why this is such an important detail," Jared said.

"It's not…"

"Then we don't worry."

"No… we make it happen."

"Then tell me why, Mohammed."

"I'm just a perfectionist. That's all."

"Bullshit," Jared said.

Mohammed glared at him.

"You're lying to me, Mohammed. That's a problem."

"It's not a lie. It's not something I'm allowed to talk about."

"Some amazing discovery in particle physics, huh? Some new oh-my-fucking-hell-there-is-no-god particle that is as powerful as twenty oh-my-gods and as wide as a Volkswagen."

"You need to accept my answer on this," Mohammed said. He'd lowered his voice, like he was passing along a secret. "That's how this needs to be."

"Okay," Jared said.

He knew it was a bad position for Mohammed to be in. And he'd probably said too much already. Mohammed was a good guy, even if he could be an ass to Chloe, or to anyone else he came across. He was the kind of guy who could make a real difference, if he wanted to. He could have hitched his wagon to Elgin and SolRescue.

Jared knew what that really meant, when he thought that way. He knew that he'd also hitched his wagon to the wrong… oxen? Mohammed wasn't the only one playing for the wrong team.

And besides all that, Jared didn't need to press Mohammed for the answer. He had another source if he really wanted to know.

There was something exciting about the top-secret world of government blunders. And it gave him the perfect excuse to rekindle things with the always-mysterious Rachael Duck.

Chloe came in just after 11 AM, which was officially late enough for her to be later than usual.

She smiled at Jared and gave him and Mohammed a wave, before taking a seat at the far corner of the lab and plugging her tablet into the workdock.

That was less conversation than they'd usually get from her on arrival.

Jared had decided to push forward with Mohammed's shielding problem, despite knowing that there was something secretive about it that Jared was apparently not important enough to know.

The solution he was thinking of involved a three-part hybrid. In addition to the magnetic coils and generic shield fabric they'd already included in the make, they'd add an electrostatic shield that fed off a portion of the solar energy.

It would reduce the portion available to transmit to earth-based rectennas (or some the evil superweapon), but if they made it variable, controllable... they could turn it up when needed, when a burst of cosmic or solar radiation was incoming.

But he wasn't sure how they'd know when they'd need to boost the shielding; by the time they detected an event on Earth—if they detected it at all—it would have already made contact with the solar shield. If you thought tracking NEOs was hard...

And putting some kind of detection system aboard, some yet undersigned system that would also need to be printed in situ from whatever's available from that rock Elgin and Singhal had shot out to STeLa-1—or whatever other rocks may be nearby, or en route, maybe—that was just a big enough challenge for Jared that it was effectively impossible.

So that left them with electrostatic shielding that would either be cranked up all the time, cutting what SolRescue provides to the three big collectors back on Earth, or leaving it at a level that would make them little more effective than being non-existent.

By the time he'd explained the idea to Mohammed, he regretted having opened his big dumb mouth.

"That can work," Mohammed said.

"The requirements don't allow for a permanent reduction in solar energy collection," Jared said. "They give us a ninety day window for the transition. Then we have to reach at least 90% of original output."

"Yeah... I know."

"More top secret stuff."

"Don't make this hard on me, Jared. You know I don't like it."

"I don't see how this'll work," Chloe said from her place in the corner. "Jared needs to know enough to get the job done. And I ought to know, too."

"It's okay," Jared said. "It doesn't matter. We'll do it because Mohammed knows enough."

"I'm going to talk to Colonel Begtang," she said. "I'll ask what it'll take to get clearance."

"It's fine."

"No," Mohammed said, "it would be great if you knew more, Jared. It would make things easier for me."

"And if I also knew?" Chloe asked. "Would that be a good thing or a bad thing?"

Mohammed shrugged. "It's more for engineers to know."

"Yeah, okay." She looked over to Jared. "We going into town for lunch today? I didn't pack anything."

"Well, you have put in a solid twenty minutes," Jared said.

She nodded. "I guess I just don't know any better. How to tell time… I mean, I'm not an engineer or anything."

"I don't care if you get clearance or not," Mohammed said. "That's all it is, okay?"

"She's just kidding around," Jared said.

Mohammed groaned. "Maybe I'll take my lunch right now. Then you guys can talk about me while I'm gone. What an asshole I am and so forth."

"I do deserve some respect," Chloe said. "To be treated like I'm a part of this team."

"You're not an engineer," Mohammed said. "So you're not on the team. It's not personal, okay?"

"I'll let the colonel know it isn't personal, then," she said.

"What the hell is that supposed to mean?"

"I don't know. It doesn't matter."

He shook his head at her.

Then he grabbed his backpack and left the lab.

"I messed that up," she said. "He looks pissed."

"He'll cool down," Jared said. "He's a good guy, Chloe. He doesn't need that kind of crap."

"And I don't need it from him, either. Whose side are you on here?"

"Why are their sides?"

"God," she said. "You can be really stupid sometimes, Jared. You know that?"

"I *so* want to have lunch with you now."

"Shut up."

He started to laugh.

"It's not funny," she said, as she tried to hold back a smile.

"I think we've fucked things up a little, haven't we?"

"Something got fucked…" She sighed. "I know it doesn't need to mean anything."

"It means something," Jared said. "That we're friends. Friends who like each other. In a couple different ways. And… well, I guess we have to figure out how this works."

"You act like this is all new to you."

"It's pretty new, yeah. I've never done the, uh, fuckbuddy thing."

"Well," she said, "it's like shoving a grenade up your ass… you only get so long before it blows up, and all your shit's spread out for everyone to see."

"I don't remember you being this poetic before."

She laughed. "I guess I've never felt this inspired."

Jared drove Chloe into town in his jeep, picking the bakery without asking for her opinion. He knew Rachael would be working, since she was apparently off the day before. And she wouldn't be taking two days off in a row.

When he got out of the vehicle, he noticed pretty quickly that she hadn't budged.

"There are only like five decent restaurants in town," Jared said. "We did that weird pseudo-pizza last time we ate out."

"To be honest, I really don't like her," Chloe said. "I don't like the way she talks to you. Or the way she looks at me."

"She doesn't look at you."

"Yeah. She won't even make eye contact."

"I don't think it means what you think it means, Chloe."

"I don't want to eat here."

Jared smirked. "Then I guess I have some reading to catch up on. You wanna wait in the jeep?"

She glared at him.

"I'm kidding," he said. "We'll eat fake pizza or something."

"And you can flirt with Rachael Duck some other time."

Jared didn't comment; he knew it wouldn't help. He knew Chloe had never liked Rachael, had always taken everything Rachael did as some kind of personal insult… but with what had happened the night before, it felt like she couldn't take that role anymore. She couldn't be the friend who doesn't like that chick you're going for. That road should have been closed off the moment they added those tangible benefits to their friendship, which, if he were honest with himself, was never really a friendship outside of a friendly work relationship.

He'd fucked a cute girl he worked with. And he expected that to maintain, to stay compartmentalized?

He knew he'd made a mistake.

But he also knew he wouldn't say no to another round of stupid.

Jared messaged Rachael that evening, telling her he wanted to talk.

She replied less than a minute later, asking him if it was something that would be "prudent" to discuss over messaging.

He knew that it wouldn't be, and there was definitely some allure to seeing her in person, even if she was still working through a cool phase with him, the cold side of the weird back-and-forth attitude she fed him.

Sometimes he wondered if she knew exactly what she was doing, if it was all just strategy, a way of locking up a guy's interest, keeping him on the line.

She agreed to meet him, to take a drive with him.

He thanked her then agonized in front of the hotel room mirror for a few minutes.

His face felt too stubbly, but he only had the razor; he didn't want to go all babyfaced to see her. Unless she liked him babyfaced.

He went with the overgrown facial hair motif, thinking it had less risk than looking like an overgrown altar boy.

He picked her up at her wood-frame townhouse on Hearne Street. She was dressed in a red sweater and jeans, her hair up in its ubiquitous pony-tail, with dozens of strands of jet black hair curling out from the queue.

It was clearly meant as a message, that she wasn't interested in the Kos-kela Charm, so Jared made a mental note to pour on a little extra.

It was like a stare-down with Russia.

"Where are you taking me?" she asked. "The best places to hide a body are down the highway a ways."

"You been to Bird Cove?"

"Of course I've been to Bird Cove. I've lived here my whole life, idiot. Why don't you ask me if I've seen Miss Piggy, or the fort?"

"You've been out to the fort?"

"Shut up."

"Then tell me where to go," he said.

"Why don't I show you something you haven't seen," she said.

"Ooh… the fort."

She laughed. "You're embarrassing yourself. Head south, to the high-way."

"You want me to drive back down to Chicago," Jared said. "Meet my parents, huh?"

She punched him on the shoulder.

The cold war was turning nice and hot.

He drove down toward Highway 6, the ribbon of asphalt that bumped along the half-melted permafrost along the Churchill River, crossing a ways south of town and heading almost due west to the higher ridges. From there it went down to the boom and bust mining city of Thompson, carrying the convoys of driverfree semis that had mostly replaced the trains, which until just a couple years before had still been plying the old ramshackle tracks that would always be closed down a dozen times a year.

Churchill had always been remote.

From Thompson the highway headed the long, long way down to Winnipeg, to the US border, and yes, even to Chicago if you knew which exit to take in Fargo.

Jared already had a feeling of where she'd want him to turn off.

They pulled onto a still-half-frozen gravel road and she had him park the jeep next to a bench and a large boulder.

Dene Village.

"Do you know the story?" she asked him as they got out and walked through the soft crusty snow, over to the plaque.

"A little. About what the plaque says, basically."

"My family is part of the Sayisi Dene Nation. Back in the twentieth century, the Government of Manitoba thought we were killing off the caribou herds, so they forced us to move here. Four hundred kilometers from our home. Into shacks they threw together here." She pointed down the road, to where all Jared could see were evergreen trees. "They expected us to let our culture die. To be like them, just a whole lot poorer. A third of our people died here."

"I'm sorry…"

"I don't expect you to be sorry, Jared. I just expect you to pay attention to what causes these kinds of horrors."

"What?"

"They thought they knew better than us. A bunch of old white guys who'd never even seen our land. They took control and they beat us over the head. And they still do it, again and again."

"The old white guys who died last century?"

"Don't start that. We get it from everyone, everyone who thinks they know better. All the so-called saviors. Like the people you work for."

"So this is about me, then…"

"The American Government thinks it knows better. That it should take control of everything that keeps this planet alive. You know what? They don't know better than the people."

"So you're a fan of SolRescue, I take it."

"It's too much power for anyone," she said. "Too much power for Carter Elgin."

"Well, that sounds like a great solution."

"What?"

"Oh… you didn't actually have a solution, did you? Let's just sit around and not trust anyone. That'll fix it."

"You think I sit around?" she said, almost growling.

"No... I know you don't."

"You know what kind of work I've been doing."

"I don't know," he said. "Not really."

"No," she said, "I guess you don't."

"So will you tell me, then?"

"What did you want to ask me, Jared?"

"Mohammed Najjar is at least one level of clearance above me. He's working on something that he can't tell me about."

"And you think I would know what that is," she said.

"I don't know. But I thought maybe you could ask some of your people."

"My people? Who are my people, exactly?"

"Is this some kind of test?"

"No," she said, "I really want to know. Who do you think I'm working with? Some secret league of girls with resting bitch face?"

"I honestly have no idea. All I know is that you know more than you're telling me. And sometimes I wonder if this is all some big trap."

"Big trap? I want to ensnare you, do I?"

"I think those are two different things," he said. "Trap versus snare."

"I'm the indian here, douchebag." And then she smiled. "I like that you don't know everything about me."

"I know next to nothing about you."

"Well, for starters, I'm not a fan of cultural genocide. And I really hate olives, which hasn't affected my life that much so far."

"Do you think you can tell me something about it? About what Mohammed is doing, I mean?"

"I can," she said. "But is that the right thing for me to do?"

"Uh... yes?"

"You're expecting a level of trust here, Jared. That you won't just feed this information to Chloe."

"What's wrong with Chloe?"

"Aside from the fact that she eyefucks you like a horny toad?"

"Come on."

"Mohammed has been told that the bots need to withstand a gamma ray burst."

"That doesn't make any sense," Jared said.

"What?"

"A gamma ray burst powerful enough to take out the sunshield would be unlikely to hit any time in the next five thousand years. It's far less likely than pretty much any other event that could damage the bots."

"Well, that's what he was told. To prepare for the gamma ray burst."

"The burst? Like they penciled one in?"

"That's what it sounds like. I know, it's not like you can plan for something like that, right?"

Jared thought about it for a moment. "There are two possibilities," he said. "Either there's a gamma ray on its way to us that somehow managed to get missed by everyone else, or…"

But that wasn't possible, was it? Between earth-based tracking and every manmade object orbiting the sun and everything else in the system… someone would have detected it and asked for confirmation.

You can't keep something like that a secret.

"Or what?" she asked.

"Or they're using that as some kind of shorthand for something else."

"Something else? Like what, exactly?"

"I don't know," he said. *And he really didn't.* "But maybe that's the plan."

"The plan? What Mohammed is working on?"

"No, not Mohammed. His stuff doesn't include anything like that. I'd know. Probably."

"So there's another big piece to this project that you don't know about," she said.

"And that you apparently don't know about?"

"You're not sure about that."

"No, I'm not."

"You know about that European space station, that it wasn't an accident, right?"

"It's been confirmed?"

"Not really, no," she said. "But it happened. Once people started realizing that the station was meant to protect the sunshield, to move it under European sovereignty. You can't build artificial islands in the ocean for making claims, but you can in outer space. Or that's what the Europeans want to believe."

"And you're saying I'm part of that accident somehow."

She sighed. "It's a big operation." She nodded over to the plaque on the boulder. "They think they know better than us, all over again. So they destroy someone else's space station. And you and Mohammed are going to replace the sunshield, the thing that's next on the hit list."

"So what do you expect me to do, Rachael? Walk away?"

"I'm just telling you what is happening. I'm not telling you what to do."

But he could see it in how she was looking at him. She expected something from him. She expected more.

"There are good reasons for an American sunshield," he said. "Keep it from being co-opted by the Chinese military government, or by anyone else."

"That's why the Europeans wanted that station up there. To protect what was already working. To keep the two big pissing-contest countries from fighting over it."

It seemed like she was close to laughing.

"Why is that funny?" he asked her.

"It's funny because the Europeans got it completely wrong. The US and China aren't fighting to each get their own sunshield up there. They've already struck a deal. They're in this together."

"There's no way you can prove that," Jared said. He was surprised himself by how defensive he was getting.

"I've seen the messages. And the photos."

"What?"

"The Chinese are working on a stealth satellite program. Hiding extra payloads on their launches and sneaking them out the capsule doors. I don't know much about gamma bursts or how to blow shit up in space, but I'm pretty sure China's part of working that out."

"So what am I supposed to do, Rachael? Can you give me a hint, at least?"

"There's a lot you can do," she said. "You can build a launcher that'll fail, you can make sure Mohammed's robots have unexpected problems."

"It won't work."

"Then why did I risk my ass telling you? So you could just sulk about it? Feel sorry for yourself?"

"I don't know."

"Just think it through, Jared. Try to figure out a way that you can make a difference. A positive difference, this time. Can you do that, at least?"

"Yeah. I can do that."

"Good. Now I need to get home."

"Already?"

"You already have a fuckbuddy, Jared. Don't waste your time trying to get another one."

He didn't know how to respond.

He wanted to kiss her. He wanted her. The more acid she gave him, the more he needed to have her.

"Just take me back home," she said.

He nodded.

And wondered what it was about her that had tied him all up. Or trapped him, or ensnared him, or whatever the hell was happening to him. She would treat him like that, and he'd just want more.

That wasn't who he thought he was.

Not at all.

111

After dropping Rachael off Jared went back to his hotel room.

And sat.

And stewed.

And felt far too alone.

After five minutes, he sent a message to Chloe.

You still up?

She replied after a couple of minutes.

LOL. It's nine in the evening.

He asked if he could come over and see her, but she told him she was tired and not really up for any company. He kept pressing, and she kept shutting him down.

He felt the urge to tell her what he'd learned. Not all of it… but maybe if he dangled a little, she'd come over.

He knew it wasn't just conversation he was looking for…

I know why Mohammed needs that rad shielding.

She didn't reply.

He waited five more minutes. Then messaged again.

Apparently we're working with the Chinese.

That got her attention, and she replied that she would come over to his room. She arrived within ten minutes, probably just enough time for her to get dressed and put on the makeup he'd never seen her without.

"This better not be a booty call," he said as he let her in.

"You wish." She sat down on his bed, her Celtic Cross flitting through her fingers. "So how do you know? About the Chinese?"

"I have a guy who owed me a favor. So I asked."

She nodded.

He couldn't tell if she believed him. How did that work; was it too much detail that meant you're lying? Or being too vague?

"I guess we knew the plan was to destroy the existing sunshield," she said. "We just didn't know how they'd pull it off."

"It wasn't like they could just shoot something out there to blow it up. Aside from pissing off the entire planet, they'd be left with more space junk than we'd ever had orbiting Earth."

"So they want to hit it with radiation? Some kind of solar event?"

"I'm not sure what it would be," Jared said, not getting into any details.

"And even if they managed to concoct some phony burst of radiation, that wouldn't be enough to just short out every bot."

"Why not?"

"Because anything powerful enough to cause that much charging… anything powerful enough to take out enough of those bots to permanently disable the SolRescue shield… it would have to be powerful enough to take out Earth sats and power grids, as well. And there's no way they could create that much energy in the first place."

"So the best minds in the two most powerful countries on Earth came up with a plan that makes no sense?"

"I know," he said, "I'm missing something. There's more to it."

"Why are you telling me?"

"What do you mean? Aren't we friends?"

"Fuckbuddies?"

"Yeah, friends who fuck. I trust you, Chloe."

She nodded. Then smiled.

"So this isn't a booty call?" she said.

"It doesn't have to be."

"But it can be."

Jared laughed. "We don't need to keep talking about it."

And then he sat down on the bed beside her.

She kissed him.

That seemed counter to the no holding convention, but he wasn't about to interject. They were her rules, not his. Her hangups.

He kissed her back.

And then did all the other stuff he'd wanted to do with Rachael Duck.

11

BRIDGET HAD talked up the project to a couple professors, a faculty advisor, and two deans, including the one up in Ithaca, and had arranged to share a lab with some uppity TAs.

Anita had come up with SORARE as the name for the project, from SOlar RAdiation REduction project, but that name lasted less than a month before Bridget sold Carter on a new name.

"SolRescue," she'd told them in the cafeteria, standing up and waving her arms like she'd just made a rabbit disappear.

"We're not rescuing the sun," was the first thing Anita had said. She realized right after saying it that she sounded overly hostile.

She just hoped no one took it for jealousy.

"I get it," Carter said, as Bridget sat back down beside him.

Anita couldn't not notice him giving her thighs a squeeze. It annoyed her that she was bothered by it. That it mattered to her at all.

"I don't get it," Anita said. "Sorry."

"It's an action and a descriptor," Bridget said. "People give us support, be it hard cash or back massages, and so they want the name to sound like it's already doing something."

"You need more buzzwords if you're going to start spewing that crap."

"It has two meanings, too," Carter said. "That's what works about it. The shield bots rescue us from solar radiation and all that bad voodoo, but at the same time, we can take that same solar radiation and harness it as energy."

"That's a tall order," Anita said. "It's one thing to deflect some of the heat, but it's a whole other deal to try and convert it to microwave and build something to receive it."

"If it's microwave at all," Bridget said.

Anita rolled her eyes. "What else would it be?"

"What's with you two?" Carter asked.

But Anita could tell that he knew.

Just like she knew that this announcement had been for her "benefit", that Bridget and Carter had probably been talking it over for days, trying to figure out the best way to force Anita to swallow it.

And that was the best they'd come up with.

"SolRescue is a name that will bring in the funding," Bridget said.

"Yeah, so on that note…" Anita said. "Getting funding…"

Bridget nodded. "My cousin's a graphic designer, and she's already drawn up some sketches of the logo. Back of a napkin or whatever, but I think they're really good." She pulled out what was literally a small stack of napkins, handing them to Anita.

"It looks like the little blue circle wants to eat the big yellow one," Anita said. "I don't know."

"No," Carter said, "I can tell you like it."

"Yeah… I guess it's pretty good. But logos aren't really a big part of grant applications."

"No grants," Bridget said. "Remember? We're going to crowdfund it, keep full control. No stuffy admins telling us to dial it back or to wear pants in the lab."

"I don't see how we'll get enough funding that way," Anita said.

"Don't worry… I got this, Nitsy."

"Nitsy?" Carter said, laughing.

"She knows I hate pet names," Anita said.

"We're going to be making that video," Bridget said, talking a little too fast. "My cousin's good with that stuff, too. We just need an animated model of what we're going to be doing, to throw that in. Make this all legit and shit."

Anita smirked. "Let's be sure to use that phrase in the video. 'Legit and shit.'"

"I know you're joking, but that could actually work. We're trying to show that we're smart and able, but that we're also anti-establishment."

"That we're the new wave of engineers," Carter said. "Not afraid to take the risks we need to take, to save the planet."

"But you don't even mean most of it," Anita said.

Carter looked at her with a little disappointment. "Hey… I do mean it. You don't need to be an optimist to do your part, do you… Nitsy?"

"Shut up," Anita said, trying not to laugh. The way he'd sait it…

"So are we on track?" Bridget asked. "SolRescue, saving the planet while destroying any hope of us having a social life?"

"We don't need a social life," Carter said. "Not when we have such a fancy lab to play in."

After the big unveiling, Bridget and Anita went to the lab to work on the positioning software, while Carter disappeared for one of his "inspiration walks", which probably meant taking the subway downtown to ogle the *Enterprise* shuttle.

The reason for choosing the L1 Lagrangian Point between the Sun and

Earth was not just that it was the obvious frontline for blocking the sun, but also because of the relatively stable orbit they could expect their bots to have.

From the first few days of thinking over the problem, Anita had known there were two ways to approach the design, not just with where the bots would orbit, but with the core philosophy of what they were building.

When you build a tall tower, you can make it rigid or you can let it sway in the wind, giving it enough give that it won't be pushed to snap under the pressure.

Anita remembered when she and Bridget had argued about that, when Anita had spent almost half an hour explaining to an undergraduate engineering student why strength and rigidity are two different things.

She hoped she wouldn't ever have to try explaining the sunshield to Bridget.

The word "shield" would only be a misnomer if you thought of a shield like Bridget had, a solid mass that would stand motionless, a hunk of rigidity—there's that word—that would never yield. But any middle school kid could tell you that nothing in the world is unmoving, not just because the whole universe is in motion, but because everything is just a collection of atoms, which themselves are nowhere near a hard hunk of anything.

So a sunshield would be in motion, too, not just as a collection of protons and electrons and magic fairy dust, but as an orbiting array that constantly shifts position against the sun. Like ink dots in a photograph or pixels on a tablet screen, each bot was just a tiny dot in the overall structure, and as each bot moved along in its orbit, the other bots would be moving, too, and the macro result was something that functioned like a big slab of hard metal, only it wouldn't need the same ridiculously high amount of stationkeeping as a stationary array would require.

So the biggest piece of consistent operation would be the positioning software, the automated formation—with manual influence at times—of bots in orbit that would provide the coverage of a shield. Whether you built in situ—like Carter the crackpot thought he could pull off—or you spent the GDP of Mexico trying to boost it all from Earth, you'd need that positioning software, and you'd need it to work as good or better than the stuff that landed airplanes or docked space capsules to the ISS or told Netflix which Adam Sandler movies it's best to avoid.

Anita would be building that software from scratch, not because she wouldn't trust the work of other people, but because she couldn't manage to find anything similar that had come before.

Lagrangian colonization models had consistently assumed there'd be one sad and lonely torus, with no thought to how a horde of small bodies would interact with one another. Even the University of Pretoria's famous space-based solar project design gave her nothing when it came to establishing coverage against the sunlight with those multiple bodies, since it had assumed a single orbiting wedge that would hold heliostats made to point at the sun.

By the time she would've tried to adapt it all into something close to what she was trying to achieve, she could have done it all on her own. At least that's what she'd told herself, and on good days she agreed with last-month-Anita's decision.

But most days weren't the good days.

So she'd reluctantly asked Bridget for help.

After twenty minutes of withstanding the usual gossip and bad jokes about sunburn and freckles, Bridget started whiteboarding the problem.

She drew out the expected orbit, not that there was any real guarantee of what they'd end up with. There'd been enough dead Mars Landers to show that it's more often the plans that expect nothing to go *as planned* that are the ones to end up working.

"So what we really want is an automatic car wash," Bridget said.

Anita started chuckling. "How is that even comparable?"

"Those big rotating brushes. Each makes contact for only a second or so, then the next one takes its place."

"I don't see how that helps."

Bridget laughed. "You just need to go with me on this, okay?"

"Yeah… okay…"

"So the brushes spin and wave around and scrub and all that…"

Anita looked back down at her screen, leaving Bridget to figure out whatever she thought she was figuring out.

Bridget was sketching things out, then wiping them away with her sleeve, not really thinking about what that would do to the aforementioned sleeve, or realizing that there was a perfectly good whiteboard brush sitting on the little ledge at the bottom.

She kept talking. "So the sunlight will poke through", "there's a axis in the middle", "it's all about opacity"…

"What do you mean, opacity?" Anita asked.

"The whole surface collects," Bridget said. "Like a cloud."

"Which is also like a car wash?"

Bridget grinned. "You're thinking like I ought to be," she said. "It's not a shield, it's a cloud. Whatever gets through the outer layer will bing and bounce around like a pinball machine."

"And all we want to do is keep it in play," Anita said. "And keep it from passing through to the Earth."

They weren't multiple small bodies in orbit. There was a very large, low density object… a cloud. She was focused on individual position, individual routing, but that was a red herring and a complete waste of time. Let the simulation determine the levels of sunlight hitting each bot. It didn't matter, as long as she could maintain a somewhat consistent level of density through the cloud, while assuming that all sides of the bot will need to deflect—and maybe one day absorb and convert—the sunlight coming its way.

The bots weren't heliostats and they weren't slim panels.

They were polyhedral dice. Twenty-sided, thirty-sided, a hundred sided...

A cloud of polyhedral dice.

The design felt right to her. And not at all like a car wash.

But somehow Bridget had led her there.

She was more than just a cute blonde girl with ridiculous freckles and a surprisingly talented cousin.

A 7 AM meeting on Thursday morning had sounded impressive when Danny Pyke had first suggested it, but back during that moment in the crusty seafood shack, Anita hadn't really considered what time she'd have to wake up in order to make it to Alphabet City with enough buffer for coffee and touching up her makeup.

A woman who was used to early morning meetings would have asked her tablet for that answer the moment the time had been proposed. Anita didn't actually look into it until she'd been lying in bed on Wednesday night.

She eschewed the ferry for the Verrazano, with two buses and the L train, which had meant setting her alarm for 4:45, ridiculous even for commuting in New York.

Especially ridiculous for a Staten Island Basic.

But she managed to be early for what she was almost convinced was the first time in her life, and the look on Danny's face seemed to confirm her suspicion.

"I'm impressed," he said. "I'd compliment you on your timeliness or appearance but I don't want you to kick me in the crotch."

"I think that was somehow an even dumber choice of words," she said as she made her way to the coffee machine.

"Are you ready to make this better?"

She turned and looked at him.

"I want you to do whatever it takes," he said. "Whip me into shape. Inspire the team. Kick some ass."

"Don't oversell this meeting," she said. "Just let us start it off at a reasonable pace. No fireworks or anything. Just... just breathe, Danny."

He smiled. "I like how we go together. Like back in the day with you and—"

"Don't fucking say it."

He laughed. "I know, I'm only like Carter Elgin when it's the bad parts."

"I need my coffee now."

He nodded, then left her to it.

She maxed the caffeine on the selection screen. And added some mint, to give her feel like she was doing more than just jabbing a stimulant into her brainstem.

She took a sip and relished the harshness.

Then she made her way to the conference room.

There were six people total in the room, herself included, which seemed a good fit since two chairs were mismatched and had clearly been rolled in for the extra load.

They were arrayed around a round table but all facing the curved wall that served as the conference screen. It seemed like an unusual flourish for Danny Pyke, that fancy surround edge that you'd see in other offices; there was little practical reason for that extra five feet of screen space on either side of the center, to show a panorama of people at some other table, so you'd feel like you really were all in the same room.

Anita wondered if Danny had made sure the joined room had the same color paint on the wall.

Danny clicked on the feed without any warning, and five more faces appeared at the front of the room, the office in Frankfurt where they'd sited the people Danny had poached from various companies and agencies in Europe.

There would be more dialing in, she knew, some in India and a handful on the West Coast of the US. She wasn't sure if they'd pop up in little windows on the screen whenever they had something important to say.

She certainly hoped it wasn't set up like that.

They say that anyone born after 2015 or so has a brain wired for the extra electronic chaff that comes up every few seconds. Anita wasn't sure on the hypothesis, but she definitely did feel like she was born a few years too early to fit in.

At some point the world decided that real work should be done like they'd show in the movies, video screens on, bright colors and flashing images…

"Good morning, everyone," Danny said. "Or afternoon, evening, middle of the freaking night…" He got the standard light murmur of fake laughter. "As you have all heard, we have officially snagged someone very special to be a part of our team. I wanna say full time, but you never know with someone like Anita Singhal."

He looked over to her.

Apparently that was an introduction.

"Hi," Anita said, not sure what else she could say.

"I don't want to waste anyone's time," Danny said. "So I'll just come clean: I am not the one to lead this project. I am the CEO, but I'm not the visionary. I'm just the guy to keep the lights on."

He looked at Anita again.

"That's the speech?" she asked.

"Yup."

"Inspiring."

He chuckled.

"I don't want anyone to hate me," Anita said, "but let's not start thinking that hating me is that big of a deal, that I'll lose sleep or anything. But I think we need to make some changes. Some pretty big ones. Now I've taken the position from the start that this project has problems, that there are things that need to be done differently. It's my job to poke holes in our theories, to point out the trouble spots, the places where you really need to show me why I'm wrong to doubt you."

There was no noise in response. Not up to that point. People were watching, staring at her. A few had smiles, while most looked slightly anxious. Or irritated? She wasn't sure.

So she kept going, doing what she figured people expected of her.

"I don't believe it's safe to orbit a critical component of the communications array so close to the sun. We've had more than enough trouble with solar weather at STeLa-1 with the sunshield, and those little bots are way simpler to program and fix than what we're intending to do."

A hand went up, from Frankfurt.

She nodded to the woman, who looked more Russian than Western European.

"You'd mentioned to Danny that we'll save on redundancy by putting it farther out," the woman said. "But we chose a vulcanoid orbit for a reason."

"I know. You don't like the extra lag of tracking all the way out to Venus orbit; you think it's a waste of time. But we're talking about the Rebote transmit, the worst of the worst. Only for when the destinations are in completely opposite positions. So how often is that in the case of going from Earth to Mars?"

"As much as ninety days."

"That's pessimistic. But even still, that's ninety days every two years."

"A little less often," Danny said.

Anita ignored him. "We're looking at the last ditch routing of communications when no other option is available. When you're talking last ditch, and forty or even forty five minutes round trip, it isn't speed that matters anymore, right? It's all about consistency. Being able to say that no matter what happens, your laser light pizza will get delivered from Mars in forty five minutes or less."

"Pizza?" the woman in Frankfurt asked.

"It's old person talk," Anita said.

A man's voice came through the speakers; not from Frankfurt, and from the accent, probably from India. "But if we accept delay here and in the other areas, it will all start to add up. I ask you what kind of philosophy that is?"

Anita felt herself smiling. She was starting to have a little fun with it. "There's only one philosophy offplanet. It's called pragmatism. You do whatever works, whatever has the best chance of success. You prove the concept, get the thing started, and then you can look at improvements."

"That's not how I like to work," the Indian man said, still not popping up in video.

"It's how we'll win," she said. "And like I've already said, Rebote is last chance communication. You better believe there will be a faster route ninety five percent of the time. But when there isn't, we need to make sure it works. That's why you pick Venus. That's why when someone bitches to you about those three extra minutes, you tell them to shut the hell up."

She heard some murmurs, a couple whispers, nothing she could make out. But they didn't seem... hostile.

"But there's more," she said. "I've looked at the list of assemblers you've tapped for this, and to be honest, they're all bunk."

"Bunk?" the woman in Frankfurt said. "Is that the old person word for shit?"

"Exactly. You used eight different types of assembly bots in the design and so you're looking at eight different kinds of species to diagnose every time one gets the sniffles. Not to mention how unreliable a multi-purpose probe can be compared to a single-function one."

"That sounds like a misunderstanding," the faceless man from India said. "Like you don't understand the latest advances."

"Maybe not... but I do understand presumption."

"What?"

"Poor old Anita Singhal. Washed up. Probably doesn't even keep track of what's happening these days. Probably misplaces her purse on a weekly basis."

"My doctoral thesis is on the multi-purposing of autonomous robotics."

"Then you should have a long talk with your advisor."

"Ms. Singhal," Danny said.

Anita rolled her eyes at him. She couldn't stop herself. "We learned lessons with the sunshield that are still applicable today," she said. "One of the biggest lessons was about consistency. Consistency in hardware, consistency in software, consistency in everything."

"So as long as we use the same type of multi-purpose bots," the woman in Frankfurt said, "then we should be fine, yes?"

Anita sighed. "Multi-purpose bots are inconsistent by nature. It's bad enough to require each bot to have propulsion and anchoring capability. That's the price you pay for decentralization and redundancy. But then you expect a miner cum refiner to become a printer, and you wonder why there's too much going on in that one little machine? Complexity is the death of autonomous systems."

"That's just more philosophy," the Indian man said. "Pragmatism should be going with what we've been using in our design for these past four months."

"You need to convince me," Anita said. "That's what need to happen. Show me why my perception is flawed, why overprogramming one bot to do the work of two or three makes sense."

"Lighter payload."

"I've ran those numbers. Less than twenty percent more mass. That doesn't make up for the inconsistency."

"Alleged inconsistency," the woman from Frankfurt said.

Anita tried not to feel like they were ganging up. But she'd already felt out of her element. She was halfway to obsolete…

"I think it's something worth debating," a guy sitting at the same table as Anita said, looking over at her. He looked young enough to be her kid. Like he should still be in school, fauxhawk and all. "If we use what's up there already, the launch cost is effectively nil. So bringing new machines up into orbit—"

"It will cost a shitload more money to do everything over again," Anita said, "when this half-assed job falls flat."

Danny glared at her, but didn't say anything for an actual rebuke.

"Your current design includes nine spacecraft," Anita said. "Four you wanted to site in vulcanoid orbit, two over Earth, two over Mars, and one at TeLuLa-2, for the dark side of the moon."

She paused, watching some people nod and others simply stare.

"And then your future phases would include two for Venus and six around the main belt. Seventeen craft, assuming no need for redundancy."

"That includes redundancy," the woman from Frankfurt said. "That's why we have four inside Mercury and not three."

"We expect that craft will be lost," Anita said. "That's how we make sure the West Antarctic Ice Sheet keeps existing. By expecting the worst."

"You talk like you are still involved with SolRescue," the young man at her table said. "But that's not really true, is it?"

Anita groaned. "I'm still involved. Peripherally." She still talked to Bridget, sometimes to Carter. Sometimes about the shield. Usually they just kept asking her how she was doing. "That doesn't matter, though. What matters is that we need to double up the craft, at minimum. Two operational satellites in each location, sharing the load, but each equipped to handle the whole when needed."

"So we will just build thirty four satellites," the man from India said. "And we double up the number of assemblers we need, as well. Since you have no faith in the latest innovations."

"I know you won't agree with it," Anita said. "No... wait... I know you'll begrudgingly come around and say you'll agree, but then you'll look to sabotage what I want to do."

"Ms. Singhal," Danny said. "I don't think Mr. Chandratrey deserves that kind of assumption."

Anita shook her head. "Carter Elgin is an expert on pattern recognition. I'm not. But I spent a lot of time with him. And you know, Danny... you know that I understand this kind of situation. And I will call people on their bullshit."

"I don't need to accept this," Chandratrey said. Still no video, but she could imagine how ridiculously angry he'd look, face all red like her Uncle Anish whenever Pakistan won the World Twenty20. "I expect Ms. Singhal to treat me with a modicum of respect."

"Then treat me like a subject matter expert," Anita said. "Not like some grizzled old *Keeda* buzzing around you."

"You're an expert on twenty years ago."

"That doesn't sound like respect, Prasad," Danny said. "Not that Ms. Singhal is being particularly friendly."

"It's not my job to be friendly," Anita said. "Or is it?"

"Can we just get back to the topic?" the younger man at the table said. "On why everything sucks and we all suck by association."

"I like the redundancy," the woman from Frankfurt said. "I think it's something to consider."

"It will cost more," Anita said. "There's no denying that. But we can find a way to pay for it."

"We're listening," Danny said.

"I'm not a marketer."

He smiled. "Still listening, but losing patience..."

"You sold people on SolRescue," the young man said. "Made that video with Bridget Hawn and Carter Elgin. The one with the lighthouse and the sunrise. My father still talks about it."

"We've made a video for Turnpike," Danny said.

"A very dull video," Anita said.

"I remember that video," the woman from Frankfurt said. "Not the new one... that one with the sunrise."

"'The sun is everything,'" the man from India said over the speaker.

"'It sustains us,'" Danny said.

"'And if we don't do something it will destroy us,'" Anita said. "I remember. I was there."

Danny laughed. So did the younger man at the table.

"That passion," the woman from Frankfurt said. "The conviction. It was so raw. So... sexy."

Danny laughed a little louder.

Anita glared at him.

"No," Danny said, "she's right. I remember watching that video in junior high. In the frozen wastes of Northern Alberta... we used to joke about global warming being a good thing. Before we started getting screwed by the weather." His face looked a little red. Not like with Uncle Anish and the Pakistani cricketers. He was blushing.

"You told me that story," the younger man said. "That you took a screenshot and made a wall poster from it."

"I hated that," Anita said.

"What?" Danny said.

"The way guys would carry on about how we looked."

"You looked *good*."

"It wasn't about that."

"Sexy isn't a four letter word," the woman from Frankfurt said. She started chuckling to herself. "You made me proud to like science. You made it seem so cool."

"Science was cool long before I came along," Anita said. "Carl Sagan. Neil Degrasse Tyson. And I didn't appreciate being objectified."

"Even men can be objectified sometimes," Danny said. "Pass or fail, really. Not all of us see much benefit from it. No one ever booked me on late night talk shows."

"They don't have late night talk shows."

Danny kept going. "I remember when you were on that Late Night Show with... I don't remember his name. He asked if he could join with you guys because it was all so cool."

"He asked if he could join Carter's Angels," Anita said. "Pretty subpar joke."

"I didn't get it. But I liked how you talked about the project."

"Carter did the talking."

"Not all of it," Danny said. "He mentioned the rocket launches and handed it over to you... and then you started describing what it would take..."

"Bridget had told me to do that, to just let it all out like I was vomiting design specs."

"It was pretty awesome. Like you just knew it was near impossible, but still… you knew you could do it."

She was starting to feel like she was blushing, too.

"I went on that night and donated fifty bucks," Danny said. "Fifty US Dollars. That was a big deal for me. Some serious iTunes money."

"My father donated right away, too," the young man said, continuing his noble crusade to make Anita feel perfectly Jurassic.

"Are we done with the accolades?" Chandratrey asked. "We still have important matters to discuss."

"We can discuss them," Anita said. "Respectfully."

"We should do it all again," Danny said. "Heck… we got it wrong with that shiny investor pitch."

"You can't out-compete SolRescue," the younger man said. "They're still the heavyweight."

"It's a done deal," Anita said. "Shield in place, end of story. And no one's doing a thing about the ocean die-off. There are some groups that should be doing better with fundraising, but just haven't gotten it right." She was starting to channel her inner Bridget. "There's room for something new and exciting."

"But this isn't new and exciting," the younger man said. "It's dry and practical."

"So let's redo the whole business model," Danny said with a smirk. "Save the Mighty Moon Worm. Or t-shirts with glitter."

"It's not practical if we sell people on the parts that aren't," Anita said.

"What is that supposed to mean?" Chandratrey asked.

"SolRescue was about saving the world, or at least buying the world some time. So we make Turnpike about something just as good."

"And what's just as good as saving the world?" Danny asked.

It's not like Anita had an answer.

So she shrugged. Very leader-like.

"Turnpike is about getting people into space," the woman from Frankfurt said. "And resupplying them."

"No, it's about relaying communication," Chandratrey said. "And multi-purpose robotics. We need focus."

"No," Anita said. "She's right. We crowdfund colonization."

"That's not the same thing," Danny said. "We're not sending up manned capsules."

Anita nodded. "Not yet. But someday we will. If we do things right. Turnpike is humanity's road into space. Starting with the communication system we'll need, to allow the whole world to work together."

"The whole system," the woman in Frankfurt said. "Once people are out there."

"Exactly. I know you guys are already thinking about bidding for the next round of Mars Research Station supply runs. We should sell that as part of the dream. Helping to explore a new world. Asking the rest of humanity to sign on with us."

"None of us are marketers," Danny said. "I can secure a Series C, but I don't know a single thing about crowdfunding. And this goes against our original plan."

"Whatever it takes," Anita said. "That's what you told me."

"I told you to sell me on it. Sell me on it, Anita."

"She's sold me on it," the young man at the table said.

The woman in Frankfurt started clapping her hands together.

No one joined in, and Anita felt a little embarrassed for her.

But the woman grinned. "You deserve some applause," she said. "I think this can work."

"It's a waste of time," Chandratrey said. "And a dangerous waste of our limited resources."

"I'm willing to explore it some more," Danny said. "Take a step back. Take a breath."

Anita could hear Chandratrey seething.

He wasn't about to give in.

"We can take this in steps," Anita said. "Let's pick one thing we can agree on, so we know where to keep our focus... while we rethink everything else."

"You want to change everything," Chandratrey said. "What we launch, how we build, where we place it. You want to take our four months of progress and throw it all away. I cannot accept that, Ms. Singhal."

"Then you should look for a new project."

"Is that a threat?"

Anita looked over to Danny.

He was rolling his eyes. Maybe at her.

Not really giving her any direction...

So she made her own choice.

"If you honestly can't think of any way you can continue to advance this project, Mr. Chandratrey... you should probably move on."

She looked to Danny again.

He was looking back at her.

He was watching her, and not much else.

"Mr. Chandratrey," she said. "Do you have any thoughts on this?"

"*Rundi ko choud*," Chandratrey said.

Screw a hooker.

Anita laughed.

She was pretty sure Chandratrey was laughing, as well.

"Good meeting," she said, looking around at the confused faces from New York City and Frankfurt.

That last part made Danny laugh, too.

Anita had not been the least bit comfortable with the wardrobe Bridget had picked out for all of them for the video shoot. And she was angry at herself for going along with the idea of letting Bridget make the call.

They were getting changed in Anita and Bridget's suite in residence, with Carter and Bridget's renaissance cousin, Medora, the one-woman film crew; they needed to be at the other end of Long Island somewhere between five and six AM, since the sun would be rising around seven, and Bridget had wanted at least two on-site run-throughs before the real thing. So rather than set an alarm for a four am wakeup, they'd decided to stay up through the night, expecting to nap in the rental car before heading back to Roosevelt Island and possibly pancakes.

Bridget modeled a very short black sundress, the kind that could be mistaken for lingerie. She'd curled her hair with what she liked to call her come-fuck-me curls, playful little twirls that started just above her ears that really did seem to send that message. And she'd gone heavy on the makeup, plumping her lips and lashes, while apparently adding something to enhance the freckles on her cheeks.

Bridget had given Carter a decidedly un-Carter outfit, a long blue button-down shirt and khaki pants; dull to a fault, which highlighted the open buttons at the top and the upper reaches of a bare chest.

It was weird seeing the two of them in costume; Bridget wore blue jeans as a general rule, while Carter tended to go as loud as humanly possible for every speck of clothing.

But it was Bridget's choice for Anita that was crossing the line.

So she made it clear that she wouldn't wear it.

"It's sexy, Anita," Bridget said, as she held up the dress, gold lamé and probably as low cut as the black one. More low cut, in away, since the two push-up bra cups had a frighteningly large gap between them. "I borrowed it from a girl on the third floor. It's based on a dress from *Cleopatra*. Like a modern update."

"I'm not some exotic animal," Anita said. "And we'll be way over-dressed for saving the planet."

"Just try it," Carter said. "We want to see it."

That made her say yes.

She hated that she wanted to make him like her.

He should like her enough as it is.

She changed into the dress in the bathroom.

There were things about her body that she would change, maybe, the size of her nose, the shit-brown shade of her eyes—which was why she usually wore her green contact lenses—but overall, she knew that she was pretty enough… enough for what, she'd never really been sure.

But with that ridiculous dress, and the emerald necklace Bridget had found down at Fort Greene Flea in Brooklyn, Anita knew that she looked about as good as she could ever hope, even without any come-fuck-me curls in her jet black hair.

She wasn't upset that Bridget had been right, that exotic looked good one her… if anything, she was worried that Bridget overdid it, that now there'd be two girls fighting to be the focal point.

Not that Anita wanted anyone to focus on her… except maybe the one…

She came out of the bathroom.

"Fuck," Carter said.

Anita laughed.

"Very, very hot," Medora said.

"You are a freaking goddess, Anita," Bridget said. "A goddess."

"We should just cut me from the video," Carter said. "I shouldn't be getting in the way of all of this."

"You look good, too, Carter," Anita said.

"Good enough to eat," Bridget said. "Like a pastrami on rye, with extra brain."

"That is so many kinds of weird," Carter said. "You should write it down."

"I still feel overdressed," Anita said. "Like how will people take us seriously when we look like we're doing a photoshoot?"

"Eclectic hipster is overdone," Bridget said. "Classy as fuck is the next big thing. People will know we know our shit when we open our sexy mouths."

"And say we're going to save the world," Carter said, "and that we're all…"

"Legit and shit," Anita said.

Carter laughed.

Bridget looked confused.

Medora didn't appear to be paying attention.

"We need to get your makeup done, Anita," Bridget said. "Make your eyes pop on camera."

"I think she looks great," Carter said.

Anita gave him a quick smile.

"It's for the camera," Bridget said. "Just like mine. Anita's beautiful green eyes, and my cute little freckles… pop, pop, pop, motherfucker."

Carter laughed again. "I like you, Bridget Hawn."

Anita didn't want to feel jealous.

But she did. And looked pretty damn good while feeling it.

᧦

They were officially trespassing by hitting the state park before sunrise, but there was no gate blocking the road, so it seemed like an unenforced rule.

They parked the rental in the big lot and walked toward the brown and white lighthouse on Montauk Point. It was still dark, that twilight that comes before the orange starts poking above the horizon. Anita was feeling tired, despite the so-called energy drinks loaded with friggin alcohol, and she was glad that Bridget had covered up any dark circles with what seemed like a wedding party's worth of foundation.

Medora had brought the one camera, and that was it; Bridget had asked about microphones and lightstands, but Medora was confident in her approach.

She did seem to know what she was doing, and Anita felt comfortable enough with her. Like because she knew Bridget, that she could be trusted to really care about the work.

"So you three should get in place right here," Medora said, standing along the paved trail that led up the hill to the lighthouse. "If we frame this right, that ugly white tower won't show up in the shot."

"The lighthouse?" Bridget said.

"No, behind the lighthouse."

"So Carter goes in the middle?" Anita asked.

"Nope," Medora said. "Guy goes on a side. We don't want it to look like he's flanked by a couple of hussies."

"So my hussies just go on one side?" Carter asked.

Medora grinned. "Anita should go in the middle."

"Anita?" Bridget said. She seemed shocked more than anything else.

"She looks great," Medora said. "And she should be the face of Sol-Rescue."

Bridget looked over to Anita.

"I'm not the face of this," Anita said. "I don't see how anyone would think that."

"You're a beautiful woman of colour," Medora said. "And smart as all heck. And charming, well spoken…"

"You girls want to be alone?" Carter asked. "Because I can go watch from behind some bushes if things are going to get intimate."

"I thought Carter was the guy," Bridget said.

"Yes," Anita said, smirking, "Carter is a guy. Excellent work, Bridget."

Bridget glared at her. "Just shut up, okay?"

"Whoa," Medora said, "that's not a very helpful energy, Bridget."

"I think Carter should be in the middle," Bridget said. "He's the genius, isn't he?"

"Do we need to set up a pan to catch all my drool?" Anita said.

"If she stands in the middle," Carter said, "she'll need to talk more. She'll be the main actor, won't she? Which is fine by me, actually."

"Fine by you?" Bridget asked. "Did anyone ask for an uninformed opinion?"

"What the hell is going on with you?" Anita asked her. "You take the middle if it's such a big deal."

Bridget nodded. "Yeah... okay. I'll take the middle."

"What about Carter?" Medora asked.

Bridget sighed. "I'm sorry... I'm acting a little bridezilla here, aren't I..."

"Might be the Twelve Loko," Carter said, counting on his fingers for effect."

"I should have brought you guys something less freakout-inducing," Medora said.

"I still do want to be in the middle," Bridget said. "I'm sorry, but that's what I want."

"You can be in the middle," Anita said. "I don't care."

"It's for the best," Carter said. "Because whoever ends up standing beside me won't be getting the ol' hoverhand. I'll be grabbing that ass with gusto."

Medora giggled.

"Don't encourage him," Anita said. "He's a terrible human being."

"I love you, too," he said.

He gave her a wink. Like Bridget would always do.

Anita smiled.

And Bridget didn't seem to like any of it.

The rehearsal was painful, both run throughs, but in the end they did the video in one long take with only two small messups—one from Bridget and one from Carter—which Medora waved away. Anita had expected some silly line about fixing it in post, but Medora told them that the flubs added to the overall effect, showing that while classy, they weren't over-produced.

They were all exhausted, but since the rental was one that could go driverfree on most freeways, they headed back to the city on the enabled routes, Carter only having to take control the car to find some on-street parking across the tramway on Manhattan Island.

Bridget, still at least one-tenth bridezilla, went with Medora to the lab to start work on the edits, while Carter told them that he was interested more in taking a nap.

Anita agreed, and he walked with her back to her suite.

"I thought you were going home," Anita said as they reached the second floor. "For that beauty sleep you so clearly need."

"Hey," he said, "you told me I look good. No takebacks, biatch."

"You can't say that to a girl, jackass."

He smiled. "I can say whatever I want. It's a free country for jackasses like me."

"Are you looking to nap here?" she asked him. "Are you really too lazy to go back to your dorm?"

"I share a room with three other guys and two Xbox Ones. You haven't experienced gaming addiction until you enjoy it in real-life surround sound."

"I don't think Bridget would want us to nap together."

"Even if you get to be the big spoon?"

"I'm serious, Carter. I don't know what you two are moving toward, but I don't think she wants me getting in the way."

"Let's just go in and have a drink," he said. "Celebratory screw drivers."

"We have two more Four Lokos that Medora smuggled in from Pennsylvania. And maybe some cranberry juice?"

He grinned. "Close enough."

She let him come inside. It wasn't like she could figure out a way to stop him, not without making it a big deal. She'd already felt like a third wheel more times than she could keep track; it'd be that much worse if he started getting his nose out of joint with something so minor.

He sat down on the couch.

Anita made her way to her bedroom to change.

"Don't," he said.

"What?"

"I like that dress. A lot."

"It's not mine," Anita said. "So I can't let you try it on, in case you stretch it out or something."

"I like you, Anita."

"Yeah… that's wonderful to hear."

"Keep the dress on."

She wasn't stupid. She could see how he was looking at her, looking her over. Checking her out.

It felt really fucking good. Because she like Carter, and respected him, and to be honest, there weren't many guys she could say that about. She remembered hearing about the "spinsters" in China, successful women who'd given up hope on ever finding a man, that they had to "marry up" to a guy who was more educated, more successful… and that those men just didn't exist.

Cornell Tech had a lot of smart guys. A lot of educated and successful-seeming guys, since that was the whole concept behind an Ivy League school.

But there was no one like Carter. Even when he was acting like a twit, he still outshone the other guys. He was special.

She wasn't sure he knew that, but she had her suspicions.

She walked back over and sat down on the couch, beside him.

"I think you may be the most beautiful woman in New York," he said.

"Plain and simple. To match your new style."

He smiled. "I do think she's onto something. I feel so pretty."

"Bridget likes you," Anita said. "Obviously you know that."

"I know that. But I'm thinking about you, Anita."

She could feel him leaning in, just a little. Not really making a move, just... testing things out?

"I like you, Anita. I want you to know that." He grinned. "I want that to be obvious."

"It's getting there."

He went in, kissing her on the lips.

He wasn't very good at it.

She pulled back a little, and he followed.

Then she stopped pulling back.

He kept going, too eagerly, reaching for her padded cups.

"No," she said.

"I can't help it."

"Then do a better job with it."

He laughed. And put one hand on her thigh.

She gave him a little concession moan.

He got a little too eager again.

"I shouldn't have to steer you so much," she said. "You're coming in too fast and too hot."

"That landing scene in *Die Hard 2*," he said.

She kissed him. She didn't want to know what he was talking about. She didn't want him to talk at all.

She'd have to take control, show him what she wanted.

That was okay, really.

Kinda hot.

So she showed him where to touch her, guiding his hands. Then did the same for his lips.

And after a few minutes she started taking off the dress, and Carter Elgin wasn't anywhere near complaining at that point.

He wasn't the first man she'd slept with, though there hadn't been too many before him. And she wouldn't call him the best when it came down to technique.

But there was something raw and primitive about it, about going up against that other girl, that flashy blonde who just seemed to much sexier… Anita hadn't even challenged Bridget, hadn't tried to get in the way.

But Carter was choosing her. He wanted Anita Singhal, the naive idealist, the brainy and confident girl with a nose that was a little too big for her face.

She didn't know what would happen with Bridget.

But that wasn't something she wanted to worry about.

After her Turnpike debut, Danny had introduced Anita to the team, one by one. Chandratrey still didn't like her much, the woman in Frankfurt—Annika or something—seemed to be warming up to her quite well, while the young man with the fauxhawk seemed warmest of all.

Too warm, maybe, since he'd acted like he knew her personally.

"I'm Vasily," he said, gripping her hand. "My father's been a supporter of SolRescue since… well, since that video came along."

"Good to meet you… and good to know," Anita said.

"Vasily's father is a pretty big supporter, actually," Danny said.

Vasily looked away. He was uncomfortable.

Anita figured it out quickly enough. The family resemblance. "Your father is Viktor Utkin." The oligarch, one of the last surviving ones.

"Yes," Vasily said. "He is currently on extended stay in Siberia."

"The gulag," Danny said, tonedeaf.

"So we should be friends," Anita said.

"I believe we are friends," Vasily said, with a smile.

12

IT TAKES three flights to get from Salt Lake City to the small town of Churchill, Manitoba. The ticket Samantha Yoon had given Benj had a departure flight at 10:30 AM. He got there early, in the hopes of clearing security while the people doing the clearing were still in a reasonably okay mood.

Benj had assumed on a fifty fifty shot at getting arrested while standing by the scanner with his shoes off.

They waved him through without a problem.

They didn't even ask to check his eyepiece.

He sat in the waiting area at the gate and read his tablet, oldschool, still feeling too much anxiety to be hungry.

That anxiety spiked again as Samantha Yoon came over and sat down beside him.

"You didn't tell me you were coming," he said.

She smiled. "I didn't think you'd show up if you knew."

"Smart lady."

"It would be ridiculous to send you up there on your own," she said. "Tell you to wait for a syrupy coded message poured on top of your breakfast waffle."

"I don't want to go anywhere with you."

"Well, I'm your assistant, Benj. You mentioned it to your new boss, and he was fine with it. You guys copied me in on the emails and everything."

"I didn't see any of that."

"It should be on your tablet soon enough," she said. "Or your eyepiece. Whatever. Don't worry about it, okay? This isn't my first day on the job."

"It is your first day, actually. As my assistant. So do you get coffee for me, pick up my dry cleaning? Send birthday cards for all my important networking contacts?"

"I'm not here to suck your dick, Benj. I'm here to keep you alive."

"Keep me alive? You know that sounds completely stupid, right?"

"Trust me, Benj. This job is a whole lot harder than you think it is."

"Nice way to talk it up."

"I've sent some reading to your tablet. I need you to go over it on the trip. All about Turnpike, about Danny Pyke himself, and about the guy in Churchill you're heading up there to poach."

"Poach? What? How is that an IT Manager thing? It sounds way more

135

Human Resources to me."

"Just read the documents, Benj."

"And this will explain everything to me, will it?"

She shook her head. "Not in the least. This is what Turnpike's hired you to do, based on a glowing recommendation from your father, of all people. But the real work is something we'll get to when we land."

"About the warning. To that engineer."

She shushed him.

"No one's listening in," he said. "Just tell me now."

She rolled her eyes at him. "People are always listening in, Benj. The secret is to be the ones who control what they hear." She glanced up, briefly, toward the ceiling.

Benj looked up for himself.

He knew there were cameras. He knew they recorded audio even more clearly than video, with enough tech to segregate each person's speech onto its own separate track, and to organize it all by position, to know who else would be part of each conversation.

Samantha obviously knew that, too.

And Benj knew that every federal security feed had been routed to the NSA grid first and foremost, and had been routed that way for well over two decades. That the NSA big data crunchers would get every snippet of intelligence even before the guys at the airport security desk.

But to strip out some of the signal, in real time... Benj had never been given a reason to believe that had been done, not that it wouldn't be possible.

A round trip from any US airport, from Guam to San Juan, would reach the data centre and back at the speed of light. The stream could be altered and returned with less than a second of delay, and it wouldn't be hard to wipe that second of delay out of the record, pushing the timestamps over to match.

Like most big anythings, the US government was usually more inept than malicious. But Benj knew that when it came to keeping secrets, the NSA was at the top of their game.

That was why he was there, wasn't it? Because Q Group was running an operation against the President of the United States?

"How late is too late to back out?" he asked.

"Would've been before we'd ever met," she said with a smirk.

And he knew she meant it.

Benj learned everything he could about the apparent target, knowing full well that once he and Samantha had reached the frozen north that she was likely to tell him that none of that even mattered.

But then why would she have told him to learn it in the first place?

The man's resume was impressive, his education, his work experience. Even his volunteering. He'd dropped what seemed like a hugely promising project in robotics and artificial emotional intelligence and spent two years overseas, as part of an geniuses without borders style program, developing some nebulous sewage treatment technology in central Africa.

Right after that he'd come to Churchill, after being singled out by the US Air Force, and it was reasonable to assume that they were paying him a great deal of money for the work.

And Benj, as head of IT for Turnpike, had been tasked to head up there and talk to the guy. Allegedly because they couldn't afford to send any of the engineers.

It sounded like bullshit. It would sound like bullshit to anyone.

If you want to poach a top talent, you send top talent to recruit him, someone he has something in common with. Not some random newly hired manager—someone who wasn't even an exec—and his Korean assistant, who seemed equal parts hot and batshit crazy.

Fuck.

A complete idiot would be able to see that there was something else at work. That Benj had another reason for being there.

What do you do if you've gotten caught up in something that's bound to fail spectacularly?

And was it really something that could get him killed?

"This won't work," he said to Samantha, as she sat next to him—window seat, while he got the middle—on their way to Denver International.

She shook her head at him, then nodded to the elderly woman asleep in the aisle seat.

"I don't think she cares," Benj said.

She sighed. "Then why won't it work? Tell me... in the vaguest terms."

"This CEO would be involved in the poaching... Danny Pyke. He would probably fly up there himself. Otherwise, the whole thing is doomed to fail, and any idiot can see that."

"Exactly," she said.

"What?"

"You're going up there to try to hire someone... not to actually succeed."

"I feel so highly regarded."

"You're going up there to keep tabs on their tech. Your father's old pal Colonel Begtang even wrote you a permission slip for a lab visit."

"So that's the actual mission?"

She sighed. "Just wait until we land," she said quietly.

"The Alchemist of Ann Arbor."

"What?"

"That's what they call this guy. There's a whole site devoted to him. To be honest, I think he's worth poaching. Imagine if I can hook this guy and bring him back to New York with us. That would make a good impression on Mr. Pyke."

She stared at him blankly.

He started chuckling.

She smiled. "I respect the attempt," she said. "But don't think you can outfox me."

"*Outfox* you. That's not one I've heard much."

"Foxy girl, foxy turns of phrase. Get used to it, bucko."

She punched him gently on the shoulder.

He kind of wanted to punch her back. But harder.

Or maybe shove her out with the landing gear.

It was a two hour layover in Denver while they waited for the rarest of creatures, the connecting flight to Winnipeg, up in Canada.

Benj had never been to Canada, had never even learned much about it outside of the Churchill launch site. For a while, when he was younger, there was talk about the Northern Tigers, and Canada was always the first to be mentioned, those countries with enough dumb luck to be positioned right next to the melting Arctic, where who knew how much oil and gold and rare earths would soon become available for the taking, under the snow and ice and permafrost.

But the Arctic didn't melt, because of SolRescue, because of people like his father, people who Benj had always known were those kinds of self-absorbed, single-minded assholes who could put their one big thing ahead of everything and everyone else.

And the people who'd been betting on that melting ice—including the US government and its sponsors in and around Prudhoe Bay—had been more than a little miffed that three university nerds in NYC had gone and thrown their business plans into the trash, without actually bothering to ask anyone for permission.

Not that Benj knew who would have been in a place to give them permission.

But that whole mess had happened over twenty years before, and those companies had gotten over it and moved on, most of them either to extracting resources from NEO or using the new flow of cheap solar to spin up recycling operations that had never made economic sense before. It was only the governments that were still stuck on the issue, the US and Canada angry about losing that new frontier, even while begrudgingly accepting that runaway climate change was a good thing to avoid if at all possible.

Benj wasn't usually privy to the data that went through the data center, not without jumping the serious hoops he'd jumped to grab those messages for his me-first father. But other people at the NSA had loose lips, despite the internal surveillance, and it was just expected that some basic information would get passed around at coffee breaks and lunch chats.

So he knew about the US plan in Churchill, from his day job and from his late nights reading all the various conspiracy theories. He hadn't known as much as Samantha, about the Chinese launches and secret satellites, but he'd known that what Mohammed Najjar had been tasked to do was more than what was easily found out.

Yes, he was working on replacing the sunshield. Which made no sense as long as the existing sunshield was still in place.

And all while the US government still refused to even acknowledge that SolRescue should be negotiated with, that they had a place at the table.

So it wasn't like the US Air Force's next generation sunshield tech would be ever-so-gently eased into place while SolRescue gracefully steps aside.

There wouldn't be some brokered deal.

So was that what Samantha expected Benj to work on? Some kind of black ops sabotage, making sure Mohammed's next gen sunshield bots never get assembled? Just to stick it to the US Executive for overstepping for the billionth time?

She still wouldn't tell him; she sat "working" with her tablet beside him, looking every bit like a frazzled assistant as her self-important senior report seemed ready to take his nap.

Without a word, she stood up.

She started walking away, holding her tablet in her hands, but leaving her carry-on suitcase behind.

"What about your bag?" he asked her.

"I have to go to the bathroom," she said. "Just wait here, okay?"

He watched as she headed down the corridor, moving toward the central court.

Not a bathroom break.

He grabbed her suitcase and his duffel bag, and started off behind her.

Benj hesitated to keep following once Samantha passed through the metal gates that marked the edge of the secure area; she'd have to go through DIA security to get back in, and Benj didn't like the idea of risking more scrutiny.

But she was hiding something from him—well, one more something to go with however much else—and he needed to know what.

He followed her to the baggage carousels, trying to stay back far enough that she wouldn't notice him.

She walked up to a couple sitting in a bank of chairs. A man and a dark-haired woman, both white, the woman at least ten years too young and—from what Benj could see—two or three ranks too attractive to be with the older man, who apparently wasn't well versed on the ridiculousness of combovers.

The dark-haired woman stood up. She was thin and pretty, with long dark hair.

She gave Samantha a hug.

Like they were friends.

He suddenly felt uncomfortable with himself, watching old friends meet up in an airport. Why they met up, he couldn't guess; he'd run into friends before just by seeing their location updates flashing on his lens feed. Maybe that was all it was.

And then he felt like an idiot.

She wouldn't advertise herself to some random acquaintances, hoping to catch up for a few minutes.

He walked toward them.

He heard them talking, something about the heat.

Samantha reached into her pocket and pulled out a slip of paper.

Then she stopped moving. And turned to look at him.

And put the paper back in her pocket.

"You're nosy," she said, as he approached the chairs. "Just trust a girl the next time she says she has to poop."

"Hello," the other woman said, extending her hand. "You're working with Sam—"

Samantha interrupted. "It doesn't matter. He doesn't matter."

"That's harsh," Benj said. He shook the other woman's hand.

"I'm Mireia," she said. "I worked with Sam back in Stockholm."

"This isn't a social visit," Sam said. "And your name isn't Mireia."

"Shoot," Mireia said. "I assumed he was with you—"

"That's exactly what you aren't supposed to do. You aren't supposed to assume anything."

"Don't worry," Benj said, "Samantha treats me like trash, too."

"Wait," the man with the combover said. "Your voice. It's familiar."

He sounded European. German, or French. Or Dutch.

Benj shook his head. "I doubt we've met. I don't get out much."

"I need you to go back to the gate, Benj," Samantha said.

"I don't care what you need."

"You look and sound just like him," the man said. "Like Derrick Mc-Pherson."

"What the hell is wrong with you guys?" Samantha said. "This is not a goddamn social visit."

"I'm his son," Benj said. "I doubt he mentions me."

"You're Benjamin," Mireia said.

"Yeah... Benj..."

"Okay," Samantha said, "we'll go through this. You are Benj and you are Mireia." She pointed at the European man. "And you were smart enough not to introduce yourself to the weird stranger at the airport."

"Sorry," the man said. "I'm Nicolas."

"Fucking hell."

Benj started chuckling.

"Shut up, Benj," she said.

"So we aren't supposed to meet," Benj said. "And now we have. The whole operation is in jeopardy."

"Derrick didn't mention that you'd be helping us," Mireia said. "I didn't think you worked with us."

"With the NSA?"

"God-fucking-dammit," Samantha said.

"This is fun," Benj said. "I love seeing you lose your shit. Putting you on the receiving end for once."

"How many times do I have to explain this to you? That this isn't a game?"

"You're with the NSA now?" Mireia asked Samanatha.

Benj shook his head.

Samantha the superspy. Blowing everyone's cover, apparently.

He chuckled some more.

"I don't get it," Nicolas said. "Why is this so funny?"

"Benj is like a small child," Samantha said. "He also enjoys people slipping on banana peels, or anything involving cream pies."

Mireia started giggling. "Cream pies..."

"Like *throwing* a cream pie," Samantha said. "*Gawd.*"

"You may seriously be the worst spy of all time," Benj said.

Samantha reached back into her pocket and grabbed the slip of paper. She threw it toward Benj, who snapped it from the air as it drifted toward the floor.

"You handle it, then," she said.

She stormed off, heading toward the security gate.

Benj unfolded the small scrap.

"19154 East 66th Drive," he said. "I assume that's close by." His eyepiece had already started displaying the route.

"I have no idea," Mireia said. "I think we pissed her off."

"Couldn't happen to a more deserving person."

"She's my friend, you know."

"Yeah," Benj said. "From Stockholm, apparently."

"Yes."

"Where you guys both worked with my father, I take it."

"Sam did. I'd only met him a few times."

The woman had confirmed it. SolRescue and the NSA. Samantha Yoon was playing both sides.

Benj knew enough about Carter Elgin to guess that SolRescue was the group that was pulling her strings. Or Benj's father. Or Carter Elgin might even be doing it, personally.

Benj knew all of the conspiracy theories about Carter Elgin.

"And you still work in Stockholm?" he asked Mireia.

"We worked in Guyane," Nicolas said. "For the space station."

"Oh," Benj said. "Sorry."

"And now they think I'm responsible for what happened."

"So that Nicolas. Clou-something…"

"Clouatre, yes."

"Shit."

"Yes. Shit is an accurate description."

"You should go after her," Mireia said to Benj. "We can't get through security without boarding passes."

"Oh," Benj said. "You're not coming with us, I take it."

"I don't even know where you're going. I didn't even know Samantha was going to meet us here. I haven't seen her in like five years."

"We didn't even know we were coming to Denver," Nicolas said.

"This is a shitshow," Benj said.

"It's a Jackson Pollock," Mireia said.

"What?"

"Most overrated artist, in my view."

"So?"

"So he's Carter Elgin's favorite. Because of the 'chaotic complexity'."

"I like Pollocks," Nicolas said.

"Carter has one hanging up in the office in Stockholm. Not really a painting, though. A mosaic. So a strange Jackson Pollock, who himself was very strange."

"Messy on purpose," Benj said. "Like they always say about Elgin's own work."

"Yes. Possibly."

"I think I understand the concept," Nicolas said. "Hiding by breaking the pattern."

"I don't understand it," Benj said. "I didn't sign up for any of this."

"I don't think any of us signed up," Mireia said. "It just happens."

"What happens?"

"I don't know. History, I imagine."

"We're just in the way," Nicolas said.

"But you need to find Sam," Mireia said.

"It's okay," Benj said. "I know where she'll end up."

"Wherever you're flying to."

"Yeah."

"Where are you flying to?" Nicolas asked.

"There's no point in telling you," Benj said. "Since Samantha isn't here to bitch me out for saying it."

Benj sat down beside Samantha, back at the gate for the flight to Winnipeg. He felt angry just seeing her.

She didn't look up from her tablet.

Mireia and Nicolas had taken their small and matching backpacks and walked out the doors of DIA, heading toward the address Samantha had written on the scrap of paper.

It wasn't far, but it wasn't that close, either. Not that anything's close to the Denver airport.

Benj didn't understand why SolRescue would care about two disgraced ESA workers, as juicy as the rumors about them were, a trio of lovers bought and paid for by some sinister group. He didn't know where that third person was, the other man, Mireia's husband.

What a rumor could be started on that.

The way it had been described in the more mainstream media that Benj did his best to avoid had clued him in on where the truth probably was, that neither Nicolas nor Mireia had anything to do with the sabotage, that it was a smokescreen for someone else.

But who was that someone else? Benj had been on the road; he hadn't had time to crunch the data, get the viewpoints of people he trusted.

But he couldn't shake the feeling in his gut.

That the space station would fit very well as part of Carter Elgin's "chaotic complexity". And maybe the NSA had known what SolRescue was up to, and maybe Benj's dear father had planned it out all with Elgin.

Was that possible?

And if it was, did Derrick McPherson understand that by asking his son to provide those messages from Guyana, he'd given the NSA just enough to blackmail Benj into doing whatever Samantha Yoon told him to do?

Samantha Yoon, the same person who'd acted like she was investigating

SolRescue's knowledge of the space station attack, while being some kind of SolRescue operative the whole time?

Fuck.

He looked over to her. His jaw was clenched. He was glaring at her. *At that lying bitch.*

He knew she felt him watching, but she didn't look up.

He had to confront her. But not right then. Not there.

He'd have to wait for the right moment.

And then he'd show her that Benj McPherson isn't some idiot she can fuck over.

He's way too smart for that.

Growing up in Woodson Terrace, Missouri, had never been a big problem; it was never the worst of neighborhoods, and it had never had a Ferguson-style clusterfuck, where white cops would shoot young black men and expect to get away with it somehow. Benji McPherson had never been to Ferguson, since there was no reason to go to Ferguson, but he had a sneaking suspicion that it didn't look much different than Woodson Terrace, probably with its own strips of Waffle Houses and liquor stores and places that give title loans for people who still couldn't manage, even with the universal income that had started coming in.

Benji's Mom had worked hard, but because of the basic, she could keep it down to one job, no longer having to hustle Benji to grandma's or getting him to spend the evening at the McDonald's playground while she tapped away on her laptop.

But it hadn't stopped Benji from doing stupid shit.

Because even when your mother thinks she knows what you're up to, she doesn't *really* know.

And it had started as a way to hang out with the two older guys—fraternal twins, actually—who lived a couple blocks down on the other stretch of Tutwiler. It wasn't like they were his only friends; they were black and he was black and the other kids he hung around with mostly were white and Asian, but that wasn't it. It wasn't like that made them understand him better, like you need to be black to get it.

It was just that they were cool, and they knew it, and the girls seemed to know it, too, and Benji had always been a big fan of girls, particularly the ones who'd wear those black pants with the orange "Huskies" written out across the ass.

And that was most girls at Ritenour High, who were the same demographic who'd paid little to no attention to the slightly overweight black

McPherson kid, who'd always spent more time trying to make his own video games rather than play them.

So Benji started hanging out with the Washington boys, trying to pretend that he didn't realize that he was really just the first recruit for their entourage, not someone they counted on for anything more than taking up space.

The Washingtons, unlike the McPhersons, were Basics, which mean that their household didn't have any extra income; their father had died in Afghanistan when they were little kids, and their mother had never been able to find work outside of waitressing. So once the universal income started, she quit her minimum wage plus minimal tips job and devoted her time to what she'd always wanted to do. Somehow that had resulted in even less supervision for Anthony and Ames, since wildlife photography kept their mother outside the Greater St. Louis area about as often as she could manage it.

So Anthony and Ames Washington took care of themselves as most fifteen-year-old boys would, trying their best to act like they were a lot older and smarter than everyone knew them to be.

And fourteen-year-old Benji McPherson had followed along with them.

Teenagers in the 2030s didn't bother with stupid bullshit like smoking homemade cigarettes, or trying to get a hold of marijuana from older brothers or "cool" uncles, or ordering fake IDs from some state out west; the big play was trying to get more money, to buy the top-shelf shit that Basics and barely-over types just couldn't afford.

The Washingtons had their collective eyes on buying a car, not that they were old enough to get a driver's license. But you pick up a used but not-too-crappy ride and you print off some phony tags, and you'd likely get away with it, at least for long enough to be the coolest fucking guys in dull-as-shit Woodson Terrace.

Only you can't buy a car without money, and it wasn't like you could get much extra spending in a town where sixty percent of your neighbors are looking for the same damn thing.

So the path of least resistance for Benji and the Washingtons was to scam that extra money loose from somewhere. And the best somewhere involved finding a loophole in the brand new income plan that no one else had located right yet.

And Benji was the one to come up with the idea.

He remembered reading about the disappearing dependents, a weird story when seven million children went missing once the IRS started requiring social security numbers, for every dependent listed on tax returns. Some had been divorced parents each listing the kid, but others were kids who'd never actually been born.

He knew there had to be a way to do the same thing, to get universal basic income paid out for people who didn't exist.

Or… maybe for people who did exist, but hadn't filled out their registration forms.

Like the people who'd fought against that universal income in the first place.

It hadn't taken much for Benji, a little bit of script-kiddie-level stuff, mixed with a big dose of social engineering; his voice was deep enough to sound older if he remembered to pretend he was as stuck up as his absentee father.

By picking just a handful of people from obscure news articles, man-in-the-street style quotes mostly, Benji identified five people in five different states—none of them near Missouri—who had stated in no uncertain terms that they would never sign up for the socialist—yet somehow also fascist—government's welfare plan.

After two hours of phone calls to four separate regional offices for the UBI, Benji managed to get two by-your-bootstrap-loving Americans registered for the basic income, and routed those funds to that very libertarian-oriented crypto currency they always advertised on the Fox News channels.

He then set up the shell game with the crypto currency, automatic transfers to other anonymized holders, until those full age-of-majority payments ended up in Benji's bank account… or rather, a private banking account that accepted a fake ID from Oregon and a borrowed social security number to match.

Split three ways, Benji and the Washington boys would have enough for three cars. And a shitload of extra spending. And anything else you need to get those "items" almost every teenage boy would want, their school spirit sweatpants optional.

Benji McPherson had learned the first big lesson of his life; that it's not that hard to outsmart the system, since the people in the system are too damn self-centered to pay attention to what a clever few on the outside happen to be doing.

There was always a way to get what you want. If you took the time to figure out how to make it happen.

13

MIREIA GAVE the cabbie an address a few blocks off from East 66th Drive, and Nicolas followed her as she made her way to the address from the scrap of paper.

She had more energy than him; that wasn't really a surprise.

The garage door to the two story house was open, a white pickup truck parked on one side.

Montana license plate.

"This feels like a trap," Mireia said.

"It does," Nicolas said, "but we know it isn't. Don't we?"

"I really miss my stun gun."

Nicolas chuckled.

She gave him a look that made it clear she didn't think it was funny.

He stepped in front of her and made his way into the garage. He paused for a moment, then walked up the wood stairs and opened a door to the house.

He went inside.

The furniture looked untouched, staged, like you'd see in a model home, right down to a bowl of fruit on the kitchen counter that was composed entirely of colorful plastics.

Mireia had followed in behind him, closing the door.

"I don't think anyone's here," Nicolas said.

"So we wait?"

Nicolas shrugged.

Mireia pulled out the scrap of paper. She looked it over than put it back. "Don't know what I expected to find," she said.

"They're giving us too much credit."

"What?"

"McPherson and all of them. We're supposed to just know what comes next."

"I would think that the default is to wait."

Nicolas nodded.

They could wait. Maybe there was food in the refrigerator. Maybe there were some movies loaded up to watch on the TV. Maybe Mireia would like to take a shower and… he felt his heart beating a little faster. He felt bad for it.

It wasn't like she wanted anything to do with being there. Or being with him.

She'd slip away the first chance she got, if she could.

Maybe that was coming soon.

"Maybe there are keys in the car," he said. "Maybe that's what we're supposed to do."

Mireia started walking toward the garage. "Not in the car," she said. She reached over to a key rack by the door to the garage. A gray fob with a Ram on it.

The pickup keys.

"But it still doesn't tell us where we're going," she said.

But Nicolas had figured it out.

He held out his hand, and she handed him the fob.

He walked out into the garage and climbed into the driver's seat of the pickup.

The console lit up.

Mireia climbed into the passenger side.

She looked at Nicolas.

"That's a stupid grin on your face," she said.

Nicolas laughed. "I know."

"And so?"

"So the truck knows where its going."

"And where is that?"

"Somewhere in Wyoming."

The driverfree in the pickup took them north, around Denver and up through the Front Range corridor, and kept on, into the emptiest parts of Wyoming.

It looked exactly like Nicolas would have expected from a Clint Eastwood western, scrublands with light brown mountains in the distance, the place you'd see tumbleweeds and barbed wire fences and maybe even stampeding bison.

Exactly what America is supposed to look like. To a Frenchman, anyway.

It took just under five hours at driverfree speeds to reach their destination. The middle of nowhere.

"Now we wait?" Mireia asked.

"I guess so," Nicolas said. "The old vehicle switch?"

"A bad cliche."

"Yes."

She sighed. "I'm already bored."

"You know what they say," Nicolas said, not really giving it any thought. "If you're bored, it's because you're boring."

"Thanks."

"Sorry."

"So you haven't asked me," she said. "About Stockholm."

"You don't look Swedish."

"Neither does Samantha. Derrick recruited her, and she recruited me."

"But you're from Barcelona."

"I met Samantha there, on La Rambla. She used to be a lot more easy-going."

"Must be the spycraft."

"Spycraft? Really?"

"I guess you're the same way, Mireia."

"The same way? I think you need to make less assumptions."

"Yes, okay. But there is some duplicity there. You work for the ESA but also for SolRescue. And Samantha works for SolRescue, and which else? The CIA?"

"He said NSA," she said. "Derrick's son. And she didn't deny it."

"And you don't work for the NSA. Or whatever the Spanish version of the NSA happens to be."

"I'd rip out my own fingernails before I worked for the Spanish government. This is usually where I spit on the floor, but this truck is borrowed." She looked over at the console. "So this is where, exactly? Kaycee, Wyoming?"

"This isn't a town."

"There's some kind of sign out there," she said. "Can't tell what it's for."

"Historic site."

"Let's take a look."

They climbed out and walked up a dirt road to the stone marker.

"Fort Reno," Mireia said. "Not much left of it."

"I guess it wasn't that important."

"I've never been somewhere this quiet. All I can hear is wind."

"Nothing like Guyane." Nicolas realized that he missed it. The provincialness, the humidity, the torrential rains.

He missed it, and he knew he'd probably never go back.

"There's someone coming," Mireia said.

Nicolas followed her gaze.

Clouds of dust coming from the south.

They both watched as the vehicles started coming up over the horizon. Vans, a stream of them, boosted higher than what you'd expect, with rugged-looking tires. Most of the vans were white, with some gray and navy blue, and a few painted in much wilder colors and patterns.

At least a dozen vans.

More…

"What is going on?" Mireia asked. "Who are these people?"

"They're quiet," Nicolas said. "Likely electric."

"Electric vans… are they caravans?"

Nicolas nodded.

"It's a maker camp," Mireia said.

It made sense. A line of electric vans in the middle of nowhere. What else could it be?

The vans slowed down a few meters behind their borrowed pickup truck. Nicolas watched as the telltale signs of driverfree appeared during the parking; each van jockeying for a place on the dirt turnoff, but with a rhythm and order that you'd never see from human beings. By the time the final few vans had ventured off the dirt path and onto the dry prairie sod, Nicolas could count eighteen of them in total.

The vehicle doors opened, and a stream of young men and women climbed out, probably not one over the age of forty.

Most were dressed like you'd expect a wandering maker to be dressed, as casual and comfortable as possible, running shoes for some, sandals for others, a lot of tilly hats and a handful of oddly-colored sombreros.

A thirtysomething woman with half blue and half pink hair, short-cropped, walked up to Mireia and Nicolas.

She gave them a wave, rather than extending her hand.

"David and Natália, I presume," she said.

Nicolas had forgotten, but Mireia nodded and said hello.

"I'm Nikki," the woman said. "I'm the organizer. Welcome to Leonardo."

"Leonardo," Mireia said. "Beautiful. Named for Da Vinci."

Nikki smiled. "Da Vinci wasn't his last name. And we're actually named after the Ninja Turtles. Except for Mercator. That one was supposed to be called Shredder."

He had no idea what she was talking about. So he ignored it.

"How many of these camps are there?" he asked.

"From four to eight," Nikki said. "Depending on how many organizers are in play. Things shift pretty fast around here. I was just outside the village of Fishtail, Montana this morning."

"So Leonardo moves around a lot," Mireia said.

"Yeah. And people move in and people move out. We change states at least every five days, but not every five days, because that would be too obvious."

"Too obvious to whom?" Nicolas asked.

Mireia chuckled.

Nikki smiled. "A lot of people are scared of makers. Not just the federal government. We get most of our trouble from locals, actually. People who just don't understand what we do. So it's best not to wear out our welcome. And it's best if no one really knows what we're making or how much progress we've made. I think you guys understand that, after Guyane."

"I don't really get it," Nicolas said. "What are you making? I just see the vans."

"We try to keep everything in the vans, if we can. Most semis still run on diesel, and that's not as easy to provide. But Donatello has two Peterbilt tractors with hella-long flatbeds. That's where the beads go."

"The beads? Like with *Nisi?*"

"Derrick didn't tell you much," Nikki said. "I guess I can understand that. We weren't sure you'd make it here."

"No, he told us," Mireia said. "I think *David* is a little overtired."

Nicolas felt a little stupid. "If another camp has the beads, why are we with you?"

Nikki gave him a frown. "You telling me how to do my job?" she asked.

"Sorry."

She laughed. "I'm just kidding. Don't worry."

"I wasn't worried..."

"We've got you two a van; you'll need to share the sleeping arrangements, which would make sense if you actually were married or something. Each van has two docks for your tablets, and is hooked to the network, so you can get started on your tasks as soon as you're ready. A few places we're stuck with satellite, but I think Fort Reno picks up radio WiFi if we get the antennas high enough. I sent the comm. truck out to North Butte to get that signal."

"So you do have a truck," Nicolas said. "Not just vans."

Nikki chuckled. "Nope. It's a van, too. But comm. van sounds like... I don't know... doesn't sound good, anyway. But anywho... you'll know when we're about to move again, and when it happens, you'll likely end up meeting up with people from the other teams, probably at some other location, and it might include those two flatbeds. I'm not even sure I'll be headed to the same spot."

"I still don't see how this is efficient. You lose so much time moving from place to place."

"It's safer than setting up in one permanent place that can be easily raided or worse. And since I'm the organizer, I'm the one who loses time. Getting me and three other people to set up and take down. Everyone else just gets the important stuff done, working at their docks while the vans drive them to the next site. But we usually travel by night, so people can sleep through most of the trip; you guys made this a special case."

"Sorry about that," Mireia said.

"You guys are worth it," Nikki said. "From what Derrick tells me. So...

you guys wanna give me a hand? Usually helps get people grounded with the whole endeavor."

They spent the next forty-five minutes doing what Nikki directed them to do, including setting up a small bank of solar collectors and cabling to each van, and erecting four latrine tents a few hundred meters away from anything else, lightweight canvas shells over portable composting toilets.

Nicolas made note of the lack of shower facilities.

While they worked, Nicolas saw the other setup workers, assembling what looked like a pretty impressive outdoor kitchen, with a long line of folding tables and chairs that could serve half a wedding.

After those forty-five minutes of setup, the setup was done.

"Now I usually get to do whatever the heck I want," Nikki said. "Sometimes I go on hikes, even. They just ping me if they need anything. I'll take you over to your van."

It was one of the white vans, which made Nicolas feel a little better. The last thing he wanted was something as conspicuous as the van right next to it, with a giant pink tuna painted on one side, and a fat black cat on the other.

He didn't understand why these people who were so proud to be called makers would think they needed to dash around like wanted fugitives. But even assuming that there was a reason, the weird van murals didn't seem like a good way to hide in plain sight.

Nikki took them on the tour of the inside. Two rows of two seats, the first including the seat for a driver if a driver is ever needed. She folded down the seats, turning the two rows into one queen-sized bed.

"There are sheets in the back," she said, nodding to the assortment of plastic crates behind the seating area. Now... the docks..."

She set the seating back into their upright positioning, then pulled on a handle between the rows. The docks were two foldout fake leather benches, with velcro covers over to docking ports. She unzipped one of two strips near the front of the bench, opening a crevice. She lifted up a thin screen with only the slightest of surround curves.

"Two screens, of course," she said. "Power should never be a problem; enough battery to run off three days of night if you had to. And we've got a couple of wind turbines we can set up if the sun quits on us for a long while."

"And it's all electric?" Nicolas asked. "No backup generation?"

"There's no need for backups," Nikki said with a grin. "If the sun goes out long enough to screw us, we're talking supervolcano-level extinction event. So then our little projects don't matter that much anymore."

"Thanks, Nikki," Mireia said.

"It's my pleasure. Really."

After handing a key fob to both Mireia and Nicolas, Nikki left.

Mireia immediately switched the setup back to the bed.

Nicolas wasn't about to argue with lying down; he was exhausted.

"I'll get you two confused," Mireia said. "Nic, Nikki... and you even look alike."

"She was trying to cut her hair short and it's still way thicker than mine."

"It's all that testosterone. You're just too rugged."

He smiled. "I wanted to say that I appreciate this, Mireia. I know you didn't want to come here."

She finished setting up and lay down on the fake leather bed. "We're still friends, Nicolas. I do like you, outside of any ulterior motive."

"You mean outside of Derrick telling you to keep an eye on me."

"Yeah."

Nicolas sighed. "That's the first time you've admitted that to me."

"I never denied it," she said. "And you never asked."

"I didn't want to think about it. I really thought..."

"We're friends, Nicolas."

He lay down beside her. Not too close. "No... not that." He felt a little ridiculous.

"What?"

"Nothing."

"No," she said. She grabbed his hand and gave is a quick squeeze. "You can tell me. We're supposed to be married, you know."

"I thought maybe you guys were coming on to me."

She started chuckling.

"Or maybe you weren't," he said.

"I never thought of it... but now that I do... it was a little heavy-handed of us. And all that cava we kept pouring down your throat... I'm sorry, Nicolas. That was ridiculous of us."

He felt old. And ugly. And pudgy. And bald.

And pretty much the opposite of her dead husband.

"Now I'm embarrassed," Mireia said.

"Don't be embarrassed. I understand now."

"You're a good man, Nicolas. And a good friend."

That made him feel worse.

Like she pitied him and his combover.

"She said we had tasks," he said.

"I thought we'd just relax for a few minutes. Catch our breaths."

"I want to get to work, Mireia. I can't just lie around and think about things."

"Okay," she said.

"I'm sorry."

"There's no need. You're right. We need to do something again. No more waiting for the next thing to happen."

Nicolas nodded.
And they both got up to take apart the bed.

14

IT WAS halfway through the flight to Winnipeg when Benj spotted the right moment. The flight attendants had finished the drink run, and Samantha had made her way back to the lavatories.

Benj waited until she went inside the lavatory on the left before he got out of his seat.

He walked down the aisle and up to the door on the left.

He knew she would have locked it.

He lifted up the metal sign on the door, and slid the knob underneath, from locked to unlocked.

He opened the door and pushed his way in.

Samantha was sitting on the toilet with her pants down.

She didn't make any noise when he came in, but she made her disgust well enough known with how she was looking at him.

"We need to talk this out," he told her, keeping his voice low but trying to sound menacing.

"If you wanted to join the mile high club we could have just got it on in Denver."

"I don't trust you, Samantha. And since you seem to be playing both sides, there's a good chance you're a goddamn traitor to your country."

"You're the one sending classified data to other nations. Remember? I have the evidence."

Benj couldn't let her do it. He couldn't let her threaten him, like he was some fucking fat little bitch. He wasn't anyone's bitch. He'd made a fucking life for himself, gotten his record expunged and taken a job for the goddamn National Security Agency.

And he'd done his best to do it with as little involvement as possible from his father.

To do it with his own fucking wits.

And she'd come along and decided that it wasn't worth anything, that she could just fuck him over and get away with it. And not for the NSA, or Q Group. For who knows what reason.

Probably because his goddamn father put her up to it. Because even though he couldn't be bothered to give a shit about anything in Benj's life, he could certainly burst in and take what he wanted. He could ruin Benj's career and the entire lives of his friends, and there was nothing Benj could do to fix it.

But he'd be damned if he'd let some stupid Korean *cunt* hold that all over him.

He took his left hand and shoved it over her mouth, half of it a slap that caught her off guard, pushing her against the back of the wall, but mostly he'd done it to keep her quiet.

He took his right hand and clamped it down over her nostrils. So she couldn't breathe.

He'd done that before, in his previous life. You did it in fast enough, hard enough, and a person more likely than not just freezes, like they don't know what to do. By the time they even think to fight back, they're already running out of breath. They might swing out at you, but usually it's too poorly planned to stop you.

And Benj had always been strong enough to keep them pinned. Or had whatever backup he'd needed to get the job done.

He felt the doubt in his head, the shame lurking in the back somewhere. To go back to that shit, and back to doing it to yet another woman. Even a woman like Samantha Yoon.

Fuck.

But he had to send her the message.

"Listen here, you little bitch," he said. "You fucking listen."

She tried to respond, his hand still muffling her, her airway blocked.

But she wasn't trying to scream.

She didn't want anyone to come.

"I'm in this because you and my father fucked me over," he said, "and that means that I fucking hate you. You understand? I hate you, Samantha. And I'm not going to put up with any more shit from you. You treat me with respect… you treat me like I'm in charge. Because from this point on, I *am* in charge. Do you get what I'm saying?"

She didn't try to say anything.

He pulled his right hand off her mouth.

"Hurting me won't change anything," she said. "Killing me won't fix this."

There were tears in her eyes.

Pulse elevated, heart pounding.

She was terrified.

Benj wanted to apologize. But he had to fight that.

It's not like it would make things better somehow.

And he couldn't waver, couldn't show weakness. He had to assert his dominance. His control. His authority.

"I'm not going to be some stupid pawn," he said. "You're going to tell me everything you know, and you're going to tell me who you're really working for. And you'd better hope that I believe you."

"Or… or what will you do?"

"We both know what I'll do. If I'm going down, I might as well make sure you can't get back up, either."

"Please," she said.

"Please, what?"

"I don't know."

"I'm going to leave first. You give me thirty seconds, then you come back to the seat. And then you tell me why I shouldn't call the FBI and let them know about the SolRescue mole at the NSA."

She nodded.

He went back to his seat and counted down in his head.

She was right on time.

Several passengers noticed the redness of her eyes, the traces of mascara running down her face.

It didn't matter what they thought of him.

"So who is it?" he asked her. "Who do you work for?"

"Carter Elgin," she said, in a hushed voice. "I work for Carter Elgin. Directly."

"What about my father?"

"He's usually the one to gives me tasks, yeah. But Carter also tells me when something needs to be done."

"And how did you get into the NSA?"

"Same way you did. Through your father."

"I didn't get that job through my father."

"Okay."

"Are you really with Q Group?"

"No," she said. "But we have someone in there who helped with this operation."

"Who?"

"I don't know. Your father set it up. I was just supposed to get in there, keep tabs on you, and wait for further instructions."

"And further instructions just happened to be my father telling you to destroy my career?"

"Yeah," she said. "And I wish it hadn't happened. But it's what I signed up for."

"What about Laila and Malik?"

"I wasn't lying about that. From what I was told, they've been taken to detention. That whole are is not my responsibility."

"How could you even manage that? Getting them detained?"

She nodded to the seat in front of her.

Benj looked over.

The man was trying to look like he wasn't listening in.

A clear sign that it was time to table the discussion.

"We'll talk about this more when we get there," Benj said.

"I know," she said.

She looked down at her tablet.

But she wasn't doing anything with it.

She was still shaking.

Still scared of him.

Is it possible to regret something while still being glad you did it?

The final flight—from Winnipeg to Churchill—was on a twin turboprop that was probably the smallest plane Benj had ever flown on, smaller even than the tiniest of regional jets he'd taken between Salt Lake City and St. Louis each year for Christmas with his mother, at that same old house in Woodson Terrace.

It was just Benj, Samantha and maybe ten other passengers on a place that could seat at least two or three dozen more. Samantha kept her seat beside him, but did her best to avoid any eye contact.

And he spent the two-and-a-half-hour trip fighting the urge to apologize.

They arrived in Churchill—which was still half-covered in a light blanket of snow—around dinnertime, and took a taxi to the B&B, which was an unadorned bungalow in a small row of unadorned bungalows, next to a row of even less appealing townhouses.

The town looked like it was still trapped in the first few days of a cold spring, despite it being the middle of May. And Benj noticed that only the saddest little evergreen trees and scrubby bushes survived, few of them coming close to reaching the rooflines.

He knew there were polar bears in the area, not that he knew where, or how close they'd come to the middle of town.

Did people get eaten by polar bears?

Or just half-heartedly mauled?

They checked into the bed and breakfast, Samantha having booked both of the rooms available; it wouldn't make sense for a boss and an assistant to share a room… well, sometimes it could make sense.

But not in this case.

He brought his duffel bag up to his room, then headed straight for hers.

He knocked on the door; force of habit.

She didn't answer.

He opened the door and walked in.

She was sitting on the bed with her shirt off, unhooking her bra from the back.

"You heard me knock," he said.

"I was hoping you'd wait."

He walked over to the bed and sat down, pretending to be uninterested in anything involving her lack of a shirt. "I need your tablet, Samantha."

"Why?"

"I don't trust you. I don't think I need to tie you to your bed, but I should at least keep track of your communications. You know, so you don't fuck me over again."

"They have a telephone downstairs," she said. "Probably plugged in and everything."

"Give me your tablet."

She got up off the bed and pulled her tablet out of her jacket pocket. She handed it to him, then returned to her seat on the bed.

"So what is the next step?" he asked her. "Or are we waiting on something from that father of the year of mine?"

"I... I already mentioned it. I've got a signed letter from Colonel Begtang. Hard copy. Promising us unrestricted access to the project Mohammed Najjar is working on."

"An authentic letter?"

"I don't think it matters," she said.

"So is this really the plan? To snoop around? Pretend to want to poach this Najjar guy?"

"Someone connected to that project knows about the space station attack."

"You think."

"What do you mean?"

"Well, you talked about chatter from Churchill, and we know that Najjar is working in Churchill for the US Air Force. But that's all you've got, isn't it? No real link."

"That's enough of a link," she said. "At least, Carter thinks it is. And last time I checked, he's one of the smartest people on the planet."

"At least according to the members of his cult. Which includes you, of course."

"And your father."

"Yeah. And my father. You and him. The two people I most wish I'd never met."

"It can be a real job, you know," she said.

"What?"

"This job with Turnpike. You're more than qualified."

"IT Manager? Yeah. I can't even manage my own life."

"The thing about our little cult is that we take care of our people."

"Pretty sure I'm not your people," Benj said. "You know, since I attacked you in an airplane bathroom."

She shook her head. "Your Derrick McPherson's son. You've always been one of our people, even if you don't want to be."

"I don't want to be. And I think we're done with that bullshit."

"I'm sorry," she said. "I just think you can do great things, Benj. Great things for the right kind of organizations. Like Turnpike."

"I thought you worked for SolRescue, Samantha. Or wait... maybe the NSA? You can't even keep your story straight."

She leaned back a little on the bed, putting her hands behind her. It pushed her chest forward.

She caught him looking.

He couldn't *not* look.

"Are you attracted to me, Benjamin?" she asked. "Because that's okay, you know, if you do."

"I find you very punchable. Which is a very strange feeling to have."

"Come on... you were interested in me before. And you know I'm interested in you."

"I'm not buying it."

"I want you to know that I'm not upset. About the bathroom. I know why you did it. I *understand* why you did it."

"I'm not an idiot, Samantha. You can't just flash your breasts at me and expect me to forget who you are. How completely disgusting you are as a human being."

He heard her sniffle.

She'd started to cry.

"The fuck?" he said.

"I'm sorry... It's been a messed up day. I'm just... I don't know..."

He leaned in closer to her.

"Shh..." he said.

He put his hand up and swept a tuft of hair off from her forehead.

"Listen, Samantha... you need to get your shit together. You need to stop with the bullshit and the crocodile tears. I told you, I'm not buying it. So shut the fuck up."

She kept crying.

He got up and left her room.

She was still trying to fuck him over.

15

IT FELT strange to Jared, spending the morning working alongside Mohammed on his radiation shielding problem, knowing that he didn't understand the reasons.

He tried on a few occasions to drop hints to Mohammed that the five-hundred-year event didn't make a lot of sense, that it would mean more trouble for Earth beyond the sunshield getting whacked. It's not like the power grids and comm. systems are hardened for something like that.

If there was really something that bad coming, they might be focusing on the wrong problem.

But Mohammed ignored those little comments, as if Jared hadn't even spoke. The "Alchemist of Ann Arbor" would then wait a few minutes more before bringing up some other topic, like some video with talking hand puppets he saw the night before.

The timeline didn't fit; there was no way Mohammed stumbled on twenty random conversation topics the night before. If he was recounting a lifetime of inane bullshit all at once, he'd run out of gas pretty quick.

And then what would they talk about?

Obviously not the one thing that they ought to.

Chloe had messaged to say that Colonel Begtang had agreed to a meeting, and that she'd booked the teleconference room at the Northern Studies Centre for noon and would come to the lab after that.

Jared was glad she was out, since she and Mohammed weren't getting along particularly well of late.

They didn't make much progress on the work, since Mohammed had chosen to hold firm on using the rad shielding material without a license, and Jared was having problems enough just trying to find a shadowy enough place for the recipe to be posted. He wasn't anonymous enough from his dock at the lab, and he certainly didn't have the setup back in his hotel room.

So they either found some way to defy common sense, or they'd continue beating their heads against the wall.

Not that Mohammed's ideas weren't novel; he'd sketched out a handful on the whiteboard, the most promising being what he'd called the triceratops ring: using the existing shield bots to form a temporary barrier between the sun and the replacement shield, the older bots being like the older dinosaurs circling around their young. Like a wagon train circling around the rifle-toting pioneers, but with the appeal of dinosaurs.

A non-triceratops portion would be required, sensors placed in advance to "spot" the radiation. Because the radiation would be travelling significantly slower than the speed of light, it was possible—though not anywhere near simple—for those sensor craft to signal the elder shield bots with a warning, and then for those shield bots to form their barrier in the required formation.

"So many moving parts," Jared said. "Inelegant."

Mohammed chuckled. "There's very little that's elegant about the noble triceratops. But the shield itself is moving parts. Millions of them."

"Millions of parts, but no single point of failure. The beauty of the cloud."

"Except the original problem," Mohammed said, "the weakness of each bot, to radiation and everything else."

"The everything else is what baffles me."

Again, Mohammed didn't take the bait.

"I mean," Jared continued, "it's either there's some secret cosmic blast coming, some supernova that everyone but the US Air Force seems to have missed, or there's some secret component to this plan that you and I wouldn't be okay with. What if we're working on a project that includes the destabilization and destruction of the existing sunshield? It doesn't seem like SolRescue will consent to being put out of operation."

"Enough, Jared," Mohammed said.

"What?"

"We can't talk about this. It's not our job."

"I won't be a part of something that isn't right."

"Then you work for the wrong government." He looked away. He seemed to regret saying it.

"I don't want to be the bad guy," Jared said. "But this is really messed up."

Mohammed shook his head. "I don't think you understand what's happening. This isn't like working for Boeing or SpaceX, Jared. You don't just resign in protest and hope for a neutral work reference. This is a classified project."

"No, it isn't. What we're doing here isn't classified. Everyone in town knows we're here."

"What did Colonel Begtang tell you? Did he tell you that this project was an open book?"

"Obviously not."

"As far as anyone outside of this lab knows, we have nothing to do with replacing the sunshield. And no one is working to replace it. SolRescue might know what's coming, but no one is making that knowledge public. It's backchannel stuff, Jared. And we can't be messing that up."

"I'm not talking about messing it up," Jared said. "I'm talking about making sure we're doing the right thing."

"I'm not being clear enough. You are part of a classified program that the world is not supposed to know about. You can't just quit and go home."

"Because they'll have to terminate me? With extreme prejudice?"

"It's not a joke, Jared. I mean it. You want to drive back down to the border, you to ahead. But don't be surprised if you're picked up on the way."

"Picked up? And then what?"

"And they'll stuff you away somewhere."

"Some secret prison? You really believe that?"

"It's real, Jared. I know. I've had to go there before."

"What?"

"I created something that led the FBI to my apartment," he said. "I guess when you livestream your experiments, you're pretty much asking for outside interference."

"MechaTeacher," Jared said, recalling the patently ridiculous name for Mohammed's robot instructor.

"You're familiar with it?"

"I watched the experiments. They were a pretty big deal when I was in school."

"I'm not that much older than you," Mohammed said.

"Old enough."

"We've had robot teaching assistants for years. I remember them bringing them out in elementary school to help teach us Mandarin. Not that I remember any Chinese from it. But those TAs always relied on the human monitoring—the real instructor—because their judgments were always a little off."

"Yeah. Facial and tone recognition, understanding sarcasm and humor. I remember you talking about that."

"So MechaTeacher had something unique about it," Mohammed said. "Aside from the completely awesome name. I adapted an old notation technique from the 1950s to rewrite human language patterns to create context-free grammars. Backus-Naur Form. It used to make a splash in the news every once in a while, but would quickly fade into the background. But it was just what I needed. I blended it together with what I'd done already, figuring out a way to detect minute changes in facial expression and tone of voice, the process of change being the important determinant, rather than the end state."

"Like dance steps."

"That's what I'd said, yeah. Both together gave MechaTeacher something no other interactive AI had. And the US government was interested in my work, and they didn't want me livestreaming it anymore."

"That's why you gave up," Jared said. "With no explanation."

"I didn't give up. I kept working on it, until I stopped."

"Why?"

Mohammed sighed. "DARPA was the main sponsor. They wanted me to relocate to Arlington, Virginia. They wanted me to drop everything else and focus on MechaTeacher. But not to actually build a teacher. To build a UGCV. An autonomous land drone. For counterinsurgency, they said."

"Oh."

"Some things are too far, whether you're an Arab or not. I knew that MechaTeacher was going to be used to kill non-combatants all over the world, that one error in my programming could murder a child."

"They're still developing it, though," Jared said. "Aren't they?"

"I think they've tested it. I think it will be sent in on the next so-called intervention. I couldn't stop it. All I could do was delay it and try to minimize my culpability." He looked down at his feet. "It didn't work."

"I don't understand, Mohammed. You told them you were quitting and they took you somewhere? Detained you?"

"Highland County, Virginia. So I relocated to Virginia anyway, just not by choice. They have a little subdivision there, right along the Jackson River. No radio, no network, but lots of civil war history if you're a buff."

"And now you're working with them again?"

"It's still my country, Jared. Even if it's run by self-important douchebags who don't mind killing a few innocents now and again. And the sunshield is important."

"That's what I always tell myself. But then, why are we trying to destroy what's already there?"

"Because of the Chinese military. Because ever since they took control from the Communist Party, they've become a threat to the entire planet."

"That's what they tell us," Jared said.

And it was apparently what Mohammed believed. Unless he was just lying. Just trying to shut Jared up.

But Rachael hadn't mentioned anything about Mohammed knowing about the partnership with China. He knew about rad shielding, but was there more to it? What else was he working on?

It wasn't like he was keeping Jared out of it. They were working on Mohammed's project together.

Chloe was out at the North Studies conference room, looking to get her and Jared access to what Mohammed knows. And maybe that's all Mohammed knows.

How would Jared know?

"They say China's working on their own project," Jared said. "That they want to take control of the shield from SolRescue. You hear anything about that?"

"I try not to pay attention," Mohammed said. "You should do the same, Jared. There's no good coming out of rumors like that." He stood up from his workdock. "I spent two years in detention, while the US government forged my personal messaging to make it seem like I was out volunteering for some African NGO. Sharing a house with two Iranian-American Shias, because I guess they figured us brown guys were all the same. I think those two guys are still there, and it's possible they'll never be allowed to leave. And I'm just lucky they didn't tell me why they were there. Otherwise I'd probably be right there with them."

"It seems like a lot of trouble."

"The US no longer kills its citizens," Mohammed said. "The 31st Amendment, remember? But keeping them in some backwater for the rest of their lives is perfectly legit. If you try to back out of this project, Jared, they will send you to Highland County. Or worse."

"What's worse? Indianapolis?"

Mohammed sighed again. Deeply. "If you know anything about our country, you know that they don't always listen to the constitution."

"Nah... not for this. They wouldn't bother."

"Just keep quiet about China, Jared. If you're smart." He smiled. "Of course, if you were smart, we'd have this radiation problem fixed by now."

Jared didn't smile back.

For some reason, Mohammed opening up made Jared more suspicious than ever before.

Chloe showed up just before two PM, mentioning that the Colonel was "thinking about it" when it came to granting access.

Mohammed made an excuse for being gone by 3:30.

So Jared continued to look at the shielding problem until Chloe came over to his dock, for the conversation he'd known was coming.

"What did Mohammed tell you?" she asked. "Did he say anything?"

"He's just paranoid. Thinks if we ask questions we'll run into trouble."

"What kind of trouble?"

Jared told her what Mohammed had said, about Highland County, and about what else could happen. That Mohammed honestly believed the government would kill someone over the project.

"He's trying to shake you," Chloe said. "He knows we're onto him."

"We're onto him?"

"I know, it sounds stupid. But like you told me, he knows more than we do. And Colonel Begtang isn't going to give us clearance."

"You said he was thinking on it."

"That was bullshit." She grinned. "If anyone should know the smell, it should be you, Jared Koskela." She put her hand on his shoulder. "So what do we do about this?"

"About what?"

"Come on. I know you don't want to stay with this project."

"I never said that," he said. Had he?

"I know you, Jared. You were already having doubts before this rad shielding stuff. I mean, we both thought the Chinese military was the big threat."

"And now we know different."

"No," she said. "They're still the threat. But so is our own government. My god. What the heck are we going to do?"

He reached up and put his hand on his shoulder, cupping hers. "We don't do anything yet," he said. "We think it through. Whatever is going to happen is still like half a year away, isn't it? We have time to figure this out."

"And in the meantime we keep working for the corrupt military junta that's taken control of the largest country on Earth?"

"It's good for our resumes," Jared said, with a smirk.

"There might be more we can do."

"Like what?"

"I want to show you something," she said.

She walked over to her station, where her tablet was still docked. She sat down and started typing on the keyboard.

Jared watched, but couldn't help but glance down her neck and to her chest, her silver cross lightly bouncing against her cleavage as she worked.

"This is a list of SolRescue members," she said. "Publicly available, so it's no big secret."

"There are thousands of members. It's a hobby for most of them, like a Carter Elgin fan club."

"You ought to be a member. Send him scented letters with lipstick kisses."

"So what? You want to contact some random member and tell them what, exactly?"

"Look at this list, Jared. Look closely. I've filtered it down."

"To the province of Manitoba."

"And here's someone who lives in town," she said. "You may recognize the name."

"Rachael Duck."

"I already messaged her," Chloe said. "Told her we had some information."

"What? What did you send her? I need to see it."

"Why?"

"Because, Chloe. Just show me."

She pulled up her message log. She clicked on Rachael's name.

SolRescue is in danger. The US and Chinese are working to dismantle the shield.

"Fuck, Chloe," Jared said. "You spelt it all out, didn't you…"

"I didn't think you'd have a problem with that. I figured you'd want us to talk to her. You trust her, don't you? Tell me you trust her, at least."

"Fuck. I can't believe this. You just sent a message in the clear to a Sol-Rescue member, giving her privileged information. Telling her something that we're not even supposed to know."

"Do you really think she'll report us to the authorities?"

"It's not that. It's in the clear. Who knows who could intercept it."

"You messaged me about it," Chloe said.

"What?"

"Last night. In the clear."

Shit.

"Well, I guess we've just reserved ourselves a couple of bunks in Highland County, Virginia."

"She needed to know, Jared. We had to tell her."

"You didn't have to tell her," Jared said. "Not yet. Not without talking to me first. Why the hell would you think this was okay?"

She threw up her hands. "I thought we were on the same page."

"But this is… just *stupid*, Chloe."

"I guess there's a lot of stupid going around," she said.

"I don't know what to do now."

"She wants to meet us. Tonight. Some guy at the Northern Studies Centre told me."

"Oh, so you didn't book the teleconference room for it?"

"Shut up. This can work, Jared. You have no reason to believe that anyone's keeping track of our messages."

"Where do we meet her?"

"The Tundra Buggy Lodge at Polar Bear Point. Apparently she works for them during bear season."

"Yeah. I know."

"I guess you would."

She'd looked a little smug when she'd said it.

The Tundra Buggy Lodge was a collection of connected train cars that had been converted into surprisingly comfortable accommodations; the setup was close to being antique, but somehow they kept it together in conditions not much less harsh than you'd find at those British and Chilean anchor towns in Antarctica. In late October or usually November, the tour company would tow the cars out over the tundra flats to Cape Churchill, a slab of land even more remote than the town or the launch site.

Rachael had showed him pictures of the lodge, and you could tour it online if you wanted, but he'd never been up to Polar Bear Point. Jared had always assumed she'd take him out there before he left, making a secondary assumption that she'd be talking to him at all at that time.

He and Chloe headed up for the meeting just after eight PM, having spent an awkward early evening in the lab, each pretending they weren't pissed off at the other.

There was no point in rehashing stupid; they'd both done it, they both were partly responsible. If Jared had been thinking straight, he wouldn't have messaged Chloe about the Chinese. And probably wouldn't have messaged her at all. Or slept with her.

He knew Rachael would blame him.

So maybe it was good he was making the trip up there before she murdered him.

The Hudson Bay flats reminded Jared of Lake Michigan in winter, but maybe a little choppier, since the flats were land and not ice, though the breaking up sea ice of Hudson Bay was just beyond.

The snow was on its last legs, and there were plenty of patches of bare ground, which had low brown grasses interspersed with rock and icy ponds and what looked like gravel.

The sun was still at least an hour above the horizon; Rachael would have chosen the time in the hope of no one seeing, just close enough to nightfall that there was little chance of anyone else hanging out in polar bear country. While the chance of running into bears wasn't all that high in May, it wasn't anywhere close to impossible, and from what Jared had read of the warning pamphlets, the worst time to run into a polar bear was at night.

They arrived at the collection of train cars a few minutes before 8:30. He saw a white pickup parked by the buggies; Rachael had borrowed a vehicle from someone, which now seemed obvious considering that twenty miles from town was a little far for her to walk.

Jared parked his jeep beside the truck and he and Chloe walked up to what looked like the entrance, an elevated dock with an open door.

"No ladder," Chloe said. "How do we climb up?"

Jared saw Rachael poking her head through the door.

"You bring a ladder," she said. "Otherwise you don't get in."

He watched as Rachael lowered a small metal utility ladder.

"I had to bring it with me," she said. "They don't really want people playing around up here."

Chloe climbed up first, Jared following behind.

Rachael gave him a cold stare once he reached the deck.

"I'm sorry," he said.

"I thought I told you not to tell anyone," she said. She nodded to Chloe. She meant that she hadn't wanted him to tell Chloe.

Which he'd promptly gone and did.

Because he was untrustworthy. And because he'd been horny.

They went inside the train cars and she led them to a dining area, rows of booths that looked unsurprisingly like a dining car on a train.

They sat down, Jared sitting beside Chloe, and Rachael still glaring.

"You two are idiots," Rachael said as she sat down across from them. "If the USAF didn't already know about you having doubts, they will now. And you've dragged me into it, too."

"The USAF doesn't monitor our communications," Jared said. "Do they?"

"Network communication is monitored. That's Technology 101. Just because it's Five Eyes and not the Air Force doesn't mean it won't get where it needs to go to fuck us all."

"Ten Eyes?"

"The NSA, dumbass," Rachael said. "And everyone else. The UK, Canada, Germany…"

"So how long until it filters down?" Chloe asked.

Rachael shook her head. "It's not an exact science. All I know is that there should be enough red flags for someone to start paying attention."

"So what do we do?" Jared asked.

"You leave me the fuck alone," Rachael said. "That's it. Don't message me, don't talk to me, don't look in my direction if someone's set me on fire."

"How does that solve anything?"

"It doesn't," Chloe said. "Not for us."

"Don't worry," Rachael said, "I'm royally fucked, too. Remember that you messaged me, okay?"

"And you didn't reply to that message. You sent someone to talk to me."

"Someone I can trust. So someone who's nothing like Jared."

"So you'll be fine," Jared said. "Some crazy woman sends you a message because you're the closest person she can find to SolRescue."

"No, I won't be fine. I now have to give up on the work I was doing, because they'll be watching everything I do."

"What work?" Chloe asked.

"It doesn't matter now, does it?"

"So how do we fix this?" Jared asked. "There's got to be a way."

"There isn't," Rachael said. "It's done. I fucked up. It's over. And now you need to get the fuck out of here."

He nodded and climbed up out of the booth.

"We won't go," Chloe said. "Not until you explain something to us."

"I'm not involved," Rachael said. "Just implicated."

"No, you're involved. I can tell. You know exactly what's going on. You're too in control. You're clearly driving this exchange."

"I'm just wanting to stay away from this. You guys want to spin some crazy theories, you go ahead. But don't include me."

"You're the one who told Jared about Mohammed's instructions for the shielding and that gamma ray burst," Chloe said. "I'm pretty sure of that. I'm just not sure why he didn't want me to know…"

"Chloe," Jared said, "just leave her out of it."

"No, she's in it. All the way. So let's figure something out. Let's come up with an actual plan."

"I don't want anything to do with either of you," Rachael said. "Just leave, alright?"

"They come for us and we'll point them to you," Chloe said.

"Shut up, Chloe," Jared said.

But she kept it up. "We need to let SolRescue know what's happening here. What Mohammed is planning to do."

"Again," Rachael said, "you two are idiots. You don't know a single thing they don't already know. Now, if you'd kept your gaping mouths shut, maybe you could have found out something of value. Maybe. Instead of broadcasting to the whole world that you're wanting to blow the whistle."

"That's not fair," Jared said. "How could she have known?"

"Known not to send open communications about top secret projects? Hmm… let me think…"

"So what do we do?" Chloe asked. "We're in this together now, Rachael."

"Fuck," Rachael said. She looked over to Jared. "Fuck!"

"Well?" Chloe said.

"Just hold on, Chloe," Jared said. "Just try to ease the tension, you know?"

"I can ask about it," Rachael said. "Find out if the messages can be scrubbed before they're analysed."

"What?" Chloe said. "How the heck would you be able to do that?"

"There are petabytes of data, sent every minute over the various networks they monitor. The system isn't perfect; they're always trying to catch up. But I doubt they ever will."

Chloe grinned. "So there's a delay."

"Maybe not enough of one," Rachael said. "By the time I get the request to the right people…"

"But you can try?" Jared asked.

Rachael sighed. "I'll try. But I'm not changing my mind on this. We're done, Jared. We don't know each other any longer. So get back in your jeep and go."

"Okay."

Chloe stood up. "Thank you, Rachael."

"Go fuck yourself, Chloe," Rachael said.

She followed Jared and Chloe out to the deck, and after they'd climbed down, she pulled up the ladder.

"You're not leaving, too?" Jared asked.

"I'll be putting some space between us," Rachael said. "A whole lot of space."

Jared nodded.

He and Chloe got into the jeep and drove back toward the town of Churchill.

After three minutes or so, the jeep stalled and drifted to a stop.

Jared restarted the engine.

It stalled again.

"There's something wrong," Chloe said.

"You think?"

"Don't get mad at me."

"I've been mad at you for a while now, Chloe."

He tried started the engine again. It wouldn't turn over.

"Really bad timing," he said. "Really bad."

"I've got my tablet," Chloe said. "Shit."

"No service, right?"

"I thought there was service everywhere along these trails. For emergency calls, at least."

"Well, try it."

She started dialing. "Shit."

"This isn't that complicated," Jared said. "Thirty minutes to sunset in polar bear country. We don't leave the vehicle."

"The vehicle isn't exactly bearproof."

"It's more bearproof than your jacket. Besides, Rachael should be along. There are only two trails she could take. So… fifty/fifty chance…"

"Seriously?"

"It can't be more than a couple hours' walk to the Northern Studies Centre. We can go once it's daylight again. I'm pretty sure we won't freeze to death overnight."

"Pretty sure?"

"We'll be fine, Chloe."

"Okay," she said. "We'll be fine."

Like she'd just decided on it.

It only took twenty minutes for headlights to show up behind them.

"It's gotta be Rachael," Chloe said.

"It doesn't matter who. I'll take anyone at this point."

As it came closer, they could see that it was a pickup. It was still light enough to tell that it was white, just like the one Rachael had brought to Polar Bear Point.

"Thank god," Chloe said.

The truck slowed down behind them.

It stopped a few feet behind.

Jared climbed out of the jeep.

He gave a wave as the truck door opened.

But whoever came out didn't look like Rachael. Too tall and dressed all in white, with a white balaclava.

He couldn't see a face.

But he could see a rifle slung over the shoulders. Even in the twilight he picked out the telltale signs of a homebrewed gun. 3d printed in a workshop. No registration, no trace.

Perfect for polar bears, or for any other targets.

"Car's dead," Jared said, trying to sound at ease. There was something anxiety-inducing about ski masks, even in the arctic.

"Start walking." A man's voice.

"Funny."

The man pulled his rifle from his shoulders, pointing it down at the snow.

"What's the hell?" Jared said. "Who are you, anyway?"

The man lifted the barrel higher, pointing it at Jared.

"Start walking," he said again.

Jared heard the other door to the jeep open.

"Stay in the car," he said to Chloe.

"Both of you," the man said. "Shut up and walk. Head west."

Jared slowly turned around, to face west. He saw Chloe slowly moving over to him.

She reached him and grabbed his hand.

"I'm scared," she said.

"You think?"

They walked down the gravel road, past the smooth ice of a large lake. The sun was setting, and Jared could feel the wind picking up. From the north, so definitely cold enough.

He and Chloe walked several hundred paces, before he got up the nerve to look back.

The man hadn't been following him.

He was standing by the jeep, still pointing the rifle.

"He isn't bringing us anywhere," Jared said. "I don't know what he thinks is going to happen."

Was the man with the gun hoping they'd chance on a hungry bear or two? He couldn't be expecting them to collapse into the melting snow of late May, freezing to death in slightly below zero degrees Celsius.

Or was someone else waiting out in the distance to ambush them? During the day you could see well ahead of you in every direction, but at night...

"We should make a run for it," Chloe said. "Once we're out of range. Not sure when we're out of range..."

"He wants us to run."

"What?"

"Walk or run, doesn't matter. As long as don't make it back to my jeep."

"What about Rachael? Was that the truck she came up here in?"

"I don't know. Looked like it. But white pickups aren't exactly rare."

"So if we wait by the road, she might come by."

"Or they might have gotten to her first."

"And done what?" Chloe asked.

"I don't know. This isn't something I'm used to."

"So what the heck do we do, Jared?"

"We keep walking, I guess."

They reached the junction in the trail, where right went up to the edge of the bay, and left headed back to the Northern Studies Centre and the edge of civilization.

There was no point in heading to the right, even if that happened to be counter to what the man with the rifle would want them to do.

So Jared led Chloe south, along the shore of Hudson Bay.

And he saw the headlights of another vehicle.

"Rachael?" Chloe asked.

"I doubt it," he said. "That truck doesn't seem to be moving. I doubt she'd see us from that far away."

"It's the same truck from before. Coming around..."

"I don't think he had time for that," Jared said. "He's probably still waiting by the jeep, in case we head back. Because that's definitely an option to consider."

"You think there's another guy up there... with a gun..."

"I don't know. But I don't think it's Rachael."

He saw something else, behind the vehicle, the taillights bouncing off of it.

A trailer... a cylinder...

He'd seen some of those around.

"A bear trap," he said.

"What?"

"There's a bear trap behind that vehicle. Might be towing it."

"So maybe it's a conservation officer," Chloe said.

"I don't know... maybe."

Chloe picked up her pace, waving both arms over her head.

"I don't know, Chloe," he said. "We can't be sure."

"We'll find out soon enough."

They reached a point where Jared could make out the truck. Not the green color of the conservation branch. Another white pickup.

There were too many of the goddamn things.

The truck started driving.

The trap didn't follow behind.

The truck turned around and started moving south.

"He should have seen us," Chloe said. "Why didn't he see us?"

"I'm not sure he didn't."

"What do you mean?"

"I don't know, Chloe. I just don't."

The trap.

He could see that the trap door was up. The trap was open.

Were there bears nearby?

He saw movement.

Hard to see in the darkening skies.

White against the grays of the trap and the barren ground and the dirty snow.

Movement out of the trap.

They'd let something out.

"Holy shit," Jared said. "There's a bear in that trap."

"A polar bear?"

"Holy shit."

"Okay," Chloe said, "we just need to stay calm. We just need to keep our distance. Stay downwind."

"We're not downwind."

"We've read the handouts, Jared. We can figure this out. There's two of us, so that's a good thing. Maybe we can scare him off."

"No... we're supposed to walk away..."

"Not if he can smell us."

"Just hold on, okay?"

Jared tried to watch. His eyes were trying to adjust, but the light was changing as it darkened.

The bear had climbed back down from the trap, and was moving around the side of the trap, toward Jared and Chloe.

At that moment, the bear seemed more interested in the trap than anything else. It looked smaller than Jared would have expected, smaller than the bears he'd seen in the pictures hanging around town, in the videos he'd watched about protecting from bear attacks.

Maybe not smaller, but thinner... Jared knew enough to know that thin bears weren't a good kind of polar bear to run into. Especially at night.

The bear stopped.

Then reared up on its hind legs.

It was sniffing the air.

Wondering what they were.

"We show him we're human," Chloe said. "That'll make him less likely to attack."

"Unless it doesn't."

"Yeah."

Jared waved his arms above his head.

"Hello," he said, trying to keep his voice low and calm. "We are human. A couple of humans."

The bear dropped back down onto four legs. It took several slow steps forward.

"Now we move back," Chloe said.

She started stepping backward.

Jared did the same, keeping his gaze on the bear.

At least it was dark enough that his eyes could adjust.

The bear stopped and raised its head. Sniffing some more.

It started moving again. But turning a little to Jared's left.

They kept walking backward.

"I think it's leaving," Jared said.

"No... it's circling."

"I don't know."

"Oh my god, Jared. Oh my god..."

"Just wait, Chloe... we don't know yet."

The bear moved a little closer, but still circling to the north, looping inward.

Jared waved his arms again.

"Don't come any closer," he said to the bear.

The bear kept moving, still circling, walking down by the edge of the frozen lake. The ice wouldn't be thick enough for the bear to walk on; Jared knew that if the bear kept heading north, he'd have to close in on them.

Which the bear was slowly starting to do.

"If he charges," Jared said, "don't run."

"You're hoping he'll go after me… oh my god…"

"Come on, Chloe. We know what to do. If he charges, we stand our ground."

"And then what?"

"And we fight."

The bear turned to face them.

And started its charge.

"Holy shit," Jared said.

He saw Chloe take a couple steps behind him.

He understood the concept.

Jared started yelling. As loud as he could. Cursing out the goddamn polar bear.

The bear kept coming.

Jared held out his fists; he'd never even been in a fight with another person.

The bear lunged, throwing a claw into Jared's shoulder.

Jared shoved his right fist out, aiming for the bear's head. He hit it on the lower jaw.

The bear grasped at him with its mouth; Jared threw out a left, striking the bear between the eyes. The bear pulled its head back, then sent out its other claw.

Jared felt the scrape in his arm; it felt like a warm gust of wind over the arctic chill.

He lost his balance, falling backward.

He saw Chloe throw her hands at the bear, hitting with both fists against its head. Then he saw her go down.

The bear had her, its mouth clamped over her leg.

Jared pulled himself up.

The bear was dragging her along the ground.

He threw his left elbow into the bear's thick neck.

He punched his right fist into the bear's left eye.

And elbowed the bear again.

He screamed as loud as he could.

The bear pulled back, letting go of Chloe's leg.

Jared kept driving, throwing his elbows, his fists, yelling and shrieking.

The bear started moving off.

Jared yelled again.

The bear kept moving.

"Chloe," he said. "Are you okay?"

She was breathing heavily. Heaving.

He could see blood dripping through her pants, a small puddle forming in a bank of snow under her leg.

"Chloe…"

"I'm okay," she said. "But what… what if he comes back?"

"I know."

Jared wanted to reach down and help her.

But he had to stay upright. He had to make more noise.

He yelled again.

The bear was moving south again, back upwind.

"Do you think you can walk?" he asked her.

"I don't know. It really hurts."

Jared could feel the cuts, his shoulder and his arm. He wasn't sure he had the strength to help Chloe up.

She started getting up on her own.

"This fucking hurts," she said.

He'd never heard her swear before.

She helped her throw an arm over his shoulder.

He groaned from the pain.

"We need to move north," he said. "Away from the bear."

"And back to the guy with the gun," she said.

"Back to the guy with the gun."

They walked slowly along the road, the cold biting through their shredded clothing. He could feel Chloe shiver as they took each step.

It didn't feel like they were going to make it.

He felt like he was thirty seconds away from nose-diving onto the gravel.

He knew it was too perfect to be an accident; the man with the rifle had forced them toward the bear trap.

Where they'd had a hungry bear.

Which they then let out just in time for a late night snack.

Fuck.

They'd planned it all, right down to having a bear *on hand*. Who the hell has a starving bear on hand?

Someone who'd wanted it to look like bad luck, Jared and Chloe running into car trouble just as the sun was setting on the Hudson Bay Flats.

He couldn't shake the feeling that Rachael had been involved.

Jared stopped walking.

He helped lower Chloe down to the ground.

"What are we doing?" she asked. "You think it's safe to rest here?"

"I don't know. We just need to rest."

He sat down beside her.

She leaned her head against his shoulder.

He grimaced from the pain, but tried to hide it from her.

She hadn't noticed it.

"We either go back up to where the jeep stalled out," he said, "or we make our way up and along the bay, looping around to where we'd met Rachael."

"How long would that take?"

"Probably too long. I don't know if we can make it that far."

"We can make it," she said. "I know we can."

"I don't think so."

"Let's go," she said, slowly standing up. "And I'll prove it to you."

He chuckled a little.

She'd prove it to him.

He followed along as she trudged up the road in front of him.

He wasn't leaning on her.

He felt like maybe he could keep going for a little while longer.

They passed the junction to the jeep and the gunman and kept moving straight to the north, toward the point on the bay.

Chloe had started humming, some song that Jared had never heard before. It sounded like a hymn, and he didn't question her newfound faith.

Surviving a bear attack could be considered a religious experience. So could not surviving, in theory, depending on your worldview.

Jared knew he was beyond exhausted by his legs; they were now aching enough to almost rival the open cuts on his shoulder and arm. He shouldn't have been this tired. He could see the bloodstains on his jacket. He looked back and saw the drips in the snow and gravel.

He was losing more blood than he'd thought.

He needed to close the wounds.

He took off his jacket and his shirt. He ripped several lengths from the shirt.

Chloe helped him tie the tourniquet around his shoulder, and another around his arms.

He was glad for it; he wasn't sure he would have pulled them tight enough.

"We need to tie you off," he told her.

She nodded.

He wrapped two strips of fabric over the cuts on her forearms. There were scrapes on her hands and up her arms, but they weren't as bad as the two deeper gashes.

And she wasn't bleeding as much as he had been.

"I've lost a lot," he said. "Maybe too much."

"You can make it, Jared. You can lean on my shoulder."

Jared knew that it was ridiculous that he was feeling ashamed; they'd fought off a thousand pound polar bear. You don't just skip away from that.

And he'd bore the brunt; he'd like to think he saved their lives, but Chloe had helped more than a little. He wasn't the hero of the story.

He was just feeling weak and cold and a little embarrassed.

There was a gunshot. To the south.

"Someone shoot at the bear?" Chloe asked.

"I think so."

"We should keep moving."

Jared slowly stood up. He started walking.

Chloe offered her shoulder, but he shook his head.

It wouldn't help for him to sap all of her energy.

Worst case, she'd have to leave him and go for help.

They kept heading north, and after a few more minutes they reached the edge of the small point, where the road took a turn to the southeast.

All Jared wanted to do was rest.

But Chloe kept moving, so he followed behind.

And then he fell.

Onto the gravel, scraping his arms, his wounds, his face.

Chloe turned back, kneeling down beside him.

"You have to keep going," he said.

"I know." She knelt a little lower, kissing him on the forehead. "I love you, Jared. Fuckbuddy or regular buddy or who knows. But I do."

Jared nodded. He didn't know what to say to that.

She smiled.

Then she stood up and continued moving along the trail.

Jared closed his eyes.

16

SAMANTHA WASN'T around on Friday morning.

Benj still had her tablet, and she wasn't in her room. She was avoiding him. Maybe she was embarrassed for coming on to him, after he'd made it clear how much he hated her guts.

But he didn't hold that against her; it was every other thing she'd done that was the problem. That a suddenly intimidated Samantha had tried to restore some sense of balance by trying to manipulate him... that he understood.

He'd done the same kind of thing to her in an airplane bathroom.

Something he was never planning on doing again. He'd had trouble sleeping over it. He'd crossed the line, and he couldn't just swallow it.

It was eating away at him.

And he didn't know how to stop it.

From before he'd even left Utah, Benj had been sending messages to all of the members of his famed Afro-American Contingent, including Laila and Malik.

None had replied, until he received a message from Taylor.

Haven't been able to contact Malik or Laila. Tell me where you are.

He didn't reply.

He couldn't tell her anything; Laila and Malik really had disappeared, and she'd be next.

Assuming that simply replying to him wasn't enough for that outpatient detention Samantha had talked about.

Benj knew enough about that little patch of land in rural Virginia. It was the latest place where the US government would hold the citizens they didn't feel they should kill, but who couldn't be allowed to tell anyone what they knew.

The constitution had been amended over ten years before to ban killing US Citizens, and that included death penalties, drone attacks, and especially whistleblowers. Not that Benj believed the US government would shy away from bending the rules every once in a while.

He just hoped that Laila and Malik weren't important enough for that kind of fudging.

181

⤧

Samantha finally knocked on his hotel room door at 12:30 PM. She came in with a friendly-looking smile and a paper bag.

"Sandwiches," she said. "I hope that's okay."

"Depends what's in them," he said from his place on the desk chair. He didn't smile back.

But he felt like shit. About all of it.

Even if he hated her.

She sat down on his bed and started unpacking the lunch.

He realized that she could see the screen of his tablet.

"I see Taylor still cares about you," she said.

"No surprise there. That you'd still be trying to spy on me, I mean."

"So why did you break it off with her, anyway? I mean, she's really great, isn't she?"

"She just doesn't pack the same appeal as psychotic Korean girls."

"Ha," she said. Not really a laugh, *per se.*

"So you really did manage to get them detained. Laila and Malik."

She nodded. "We didn't have a choice. I'm sorry, Benj. There was nothing I could do to prevent that."

"I'm sure there was," he said. "You just didn't care."

"That's harsh. But it doesn't matter what you think of me, does it? As if you could think any less of me."

"I'm always willing to hate someone even more."

She nodded again. "I need to send a message to the project manager up here. She's ignored everything I've sent so far."

"Get your colonel to message her. Not that you have a way of doing that…"

"I think we'll just drop in unannounced."

"And you'll blow them all away with your charm?"

"Mostly with my fancy letter from Colonel Begtang. And your charm, Benj. I'm sure you can flirt a little with this project manager, show her the goods."

"I'm not really the type, Samantha. Maybe you should handle that. It's almost summer, so you could just leave your shirt back at the room."

"I know you think I was just trying to play you, Benj. But that's not what that was."

"Oh, come on," he said. "There's no way you think I'm that stupid."

"I don't know… I just… I liked it."

"What?"

"When you showed me your balls."

"What?"

"On the plane," she said. "You held me down and you showed me who you are."

"What the hell is wrong with you?"

She smiled. "I'm a little messed up."

"I honestly can't trust anything you say," he said.

"I know. I like that, too."

Samantha had rented a large 4x4 pickup truck from the local outfit, and she drove Benj out of town, past the airport, and out into the pock-marked lowlands along the bay.

After a long stretch of lifeless wilderness, she drove them past a large white and blue building that was more than a little out of place on the bare tundra. A research facility.

After that, the emptiness came back, but with more and more short little evergreens colonizing the tundra.

And a small inflatable hab in the middle of a barren patch, not much bigger than a one-car garage, with a small solar array to the side.

"Where the magic treason happens," Samantha said.

She pulled a little to the side of the gravel road and parked.

They walked up to the canvas door.

There was nothing to knock on, so Samantha called out hello and unhooked the latch.

She walked in, and Benj followed behind.

It was a lab, the kind of disorganized mess you'd see in a hardware shop, benches with machinery and scattered bits of electronics, but with several large printers along one wall.

Bigger than what Benj had seen before.

And beside one printer were rounded metal plates.

Like parts of a fuselage.

There was a man at the far end of the lab, sitting at a workdock.

He'd turned around in his chair, but hadn't stood up.

"This is a private lab," the man said.

He had dark curly hair and a clean-shaven face.

Benj recognized him from his photograph. The Alchemist of Ann Arbor.

"Dr. Najjar," Samantha said.

"Not a doctor yet," Najjar said. "Maybe never. But again. Private lab."

Samantha took a few steps deeper into the building. "We're sorry to intrude... but we have a letter from Colonel Begtang."

"I doubt it."

"Excuse me?"

"We don't give tours," Najjar said. "I'm sorry to disappoint."

Samantha smirked. "I'm sorry to insist." She pulled an envelope out of her jacket pocket. It seemed too small to be something official.

She walked over to the workdock and handed it to Najjar.

He opened it and pulled out the folded letter. A small business card dropped to the floor.

Najjar let out a long and deep sigh.

"Turnpike," Najjar said. "Another one of Carter Elgin's arms-length companies. Sounds like corporate espionage to me."

"That's not really your concern, Mr. Najjar," Samantha said.

"Don't antagonize me. This will go better if I don't have to dislike you."

Samantha looked back to Benj, who was still just a couple steps in from the door. She was pressing him.

He was supposed to be the one in charge.

And he had no reason not to play the part.

He swept forward and stuck out his hand. "Mr. Najjar," he said. "Or Mohammed? I'm Benj McPherson."

"Director of ICT," Najjar said. "Nice title."

Benj hadn't actually heard it before. It sounded like it required more pomp than IT Manager would.

"We don't want to antagonize you," Benj said. "In fact, let's get to the point, since you've got shit to do."

Najjar flinched a little at that. "And that point, McPherson?"

"We want you to work for us."

He heard a barely audible groan from Samantha. Apparently his spycraft wasn't up to snuff.

"I won't work for Elgin," Najjar said. "I have too much self respect."

"It's not Elgin," Samantha said. She stopped herself.

Najjar shook his head. "It doesn't matter, anyway. A man can't quit a project like this."

"Why not?" Benj asked.

"You know why not," Najjar said, almost growling.

"This project isn't high clearance," Samantha said. "Otherwise we wouldn't be allowed here in the first place."

"You aren't allowed here. Some letter from an easily-impressed colonel doesn't change the facts. This is high clearance enough. And I'm not going to anger the powers that be by stepping away."

"There's no impressive tech here," Benj said. "Nothing like what we want to do."

"Is that what you think?" Najjar asked. "That I am some kind of mercenary looking for the next big thrill? You should respect me enough to try to understand my motivations."

Benj gave a little nod. Trying to show he understood.

"I'm not interested in your offer," Najjar said.

"We haven't made an offer," Samantha said.

"Why did you quit the MechaTeacher project?" Benj asked.

Najjar glared at him.

"It doesn't make sense," Benj said. "You were making good progress, really starting to get some attention, then poof!"

"Poof?" Najjar said. "Is that how you'd describe it?"

"You ran off to Africa and didn't even tell people why you'd dropped it."

"It was a failure. Not something I usually bring up with people who want to hire me."

"But less than two years later the Defense Department shows off a un-manned combat vehicle that seems to have the same emotional intelligence that you were working on."

"So they followed up on my research," Najjar said. "And they were smarter than me."

"What part of Africa, Mr. Najjar?"

"What?"

"I read it was somewhere central. So would that be the Congo, maybe, or Northwest Virginia?"

Najjar didn't reply.

"Benj," Samantha said. "Drop it, alright?"

"You won't get detained if we do this right," Benj said. "We take you away from here and then we make the announcement. It's a combination of 'too-public-to-sweep-away' and 'too-hard-to-reach'."

Najjar shook his head.

Samantha didn't say anything else. Benj couldn't tell if she knew she couldn't stop him, or if she was just genuinely curious in what he was trying to do.

"You know this project isn't a good thing," Benj said. "Copying existing tech in order to destroy something that, quite honestly, saved the planet."

"The Chinese will destroy it eventually," Najjar said. "We need to get there first."

"You're working with the Chinese military. You just don't know it."

"Working with the Chinese? What are you trying to do here?"

"We have evidence," Benj said.

"Evidence... maybe some fake photographs or doctored conver-sations?"

"Okay," Samantha said. "I think that's enough."

"This is why Carter Elgin has too much reach," Najjar said. "You think I don't know what this is? That I don't know who you are and why you're here? Benj *McPherson*. You might as well be named Carter Elgin, Jr."

"I think I'm a little too tanned," Benj said.

"This isn't funny, McPherson. This is disgusting. Two SolRescue agents using their organization's influence to circumvent national security protocol. In an attempt to sabotage a US government project."

Benj shook his head. "We just want your beautiful brain. And to throw wads of money at you."

"Forget it," Samantha said. "We need to go."

"And that's the smartest thing you've come up with," Najjar said. "Please leave and don't come back. And I will be reporting this breach of security to Colonel Begtang's superior officer."

Samantha turned to leave.

"Don't be the bad guy, Mohammed," Benj said. "You know better than to trust the government."

"We need to go, Benj," Samantha said. "Please."

"Listen to your assistant, McPherson," Najjar said.

Benj nodded.

"You've got our contact information, Mr. Najjar," Samantha said. "Please think on it."

Najjar didn't respond.

Benj and Samantha left the inflatable lab.

They walked silently to the truck.

Samantha drove them back toward the town.

She started chuckling.

"What's going on?" Benj asked.

"That was perfect," she said.

"What the hell is wrong with you?"

"One clumsy attempt by SolRescue to derail the project. *Check*."

"Clumsy attempt?"

"You didn't think that would work," she said, "did you? That two random people who are clearly affiliated with SolRescue could just swoop in and convince him that there's some secret partnership with China?"

"So what was the point? To piss him off?"

"Exactly."

"You think he was involved with the attack on the European station."

"Not at all. He doesn't know any of that."

"This isn't how this works," Benj said. "Or have you forgotten? I wasn't going to be fucked with anymore."

"I told you it wasn't about poaching Najjar. I wasn't lying."

"But you didn't tell me what we were doing."

"Oh, my bad," she said. "We're messing with Najjar."

"Fuck. This isn't okay with me. You understand?"

"Yeah. I know."

"No," Benj said. "I'm saying that this is the kind of behavior that causes problems between us."

"Like you're going to corner me in another tiny bathroom?"

She wasn't the least bit intimidated by him.

He was a fucking joke to Samantha Yoon.

"I'm sorry, Benj," she said. "I meant all that I said. That I like you, that I like when you act all gangsta."

"Gangsta?"

"You know. You get that tone in your voice, that look in your eyes…"

"That's incredibly racist."

"I'm not sure it's racist. I'm not white."

That made Benj chuckle. He wished it hadn't.

He knew that he should be angry with her. She'd been fucking him over from the day they'd met. For months and months, and he'd had no clue until she'd gotten his ass fired.

Fucking bitch.

What a fucking bitch.

Benj knew that deep down, like way deep down… part of him liked it.

17

ANITA HAD gotten her first inkling of what Carter Elgin was up about three minutes after he'd finished inside of her in her and Bridget's suite in the residences of Cornell Tech.

He got a text on his phone. He disentangled from his cuddle with her, then lazily grabbed the phone from the pocket of his khaki pants, hanging over the side of the bed without getting up.

He read the message.

He shot up.

"What is it?" Anita asked. "Is everything okay?"

"Yeah, good," he said, quickly starting to dress himself. "Good, good, good. Look... I gotta go."

"Yeah, okay."

"This was... wonderful, Anita. I mean, really wonderful."

"Um—"

"I'll talk to you tonight, okay? After your nap?"

He walked out of the suite.

Anita didn't feel like napping.

She knew he was on his way to the lab, to see Bridget.

Anita wasn't sure she had the guts to follow him.

But she didn't really have the stomach to sit back and wait.

She got dressed, not in the ostentatious dress she'd been wearing when he'd come onto her, but in simple jeans-and-sweater, not classy but not slouchy, either.

In practically every other species of animal, the male had to win over the female. The bowerbird would decorate his giant nest, the peacock would flash his colorful array of tailfeathers, the narwhal would grow the world's longest overbite.

But Anita knew that humans were different.

That's why she had breasts instead of an ass that would glow red on special occasions. Because she had to compete. Because one day soon she'd grow too old, and it would be that much harder to get anyone to pay attention to her.

Because women were always on the losing side.

She checked her hair in the mirror. She teased it a little, trying to make it look less like bedhead, but not *completely unlike* bedhead.

She hadn't washed off the makeup from the shoot; the running mascara and blotchy foundation sent a significantly different signal than the messy hair.

She took a minute to clean herself up.

Then she made her way down the Tech Walk to the Mae Jemison Building, and over to the lab.

The blinds were down; she couldn't see into the front bank of windows. Bridget was never one to turn her back on natural light.

Anita opened the door and stepped inside.

Only Medora was there, sitting at a workstation, fiddling with some cables.

"Where's Bridget?" Anita asked.

"She went for a walk with Carter," Medora said. "Just text her. She's got her cell."

Anita thanked her, then left the lab.

A walk with Carter.

So Bridget had texted him, and he'd jumped up like there was a lobster in his boxer shorts.

At her beck and call.

She'd already lost, and she felt stupid for even playing.

And she felt even stupider for caring, for thinking that the attention of some goofy guy should matter. Her mother had raised her to know better. She'd said that most men were no better than "unreasoning animals", that they were controlled by the same external stimuli that would work on a dog or a rat.

Anita still didn't know if her mother was right.

Maybe she was.

And maybe the fact that Carter Elgin was different than those other men was exactly why Anita couldn't get him out of her mind.

Lawyers still send paper letters, a half century after email had become a thing for most people.

Anita had a theory about that—like most cynics—that it was just a way of adding another $100 service charge, that sending electronic correspondence didn't seem tangible enough for the price.

But most lawyers, including Anita's, would send a text message to their clients as well, which would arrive anywhere from three hours to three days before the paper letter, depending on what kind of courier was used.

Anita tended to ignore those messages she received on her tablet. It was only when the drone would drop off the hard copy that the letter would seem real.

And one was dropped off first thing Friday morning. Or possibly late Thursday night.

A settlement offer.

Cynical old Anita figured that Bridget must've gotten wind of Anita's new income stream.

Five hundred thousand dollars. Down from a million three months before. And nothing for legal costs.

Bridget wanted it to be done.

But she still wanted Anita to admit wrongdoing as part of it. She could ask for a dollar and the price would be too goddamn high.

Anita would have to say no, which meant that the cycle would continue, and the lawyer fees would pile up.

Not that Anita had to pay them. That's what the legal fund was for, a shell under some distant cousin of hers' name, that Anita knew was really fed from anonymous donations from one donor in particular.

Carter was funding the lawyers to defend against the suit. The suit that he and Bridget had filed against her. He was still playing both sides with them, still trying to take care of both of his "girls".

Anita was tempted to tell her cousin to shut down the fund, that she'd pay her own defense. A big fuck you to Carter, because she doesn't need him to save her from Bridget. Or from him.

Or from herself.

But she didn't message her cousin.

She just messaged her lawyer instead, to tell her to try again.

To send back the offer with a counteroffer: five hundred thousand dollars that Anita didn't have, and no wrongdoing on either side.

She wanted it to be over, too. But not enough to take the blame. Not for something that wasn't her fault.

Anita had decided to talk to Bridget before she'd talk to Carter. She and Bridget had been friends since the day Anita had arrived in New York City—or maybe the day after, come to think of it—and Carter was new, an encroachment, really.

She'd asked Bridget to meet her at the Starbuck's, since she knew that neither of them had yet recovered from the video shoot earlier in the week.

Medora would be sending them the final version soon; then if Bridget was right, they'd get lucky and things would start taking off, and there wouldn't be time for just two girls and eggnog lattes.

Or everything would go nowhere.

And Anita wasn't sure that would be a bad thing.

"I know this Carter stuff is getting weird," Bridget said, bringing the subject up before Anita had thought either of them was ready. "I feel like he wants to come between us, you know?"

"I know," Anita said. "I think that's just his personality."

"He kissed me. That day we came back from the shoot. We were out for a walk, and—"

"And he kissed you."

"Yeah. Does that upset you?"

"What?"

"I don't know. Is this a problem? Like, we're supposed to be all three of us together, and then Carter and me..."

"It's fine," Anita said, not that she felt it ever could be. Which was stupid. But still. That's what it was.

Bridget sighed. "I don't know if it is. I mean, what if it doesn't work? Then we break up, and we hate each other..."

"So it's a whole relationship, is it?"

"Well, yeah. I'd say so."

"Yeah, okay."

"Okay?"

"I think it's fine," Anita said.

She took a gulp of her drink. Still too hot. She took another sip. She just wanted to be done.

"We can go walk or something," Bridget said. "You seem restless."

"Yeah, okay."

They walked through the campus greenspace, heading south to the park.

Anita didn't have anything to say. She felt like Bridget had punched her in the throat, and she was having trouble not wanting to hit back.

But it wasn't Bridget's fault.

It's not like Anita called dibs or anything. Or that dibs was even a thing.

And it wasn't like Carter wasn't playing both of them. He'd had sex with Anita then high-tailed it over to Smoochfest with Bridget.

But Anita couldn't say anything... *she just couldn't.*

She was embarrassed, and she knew that it wouldn't make anything better. Calling Carter out would kill the thing with Bridget, sure, but it would kill the project, too. Right before the big SolRescue video came out, before they found out if they were going to sink or swim. Or at least if people wanted to throw money at the problem.

She could wait, couldn't she? Sure, she could tell Carter that he's a worthless piece of shit, but she wouldn't ruin it for Bridget. Not while they didn't know what could be.

Saving the planet was worth a few ruffled feathers.

And letting a two-timing asshole play his game for a few more days.

18

JARED WOKE up feeling dizzy.

Not in pain, just dizzy.

He was in a hospital room.

He looked at the window, not sitting up. He could see a cloudy sky. Nothing else.

He slowly sat up.

He could feel a twinge of pain in his shoulder, something the dizzying drugs weren't able to cover up completely. Probably for the best, as it made him rise a little more gingerly.

Out the window was the steel expanse of Hudson Bay, with the supertankers and the offshore gas rig across the line in Nunavut.

They hadn't airlifted him to Winnipeg.

A good sign that he wasn't about to die from his injuries.

He looked around.

And saw Rachael Duck.

"You're alright," she said. "I'm glad."

"What are you doing here?"

"Some guy I know got attacked by a polar bear."

"I thought you were done with me," he said.

"It's not a big deal. We went on a few dates, and you don't have anyone else to look out for you."

"How's Chloe?"

"Well, she isn't here, so that should give you a clear answer."

"What the hell, Rachael? Is that some kind of joke?"

"I haven't heard from her," Rachael said. "I'm sorry. I didn't think that would upset you."

"She was with me."

"No she wasn't."

"Yes, she was. In the jeep. When we were forced out. When the bear attacked."

Rachael shook her head. "I don't understand, Jared. She didn't leave her truck at the lodge."

"Her truck?"

"The white pickup. I saw it parked out front at the lodge."

"Shit."

"That wasn't her truck."

"And it wasn't your truck," Jared said. "It was the guy who followed us. The guy who fucked up my jeep while we were talking, so it would stall out on the way back. The guy with the rifle."

"What rifle?"

"Why else would we get out and walk, Rachael? Some guy came up behind us. Told us to get moving. Listen, Chloe's gotta be here, too. Or she was taken to Winnipeg for treatment. She was mauled by the polar bear, too."

"I'm sorry, Jared," she said. "They didn't find her."

"She's still out there."

"I don't know. My ride saw the jeep on their way to come get me. They drove around and found you, brought you in. You'd lost a shitload of blood."

They'd found him and stopped looking. They'd only been looking for him.

"She's still out there, Rachael."

"I'll tell them," she said.

She got up and rushed out of the room.

Jared looked at the IV in his arm. He slowly pulled out the syringe.

He climbed out of bed.

He found his clothes in the dresser, and started getting dressed.

A healthcare worker came in, a heavyset aboriginal man.

"I'm leaving," Jared said.

"You should be in bed," the man said.

"I know."

The man didn't try to stop him as he slowly stumbled out the door.

Rachael caught up to him as he walked down the hospital corridor.

"I've got my brother's truck," she said. "We can take that out to look."

"He's the one who found me?"

"No. He's not big on driving those trails. My boss picked you up in the Tundra Buggy. He said you're lucky to be alive."

"We need to find Chloe," Jared said.

"I know."

She reached over to help steady him.

And helped him out to the waiting white pickup truck.

They spent three hours driving the trails, starting with where Jared had been found, then following the road where Chloe had walked. There'd been footsteps for some of the way, but the ground was the wrong mix of frozen and snowless, leaving the tracks to disappear every few paces before reappearing again further up the road. And the tracks disappeared for good long before reaching Polar Bear Point.

Jared couldn't tell if Chloe had been picked up, or if she'd veered away from the trails.

All he knew was that she wasn't there.

And neither was his jeep.

They expanded their search, covering Bird Cove, the Northern Studies Centre and the area near the lab, and even down around Miss Piggy and the airport.

There was no sign of Chloe. And no sign of the bear, who from Rachael had said hadn't been reported by anyone else.

It was still a good four hours until sunset, but Jared knew there was no point.

The trails covered most of the area, the ground was flat enough, the kettle lakes still covered in a thin layer of ice.

They would have seen her.

He knew they would have seen her.

"I think that's it," he said.

"I'm sorry," Rachael said. She reached over and put a hand on his lap. "I really am."

"Someone picked her up. I can't see what else could have happened."

"I don't know…"

"Did you find out?" he asked. "About those messages. If anyone was listening in."

"I haven't had time, Jared."

"Maybe they saw her as the threat. They saw she wasn't killed, so they grabbed her."

"I still don't understand this," she said. "You're saying someone knew that polar bear was out there, and that he'd attack?"

"No… they'd trapped a polar bear and released it on us."

"Trapped a polar bear? Do you have any idea how crazy that sounds?"

"They have traps all over, Rachael."

"Not just anyone can rent one and grab themselves a bear."

"It happened," he said. "I was there."

"Okay."

"So what does this mean? If they took her, if they'd wanted her out of the way… shit."

"We don't know anything, Jared."

But he knew. If the hospital didn't have her…

"They'll have taken her somewhere. Somewhere we'd never find her."

"Jared…"

"Drive down Highway 6, toss her just half a mile off the road."

"We don't know that," she said.

"I know we'll never find her."

And that was how Jared knew how much he cared about Chloe. Just in time to know he'd let her down, and it had cost Chloe her life.

ဆ

Mohammed messaged Jared as Rachael was driving him back into town. Apparently Mohammed hadn't heard until that moment.

And he said he wanted to meet, at the lab.

"Just put him off," Rachael said. "You're exhausted."

"Come with me," Jared said. "Please."

"I doubt that invitation is meant to include me."

"I don't give a flying fuck."

She nodded.

Then she turned the truck around.

ဆ

Mohammed was working at his dock when they arrived.

He'd still been productive, apparently.

He looked less than impressed that Rachael was there, but he didn't comment on it.

"I need to know," Mohammed said. "Tell me how it happened."

"Is this just some morbid curiosity?" Rachael asked.

"Just tell me, Jared."

"We were up by Polar Bear Point," Jared said. "Chloe and I."

"Why?"

"To see the bears."

"Bullshit."

"They were meeting with me," Rachael said. "I invited them to the Tundra Buggy Lodge."

"Why?" Mohammed asked.

"If you have to ask why," she said, "then you're a lot more sheltered than I would have thought."

Mohammed looked over at Jared. "Seriously?"

He seemed impressed. And jealous, unsurprisingly.

"Chloe and I left together in my jeep. There was a white pickup truck parked outside, but we'd thought that Rachael had driven it up."

"But I'd gotten a ride," Rachael said. "So I thought they'd come up in separate vehicles. That Jared was driving the jeep by himself."

"And you had car trouble," Mohammed said. "Kept stalling out. Magically."

"Yeah," Jared said. "You seem oddly familiar with that."

"I have my suspicions. So the car stalled, and then you decided to walk?"

Jared shook his head. "No. Not at all. We were going to stay in the jeep, wait for someone to find us. We figured Rachael would probably be driving by soon enough."

"So what happened?"

"He's getting to that," Rachael said.

"A white pickup showed up behind us," Jared said. "I thought it was Rachael. But it wasn't. It was a guy in a ski mask, with a rifle. He told us to start walking."

"So you did," Mohammed said.

"He had a gun."

"Okay."

"So we walked a ways, trying to get to the Northern Studies Centre, to get some help. And then we saw the second truck."

"A different truck? Or the same one."

"White pickup, but probably a different one. I don't see how he would have moved around so quickly. But it's possible."

"You guys are driving a white pickup," Mohammed said.

"How the hell do you know that?" Rachael asked.

"Surveillance cameras," Jared said. "No reason not to have them."

"It's my brother's truck," Rachael said. "There are a shitload of white pickups in Churchill."

"I understand," Mohammed said. "So what happened next?"

"There was a polar bear trap," Jared said. "Then the truck drove away, and I realized the trap was open."

He described the attack, how he and Chloe had worked together to fight off the bear. And how he'd collapsed, and Chloe had kept going.

And that she'd disappeared.

"I'm worried we won't see Chloe again," Mohammed said. "I'm sorry to say."

He did seem sorry, saddened. Like he'd forgotten any of the problems he may have had with Chloe.

"You weren't here that night," Rachael said to Mohammed. "Is that right?"

"I was at the hotel," he said, "talking to my family."

"Your family?"

"I videoed with them. My brother and his family, in Farmington Hills. Would you like to confirm with them, inspector?"

"We're all a little upset," Rachael said.

"No," Mohammed said, "I'm not upset. I'm terrified. We're obviously being targeted."

Rachael shook her head. "You don't know that you're a target."

"Two people came here today," he said. "They said they're from a company called Turnpike, which is just another SolRescue shell. A man named Benj McPherson. You heard of him?"

"Derrick McPherson's son," Rachael said.

Mohammed nodded. "So… SolRescue. Hoping to sabotage the project."

"And you honestly think they would try to kill us?" Jared said.

"Yes. I honestly think that Carter Elgin would kill us if he had the slightest inclination."

"Says the guy who was detained by the US government for two years. And it's Carter Elgin you don't trust?"

"I know you're unsure," Mohammed said. "You look up to Elgin. You think the sunshield is something wonderful."

"Yeah," Rachael said. "Jared's one of those jackasses who likes his Earth untoasted."

"They told me some lies," Mohammed said, "that we're working with the Chinese. They were saying they wanted to hire me away from the project. McPherson even told me that they could protect me from detention."

"And I take it you didn't believe him," Jared said.

"I didn't believe a single thing they said. And you shouldn't, either."

"They didn't come talk to me."

"I'm not sure they wanted to bother with you," Mohammed said.

"So in your mind, they would hire you and murder me?"

"I don't know. I think now they'll want me dead. We're all targets." He pointed a finger at Rachael. "Except you. I'm not sure why you're here."

"Because I'm a SolRescue spy," she said. "I'm going to strangle you with your own intestines."

"You think you're clever. But you're just some stupid girl who think she knows everything."

"Easy, Mohammed," Jared said.

"Don't worry about it," Rachael said. "He's scared. I get it."

"We need to find them," Mohammed said. "These two from SolRescue."

"And do what?" Jared asked.

"We get their confession."

"What the hell is wrong with you?" Rachael said. "You think you're Batman?"

Mohammed sighed. "We can't prove they did this. So we wait for them to try again to kill us, or we run away?"

"We run away," Rachael said. "That's what smart people do. We pack our shit and we head south and we don't look back."

Mohammed eyed her warily. "Why are you running away? They're not after you."

"I can't run away," Jared said. "We don't know what happened to Chloe."

"There's a good chance you'll never know what happened to Chloe," Rachael said. "You need to understand that, Jared."

"I serve my country," Mohammed said. "I won't abandon this project."

"Your country fucked you in the ass," Jared said.

Mohammed stood up from his chair. He walked over to Jared, leaning in. "I will hurt you, Jared," he said. "I don't care that you just came out of the hospital."

Jared stood his ground, even with his drugs having started to wear off.

"I honestly don't get it, Mohammed. That's all. Why do you think you owe them something?"

"I don't owe them. But what we're doing is important. We're fighting a war."

"Najjar's right," Rachael said. "He shouldn't have to run away."

"So we stay and we fight," Mohammed said. "We find them and we get them before they get us."

"No... Jared and I won't be a part of this. We'll be leaving."

"I can't leave," Jared said. "Not yet..."

"I'll report you," Mohammed said. "I will let them know you are fleeing with classified documents. You won't get far."

Jared shook his head. "Seriously? You're threatening me?"

"I can't do it without you, Jared. Clearance or no clearance, I need your help with the robotics. A second set of eyes. And I don't care if you want to be a coward. I'm not giving you that choice."

"Don't make this ugly," Rachael said.

"Shut up," Mohammed said. "This doesn't concern you."

"You can't threaten us," Jared said. "It won't work."

"We grab those two and we get the answers we need. We do it for Chloe."

"If those people are trained killers," Rachael said, "you guys won't stand a chance."

"We don't know what they are," Mohammed said. "But I doubt Derrick McPherson's son and some Asian-American woman are a couple of assassins."

"They might have done something to Chloe," Jared said. "I don't know what that makes them."

Mohammed nodded. "There is a very small chance she's still alive. If they wanted information from her..."

Jared wanted to believe that.

And he wanted to buy more of what Mohammed was selling.

Mohammed was offering him a solid lead. A chance. A hope that Chloe wasn't gone.

Jared couldn't handle believing anything else.

Mohammed rattled off his plan, which was mostly a combination of willful ignorance and wishful thinking. He'd assumed the two operatives didn't have guns, that they weren't skilled in any kind of combat, and that they didn't expect any sudden retaliation.

His plan was to show up at the bed and breakfast the Asian woman had scrawled onto her business card, restrain both operatives, including one 200-plus pound black man, and bring them to an as-yet-undetermined location for some as-yet-undecided interrogation method. And that would somehow lead to Chloe's rescue and enough hard evidence to convict the two SolRescue spies of... high treason, maybe?

Mohammed Najjar seemed to be doing his best to prove the axiom that oftentimes the smartest guys in the room can end up with the dumbest trains of thought.

Rachael listened in, but stood off to the side, as if she was making some statement that she wasn't really part of the conspiracy.

Jared wasn't sure what she would do, in the end. He had trouble imagining her helping with an attempted abduction, particularly since Mohammed's evidence was several hundred yards short of circumstantial. And he had trouble imagining himself being involved, either.

Mohammed was making some random guess, that because two people showed up on the same day Jared and Chloe were attacked, that somehow those two newcomers were responsible. Or, if not responsible, that they obviously must know something about it.

The way Mohammed was talking... he sounded like his perspective was slipping, that he was losing his grip on reality. Something had clicked on in that high-octane brain of his, some genius/crackpot switch.

He honestly thought that SolRescue wanted to fight a war against the United States. And that if China's military junta was involved at all, it was probably on SolRescue's side. Somehow.

Mohammed hated Carter Elgin and the Chinese so much that they had to be working on some new form of evil together.

Jared wasn't sure what to do.

He knew he couldn't just step away and let Mohammed lose his mind.

"We should try some kind of parley," Jared said.

"What are you talking about?" Mohammed asked.

"We contact the two of them, tell them we want to talk. Some neutral place."

"That's a good idea," Rachael said. "We can size them up."

"And they'll size us up, too," Mohammed said. "And see that we're all talk."

"We are all talk," Jared said. "We don't know anything about this cloak and dagger bullshit. I build rockets and you build robots. And Rachael…"

"I wait tables and change sheets," she said. "And look good doing it."

"So what do you expect will happen?" Mohammed said. "We meet them and they realize that we're good people, and offer to give us back our project manager?"

"We won't help you until we're convinced," Jared said. "I need to see these people firsthand before I risk my career and maybe my life."

"So what, then," Mohammed said. "They give us nothing, dance around the questions, and then you're ready to do things my way?"

Jared shook his head. "No promises. But it's the best I'm willing to do."

"You're a coward."

"Doesn't matter if I am. It's the only option, Mohammed. We talk to them first, or we do nothing. You can't threaten me into hurting people."

"Okay," Mohammed said. "We talk to them first. And then I'll be going after them, with or without you."

"Okay."

Rachael was shaking her head.

"You got a problem?" Mohammed asked her.

She smirked. "I've had nothing but problems since you assholes got here."

19

BENJ KNEW things were about to get dicey.

The message had come through the bed and breakfast hosts, to "meet the rocketeers", and asking for him and Samantha to choose the time and place.

Samantha didn't take long to come up with the answer.

At seven PM. At Miss Piggy.

Naturally, Benj hadn't had any idea what Miss Piggy was, until his eyepiece filled him in. Location, and then once he tapped the right frame, a short history.

A Curtiss C-46 Commando that had crash landed almost a hundred years before, in 1979. Apparently it had been used for many a cargo run, including at one point, a load of real, live pigs. At first after the crash, no one had bothered to attempt any kind of salvage operation, and over the years, the wreckage had become such a landmark that any thought of cleaning up the mess was dead on arrival.

Most places had battlefields and historic buildings; Churchill just had a massive collection of ruined shit.

"It's the perfect place to set the scene," Samantha said. "Two groups of people, at war with each other. Scorched earth."

"What?"

"You need to have a sense of the theatric. But either way... Najjar's rattled."

"It's not just him," Benj said. "Who else will be there?"

"Jared Koskela. He's nobody important."

"He's still somebody, though. Two on two."

"Don't worry, Benj," Samantha said. "We won't be armed, so we'll be completely outmatched."

She was grinning.

"You think this is fun," Benj said.

"I like making progress. Setting the stage."

"How is this even progress? What is the end goal here? If you don't think these guys actually know anything..."

"I received a message a few hours ago," she said. "From a friend at the NSA."

"Wait... there's someone at the NSA you didn't fuck over completely?"

"More chatter. Messages between the project manager and someone named Rachael Duck. Mentioning exactly what we've been looking into, a partnership between the US Executive and the Chinese junta. I'm trying to get it wiped, like the other stuff. Just in case."

"Just in case of what?"

"I think this Rachael Duck's the one we're looking for. I don't want someone else getting to her before we do."

"By getting to her…" Benj said.

"I don't think anyone's up here, but I can't be sure."

"You think someone might come up here and start killing people?"

"That's what they did in French Guiana, remember?"

"That's a long way from here."

"Probably not the *exact same people*," she said. "Global conspiracies often involve more than a couple of lackeys. Haven't you ever watched a James Bond movie?"

"I'm imagining that's what your training consisted of. Just hours and hours of spy films. So no actual training or anything."

"You being an asshole doesn't increase our chance of success."

"So you want us to just show up at some wrecked plane and hope these two guys can be trusted."

"And hope there aren't any bears around," she said. "You heard there was an attack last night…"

"No."

"Some researcher or something. They haven't released his name. Guy's at the hospital in town, should be fine."

"So the bear didn't get anything to eat."

"Probably still pretty damned hungry."

"You know I'll fucking trip you if I see that bear," Benj said. "I will climb to the top of Miss Piggy and watch the feast. Korean barbecue, without the grill."

She nodded. "Good to know."

"I'm saying that I hate you."

She just laughed.

There was only one truck parked near Miss Piggy, a white pickup like theirs, just a little lighter duty. No one was sitting inside of it.

The plane itself was more impressive than Benj had expected from the photos on his tablet, a long bare and gray fuselage, open to the elements. It sat on a crown of granite outcropping, almost like it had been positioned there like a monument, its nose lifted higher than its tail, as if it was about to lift off again despite its gaping holes and smashed wings.

His eyepiece had started giving him too much information, photos of Miss Piggy from over the years. He tapped it away.

Samantha led the way to the plane, strolling in front as if she'd been there before, even though there was very little chance she could have been.

She walked up to the large opening where the cargo doors would have been. He saw her grin. "Rachael Duck, I presume."

Benj hurried up to the entrance.

Najjar was there, as was a somewhat younger man with light brown hair styled a little too perfectly, and a pretty and petite aboriginal woman, with her long dark hair tied in a high and tight ponytail.

"And I'm Jared Koskela," the other man said, walking in front to shake hands with Samantha.

There was little room to maneuver, considering the low ceiling, but Koskela seemed to have a handle on it.

Samantha took his hand, and then the man offered it to Benj.

"Benj McPherson," Benj said, "and my assistant, Samantha Yoon."

"Let's get on with this," Najjar said from the back. Or the front of the plane, rather, standing just shy of the cockpit. "Our project manager, Chloe Nielson-Brown, is currently missing. Someone tried to set up a polar bear attack on Chloe and Jared, here."

"Wait," Samantha said, looking over at Koskela, "that was you?"

Jared Koskela unzipped his jacket.

It was mostly bandages that could be seen. No blood, and just a few scratches aside from the wrapping.

Not that Benj knew how deep a mauling actually went.

His eyepiece didn't seem to know, either. Not unprompted, at least.

"So you'd like our help?" Samantha asked. "I'm not sure what we can do, to be honest."

"Mohammed thinks you had something to do with it," the woman, Rachael Duck, said.

"To do with a polar bear attack?" Benj said. "Is that a joke?"

"It's not a joke," Najjar said. "You think we don't know why you're really up here?"

"To train an unholy army of polar bears?" Samantha asked.

"You're not taking this seriously," Jared Koskela said. "I almost bled to death on the flats. And Chloe is missing, and we're not sure she's still alive."

"We had nothing to do with that," Benj said. "I'm sorry it happened, but I can't even imagine how Samantha and I could be involved. I'm from Missouri. We don't even have regular bears."

"No, we have bears," Samantha said. "Black bears, down near Arkansas."

Benj hadn't given any thought to where Samantha was from.

"No one gives a shit about Missouri," Rachael Duck said.

"Not even people from Missouri," Samantha said.

"I'm losing my patience," Mohammed Najjar said.

"They're just trying to get a rise out of you," Koskela said.

"Not really," Benj said. "Or, well, I'm not… but we truly have nothing to do with what happened to your project manager."

"I believe him," Rachael Duck said. "Not sure I'm a fan of this one, though." She was pointing at Samantha, not that her visual aid was a requirement.

Benj nodded. "We see a lot of that. It's generally because Samantha is an asshole."

Rachael Duck started laughing.

"He's not joking," Samantha said, chuckling a little herself.

"So that's what we're supposed to think?" Najjar asked. "That you guys showed up—total coincidence—and that there's some other group of people out to kill us?"

"That's why we're here," Benj said. "To find out what's happening."

Samantha shook her head at him, but didn't deny it.

"You're here for what, exactly?" Koskela asked.

"We know about the Chinese government," Benj said. "That they're partnering on this project."

"That's a lie," Najjar said.

"We believe the Chinese may have been involved with the attacks in French Guiana," Samantha said.

"Attacks?" Rachael Duck said. "You mean the space station? Was there another attack there?"

Samantha nodded. "A couple of murders. And if SolRescue hadn't pulled people out, there would have been two or three more."

"So you admit it," Najjar said. "That you work for SolRescue."

"Everyone either works for SolRescue or they work for the bad guys," Samantha said. "And we don't work for the bad guys."

Najjar stamped his foot. "You're here to sabotage our work. And I think you're also here to kill us."

"With polar bears?" Rachael Duck said. "Come on, Mohammed. How could they have arranged that?"

"We've been here for maybe twenty four hours," Samantha said. "Not a lot of time for, you know, teaching bears how to develop a taste for blood."

"Shut up, Samantha," Benj said. "You're not helping this along."

"You believe we were involved in the attack in French Guiana," Najjar said. "That's why you came here. For revenge."

Benj shook his head. "No one thinks you're involved." He looked over to Rachael Duck. "But *you* might be involved."

He heard Samantha groan. Not a fan of his full disclosure strategy.

"Involved in what, exactly?" Rachael asked. "In secretly working with the generals who've killed thousands of Chinese protesters? Or are we talking about me sneaking down to South America to murder people?"

"We think you knew it was coming," Samantha said. "That you sent a warning to a man named Alex Vives, an engineer who worked for the ESA. And you mentioned thermal runaway, and you mentioned someone triggering it remotely. So… exactly what ended up happening."

Rachael Duck smirked. "Not a very effective warning, was it? Since the station's not really in working order anymore."

"You could be a target," Benj said. "If we know, they might know. Even if we did scrub the records."

He saw Jared Koskela look over to Rachael Duck. Look over quizzically, is how Benj would describe it.

"I want to hear you admit it, Rachael," Samantha said. "Tell me you sent that message to Alex."

Benj was thrown off by the sudden familiarity.

"You already know I did," Rachael Duck said. "That's why you're here, isn't it? You're hoping to drag me down to god knows where, get Derrick to give me shit."

"They know each other," Najjar said. "What is this?"

"Yeah, Rachael," Koskela said. "You need to explain what the fuck is going on."

"Alex didn't stop it," Rachael Duck said. "He said he'd stop it, and he didn't. Can you tell me why he didn't stop it, Sam?"

"I guess he couldn't stop it in time," Samantha said.

"You should be explaining this to me," Najjar said. "Explaining to me why I shouldn't report each and every one of you to the United States Air Force."

Samantha grinned. "I thought you were worried about me murdering you, Mr. Najjar."

"Someone took Chloe," Koskela said. "Someone wants us dead."

"Maybe all of us," Rachael Duck said. "Depends on just how well they're paying attention."

"But who the fuck are they?"

"We need to figure that out," Samantha said.

"And how many of us are part of that 'we'?" Rachael Duck asked.

"I'm reporting all of this," Najjar said. "Let the US government sort you all out."

"Great plan, Najjar," Benj said. "You must really miss that detention center."

"They won't detain me. I'm not responsible for any of this."

"I'll report you right back, Mohammed," Koskela said.

Mohammed Najjar took several steps forward, coming within a few paces of Jared Koskela. "What was that?"

"I can cast some doubts on you. No problem there. Maybe they'll put us all in the same quarters. That would be some kind of zany comedy routine right there."

Najjar gave Koskela a shove, pushing him hard against the side of the fuselage.

Rachael Duck rushed in.

Najjar punched her in the face.

Benj took a step forward.

Samantha stuck her arm in front of him. "Hold on," she said.

He shoved her arm out of the way.

But by that point Najjar had pulled back, pacing toward the cockpit.

"No one reports anyone," Samantha said. "No one breathes a word of any of this. No one finds out."

"Why?" Koskela asked as he regained his balance. "How does keeping this quiet keep us safe?"

"Just trust her," Rachael Duck told him. "And trust me."

"No one should ever trust people like you," Najjar said. "Nothing you've said so far is true. You or that other woman. Or McPherson. You are all liars. It's disgusting."

"Fine," Samantha said. "Be disgusted. But do it quietly, okay?"

Najjar grumbled something. He walked past Koskela, toward Rachael Duck.

Benj moved closer.

Najjar spat at the feet of the aboriginal woman.

And kept walking.

"Now don't you fucking spit on me," Benj said. "That's happened to me already this week."

Najjar shook his head.

And he continued on, past Samantha, and out the door.

"So I don't get any spit?" Samantha called out after him.

Najjar didn't answer.

"He came with us," Koskela said. "Where the hell is he going?"

"Anywhere else, I guess," Benj said.

"Maybe we'll get lucky," Samantha said. "Maybe our pal Mohammed will run into that hungry polar bear."

Benj shook his head. "Fuck, Samantha. For the love of all that's holy, just shut up."

Rachael Duck and Jordan Koskela left first, leaving just Benj and Samantha in the old wrecked cargo plane.

"I'll bet you want to threaten me a little right now," Samantha said. "We should look for a portapotty."

"You knew it was her," Benj said. "The whole time. Not some vague suspicion about *someone* in Churchill sending a warning. Why all the lying? And why did you drag me up here?"

"We're not done, Benj. Not by a long shot."

"But why? Why did you put me in the middle of this? Just because my father told you to?"

"You were supposed to maintain your cover. Which you didn't do."

"Because it didn't matter," Benj said. "Because Najjar saw through it the moment we walked into that lab."

"Exactly."

"What?"

"You're our red herring, Benj. Everyone thinks you're connected all the way to Carter Elgin."

"And that matters?"

"It matters," she said.

"Why?"

"I can't tell you that."

"I told you I wouldn't go along with this need-to-know bullshit."

"You never said that. You just shoved your hands over my face and started muttering something about you being in charge, and you needing respect..."

"Tell me why I'm here," he said.

"Or you'll crush me like a bug?"

"Maybe I could hurt you, Samantha. Maybe I could dump your body wherever they dumped that project manager."

"Don't waste all that sexy threatening," she said. "Let's wait until we get back to the ol' B&B."

"Tell me why I'm here. The real reason."

"To protect me."

She wasn't smirking, or grinning. Or rolling her eyes.

She was acting all serious.

"I don't believe you," Benj said.

"Derrick couldn't come with me. It was too risky, he's too high profile. But you're the next best thing."

"Mohammed Najjar didn't seem the least bit intimidated by me being a McPherson."

"I'm not worried about Mohammed Najjar," she said.

"Then who?"

She sighed. "Rachael Duck. Honestly, Benj... if you weren't here, I think she'd have already tried to kill me."

"No... that doesn't make any sense. She'd kill you because you know she sent some warning message? And aren't you on the same team?"

"I don't think Rachael is working with us," Samantha said. "I think she's working for them."

"The US government?"

"No. The Chinese junta."

"Based on what, exactly?"

"We don't have any hard evidence," she said. "Not yet. But we will."

"And when will that hard evidence come along?"

She smiled. "When you help me get it."

20

WILLIAM YEUNG Huan was exhausted, but no more than usual. He estimated that he was operating at around 40% capacity, which for most people would be a problem.

But there were two things about Huan that most people didn't know:

1. *He was smarter than anyone realized*

2. *His job was a complete farce*

Because there was no need to inspect local democracy in the far-flung provinces of China. Local democracy had never been the problem. Give the peasants a council and they'll make it work.

That was assuming, of course, that the People's Convocation kept those councils in place, and Huan had seen no indication either way.

But the job was his, and he made good on filling out the needless reports, and then he'd get on the train and try not to fall asleep in the comfortable chair.

The travel was what gave Huan a chance to do his real work.

It still took four to six hours to get from Urumqi in the northwest to anywhere else, and for whatever reason the conductor had decided to pipe in a constant flow of inane Mandopop over the sound system.

All the world in Mandarin. That's what they wanted.

Huan had to throw on his headphones to drown out the Great Unity under construction. He had too much work to do.

The People's Convocation was always subtle enough; most people didn't notice the ways it seeped into everything, probably because they'd gotten used to the heavy hand of the Party.

But the Convocation was nothing like the Party, and everything like it, too. The generals had seen the weakness in the market reforms, watching the peasants sink further into hopelessness while a small coterie of the prosperous pretended the system worked just fine as it was. They'd seen the concessions granted to Hong Kong—and extended to Shanghai—as a sign of weakness from the Party, that the new guard didn't have the stomach to keep China together.

So they stepped in.

And the Party learned that the People's Liberation Army preferred the People's Convocation to the old way of doing things, and the trials and exe-

211

cutions picked up their pace.

And the Convocation started trying to gain favour with the South and the West, all while quietly pushing the Beijing way of life.

And they'd hired southerners like Huan to "keep them honest", and to make sure the peasants were seeing progress.

The dynastic cycle continues, as it always does.

The only question for Huan was whether the Convocation was chaos or order, war or empire.

Huan started his real workday with a couple of caffeine tablets, then he began assembling his workspace. The dock went on his knees, with the understrap he never used due to a lack of air turbulence on China Railways. The tablet secured to the dock as a matter of course, serving as his screen, tilted in from of the built-in keyboard. Under his feet was where the sat terminal went; some idiots thought you needed to practically hang it out the window to get a signal, but Huan was far from being an idiot.

And the conductor would be checking up on him; it's a little strange for a traveller to eschew the onboard WiFi.

Once he had a signal, he opened up the secure messenger. It had been almost 24 hours since he'd last checked in.

He separated the germ from the husk; only three messages that mattered, in the end:

1. *Jia was going to send in a whitewashed account of the corruption in Tibet*

2. *Tan Fuhua had sent him a copy of the Little March designs.*

3. *Alex Vives had suffered a fatal accident while attempting to flee French Guiana*

He'd told Jia to be honest, and she hadn't listened. He typed off a quite reply, telling her that whitewashes are always eroded away in time. The truth would out eventually, and Jia would be found out.

The Little March design was more interesting than Jia's moral dilemma. They'd launched at least one from Wenchang already, with a secret payload that Huan still didn't know anything about.

He'd need to find out. But he didn't know how... not yet.

He focused his attention on Alex Vives.

His wife Mireia Lona was still missing, along with Nicolas Clouatre, the chosen scapegoat. If Huan had to guess, he'd say they made it out of French Guiana, into Brazil. From there they could have gone anywhere, but his money was on the United States.

SolRescue had the most influence there, in the one country that officially seemed to despise crowdOrgs the most. And Derrick McPherson would have put the two fugitives to work, if he was the one who'd helped them.

And Derrick McPherson seemed to always be the one in the middle of it.

He forwarded the message to Archie, in San Jose. He didn't need to provide an itemized list; Archie would know how to find them, if they could be found.

But if Huan was wrong, and McPherson had caught on to his pattern being tracked, or if he'd taken Carter Elgin's advice to avoid creating those patterns in the first place...

He forwarded the message again, to his Canadian contact. McPherson may have sent them further north, probably not up to his contact's neck of the woods, but anywhere in Canada was somewhere she could track them.

Rachael Duck didn't have the same experience as Archie in San Jose, but lately she seemed to have made up for it with sheer luck.

21

THE MESSAGE had come late Friday night; Anita didn't see it until early Saturday morning, as she was getting ready to head into the city.

Not that she had anywhere to be on a Saturday. She just had to not be on Staten Island.

It was from Bridget, and it wasn't the boilerplate "let's pretend we're still friends" message that she'd always wondered if Carter had continually put her up to sending; it was Bridget asking for a favor.

I need you to come to the seastead to see Carter. He needs your point of view. Please, Anita. We could really use your help.

Not something she'd ever have expected to receive. A far cry from the usual pitying check-ups from the two of them.

A favor.

Anita would think about it on her way to Manhattan.

Despite the influx of basics from other boroughs, Tompkinsville on Staten Island still had a large community of Sri Lankans, which made Anita feel more uncomfortable than welcome. As she walked to the SIR station, she saw a group of Tamil-looking kids playing football—or soccer, if Anita felt particularly 'Murican—on the street.

A half dozen boys and one little girl.

Maybe eight years old, with her hair done up in a shoddy ponytail.

It reminded Anita of home.

Not India, a place she'd never been, but La Crosse, Wisconsin. The part of Wisconsin that was definitely more about the beer than the cheese.

Her mother used to take eight-year-old Anita to the football pitches at the university, and sometimes the big kids would let her play with them, getting her stand in goal and lobbing soft shots directly at her feet.

Looking back it seemed like Mama had started the push even then, of getting Anita used to the notion of going to school somewhere close to home.

Anita had promised her mother that she'd come back after Cornell Tech; even when she'd said the words, she'd known it was a lie.

And Mama had known it, too.

Anita hadn't originally planned on returning the phone call, and she hadn't planned on going to the interview.

But as winter and the SolRescue project had continued on, she'd felt further away from both Bridget and Carter, a third wheel at best and more probably a roadblock.

The video had gone viral back in December; the coverage had been more than even Bridget had hoped for, including spots on three national morning shows, nine in total if you included Canada, the UK and Germany, along with a hilariously awkward segment in Ireland where Carter unconsciously began to mimic the interviewer's accent.

The funding had come in, more than enough in big part due to the strangest of donors, Arabian emirs, Nigerian startup founders, and a large contribution for Viktor Utkin, one of the biggest of the big Russian oligarchs.

But what was more important were the memberships.

People didn't want to send money and sit on the sidelines; they wanted to be a part of it, whether that meant the mostly useless armchair quarterbacking you get—people with no practical experience claiming that they understood propulsion or refining in microgravity or how to alienproof the printer bots with a thick layer of tinfoil—or actual tangible assistance, people trying out slight variations based on what Bridget or Carter would post on the progress blog, reporting back on possible improvements (rare) or pitfalls (common).

That was the start of SolRescue as a crowdOrg, a structure that had been toyed with for years but that had never been set up under the same publicity glare.

December had been like a waking dream, but after missing the holidays in La Crosse and sitting through the inevitable blowback that came in January, Anita had felt battered and worn by all of it—it being just too much, good or bad—and she'd realized that she wasn't really in it with Bridget and Carter. They were on one side, weathering the storm, while she was drifting further away, closer and closer to dropping under the waves and drowning.

So she'd returned the call, she'd taken the interview... and when the offer had been emailed to her, she'd realized just how tempted she was to accept.

Of course it was tempting. She hadn't even finished her engineering degree, and they still wanted her. As many hours as she felt she could give them, as remote as she needed it to be.

She'd called her mother to talk it over, and had received the advice through the usual tint of Mama wanting her little girl to come home.

Mama had wanted her daughter to take the job, then finish her degree, in NYC if she must, and then find a way to relocate somewhere closer, be it Chicago or the Twin Cities. Or even scenic La Crosse, Wisconsin.

Anita had been through enough. And she'd given Carter and Bridget the support and the boost they'd needed.

The whole world was behind them, save for the US government, which was already lobbying to prevent them from ever launching. The whole world would help out, join the cause, run the tests.

Anita had done her bit for king and country.

And she'd needed to get away from the two people she felt the closest to, because the pain of watching them move on without her was decimating her.

The other two directors of SolRescue first learned of Anita's departure from a press release.

She hadn't known it was newsworthy, some random engineering student taking a part time consulting gig with an established aerospace company. She'd been naive, obviously.

And Bridget had been the first one to track her down when the news had broken.

Anita had realized too late that hiding out in Starbuck's was nowhere close to brilliant.

"You bitch traitor," Bridget said, leading to hushed gasps from most of the patrons. "You're trying to kill it."

She'd stormed in off the street and right to Anita's table.

She hadn't even sat down.

"I'm not trying to kill anything," Anita said. "I just need a break from this."

"From what? From doing something worthwhile? From not selling out to some military-industrial monstrosity?"

"Can we just talk about it? At a lower volume?"

Bridget sat down.

She dropped her head into her hands.

"I don't see why it matters with Carter," she said. "Why can't you just be happy for us?"

"It's not that at all. It's not."

"Except that it is, Anita. I know you've come onto him."

"What?"

"You think I'm an idiot? That I don't see your pathetic attempt at flirting with him?"

"He's flirting with me."

"What are you talking about?"

"He's playing us," Anita said, "he's been playing us from the start. He wants us to fawn over him… to fight over him."

"You're fucking delusional. He chose me from the start, Anita."

"Shit… I can't believe we're fighting over a guy. What the hell is wrong with us?"

"No… this is not a time for reflection. This is you turning your back on the project we started as a team."

"I'm not turning my back," Anita said. "I'm moving on. Just like you and Carter."

"What the hell is that supposed to mean?"

"We're not a team anymore, Bridget. There's me, and then there's you and Carter. Two separate teams."

"You signed a non-compete, Anita."

"I'm not competing."

"Do you even understand the concept? You're taking a job with another company that makes rockets. This little crowdOrg of ours? A member-run company that makes rockets."

"The US will ban those launches."

"We'll find a way, Anita. Because Carter and I don't believe in jumping ship."

"I've made up my mind, Bridget."

"We'll take you to court."

"That is so fucking petty. You're going to ruin our friendship over this."

"Me ruin the friendship?" She laughed, almost a cackle. "I'd say you're doing that all on your own. God… I really thought you were somebody else. You're such a disappointment, Anita."

"Fuck you," Anita said.

She got up and left the Starbuck's, trying not to notice the stares. Everyone knew who they were; the whole world would be gossiping about it.

She'd hoped that the rumors and reports would be kind to her; she'd found out before she even got back to her suite that both she and Bridget took the hit.

After seeing over a dozen tweets about the #SolRescue "Starbuck's Spat", Anita had started packing her stuff.

She'd ended up spending the night down the hall. By the next night, she'd moved in with a friend at Columbia.

As far as she'd been concerned, there was no point in maintaining contact with either of them. Bridget and Carter could go their own way.

Danny Pyke had scheduled a late meeting, 5 PM.

Anita didn't mind staying after most of the team had left, not that those same team members wouldn't be putting in more hours from home as the night wore on; she had a problem with the assumption that she'd stay, a meeting request sent without any kind of polite preamble.

He was treating her like she was just another employee.

That wasn't acceptable.

But she showed up to his office on time, to set him straight in person.

"It's quite the expectation," she said, as he offered her a chair with a wave of his hand. "Does everyone just follow Danny's hours?"

She was still standing, bearing down on his desk.

"My team does, yeah," he said. "And I was hoping you'd indulge me this time."

She couldn't help but smile a little at that. "That sets a precedent, Mr. Pyke."

"I won't tell anyone, Ms. Singhal. Not if you won't."

She decided to take the seat. "So what's this about?" she asked.

"It's the top secret part of the job. Not sure if you knew it was coming."

"Is this a joke?"

"They're not just for data transmission," he said. "We're also going to be doing a bit of data collection."

"Oh, lovely. So let's add the completely unnecessary complexity of some non-critical equipment."

He laughed.

"Not funny," she said.

"Video surveillance, Anita."

His tone had changed. Less goofball and more... intimacy?

She wasn't sure she liked that.

"Have you ever heard of space telescopes?" she asked him. "They do the coolest thing, where they take still photos and even video of shit you'll see in space."

"No one has space telescopes trained on the sunshield."

"Seriously?"

"Protecting humanity's assets," he said.

"Protecting Carter Elgin's assets. For free, is it?"

"You're running this now, Anita."

"Hence the presumptuous familiarity you're throwing at me."

"Carter doesn't own a speck of Turnpike. And he doesn't own me."

"But you do what he tells you."

"I do what he asks, because he's a friend."

"And did he ask you to weasel your way into my life?"

"Weasel? You mean offer you an advisory position? Give you more influence on real project work than you've had in twenty years?"

"You're too familiar with me, Mr. Pyke," she said. "Quite honestly, it's rude."

"I'm sorry, Anita, but yeah… I'm familiar with you. I'm familiar with how you'd just given up on your work. Sitting on Basic like you've got nothing to contribute."

"I think you need to rethink your approach. The 'babbling asshole' is not the most effective technique to use on me."

"You haven't walked out."

"What?"

"You want to be here, don't you? Making a difference again."

"I'm not the one who took me out of the work," she said. "Talk to your buddy Carter about that."

"You know he cares about you. He wants the best for you. Just like I do."

"Too fucking familiar, Pyke. Or are you hard of hearing?"

She stood up.

But she didn't storm out.

She knew he was right, that there was a small slice of Anita Singhal that worried that walking out one more time might result in not being wanted back.

Her father used to say something about her, probably the truest thing he ever said. That it took forever to get her started on something, but once she'd started, it was impossible to get her to stop.

"So each satellite will take video," she said. "But it's not as easy as a single lens sticking out the side, is it…"

He smiled. "It's how you want to do it, Ms. Singhal. Track the targets with one or two lenses on each, or try to get a panoramic view of everything."

"Targets… more than just the shield."

"The shield is today. But you know there's a big tomorrow."

She nodded. "What's a startup without the outsized ambition?"

"You got it," he said.

"And this is how secret?"

"Open book internally. But no trails for investors to sniff out. I know you understand that kind of thing."

"The kind of thing I railed against with SolRescue. When Carter wanted to keep secrets about the microwave converter prototypes, how the magnetic scoop would work… the man acted like we were racing the Soviets on that thing."

"Racing the Soviets," he said, grinning. "I like that."

"So how much of this is Carter?"

"How much of the video? Maybe sixty percent. It's not like it's bad for us long term. Just not good for short term business plans."

"No… the whole company. How much of Turnpike is Danny Pyke, and how much is Carter Elgin?"

He shrugged. "Like I said, Carter doesn't own any of it."

She shook her head at him. "Never forget your audience," she said.

"Bridget Hawn's in for ten percent."

Ten times more than Anita's share.

"And the rich get richer," Anita said.

"It's never been about the money with you," Danny said. "Never will be."

She nodded.

She liked that he was going along with the ruse.

That Anita Singhal didn't need the money. That the lawsuit was the only source of strain in her life.

That her rapidly decaying house in Tompkinsville was good enough.

That she didn't see herself in the mirror, getting older, getting worn, while every photo she'd seen of Bridget Hawn showed a perpetually beautiful woman who almost seemed to be getting younger, drinking in all the benefits of money and a team of image consultants. Anita looked worse today than she had yesterday, and she'd never look as good as she looked today, not ever again.

She was crumbling away, while Bridget was still shining like the goddamn sun.

22

THE POLAR Bear Holding Facility looked more like a machine shed than a prison or a zoo. Jared had never seen it before, as close as it was to the airport where he'd first landed in Churchill.

Rachael knew some of the conservation officers, which made sense in a small town that's over four hundred kilometers away from any other small town.

One of the officers, a middle aged man named Cannae Friesen—with a heavy beard that seemed to suit—was waiting for them by the small red door.

"I guess the polar bears go through the big door," Jared said as he shook Cannae's hand.

"Too much seal blubber," Cannae replied with a grin. "We only have one resident inside at the moment. But she's been here for over a week, so I doubt she's the one you ran into out there."

"So no other bears in or out lately?" Rachael asked.

Cannae shook his head. "Been quiet so far. Things should start getting busier in a week or so, and even busier as we head towards fall."

"Can we see her?" Jared asked.

"Sure."

Cannae led them inside.

The corridor felt like a dog kennel, just larger. And instead of a wall of bars, there were mostly concrete blocks, the openings to the pens being smaller than a bay window. Most openings were closed up, strongly resembling walk-in freezers.

Cannae led them to a bear peering out through the metal bars.

"I call her Brown Betty," he said. "It's okay to name them, since we're not gonna eat them."

"Why Brown Betty?" Jared asked.

"That brown patch on her back."

"Looks like yellow snow," Rachael said.

Cannae smiled at her. "Too late, Rachael. She already has a name." He looked over to Jared. "Not your bear, I take it?"

"Not my bear," Jared said.

"That's a good thing," Rachael said. "I don't know what we'd do if these bears were sneaking out of jail at night."

"Did your bear have those tags?" Cannae asked, pointing at the white clips in both ears.

"I don't remember seeing them," Jared said, "but it was dark and a little near-death-experience-ish."

"Of course, we do release these bears eventually. Brown Betty was found in a snare trap... messed up her foot something awful. She should be good to go in a few more days."

"Go where?"

"We fly them away from town for release. Betty wasn't a problem bear, far as we know, but she'll still get a free trip somewhere else. So you wanted to see the traps."

Rachael nodded.

Cannae led them back outside.

He seemed really prepared for the visit.

"We've got ten culvert traps at the moment," he said, waving to the collection of metal cylinders to the side of the building. "We've lent one of them out."

"I didn't think you lent them out," Rachael said.

"Usually we don't. If there's a problem bear report, we take the trap out and we set it up. No one else is allowed to touch them. Usually."

"So who managed to bend that rule?" Jared asked.

"A research team from China," Cannae said. "They apparently have some kind of *special dispensation*, whatever that means. Seems a little shifty to me."

"From China? Since when do the Chinese come up here to study polar bears?"

"Since so many Chinese nationals started moving up to Siberia," Rachael said. "Won't be long and the Chinese government will stage a 'Russian intervention' on Russia itself."

"None of it's good for us," Cannae said. "The Passage is crawling with Americans and Russians, and now the Chinese." He looked at Jared. "You're American, aren't you?"

"Chicago," Jared said. "Never been on a boat bigger than a canoe."

"Use it or lose it," Rachael said. "And I guess we just haven't used it enough."

"Be worse if the sea ice had kept melting," Cannae said. "Even if that big change in direction did pound my retirement fund in the rear."

"So the Chinese researchers," Jared said, "are they over at the Northern Studies Centre?"

"They have their own temporary hab. I guess they weren't interested in close quarters with Canadian and US teams. They're up along the bay, about halfway between here and Bird Cove. You got a tablet?"

Rachael passed him her tablet.

Cannae swiped and pinched for a few seconds.

"Right here," he said, pointing to a little offshoot of road. "Behind that bank of trees."

"They're acting a little suspiciously, eh?" Rachael said.

Cannae frowned. "They know we don't trust them."

"Well, you were nice enough to give them a bear trap," Jared said. "Not sure what shit they pulled with it, though."

"I'm not sure they were involved," Cannae said.

"Why not?"

"Because it's a pretty crazy thing to do. You don't just tow that trap out and throw a rotisserie chicken inside."

"Don't you?" Rachael asked.

"Well, we do, but it's not something you'd want to try on a lark. Suppose the trap doesn't close automatically, or the bear won't enter it and just hangs around. It could get pretty dangerous if you don't know what you're doing. And then you need to know how to let the bear out again."

"I don't see how that's impossible for any biologist to figure out," Rachael said. She seemed annoyed with the man, like he'd overstepped his bounds with all of the theorizing.

Like it wasn't his place to tell them what the Chinese researchers may or may not do.

"I've seen people do crazier things," Jared said. "And it was definitely a trap like this. So unless there are others in town…"

"Not that I've seen," Cannae said. "We've got a monopoly on bear trapping. Lucky us."

"Yeah," Rachael said, "thanks, Cannae."

She still seemed miffed.

He gave her a nod.

Rachael and Jared got back in her brother's truck.

"So we head out there," she said. "Check that other trap."

"I know it's not realistic," Jared said. "I know we won't pull up there and see Chloe handcuffed to a pine tree."

Rachael nodded. "We just keep going. That's all we can do."

There was no marker on the turnoff toward the Chinese research hab, just a narrow gravel road keeping to the shore of the bay as the main road swung south on a jog before it continued east to the Northern Studies Centre and Jared's own portable hab.

There were so many unmarked roads to nowhere that he'd never even noticed the one they were now exploring.

Rachael drove them past the bank of trees.

There was an inflatable hab, maybe half again as big as the Jared and Mohammed's lab. And a small plastic shed beside it. Two more pickups were parked out front, one white and the other a conspicuous dark red.

And behind them, a jeep.

Jared's jeep.

"Holy shit," he said.

"Holy smoking gun," Rachael said. "Too much of one, actually."

He couldn't tell from looking if someone had managed to get the jeep running again, even temporarily, or if they'd just hooked up a tow cable and dragged it to their research station.

Rachael drove a little farther up the road.

The bear trap was at the side of the road, a few dozen yards away from the hab and the vehicles.

Rachael stopped the truck.

Jared hopped out and jogged over to the trap.

He hadn't expected anything to be inside, particularly since the red trap door was open, set above the culvert.

But there was something inside.

"Holy fucking shit," he said.

Rachael came up beside him.

He reached into the trap and pulled out a silver pendant. The Celtic Cross.

"That's hers, isn't it," Rachael said.

"I think she may have left it here on purpose."

"They put her in the trap?"

"Fuck," Jared said.

There was nothing else in the trap, aside from some pine needles and specks of dirt. No sign of whatever bait they'd used to get the bear to climb inside.

Bait.

He didn't think they could have used her like that. The fear was ridiculous. But the fear was there; he could feel it, and it was crushing him. The idea of Chloe in that trap, terrified, knowing that she'd probably never get home again.

"I bet that bear is still out there," Rachael said. "They locked Chloe in the trap and left the bear."

"Can't a person release themselves from one of these?"

"Not really, no. Anything a person could figure out a bear might, too. Those guys are smarter than most of you southerners."

He shook his head at her. It wasn't the time for that kind of banter.

Jared started marching back toward the Chinese hab.

"I guess you're hoping they speak English," Rachael said, following behind.

"Maybe they speak Dene," Jared said.

Rachael smirked. "I barely speak it. But look, Jared… you can't just confront them."

"Why not?"

"Because either they aren't involved—"

"Come on."

"Or maybe they're dangerous. Since, you know, they may have already tried to kill you. And may have…"

"May have killed Chloe," Jared said.

He stopped walking.

"Yeah."

"Then what do you expect me to do, Rachael? Call the Mounties and tell them the Chinese are attacking innocent Americans with polar bears?"

"We can talk to Sam," she said. "And Benj McPherson. We tell them what we've found out."

"So you trust them now? Seemed like you weren't too friendly with that woman."

"I'd trust them more than I'd trust the people we've found with Chloe's pendant and your broken-down jeep."

Jared turned around, heading back toward the pickup, still out by the trap.

"What are we expecting those two to actually do for us?" he asked. "I know Mohammed thinks they're bad news, but they aren't exactly intimidating, are they?"

"Were you expecting something else from SolRescue? Navy SEALs?"

"I don't feel any safer with those two around."

"Neither do I," Rachael said. "But we have to work with them."

"Because they're all we've got? I don't think that's a good enough reason."

They climbed back into the truck.

Rachael started driving them back to the main road.

"That hab has no windows," she said. "Do you think they saw us?"

"I'm sure they saw us. They'd have surveillance."

"But they didn't come out. If they want us out of the way…"

"I don't know, Rachael. I have trouble believing they're innocent bystanders."

"But you don't trust Samantha Yoon, either."

"No, I don't. For all we know, those two are working with the Chinese. Hell, I'm apparently working with the Chinese. I just didn't know it until earlier this week."

Rachael sighed. "So everyone works for everyone else, and no one trusts a soul."

"I think I trust you, Rachael."

"Heh," she said. "And I thought I could trust you. So…"

Jared nodded. He felt like an ass, but he couldn't change his past stupid. He could just try to be less stupid going forward. *He could try.*

"We should go back to my lab," he said.

"Mohammed might be there. You really want a confrontation?"

Jared chuckled.

"What?" she asked him.

"It's funny. He is so pissed at us. Goes to show that Mohammed Najjar is the one guy I honestly think we can all trust."

Rachael hung back in the truck while Jared checked the lab. Mohammed's rental van was still parked outside, but since they'd taken Rachael's brother's truck the night before for the meeting at Miss Piggy, there was no way to know for sure that Mohammed have ever found his way back.

He hadn't. Not from what Jared could see.

He went back out to the pickup.

"I don't think he's come back," he said.

"It's Saturday," Rachel said. "Maybe he's taking the weekend off."

"We don't do weekends very often."

"I'm aware."

"So where is he?"

"Maybe you should message him. Like people normally would do in just this situation."

Jared pulled out his tablet and sent the message.

"More waiting," Jared said. "There's a chance Chloe's in that Chinese hab and we're just standing around."

"So what did you want us to do? Are you seriously hinting that we should go there and look for her?"

"I couldn't live with myself if I'd just left her there."

Rachael nodded. "We need to do it right, then. We need to expect them to fight back."

"Fight back. You think they're armed?"

"You should know that anyone can fashion themselves a weapon these days."

"Worst I've made is an airsoft gun," Jared said. "That's a far cry from manufacturing an arsenal."

Rachael restarted the engine. "I've got something that can work."

"You're serious."

"Yeah. We can get Sam and Benj McPherson in on this. We can get some answers from the Chinese. But let me be clear about this. You can't unsee it. So you can't just pretend you're not involved. And you can't go spouting off about it, either."

"Yeah, okay…"

"Fuck," she said. "I really wish I trusted you."

She gunned the engine and started back up the road to Churchill.

23

BENJ COULDN'T get a hold of his father.

That wasn't too unusual, since Derrick McPherson only seemed to be reachable when he was the one who wanted something. So Benj pulled the coded contact list from his datastore and reached out to the person he believed was the next best thing.

He knew she'd want to see how he was doing, so he used his tablet instead of the eyepiece, turning on the video screen before he'd even sent the request. He sat down on the bed and tried to look a little less panicked.

Bridget Hawn was sitting on a deck chair, an ocean and overcast sky behind her. She was dressed in what looked like a winter jacket, with a black toque with the blue and yellow circles of the SolRescue logo.

She was still *stunning*. That was the right word to use.

"It looks like you're freezing to death," Benj said.

"It's called sunbathing," Bridget replied with a chuckle. "It's great to see you, Benjamin."

"You're out on *Basilica?*"

"Where else? We go where he goes." Her smile faded. "What's wrong, Benjamin?"

"I can't reach my father."

"That's nothing new. Last I heard he was on the road."

On the road.

The euphemism everyone used for Derrick McPherson and his extra-legal activities. When you wanted something done that this or that government or international organization didn't want done, Derrick was your guy.

And yet he'd started off as Carter Elgin's compliance expert.

Maybe you had to understand the labyrinth of bureaucracy to consistently break all of its rules. To do it and get out before anyone caught on.

Benj hated that his father could be that impressive.

Deadbeat dads are supposed to wear stained wife-beaters and float between low-paying jobs and straight up stints on basic.

But Derrick McPherson had forced his wife and kid to live one tiny step above basic, while he'd become Carter Elgin's right hand man and the face of SolRescue's backroom power.

And now Benj needed his help.

"I think I'm in over my head," he said to Bridget. "I'm getting pushed around and... and I think my father's a part of it."

231

"I don't think he'd pull you into something," Bridget said. "He wouldn't want to risk you getting in trouble."

"I'm way beyond being in trouble."

"Don't give me any details. Not like this."

"I don't have any other way, Bridget."

"I'll track him down. I'll let him know you need him."

"Thanks," he said.

Benj heard a knock on the door to his room.

"I've got to go," he said to Bridget. "Thanks."

She nodded as he disconnected the video call.

Samantha opened the door and walked in.

"Why bother knocking?" he asked her.

She sat down on his bed, beside him.

She looked over at the tablet set up on the nightstand. "Who did you call?"

"You're the one monitoring everything I do."

She rolled her eyes at him.

"What?" he said.

"I don't have my tablet, remember? And I'm sure even if I did, I wouldn't be able to trace it."

"Wouldn't have been my doing, Samantha. It's how all those calls go."

"You called your father."

"Sure."

"Wait," she said. "Not your father. But… there's no way…"

"It wasn't Carter Elgin. It was Bridget."

"You didn't mention me…"

"No. I guess I should have."

"She doesn't know," Samantha said. "She's not involved in the day-to-day anymore."

"You mean the super secret shit? The shit that isn't anywhere near legal?"

"I do my job, Benj. Just like your father does his."

"And you guys are what's wrong with SolRescue."

"I hear that bullshit all the time," she said. "But I don't have to listen to it."

"You could stand to listen more often."

She shook her head. "Don't start on that, Benj. Your father—"

"My father did all sort of shady stuff that no one talks about. I know that. Fuck, we both know I helped him with some of it. And then I lost my job. And my freedom. Not to mention what happened to Laila and Malik."

"You're a broken record, Benj."

"You're a psychotic bitch."

"Is that how your mother raised you? To go and call women bitches if you don't like what they're telling you?"

"You have fucked up everything in my life," he said. "I don't know what else to call you, honestly."

"I've told you before. It doesn't matter how you feel about me. All that matters is that we get the job done."

"The job you won't tell me about."

"I'm telling you now," she said.

"Not really."

"No... really. So let me talk, okay?"

He nodded.

"Rachael messaged me a few minutes ago. Rachael Duck."

"I know who she is. Wait... I have your tablet."

"No," she said with a smile. "I took it back and you didn't notice. Idiot."

"Shit." He felt like an idiot.

"She and Jared Koskela have allegedly found more than enough evidence that a group of Chinese researchers were involved in the attack and in their project manager's disappearance."

"Allegedly?"

"Oh, I'm sure Koskela believes it. But I'll tell you, Benj, it's a total snowjob. Get it, snowjob?"

"Like Rachael is setting them up?"

"She's setting us up."

"What?"

"She set up the bear attack. I've been sent the messages to prove it. Between her brother and some conservation officer named Cannabis or something."

"Cannae."

"Yeah."

Shit. That one he didn't say out loud.

"And she's probably leading us into a trap," Samantha said. "We go with her and Koskela to that Chinese hab, and things go really wrong. Before you know it you and I are both dead on the ground with two well-placed gunshots each. Probably Koskela, too."

"And then what?" he asked.

"Well, you'd be dead, so not much for you. But then I imagine Rachael and whichever of those Chinese researchers aren't really researchers would disappear for good. And again, you and I and probably Koskela would all be dead."

"Yeah. I got that part. But it doesn't make sense."

"What? Why?"

"Because it's a little obvious, isn't it?" Benj said. "We're assassinated and Rachael disappears? Slam dunk case."

"It won't matter if the Chinese show their hand."

"Why not?"

"Because if we're right about the partnership between them and the US Executive, no one will ever know what happened here."

"Then why bother with the polar bear in the first place? Why not just double tap us the moment we got off the plane?"

"Oh, double tap. I like how you say that."

"Seriously, Samantha…"

"They didn't want to blow Rachael's cover. She's a high-value member of SolRescue, Benj. Someone Carter Elgin trusts. Not just some groupie they turned. The Chinese must have spent some serious treasure bringing her on side. They can't just go down to the supermarket and pick up another Rachael Duck."

"So if this is what's really happening," he said, "then what are we supposed to do?"

"You're right… I don't know for sure that she has an actual plan here. But I don't see how us confronting the very people she's working with will turn into handjobs and ice cream."

"So what do you expect us to do?"

"I'm supposed to get evidence on Rachael," she said. "That's what Derrick asked me to do. I'm supposed to be able to prove to your father that she's been bought by the Chinese."

"And then what?"

"And then it doesn't matter if I kill her."

Benj laughed.

Samantha gave him a little smile.

"Seriously, though," he said.

"We go along with it for now. She wants us to meet us at her place, just a few blocks away from here. All we need to do is get Koskela out of the way, and then we'll deal with her. We'll get the evidence. Whatever it takes."

"You think it's that easy?" Benj asked. "We just strongarm her into confessing everything?"

"No, you're right," she said. "Let's just go with her plan. We'll get ourselves murdered instead. Listen, she lives with her brother. He's low priority and we need him to not be there. And we need Jared gone, too. We go in, search her place, take her and her tablet and filebox out. Maybe take her to Najjar and Koskela's lab. If she's getting payments from the Chinese we'll find it." She grinned. "Actually, you'll find it, Benj."

"Me?"

"Ah, the final piece of the puzzle."

"You want me to check out her tablet and filebox, and her profiles and accounts. She'll have extra levels of security, maybe biometrics, even a time bomb."

"A time bomb?"

"Accessing certain booby trapped items will trigger a countdown for the data to get wiped. And then you need the workaround."

"I know you can handle it. I want you to reverse engineer what she's done. To find the money trail and to find out how she's been passing information to the Chinese. You were smart enough to trick the Universal Income program, so I'm sure you can handle this."

"For a system audit? That's why you destroyed my career?"

"You still don't get it, Benj."

"Get what? That you're a sociopath?"

"Your father's called you up to the majors," she said. "He wants you on board."

"This is a really fucked up way of recruiting."

"It's the family business, Benj. It's what the McPherson men do. You know that. And you knew it when you joined the NSA. And when you started digging into all those ridiculous conspiracy theories with your little home anonymizer. You're just like your father. And I'm glad."

"Because you also want *my father to fuck you?*"

She laughed.

"I don't trust you, Samantha. You know that. There is no goddamn way I am going to help you kidnap Rachael Duck and search all her systems."

"I've got the messages. Proof she tried to kill two people with an eight-hundred pound set of walking steak knives."

"It doesn't matter. I didn't sign up for this."

"You'll do it if the right person asks," she said.

"You mean my father? I doubt it."

"What about Laila? What if she asked you?"

"Get her to try, then."

"Can't call her where she is. You know that. And she hates your guts right now, Benj. I've heard she curses you out in her sleep. You know why?"

"We both know why. Not that I believe you."

"You do this and Laila can go home. Malik, too."

"Fuck, Samantha. Do you really not get this? I don't trust you. So you trying to make some deal, making some flimsy guarantee about a girl I had a thing for... it's not something that would ever work."

There was a noise out in the hallway.

Yelling. An argument.

"Domestic bliss," Samantha said.

"No... it's something else."

Heavy and rushed footsteps, coming up the hallway.

The door to Benj's room swung open.

It was Mohammed Najjar.

No weapon that Benj could see.

But Najjar would still be a problem.

"You had no permission to investigate our lab," Najjar said. "No access grant from Colonel Begtang. Just more lies." He was looking directly at Benj.

"Stop stirring the pot, Mohammed," Samantha said.

But Najjar wasn't distracted by that. He came up to Benj and leaned right in. He was probably two inches shorter and thirty pounds lighter; that was not enough of a gap.

Benj knew where things were likely to go.

"You need to calm down," Benj told him. "There's no upside to a physical confrontation."

"Is that a threat?" Najjar asked. "Are you threatening me?"

"You shouldn't have contacted the colonel," Samantha said.

Najjar groaned. "I didn't contact the colonel. I contacted the colonel's colonel. A brigadier general, actually. I told them about your little sabotage mission."

"And what was the response?" Benj asked.

"As if I'd tell you."

"Loose lips sink ships," Samantha said.

"Can you tell her to shut up?" Najjar said.

Samantha grinned. "That's like every second sentence out of his mouth. Hasn't worked so far."

"We're up here looking for a real saboteur," Benj said.

"Oh, yeah," Najjar said, "the space station. Because Jared and I had nothing better to do than attack some European boondoggle."

"Boondoggle?" Samantha said.

"We think Rachael Duck is involved," Benj said. He had a feeling that Samantha had seen that particular admission coming from him.

"We have evidence that she coordinated the polar bear attack," Samantha said.

"You think she's working with who, exactly?" Najjar said. "She doesn't work with me."

"The Chinese government," Samantha said. "Maybe we're wrong about the partnership with the US Executive. Maybe China's acting on its own."

Najjar nodded. "Would make more sense, but—"

"We're not sure. All I know, aside from the goddamn bear, is that Rachael knew what the Chinese were up to with the space station, and she claims she warned her contacts in French Guiana in time. I think that's a lie, that she found a way to alter the timestamps."

That was the first Benj had heard of that theory. He wasn't sure Samantha was telling the truth.

"Wait," Najjar said. "Why would she admit to knowing about a plan to attack?"

"We don't know that yet," she said. "It's possible she's looking to finger someone else, or maybe the Chinese *wanted* SolRescue to know they did it. Unofficially, of course."

Najjar nodded. Pensively?

Somehow he'd calmed down a little, simply by being included in the call to order of the tinfoil hat club.

Samantha was jumping to conclusions. Her suspicions about Rachael and the Chinese military government were completely unfounded.

But maybe that was just some bias of his, maybe because Rachael Duck didn't seem like a double-crosser. She seemed like a battered idealist to him, made cynical by everything she'd learned about the world, but still trying her best to see a way through.

And no one could honestly believe that the rise of the Chinese People's Convocation would appeal to a Native Indian girl on the other side of the world.

She'd believe in SolRescue, about the decentralization of power and the progress of equality. She wouldn't fall in line with some shadowy opposition to what she cared about, even if she believed—like many seemed to, including Benj—that SolRescue had started to lose its way.

But still... he could see that Najjar was starting to buy into it.

Samantha had gone to work on him, that sexy-smiley sarcasm thing she did, half a flirt and half a jab. She'd tried it time and again on Benj, and he liked to think it hadn't worked, that he'd never had the goofy look on his face that he now saw on Najjar's.

He'd like to think it, at least.

"Who do you work for?" Najjar asked her. "For real. Is it SolRescue, or are you not telling me the whole story?"

"I know what you're asking," she said.

"I don't," Benj said.

"I work for a cause more than one specific organization," Samantha said. "When values align, I go to work."

"And your values align with how many groups at the moment?" Najjar asked.

"At the moment, almost all of them. SolRescue, the NSA, probably the US Air Force, even if Colonel Begtang has never heard of me. I just don't work for the Chinese junta. That's a line I'll never cross."

Najjar nodded.

The brilliant Alchemist of Ann Arbor was eating it up.

Benj felt weird watching it so passively. Was he supposed to step in and knock some sense into the man?

"Will you work with us, Mohammed?" she asked. "If we can prove that Rachael Duck is an agent for the People's Convocation, we can kill five hundred birds with one stone. No more doubts about Chinese involvement in your project, and case closed for the attack on the space station."

"But I still haven't seen any evidence," Najjar said.

But he was teetering already.

"We'll get that evidence," Samantha said. "Benj will find it for us."

Najjar looked back to Benj. "You can do that?" he asked.

"Maybe," Benj said. "But I haven't agreed to it."

"Haven't agreed to it? What does that mean?"

"He's worried about Rachael's rights," Samantha said. "Benj is a by-the-book kind of guy."

Najjar sighed. "And which book is that?"

"You know who his father is."

Najjar chuckled. "So it's not about the girl's rights at all," he said. "It's about not getting caught."

Samantha smiled.

"It's not about any of that," Benj said.

"Your turn to shut up, Benj," Samantha said.

"No," Najjar said, "I want to hear this."

Samantha looked over to Benj. "Go ahead," she said. "Tell him all about your moral reservations."

That's how she was going to frame it.

And trying to cast doubt on whether or not Samantha could be trusted... it brought no advantage. Najjar on board was safer than Najjar going off the reservation.

This was a man who'd punched Koskela and spit on Rachael Duck. Najjar just getting started.

"Sometimes we go too far," Benj said. "I want to make sure we treat Ms. Duck with a little sympathy. I think once we know the whole story, we'll know why she felt she had no choice but to cooperate with the Chinese operatives."

"Because she's pretty," Samantha said, with a smirk.

Benj swallowed his self-respect. "You know me too well," he said.

Samantha chuckled a little before continuing her play. "So I think we know what we need to do, guys. I believe Rachael is hoping to lead us into a trap. We need to use this opportunity to trap her instead. And get Benj access to her systems while Mohammed and I search her house."

"Will we have to hurt her?" Najjar asked.

"I hope to god we won't have to," Samantha said. "But that's going to be up to her."

24

NICOLAS HAD gotten used to the idea of Mireia Lona—Mireia Lona *de Vives*, she often reminded him—being his friend.

The only friend he had left who he could speak to in his native tongue, since she knew French almost as good as English.

They'd started working more closely than they'd ever had at CSG, since he was heading up the overall launch while she was cloistered in environmentals with her husband and a few other engineers.

He was amazed at how easy it had been to forgive Mireia for everything that had come before; that alone was almost as amazing as the speed of the work they were doing.

The maker camp Leonardo worked wonders, and he wasn't sure exactly why. The engineers were mostly segregated, two or three to a camper van, working away on their tasks, seemingly oblivious to everyone else.

They hadn't moved yet from their stop at Fort Reno, Wyoming, but Nicolas had a feeling that his first big pack-up would be something he barely noticed, aside from a few hours of data throttling and the occasional bump on the highway.

The biggest problem Nicolas had was that he didn't think he could keep up with everyone else.

In the ESA, it was understood that while occasional overtime might happen, that six hours or productivity was more than you could hope for. It was a philosophy he'd believed in, that it was only by getting away from the work, washing dishes or walking along the beach… that was how you refined your ideas, simplified your problems.

But the makers never stopped.

They never wanted to stop.

Nikki had tried to explain it to him, about how there were busy times and slack times, and that when people were busy, because they were passionate they worked as much as they could, not just from the passion and their ingrained curiosity, but because they knew that when the next lull in their tasks came, they'd have plenty of time for everything else.

And you didn't need to worry about life if you worked at a maker camp. Your meals were cooked, your toilet was scrubbed. The support staff crisscrossed the camp like eerily noiseless bees, seeming to be everywhere while sounding like they were nowhere at all.

Those people seemed the most passionate of all, Nikki and her team;

maybe that was because they weren't motivated by the excitement of new tech, they had to run almost exclusively on ideology.

No one got paid, from what Nicolas could tell; everyone survived on basic, assuming no one had IP payments from previous lives. Not that their money had to be spent on anything, since there was nothing to buy in the middle of a moving nowhere.

And none of the makers seemed to notice or care about that little draw-back.

But Mireia had clearly noticed, and despite her keeping a much heavier pace than Nicolas and his nine hours, tops, she spent the bulk of her down-time complaining about not having anything to do.

And Nicolas' listened, as a friend, but grumbled quietly to himself.

She was so fervent, but could be so vapid. So brilliant, but dull. So completely attractive, yet at times just having to look at her annoyed him.

But he supposed that it was that strange duality that made her almost as interesting as she was frustrating.

In the balance, he still wanted to share that little electric camper van with her.

The day's tasks—Saturday apparently being an ordinary workday—had been laid out before Nicolas had even awoken. The organization of work-load was such a strange combination of priority and balance; it was like whoever set up the tasks understood how Nicolas worked better than he did, giving him the mundane at first, then a challenge, then as fun a reward as you could find on a tasklist, then possibly another challenge if there was time left in his unspokenly shorter workday.

He saw one task that excited him, the day's carrot: reviewing the check-list for the first launch. The first module had been completed and scruti-nized, and the launch would be coming on Monday, assuming good wea-ther and no setbacks.

On Monday!

When he and Mireia had first arrived on Thursday afternoon, it had seemed to him that the first launch would be weeks away, not that the time-line had shown up in his task lists. Everything he'd been working on invol-ved the second bead, the hab that would meet up with the first hab, which had been filled not with life support systems, but with whatever was needed for the skeleton of the toroid, the spokes between the beads, the solar array, the mining and utility tugs that would handle the actual materials gathering and in situe assembly.

Not that he'd ever seen that module, since both it and the sixth bead—the other hab—were with Donatello, and that information—again—wasn't part of his task list.

From what he knew, so what the mysterious project coordinator had shared with him via his tasks, mixed with whatever Mireia had shared about hers, the SolRescue station—the backup to the European station—was built somewhat differently than *Nisi* had been, but still a beaded toroid, the easiest way to get the dual benefits of centrifugal spin and shelter from nasty old particles.

This wasn't another ISS/2 or OPSEK or Tiangong, flitting in LEO; like *Nisi* should have been, the SolRescue station would be out there, beyond the warm fuzzies of the magnetosphere.

That meant shielding on the exterior, and even shielding on the interior, too, since the torus had more gap than fill for the time being. The habitat would have exactly zero windows, with display screens instead, like those ones on the "glass-bottom" planes that were popular with the Gulf State airlines. Those planes didn't have any windows, either, aside from the ones up at the cockpit.

Nicolas hadn't been the least bit concerned in sharing what he'd learned from *Nisi*. SolRescue and the ESA were informal partners, really, and as a wanted terrorist, Nicolas didn't really have much more to lose.

Mireia had told him she felt more or less the same way.

And now it felt like he was being rewarded for that subtle shift in loyalties. Not that he understood how he'd inspect a module that wasn't anywhere near the maker camp he was in.

He saw Nikki on his way out to the latrine. She had some very low tech mop and small bucket in her hands.

"Are the camps reconfiguring soon?" he asked her. "For the launch."

"No one's told me yet," she said. "I don't find out until just before. I don't think they even decide it until just before, actually."

"Who decides?"

She raised an eyebrow at him. "You asking if the members take a vote?"

"What?"

"Mireia was asking me about that," she said. "She's a big fan of total transparency, apparently. Not sure if maybe you feel the same way."

"I don't think about it much, to be honest. I'm not political."

"A true engineer," she said with a smile. She put down the mop and bucket. "You in a hurry to pee?"

He was taken aback by that.

He shook his head.

"Uh, listen, Nic. This is a weird question, okay?"

"Okay."

"Are you and Mireia really, uh, together?"

"The supposed threesome," Nicolas said.

"Uh, yeah."

"Complete fabrication."

"That's good."

Usually he'd take that to mean something else, a subtle declaration of interest. But he could see on her face that she had something more to say. Something she didn't want to say.

"I'm really glad you guys are here," Nikki said. "I am."

"But?"

"But I can tell Mireia doesn't believe in this project."

"What do you mean?"

"She's expressed doubts to more than one person, Nic. She's gotten to be a little negative."

"I've seen some of that. Heard some of that."

"I don't know anything yet. But I wouldn't be surprised if they rotate her out."

"Rotate her out? Is that a temporary thing, or permanent?"

"Well, she's a special case," Nikki said. "You both are. It's not like there's somewhere else she can go."

"So they can't rotate her out, can they?"

"I don't know. Like I said, I don't know anything yet. But most people who get on that train of thought..."

"Which train of thought?"

"That the organization has lost its way."

"I don't think she believes that," Nicolas said, though as he'd said it he'd realized that he wasn't so sure.

The woman had already told Derrick McPherson off about it, a few hours after he'd pulled her out of the Amazon. He'd chalked that up to grief over Alex, and the general strain of almost dying in the jungle.

"You need to talk to her," Nikki said. "Tell her she needs to rethink it."

"Rethink it?"

"We're the good guys. We've always been the good guys. So ask her, Nic. Ask her why she's so dead set against helping us?"

"It's not like that... she's just having trouble adjusting to all of this. Remember what's she'd gone through."

"I'm not in charge of it. I'm just telling you what I know, what I think is going to happen. If she can't start showing that she's an asset, they'll rotate her out. Or whatever the equivalent would be for someone like her."

"Someone like me," he said.

"It's not like you guys have a lot of options, right? You need to remind her of that."

Nicolas nodded.

And wished he would have stayed back in the camper van, bladder be damned.

He waited until Mireia had signed off from her task list.

She looked tired, and he was exhausted, but he knew he had to tell her.

"They can tell you're unhappy," he said. No flourish required.

"Of course I'm unhappy," she replied, rolling her eyes.

"I mean they might want you out of here."

She sighed. "I know. I've seen my score."

"Your score?"

"People talk to me, Nicolas. I guess they enjoy my negative energy. One of the guys on the miners used to work on the project coordinator."

"Work on?"

"Helped design it," she said. "You know it's all automated, right?"

"Automated? Which part? The task list?"

"The project. The tasks, the relocations, the team rotations."

"She didn't tell me that," Nicolas said.

"Maybe Nikki doesn't feel like telling you everything. She just likes bad-mouthing me, apparently."

"So what is your score, then?"

"Not good. He couldn't give me any numbers, but he explained how it's calculated. Basically. And it doesn't matter how much I produce; if the system determines that I've been the cause of anyone else's reduction in productivity, my score is lowered."

"So it tries to account for what? Your bad attitude?"

"Pretty much," she said. "It monitors more than you'd think. Not just messaging between team members; it monitors oral communication."

"That can't be true. They wouldn't listen in."

"Wake up, Nicolas. This isn't the organization it used to be. Or what I'd thought it was. The members don't even know about this project. You realize that, right?"

"Yeah, I know."

"So he decided to do it? Carter Elgin? Derrick? Obviously not the members."

"There's an executive, isn't there? For just such a thing?"

"Not for secret projects there isn't. They didn't list that in the bylaws."

"So what did you want to do about it, Mireia? You just want to keep complaining until they ship you out? To who knows where?"

"I speak my mind, Nicolas. That's who I am."

"Then be smart about it."

"What did you just say to me?"

"We're friends, Mireia. Real friends now, I think. We need to figure this out together."

"What are you saying?" she asked.

"I'm on your side, Mireia. I think you're right."

"You think I'm right."

"This project has its problems. It could be done better, and it ought to have membership approval."

"But you'll still work on it," she said.

"You're still working on it."

"Because I don't have a choice, do I?"

"No, you don't. Or maybe you do, since Nikki is convinced that what you're doing will get you rotated out. Whatever that will mean."

"I told Derrick that I didn't want to do this. I told *you* I didn't want to do this. I have no problem leaving. I've got this Canadian passport and a fake name. I can find a place to hide."

"We don't know how to do that," Nicolas said. "I think they'd find us."

"There is no 'we' on this, Nicolas. I'm sorry, but I need to find my own way."

"So what? So you're going to sneak out? Just start walking north?"

"I don't know," she said. "It's clear as day that we're basically prisoners here. The truck we came in's already gone, and this damned van won't take commands from me." She shook her head. "It's not a maker camp, Nicolas. For you and me, it's a gulag."

"So we escape together, Mireia."

"No. Sorry. I will figure something out. Just me." She bit her lower lip. "You won't tell her, right?"

"It's not my business."

"Thank you, Nicolas. You're a good friend."

He nodded.

And resisted the urge to tell her that she had little understanding of how friendship was supposed to work.

Nicolas had chosen a walk during sunset over awkward silence with Mireia, and the vivid orange and purple over the open Wyoming sky did something to improve on his mood.

Big skies. And wind. So much wind. He'd wondered how it was any different than everyone else's skies and everyone else's windy days, but there was a difference out there, out in the American West. The horizon wasn't flat, but there wasn't much to the rise in the hills. You couldn't see the Rocky Mountains, not from there; Nicolas had always thought of Wyoming as Yellowstone Park, the mountains and the geysers and the bears, like that shirt his friend in collège had worn, the two bears in the Yellowstone fires that had happened long before either Nicolas or his friend had been born.

Send more firefighters. The last ones were delicious.

He liked what he'd seen of America. He'd heard you would, from friends who'd done the stereotypical August trip to New York City. That America was more often the best than the worst place in the world, that the people were so confident and naive and so blindly *American*.

Nikki was American, he assumed, and she had an open air to her that matched the Wyoming skies; she wasn't all bottled up like Mireia, like all European women who seemed perfectly fine being sensual and passionate, but who still wouldn't let you in past anything on the surface.

Mireia had never been interested in Nicolas. Not that Nikki was interested, either, even if she was slightly closer in age to him and all other primordial life.

That didn't matter; there was nothing to be interested in when it came to Nicolas Clouatre.

But still... he felt free out there. Alone, but free.

And then he saw Mireia.

She'd gone out of the van as well, for her own walk. But she wasn't alone; there was a man with her, young and dark-haired, a man who reminded Nicolas of Alex, like a slightly shorter Alex with an odd moustache.

Like Alex Vives crossed with a lightweight version of Salvador Dali.

And they were huddled close as they walked, the way she wouldn't walk with Nicolas, like a woman who'd found something in the man she was beside.

It made him sick in his stomach.

And then he felt stupid.

He walked back to the camper van.

He sat and dwelled on Mireia. And on how stupid it was that he was thinking of her at all.

She came back after a half hour.

"I saw you out there," she said. "You must have seen me."

"I saw."

"A friend from back home. Mateo."

"Mateo and Mireia. Rolls off the tongue."

"A *friend*, Nicolas. It's not your job to judge me, anyway."

"Why is he here?"

"Same reason as the rest of us," she said. "He transferred in from another camp today."

"Transferred in? What a perfect coincidence."

"What are you saying?"

"I'm saying he's here for a reason, Mireia."

"I think it has something to do with a space station project," she said. "How unusual."

"You know they're concerned about you. And now a friend comes to visit?"

"You're jealous," she said.

"What?"

"I'm sorry, Nicolas. But you don't have a right to me."

"Don't be stupid, Mireia."

"We're not a couple."

"No, we're not. And that's good, because I'm pretty sure you just lost your husband."

"*Gilipollas,*" she said. "*Això és el que ets tu.*"

"*En français, s'il vous plaît.*"

"Fuck you, Nicolas. This is America. You're an asshole. I hate your French guts."

"What's going on with you, Mireia? I don't understand."

"You don't understand? That I'm sick of your advances?"

"What advances? I haven't done anything."

"I know what you want. You've wanted it from the first time we had you over. You were hoping to be with me. You wanted me."

He was angrier because she was right. Because he did want her.

Because he wanted to live in a world where he was still young and desirable enough to be with Mireia.

Because Mateo was some young shit who couldn't be trusted, and she was all over him.

"He invited me to move to his camper," she said. "I think it would be a good idea."

"I don't trust him, Mireia."

"You don't know anything about him."

"Did David know him?"

"What is that supposed to mean?"

"Don't make a hasty decision. That's all. Think of what David would want."

"David wanted to go home," she said. "But we can't do that, because of you. Because we were told to save you. Because David gave his life for yours, not that he would have, if he'd been given a choice. Not that I would have let him. If I could make you take his place in that jungle, Nicolas... I would."

"It worked out okay for Mateo."

She shook her head.

He was surprised she hadn't hit him.

"I am sick of the lies," she said. "Sick of the liars, like you."

"Like me?"

"I will find somewhere else to sleep tonight."

And she left the camper.

"Life is nothing but a joke," Nicolas muttered.

The camper door opened. Mireia stuck her head inside. "Mateo found me because he was looking for me," she said. "Why don't you think about that."

Nicolas tried to reply, but she was gone.

He wasn't sure why she'd said it. She knew they were in hiding, that it was a problem if random people were dropping in to visit.

Maybe she'd made it up, just to anger him.

But why?

Why did he matter to Mireia at all?

He went for a walk.

Being in the van alone wasn't making him feel better.

He didn't want to be alone.

So he pulled out his tablet and looked up Nikki up on the contact list. He'd never sent anything to her before.

By proximity she was ranked close by, not that the list gave an exact location for regular contacts.

What did he have to lose? All she'd do is say no thanks, that she's busy with something. She wasn't going to tear him down.

He'd gotten to know her well enough to know that.

So he messaged her, asking if she'd be interested in going for a treacherous walk in the middle of the night.

She replied with a quaint LOL and a yes.

He told her to meet him by the outdoor kitchen.

"Nic and Nikki," she said as she found him. "Hard to tell us apart. Only you have longer hair." She walked up and tousled the little wisp on his forehead.

"I should just shave it off," Nicolas said. "But I have this weird little indent on the back of my skull."

"You're worried people'll think a big ol' chunk of your brain is missing?"

He grinned. "They can usually tell that after a few minutes of casual conversation."

Nikki laughed. "I like you, Nic. It's nice to have someone here who's been around the block. Lived a little."

"Oh, I haven't lived. Not at all."

"Bullcrap," she said. "I know you've lived. You can always tell with someone."

"Oh, really? How can you tell?"

"It's all in how someone talks."

"How they talk."

"Yeah. Is that weird?"

"It's probably more wrong than weird," Nicolas said, giving her what he hoped was a friendly-looking smirk.

She smiled. "It's like listening to music. Like comparing Mozart to Beethoven."

"I've never listened to either."

She laughed. "Me, neither. But I listen to people talk. Oh my god... do I ever have to listen to people talk."

"I guess I could... not talk?"

"Don't be ridiculous. But there's a density to people who've been through stuff, like... like you know there's more than one layer in everything they say."

"Like double entendres?" Nicolas said. "I'm French, so we're all about that kind of thing."

"I like that you're French. So cynical and world-weary, like you ought to have a cigarette hanging out of your mouth."

"Like Pepé le Pew mixed with an existential mime."

"Ha!" she said. "You get it, then."

"How attracted you are to me right now?"

She laughed.

And then she winked.

What did that mean, again?

He didn't say anything. Or do anything.

She was waiting for something from him...

"I love it here," she said, deftly sweeping that awkward pause to the side. "Not just the open country, but... the makers."

"I was wondering how it would feel... having so many primadonnas relying on your for everything."

"I feel free, actually. Like I'm here because I want to be. I'm old enough to remember what things were like before the universal income."

"You must have been young," Nicolas said, not that he couldn't do a good estimate on the math. Unofficially.

"I'd just finished six years of overpriced college. And just one BA in Communications to show for it."

"Communications..."

"Probably not how you do it in France," Nikki said.

"Probably not."

"I tried for six months to hold out for a real job, not high paying, but at least related to my field."

"And it wasn't going well."

"To put it ultra mildly. Too many people wanted to be baristas. I ended up working at the Kum & Go. That's not as dirty or as profitable as it sounds."

"What was it?"

"A gas station. The machines made the coffee, but at least I got to clean blood and puke out of the bathrooms four times a shift."

She started laughing, so Nicolas felt it was okay for him to laugh a little, too.

"You know why I'm not still working at the Kum & Go?" she asked.

"Because you hated it?"

"Well, yeah," she said, chuckling, "but mostly because I didn't have to anymore. I could do something I cared about and still be able to eat."

"I remember the arguments they'd made, that no one would work the low-paying jobs if they didn't need to."

"Great way to justify slavery."

"So what did they do at the gas station? Did everyone quit their job after a few days of free money?"

"How did it work in France?"

"Most had already been automated before the citizen's income. You'd drive in, put your card into the machine, and fill your tank."

"Well, people still work at the Kum & Go," she said. "I guess it's not such a bad job if you don't need to keep it."

"I guess not."

"It's people like you who made it happen, Nic."

"What do you mean?"

"Makers. Engineers, hobbyists, designers. Whatever. You guys took the power away from the elites."

"Wasn't me," Nicolas said. "I was designing smart thermostats in Stuttgart."

"Germany?"

"*Jawohl.* Always helped me when dealing with the ESA team in Dortmund."

"Knowing German," she said.

"Most of them spoke really good English, actually. Even French. It's more because I'd drank most of the right beers and knew all the best jokes about Bavarians."

"See? Density."

"I don't see it."

"You're too dense to see it," she said with a grin. "There's something to be said about a man with experience."

"I'll take the compliment."

"You should."

He smiled at her.

She was attractive. He was attracted to her. It seemed like Mireia had gotten in the way of that realization.

And Nikki seemed to be interested in him.

At the moment, it didn't seem so strange. She'd made him feel pretty good about himself.

"I think it's people like you who made it happen," he told her.

"People like me?"

"Pushed those engineers and makers along. Saw what they were doing and embraced it. Made it something worthwhile."

"Team effort," she said.

"Yeah. Team effort."

"I can't tell you how excited I am about this, Nic. We've been talking about offplanet habitation for almost a century. And we're really doing it."

"We're trying to do it," he said.

"You don't think we'll make it?"

"It's not about making it, Nikki. Not day to day. It's more about trying and trying again. Not letting failure get in the way of that."

"We won't fail," she said.

"Not in the end, we won't. But it's a long voyage between here and there. I thought we'd pull it off in Guyane."

"That wasn't your fault."

"We just keep trying," he said. "That's all we need to do. That's all it takes, really."

She smiled. "Exactly what I was talking about."

She leaned in.

He kissed her.

And he realized that it felt right.

25

ANITA DECIDED that she wasn't interested in seeing Carter Elgin.

It didn't matter that it was Bridget who'd asked, which would have been a very difficult thing for Bridget to do.

It had been so long since she'd been in the same room with either of them. But it still felt fresh, the way they'd made her feel. If she wasn't careful, she'd let it through, start feeling is all over again.

She'd built up a life where those kinds of feelings couldn't break back in.

She sent a simple message to Bridget, apologizing for having to decline. She didn't ask about her counteroffer on the settlement, since that wasn't something they'd ever discussed outside of their lawyers' back and forth.

She had a feeling Bridget wouldn't be sending a reply any time soon. On either item.

Anita had been humiliated.

The job had never been anything more than a way to push Anita away from SolRescue. She'd arrived on her first day to find that there was no real work for her; she didn't even have a direct report. They'd tricked her into coming on board, and they weren't even putting in a basic effort to keep up appearances.

She left after two hours and never went back.

She'd waited half a week before responding to Carter's messages.

Bridget hadn't send a single one.

She met him off campus, as far from Starbuck's as she could get without hopping the subway, assuming she was wearing comfortable shoes.

She arrived at the Shake Shack first, joining the line that was already halfway up the steps from the lower-level counter.

She ordered the 'Shroom Burger. She was back on the meatwagon. Or off of it?

She sat down at a table just off the stairs.

And waited for Carter to show up late, as usual.

He arrived just in time for the line to be all the way up the stairs and out the door, and for all Anita knew, halfway down the block.

You don't aim for lunch at Shake Shack and expect no line at noon. That's why she'd set up the time for 11:30.

He'd cut around to apologize for being late, before heading back to line up.

She had another ten minutes before he sat down across from her.

"I hate this place," he told her.

"Then you should have told me," she said.

He grinned. "I hate it because I like it. Anything with this much power of me…"

"Yeah, okay."

He leaned in. "I'm sorry about the job, Anita. I know it was supposed to be something special."

"My just desserts," she said.

"No… we made this mess together… probably mostly me."

"Does Bridget agree with that assessment?"

"She's pissed. And that's okay."

"Oh, is it?"

"She'll get over it. Eventually. We just need to work around that."

"Work around it?"

"You're still one third of our team, Anita. That hasn't changed. That's not gonna change."

"Well, eventually these kinds of companies tend to hire a few employees. Might dilute my sheer volume."

"Heh," he said. "We need you back today, after lunch, if you're available."

She hadn't expected that. Any of it, actually. She'd even considered the possibility that he wouldn't show up at all. But to want her to hop back in, like nothing had happened…

Could she even do that?

"The US government will have banned all 'new entity' launches by March," he said. Carter knew how to get her back on track. "SpaceX has said they're interested in lending a hand to get our little bots to orbit, and I think you're the one who can get us the best arrangement."

She smirked. "Does Elon prefer brunettes?"

"You speak his language, Anita. Their company language. Bridget doesn't. Not at all."

"So what do you want me to do, exactly?"

"Teleconference. 2 PM. Jemison building, third floor meeting room, that one with the fancy screen."

"You've already set this up?"

"Yeah."

"And did you tell the SpaceX guys that I was going to be there?"

"Yeah. They were glad to hear it. You know, after that Starbuck's thing."

"So you just assumed I'd come crawling back?" she said.

"It's not that—"

"Come on, Carter. At least pretend you thought I might be able to say no to you. Like you could somehow fathom that I have a mind of my own."

"That's not fair, Anita. We all knew you'd come back."

"Oh, we all did? I did? Bridget did?"

"We're trying to save the world," he said. "You sold me on it. And Bridget. And you sold the world on it. You might think you can walk away from that... but come on."

"So what if I do this? What will happen with Bridget? With you?"

"Bridget won't get in the way. I won't get in the way. Our focus is staying out of your way."

"I don't want it to keep happening, Carter. You and me."

He reached across the table. He grabbed hold of both of her hands. "I love you and me," he said. "I'm sorry, Anita. But that's how it is."

"What is that supposed to even mean? There is no you and me and Bridget. It's you and Bridget, or it's you and me."

"Or you and Bridget..."

"It's not a joke."

"It won't get in the way," he said.

"That's not an assurance."

"What do you want me to say? That I don't care about you? That I don't think about you and the video shoot and what came after?" He sighed. "I can't change any of that, and I don't want to. But that doesn't change what we're doing with this company. How important it is. And how much it still needs you to be a part of it."

She looked at him for a while, trying to not let him win.

But he was breaking her down, or more realistically, he'd broken her down long before they'd had sex.

She knew she still had feelings for him, that she couldn't stop them from happening. She knew she couldn't be sure if he was being honest with how he felt about her.

But she was watching herself wilt, watching her give up any semblance of a woman who could control her destiny. She was drawn to Carter Elgin, because of everything he was.

She couldn't stop what she knew was coming.

Sometimes when people split up there's something good that comes of it, some child you love, or memories that you still cherish even if you want to scoop that ex's temporal lobe out with a melon baller.

With Carter, with the brief fuck-up that was Anita and Carter, out and recklessly around the everlasting binary system of Carter and Bridget... with Carter it was SolRescue, and what SolRescue had brought to the world.

Anita was ashamed of being a basic, but she wasn't ashamed that there was a universal basic income. She'd grown up being one of the ones who'd feel the crush—the crash, actually—when the inequality and the bad loans reached a breaking point, when a hundred million people were supposed to retire but had no money to make it happen. She and every other student at Cornell Tech had known that the emergency would happen when they were fighting to pay off their ridiculous student debt, when they were still scurrying along as entry-levels in a world where they were lucky if they'd climbed higher than being interns.

Anita had known that the well would dry up, and that on top of that, she and everyone else in her generation would have to either pony up for their parents' golden years—taxes or otherwise—or they'd have to accept that they no longer lived in a country—in a western *civilization*—that had any kind of safety net.

They either took more from the richest one percent, a citizen's royalty that no politician had the power to push, or they bankrupted the rest of the nation.

Bankruptcy was on the menu, a train wreck that everyone but the elites saw coming, that no one had the ability to stop.

And then it changed, and she knew—though she'd never just come out and saw it—that it changed because of the sunshield.

That it changed because of Anita and Carter and Bridget.

She wouldn't call them scars, the little bits of unpleasantness she'd been left with, the guilt of falling for Carter, the guilt of turning her back on the mission. They hurt and they'd changed her, but they weren't scars, because she knew deep-down that the only reason they were permanent was because she'd let them stay.

She hadn't done anything to scrub them off.

26

RACHAEL TOOK Jared to her place and showed him what she'd done.

A half dozen 3D printed guns in her bedroom, way more than you'd need for one person. Or two, assuming that Rachael's brother had any idea what she was up to.

And since he was out at work most of the time—including that particular afternoon—there was a chance her brother had no clue.

"I've always loved the idea of building something that's completely illegal to build," she said as he examined her armory, laid out on her bed. "Even if there's nothing I can really do with the end result."

Jared sighed. "No… these are used to kill people."

She chuckled.

"I'm not joking," Jared said. "I don't know why you'd make these."

"You have to register guns in Canada. You don't have to do that in the States?"

"People are supposed to, yeah. But there are enough loopholes that it's not a done deal."

"The land of loopholes, from sea to shining sea."

"You've really got that Canadian snark down pat, eh?"

"You're getting good with those 'ehs'."

"I don't think we can use these," he said.

"What?"

"We can't start a war with China."

"You said you wanted to get Chloe back. You wanted us to go down to the hab—"

"I don't even know if she's still alive, Rachael."

"She's alive… why else would they have brought her back with them? They could have killed her and left her out in the flats."

"Why would they do any of it?" Jared asked.

"I don't know. Because of the project you're on?"

"So China sends a bunch of operatives up to Churchill and pretends they're researching polar bears. And they then know enough about that polar bear cover story that they trap a bear and set it loose on Chloe and me?"

"I don't think there's anyone else who'd want you hurt, is there?"

"But Chloe isn't just hurt. She's gone. Why?"

"That's why we need answers. That's why you'd wanted to go to that research hab and get them. So what's changed, Jared?"

He didn't know.

He couldn't let Chloe down. But attacking that inflatable hab with a homemade arsenal? Risking his life along with that crazy Korean woman and Derrick McPherson's son, not to mention Rachael...

"I don't know if you should come," he told her.

"Why? You don't trust me, now? You're the one who keeps messing this up, Jared."

"I don't want you to get hurt. This whole thing is insane."

"Well, it's a little late for caution. You put me in this. You and Chloe."

"You can stay here," he said. "Stay here. Let the rest of us go."

"Samantha won't let that happen."

"What? Why?"

"She thinks I'm working with the Chinese."

"Yeah..."

"She probably already thinks I've set up some kind of trap. She won't want to give me enough room to spring it."

"So what? So we all have to go together because some crazy bitch doesn't trust you?"

"I don't trust her, either."

The doorbell sounded.

"It's time," Rachael said.

She walked out of the bedroom, toward the front door.

She came back into the room with Samantha.

No sign of Benj McPherson.

"Benj is back at the bed and breakfast," Samantha said. "Mohammed's there. I thought things were going okay, but then he just lost it. They're still shouting at each other. I'm hoping you can help us out, Mr. Koskela."

"What do you mean?" Jared asked.

"Come back with me to the B&B. Talk to Mohammed, help him to understand what's going on here."

"I'm not sure I know what's going on here."

"Just help us out, okay?"

Jared looked over to Rachael.

"I don't think I'm wanted," she said with a shrug.

"Okay," Jared said. "But I've got no patience for this stuff."

"I know," Samantha said. "I'm sorry."

"You haven't said anything about the guns," Rachael said.

Samantha looked over at her. "I'm not sure what I can say about them. They're impressive..."

"That's it?"

"That's it."

"Are we going?" Jared asked.
Samantha nodded.
He led the way back to the front door.

27

BENJ AND Mohammed Najjar waited behind Rachael Duck's townhouse.

He heard the front door open, and listened as Samantha noisily walked back to her rental truck. She made a point of driving east on Button Street, so Benj could be sure that she'd taken Jared Koskela with her.

"It's time," Najjar said.

Benj nodded.

Benj went first, partly because Najjar seemed a little too unstable for comfort.

He tried the back door. It was locked.

"We go around front?" Najjar asked, whispering.

"Yeah."

Benj and Najjar followed along the row of townhouses, then made their way to the front street. They walked up to the door to Rachael's apartment.

Samantha had made sure it hadn't closed all the way.

They walked in.

The townhouse felt cramped, like you'd expect in a place where construction wasn't cheap and the winters were cold. They passed a kitchen and dining room combo before reaching a dark hallway.

Benj could see Rachael through her bedroom door, sitting down at her desk.

He walked as quietly as he could, coming up behind her chair.

He clamped his hands around her arms, just above the elbow.

"What the fuck?" she yelled.

He shushed her.

He worked to force her wrists behind the chair.

She fought back, but she couldn't break his grip.

"This is bullshit," she said. "Sam put you up to this."

"Najjar," Benj said, "find something for her hands."

He looked back at Najjar, who wasn't doing much of anything.

"A belt, pantyhose," Benj said. *"Something."*

After not too long Najjar, handed him a pair of black pants.

Benj did his best to bind Rachael's wrists behind the chair.

Najjar brought over a couple of belts.

"Tie her ankles," Benj told him. "I'll keep holding her."

"She's lying to you," Rachael said. "I haven't done anything wrong."

Najjar bound her ankles under the chair, looping the belt under the wheels. So only securing her feet to the chair if she couldn't manage a way to lift it off the carpet.

Najjar wrapped the other belt around Rachael's neck, looping and buckling it. He pulled on the end, whipping her head against the back of the chair.

"Easy," Benj said. "Don't hurt her."

"Fuck you," Rachael said.

"Hold this belt," Najjar said. "I will find something to tie it back, attach it to her wrists and ankles. To keep her in the chair."

Benj took the belt.

Najjar chose the cord on the window blinds, cutting a length with a knife Benj hadn't realized he had.

Najjar tied Rachael with the cord, just as he'd described.

She gasped a little from the belt wound tightly around her neck, but didn't try to say anything.

Najjar got to work searching her bedroom.

"We need you to give us your login info," Benj said. "Your passwords, all three levels. The workaround for the time bomb."

She didn't answer.

"I know these systems," Benj said. "I work on these systems. I know you'll give me some BS about not planting any bombs, not having a workaround password... but like I said, it's BS."

"I'm not telling you shit," she said.

"You're going to need to."

"Or what? Are you planning on torturing me, Mr. McPherson?"

"You're working with the Chinese government. I'm just here to prove it."

"There's nothing to prove," she said. "Samantha's wrong about me."

"I don't believe you, Rachael."

"I don't care what you think."

"You should care. I don't want to hurt you."

"You think your father would be proud of you? Tying me up and threatening me? Just because some psycho told you to?"

"You tried to kill two people," Benj said. "To murder them. You went out, and your brother and that conservation officer, and you tried to get both Jared Koskela and Chloe Nielsen-Brown killed. And you weren't as careful as you think you were."

"That was Carter Elgin. Not me."

"Oh, so Carter Elgin flew up here and captured a polar bear?" Najjar asked.

"So proximity is all the evidence you need, apparently," Rachael said. "Call the RCMP and have me arrested."

"You know they'll scrub that data," Benj said. "None of this will ever make the public record."

She tried to hide her fear, but she let out a small gasp. "None of this matters... you're going to kill me no matter what I say."

"No one is going to kill you," Najjar said.

"I'll handle this," Benj said.

"I'm still not going to give you my credentials," Rachael said.

Benj sighed. "Then talk to me, Rachael. Tell me why I should believe you over Samantha Yoon. When she has a pretty strong argument."

"I think you and Sam are here to kill me."

"I'm not here to kill anyone."

"She is."

"I don't believe that, Rachael."

"It doesn't matter what you believe. Carter Elgin told me to kill the project. I couldn't convince Jared to quit, so Carter asked me to find another way. And I knew they wouldn't die."

"You couldn't have known that."

"Two healthy people versus one weak and half-starved polar bear? No. I knew. The bear would attack, Jared and Chloe would fight if off, and then they'd be airlifted out for treatment. The project would be delayed, if not cancelled, with no one bothering to look for something more."

"And why did you take Chloe then?"

"It was Cannae Friesen, the conservation officer. The first time he messed up was by releasing the bear too late and getting seen. Then he went out to get the stupid bear after not waiting anywhere near long enough. Found Chloe on one of the trails. She figured out pretty quick that he was the bad guy."

"So he took her?"

"Locked her in the bear trap," Rachael said. "Then called my brother in the open and told him. My brother then messaged me the right way, but I guess that one open call was enough."

"It's so convoluted," Mohammed said. "You should have just drowned them in the Bay."

"That's what they did in French Guiana," Benj said.

"I didn't want to kill anyone," Rachael said.

Benj shook his head. "But once you had Chloe, you knew you'd have to kill her."

"No..."

"Come on, Rachael. She'd made you. There was no way she wasn't going to tell Jared Koskela and anyone else who'd listen about you and your pet polar bear."

"We were hoping she'd come around, that we'd convince her."

"What happened to Chloe?"

"I don't know."

Benj pulled back on the belt. Not enough to hurt her...

"Someone took her," Rachael said. "And the bear trap."

"So you guys left her in the trap?"

"We didn't know what else to do."

"She's lying," Najjar said. "She killed her but she won't admit it."

"Is that true?" Benj asked her.

"I didn't kill her," she said. She was crying.

Benj believed her. Or thought he did.

He wasn't sure. But he wanted to believe her.

"There's nothing in this room," Najjar said. "Nothing that proves any information exchange, or a payoff."

"I didn't think there would be," Benj said.

"No... that's why you need to get onto her system. I would have expected more progress from you on that front."

"I'm working on it."

"Circumvent the security," Najjar said. "You're a computer hacker, aren't you?"

"You can't beat this level of protection. Not without a supercomputer and a thousand years of waiting."

"That was the intent," Rachael said.

"Social engineering is the way to go," Najjar said.

"I don't think I can trick her into believing I'm with the gas company," Benj said.

"We get her to talk."

"I'm working on it."

"He wants you to beat it out of me," Rachael said. "Think you can do that?"

"We can do whatever needs to be done," Najjar said. He walked up to her chair.

"I'm handling this," Benj said.

"Not really."

"She'll tell us."

"We need to hurry this up."

"We need to stay calm, Najjar."

"I'm calm."

"Are you sure?"

Najjar rolled his eyes. "I'll keep looking," he said. "Search the other rooms. Check the vents..."

Benj knew it was a waste of time. But busywork was a perfect match for Mohammed Najjar. He was too intense. In all the wrong ways.

There was still no proof that Rachael was working with the Chinese. Only proof that she'd made a really bad call, allegedly at the insistence of master manipulator Carter Elgin.

Benj knew enough about Carter and SolRescue to know that Rachael wasn't the first person Carter had pushed, the first person who ended up going far beyond what they ever thought they'd do.

His father had told him once, something he'd never forgotten. That pushing people's boundaries was Carter Elgin's favorite way to pass the time.

28

SAMANTHA DROVE past the bed and breakfast. She headed to the main road and started heading out of town.

Jared wasn't sure how to bring up his abduction in progress.

"Obviously I wasn't telling the truth," Samantha said. She sounded almost playful. "I couldn't have Rachael know what we're up to."

"What are you up to?"

She smiled. "Mohammed Najjar thinks he's found Chloe."

"What? Where?" And he asked the real question. "Is she okay?"

"We think she's okay," Samantha said. "But there is a bad side to this."

"What?"

"We think Rachael was involved in the bear attack. And in Rachael's disappearance."

"Part of your conspiracy theory," he said.

"Okay… it's more than what we think. I have the proof. You know I've got people in the NSA. We've got the messages."

"We're going to Chloe now, right?"

"Yeah. Mohammed's already on his way there."

She drove them past the airport and toward the tundra trails. She passed the turn off to the Chinese research hab. Where Jared had found the bear trap. And Chloe's celtic cross.

Jared didn't say anything about it.

She seemed to know where she was going.

Headed toward the launch site.

"Mohammed will ping you, right?" he asked. "When he reaches her?"

"Don't worry, Jared. I've seen this before. I really think Chloe's okay."

He tried not to let it all overwhelm him. The fear, the hope, the uncontrollable desire to just see her again.

He needed to see her.

She turned left onto an unmarked road, heading toward Bird Cove. He could see the bulky metal wreckage of the freighter *Ithaka* sitting on its rocky bed, the water having lowered with the tide.

"There's nothing up here," he said.

"There is."

She stopped the truck at a bank of brittle trees. She climbed out of the truck and started walking.

He followed, and saw the cylinder bear trap.

"This isn't the same trap," he said. "I found it at that Chinese research hab."

"It's the same trap."

As they neared, Jared saw that the trap wasn't empty.

And not a bear.

"Oh my god," Jared said. "She's in there."

He ran up to the trap.

Chloe was on one end, near the trailer hitch, the far side from the trapdoor. She was crumpled against the grate at the end of the cylinder. Jared could see something tied over her mouth.

"I don't see Mohammed," Samantha said. "I'm worried."

Jared ran to the crank on the side of the cylinder. He started turning it, lifting the trapdoor.

"Be careful," Samantha said.

He kept turning.

"Jared," Samantha said. "Are you listening? Be careful, okay? Something's not right here."

He lifted the door. He climbed in.

Chloe's eyes were closed.

He put his hand on her forehead.

She was warm. He could hear her breathing.

Thank god.

He wrapped his arms around her.

He started pulling her backward.

He heard the slam of the trapdoor.

"Shit," he said. "Samantha... grab the crank."

"Yeah, okay," she said.

But she was already walking back to her truck.

Jared pulled out his tablet.

No network.

Not weak network. Nothing.

He knew that wasn't right. Something was blocking the signal.

"Samantha," he shouted. "Get back here!"

She didn't answer.

She got into the truck and drove away.

Jared went back to Chloe. He pulled the strip of dirty cloth out of her mouth, taking another strip of wadding out with it.

"Chloe," he said. "Please."

She didn't respond.

He felt for her pulse. It felt... normal?

He checked his own. His was definitely faster.

He took a look around the trap.

The grate was too heavy, too strong. No way he'd get an arm through the gaps.

There was no safety release, no emergency handle. The only way out was with the crank on the side, which he couldn't reach. His belt… he took it off and fed it through the reinforced bars.

There was no way he could throw it around the crank, no chance of using it to open the trapdoor.

They were stuck until someone came to let them out.

So he went back to Chloe, wrapping his arms around her, holding her close for warmth.

Hoping she'd wake up soon, even if he had nothing good to tell her.

29

SAMANTHA ARRIVED at Rachael's townhouse after just over an hour away. She walked directly into the bedroom and up to the chair where Benj and Najjar had tied her.

Benj knew she thought very little of his interrogation technique.

"Still nothing," Samantha said.

"Won't give me access," Benj said.

"You aren't very persuasive, I'll give you that."

"What did you expect us to do? Torture her?"

"Don't worry, Benj," she said. "I'll take it from here."

She pulled out a knife and cut the cord that bound Rachael's wrists and ankles. She buckled the belt around Rachael's neck. "We need to take her out of here," she said. "I have a place that would work."

"She hasn't tried to escape," Benj said. "Hasn't screamed for help."

"She knows she's fucked. But still… this might get a little too loud."

"I'm not going to help you frame me," Rachael said.

"We'll find the evidence," Samantha said. "I know you're a traitor, Rachael." She turned to Benj. "I need you to find something to put her in."

"Put her in?" Benj said.

"Like a bag or a box. We bundle her up and stuff her inside."

"That sounds like a terrible idea."

Samantha glared at him.

"So where's Koskela?" Benj asked.

"Gave him a false tip about Chloe," Samantha said. "Needed some space, you know?"

Najjar came over with a large rolling suitcase. "This can work."

"Now that's initiative," Samantha said. "Thanks, Mohammed."

Najjar knelt down and undid the belt around Rachael's ankles. He then wrapped his arms around her in a bear hug and pulled her up and off the chair, tipping it over as he lifted her body.

Rachael groaned as he dragged her over to the suitcase.

"There's duct tape in the kitchen," Najjar said.

"There's duct tape and you tied her up with belts?" Samantha asked.

"I didn't know about the tape when we did that."

Samantha looked over to Benj. "Get the tape, would you?"

Benj walked over to the kitchen. He checked the drawers and found the half-empty roll of silver duct tape.

He brought it back to Rachael's bedroom.

"Put the wrists and ankles together, like before," Najjar said. "But tighter. I hold, you tape."

"She's not fighting you," Samantha said. "She knows there's no point."

"I know you plan on killing me," Rachael said. "And since Carter himself was the one who asked me to do this, to run Jared off, it's pretty obvious that you're the one who's working for someone else." She looked over at Benj. "You understand that, don't you? She's been lying to you the whole time."

"She lies to everyone she talks to," Benj said. "So give me your passwords and show me you've got nothing to hide."

Rachael shook her head as Najjar kept pinned to the floor. "Innocent until proven guilty."

Benj wrapped the tape around her ankles.

"You know she's hiding something," Samantha said, handing him her knife to cut the duct tape.

Once he'd finished Rachael's ankles, Benj pulled them up, bending her legs at the knees. He wrapped the tape around her wrists, pulling off the shoddily-tied black pants. He then brought the length of tape from her wrists to her ankles, wrapping her feet together a few more times before cutting the tape off the roll.

"Now her mouth," Samantha said.

"That hasn't been an issue," Benj said.

"Doesn't matter."

Benj put the tape down on the floor and stood up.

"Fine," Samantha said, in a huff.

She bent down and pulled one of Rachael's socks off its foot. She stuffed it in Rachael's mouth.

Najjar was right behind her, wrapping the duct tape all the way around Rachael's head. Three layers.

"I hope she can breathe," Benj said.

Rachael tried to say something.

He couldn't understand it.

Samantha grabbed the suitcase and unzipped it. She laid it down, holding the flap up.

Najjar grabbed Rachael and tried to shove her in the suitcase.

It wasn't easy.

Samantha leaned in to help, her and Najjar trying their best to squish a grown woman inside a too-small container.

"It won't work," Samantha said. "We need to fold her up like she's in an egg, head down, hands in front, knees up."

"Her hands need to be tied around her back," Najjar said. "Or she'll free herself."

"We can tape her arms and knees together. Wrap her hands up completely."

"That could work."

Rachael muttered something through the sock shoved in her mouth.

Najjar pulled her out of the suitcase and cut the lengths of tape between Rachael's ankles and wrists. He then slowly pulled her arms down and around her feet, bringing them up to her front.

He wrapped several layers of tape around her legs and arms, forcing her knees to a sharp point. He then mummified Rachael's hands completely, from just below her elbows to her fingertips.

Then he shoved her back in the suitcase.

On the second attempt she fit, her head bent down almost to her bound hands and knees.

Samantha closed the zipper.

"Okay, Benj," she said. "You take her out and get her in the truck. I doubt she's more than a hundred and twenty pounds."

"I can do it," Najjar said.

Samantha shook her head. "I wanted to talk to you, actually. So if Benj would give us five minutes. A full five…"

Benj carefully lifted the suitcase onto its side. He grabbed the handle at the top of the case and extended it upward.

He started pulling the case down the hall toward the front door.

He needed a chance to talk to Rachael, away from the others.

He pulled the case out and across the street, to where Samantha had parked it, in front of another house. To make it seem like no one was over at Rachael's, probably.

It didn't seem like a terribly essential bit of duplicity.

He brought the case up to the back of the truck. He unzipped it, just a little at the top and down the one side, to uncover her head.

Rachael tried to speak.

He knew he couldn't take the tape off; three layers was too much to try and unwrap.

"I need to ask you some important questions," he said. "If you want me to help you, you need to tell me the truth. Yes or no questions, okay?"

She nodded, as much as she could in the confined space.

"Are you working with anyone else?"

She didn't give any kind of response.

"You need to help me," he said. "Who are you working for?"

She mumbled something through the sock and saliva and silver tape.

He realized he hadn't asked the right kind of question.

"Are you working with the Chinese government?"

She shook her head. No.

"Are you working with the US government?"

No.

"Have you betrayed SolRescue?"

No.

He thought about that last question.

He had one more.

"Have you betrayed Carter Elgin?"

She didn't answer.

"Rachael?"

She nodded.

Yes.

"So whatever you've done, you believe in it."

Yes.

"Shit, Rachael. Samantha will find out what you've done."

She gave another nod.

"What am I supposed to do?" he asked her.

Another muffled reply.

"I can't let you go. Not if you're guilty."

She shook her head.

That she didn't believe she was guilty.

He zipped up the case.

And carefully lifted it up to the box, trying not to strain his back.

Once they'd taken her away from there, to whatever place Samantha had chosen… he could talk to Rachael, and to Samantha. He could find a way to defuse the situation.

He *knew* Rachael wasn't lying to him. That she believed in what she was doing.

That she hadn't sold away her values.

Which was more than Benj could say about himself most of the time.

He walked back to the house after the requisite five minutes.

Rachael's bedroom was empty.

He saw that the bathroom door was shut.

"Are we going?" he asked.

No one answered.

He walked back toward the front door.

Samantha came out from the side of the townhouses.

She was running toward the truck.

Shit.

Benj threw open the front door. He ran toward the street.

Samantha started driving before he could get to her, the suitcase falling hard on its side as she pulled out of the opposite driveway and drove toward the main street.

He ran back into the house.

He opened the bathroom door.

Najjar was in the tub, a small cut on his forehead.

He was unconscious. But Benj didn't think that cut wouldn't have been near enough for that.

At least Najjar was breathing. Samantha could have done worst to him.

That was the moment that Benj realized it. How dangerous Samantha Yoon could be.

30

CHLOE HAD woken up in Jared's arms, having opened her eyes only a little.

Jared had been unable to reach her wrists, ziptied behind her, and attached to what he'd realized too late was the tripline for the heavy metal door that had trapped him inside with her.

"Are you okay?" he asked her.

"I'm sore," she said. "My hands."

"See if you can turn around a little. I can probably break that tie."

She slowly twisted her body.

He took his belt buckle and jabbed the metal prong into the ratchet of the ziptie. It broke open, releasing her wrists.

She brought her hands around and started rubbing the red marks.

"Thank you, Jared," she said.

"We're still stuck in here."

"I know."

He brushed a tuft of hair off her forehead. "How long have you been in here?"

"I was in some machinery shed for a while," she said. "That's where Rachael had them bring me."

"Rachael... not Samantha?"

"It was Rachael first... then Samantha. They're both in on it. Working together."

"I don't know about that," he said.

"Rachael's brother took me out of the shed and shoved me back in the trap. Then he pulled it out here. No food or water. Nothing since they took me."

"That explains why there's no pee corner."

She laughed. "I don't know why I'm laughing," she said.

"We'll be okay, Chloe."

"I know. Now that you're here."

"Now that you're not alone," he said.

"No. Now that you're here, Jared."

He heard a truck. He couldn't see it from the angle of the trap.

But it sounded like the one that had driven him there.

The truck pulled off the road, heading toward them, closer than Samantha had brought it before.

He saw it.

Backing up.

He saw Samantha in the cab.

No one else. No Benj McPherson.

She stopped the truck around half a foot in front of the cylinder trap.

Jared realized that there was no trailer hitch.

She got out of the truck.

He saw a tow rope dragging behind her.

"What the hell are you doing?" he asked her.

"Moonlighting," she said. "You can make like two hundred bucks a tow out here."

"Let us out of here!" Chloe screamed.

Samantha didn't answer.

She hooked one end of the cable to the rear of the truck, then the other to the bar of the trailer, just behind the ball.

It wouldn't be the safest towing job.

But Samantha obviously didn't give a shit about her cargo.

She got back in the truck.

And started towing them, back to the road.

"Where is she taking us?" Chloe asked.

"I don't know."

Samantha turned left at the road. Heading north to Hudson Bay, toward Bird Cove, and the gravel bank with the shipwrecked freighter.

Rachael had tried to kill them. If they were working together…

"She's taking us to the Bay," Jared said.

"Why?"

He didn't want to tell Chloe what he was thinking.

Dump the trailer into the frigid water. Wait for the people trapped inside to freeze or drown. Then open the trap and let them float away.

No fuss, no muss.

Maybe the red marks on Chloe's wrists might tell a story. When they find her body.

Or maybe they'd just be two poor idiots who'd managed to end up in Hudson Bay. Maybe they'd fallen off the dock at the port, or maybe it had happened right near there, two amateur explorers messing around the wreck of the *Ithaka*, not giving any thought to what would happen once the tide came rolling back in.

But he could see that Chloe had thought of it, too.

"We won't be able to get out of here," she said.

"We can yell for help," Jared said. "Someone might hear us."

So he did, screaming as loudly as he could. For anyone.

She drove them to the end of the road and onward, onto the dirt and rock and gravel of the Flats. The tide was still low; he could see how shallow it was, all the way out to the freighter, at least a quarter of a mile out from the shore.

She drove out onto the shallow edge of Hudson Bay. Toward the *Ithaka*. Driving them out to sea.

If she dumped them out there, out by the freighter... maybe she was going to dump them in the freighter, hoping to find some way to pin them inside. It wouldn't be that hard to do with a couple of waterlogged bodies, right?

He had to think of some way out.

Was there something he could offer her, some appeal to her vanity, some classified information, maybe... anything to save them... to save Chloe, in particular. He couldn't let this happen to her.

There had to be a way to convince Samantha not to kill them.

A way of proving that they were worth more to her alive.

She drove the truck all the way out to the shipwreck, bumping and splashing along the uneven bank of gravel and sand. She drove around the wreck, putting the bulk of the ship between them and the land. No one would know they were there. Not by sight, at least.

She turned the truck around at the tip of the spit, bringing the back bumper against the front of the trailer.

She pushed the trailer and trap into the deeper water.

"Oh, god," Chloe said.

Jared knew he was on the edge of crying.

The trailer rolled in as it bounced, down onto a deeper bed of gravel, tilting almost thirty degrees, with the trap door at the lower end.

The water swept in, several inches deep by the door.

Jared and Chloe crawled to the higher end.

Samantha climbed out of the truck.

She walked over to the edge of the bank.

She gave them a wave.

"Don't worry," she said. "The tide won't come in for hours."

"You're going to leave us in here," Jared said. "And we'll drown."

"Or freeze to death. Which is more likely, considering that there's still a shitload of ice out here."

"You're not a murderer," Chloe said. "You can't do this."

"I'm sorry," Samantha said. "But this isn't going to end well for you, Chloe. And it's not your fault. Not entirely." She went back to the truck, opening the passenger side door. She pulled out what looked like an automatic rifle. "No more screaming, guys. Or I'll just shoot you, mkay?"

"We're worth something," Jared said. "Both of us."

Samantha shook her head. "You're worth something, maybe. But Chloe is just another pencil pusher."

"Let her go and I'll do whatever you want."

"Says the guy with no options."

"Please."

"Just hold on, okay?"

She reached over the side of the pickup box, placing the rifle down inside. She then walked over and pulled down the tailgate.

She hopped up into the pickup box. There was a suitcase there.

She pulled the zipper open a little, then pushed the suitcase off the back of the truck.

Jared watched as a woman rolled out of the suitcase and crashed into the gravel bank.

Rachael.

Wrapped in duct tape. Her arms and knees bound together, her hands completely covered in silver tape.

With even more tape wrapped around her head, over her mouth.

"What the hell is wrong with you?" he yelled at Samantha. "You're a goddamn psychopath."

"We're getting some answers," Samantha said. "I'm sure we'd all like a few."

Jared turned to look at Chloe.

Her mouth was wide open.

Samantha hopped down from the truck.

She grabbed Rachael by the ankles and started dragging her along the rocks, scraping her clothes and bent body against the rough ground.

Rachael was screaming in pain, the noise stifled only a little by the gag over her mouth.

Jared could feel his stomach heaving.

Like he was going to throw up. Or hyperventilate… he wasn't sure.

He didn't know what to do.

Samantha brought Rachael to the edge of the iron hull of the *Ithaka*, then dropped her. The ship towered over Rachael's bound body, almost twenty feet from the gravel to the deck.

She walked back to the truck and pulled the tow cable off of the ground. She brought it back to where she'd left Rachael.

She pulled something out of her jacket pocket.

A knife.

She sliced along Rachael's thighs, cutting the lengths of tape between her legs and arms. Rachael's hands were still bound together despite the gaps closer to her elbow. Samantha then yanked on Rachael's wrists, forcing them down and under her knees and ankles, setting them behind Rachael's back.

She clamped one end of the cable to Rachael's taped wrists. She pulled something else out of her jacket pocket, putting together some kind of mechanism to attach the cable to the layers of tape. Probably one or more zipties, the same kind she'd used on Chloe.

Samantha threw the other end of the tow cable upward, over the top of the hull of the *Ithaka*. She then walked into the giant gap at the base of the freighter, disappearing underneath.

Rachael slowly started to struggle, trying to pull her ankles and wrists apart, writhing against the rough gravel.

She wasn't getting far.

Jared saw Samantha peek up on the deck of the *Ithaka*, carefully ambling over to where she'd thrown the tow cable.

"This ship is corroded half away," she called out. "I wonder how many years she has left."

"Make sure you don't fall and crack your skull open," Jared said. "Or do."

She reached the tow cable and looped it around some of the *Ithaka*'s metal rigging. She started pulling, straining against the weight on the end.

She was trying to lift Rachael up off the gravel, by her wrists, bound behind her back.

Samantha groaned and heaved and kept pulling, and Jared watched as Rachael's arms rose slowly into the air. Her body started twisting as it lifted, pivoting on her ripped and bloodied knees. Her head bobbed as her wrists went higher.

Rachael had started to scream again. Still muffled. Still sickening.

Jared couldn't do anything for her.

Samantha tied the cable into place, holding Rachael up on her knees, her arms pinned hard behind her and lifted into the air.

After a minute or so Samantha had climbed back down.

She walked over to Rachael and started pulling the tape off from around her head.

And pulled a wet sock from Rachael's bleeding mouth.

"It's time to tell me your passwords," Samantha said. "Including that time bomb or whatever."

Rachael didn't reply.

Samantha shoved her hand up against the base of Rachael's, slamming her victim's head back.

"Tell me, Rachael. Make this stop."

"I've got nothing now," Rachael said. "I don't care what you do."

"Aren't you a tough-as-nails bitch. No wonder Carter likes you."

"Go fuck yourself."

Samantha gave her a nod, then walked away, toward her truck.

She opened the front door.

She pulled something out, stuffing it in her jacket pocket.

Jared couldn't tell what it was.

"You tried to kill your boyfriend," Samantha said.

"I didn't try to kill anyone," Rachael said.

"I don't believe that."

"I don't care."

Samantha walked over to the bear trap.

She had the knife.

Jared and Chloe shuffled away from the grate.

"So you like Jared, do you?" Samantha asked.

"I don't care," Rachael said.

"I'll bet he's not your biggest fan right now, though. With that whole polar bear incident."

"Just forget it," Jared said. "It doesn't matter what she did. You can't undo what you're thinking of doing here."

"I'm going to take this knife," Samantha said, "and I'm going to jab it into Jared's skull. Right through his ear, like the world's sharpest Q-tip."

"I don't care," Rachael said again.

"She's going to kill us anyway," Jared said. "All of us."

"I won't kill Jared," Samantha said. "I'll let him live. I'll kill Chloe, because let's face it, who wouldn't?"

"You're a crazy bitch," Chloe said.

Samantha smiled. "And you're just another idiot."

"I'll tell you if you let them go," Rachael said.

"You'll tell me what?" Samantha asked.

"The passwords. Anything. It doesn't matter. Just let them out."

"I'll let Jared go. Once Benj finds the evidence we need."

"There isn't any evidence."

"Then there won't be a Jared, either." She dragged the knife against the grate.

"I want to see you open that trap," Rachael said. "So you can try and get in, and hollow out Jared's skull. See what happens when you open it."

"I've got the knife."

"And he's got a hundred pounds on you."

"And there's the little matter of that gun I took from your place, Rachael."

"I'm pretty sure you didn't find the magazine for that," Rachael said.

"I guess you'll have to make an assumption there."

"Cut Rachael free," Jared said. "Then put the knife down and she'll give you what you need. We can all walk away from this, can't we?"

"We won't tell anyone what happened her," Chloe said. "I just want to go home."

"I just want to plug the leaks," Samantha said. "No more information getting passed to Chinese operatives."

"You think I work with the Chinese government," Rachael said. "But it isn't me. I sent the message to save that station."

"But how did you know in the first place? About the attack. About how they were planning on doing it."

"I have a contact... from inside the Chinese government."

"And you feed him some secrets, and he'll return the favor."

"No, it's not like that at all," Rachael said.

"Then explain it to her," Jared said.

"I can't."

"Why not? You think it's better for me and Chloe to drown in Hudson Bay?"

"I just can't," she said. "I'm sorry, Jared."

"She's going to kill us," Chloe said. "All of us."

"That's an excellent point," Samantha said. "For an idiot."

"This is more important than any of us," Rachael said.

"So you sold out to the Chinese junta on principle?" Samantha asked. "Wow... that is messed up, Rachael. How backwards are your ideals if that makes sense to you?"

"I told you before," Chloe said. "But you wouldn't listen. Rachael is working against Carter Elgin. Like anyone with half a brain, she's realized that he's a danger to his own crowdOrg."

"But she follows his diktats," Jared said. "She sicked a goddamn polar bear on us because he wanted us out of the way."

"I know," Samantha said.

"She's right," Rachael said. "Chloe's right."

"What?"

Rachael sighed. "That's who I work for. A group within SolRescue that's working to remove Carter Elgin from the president's chair."

"That's hilarious," Samantha said. "You destroyed a multi-billion-dollar space station because of some insider bullshit?"

"We didn't attack the station. I told you that already. I tried to warn them. I messaged someone I thought I could trust."

"Alex Vives."

"Yeah."

"And then he just sat on the warning."

"Yeah."

"Because he's the turncoat," Chloe said. "You contacted the one person who wouldn't pass on the warning."

"Alex Vives is dead," Samantha said. "So we've lost all hope of staging an intervention."

"So you know it wasn't me," Rachael said.

"There's no evidence, Rachael. I need the evidence. And right now you're right here and you look guilty as shit."

"Give her the evidence," Chloe said.

"She'll still kill us," Rachael said.

"You don't know that," Samantha said. "If Rachael can prove it was Alex Vives and not her who was working with the Chinese, maybe I can let you guys go."

Rachael sighed. "I can't prove that. If I'd known Alex was a problem, I wouldn't have trusted him."

"So give her something, at least," Chloe said. "Give her a reason not to kill us."

"Tell me, Samantha," Jared said, "how will you explain this to Benj Mc-Pherson? And to his father? I honestly can't believe they'd be okay with what you're doing."

"No," Samantha said, "they're fine with it."

"That's why he isn't here. Because you told Benj that you were going to capture and interrogate us and he just said he'd catch up with you later?"

"Benj has other tasks."

"Bullshit. He doesn't know you've locked me up. He doesn't know you've been keeping Chloe for however long."

"He doesn't need to know."

"You'll have to kill him, too."

"What?"

"You think you know people," Jared said. "But you really don't."

"I know vastly-overconfident guys like you," she said. "Idiots like Chloe. Naive dumbfucks like Rachael Duck."

"And what kind of moron is Benj McPherson?"

She shook her head at him.

She walked back to where she'd suspended Rachael from the hull of the *Ithaka*.

"Give me the passwords," she said to Rachael. "Give me the passwords and I won't halal you right here."

"Halal me?"

"I'm going to bleed you out. Like a pig."

"Muslims don't eat pigs."

With her left hand, Samantha grabbed Rachael by the hair, lifting her head up. She brought the knife up to Rachael's throat.

"She's the only one who can give you those passwords," Jared said.

Samantha lightly moved the knife down Rachael's body, tracing an invisible line along her left side, all the way down to her stomach. "Just tell me, Rachael," she said. "Please."

"I can't."

"Please."

She didn't want to do it. Or she couldn't.

Jared couldn't tell which.

"What if we can find another way to prove it?" he asked her.

"What?"

"Obviously she won't compromise whatever operation she's involved in."

Samantha pulled the knife back, away of Rachael's stomach, but keeping it clutched in her right hand. "I need to know what she's involved in," she said. "That's the whole point of this."

"But if it's not the People's Convocation," Chloe said, "it doesn't matter."

"Oh, it matters."

"She'll pass it all on to Carter Elgin," Rachael said. "Everyone who's involved."

"And then what?" Chloe asked. "They get a firmly-worded letter? It's not like he's going to have them killed, right?"

"Depends on how many polar bears he's got," Jared said.

"Give me the passwords, Rachael," Samantha said.

"I can't trust you with that information," Rachael said. "I can't trust that it won't get into the wrong hands."

"The wrong hands? Like Carter?"

"Like the Chinese government."

"This is lunacy," Chloe said. "Sheer lunacy."

"What's your problem now?" Samantha asked her.

"You are both convinced the other is some big danger. Enough that you're probably going to kill Rachael before this is over. But you guys aren't the problem here. You never were."

"Derrick wouldn't have sent me up here if Rachael could be trusted," Samantha said. "If she really was just doing what Carter had told her."

"Maybe Derrick didn't know," Rachael said. "You ever think of that?"

"Of course he knows."

"How can you be so sure of that?" Jared asked. "Maybe Chloe's right. Maybe you guys are both just good little soldiers, and this is just fog of war type of stuff."

"Friendly fire," Chloe said.

"Then she'd tell me the passwords," Samantha said.

"I don't trust you," Rachael said. "For some strange reason."

"What about Benj McPherson?" Jared asked. "Can you trust him?"

Rachael sighed. "I don't even know him."

"But you know his father. Do you trust his father?"

She nodded. "I think so."

"Not enough to tell him what you're up to," Samantha said.

"Are you trying to kill this?" Jared asked her.

"I just want the passwords."

Jared ignored her and continued. "So Benj checks the data. Rachael gives him the passwords directly, and he doesn't share any of it with Samantha or anyone else. He finds out what he needs to know, that Rachael's clean… well, almost clean… and then he sees if there's anything there that can prove at minimum the Alex Vives received the message from Rachael. Benj takes what he finds to his father, and it goes on from there."

"And Benj just ignores everything else," Rachael said. "I don't see how he can."

"Or you give me the passwords. And Benj helps me in and I do most of the digging."

"How is that any better?"

"I can try and keep him from seeing stuff that isn't directly related. To protect you… and your people."

"Not good enough," Samantha said. "I don't want some whitewashed version of Rachael's lies. I want to be there when Benj examines it all. I need to see it for myself." She brought the knife back against Rachael's throat. "And I don't know how this could ever be considered a negotiation."

"Benj won't help you kill me and Chloe," Jared said. "I know that much. So I'd call this a stalemate."

"I will kill you, Jared. If she doesn't tell me what I need to know."

"Come on."

"I can reach you in there."

"No… not unless you climb in for a visit. And then you know it's not a sure thing. There's no one here to help you, Samantha. You're on your own."

"And my fancy new rifle?"

"With no bullets?" Rachael said. "You *are* on your own, Sam."

Samantha didn't answer right away. She looked over at Rachael, then back at the trap and to Jared. Then at the truck…

He was close to convinced that there were no bullets in that rifle lying in the back of the pickup.

"So I'm not completely on my own," Samantha said, after a while. "I have the tides."

"That could take a while," Jared said.

"You'll be dead sooner than you think. That water's cold enough to kill you, long before it reaches the top of that cylinder. I guess you could beat Chloe to death and just lie on top of her corpse. Could buy you an hour. Maybe some sightseers will come along to rescue you. Of course, I could just kill them."

"You're not a murderer," Jared said. "I know you aren't."

She shook her head. "You don't know me at all."

Chloe started shouting, calling for help. She'd apparently reached the same conclusion about the gun.

"Shut her up," Samantha said.

"She doesn't want to die here," Jared said. "I don't blame her."

"She can scream until she passes out, then. It's not like anyone's coming out to visit."

"People will come," Rachael said. "There's always someone wanting to see the sunset out this way."

Samantha smirked. "Not with the road closed off. Two pylons across the turnoff can do that, you know. So I guess they'll all just head someplace else, or take a few photos from the main road. Face it, guys. This is a pretty exclusive engagement."

Chloe gave another shout. She was starting to sob a little as she called.

"Tell Benj to come here," Rachael said. "I'll give him what he needs in person. I'll even go back with him to my place, to show him what he wants." She sighed. "I'll show you, too. Just let them go."

"I'll let them go," Samantha said. "Once we have what we need."

"I don't trust you. Not in the least."

"Then we don't have a deal, Rachael."

"Let Chloe go first," Jared said. "Hold onto me for now. Take me to Benj. Once you have what you want, he can let me go."

"And so Chloe will run to the cops."

"I can't," Chloe said. "I can't risk Jared's life."

"We make Benj the go-between," Jared said. "You give him the knife, you put him in control. We all get what we need. No one gets hurt."

"And no one else needs to know about this," Rachael said. "Any of it."

Samantha spent some more time looking things over, Rachael and her stress tie, Jared and the bear trap, the pickup truck with the empty rifle.

He knew she wanted it to work.

She just had to take the first step.

"Okay," she said. "We hand this over to Benj."

"We get him to come here," Rachael said.

Samantha nodded.

And Jared looked over to Chloe.

"I want to think this can work out," she whispered.

But he could tell she didn't believe it.

31

SAMANTHA HAD sounded upset when she'd given Benj the call. But she hadn't sounded apologetic.

Just upset.

She'd asked him to come out to a shipwreck east of town, past the airport. The *Ithaka*.

He'd never heard of it before.

Some freighter that had run aground, on a gravel bank not far from the shore of Hudson Bay.

A shipwreck. How dramatic. How grandiose.

Exactly what Samantha seemed to want in her life story.

She'd asked that Najjar stay back, but had also told Benj to unplug the small filebox plugged into Rachael's work dock. So it would have made just as much sense to bring Najjar along, assuming that Samantha felt they could trust the man.

Benj wasn't sure they could, so he didn't push for a travelling companion.

That and the fact that Najjar was still passed out from whatever she'd done to him.

Benj took the pickup parked outside Rachael's townhouse; he'd thought he'd heard it belonged to her brother, but it was still there with the keys hanging on a rack by the door.

He drove past the airport and out toward the coordinates she'd sent him, steering around two orange pylons that were stuck out in the middle of the turnoff.

He could see the *Ithaka*, out in the water.

He drove to the end of the road, near the edge of the bay.

She'd said he could drive all the way to the freighter. But it was out on the water.

He parked the truck.

He tried calling Samantha.

It didn't go through. But she'd just called him, apparently from out by the *Ithaka*.

But he couldn't see any sign of life out by the shipwrecked boat, even zooming in as much as he could with his glasses.

He started to wonder if it was another ruse, if she'd brought him out there so she could sneak back into Rachael's house.

But she'd told him to bring the filebox. Which in all likelihood was where Rachael kept her data.

If she'd wanted to circle around him to get that data, she wouldn't have had him bring it to the middle of nowhere.

Unless she was framing him; if she'd reported him to someone, the Royal Canadian Mounted Police, the US Air Force... would a string of black SUVs show up to whisk him off to some black site?

Or to Highland County, Virginia?

But what had happened to Jared Koskela? To Rachael Duck?

What had she done with them?

He got out of the truck and started walking toward the beach.

The water looked shallow enough, all the way out to the wreck. He'd get wet, and he'd freeze a few toes halfway off, but he could make it out there in one piece.

His eyepiece brought up a message from Samantha.

Sorry. Had a signal jammer on. Bring the truck out to the boat.

He replied by voice, telling her he was worried it would get stuck.

It won't get stuck, she replied. *I've already driven one truck out and there wasn't anything close to a problem.*

So he climbed back in the truck and headed toward the *Ithaka*.

He stopped the truck the moment he saw what Samantha had done.

He climbed out and ran over to Rachael.

Samantha had suspended her from a motherfucking tow cable, wrists raised up behind her back, likely yanking her arms halfway out of their sockets. She'd roughed her up to, Rachael's body covered in cuts and bruises, her knees sliced up like goddamn pulled pork.

"What the fuck is wrong with you?" he asked. "You would do this to someone? I can't fucking believe this."

The wrists were taped up and ziptied; he didn't have anything to break the ties, one around her hands and one wrapped like a chain between that tie and the tow cable, too tightly to pull off the metal clamp.

"Help me cut her down," he said.

Samantha slowly walked over.

Taking her time.

She handed him a knife, blade forward.

Like she'd wanted him to slice open his palm.

He took the knife and cut the one tie from the tow cable.

Rachael fell against him.

He wrapped his arms around her for a moment. To help steady her.

He cut the tape from her wrists, then her ankles.

"I'm sorry," he said. "I didn't know she would do this."

"Don't apologize to her," Samantha said.

Benj knew he would have hit her if he hadn't had Rachael leaning against him.

He wanted to kill Samantha. He did.

"I ought to tie you up like that," he told her. "See how you like it. Or should we stuff you in that suitcase first?"

"It's a legitimate technique," she said. "Nothing your father wouldn't have done if he'd felt it was necessary."

"I'd kill my father if I found out he was doing this to people."

"Bad news, then."

"You're supposed to let Chloe out now," someone said. A man.

He turned to look.

And saw Jared Koskela staring back at them through the grate in a half-sunken polar bear trap.

Benj saw another person behind Jared.

Chloe Nielson-Brown, he presumed.

Samantha had taken her.

Rachael's brother and the conservation officer had taken her first, but Samantha had swooped in behind.

And abducted an abductee.

It was so messed up. All of it.

"We let them both out," Benj said to Samantha. "No more captives."

"That's not the deal," she said. "Chloe gets to leave, and Jared has to wait."

"No... that's not how this works. I've let this go on for too long already. Come on, Samantha, look at what you've done. You've lost your goddamn mind."

"We should stick with the deal," Rachael said. She pulled away from Benj and sat down on a rock poking above the waterline.

"You don't need to stick with the deal," he told her. "The deal is shit."

She shook her head. "I just want this to be over. Take Jared and me back to my place. Let Chloe go."

Benj nodded. He didn't feel like arguing with a woman who'd just been through eight layers of hell and duct tape.

Samantha pulled a length of plastic from her jacket pocket. Another zip tie. Apparently she'd planned for multiple uses.

She brought it over to the cylinder. She stuck it through the grate.

"Chloe," she said. "Tie Jared's hands behind his back. Don't fuck this up."

Chloe bound Koskela as Samantha had ordered.

"Now Rachael," Samantha said. "Come open the trap, would you?"

Rachael slowly got up and limped over to the trap.

She started turning the crank.

Benj jogged over. "I'll do it," he said.

Rachael nodded and stepped back, sticking a hand against the cylinder to steady herself.

Benj turned the crank all the way, lifting the trapdoor.

Chloe climbed out first, before helping Jared out with his tied hands.

Samantha opened the door to the crew cab.

Chloe helped Jared into the backseat. "I'm coming, too," she said.

"You're not wanted," Samantha said.

"I'm still coming."

"She's coming," Benj said.

Samantha seemed to let the matter drop.

Benj stuck a hand out for Rachael.

She took it.

He helped her over to her truck.

Samantha had already started heading back to the shore.

Benj drove the smaller white pickup behind her.

Mohammed Najjar was not at Rachael Duck's townhouse.

Benj tried calling Najjar with Jared's tablet, but there was no response. So he sent a quick message to get in touch.

Then he sat down at Rachael's dock, on a chair from her kitchen, having given her the more comfortable desk chair. Chloe Nielson-Brown and Jared Koskela were sitting on the floor, up against the wall, Koskela's wrists still tied behind his back.

Rachael logged in through both security levels, then opened the hidden app to disable the timebomb. Benj made it obvious that he wasn't watching her keystrokes; it was enough that she was letting him see the data.

Samantha Yoon was lying on Rachael's bed, kicking one foot every few seconds. It felt like she was doing her best to emphasize how at ease she was. That she didn't regret what she'd done to Rachael or anyone else, that she wasn't the least worried about any consequences from Benj or the world at large.

He'd run into true believers in the darkest of online forums, people who'd claimed that they'd do whatever it took to defend themselves and their points of view.

But Samantha was the first person who'd demonstrated it, the first person to gleefully destroy everything and anything she wanted, to reach what she'd set her mind to.

He hated her, more than anyone else.

More than he'd ever thought possible.

He'd learned that Samantha Yoon was dangerous, that she could kill if she'd felt the need. And he'd learned that there's a level of hate that he could feel that could lead him to the same place.

He didn't know how guilty Rachael was, beyond the attack on Jared and Chloe. But there was no forgiving what Samantha had done.

He had trouble focusing as he scanned the messages in Rachael's secure inbox. But then he saw what he was there to find.

"William Yeung Huan," he said. "Chinese national?"

Rachael nodded.

"A member of the People's Convocation," Samantha said.

"You know him?" Benj asked.

"I just know he is. I know what we'll find."

"He's not what you think he is," Rachael said.

"Oh, that's a relief. So he's totally not part of the Chinese junta. He just drives an ice cream truck around Beijing."

"He's from Hong Kong. And he's a member of the Convocation. Low-level. But that's not what we work together on."

"So this smoking gun isn't really smoking us out of the room?"

"Why are you tasked with locating Nicolas Clouatre and Mireia Lona?" Benj asked.

"I don't know," Rachael said.

"Bull-fucking-shit you goddamn ditchpig," Samantha said. She started chuckling.

"What the heck is wrong with you?" Chloe said.

Samantha sneered. "Shut up, stupid."

"What were you supposed to do if you found them?" Benj asked. "Nicolas and Mireia."

"Nothing," Rachael said. "Tell him where they are."

Benj looked over the other names in the message. Alex Vives, no surprise. The others were first names, and when he tapped for suggestions, found they were connected to coded recipient addresses and nothing more, alphanumeric strings with no real pattern. Some guy named Archie, a woman named Jia.

There were no other messages in the inbox. No saved folders. No trash bin for restores.

"There needs to be more," he told Rachael. "This is too vague, and it makes you look guilty."

291

"Looks don't matter," she said. "It proves nothing."

"This isn't innocent until proven guilty," Samantha said. "It's already confessed to one thing so almost definitely connected to the rest of it."

"Rachael's right," Benj said. "It proves nothing."

"So we pass the names up the chain. I'm sure Derrick McPherson will know who this Archie guy is, where he's from."

"He's in San Jose," Rachael said. "He does what I do. Tracks what Carter Elgin's up to and passes it along to Huen."

"And Jia?" Benj asked.

"I don't know her."

"So this is seriously just about keeping tabs on Carter?" Samantha asked. "That sounds like a lie to me."

Rachael groaned. "So the guy's Chinese and I'm obviously selling secrets? You only want the one answer, Sam."

"She's given you what you wanted," Jared said from his seat on the floor. "Full access."

"We're not done," Benj said. "There must be more… somewhere."

"I don't keep anything for long," Rachael said.

"So this Huen guy asks you to find someone, and you do, and then what?"

"I've told you what I know."

"So when Mr. Clouatre ends up dead in a ditch somewhere, you won't care?" Samantha said. "That's cold, Rachael. Even for you. Do you feel bad about those two guys your friends killed in South America?"

"That wasn't us," Rachael said.

"Oh, so that was the other bunch of Chinese junta members. Some other gang of clandestine operatives who also happen to be looking for Nicolas Clouatre and the wife of Alex Vives."

"Is my father involved?" Benj asked. "Does he know what you're doing, Rachael?"

She shook her head. "He's too close to Carter." She nodded to Samantha. "Like she is."

"You were close enough to Carter to try and kill us," Chloe said. "Or have you forgotten that already?"

"So you keep tabs on my father?" Benj asked. "You report in whenever he's up to something?"

"Your father's not the problem," Rachael said. "But that doesn't mean he'd be willing to listen to any of this."

"Not that you talked to him. You guys just went behind his back."

"Because Huen is junta," Samantha said. "And that Jia person probably is, too. And Rachael sends them information and does little favors for them. Do I have to spell this out for you, Benj? The girl is a traitor."

"I'm done with this," Koskela said.

He stood up.

Benj noticed that his hands weren't bound.

"Rachael isn't working for the Chinese," Koskela said. "And neither is Samantha. Chloe's right. The Chinese agent died in the rainforest. Alex Vives. He killed those men in French Guiana. He provided the access to the Chinese cyberattackers, assuming he didn't program the overload on his own."

"And we're running around in circles," Chloe said, standing up beside Koskela. "Carter Elgin asked Rachael to sabotage our project. But I'm thinking he didn't let Derrick McPherson in on the plan."

"And Rachael's chatter from Churchill looked pretty suspicious to him," Benj said.

Chloe smiled. "Exactly."

"Prove it," Samantha said.

"How can we prove a negative?" Jared asked. "Rachael didn't send information to the Chinese. She wasn't responsible for the attack on the ESA station."

"She just tried to get us mauled by a polar bear," Chloe said.

"I'm sorry," Rachael said. "I had to kill the project. And…"

"And what?" Benj asked.

"Carter told me I had to kill the project."

Benj shook his head. "No, Rachael. There's more to it. You need to tell us."

She gave out a long sigh. "Carter Elgin gave me two options. Either I got Jared off the project, or… or he'd have to find someone else to handle it."

"To handle it," Jared said. "What the hell does that mean?"

"I don't know," Rachael said. "Nothing good."

"You're trying to paint quite the picture here," Samantha said. "That Carter Elgin would gotten someone to kill Jared. That you saved his life by siccing a hungry bear on him."

"I can't say that for sure," Rachael said. "He didn't say it."

"But that's what you thought he meant," Benj said.

Rachael nodded.

"A little overdone, Rachael," Samantha said.

"I didn't explain it to Carter," Rachael said.

"What do you mean?" Benj asked.

"I've got the messages. To Carter. From Carter."

"Where?"

She tapped on the screen. A hidden folder. A prompt came up.

She typed in a password, too quickly for Benj to track it, had he tried.

Another inbox opened on the screen.

From Carter Elgin.

Dozens of messages, at least.

"This is the smoking gun," Rachael said. "He asked me if the polar bear would kill Jared. I told him it would. I said that I'd make sure it did."

"But you knew he'd find out," Benj said. "That Jared didn't die."

"That doesn't matter. The message is what matters. The evidence that Carter Elgin's crossed the line."

"Evidence that doesn't make you look particularly innocent," Jared said.

Rachael nodded. "That's why I haven't sent it to Huen. I know what it will mean for me."

"You shouldn't have kept this from me," Samantha said. "You god-damn idiot. God. What if I'd killed you?"

"You did enough," Benj said. "Unforgivable, actually."

"They both did," Chloe said. "They both deserve to rot in a dark cell somewhere."

"I did what I thought I needed to do," Samantha said. "To find the leak. And I'm still not convinced on this."

"No one gives a shit if you're convinced," Jared said. "No one. I'd say this room is about evenly split, between those of us who hate your guts and those of us who would actually like to drown you in Hudson Bay. And that's not a joke, Samantha."

"Plenty of people hate me," she said. "I'm used to it."

"Boo-fucking-hoo," Benj said.

"So what happens now?" Rachael asked.

"We find Mohammed," Jared said. "And he and Chloe and I get back to work. I honestly don't give a shit what happens to the rest of you."

"You're not concerned about the project?" Samantha asked. "About the real purpose? About taking control of something that should belong to all of us?"

"Shut up, Samantha," Benj said. "Just shut up."

She glared at him.

Then she climbed off the bed and walked down the hall, and out the front door.

"Looks like you may have just lost your ride," Jared said.

Benj nodded.

He turned to Rachael. "I'm really sorry," he said. "About all of this." He looked over to Jared. "We should take her to the hospital."

Jared shook his head. "You can take her wherever you want. I don't care. I'm done with her."

"I'm sorry," Rachael said.

"No one cares," Chloe said.

Jared reached out for Chloe's hand.

They walked out together.

Benj looked back at Rachael.

She was crying.

"I'll walk you to the hospital," he said.

"You don't need to."

"I know."

She nodded. "I can't come back from what I've done."

He didn't answer.

He wasn't going to lie.

Benji McPherson could have waited and had his first time at home, once his mother was out for an evening.

But there's a hundred-year-old tradition of car sex that he was willing to respect. And Valeri Timms had shown clear interest, and was at least a solid seven—with light blond hair and the slightest chin dimple—so Benji had taken her on a drive out to that spot at the end of Ridge Avenue, right after the "no trespassing" sign, and after waiting five minutes to make sure none of the local busybodies had called the cops, he started with some light petting around Valeri's thighs, and move under and up from there.

He managed to reach third base before first, and was proud of it.

There was a strong chance he would have never had a chance to see or touch anything close to Valeri Timms without that car and the ill-gotten money that had bought it; that didn't bother Benji as much as he would have expected, probably because he'd earned that money. Earned it the only way you could earn money most of the time, by being smarter and working harder than everyone else.

After Valeri he'd crassly upgraded to Monique, who was a strong eight and definitely the hottest black girl at Ritenour, which had never been a stronghold of hot black girls.

After Monique he was back to blondes with Jenna, and then he was on to Jenna's older sister, back when older universally meant better. From there he actually made out—not much past second, that time—with an incredibly hot Japanese-American girl from Wash. U.

That was the highlight of his high school years, at the grand old age of seventeen.

From there things went to shit.

The problem with Anthony Washington was mainly a lack of improveisation skills; when girls asked Benji or even Anthony's brother Ames where they got the money for the nice cars and new clothes, they came back with some confident bluster about knowing how to make a buck, without giving any detail or saying anything that would lead someone to question it further.

But Anthony told too many people about the scam, starting off with the poorly chosen phrase "so we've come up with this scam..."

And by the time Benji had gotten that hot Japanese girl out to the make-out spot, the FBI had already started looking into two suspicious UBI registrations, based on following the trail of an bank account in Oregon that was continually being withdrawn from a completely unaffiliated bank located in St. Ann, Missouri.

Benji found out on his tablet, after dropping the college girl off at residence. An alert that the Oregon account had been frozen. He'd known right away what that meant.

And he'd realized how careless he'd been. All three of them had gone to the ATM for the cash, connecting with the burner phone Benji had set up for the mysterious man from Oregon. That meant all three would have appeared in the surveillance feed.

In the end, it had all seemed ridiculous. Thinking that it would work, that there wouldn't be consequences.

But Benji didn't want to give up; he was smarter than the Washington boys. He was no longer the pudgy loser they'd put up with just to boost their numbers. He was an equal.

Or better.

Because he was smarter, and yes, because he worked harder than the two of them put together.

So Benji McPherson knew he had to come up with a plan.

Step One was to make a list of the laws he'd most likely broken, the various flavors of fraud he'd committed. Step Two was to determine which ones he could build an aura of deniability around.

If he tried to pin either of the Washington boys as a mastermind, the whole thing would fall apart. He had to find someone else to take the lead.

Someone who seemed smart enough to pull it off, but who was dumb enough to let Benji push them into it. And preferably, someone who'd get some sympathy from the justice system, which meant that their skin would need to be a lot lighter than his.

Benji chose Valeri Timms: white, blond hair, cute but not overtly sexy—hence that solid rating of seven—and not particularly well supported by friends and family. She was a foster child with a foster mother, living in apartments that should have been shut down years before. And a Basic, obviously, but a sympathetic one.

Benji had been moving money out of that Oregon account and putting it into hard currency, twenty and fifty dollar bills that he had split 50/50 with the Washingtons, which meant that each of the twins was getting a quarter of the goods.

After the cars and the clothes and the Grey Goose Vodka, Benji had been left with a surprisingly large portion of leftover cash. He packed that cash into a duffel bag and went to see the first girl he'd ever fondled.

The first thing he did was pass her the bag of money.

She'd opened it and then dropped it; no one takes that kind of thing well.

He then started on lying to Valeri, telling her that there were four sources for the UBI money, and that he was willing to give her all of the money they had left if she'd take the lead. He told her that she'd be protected by a loophole that had yet to be closed, and that the only law they'd broken was identity theft, which was a Class C felony in Missouri and punishable by probation.

None of it was true, since the amount made it Class B, since Class Bs rarely resulted in probation alone, and since there was quite a bit more at play than just the identity theft.

And while Valeri seemed to believe him, she'd made it clear that she wasn't the least bit interested in being involved.

And then the shit got shittier.

"I can't even believe you'd try this on me," she told him. "I mean, even telling me about it puts me in danger."

"In danger?" he said. "Come on, Valeri. Don't be stupid."

She shook her head. "I'm going to talk to my mother."

"You don't have a mother."

"Screw you, Benji."

"You're right, though," he said.

"What?"

"You're already involved."

"No, I'm not."

"You're the one with the bag of money. The one we're all going to tell the cops about. The brains of the operation. The clever white girl."

She started to cry.

Benj kept going, telling her that he'd already talked to all the other guys, that they'd all gotten their stories straight. That she'd brought them all on board with blowjobs and the other stuff, pushing Benji to help her work out the scripting, which he'd thought was just a harmless prank.

"This is the one thing black guys can get away with," he said. "Judge knows we's too stoopid to figure out a crime like dis."

"I'm not doing it, Benji."

"I'm all busted up on purple drank, bitch. I'm not even listening."

"This isn't funny."

"Just do this, Valeri, okay? You're only sixteen and you're white as a toilet. They'll send you for a few weekends out at Camp Fischer and that'll be it."

"And you guys will get off with a slap on the wrist, right?"

"Shit, Valeri. We'll be lucky if we can stay in the juvenile court."

"I had nothing to do with this," she said.

"I know. But we need your help. And it wouldn't be for free…"

"No way, Benji. I'm not comfortable with this at all."

She pulled out her tablet.

"What are you doing?" he asked.

"I'm asking my mom to come home. Or my foster mom, since that's an important distinction to you."

"You can't tell her."

"I'm gonna tell her, Benji. Because this is stupid."

And that was when Benji had decided to shift his approach.

He'd started with his right hand around her throat, pushing her down onto the couch in her living room. The other hand went over her mouth.

"I'm not playing, Valeri," he said. "This is important."

She started sobbing.

"You'll do this or I swear to Jesus I'll kill you. And your fucking foster mom won't waste her time looking for the body."

She tried to tell him to screw off again, through his clamped hand.

"We're in this together, Valeri. A few days of juvie rehab is better than the alternative. Do you understand what I'm saying here?"

He lifted his left hand from her mouth.

"Okay," she said.

"Are you lying to me?"

"No." She hadn't stopped sobbing.

"I'm sorry that we gotta do this," he told her. "But it's the best way out. And you still get the money."

"I don't want the money."

"The money stays with you, Valeri. End of story. Now I'm going to head out now, and you're going to take some of this money and buy something for yourself."

"I don't want the money," she said.

"I don't care. You do what I say. You go and you buy something nice for yourself. Do you understand."

She nodded.

And Benji left her there, on the living room couch.

Still sobbing. And terrified.

He got in his car and drove home, his hands shaking on the steering wheel.

He went to his room and crawled under the sheets and cried.

He'd known before he'd packed up that duffel bag what he'd have to do. And he'd done it.

And he'd never be able to undo it. He just had to find a way to live with it.

32

MOHAMMED HAD started cleaning Rachael Duck's bedroom, hoping that the work would help both to calm his nerves and to make him feel better about what they'd done to her.

He was no stranger to mistakes, to losing his temper and losing control. He'd punched his older sister in the back of the head once, when he was fourteen, and he'd regretted it so desperately that he'd seriously considered committing some form of ritual suicide as a way of making amends. He'd broken his wrist on a 2x6 stud in his bedroom, the day he'd found out that he was being audited by the IRS for a paltry income of well under a hundred thousand dollars. And he'd once been held for sixty hours in a Dearborn city jail for spitting at a parking control officer who didn't believe him about the specific timing of a broken meter.

But he'd never done anything like what they'd just done to Rachael Duck. And he knew that this time, it had nothing to do with his temper.

He'd fallen in line with an idea, that it was up to him and McPherson and Yoon to prove Rachael's crime. And he'd committed a healthy set of his own crimes in the process.

If the RCMP were to show up and arrest him right then and there, he'd know he deserved it. He'd confess to all of it.

He'd gotten caught up in the moment, something different than his usual anger but no less destructive. Self-righteousness. Exactly the one thing he said he'd never inherit from his father, the one character flaw that he would do everything in his power to keep out of his life.

He'd focused on that instead of his temper, and he'd lost on both counts.

But he could make it right.

He could bring what he had to SolRescue, to Derrick McPherson, maybe, anyone but Carter Elgin. He could show them the specs for the shield spiders.

Help them find a way to overcome them.

He felt weird folding Rachael's clothing, particularly her underwear, but it had been neatly stowed in her dresser, so he tried to approach it like a laboratory experiment, seeing it as a collection of varied fabrics, some of which was very lacey and had that perfume smell that he tried his best not to think about.

He heard the door open.

He hoped that Rachael had come back with them. God willing she'd come back with them.

Mohammed didn't recognize the two men who came walking down the hallway. One was black and the other appeared East Asian. He couldn't help but connect them to McPherson and his Korean counterpart.

But they were armed, each with a pistol. Pointed in his direction.

Mohammed put his hands in the air.

He assumed they were FBI or CIA. Or even USAF Security Forces. Probably not RCMP, based on their black tactical clothing.

The black man holstered his weapon, then pushed Mohammed down to his knees. He pulled Mohammed's hands behind his back, then bound Mohammed's wrists with a cable tie.

Together the two men lifted him up, each having grabbed an arm just below the shoulder. They carried him into the bathroom, and pushed him back down to his knees.

The East Asian man placed the rubber plug in the drain, then turned on the water. Just the cold.

Mohammed had to assume it was for some kind of interrogation technique.

"You don't need to do that," he said. "I will tell you what you know. If you identify yourselves, who you're working for."

"No talking," the East Asian man said. Heavily-accented English. Mohammed's best guess for a mother tongue was Mandarin Chinese.

"I didn't know," Mohammed said. "I didn't know what they were planning. I just wanted to be sure this project is in good faith."

"Quiet," the black man said. "Please, Dr. Najjar."

"I'm not a doctor."

The Chinese man left the bathroom, heading toward the front door.

"We thought she was doing something really bad," Mohammed said.

"Please, Mr. Najjar," the black man said.

Mohammed decided not to say anything else, since it didn't seem to be helping.

They would submerge him in the water, to be sure he was telling the truth. And then he would tell them the same thing, and they would believe it.

He had no reason to lie, and they had no reason to distrust him. They knew who he was. That he was a good citizen.

He knew that he had to stay calm; the last thing he could allow to happen was to lose his composure, especially if that meant losing his temper along with is. You don't spout off to men with guns.

He wouldn't give them a reason to hurt him.

The Chinese man came back with a small backpack. He pulled out a plastic sack. It looked almost like decorative landscaping fill, small ground pebbles and powder and a small ribbon of liquid floating above.

The Chinese man dumped the contents of the sack into the filling bathtub.

"What is that?" Mohammed asked. "What is it for?"

Neither man replied.

Mohammed watched as the water continued to pour into the tub. The powder and pebbles had swirled around with the current, and the water had started to brown. He saw several pieces of what he was sure was algae.

Like they were turning Rachael's bathtub into a fishtank.

They'd brought water from somewhere else, to where they'd leave his body.

He knew what they were about to do.

The men grabbed him by the arms once more and lifted him into the frigid tub. Still on his knees, for the moment.

He tried to believe in it all again.

To Allah we belong and to Him we will return.

The black man grabbed Mohammed's head and pushed it down.

Mohammed felt his whole chest start to fill with the cold and dirty water.

33

MIREIA DIDN'T know where Nicolas had gone.

She'd woken up Mateo's camper. He'd let her bunk with him, and he hadn't tried anything.

So far.

She'd gone back to find Nicolas. But he'd already left.

She'd folded up the beds in their campervan, and then she'd checked her tasks at her dock.

She'd gone to the outdoor kitchen for breakfast.

She hadn't seen him.

When she'd first met Nicolas, she'd thought he was a little ridiculous, one of those fast-aging men who had trouble admitting to their hair loss and bulging stomachs.

But it hadn't taken her long to find the passion underneath that unpleasant forty-something exterior. And passion was what drew Mireia to people, to friends, to Alex, to Mateo...

And she could feel herself being drawn to Nicolas despite herself, to his flat but intelligent grey eyes, his long nose with the odd little outward bend at the base, like a Gallic fishhook.

Because he was passionate, about the work, about the future, even when the whole world was wanting him to go away.

She knew he was jealous of Mateo, just like he'd been jealous of Alex, the young, fit men from Barcelona, with their buzz cuts and hard jaws. And at first she'd wanted to make him jealous, not because she didn't still have feelings for Mateo—because she did—but because she thought it would make him decide what he wanted to do.

If he wanted to fight for her. If the way he looked at her was more than the way he'd look at some other woman.

And it looked like he'd made his choice. He'd chosen to be anywhere but next to her.

She shouldn't have cared. She still had Mateo following her around like eight years of distance had never happened, *like Alex had never happened.* And if wasn't as if there weren't more important problems in her life.

But that's just it, isn't it? When everything big is going wrong, you want to feel like you can make something little go right.

After breakfast she immersed herself in her task list.

Her main role was to merge the SolRescue designs with what they'd learned from *Nisi*, from her time at CSG. There were things that SolRescue had done better, but not everything; their water and waste system was driven completely by chemical processing, with no thought given to the biological systems the ESA had been researching.

It played well to the stereotype, that American engineers were less likely to consider anything that could be tarred with the slur of being "Gaian Greenwash", the notion of kowtowing to the pigheaded environmentalists at the expense of good old fashioned technology. New plasmas and polymers got funding in the USA; growing algae to filter waste did not.

But SolRescue wasn't beholden to the whims of the US government, so there was no reason for the new habitats to rely on and 85% efficient chemical system when Mireia and Alex had already developed a proven water and waste recycler at 98%.

Why go out to some nearby rock for water ice when you've got gallons of perfectly good pee at home?

She loved being useful; before she'd joined the ESA as a liaison with SolRescue, she'd been working for the Generalitat. It had seemed impressive enough, an advisor on resource conservation for the Catalan Minister of Sustainability, but she'd realized quickly enough that the decisions she was advising on had been made before she'd even been consulted, that most of her work was vapour, reports no one would read and advice no one cared about.

It hadn't been all bad, since she'd met Alex during one of her poorly-attended presentations, an ambitious late-bloomer who was a good five years behind her in education and career.

It was his passion that had drawn her to him. That and the throbbing veins on his forearm.

And after meeting Alex her life had started to move in the right direction, starting with his encouragement for her to do what she herself was passionate about, rather than focusing on the status of a job that meant nothing in the end.

So the Generalitat had made way to the upstart Resource Collective of La Ribera, a way of sharing between neighbours in the barri that was an eclectic mix between Basque Mondragon and Anita Singhal's Liquid Governance.

And from there she found her work, and Carter Elgin had found her. And Alex.

You can't accept the bad that comes with the good. Even if the two seem locked together.

She missed him so much. Not just the young idealist Alex, who'd pushed her to become the real Mireia. But even the slightly less young Alex who'd started to obsess over their status, who'd started shifting his passion from designing the future to planning their personal future, scrambling to find the right schemes to supplement their surprisingly marginal salary, which relied too much on the assumption that the basic income was nearly good enough, that not much extra spending money was really needed for engineers who lived their work.

She'd known for a while that Alex had crossed the line.

But she didn't realize until after he was gone just how bad it had gotten.

And she hadn't told Nicolas, because it was too awful, and because she didn't want him to think of what Alex had done every time he looked at her.

She wasn't Alex. She hadn't told him to sell his soul for the finer things. She'd tried to show him that life didn't need those extravagances, but… but she'd accepted the finer things he'd brought home, the better clothes, the expensive foods droned in directly from La Boqueria.

She should have stood against it. She should have told him to stop.

Mateo came by just before lunch. He'd always been that type of guy, the one who thought that being spontaneous meant showing up without warning.

But Mireia had never enjoyed working alone in a room, and the confined space of the campervan was worse than an office. She walked over to the outdoor kitchen with him.

Lunch had always been cold food since she'd arrived at the maker camp, with the exception of the soups, since the support crew was well aware of how many engineers and designers would keep working on a task until it was done, and would then saunter over to the kitchen as late as 1400 or even 1500, expecting there to be food that was still mostly appetizing.

The lunch line was buffet style, rather than cafeteria. There was not enough support crew to expect them to waste their time spooning out portions.

So being that they'd reached the line at 1201, it was just Mireia and Mateo and a folding table of sandwiches and vegetables and fruit.

"The bread tastes fake," Mateo said, in English. "Bleached flour."

"I think they buy it in town and bring it in," Mireia said. "Too much work to bake enough of it for everyone."

He nodded. "I wish we could go home."

"I think you can."

"They say that you and Alex saved Nicolas," he said, "that they would have killed him like the others."

She turned away from him. "I don't know. It's not something I like to think about."

"I'm sorry."

"*Val,*" she said, in Catalan. It was okay. She understood.

"We're not supposed to speak it," he said. "Because you're not Catalan anymore... *Natália.* And I don't know Portuguese."

"No one can hear us," Mireia said. But still, she'd said it in English.

"We should go for a walk. So we can be who we are."

"We have work... or at least I have work. Do you work, Mateo?"

He chuckled. "I worked too late last night. And more this morning. I need a break. And so do you."

She nodded, though she didn't agree with him. They'd taken a break the night before, when he'd spoken like an old friend but eyed her like he wanted more.

And Nicolas had seen them like that.

And she still didn't know where he was.

The trails around Fort Reno were less recreational and more utilitarian, walked by pronghorn hunters and possibly the occasional rancher looking for something he'd lost.

But still, the beauty was breathtaking to Mireia.

It reminded her of Donaña National Park, in Andalucia, a place that had been drying out in a hurry to match the arid American plains. She'd gone there once, with Mateo of all people, to catch sight of the Iberian lynx and to visit the salt marshes for as long as they lasted.

Mateo led the way, like he'd been there before, but Mireia was pretty sure he hadn't. Maybe he was trying to show how confident he'd become in the years since they'd been together, no longer the young man from Tarragona who'd always second-guessed himself.

"They have a wild bison herd out here," he told her. "On some of the BLM land."

"BLM?"

"Most of the public land out here."

"The ranchers can't be happy about the bison coming back," she said.

They reached a large patch of forest along the Powder River.

Mateo led Mireia along a path, to where the river flattened out around a large sand bank.

"We can cross here," he said.

"Why would we?"

He grinned. "Why not?"

"Because you're trying to get me alone," she said.

"Yes. That was the entire reason for this walk."

"Només un bandarra seria tan segurs." Only a cheeky bastard would be so sure. But she liked it.

"I want to make you smile, Mireia," he said, in Catalan, taking her cue to switch from English.

They were the only people around for half a mile, at least.

He started across the river, letting his shoes and pants get soaked in the water.

"I'm not getting wet," she said.

He smirked. "That's not the girl I remember from home."

"This *woman* is older and wiser."

"I'll carry you," he said, stopping in the middle of the current.

"That will not happen. It will most definitely not end well."

"Sang a la figa i merda al cul!"

She couldn't believe he'd say that. She hadn't heard anyone say that in a very long time.

"That's so vulgar," she said. "Not romantic at all, Mateo."

He grinned. "You want the romance, Mireia?"

"Not really. But I know you."

"I wasn't about to presume," he said. "I just want to be your friend." He ran back onto the bank. He grabbed her hand. "Your friend."

He started pulling her toward the water.

She punched him lightly on the shoulder.

He wrapped his arms around her, lifting her up.

She gave out a little shriek. An embarrassing little shriek.

He laughed. But didn't let go.

She punched him on both shoulders. Harder.

He lowered her down.

"Friends don't lift friends," she said. But she knew he could tell. That she liked it.

"Then how are you going to get across, Mireia?"

"I'll take a running jump."

"And fall in?"

She laughed. "And fall in."

He had such a goofy grin on his face.

Mireia thought of Alex.

And sighed.

"I remember meeting him," Mateo said. "When I ran into you two at Festa de Gracia. He seemed really great, Mireia. And he looked like he was in love with you."

"Wait, when? I'd only known him for a few weeks."

He grinned. "It doesn't take long to fall for Mireia Lona."

"Mireia Lona *de Vives*," she said. She was still Alex's wife.

He nodded. "Yes. I know."

But then he leaned in.

And kissed her.

She didn't move at first. He'd caught her by surprise.

Then she pulled away.

"I'm sorry," he said. "I couldn't help myself."

"That's a terrible excuse, Mateo. We were just talking about my husband, and then you kiss me?"

"I'm sorry."

"We need to go back," she said. "Now."

"We can't go back, Mireia."

"What?"

"We need to cross the river."

"This isn't a joke, Mateo."

He grabbed her arms. Her elbows. Pinning them against her sides.

She tried pulling them away from him. She couldn't.

So she kneed him in the balls.

She took a few steps back. She still wasn't sure what to think. This was Mateo, goofy Mateo. This was a poor attempt at flirting. That was all it was, wasn't it?

"We need to cross the river," Mateo said, still recovering from the pain. "Mireia. Please."

"Why? Tell me why."

"We need to go."

"Tell me why, Mateo. Or I'll kick you again."

He shook his head. "The camp isn't safe right now."

"Tell me why."

He took a step toward her.

"Don't," she said. "Don't touch me again."

He tried to step around her, to come around the back of her.

She knew that he wanted to try and pin her again. From behind.

He was hoping she wouldn't get another shot at his balls.

He wanted to take her into the river.

She thought of Riley Crouch.

They'd pulled him into the ocean, hadn't they? Suzanne had told her that, that Riley had invited her to see the nesting turtles. But they'd made it look like he was going for an unplanned swim.

The river wasn't deep, but it was swift, probably some snowmelt still making its way down from some mountains somewhere.

He wouldn't try to drown her in it…

And she could run…

"I thought you cared about me," she said. "Who are you working for?"

"I don't work for anyone now. Not after this."

"After what, Mateo?"

"Just wait here with me, then," he said. "We won't cross the river. We'll wait here."

"You know what happened… in Guayana Francès."

"The space station. Of course."

"No," she said. "To Riley. My friend."

"I'm trying to protect you, Mireia."

"Protect me from what?"

"Just wait here with me," he said. "Please."

She didn't know what to say.

"I love you, Mireia," Mateo said. "From a week after we first met, and it never went away. Please, Mireia. Please. Stay here with me."

He wasn't trying to pin her anymore.

He wasn't trying to charm her, either.

He looked like he was close to tears.

"Please stay here with me, Mireia."

She nodded.

She believed that he loved her.

That much she knew she could trust.

She heard the screams before anything else.

Then the gunfire. And several explosions.

From the north, not that she'd have expected it not to come from the maker's camp.

"They're killing them," she said. "My god, Mateo."

"Yes."

"And you knew."

"I couldn't let you be there," he said.

"But everyone else…"

"UCGVs… ground drones. The next big thing in paramilitary action."

"Paramilitary action? You mean mass murder."

"By parties unknown," Mateo said. "Officially unknown."

"You're from Catalunya, Mateo. You're one of us. How could you do this?"

"I didn't do it, Mireia."

"You knew… I have to get back there."

309

"You know there's no use in that. Those vehicles won't leave the area until there are no more heat signatures."

"Heat signatures," she said. "You mean until everyone is dead. So just say what you mean."

She thought of the people she'd met over the past few days, other engineers and designers, the support crew, Nikki with her wide smile. And Nicolas.

She hadn't seen him since the night before, when she'd left in a huff, like some stupid child.

And now...

"We cannot go back there, Mireia," Mateo said. "I scouted some of the ranches on the other side of the river. I found a place we can stay, until we figure out what to do next."

"I'm not going anywhere with you."

"It's not safe, Mireia. They won't just assume you're dead. Not unless they have the body."

"Then give them the body, Mateo. Finish the job."

He shook his head. "Come on, *meu carbassa especie.*"

His pumpkin spice. A pet name that had died eight years before.

And needed to stay good and dead.

"Fuck you, Mateo," she said, in English. She *screamed* in English. "You are a piece of shit."

"I love you, Mireia. I'm risking my life for you."

"I hope you lose it. I hope those ground drones find you and kill you."

"Mireia..."

"Fuck you."

She started running, back toward the camp.

She looked back, and saw that he wasn't coming after her.

He'd meant it. That the unmanned combat vehicles would make sure everyone was dead. He wasn't going to get any closer, not even for his dear pumpkin spice.

But she had to go.

She had to see.

She had to know if anyone else was still alive.

She cleared the trees and started walking along the bank of the river, keeping as low as she could while still upright.

She could see flames, from campervans and outside equipment on fire.

And she saw one of the ground drones, moving along the edge of the camp. Searching for more targets. And a couple more, a little farther away, deeper into the wreckage.

She'd seen footage of the drones before, out against the latest gang of Jihadists, and a few videos of non-combat roles, searching for survivors after the Ankara earthquake and the fires in Perth, Australia.

But she knew these weren't regular forces, backed by US Army remote operators in some military-grade warehouse. They were less advanced, for one thing, looking like big blocky tanks rather than the sleek Mars rover style you'd see from the Americans and the Chinese.

Illegal loggers and miners had used primitive combat vehicles like those in Brazil, to hunt and kill anyone the machines encountered on their "death runs".

She remembered hearing the news, across the border in La belle république française. Some activists in Brazil had blamed local politicians, saying that they were complicit, if not directly responsible.

And now the same types of machines were killing the people she'd worked with, and would have killed her, too, if Mateo hadn't taken her out on a walk.

She lowered herself down on all fours, to get closer, creeping through the brush. She reached an old piece of metal farm equipment, a plow or a tiller or something, and she paused.

She realized that it was her heat signature the operators would be looking for, at least that's what Mateo had said. So being low wouldn't save her from being noticed.

She saw someone running toward her, past the cairn from Fort Reno.

Someone had seen her.

A woman, with long, red hair.

Mireia thought she recognized her, from the support crew.

The woman called out to her, telling her to run.

Mireia didn't move.

She saw the ground drone change course, moving toward them.

The redheaded woman was leading the tank over to Mireia. She'd get them both killed.

Mireia started crawling back toward the river. Heat signature or not, she figured that jumping up to run would get the operator's attention. Assuming there was an operator.

The woman was gaining on Mireia, just as the drone was advancing on her.

The drone began to fire.

Mireia got up and started running.

She didn't look back to see the woman fall.

She heard the gunfire stop, and that was enough to know.

She ran down the short bluffs toward the riverbank.

And found Mateo crouched down at the side of the river.

"Get in the water," he told her.

She did as he said.

"Keep low," he said. "I'm hoping it'll mask your body heat."

She submerged most of her body, leaning her head back, only her eyes and nose poking above the waterline.

She watched as Mateo climbed up over the bluff, heading almost due west. Whoever was operating that drone would see him, just as she began to lose sight of him.

She heard the gunfire again.

She didn't move, trying to stay still in the water, not sure what would happen next.

The water was cold, like you'd expect in the last few weeks of May, and she wondered how long she could last.

She had to stay there.

She had to bear it.

The drones wouldn't stay forever, not that she knew how long the operators would feel they needed to guarantee that no one had walked away.

Would they go through the ruined camp, counting the bodies?

Would they even know how many bodies to expect, since the whole idea of the camps was to keep outsiders guessing?

They'd know about her and about Nicolas. That was the impression Mateo had given her, that they'd be looking to confirm that she was dead.

Unless he was overstating it.

Maybe it was about the impending launches, and nothing more. A complete solution for destroying the SolRescue space habitat.

Mireia wondered if the same thing was happening to the other camps, if there were other places in the wide open American west where men and women were being gunned down, if the habs themselves were being destroyed out at Donatello or Michelangelo or wherever.

Was there more than that, too? Were people like Derrick McPherson and Carter Elgin in danger?

Was this a move to destroy the entire organization?

She felt her shivering grow worse. She felt lightheaded.

She couldn't stay in the water any longer.

She slowly crawled out of the Powder River, keeping below the low-lying bluffs by the bank.

None of the drones had come down to the water.

The remote operator had seen the redheaded woman and Mateo. Had they not seen Mireia?

Or had they thought that Mateo was the one who'd run down to the river, that he'd changed his mind and tried to take off across the open prairie?

Had he really done that?

Given himself up for her?

She was still shivering, still feeling like she was fading.

It wasn't warm enough that day, not after the cold water.

She didn't know enough about hypothermia, how it felt, how long it took to come on, how long it took to kill.

She wasn't sure if she had it.

But she felt weak, like her body couldn't function with the cold that had surrounded her.

She didn't know if the drones had left.

She didn't know if anyone had survived.

She closed her eyes and rested on the sand and gravel riverbank.

34

WILLIAM YEUNG Huan was exhausted, but no more than usual.

His day was ending soon, since it was well past midnight, and it had gone well, thanks to three pieces of good news:

1. *Archie had located Nicolas Clouatre and Mireia Lona, at a SolRescue maker camp in Wyoming. Archie himself had dispatched someone he trusted personally to intercept. Huan was better off not knowing the name.*

2. *Jia had listened to him at long last, choosing honesty over the seemingly safe choice of minimizing the issues in Tibet.*

3. *Fuhua didn't have any answers or designs for the Little March's payload, but he would have it soon. And then Huan would be able to send the information on to Hampus in Stockholm, who'd find the right way to provide it to Carter Elgin.*

Huan had to accept that Elgin would still be in charge in the short term.

He hadn't received a reply from Rachael Duck, which was odd, even if it was clear that Clouatre and Lona were in the United States.

He sent a message to Margie, a trusted friend in Winnipeg, Canada, asking her to find a way to check up on Rachael as soon as they could.

There was no reason to worry about Rachael Duck. Not yet.

An unusual result does not require immediate concern.

He felt the train braking.

Far too early.

They were still over twenty minutes from the next stop, at Shaoguan.

Unscheduled stop on a late-night high speed train.

Huan began to delete the local copies of his data.

The train stopped at Humen Railway Station.

Three People's Armed Police officers came to take Huan into custody.

He didn't offer any resistance; he knew he still had some chance of being released. He had many friends.

The officers seemed to know that; they carefully cuffed his hands in front, rather than behind.

He was taken to a massive government building in the center of the city of Dongguan, itself the focal point of a surprisingly quiet concrete mall.

Huan had never heard much about Dongguan, aside from it never having enough money to meets its commitments. Looking at the towering People's Government Building, he was starting to understand.

He was ushered inside, to a small conference room on the thirteenth floor. Being as late as it was, the building was almost completely empty of workers.

There were three more men waiting there for him, sitting around the far end of a long table.

Two from the local government, he guessed.

And the one at the head of the conference table was an old friend.

Huan knew that he would not be released.

The police officers sat him down at the end of the table, then left for the hallway outside.

Huan looked down at his hands, still bound with flexcuffs.

"I am disappointed in you," his old friend said.

"Tell me why, Yong."

"Because you have two masters."

"A horse with two masters is always skinny. That's the saying."

Yong nodded. "They want you to stand trial, Huan."

"On what charge?"

"I know you can guess."

"And I know it doesn't matter."

Yong nodded again.

One of the locals spoke up. "Is this man being charged?" he asked.

"It doesn't matter," Yong said. "You heard him say it."

The local official furrowed his brows. "We follow the law here, Mr. Xin. If there are no charges, is there really an arrest?"

Yong nodded. "Local demagogues. Too much power in the hands of men with small brains."

The local man groaned, but didn't respond.

Huan knew that he was Yong's only audience. The locals didn't matter. Yong was only concerned with the failings of his old friend.

"So what is it you want to say to me?" Huan asked. "I know there's something."

Yong waved the local men out.

They seemed happy enough to leave; a brave and stupid man might take shots at the arrogant men of the People's Convocation, but anyone who'd been even braver and stupider—enough to stand up to those arrogant men—had long ago been locked away or emigrated off to the unofficial Han colonies in the Russian Far East.

"I know you never believed in Marshall Nie's vision, Huan," Yong said. "I think most of the others knew, as well. But you did your job and you did it well."

"Living on the train."

"As needed." Yong frowned. "But to subvert the Nation in favor of the West... I didn't think you would ever do that."

"In favor of the world."

"What was that?"

"I did it for the world, Yong, not for the West. What's the point of restoring our greatness if all the other countries crumble?"

"China is the world. The hope for the world, at least. Why can't you see that, Huan?"

Huan sighed. "All I see is a gang of army men who think they know better."

"We're not army men, Huan. And we do know better. You could have worked within the system, to fix the problems—"

"I made my choice. I don't regret it."

Yong nodded. "That's the worst part," he said. "You should regret it." He tapped his fingers on the table. "They want a trial, Huan. But they've given me latitude, and I don't think you want that trial."

"Because we know how it ends."

"Yes."

"How did they realize what I'd done?" Huan asked.

"You know I can't tell you."

"So you will do it?"

Yong gave one slow nod. "I'm your friend."

"You are."

"I think you made a very big mistake," Yong said. "But I can't see the future. I have to realize that I could be wrong."

Yong stood up from his chair.

He walked over to Huan.

He put his hand on Huan's shoulder.

Together they walked out of the conference room.

They went down to the basement of the building, to an unadorned section with the utility equipment, and storage of the signage of last year's China.

Yong had already placed a large plastic bucket in the middle of the concrete floor.

"Better than a toilet," he said.

Huan nodded. "But not better than a firing squad."

"We're not army men, Huan."

Huan knelt down beside the bucket. He gripped the sides with both hands.

"Where will they find me?" he asked.

"In the fountain outside. That's where I got this water."

Huan sighed. "With how people die by the Convocation's hand... it should tell you something, Yong."

"That we're on the wrong side of history."

"Yes."

"You might be right," Yong said. "I don't know."

"That's the difference between our sides. I know I'm right."

"That's funny. Marshall Nie knows he's right as well. And so does your other master, Carter Elgin. It's all the same problem, Huan."

"Carter Elgin is not my master."

"I wish he wasn't."

Huan thought of his other life, the one he should have had, without the politics, without all of the lies. Just a simple career, a small family, a perfect life.

In another bubble universe, there was another Huan. Who had a son. And had a herb garden hanging off his bedroom window.

William Yeung Huan dunked his head into the bucket of cold and chlorinated water. He felt his old friend's hands grip the top of his scalp, to help keep his survival instinct from getting the better of him.

His last thought was gratitude for a friend like Xin Yong. A friend who would let the secrets die with Huan in that bucket.

35

SAMANTHA HAD booked one full week at the B&B, and since there weren't many other options available, Benj continued to stay in his room, while Samantha confined herself to the other.

He still had her tablet.

So from what he could tell, she was sitting in a small bedroom doing pretty much nothing.

And had been doing that since the evening before, apparently not having left to eat during the night (since Churchill closes up around 9 PM) while also skipping out on breakfast.

If Samantha had been any other woman—any other person—Benj had ever known, he would have been worried that she was planning on harming herself.

But not Samantha Yoon.

Not because he hated her, which he did, but because he'd gotten to understand how she functioned.

She'd isolated herself in her room because she knew it would bother him. Because she knew it was her best shot at some kind of rapprochement.

So Benj had to do his best not to fall into her trap.

He was amazed at how hard he had to fight.

Benj had taken Rachael's filebox, but had allowed her to hold on to her tablet. He'd stayed up half the night looking over the messages from Carter Elgin he'd transferred to his own tablet, using the antiglare on his eyepiece in an attempt to keep his head from exploding, and after the eight AM breakfast he'd gotten right back to it.

And he'd been amazed by what he'd read.

There were three Carter Elgins, if you wanted to create some kind of classification.

There was the public Carter, the mostly serious man of intense intellect who seemed perfectly content with his role of managing the sunshield, who would happily give interviews on the topics of offplanet resources, offplanet colonization, basically anything *offplanet*. Most of the messages Benj had seen belonged to this well-known Carter.

The second Carter was the more candid one, making the occasional off-color jokes and sarcastic remarks, unguarded enough that he could come off as a bit of an ass, arrogant, conceited... all the stuff the public Carter had figured out how to suppress whenever the world was paying attention. Benj liked that Carter; it reminded him of the handful of times he'd been around him as a child, the Carter who would even play tricks on little Benji, like when he'd replaced Benj's handheld game console with a near-exact duplicate with the buttons mixed up, where A meant B and Start meant Finish. That second Carter was overjoyed when he saw little seven-year-old Benji adapting, quickly relearning what each button now did.

But the third Carter was something Benj had never seen, a paranoid, self-absorbed Carter whose messages to Rachael had often crossed the line from offcolor to creepy; a few notes he'd sent were unlike all others, like they were written by someone who'd long ago lost touch with reality.

You need to come see me in St. Pierre, the third Carter had written, over a year before. *I've tried to keep that distance, but I cannot. Tickets are booked and attached. Saturday. You know that I love you.*

That he loved her.

Had he ever met her?

Rachael's response had been the same as all the others to messages from that third Carter; she'd simply ignored them, and when a more important message had come to her from the other Carters, but had carried a weird sentence or two from Carter #3, she simply responded to everything else, tersely but politely, as usual, pretending that he hadn't made any comments about her "perfect face" or "boundless spirit".

From what Benj could see, Carter had been obsessing over Rachael Duck for several years.

That was unsettling.

But it was the first Carter, the one the whole world had heard of, who'd crossed the line that mattered.

Have arranged an incident for Koskela. A man named Cannae Friesen will be coming to your restaurant tonight. If you get the feeling he is not reliable, let me know ASAP.

And after Rachael's reply, that Friesen seemed reliable enough:

Friesen will handle bear. You will handle Koskela. Please advise if attack likely to be fatal.

And Rachael did advise, saying that Jared Koskela would almost definitely be killed.

But Benj didn't find the other part that Rachael had mentioned. There was no threat of what would happen if she hadn't gone along with the plan.

From what Benj could read, Rachael had done nothing to stop the attack on Koskela. She could have torpedoed the idea from the moment she'd spoken with Cannae Friesen.

She hadn't.

And she'd brought Chloe Nielsen-Brown into it, as well, risking a second person's life along with Koskela.

Rachael Duck wasn't a victim. And she hadn't tried to stop Elgin's attack on the project team.

She was just trying to cover her own ass.

Benj couldn't let that sit.

He went back to Rachael's townhouse.

She met him at the door, before he'd had a chance to knock.

"You shouldn't be here," she said. "We have no good reason to know each other."

"I'm coming in," he told her.

She nodded.

She brought him back to her bedroom.

She sat down on her bed.

"I think Mohammed cleaned up a little," she said. "Before he left."

"He wasn't comfortable with what happened."

"What about you? Are you comfortable with it?"

He sighed. He wasn't sure how he felt about it.

But that wasn't the issue.

"You said that Carter threatened to kill Jared if you didn't," Benj said. "That he gave you the choice. But it's not there, Rachael."

"What's not there? I gave you the messages."

"You went along with it. You didn't argue."

"What?"

"Carter told you the plan, and you made it happen. No resistance on your end."

"That's not how it went," she said. "He told me that Jared would be killed."

"No, Rachael, he didn't."

"Why did you come here? Why bother confronting me on this?"

"I want to know the truth," he said.

"You have the messages."

"So that's all there is? Those messages?"

She nodded.

"He didn't give you some kind of ultimatum, Rachael. He told you to set up the attack on Jared and you did it. No questions asked."

"If that's what it looks like."

"Why would you agree to that?"

"I told you," she said. "If I'd said no, Carter would have found another way. Or the same way, just without me."

"So why did you help? Did you care about Jared at all?"

"Of course I care about him," she said. "Of course I do. God. Are you really that stupid?"

"How am I stupid?"

"I've lived here all my life. I know about living here. You don't. And Carter doesn't. If I'd let them do it without me, Jared would have been out there by himself. And he would probably have been drunk, since that was what Carter had wanted me to do, what Cannae Friesen had told me to do. He wanted me to feed Jared drinks, get him wasted. Then I was supposed to pick a fight with him, call him a drunk, and take his keys away. And then I was supposed to send him on his way, on foot. Guess what the chance of survival would have been."

Benj shook his head. He didn't know what to say.

"I brought my brother in on it, didn't tell Carter beforehand. Disabled Jared's jeep, instead of getting him drunk. And I made sure Chloe was with him."

"Because you thought the bear would get her instead?"

"Fuck, no," she said. "Because two sober people versus one polar bear gives pretty good odds for survival. As opposed to the death sentence they would have handed out to Jared. Rule Number One in Churchill: don't walk home drunk."

"But the plan blew up in your face," Benj said. "Cannae messed it up, then your brother got involved. Then you were screwed."

Rachael nodded. "But no one died."

"No one died."

"You don't believe me."

"I honestly don't know what to believe, Rachael. I still don't see why you couldn't just stop him. Tell Carter Elgin not to do it."

"You want me to stop Carter Elgin. What the hell do you think I'm trying to do? I've put up with his conspiracies, his paranoia, his creepy bull-shit... for years, mind you. So we could get the evidence we need. To show your father..." She sighed. "To show his wife."

"And you have that evidence," Benj said. "I have that evidence."

"And you're the one person I can trust."

"Because of my father."

"No," she said. "Because I can tell with you. There's no bullshit with you, Benj. You won't let it in."

Benj's lens flickered. Incoming voice call.

From his father. In the clear.

That didn't make much sense.

He hesitated for a moment, then tapped to answer.

"Benji," his father said. "You need to listen to me."

"This isn't protected," Benj said.

"I know. But you need to go."

"Go?"

"Get out of Churchill. Right now. As in right this second."

"What? What's going on?"

"Get out of Churchill. Now. I gotta go."

And the call ended.

"What just happened here?" Rachael asked. "I'm having trouble processing this."

"We need to go," Benj said. "Like the man said."

"He didn't mention me."

"He wouldn't have mentioned you, whether he knows about you or not. Not in the open like that."

"So you'll take me with you?" she asked.

"Shit, Rachael. I need you to come with me. You're the one who needs to bring this to my father."

"You don't need me for that."

"I'm pretty sure I do. You're a big piece of this evidence, Rachael. I need you to come with me and I need you to be safe."

She gave him a nod. And the faintest of smiles. "Thank you," she said. "For helping me."

Benj didn't have the heart to tell her how completely unqualified he was to help her or anyone else.

Rachael had brought up her brother, and Benj had explained as best he could that her brother would be a lot safer if he found a place to go that was nowhere near his sister.

She'd reluctantly agreed, but that had created the question of how they would get out of town. Rachael didn't have her own vehicle, and taking her brother's truck would have meant that he'd get dropped off from work and find his sister and his pickup missing.

But renting a truck and the related electronic trail wasn't necessarily the best idea, either.

If his father had called on an open connection, that meant he was putting his own whereabouts out in the open, something Derrick McPherson rarely did outside of a few trusted countries on the other side of the Atlantic.

So the danger was big and it was immediate.

So Benj had decided to rent a car, credit card and all.

They loaded up their rental, a mid-sized Toyota sedan, placing Rachael's printed weapons in the trunk along with several boxes of .223 ammo that she'd kept well-hidden from Mohammed's search in a turntable sitting in plain sight on her dresser; he'd never thought to look under the platter to find the large gap she'd cut into the record player.

Rachael had little food or water, but they didn't have time to shop; it was four and a half hours to the next town, the small mining city of Thompson. They wouldn't starve on the way.

Benj had the map as a layer on his left lens, to cycle through with the other views. The highway, like most in the Canadian province of Manitoba, was only two lanes, one in each direction, with a speed limit of 90 kph standard and 110 kph driverfree.

Benj wasn't comfortable switching over to the driverfree controls; he needed to be alert to his surroundings, every mile of the way. Driverfree would entice him into dropping his guard.

So he went standard, trying to ignore the periodic alert beeps from the speedometer as they headed south.

Highway 6 went from Churchill all the way to the provincial capital at Winnipeg, most of it almost as empty as that first stretch leaving Hudson Bay, crossing the Churchill River a few miles south of town, then following along the north bank of that river into the interior of the province, moving southwest for most of the way before making a turn to full-on south, to Thompson, and from there around the west shore of the huge and long expanse of Lake Winnipeg, down to the city of a million and change that shared that lake's name.

"This highway's only been here twenty years," Rachael said, as they reached the bridge over the Churchill River. "Everything used to come up by train. You'd spend twenty times as much for a carton of milk as you would in the south."

"Train's not so bad, is it?" Benj said. "European, really."

"It would take two days if you were lucky. As the permafrost melt got more unpredictable, the track got worse and worse. If the track got shut down, you could be stranded in Churchill for weeks."

"Not really stranded if you live there."

"I've left exactly once," she said.

"Once?"

"Yeah. People used to have more reason to go to the south, but I just couldn't justify the expense of flying or the pain of the twelve hour drive to Winnipeg."

"Twelve hours? Shit. I could drive home in sixteen if I pushed it. Utah to St. Louis, Missouri."

"Utah?"

"Yeah. The NSA Data Center."

"Oh, I guess so."

"But you grew up in St. Louis," she said.

"Same place as the famous Carter Elgin."

"Yeah. Famous."

Benj realized what he'd said. What it meant to her.

"I'm sorry," he said. "That was a thoughtless thing to say."

"I met him. That's where I'd gone. A SolRescue conference in Vancouver."

"You met him."

"Yeah. I guess you've met him, too."

"I saw him about as often as I saw my father growing up. Not as often as you'd think."

"I still respect both of them," she said. "Your father and Carter. Even if I don't agree with what Carter told me to do."

"We don't need to talk about it."

"I don't mind."

"I never really talk about my father. Or Carter Elgin. I guess no one who knows me ever asks about them. Samantha used my father as a button to press."

"Samantha's an asshole," Rachael said.

"Understatement of the month."

"I don't know if I can blame her for what she did."

"Are you serious?"

"I mean, I'm angry, sure, but I understand. She thought I'd been partly responsible for what's happened. And she knew what I'd done to Jared and Chloe."

"She might have killed you," Benj said. "Like all the way dead."

"Maybe, but probably not. She wanted to know why it happened. Why the space station was destroyed."

"Do we know why? Any of us?"

"To destroy the sunshield, obviously. Like everything else they've been doing. The United States, the People's Convocation of China…"

"The Europeans were working with SolRescue," Benj said. "To establish some kind of sovereignty up there. But would that have done anything? Would it have protected the sunshield? Really?"

"I don't know. But you put people up there, 24/7, and you make it a lot easier to watch over those little bots."

"Watch over? Was that all they were planning on doing?"

"There's no ban on conventional weapons in space," Rachael said.

"So what does that mean?"

"I didn't work on it, Benj. I wasn't there."

"You know enough."

"So do you."

"Yeah, okay. But come on…"

"Anything is a weapon in space," Rachael said. "I'm no expert but I've read a little on the subject. SolRescue has more than enough studies on it, starting with the original Phase Two plan that Anita Singhal came up with. You collect some rocks, put them in a Lagrange orbit. Keep a few mining bots nearby to scoop off and toss little pieces at anything that's coming your way. You throw it with enough velocity and it's not space junk you can easily avoid."

"Read a little on it, huh?"

"I read all of her papers."

"Singhal's?"

"Yeah." She started chuckling.

"What is it?"

"Jared," she said. "He tells pretty much everyone that Carter Elgin was his personal hero. I never tell people about Anita Singhal."

"Personal hero."

"Partly. And part personal cautionary tale. To never give up on what you believe in. Fuck… I was going to watch out for that. And I fell right into it with Carter Elgin. The same goddamn guy who messed it up for her."

"You thought you were doing the right thing," Benj said. "Not that you were. So… what did he say to you when you met him?"

"Who, Carter?"

"Yeah."

"Nothing. We didn't really talk. Shook hands, got a photo with him. That was it."

"That was it?"

"Yeah. He started messaging me a few months later; didn't seem like he remember me at all. Just wanted me to keep an eye on the project that was starting up."

"Najjar and Koskela's project."

"That's the one. Only because I live in Churchill. First on the list. Same reason Chloe messaged me, too."

"First on the list," Benj said. He found it funny.

Funny for a few reasons.

But mostly he didn't understand the messages that Carter had sent to Rachael. The earliest one he'd found had made it clear they'd been talking back and forth for a while; either she'd cleared them out or they'd come through another system.

Elgin had become so obsessed with her.

How had it happened?

So Benj decided to do what Benj does.

"Why did he get all weird with you?" he asked her. "Do you know?"

"Like I said, I don't think he even remembered meeting me in Vancouver."

"But he probably saw your picture at some point."

"Yeah. I even took one to send him. They had this sign up at the hospital that said something like 'do not pass this point unless you wanna get eaten by a freaking polar bear', and right behind that was their picnic table for smoke breaks and whatever. I thought it was pretty funny."

"So he knew what you looked like," Benj said. "That you're…"

"That I'm native?"

Benj laughed. "No… that you're hot."

She started laughing as well. "I'm not sure I qualify as that," she said.

"No, you definitely do. And I've been to enough places to have a representative sample of independent and identically distributed random variables."

"I'd blush if I understood what the hell you're saying. Only it does smell a lot like bullshit…"

"Some girls think I'm smart," Benj said.

And then he realized who she had to compare him against in her *particularly puny* purposive sample. The Alchemist of Ann Arbor, Koskela the goddamn Rocket Scientist, and Nobel Laureate Carter Elgin.

"You're smart enough to be nice to me," Rachael said. "That's definitely a plus."

They were an hour outside of Churchill, so just over three hours away from Thompson and the start of the rest of the world, skirting the edge of Nuymaykoos Lake Provincial Wilderness Park, which was apparently set up *because* it was a wilderness. There'd been no buildings and no roads, the only sign of life aside from the highway being the rail line, which they'd crisscrossed a couple of times in the past half hour.

Rachael picked something up on her tablet, judging from the notifycation sound.

"Didn't know there was network out here," Benj said.

"Not network," she replied. "Radio signal. Some of us have some extra components stuff into our little box."

"What kind of signal?" He knew she wasn't talking about some out-of-the-way radio station.

"Says 144 MHz. Some kind of amateur signal. But no noise, no static."

"Digital encryption."

"I think so."

"There aren't many cars on this trip today," Benj said. "You think this is about us?"

"Could be a couple of truckers."

"Do they have a lot of truckers on this route? Or just driverfree?"

"You're right," she said. "Probably not truckers."

Benj tapped the frame on his eyepiece, bringing the map onto his lens.

"We're a long way from any settlements," he said. "Just one lonely service station up ahead, with the boat launch for the park. Little Beaver Station. Four miles on our left."

"I don't know this road. Not at all."

"We're just a couple of tourists."

"Pretty much."

Benj knew he was being paranoid, that an encrypted signal could mean anything in the wilderness; there could be trappers or loggers or miners or whoever out there, just not marked on the map. There could be some Canadian Army survival training for all he knew.

But his father had told him to get his ass out of Churchill ASAP.

That meant that someone wanted at him, whether that meant grabbing him and throwing him in the back of the car, or shooting him in the back of the head.

And maybe Rachael, too, not that his father had said anything about her.

They were in the middle of the boreal forest, just one long ribbon of two-lane highway and nothing else.

"We should stop at the service station," Benj said. "Find a way to get in touch with my father. Or someone else we can trust."

"You're assuming the service station is safe."

"I'm not sure what else we can do. Turning around could be an even stupider choice."

"I know," she said.

"We just have to keep our eyes open, watch for anything else that seems out of place. If that radio transmission has anything to do with us, they don't know we know."

"That's irony, isn't it?"

"What?"

"Sam almost kills me yesterday, just so I can end up dead."

"I won't let that happen, Rachael."

She chuckled nervously. "You have a superpower you haven't mentioned before?"

"I have certain skills," Benj said. "I have a life outside of you."

"Like what?"

"It doesn't matter. Just keep an eye out. And we'll get through this, alright?"

She didn't answer.

"Alright?" he said.

"I nodded."

"To a guy who's supposed to keeping an eye on the road."

"From a girl who's not really used to road trips."

They rounded a corner and crossed the small but swift Smith River, climbing a ridge on the other side that curved a little to the south.

"I can see the sign," Rachael said. "Manitoba government. Yellow bison."

"That's a gas station?"

"Do you expect anyone else to run a business out here? It's probably just a bunch of automated pumps and vending machines. Wait..."

"What?"

"The road's blocked."

"I'll zoom in," Benj said. His eyepiece responded from his voice suggestion alone, slowly bringing the view closer. Once of those features that seemed less than ideal when driving; of course, you aren't supposed to wear smart glasses when driving.

The road was blocked by three barricades, evenly stretched across both lanes.

No road worker. No other signage.

"This is it," Benj said. "Whatever they've been planning."

He slowed down, to around 20 mph, or just over thirty kilometers per hour on the dial.

"Turn around?" Rachael asked.

"I think there's someone waiting for that."

"Whoever sent the radio signal. Told these guys to block the road..."

"They expect us to turn around," Benj said. "But I'll bet they're prepared for either option."

"So we come up with option number three."

"Which is?"

"I don't know," she said.

"Can't go on foot."

"So turn around or we go forward."

"Or we aim for the railroad tracks."

"The tracks?" she said. "I don't think we'll get far without getting stuck."

"I think it's an option, at least."

"That it is. Just a really bad one."

Benj started turning the sedan around.

"This won't work," Rachael said. "Maybe with a pickup truck. But you see how low this thing is?"

"There should be room along the side of the rail."

"Are you sure?"

"The right of way," Benj said. "Room for maintenance, for cuts or whatever. It's our best bet."

"Okay."

He drove up north to the most recent crossing with the tracks, reaching as high as the 119 kph ceiling before the car would automatically begin to decelerate.

He reached the tracks and confirmed on his map before turning to the right.

There was room between the track and the end of the gravel, but not wide enough for the far side of the car, which would run over the dirt and moss and tall grasses as they headed down the line.

It wouldn't take much wet to stop them. And they could drive onto the tracks, as the rails were high enough to pull parts off the undercarriage, assuming they even had enough power in that sedan to climb up over the righthand rail in the first place.

They drove over several culverts, the passenger side of the car a few inches from the edge, where the gravel and grass fell off to the small and reedy northern creeks.

On the straightest stretches Benj was able to accelerate as high as 30 mph; at that rate they'd be in Thompson long after dark. And pulling off the rail line was risky, since whoever was tracking them on the highway could move a lot faster than they could; there was no reason not to expect a reception at the next road crossing.

Benj wondered if he hadn't thought it through.

Maybe the tracks weren't any safer than the highway.

"You have a map on your tablet," he said. "Can you check for the next time we meet back up with the road?"

It didn't take long for Rachael to reply. "We'll cross the road just before we cross the Churchill River again, just west of Billard Lake."

"So if they really are after us—"

"That's where they'll be," she said. "But there's a siding just north of there."

"A siding..."

"Some kind of building, too. Not sure for what."

"We don't need a building," Benj said. "We need another way out of here."

"I know... I'm trying here."

"We both are."

He noticed the road turning away from the Little Beaver River, which they'd been following since leaving the banks of the Churchill. A slight climb, then another curve, back toward the water.

A bridge over the river.

He stopped the car.

There was no room to the side of the track; the gravel edge of the ballast was replaced by less than a foot of wood planking leading to and over the large steel girders that crossed the Little Beaver and two concrete piers.

"There's no way to get across," Benj said. "We'll get hung up on the rails."

"So what? We turn around?"

"Maybe... I'm not sure they've thought it through, either. If they are expecting us to have taken the tracks, they might not know we'd get stuck at this bridge. Or known there was a bridge here."

"They've got maps," Rachael said.

"But we didn't know."

"So again... what the fuck do we do?"

"Three options once again," Benj said. "We turn around and hope we don't get stuck trying, or we ditch the car and keep following the track on foot..."

"That's two options. What's the third one?"

"I'm thinking. I know there's a third option. Right?"

"Swim?"

Benj held up his hand, hoping she'd take the cue to give him a minute. He just needed to think it through, he knew that. He had to stay calm and consider the possibilities.

If he was back home he'd hitchhike. Not impossible in St. Louis, but not nearly as easy for a black man in Utah... but again, not impossible. But there wasn't much traffic on Highway 6, and most of it was driverfree. So even if it was a passenger car they came across, rather than a freight truck, there was little chance the people in that car would even notice two people standing on the shoulder.

The only way those people would notice was if those people were the ones looking for Benj and Rachael.

Goddamn driverfree.

But he thought about it. Two lane highway. Automatic collision avoidance.

If they blocked the road, a driverfree truck would stop. There was a chance that truck had an attendant, and an about equal chance it wouldn't.

If they blocked the road, the truck would stop until the debris was cleared. Maybe that would give them enough time to hitch a ride.

Probably the second craziest idea Benjamin McPherson had ever had.

In retrospect, that first one he'd gotten—the UBI fraud—had almost ruined his life... but not quite. Crazy ideas weren't the end of the world.

❧

It was a hard walk through the bush from the rail line back to the high-way, particularly since they had two of the rifles on their shoulders along with two backpacks and a mid-sized suitcase—that matched Rachael's earlier enclosure—to hump down the nonexistent trail.

But Rachael had surprised Benj by being on board with the plan; in fact, she seemed more convinced of its chances than he was, which impressed him even as it made him concerned for her mental state.

They reached the road after twenty minutes.

They hid their bags and guns in the ditch, a couple inches above the dark green water that half-filled the trench. Then they walked back to grab the longest log they'd seen on their hike, at least ten feet, but weathered and eaten away by enough time that it wasn't as heavy as some of the newer falls.

Benj pulled and Rachael pushed, bringing the dead trunk out onto the pavement, dead center.

"I'm not sure it's enough," Rachael said. "Wouldn't be hard to swerve around, onto the shoulder."

"Does that happen with driverfree?"

"I have no idea. Try to remember my personal history."

He laughed.

"We get two smaller logs for both sides," Rachael said. "It's not like the sensors can detect 'might be a trap'."

"They might, actually. Hijacking a driverless truck seems like a good income stream."

"So what are you suggesting?"

"Not sure," Benj said. "And there's a chance we'll meet a truck with an attendant, or some black van with people who want us to disappear."

"I'll stand out on the highway," Rachael said.

"What?"

"Like I was trying to move the log, but then I saw the truck coming."

"That's a bad plan."

"I'm just some random indian in the middle of the wilderness. Makes more sense than a black guy in Northern Manitoba."

"You don't have black guys here?"

"Did you see any?"

"What if they grab you, Rachael?"

"We have the rifles. You can defend my honor."

"So it's a driverfree and it stops," Benj said. "Then we'll need to figure out a way to get on board. Those cabs are probably secure, trailers, too."

"We might be better off with an attendant," Rachael said. "I'll be the damsel in distress. Think I can pull it off?"

"So we're hoping the attendant comes out, and then…"

"Not really defending my honor at that point. But we need to hitch a ride. Doesn't matter how."

Benj nodded.

He'd crossed back over that line with Samantha, to start, making threats in an airplane bathroom. Then he'd helped to kidnap Rachael, knowing that Samantha wasn't someone he could trust.

And now he'd have to do whatever it takes to get south, unintended consequences be damned.

Like he'd never learned his lesson from what he'd done to Valeri Timms.

Benj was knelt down in the ditch, covered from view by a stand of tall grass. He had the rifle trained on what the log itself, hoping that his video game experience would transfer well enough to keep him from accidentally shooting Rachael.

She was posed by the log, in the southbound lane, wearing Benj's eyepiece extended to full zoom as she stared up the highway. Any sign of anything other than a semi truck meant she should take a dive into the ditch, risking the wet for not getting spotted by the wrong crowd.

The zoom would make it so she'd see anything coming up over the horizon, hopefully clear enough to get hidden as needed.

They waited for twenty minutes before anything happened.

The first vehicle—a tractor-trailer—came from the south, heading toward Churchill and the bay.

Rachael went for the ditch; they hadn't discussed every scenario, but Benj didn't argue with the decision. It made sense to see what would happen with the first driverfree, and it wasn't as much of a waste if it was driving the wrong way.

The truck slowed as it approached the log, an even deceleration you'd expect from a driverfree.

Benj didn't see an attendant in the cab, but that didn't mean there wasn't one in the berth.

The truck swerved onto the shoulder at maybe forty miles per, before righting itself in the lane and accelerating back to its usual speed.

Benj knew that the avoidance might not be universal; other breeds of semis might not take to the gravel shoulder as easily.

They waited another ten minutes, Rachael back out by the log.

Another vehicle. Northbound.

A white pickup truck.

Rachael made for the ditch, dropping down around ten feet away from Benj's hiding spot.

She looked over at him.

He gave her a nod, hoping she'd stay calm.

Hoping he'd be able to stay calm, too.

The pickup stopped a few feet short of the log.

No swerve onto the shoulder.

Two passengers inside.

A man got out of the driver's side.

A second black man in Northern Manitoba, but another transplant from Utah.

It was Malik.

Dressed in a navy blue tactical jacket, bullet-resistant to a point, from what Benj had seen *in the movies*.

"Get out of the ditch, Rachael," Malik said. "You in that ditch, too, Benj? Leave the rifles where they are, alright?"

Rachael was looking to him. Wanting him to lead.

Made sense.

But Benj wasn't big on climbing out.

"We've been keeping an eye on you guys," Malik said. "Your eyepiece, Benj. Like living behind your eyeball, really."

If that was true... Malik would have seen everything. Including what they'd done to Rachael, including the messages to her from Carter Elgin.

And Benj had no idea who Malik was working for.

Q Group from the NSA? The US Air Force? The Chinese junta? Google?

Benj stood up, leaving the gun in the ditch.

"Good choice," Malik said.

"I'm guessing you won't tell me whose side you're on," Benj said.

Malik smiled. "I'm on your side."

"Come on, Malik."

"Samantha isn't with Q Group. You know that. She's with SolRescue, but you know that, too."

"And you know what toothpaste I use."

"Tell Rachael to stand up."

"You tell her."

Rachael stood up.

"I have a gun," Malik said, waving his hand at the bulge under his jacket, "but you can see that it's not drawn. My partner in the truck also has a gun. I'm not sure if he's whipped it out."

"Are you planning on shooting us?" Rachael asked.

Malik shook his head. "No one's getting shot. No one. So what did you do with your rental car?"

"Left it by the rail bridge," Benj said.

"Did you pay for the extra insurance? Not sure there's a hit by a train clause."

"So who do you work for?" Rachael asked.

"I actually do work for Q Group," Malik said. "I'm the guy who hooked Samantha up with all her so-called connections at the NSA."

"Like entrapment?" Benj asked.

"No law against it. No laws at all when it comes to national security. Except for that 'no killing citizens' thing."

"Loosely followed," Rachael said.

"We've taken Samantha into custody," Malik said. "And we're hoping to do the same with you guys. Head back across the border for a debrief."

"I don't trust you," Benj said.

"Because your father tried to warn you about me. I understand. He's worried about what comes next."

"Which is what, exactly?"

"Highland County, I would imagine. Not the worst place to spend your summer vacation. Although I think it might be tick season."

"And you expect us to trust you?" Rachael said. "With no good reason to do so."

"I expect you to make a decision based on the factors at hand," Malik said. "Namely, that my partner and I have been thoroughly trained in the operation of our handguns. And that it's a long fucking walk to the next town from here."

"You want us all to squish into that pickup?" Benj asked.

"You and I will ride in the box," Malik said. He reached into a pouch on his tactical jacket. He threw a zip tie toward the ditch, almost reaching the gravel shoulder. "Rachael, you can figure this out. Put his hands behind his back."

She looked over to Benj.

He gave her a nod. It seemed like they'd reached the point where they were fresh out of options.

She picked up the zip tie and walked over to Benj, who'd taken a couple steps out of the ditch to meet her.

He placed his hands behind his back.

"Turn around," Malik said. "Back to me, Benj. Cup one hand in the other."

Benj did as instructed.

Rachael bound his wrists.

"All the way tight," Malik said.

She pulled the tie tighter.

"Now help him into the back of the truck."

Benj made his way to the tailgate, Rachael following behind.

She opened the gate and helped him up into the box.

"Sit down, Benj," Malik said. "Don't want you to fall out."

Benj lowered himself down carefully as Malik walked closer.

Malik stopped ten feet from the back of the truck, waving Rachael over.

Once she'd reached him, he bound her hands behind her back.

He then led her to the passenger side of the cab.

The other man got out.

"Yes," Malik said, "my partner is of East Asian descent. How very suspicious."

The other man grabbed Rachael by the elbow and pushed her into the cab.

He walked around the front of the pickup while Malik made his way toward the back.

"It's going to be a long trip," Malik said once he'd climbed into the box. "Good thing you're wearing layers, Benj."

"Rachael doesn't deserve this," Benj said. "She's been through a lot."

"I've seen what she's been through. And I don't disagree. But this is the safest option for both of you right now."

"You know I don't trust you. You were supposed to be my friend, Malik."

"You got me fired, man. Well, kind of. And Laila."

"Is Laila okay?"

"Fuck you, is Laila okay. You fucking killed her."

"What the hell are you talking about?"

"Yeah, good. Play dumb with me, you dumbass piece of shit. Laila didn't deserve what she got, not in the least. And you know what, asshole? Karma's a bitch."

36

THE RCMP hadn't needed much by way of confirmation; they'd found Mohammed Najjar's body in the Churchill River, just downriver from the weir, with his wallet and ID still jammed into his pants pocket. And there was a good chance his DNA would be freely available to the Canadians.

So when Corporal Pasteen had come by the lab to talk to Chloe and Jared, there'd been no talk of needing some kind of positive ID from either of them.

Corporal Pasteen had made it clear that they were confident Mohammed had drowned. He'd been less clear on the notion of foul play.

But Jared wasn't about to mention the possibility; he wasn't expecting much help from the RCMP on what was likely a play by *someone's* national security operatives.

So he and Chloe had looked appropriately shocked and upset, and Corporal Pasteen had gone on his way.

"I honestly don't know why they haven't come for us," Jared said, as he and Chloe sat at their docks staring at one another. "I don't know why they'd chosen Mohammed."

"We'd been with those other two," Chloe said. "If they're working with whoever did this…"

"I wouldn't be surprised if something's happened to them."

Chloe sighed. "Maybe two more bodies to wash up."

Jared took out his tablet and called the bed and breakfast where Samantha and Benj had been staying.

Still officially checked in. That was all the hostess would tell him.

"I'm not sure how to get a hold of them," he said. "Mohammed was the one with their contact info."

"Search brings up nothing," Chloe said.

"I don't want to ask Rachael if she's got a line on them."

"What about the Chinese researchers?"

"What about them?"

"For a while Samantha had kept me in some kind of shed, right outside their lab. They might know what happened to her and Benj McPherson."

"You were there? In some shed? I walked right by."

"I thought I'd heard you," she said. "But I was gagged… and probably drugged…"

"I'm sorry, Chloe. I'm sorry I couldn't save you."

"You did save me, dumbass."

She leaned in and gave him a kiss.

They took Chloe's long-standing rental car to the Chinese research hab. The two pickups were still parked outside, along with Jared's jeep.

He still hadn't claimed it.

He wasn't sure how to even begin.

He saw the shed where Chloe had been, not even a football field away from where Jared had checked out the trap. Where he'd found her Celtic Cross pendant, and then he'd ran back to the lab with his tail between his legs.

He could have brought her home that much sooner.

"Do you think this is safe?" Chloe asked, as she pulled up alongside the white pickup truck.

"Rachael had thought it might be a trap. Samantha thought that too, for other reasons."

"They must have known about me. In that shed."

"I don't know, Chloe."

She nodded. "I'm going in."

She started walking toward the entrance.

Jared rushed to keep up.

Chloe knocked on the hard plastic door.

They waited.

No answer.

She tried to pull open the hatch.

"Locked," she said. "Don't see why they bother. Can't we just cut a hole in the side?"

"It's stronger than that," Jared said. "This material is built to withstand some pretty harsh conditions. Like Antarctica. And that's assuming it's not using the stuff they've developed for going to Mars. That stuff's hard as concrete once it's inflated."

"So how do we get in?"

"Not sure."

He walked along the side, then back to the front. The hab had all of the signs of being not just strong, but airtight. The door itself looked like an airlock, jutting out from the main mass of the building.

It made sense, not just because of the cold; because the best way to improve on tech for the Moon and Mars was to actually use it for real once in a while.

"What was in that shed, Chloe?" he asked. "Do you remember? Any equipment?"

"Like shovels or axes or something?"

"Like any big, mechanical boxes. Like a big air exchanger or some supply tanks or something. I'm not really an expert on this stuff."

"I don't think so... why?"

"Airtight means they get their fresh oxygen from somewhere. And I don't see any filters or anything attached to the hab. And I doubt they'd have big tanks of O2 just sitting around inside."

"You were hoping that cutting the air supply would get that door open?" she asked.

"Thought it was worth a try. Not that I can see any lines leading from that shed into the hab. Unless they buried them..."

"I'm not sure they're even in there. You'd think they'd just come out and confront us."

"They didn't when we were here before," Jared said. "Rachael and I."

"So no way to force them out and no way to get inside. Bullocks."

"Bullocks?"

She smirked. "Yeah. Bullocks."

"I'd say the only way we're getting in is if we ram one of these trucks into the side of it."

"Then we'd better hope no one's standing by that particular side," she said.

"So not the best idea."

"Not even compared to most of your ideas."

Jared knew these habs, almost. This was not the same as what he'd been working in for the past three months, not just because of the airlocks, but because it was a Chinese hab, as opposed to the Bigelow habs from Lockheed Martin that the USAF put into the field.

But the design was similar, and similar might give him the right point of attack. The weakness in the Bigelows came in two places; joins and outlets. The joins had always gotten the most attention, based on the primal human understanding that when you stuff too much air into a cartoon pig, the first thing to come apart is that cartoon pig's clothing. At the seams.

So that's where the effort had gone, to keep those seams strong.

But the outlets, the little holes for cabling and piping... those weren't as well-protected. Especially since those cables and pipes were often the weakest parts of the whole operation.

You wouldn't use that design offplanet, unless absolutely necessary. So he knew there was a chance there'd be no visible outlets on the Chinese model, given it was blessed with what looked like airlocks.

But he had to check.

Jared followed the side of the hab. It rounded a little as the sidewalls became the flooring, and he had a sinking feeling that the Chinese had chosen wireless transmission for their power needs.

But then he reached the power cables. There was no connection to the shed, but there was a clear connection from the hab to the solar stand. And it appeared to have its own battery bank underneath, most likely an extra boost to the batteries they'd have inside the hab itself; that was just like the hab Jared worked in.

Four different cables entering through four separate holes in the hab, arranged in a straight line, six inches between each outlet. An improvisation for the Earth-based model? A patch of hard plastic sewn into the layers of Nextel and open-cell foam.

Connecting that panel was the one set of seams that probably hadn't been included in the offplanet version.

The weak spot.

He walked over to the array.

He'd had to do a little bit of improvisation with their own hab, having once had to change out the entire cabling. So he was comfortable enough in the process of yanking out plugs from the small hard-plastic battery case; he made sure there would be no current in the wire that made its way into the hab. Or at least he hoped there wouldn't be.

And then he went back to the outlet by the inflatable lab. He took his small utility knife and started slicing at the seams.

"What are you doing?" Chloe asked. "You think cutting the lights will force them to open up? In like a day or two when the batteries run dry?"

"I've got a plan."

"Ah... so this is how we die."

Jared wasn't getting far with a gentle sawing of this knife, so he started going with hard jabs, all the while doing his best not to slip and slice through one of the power cables, just in case there was some weird Chinese system of cycling power between the two battery banks.

He made a tiny hole in the top seam of the panel.

"They should be trying to stop you," Chloe said. "Why aren't they trying to stop you?"

"I don't know, Chloe."

He kept working, and after ten minutes of cutting and jabbing and grunting, he managed to slice the top and side seams.

He started pulling, hoping that the cabling wouldn't keep him from making a hole.

But the panel was wedged in with the cables.

"I'm going to have to cut them," he said.

"That's fine, right? You disconnected them..."

"So you want to cut them?"

She stepped forward.

"I was kidding," he said.

"Team effort," she told him.

She held out her hand.

He passed her the knife.

She knelt down and sliced the first wire.

So far, so good.

She cut the others, then the two of them pulled the hard plastic panel clear off the hab, creating a gap that was maybe two by three feet.

Jared didn't think he could make it through.

"I can get in there," Chloe said. "God and genetics blessed me with small knockers."

Jared caught himself looking at her chest... for confirmation.

Chloe laughed.

He couldn't see anything through the gap; the battery bank was blocking the view. There was no sound from inside, aside from the usual hum of electronics.

Maybe there was no one in there.

The one thing that stood out was how cold it seemed. Not cold like outside, a late winter coming into a short spring, but colder. Like a walk-in freezer.

Like something had gone wrong with their environmental controls.

Chloe stuck out her arms like she was about to dive into a swimming pool, and started pushing her way through the gap.

"Be careful," Jared said.

He heard her chuckle. "Little late for that."

Then she started swearing.

"What's going on?" he asked.

"No," she said. "My god."

"Chloe... what is it?"

She didn't answer.

He looked through the gap. He couldn't see her. Just the battery bank.

He had to go in after her.

He took a deep breath, not that it would do much, and started trying to force his way through.

He had a strong feeling he was going to end up getting stuck.

He couldn't do it.

He pulled back.

He had to think.

There was a noise to his left. Back by the entrance.

He turned to see.

It was Chloe; she'd opened the front hatch and was walking toward him.

She looked like she had when they'd been locked in the bear trap.

Terrified.

He wrapped his arms around her.

"Did you want to wait in the car?" he asked.

She shook her head.

He led her back to the front door.

She'd left the airlock open.

As they crossed through Jared felt the temperature drop by at least ten degrees.

It was maybe thirty degrees Fahrenheit. Maybe.

Below freezing.

The hab looked like you'd expect, work docks and work docks and a small kitchen, a bar fridge and microwave and portable wash basin. But there were no chairs at the work docks, or pulled around the small folding table by the kitchenette.

He saw them in the far end of the room.

And he saw two Chinese men and two Chinese women, bound to those rolling chairs. With one chair to spare, second from the right.

And he saw that their clothes were soaked in blood, from small cuts across their throats.

"I've seen this before," Chloe said.

"What?"

"In Vietnam. The hydro project on the Hieu River. I walked in on something like this before."

She was shaking. He reached for her.

She pushed him away. "Don't," she said. "I was supposed to be there when it happened. I'd been called up to one of the other worksites, up-river... I came back and found all of my engineers murdered. All but one."

She pointed to the empty chair.

Jared looked closer.

He could see the stream of ice, the puddle on the floor.

Whoever'd been sitting there had pissed themselves.

And been taken away.

"They found the other engineer long after I came back home," Chloe said. "Parts of him."

"Who was responsible?"

"We didn't know. Some people thought it was the Chinese, but that wasn't something the Chinese had ever done before. That was before the hardliners, before the coup."

"Could it have been the US government?" Jared asked.

She turned away.

"Chloe..."

"This wasn't us," she said. "You ought to know that, Jared."

"I don't mean us."

"You mean our country. That's pretty much the same thing."

"Not the same thing."

"I don't want to talk about this," she said. "I just want to go."

Jared nodded.

They left the hab.

"We call the RCMP," he said.

"We broke in."

"With our bare hands and stupid fingerprints."

"And video surveillance, I'll bet."

"Shit," Jared said.

"They'll hold us if we report this."

"They'll find us if we don't."

"We need to go," she said.

"Are you hearing me, Chloe? They're going to know we were here."

"Yeah. We need to get back across the border. Get to Wright-Patterson, if we can. To Colonel Begtang."

"What about the project?"

"Mohammed's dead. These people are dead. Yesterday you and I came close to being dead. I'd say this project is probably dead, too."

"Probably."

"Maybe we can get things back on track in the Marshalls. I don't know."

"Or we move on," Jared said.

"Move on. I know what that means."

"Shit, Chloe…"

"I know… I don't want to talk about that, either."

They got in Chloe's rental car and headed back to the lab.

Where they'd pack up what they needed, giving up on finding out what happened to Samantha Yoon and Benj McPherson. And not knowing if Rachael was okay.

And hoping that Corporal Pasteen of the RCMP didn't show up to arrest the two of them.

They took the filebox, after Jared had checked it over enough to know that he wouldn't be getting into Mohammed's secret files without outside help… like Benj McPherson, maybe.

They couldn't take the big stuff in Rachael's rental car, which meant that both Turaco and the prototype printer bot had to stay behind. They'd take the quarter-scale bot models instead, the scooper, the assembler, and the example of the end result, a partially-hardened—only partially, so far—shield bot.

And Chloe found something else, Mohammed's backpack; he'd left it at the lab, rather than bring it to Rachael's townhouse.

Inside they'd found something that shouldn't have been there.

Another bot, much smaller than the others. Small enough to fit in the palm of his hand.

It looked like an octopus, or maybe a spider, eight legs with sharp metal points on the ends.

A personal project?

It didn't feel like it.

Jared knew it was part of the big secret.

He wouldn't have time to examine it as much as he'd need to.

He'd have to wait, until they were somewhere safe.

"I'll take it," Chloe said.

"What?"

"You know we might lose the filebox. If anyone searches us, for any reason. I can keep that thing from being found."

"Do I want to know?" he asked, giving her a smirk.

"Pass it to me."

He gave her the little spider bot.

She reached into her pocket with her left hand. She pulled out a small elastic band.

She put the bot on top of her head. Then she carefully weaved it into her hair, pulling the strands into a low and unkempt ponytail.

She wrapped the elastic band around her hair.

She held up her hands, for judgement.

"I don't think it will stay in there," he said.

"Just keep an eye on me... make sure there's nothing falling out of my golden locks. It's not like it'll break if it hits the floor, right?"

"I don't know... it doesn't feel that tough, actually."

"Let's try it," she said. "Okay?"

"Yeah. Okay."

She leaned in and gave him a kiss. "I love that we have these death-defying adventures together."

He laughed.

37

THERE ARE a handful of good things about getting old. Not stupid things, like the notion that frequent urination being an excellent way to remember more dreams, but actual, good things.

Good thing #1: you don't give a shit what people think.

Or less of a shit.

Nicolas had only known Nikki Taunton for how many days?

But he felt something for her, something he knew was infatuation but was perfectly happy calling love.

And when they'd snuggled together watching the sunrise from the top of North Butte… it was a feeling Nicolas hadn't felt since years ago in France, before he'd fucked things up with Madeleine, before he'd volunteered for exile in South America.

It didn't matter how Nikki felt about him, if he was just the default guy because there was no one else. He liked being there with her, and for as long as he could, he'd enjoy it.

She'd asked him again about the rumours, as they were cradled together, about if he and Mireia had known about Alex, even if he hadn't been involved in something physical with the two of them.

He'd told her the truth, that they'd gotten close to him, that it had been suspicious, but that it had never gone further than too much wine.

And that Mireia knew enough to regret not speaking out, but not enough to be… responsible, maybe?

Nikki had listened to it all, kindly, gently.

She didn't seem to be judging him.

He felt like maybe she should be judging him a tiny bit.

"We should get back," she said. "We already missed breakfast."

"They can't fire you… since they don't pay you."

"No, they can fire me. Not that they would." She smiled. "But let's head back just in case."

"Okay," he said. He gave her a kiss on the forehead.

She smiled again. "I liked that."

"Me, too."

She drove them back, slowly moving down the steep curve that descended the site of the high bluff. There was no driverfree option along the nameless tracks that led back to Fort Reno; as far as the navigation system was concerned, there weren't any roads out as far as they were.

It was a long enough trip; it would be an hour before they forded the Powder River, crossing at the shallows where no one had bothered to build a bridge.

And Nicolas was spending that trip so far watching her drive, like a goof.

Nikki had been the first to notice the smoke.

"Wildfire?" she said, not that Nicolas would have had an answer. "No... it's not that..."

She started fidgeting with the console, tapping away as she drove past an abandoned ranch.

"I can do that," Nicolas said.

"You don't know what I'm doing."

She was upset.

"I don't think it's near the camp," Nicolas said.

"You don't know that."

She started a voice call.

Nicolas stayed silent as the console pinged.

No response.

"He never answers," Nikki said. "Of course he doesn't answer."

Nicolas read the number. No name listed. That was unusual in itself

"Who are you trying to reach?" he asked her.

"Derrick McPherson. Who else?" She sighed. She stopped the van.

"What's going on?"

She was tapping on the console.

She didn't answer.

"Nikki, please," he said. "Tell me what's happening."

"That smoke," she said. "That's not grass burning. I've seen what it looks like when the grass burns out here. Lots of flame, spreads wide and fast."

Nicolas looked at the plumes of smoke. There was more than one. There were more than a dozen, coming up over the horizon and meeting in the sky.

"You think it's an attack," Nicolas said. "On the camp."

She nodded.

"So we need to get there," he said.

"We don't know what we'll find. It might not be safe, Nic. We need to know what's happening."

"So call the camp."

"I already called the camp. The network's down. Obviously I can hit North Butte, but I can't ping anyone at Fort Reno. And McPherson isn't answering his phone. *Darn* it."

That almost made him laugh, the way she didn't swear.

"So we check out the camp," Nicolas said. "We do it carefully, but we do it."

"We can't stop what's already happened."

"We don't know what's happened. We don't know if people might need our help."

"You're right," she said, like she'd hoped he wasn't.

She started driving again.

They reached the large ranch house at the Powder River and stopped. The road officially bent left, to the south, with a small track—through the middle of the yardsite—that forded the river and led to the road that would bring them to Fort Reno.

"They'll see us coming on the road," she said.

"If they're still there."

Nicolas noticed a woman coming out of the ranch house.

She was waving her hands in the air.

Nicolas opened his window.

"My husband went across to see," she said. "He hasn't come back."

"Is he armed?" Nikki asked, leaning in over Nicolas.

The woman nodded. "He's careful."

"Do you know what happened?"

"The explosions. And gunfire."

Nikki nodded.

Nicolas thanked the woman, and she headed back inside.

"There are two more houses across that river," Nikki said. "Might have more good samaritans out there."

"With guns," Nicolas said.

Nikki nodded.

"We sneak up from some weird place and we might get shot by one of them," Nicolas said.

"So we head in on the road."

"Yeah."

She drove them across the river, along the Streeter Road crossing. They reached the intersection with Lower Sussex Road, and Nikki took them to the left, toward the site of the old fort and plumes of black smoke.

Nicolas saw two men walking back up the road.

They looked like locals, armed with long barreled guns, rifles or shotguns, from what he could tell.

But if they weren't...

Nikki stopped the van.

"We don't have any way to defend ourselves," Nicolas said.

"I know."

She opened her door.

She stepped out, leaving the door ajar.

Nicolas decided to stay where he was.

He told himself it wasn't cowardice. He was a man, more likely to be regarded as a threat.

He would wait. And listen.

And see if he had to get involved.

"It's bad," one of the men said. "Really bad."

"Is anyone still out there?" Nikki asked.

The man shook his head.

The other man told her he was sorry.

Nicolas climbed out of the van.

"This is a strange request," he said, "but can we borrow one of your guns?"

Both men looked over to him, but neither gave him an answer.

Which was probably an answer in itself.

"We can go with you," the first man said, talking to Nikki.

"That would be great," she said. She walked back to the van, pulling open the sliding door on the side. "Nic… you can get in the back, okay?"

He nodded.

And climbed into the back along with the second of the local men.

Nikki drove farther up the road.

To the edge of the maker camp.

Nicolas couldn't see much from the back, but he could see enough.

Whoever had attacked had been thorough. Each van had been hit with some kind of explosive shell, ripped open and smoldering.

He could see some of the bodies, some burnt by fire, most brought down by what was probably shrapnel or bullets.

Nikki stopped the van.

All four of them climbed out.

"I think we were pretty thorough," the first man said. "We didn't find anyone we could help."

"I'd like to look again," Nikki said.

"Yeah. That's fine."

They walked in a circle around the outer camp, then a second circle nearer to the middle, in case they'd missed something or someone.

Nothing was left.

There was little chance of anyone still being alive, and even if they were, they'd be dead long before they could be moved out of there.

Nicolas didn't know how many people; he hadn't counted the bodies.

There was only one person he'd been looking for.

And he hadn't found her.

"Mireia," Nikki said. "I haven't seen her, either."

"She could have run off," the man said. "We can split off into two groups, try to cover some more ground."

"We should stay together," Nicolas said.

Nikki nodded.

They walked past an old tiller, sitting abandoned in the grass.

And found another body. A woman. She'd been hit in the chest and stomach. Gunshots.

"That's Emily," Nikki said. She knelt down beside the body. She leaned in and checked for a pulse.

She stood back up.

They kept moving, toward the river.

And found another body.

A man. Also shot in the chest and stomach.

Nicolas recognized him.

"Mateo," Nikki said.

"He might have been with her," Nicolas said. "When it happened."

"She could have made it down to the river."

Nicolas started running.

"Hold on," one of the men called out.

He didn't slow down.

He ran down to the water.

And he found her.

Lying along the gravel bank.

"Mireia," he said.

He fell down on his knees beside her body.

No wounds in her chest. Or her stomach.

He could see that she was breathing.

He tried to wake her.

"She's cold," he said. "Wet."

"Hypothermia," the first man said as he came down to the riverbank. "You need to be careful with what you do here."

"I know what to do," Nikki said. "We need to get her back to the van."

Nicolas reached for her shoulders.

Nikki grabbed Mireia's ankles.

They carried her up from the bank of the Powder River, back toward the vehicle.

He made sure not to bump her on anything as they walked.

He remembered having cursed Mireia out for dropping his feet on his staircase in Guyane.

When you go through so much with someone, you build a connection that doesn't sever easily. Nicolas knew that he couldn't lose Mireia Lona. She meant too much to him.

❧

Nikki had established an operating base in the nearest ranch house, where one of the good samaritans lived with his teenage son.

The other local had headed back home to check on his family, but promised to come back if needed.

But there wasn't much else they could do.

Mireia was still unconscious, or sleeping, really, her body having needed to slow down as much as it could as its temperature had dropped.

It didn't take ice to make water too cold for the human body. The Powder River in May was still cold enough to kill if you spent enough time in it.

And that seemed to be what Mireia had done, hiding in the water while the camp was attacked. It looked like Mateo had been heading toward the camp when he'd been shot; it was possible that they'd been away when the attack had happened, that Mateo had climbed the bank to check, and that Mireia had heard the shots on her old suitor and known that she had to find a place to conceal herself.

Nikki assured Nicolas that Mireia would be okay. Hiding in the cold water had saved Mireia's life.

The rancher's son had contacted the Sheriff's Office, but they would be at least a half hour, if not longer.

And Nicolas wasn't particularly interested in getting involved with local policing, mostly due to his fake ID; European Arrest Warrants didn't mean automatic US compliance, but he wasn't confident his phony Canadian passport—or Mireia's—would stand up to any scrutiny.

And from what he knew of US Immigration Policy, which wasn't much, even being part of a maker's camp was probably in violation of his tourist visa.

Not that he knew what that would mean.

"We need to go," he said to Nikki, once it was just them and Mireia in the unadorned guest bedroom. "We can't stay here."

"They think the job is done," Nikki replied, "whoever this was. They'll be long gone."

"I don't see how you can know that."

"I don't know. But they wanted to stop us from pulling off that launch tomorrow."

"But that launch wasn't going to be here, was it?"

"No," she said. Her face darkened. "I need to get a hold of Donatello."

She pulled out her tablet and got to work.

"You didn't already try to contact the other camps?" Nicolas asked. Not that he'd seen her doing it.

"I'm not supposed to contact the other camps. It's supposed to go through McPherson."

"The guy who doesn't answer messages."

"Or through the emergency line."

"There's an emergency line? Isn't this an emergency?"

"I tried the emergency line already. While we were driving."

"I thought you only tried McPherson."

"I couldn't even ping the emergency line," she said.

"And you didn't tell me this."

"I didn't know what it meant. And I didn't know…"

"You didn't know…"

"You're not officially part of SolRescue, Nic."

"You're not supposed to be included in this insider stuff."

"Can you get a hold of Donatello?" he asked. There was no point in telling her how excluded she'd made him feel.

"I'll have to call Tyler directly."

"I don't know who that is."

"He's the camp organizer, like me. We're not supposed to have each other's numbers."

"But you do."

"We're friends," she said. "Friends who like to break the rules, apparently. I'm not supposed to call him directly from my tablet. It'll get reported."

"And that's a big deal?"

"Yeah."

"I can call him," Nicolas said. "Is that any better?"

"Maybe… you got your tablet from where?"

"McPherson."

"Yeah, okay. Might not have the same kind of auditing."

She held out her hand.

He passed her his tablet.

She typed in the numbers. She'd gone to the trouble of memorizing them.

Nicolas couldn't remember the last time he'd *dialed* someone.

She specified voice.

Not speaker, but he could hear the pings.

No answer.

"Maybe he didn't want to take a call from some random person," Nicolas said.

She nodded.

But he could tell she didn't agree.

"I can call someone," Nicolas said.

"You're a fugitive," she replied, just slightly above a whisper.

"This is important."

She nodded.

"Do you know where Donatello should be located right now?" he asked her.

She hesitated.

"I know," he said, "I'm not SolRescue."

"They don't tell me, but I can guess. I know the two camps would need to be close enough to share physical resources for the launch, and since didn't relocate last night…"

"You think they've moved close to us."

"Probably set up this morning… within fifty miles."

"That might be enough to figure this out," Nicolas said.

It was his turn to dial, the one number he had memorized.

The one person he'd promised never to contact again.

His ex-wife Madeleine answered the voice call.

"Nicolas," she said. *"Qu'est-ce qui passe?"*

He apologized, and told her it was important. He said that he needed her to connect into the ESA sats.

"You want me to risk my job for you?" she asked, in her clipped and staccato Parisian French.

He missed her so much.

"Lives depend on it," he said. "Depend on you."

That was all he'd needed to tell her.

She started the connection.

He waited.

"To where?" she asked.

"I need coordinates," he said to Nikki. He switched to speaker and held out his tablet.

She grabbed her own tablet and quickly found and read off the coordinates. "43.8275 by -106.24."

"Within eighty kilometers of that location," Nicolas said to Madeleine, "you should see smoke."

"There's smoke at your location," Madeleine replied. "Are you alright?"

"There should be more smoke," Nikki said. "A second location."

Should be. Like she expected it. For Donatello to be in ruins, for all its makers to be lying dead in the grass.

Putain.

"I see it," Madeleine said. She rattled off the coordinates, which Nikki tapped into her tablet.

She passed the tablet to Nicolas.

Empty land near something called Charlie Reservoir; it sounded like some guy named Charlie had just started damming up a creek on a lazy Sunday afternoon.

Even more remote than Fort Reno, while still surprisingly close to I-90.

He thanked his ex-wife and disconnected.

"We should head over there," Nicolas said. "See if anyone's okay."

"We can't," Nikki said. "It's too dangerous."

"You told me they were done. That they'd figured we were all dead."

"What if you're right? What if they're keeping count, if they know that the three of us are missing?"

"You think they'd have that kind of information?" he asked. "That would require some serious spying."

"They were spying," he heard Mireia say.

He looked over to her. Her eyes were still closed.

"Mateo knew it was coming," she said. "He led me away from the camp."

"To save you," Nicolas said.

"I think so."

"I don't know about that," Nikki said.

"What do you mean?" Mireia asked, opening her eyes. "He... he told me."

"She's not lying, Nikki," Nicolas said.

Mireia took a heavy breath and started to sit up. "She thinks I'm lying?"

"It's okay, Mireia." He looked over to Nikki, shaking his head.

Did she really want to start an argument with someone who'd come so close to dying?

"All of the camps are at risk," Nikki said.

"They must know that," Mireia said. "If Nicolas could find that out..."

"She's right," Nicolas said. "So we should see what we can do to help."

"We need to find a place to lay low," Nikki said. "Until we know what's happened."

"We know what's happened. Dozens of people were murdered today. Maybe hundreds. And if we can save one or two people—"

"We should go to Donatello," Mireia said. "Even if we're too late to save anyone. Someone should be a witness to what happened."

Nicolas' tablet started to ping.

Not some unprecedented call from Madeleine.

No contact information at all. Voice request.

He answered.

"David Tarbion?" the voice asked. Derrick McPherson.

"Yes," Nicolas said.

"Is your wife with you?"

"Yes."

"Good. You need to leave."

"And go where?" Nicolas asked.

"Get to I-90 and head west. I'll let you know."

The call ended.

"That was McPherson," Nicolas said. "Telling us where to go."

"I'll tell him where to go," Nikki said. "Jerk won't call me back, then he calls you."

"I don't get it, either… but we need to go."

"What about Donatello?" Mireia asked.

Nicolas shook his head. "There's no time for that. We need to go."

Mireia was looking him over. She glanced over to Nikki.

Then she gave Nicolas a nod.

And lowered her head back down to the bed.

38

THE FIRST SolRescue launch would be in late October, outside Brownsville, Texas, at SpaceX's Boca Chica facility. From what Anita had been told by her contact at SpaceX, it was specifically because they wanted to have better control of the media frenzy they expected to result, and Boca Chica was their best hope of doing that.

And they had wanted Anita to be there, not just on launch day, but for at least two weeks before. So they'd given her a suite at one of the condos on South Padre Island, the eighth floor, overlooking the cloudy Gulf of Mexico, just two blocks from the private ferry SpaceX used to bring employees and media from South Padre to the launch site, just south of the state park on Brazos Island.

Anita had only been in South Padre for half a day, but she'd already had her first taste of life outside New York City. Two autograph requests from other student-y types, and a lecture on history from a starstruck—yes, starstruck *by her*—about the old port on Brazos Island, abandoned and swept away by the storms.

No one came up to her in New York, other than fellow Cornell Tech students asking about the project, but that was New York, where celebrities could ride the subway, and you just expected to see famous people walking their dogs along The Mall in Central Park or picking up their own dry cleaning pretty much everywhere in Manhattan and certain hip slices of Brooklyn.

But Anita was famous in South Padre, and she'd been famous on the flights in, having been approached more than once in the terminal in Houston, and finally having been followed by a slightly creepy South Asian man to the car rental desk in Brownsville.

She already knew that being a celebrity—even a D-Lister—wasn't something she wanted, and on the drive to South Padre she'd started daydreaming of a Salinger-like existence on some acreage in New Hampshire.

She'd finally get her own dog, just to know what the fuss was all about, and she'd live alone with her own little home lab, and there'd be no awkward conversations about Carter, when she'd press him about Bridget, and he'd completely fail to dodge the questions.

They'd let her back in to SolRescue, but only on the edges.

She met with the Flight Director himself for lunch, at the cafeteria-channeling cafe in the control center at Boca Chica. Jack Roland was exactly what you'd expect a Flight Director to be like, an overstressed acerbic middle-aged white guy who seemed to be both annoyed and attracted by Anita.

She'd known before meeting him that he'd never been a fan of the partnership with three "publicity-whoring Cornell students", which was the exact quote she remembered from an email Carter had forwarded her, back before she'd taken that other job and pretty much ruined everything in her life.

He'd looked her up and down as she'd entered the room.

"I thought you'd be taller," he said with a grin as he shook her hand.

"Thanks," she said.

"So you're the face of SolRescue."

"I think that's Carter."

"Well, you're the prettier face, then."

"And Bridget?"

"Oh, I like Bridget," he said.

"I don't get what you're trying to do, Mr. Roland. Aside from keep me from feeling comfortable."

He laughed.

Then led her toward a table.

"They have waitresses," he said, "but you go up to get your own salad and drinks. I think it's European or something."

He sat down. No attempt at pulling out her chair, which she found herself okay with.

She sat across from him.

"I know the work should be done with you," he said. "So I don't know why they brought you here so goddamn early."

"Optics?"

"You know I wasn't a big proponent of this relationship. But it won't be a problem, Ms. Singhal. Or can I call you Anita?"

"Either's fine."

"You know I've received three phone calls this morning about you. Reporters asking me when we're meeting, where we're meeting, what we'll talk about... they act like you walked on Mars. It's pretty frustrating, actually."

"I'm sorry," Anita said, "but I don't really control that stuff."

"So you make a video with some cut-rate graphics. And that's all it took."

"Will this help you achieve something, Mr. Roland?"

"I just want to understand, Ms. Singhal. Anita. What's so special about three college kids with no real-world experience?"

"Are you angry about the ageism? Or because you guys were more focused on moving onto Mars than saving the Earth?"

He groaned. "Saving the Earth? You really believe that?"

"Um... you don't, I take it?"

"The oceans are being poisoned, the plane you came in on is still polluting the atmosphere... and you haven't actually built anything yet."

"What's your point, Mr. Roland?"

"No point, really," he said. "I'm just venting."

"Can you scream into a pillow or something instead?"

He chuckled.

"Look," Anita said, "I'm really grateful for the work you guys have been doing for us. If it wasn't for SpaceX, we would have had to launch from god knows where. If at all."

"Saved you some work, too, I hear. You could focus on two vehicle designs instead of three."

"And gave us a boost with the government."

"No," he said, "the government still hates you."

She sighed. "That's something I don't understand. I mean, I get why you don't like me."

He smiled. "I like you, Anita, except when I don't. But the government... yeah, they always hate you. Because you're doing something they don't like people doing."

"Trying to make things better?"

"Doing things on your own. Saying that you don't need the government for something like this."

"That's what you guys did," she said. "Elon Musk didn't sit back and wait on NASA."

"Elon plays ball with the government. He stays on the right side of the line. You haven't done that. You don't even know where the goddamn line is."

"You're right... I don't."

He nodded. "Here's a hint, then. You cross the line when you accept funding from non-friendly nations."

"We didn't do that."

"Donors in China, in Russia, in Iran for god's sake."

"People. Not governments."

He leaned in across the table. "There's a lot of money that's been spent on climate change, Anita. On investing in the future we've all been expecting. When you try to change that future, you're taking all of that investment and flushing it down the toilet."

"And trying to prevent the East Sheet from collapsing, stop the Gulf Stream from failing…"

"You don't need to sell me on it," Roland said.

"Sounds like I do."

"I'll do my job, Ms. Singhal. And you'll do yours."

"Okay…"

"Just don't be surprised when you find out you have almost as many enemies as friends."

"And exactly which one are you, Mr. Roland?"

"Like I said. Sometimes I like you."

She smiled.

If nothing else, she appreciated his honesty.

Danny Pyke hadn't bothered to message her.

He'd apparently decided to take the ferry down to Staten Island un-announced.

And he'd shown up at Anita's front door, early enough on Sunday morning that she hadn't had a chance to escape to the city.

"I didn't invite you over," she said, holding the door as close to her body as she could, to block him from seeing into her world.

"We can take a walk… I hear Tompkinsville is lovely this time of year."

"I don't need that kind of crap."

"Will you take a walk with me, Ms. Singhal?"

She rolled her eyes at him. With added emphasis. "I'll have to get dressed first."

"Yeah, alright."

"And you can wait out here."

He smiled.

She hated that.

That he seemed to enjoy how poorly she treated him.

Anita led Danny Pyke up Grant Street, deciding on the loop along Homer Street as a strategy to keep the visit short.

"I need you to come with me," he said. "To *Basilica*."

"To the oversized garbage scow."

He laughed. "Never heard anyone call it that."

"Then you live under a rock. Or in a startup bubble."

Another laugh from Danny Pyke.

Which forced her to roll her eyes again.

"I won't go to the seastead," Anita said. "Bridget already asked me, and I already said no."

"It's part of your job."

"Don't do that."

"What?"

"Pretend like I'm actually working for you," she said. "When you know I'm an advisor."

"I don't see the difference. Really, I don't."

"I told you, Anita. Whatever it takes to make this company work."

"You promised me, Mr. Pyke. I didn't promise you."

"Please, Anita…"

"I'm not going out there."

"You need to talk to him."

"To Carter. The answer is still no."

"Look," he said. "Something has happened. Something bad. We really need you to go out there and talk to him."

"I'm not a life coach."

"They killed a lot of people this morning. SolRescue people."

"Who did?"

"Homebrewed land drones. 3D printed. Built to fire .223s from any popup gun show in the country. To be as deniable as possible."

"Deniable. By the American government."

"We think so," he said. "Three different maker camps. Almost a hundred people gunned down, some still missing."

"The SolRescue maker camps."

"Yeah."

"The ones Carter said were only tinkering, with no official projects."

"Yeah."

"Which was a lie no one believed."

"Pretty much. Look, Anita, this attack killed any chance of mounting a sovereignty claim on STeLa-1."

"Which was far fetched as it was."

"Do you even care that this happened?" he asked her.

"What do you want me to say?"

"I want you to help us."

She shook her head. "I can't fix Carter Elgin."

"What do you mean?"

"If Bridget reached out to me about Carter, that means that Carter was already losing touch before any of this happened."

"Losing touch."

"Yeah."

"He won't even talk to me," Danny said. "Won't talk to anyone."

"Not even Bridget."

"He needs to talk to you, Anita."

"Well, I don't want to talk to him." She knew she sounded immature.

Petty. Self-absorbed.

And she knew it was her go-to defense mechanism. She'd had to build that up. She'd had to.

"Please, Anita," Danny said. "It's not about me and Turnpike, or about you and Carter and Bridget. It's about the sunshield."

"You really think it's in danger."

"Yeah. I do. We've heard things."

"We. We meaning Carter and Derrick McPherson."

"Yeah."

She was curious. She couldn't not be.

"What things?" she asked.

He stopped walking. He glanced around.

Making it pretty obvious to anyone who might actually be watching that things were about to get interesting. That eavesdropping was about to bring a big payout.

"Sovereignty wasn't about future protection," he said. "The US and Chinese governments have been actively working to take control of the sunshield by any means necessary."

"That's nothing new."

"They're going to destroy it, Anita."

"That's insane."

"Oh, they'll have a replacement ready to go. A replacement that they own. Which is a lot more dangerous than—"

"I know, Danny," she said. "I know what it can be used for. I came up with the damn thing." She and Bridget...

"The US project is faltering. Which might be a bad thing for us. The Chinese junta might have been counting on that, since they seem to be ready to take over the whole thing. No more bilateral partnership. One country running the shield."

"Not a country. A handful of unbalanced generals ruling over a fifth of the planet."

"I don't get it, Anita. You know the stakes. Why won't you help?"

Why wouldn't she... that was always the question, wasn't it? Why wouldn't she come to see Carter? Why wouldn't she settle with Bridget? Why wouldn't she come out of her self-imposed exile, and let the world worship her for something she hadn't worked on in decades?

You see, world, there's one thing you don't know about me. I fucking hate who I've become.

She felt Danny grab her hand.

He gave it a squeeze.

"I care about you, Anita," he said. "You need to do this. Please."

She pulled her hand away. "I don't need to do anything."

She turned around and started back toward home.

Visit over.

She didn't need anyone dropping by to guilt her.

"I can't go there without you," Danny called out.

She looked back to him.

"Please, Anita."

"I won't do it," she said. "End of story. End of conversation."

He threw his hands up.

But he didn't say anything else.

She made her way back home.

She glanced around for any sign of Danny Pyke, then went inside.

She sat down on her couch.

He sent her a message instead.

I don't know what happened with Carter and Bridget. I wasn't there. But we all need you now. And yes, this is about to get corny, Ms. Singhal. We need you to come back and save the world.

She didn't respond.

She searched her fridge for last night's wine.

And remember too late that she'd already finished it.

"I shouldn't have to do it," she said, out loud. "I shouldn't have to talk to him."

Her coffee table didn't come up with a cogent counterargument.

She looked over to the telescope in the corner of her living room, the one she hadn't used once since she'd moved to her place on Staten Island.

The last time she'd used it was long before she'd moved from her place in Chelsea, that mostly-glass block that fronted the High Line that she'd known she couldn't afford from the moment she'd signed the lease.

She'd taken the telescope and brought it out to where the path splits in two over 13th Street, where there's that stretch of original track purposely overgrown by a stretch of flowering bushes.

She'd set up for a view of Mars, since as impressive as the sunshield was, it was a little hard to see from New York City at night.

And she'd spent three hours there, letting people who came by peek into the eyepiece, answering their questions about Mars and telescopes and—obviously—about the sunshield.

It was one of the happiest nights of her life.

But that was New York, where you could stand out on the High Line with a telescope and a low-level celebrity status and just *be*. And that was how things were supposed to remain, just a Manhattan girl gracefully resting on her laurels, only being famous when she wanted to be famous.

And Carter had ruined that. Not Bridget, because Anita had never been foolish enough to blame Bridget for what had happened. It was because

Carter had felt entitled to everything and everyone, and he'd fucked it all up and *someone* had needed to go.

Anita Singhal's life was wrapped up in Carter Elgin.

She couldn't escape it. Just like she couldn't stop loving him, even as she hated him.

That's why she needed to stay away.

Because he still had that power over her, all the power over her.

Because somehow he still *owned* her, like she was just some dusty trophy he'd taken off his shelf and stuffed into the back of his storage room.

It disgusted her.

It made her *so goddamn angry.*

But she couldn't escape what she knew.

That she was the one who'd given herself up to that.

"And as long as I let it be like this," she said, "it just... is."

She could blame herself and she could blame Carter Elgin.

But it didn't change any other piece of the universe.

She sent a reply to Danny Pyke.

She'd go with him. She'd talk to Carter.

She'd do what she could to help.

Anita knew that she'd lost a lot of who she was since that night on the High Line.

No. That wasn't it.

She hadn't lost it.

She'd given it up.

39

BENJ RODE with Malik in the back of the pickup truck, south down Highway 6. He would occasionally look in on Rachael, not that he expected the East Asian man in the driver's seat to be doing anything sinister, even if the truck seemed to be on driverfree.

He didn't ask about Laila; he didn't know why Malik was lying, why he'd accused Benj of murdering her.

What good did that do? Was it meant to turn Rachael against him?

They turned right onto the gravel road to South Indian Lake, a name that seemed old-fashioned even to a man who'd spent a few years in a state with an overabundance of ankle-length skirts.

Only a few miles up that road they reached a white passenger van with decals for a "Great Nelson Adventures Company". Benj knew the moment the pickup started slowing down that they were about to be transferred.

"It'll be comfier," Malik said as he helped Benj out of the box. "Ridin' in style to our surprise destination."

"Which is?" Benj asked.

"I *know* you know what a surprise is, Benj."

"I just wish I knew whose side you're on."

"The right side," Malik said with a smile, "which also happens to be the winning side. A side you can still be on, if you play this right."

"I don't believe that."

Malik shook his head. "Your name is worth more than anything else about you. You're one lucky asshole, Benj. If it was up to me, you'd already be lying in a ditch with half your head blown clear off."

He loaded Benj into the van, third row. He noticed a driver and a man in the passenger seat. The passenger looked East Asian as well, while the driver looked Southern European or possibly Middle Eastern.

Neither of them spoke.

Rachael came next, put in the middle row, both she and Benj belted in for safety, among other reasons.

"You're okay?" she asked Benj.

"I'm okay," he replied, wondering if that was something he'd been supposed to ask.

"We're going on an adventure, apparently."

"An adventure?"

She nodded. "Says so right on the side of the van."

Malik climbed into the van and sat down beside Benj, while his partner took a seat next to Rachael.

"What about the truck?" Benj asked.

"That thing's diesel," Malik said. "Waste not, want not."

"Whatever."

The man beside Rachael looked back at him. But he didn't speak.

"No one talks," Rachael said. "No one but Mr. Malik. Why is that?"

"They can talk just fine," Malik said. "Maybe you're just not worth the effort, you know?"

The van started moving, turning around and heading back toward Highway 6.

"Heading to the Nelson," Rachael said.

"That's a river, right?" Benj asked.

"Yeah. Heads down to Hudson Bay, just like the Churchill."

"Don't worry," Malik said. "You're not lunch for the polar bears, Rachael. That would be a little too symmetrical, wouldn't you say?"

"I take it you know everything about me," she said.

"Rachael Duck. SolRescue groupie. Self-absorbed bitch. And Carter Elgin's latest obsession."

"You forgot to mention that I'm a morning person."

"So this is the plan, is it? Try to show us the old cool-under-pressure thing? Such wit, Rachael. Such wit."

"This is what Malik does," Benj said. "He likes to push people's buttons."

"He hasn't found my buttons," Rachael said. "Doubt he ever will."

Malik just shook his head and smiled.

That was worse than if he'd fired back.

The van turned off of Highway 6 onto a road marked 280, but with a different marker than the provincial highways; Benj took that to mean that the quality of the road could go downhill pretty quick, which was saying a lot considering the sorry state of the two-lane they'd taken from Churchill.

Maybe it was the extreme temperatures or the permafrost; all he knew was that the roads in Northern Manitoba were uniformly terrible.

They drove through a collection of houses along the road, passing a sign for Tataskweyak Cree Nation. Benj had no idea if Rachael was Cree, or something else. But he decided not to bring it up.

After a turnoff to some place named Keeyask, the paved road gave way to gravel, travelling through nothing but forest for over an hour before becoming paved again at an intersection.

The van turned left, away from the signs for the town of Gillam. Still heading east, from what Benj could tell.

He started to see the wide water of a river, likely the Nelson. The road—now marked 290 instead of 280—was following the shore, toward Hudson Bay.

They drove past a huge transformer station, along with signs for Limestone GS, which Benj assumed was the name for a nearby hydroelectric dam.

They passed by white Manitoba Hydro pickups—white being the default color for trucks, it seemed—and a few larger yellow trucks with cabling and other power-company type of equipment.

The van seemed to get little notice; "adventure" tourism was likely a common thing.

The road was still paved. They reached what looked like a work site that had just stopped.

"Conawapa," Rachael said. "Might never be finished."

"There's so much potential here," Malik said. "I've never understood why Canada never did more with all of it."

Rachael shook her head, but didn't reply.

The van drove to what looked like the end of the road, where the straight line of gravel hit a wall of evergreens, with only a little track continuing into the forest, too narrow for a truck.

The van started backing up.

"He missed the turn off," Malik said.

The van didn't turn around, just continued reversing, until it reached a gravel turnoff on the right. Then the van drove along the tight winding road, brushing against the trees as it went. And reached the banks of the Nelson River.

Where a 20 foot motorboat was waiting, still sitting on its trailer.

"Now we take to the water," Malik said.

"This is ridiculous," Rachael said. "You could have dumped our bodies two hours ago."

"Rachael..." Benj said.

"She's right," Malik said. "But this isn't about dumping bodies. It's something way cooler than that." He chuckled. "Now you're probably expecting UFOs or shit."

Malik climbed up and helped his partner bring Rachael out of the van, each grabbing an elbow; they seemed more worried about her running off than they'd been at the last transfer.

They were closer to civilization. That had to be the reason.

Once Rachael was sitting on the gravel by the river, they brought Benj out. They sat him down a good six feet away from her.

Then the four men got to work on the boat, backing the van up, hooking the trailer, then backing the boat down what a gravel boat launch, Malik and the passenger from the front seat wading into the river as the boat barely reached the waterline. That left the olive-skinned driver in the van, and the fourth man as spotter, standing to the side and signalling with his hands.

Benj watched at the boat was disconnected from the trailer, hazardously earlier than he'd remembered from the three times he'd ever been to a lake, Malik and the other man in the water guiding the boat past a series of barely submerged rocks.

Not the best boat launch.

Benj knew that it might be their only chance to escape.

He noticed Rachael was looking at him.

She was thinking the same thing.

They could make a run up the road, trying to reach the work camp, hoping someone was still there, that the project wasn't completely forgotten.

And that was about all they could do.

The river was far too wide and powerful; it wasn't like they could just swim to the other side without getting swept with the current and drowned, sooner or later.

And even if they'd somehow managed to fight across to the other bank… there was nothing there for them, and the men who'd be chasing them had a goddamn motorboat.

He shook his head at her.

She made it clear that she didn't agree.

She was going to try.

"Don't run, Rachael," he said, making sure it was loud enough for their captors to hear.

The spotter dropped his hands and came over.

The driver also stopped what he was doing, climbing out and jogging up to them.

Almost as if he was wanting to get in front of the other man.

"It's a terrible idea," the driver said to her, in an accent that reminded Benj of the Northeast US. "This doesn't need to end with you dying, Rachael. Not if you do as you're asked."

She glared at Benj.

It didn't matter how she felt.

They would have killed her.

The motorboat took them down the Nelson River, the driver of the van having taken over as the driver of the boat.

Malik cheerfully pointed out two polar bears, a mother and her cub, walking along the bank of the river. "Do you know them personally, Rachael?" he asked. "Should we consider them a threat?"

Malik reached into his jacket.

He pulled out his pistol.

"I've never had to defend myself against a polar bear," he said.

"What the hell, Malik?" Benj said.

Rachael was looking away, at the opposite bank.

She was trying to ignore him.

Which Benj knew would make Malik go farther.

"Slow the boat, captain," Malik said. "I've got some target practice coming on."

As the boat slowed, Malik pointed his gun toward the bears.

"Killing those bears won't change a thing," Rachael said. "You'll still be a pathetic loser who sold himself to the highest bidder."

"What did you just say to me?" Malik said. "Did you forget who's running this operation?"

"Malik," the man driving the boat said.

"Shut the fuck up, Dav."

"Shoot the bear, asshole," Rachael said. "Shoot them both."

"Or maybe I'll shoot you," he said.

"You'd better shoot me first," Benj said.

"My hero," Rachael said. "Just stay out of this, alright?"

"Let's drop her off on shore," Malik said. "See if these bears like her as much as she seems to like them."

"Sǐ pì yǎn," one of the East Asian men said. Angrily.

The other East Asian man said something else, and the two began to argue.

"Would you two give it a rest?" Malik said.

"Do they even speak English?" Rachael asked. "Is that a requirement for Chinese Special Ops?"

Malik sneered. "Oh, so goddamn smart. The shadowy Chinese guys are working for the Chinese government."

"And I guess you are, too," Benj said. "Pretty disappointing, Malik."

"Disappointing?" Malik said. "You're one to talk, Benj. Your whole life is a special exhibit. Disappointment on display."

"How long you been thinking that one up?" Rachael said. "You two seem to have some unfinished business."

Malik put his gun away. "You know what? We do have unfinished business."

"Yeah," Benj said. "I guess we do. Since you were obviously involved in my career being completely trashed."

"Fuck, no, Benj. You did that on your own. Feeding secrets to Daddy, fornicating with Samantha Yoon…"

"There was no fornicating, dumbass."

"You're the reason Laila's dead, Benj. That was you, not me. If I'd had the power, I would have saved her from you. You ruined her life, you know that?"

"Do you even work for any branch of the US Government?" Benj asked. "Or is it Chinese junta all the way down?"

"I answer directly to the President."

"Bullshit."

"Fuck you, Benj."

"This is going nowhere," Dav—the driver—said. "All you are doing is pissing them off, Malik."

"And what's wrong with that? Pretty dull trip otherwise. Look, a tree. Look, another goddamn polar bear."

"It's beautiful out here," Rachael said. "The fact that you can't see that—"

"Shut up," Malik said.

"How long has this been going on, Malik?" Benj asked.

"What?"

"How long have you been spying on me?"

"With your stupid eyepiece?" Malik said.

"Yeah."

"I only came to Utah to spy on you, Benj. My whole career has been spying on you."

"Is that supposed to be a joke?"

"No joke," Malik said. "McPherson's kid gets a plum job at the NSA Data Center. Oh, yeah, that's totally legit."

"Pretty boring job," Rachael said. "Spying on Benj."

Malik grinned. "We've had some good times. You were fucking Taylor for a while… and she was *nasty*."

"So what is this about?" Benj asked. "Why are you taking us all this way?"

"Just wait and see," Malik said. "Just wait and see."

The Nelson River passed several collections of small islands—and one big one—before it started widening on its way to the ocean. The ground was relatively flat, the rise from the bank being about the only change in elevation Benj could see.

He saw what looked like a manmade structure up ahead, a reasonable straight line near the horizon.

As they came closer, he realized it was a long truss bridge, leading from the shore to a small island. The island itself seemed as unnatural as the bridge, like it just didn't belong, a clump of flat land just high enough to peek above the water, sitting out in the middle of a wide river mouth.

On the far edge of that island was a large iron boat, cracked in two on the shore like a broken joint, the smaller chunk holding some kind of crane.

From one end of the island, moving upriver in their direction, was the broken up remains of some kind of improvised breakwater, built from wood and sand or dirt.

"What the hell is that?" he asked.

"Port Nelson," Rachael said. "Before Churchill took its place as the end of the Hudson Bay Railroad."

"This was a port?"

"For a little while."

"There's an old fort or something near here," Malik said. "Up the other river... the Hayes."

"York Factory," Rachael said.

"No one's there right now. Not really tourist season just yet."

"Is that where we're going?" Benj asked. "To some old fort?"

"It was a trading post," Rachael said.

"This is our stop," Malik said. "Port Nelson, like the bitch said."

Rachael didn't bite.

Dav brought the boat to the left of the breakwater, between the small island and the mainland, heading downriver toward the rail bridge, which Benj counted as having seventeen low-rising spans, a half dozen of their wood plank decks collapsed into the river.

Dav reached a small floating dock by a small white building.

Malik hopped out and tied off the boat.

One of the Chinese men helped Rachael out onto the dock, then Benj.

Malik grabbed Rachael by the shoulder, pulling her close.

She didn't speak.

He reached into his pocket and pulled out a small pocketknife.

He cut her wrists free, then gave her a light shove to the side.

He walked over to Benj.

"You aren't scared of us," Benj said.

"You have nowhere to go," Malik said. "And there's no way in hell you'd have the guts to try and take us out."

"Why's that?" Rachael asked. "Why shouldn't we take at least one or two of you down?"

"Because you don't need to die here," Dav said. "Please, Rachael. Trust me on this."

"We don't trust any of you," Benj said. "Why would we?"

"We're going to play a game on that," Malik said. "Right here, right now."

"What the fuck are you talking about?" Rachael said.

"We're going to teach you guys something. About how this is going to work. Start walking, toward that bridge."

Rachael rolled her eyes. "Go fuck yourself."

Malik stepped over to her.

He gave her a harder shove, moving her forward to the rail bridge.

Benj decided to follow along.

Rachael kept moving, too, without another shove needed.

They reached the edge of the bridge.

To where there was a six foot gap between the land and the bridge deck.

"How far can you jump?" Malik asked, looking to Rachael.

"All this way to drown me in the river," she said. "What a fucking waste of time."

"Just face the bridge and shut up."

Rachael did as she was told, which surprised Benj.

Malik turned to Benj. "You, too," he said.

Benj walked up beside Rachael. He looked over to her, but she was doing her best not to look at him.

"We'll be okay," he told her. Which he knew was a stupid thing to say.

She didn't respond.

"So I'm going to ask you both some questions," Malik said. "And each question will have a right answer and a wrong answer. Right answers are the ones we're looking for here. Wrong answers get people jabbed in the back with a pocketknife. If you're lucky, that kind of stabbing won't make you lose your balance and fall headfirst into a bridge pier."

Benj felt the blade poking at his back.

All those times when you imagine swinging around and disarming the asshole who's threatening you with a knife…

Benj knew he wouldn't be able to win.

"Okay, Benj," Malik said. "You get to go first. Tell me… what information did you pass onto you father from the NSA?"

"I don't need to tell you anything," Benj said.

"One more chance, Benj. What information did you pass onto your father?"

"Mostly recipes."

He felt the knife stab into his lower back, feeling almost like a bad burn.

"Hope that didn't knick anything important," Malik said.

It didn't *feel* that deep. It just hurt like hell.

"So that's illustrative," Malik said. "A wrong answer. Here's what we were looking for, Benj. You sent records of calls sent between two ESA workers in French Guiana. Not the content, just the logs. Does that sound right to you?"

"Yes," Benj said. "I don't know what was sent. He never asked for the content."

"Your father knew the content," Malik said. "Didn't he, Rachael?"

Benj slowly moved his head to the left, watching as Malik pressed the knife against Rachael's back, close to her lower spine.

"I asked you a question," Malik said. "Did Derrick McPherson, and by extension, Carter Elgin, know what those ESA workers were talking about?"

She didn't respond.

"Explain the game to her, Benj," Malik said.

"Just tell him, Rachael," Benj said. "It doesn't matter."

"Is that a direct order, sir?" Rachael said.

"This isn't a joke," Malik said. "You think I won't stab just because you've got ovaries?"

"You don't know if I have ovaries. Not like you can see them from there. Maybe you should cut a little opening and take a look."

"What are you doing, Rachael?" Benj asked. "He will hurt you, okay?"

"Everyone knows what was sent," she said. "It's not a secret anymore. Eduard Hubrak and Riley Crouch... those are their names, right? Everyone will know their names soon enough."

Malik pulled back.

What had seemed like a non-answer to Benj seemed to have been enough.

"Now for the hard questions," Malik said.

"We don't know anything," Rachael said.

"What?"

"We don't know anything you don't already know. We only matter if they think we matter."

"By they—"

"Yeah. Derrick and Carter. We're just a couple of hostages. No value outside of that."

Malik started to chuckle.

He put his knife back into his pocket.

"There's no point in asking why we shouldn't kill you," he said. "You seem to know what this is all about."

He said something to the other men; not English.

Probably Mandarin Chinese.

The two Chinese operatives walked over to the white shed. They opened an unlocked door and pulled a metal ladder, maybe eight feet long.

They brought it over to the bridge, laying it across the gap.

The two men each grabbed onto the bottom rung.

"Bitches first," Malik said. "I mean that in a complimentary way."

Rachael stepped toward the ladder.

"You should shimmy along on all fours," Dav said. "Should be safer that way."

Rachael nodded, then got down on hands and knees.

She slowly crossed the ladder.

"What's the point of this?" Benj asked. "There's a perfectly good boat back at the dock."

"Just cross the ladder," Malik said.

So Benj got down on his hands and knees and crossed behind Rachael.

Once he'd reached the other side, the two Chinese operatives pulled the ladder back to their side of the gap.

"So what is this, exactly?" Benj asked. "You're stranding us?"

"You guys will wait here," Malik said. "Simple as that."

"For how long?"

"For as long as it takes."

"What the hell are you talking about?" Rachael said.

"I have a life outside of you guys," Malik said. "So shut the fuck up and wait."

He started on his way back to the dock, the two Chinese operatives following behind.

Dav stayed standing beside the gap.

"You're our babysitter," Rachael said.

Dav nodded.

"You think Malik's an asshole," she said.

Dav gave a little shrug.

Then he started walking along the shore of the island, toward the wrecked ship.

"Where are you going?" Rachael asked.

He didn't answer.

Rachael didn't look like she wanted to talk.

So Benj sat down on the cold wood planks and waited.

He looked over at her every so often, and whenever he did she'd make sure she was looking the other way.

She was an expert at avoiding eye contact.

For entertainment, Benj watched Dav wander around the island, down at the boat, then back at the shed, then checking in at the foot of the bridge… he looked very much like someone who'd never been there before, or at least someone who hadn't gotten a chance to look around.

Dav wouldn't answer any questions, whether from Benj or Rachael; he wouldn't say anything at all, just shrug if anything, before wandering off again.

He didn't seem like some secret agent or whatever. He seemed like a man who hadn't gotten used to following Malik's orders.

Benj hoped that there was something there that would help, some divide between Dav and Malik, and between the two Americans and the operatives from China.

They weren't really a team.

And they probably didn't agree on much.

The sun had set before Malik returned to the island.

Dav had gone to the dock to greet the boat, and from the bridge Benj could make out six people on board. Once they'd tied off and unloaded, he realized that three of the six were ziptied like he'd been. And they had what looked like laundry bags thrown over their heads.

Benj wondered why Malik hadn't bothered with hoods for him and Rachael.

The three prisoners were marched off the dock, but weren't led over to the bridge.

Instead, the two Chinese operatives brought the ladder back, laying it across to the gap.

They didn't say anything, but Benj took the hint and started making his way across.

After almost thirty seconds of hesitation, Rachael followed.

The Chinese operatives bound both Benj and Rachael with new zipties, wrists behind their backs as before.

But no laundry bags of their own.

They were marched over to join the other three captives.

From that point Benj had no trouble figuring out who they were. Two women and one man. Chloe, Samantha, and Jared.

"We had to kill two conservation officers," Malik said. "Because of you, Rachael."

"Rachael?" Jared said.

"I'm here," she said. "I'm okay." She seemed embarrassed for saying it.

She hadn't asked about her brother.

Benj assumed it was some desperate hope on her part, that Malik had somehow overlooked Rachael's brother, that he'd just assumed it was Cannae Friesen and that other conservation officer who'd been involved.

Benj knew that Malik wouldn't have overlooked anyone.

The Chinese operatives led each captive back to the boat, one by one, loading them in.

Nine people. Seemed like too many to Benj. But he knew very little about boats.

Dav took back his job of driving, ferrying them upriver, then back downriver, circling around the breakwater and island, then moving closer to the north bank of the Nelson.

Just over a mile downriver was some kind of landing, probably built and last maintained back when the bridge had first been built.

Malik hopped out just short of the shore, grabbing a rope and tying it off on a fallen log.

Dav stood up and walked over to Jared.

He pulled off the hood.

And did the same for Chloe and Samantha.

Then he and the Chinese operatives helped the prisoners overboard, and they all waded onto shore.

There was nothing there.

No buildings, no roads.

Just gravel turning into grass, then a forest of evergreens, taller and thicker than Churchill, but not as heavy as they'd seen along Highway 6.

Malik started marching toward the trees.

There was no reason not to follow in behind.

He led the group along an overgrown trail that you wouldn't have noticed if you weren't looking for it.

The trail was straight, but there was the occasional tree disrupting the flow, fighting to sink the path back into the wilderness.

Malik turned right, onto another forgotten trail. Also straight.

They used to be roads.

It used to be a town.

After fifteen minutes of walking, they reached a wood house, both siding and shingles, still standing but obviously worn down by years of neglect.

The panes of the windows had fallen, but hadn't shattered, the glass still hanging from the sunken frames.

The door was still intact.

Malik turned the handle and opened it, then walked inside.

Benj was first in behind him.

The inside had been cleaned up.

There was a set of batteries on the floor, under a folding dock. And a screen on top of that dock, ready to go. There was a kitchen table, probably original, but with a clean tablecloth spread over. And a mismatched array of chairs, over a dozen, lined up along the wall.

"Home sweet home," Malik said.

"What is this?" Rachael asked.

"Our hideout."

"What the fuck does that mean?"

"Where they're going to hold us," Benj said. "Until they're done with us."

The Chinese operatives wordlessly led the captives to chairs, wrapping each of them around the backs with several layers of duct tape.

"Some of you have value," Malik said. "Some of you probably don't."

"He's talking about you, Sam," Rachael said.

"I've got value," Samantha said.

"Not sure you do," Malik said.

"We'll make contact with Carter Elgin," Dav said. "Discuss terms."

"Terms for what?" Jared asked.

"Succession planning," Malik said. "Carter and Derrick McPherson are nearing retirement age. It's about time we talked about what happens next."

"We know what happens next," Rachael said. "The Chinese destroy the sunshield and replace it with one of their own. And then they call the shots for everyone. I mean, after they kill off idiots like you, the ones who thought they had a future with them."

"Maybe we should find out if you have value, Malik," Samantha said. "Once this is all over."

"We don't have enough food," Malik said. "Didn't really plan for five captives. Not to mention having to keep an eye on all these assholes."

"Why did you kill Mohammed?" Benj asked. "He didn't have anything to do with SolRescue."

"So we're going to have to whittle down these numbers."

"Are you listening to me, Malik?"

"Shut up, Benj. Alright?"

"Just answer the question. Why did you kill Mohammed?"

"Mohammed was a liability," Dav said.

"Shut your mouth, Dav," Malik said.

"A liability, eh?" Rachael said. "Because he didn't like the Chinese?"

"Why would that matter?" Benj asked.

"It wouldn't," Malik said. "Now can everyone just shut up now?"

"He knew what was happening," Samantha said. "That the Chinese were involved with his project."

"Do I need to start cutting out tongues?" Malik asked.

The threat was effective enough.

No one said anything more.

One of the Chinese operatives sat down at the workdock. He connected a tablet and started to work.

Benj couldn't see the screen.

They'd clearly laid the chairs out that way for a reason.

The man at the screen gave Malik a nod.

"My friend Chuck here has sent the first message," Malik said.

"To Carter Elgin," Rachael said. "Sure he has."

"No, not to Carter. To the guys who'll send to Carter. Be a nice change from the old op, sending messages from Carter to everyone else."

"What are you talking about?"

"I never really tell people this, Rachael. But you see, we've been sending messages as Carter for quite a while now. The man's been using the same exact tablet for five years. That's like forever, really. Took the Chinese maybe a month to find a way in."

"Bullshit," Benj said.

"You've seen the messages, Benj. I watched you read them, remember? So you tell me… why would Carter Elgin set up the dirty work when your father's been doing such a bang-up job all these years? Do you really think he told some yokel conservation officer to attack people with a polar bear?"

"So what," Rachael said, "you're claiming it was you?"

Malik smiled. "Yes. Me, personally. For some of it, at least."

"And all that stuff from him, about being in love with me…"

"Ha! No… he wishes that was me. The man's a kook, Rachael, and he really has fixated on you."

"This isn't true," Samantha said. "None of it."

"Why would I lie?" Malik asked. "What's the point?"

"What's the point in telling us?" Jared asked.

He was looking at Rachael, not Malik.

"Like I said," Malik told him, "some of you are valuable. For various reasons. If we can all come to an understanding, this can end well for everyone." He looked over at Chloe. "Well, almost everyone."

"Why is he looking at me?" Chloe said.

Malik grinned. "So… about that whittling down…"

"This isn't productive," Dav said. "Elgin will negotiate."

"And what if he doesn't?" Samantha said.

It was like she wanted to give them reasons to start killing people.

"You can head back into Gillam for supplies," Malik said, looking at Dav. "That's the cost of keeping these losers past their expiry date."

One of the Chinese operatives, "Chuck", said something in Mandarin.

Malik shushed him.

That didn't work, and the man kept talking, his loud tone making his feelings known.

Malik grabbed the man by the shoulder and urged him outside. They went out, leaving Dav and the other Chinese operative with the prisoners.

Benj could hear the two men outside the building, arguing back and forth in Mandarin.

"Not the best of friends," Samantha said.

"Kinda like us," Rachael said.

"We are allies," the other Chinese operative said, his English clear, if heavily accented. "Not friends."

"We do what we need to do," Dav said.

"What is it you need to do?" Benj asked. "Was there something stopping you guys from just sitting down with SolRescue, hammering out some kind of deal?"

Dav sighed. "You think this is my issue? Something I can control?"

"What can you control?" Rachael asked him.

"Don't talk to them," the Chinese operative said.

"I'll do what I want," Dav said. He looked over to Rachael. "Remember, Rachael... there's a way out of this."

"What about the rest of us?" Chloe asked. "Is there a way out for everyone else?"

Dav shrugged.

"What the hell does that mean?" Jared asked.

"I don't know," Dav said. "Sorry."

Jared started rocking his chair, pulling against the tape.

"There's nowhere to go," the Chinese operative told him.

"Motherfucker," Jared said. He kept trying to wiggle out of the duct tape.

Dav walked over to him. "Convince them," he said.

"What?"

"Convince these men that you have value. Convince Carter Elgin that you have value. That's what you need to do to survive."

"And what if we can't?"

"I can't do anything about that," Dav said.

"Fuck you," Samantha said.

Dav gave Samantha her very own shrug.

"How long will we be here?" Benj asked. "I'm feeling like this isn't a short term arrangement."

Dav stepped a little closer to Benj. "We have until mid-June at the latest to get this done. Then we have to shut this place down. We're in that sweet spot, after the sledders and before the summer season."

"You're a local," Rachael said. "I can tell."

He smiled. "I wasn't born here, but I grew up in Thompson."

"And you're working with these people."

"We all do things we don't want to do, Ms. Duck. I think you understand that."

"So you are going to kill us," Chloe said.

"I wasn't lying," Dav said. "Show Malik that you're worth keeping alive, and he'll keep you alive. As long as Carter doesn't call his bluff."

"He can't call his bluff," Jared said. "Not with Benj being here, too."

"It's a bad idea to make assumptions," Benj said.

Dav sighed. "Benj is probably the only one here who has a get out of jail card. The rest of you need to earn yours."

377

Benj felt a flash of what he'd felt before. That feeling that you don't deserve that special treatment, that you've done something wrong by being the one who made it through when others didn't. And he's been responsible for that.

This isn't the same.

Benj knew he had no leverage, no value aside from his name, who his father happened to be. He couldn't threaten that he wouldn't cooperate, since they didn't expect him to do anything but sit and wait to go home.

He didn't have a play.

He didn't know how he'd get everyone else out safely.

But he knew he couldn't live with himself if he didn't.

Valeri Timms had been the perfect choice.

The judge had taken their guilty pleas and given Valeri a two-year suspended sentence, and had handed down a one-year of the same for Benj, mostly due to the McPherson in his name. The Washington boys had gotten six months, which sounded great, but they'd had to spend it inside, at Camp Fischer. Not just weekends, but a straight stint.

It wasn't fair, and the whole world had known it.

For a week and a half, Benj and Valeri had been national news, but mostly just a two-line mention. And the Washington boys had been the victims, black kids with no famous parent, but there'd been no move to cut back their sentence, and no appetite for the prosecutor to try and appeal for harsher punishment for Valeri or Benj; it's not like anyone got hurt.

And that had been the moment when Benj's life had turned around, his father swooping into Woodson Terrace and pulling Benj out, only to drop him off in nearby Fulton, an hour and a half away, to attend Westminster College whether he wanted to or not.

Derrick McPherson had gotten his son a spot in residence half a year before Benj's classes were even set to begin. With no lead time.

And Benj had hated his father for it, for a while, until he'd found better things to hate his father for.

The Washington boys had made the news a couple years later, while Benj was still in college. Shot and killed by police, but without much uproar, since they'd been fleeing the scene of a home invasion, each with their own stolen handgun.

Because in Missouri at that time, convicted felons had to forfeit their basic income to the state to "pay back" their legal costs, including incarceration. When the Washington boys couldn't find work, they didn't have anything to fall back on; their mother couldn't keep them fed and clothed on one person's basic.

The death of those two black kids had eventually changed Missouri's law, but that made little difference for what Benj had done.

And he'd never entertained any illusions that he wouldn't have ended up on a slab right beside the Washington boys, if it hadn't been for two very simple things: his father, and what he'd forced onto pretty but troubled Valeri Timms.

40

MALIK DALEY stepped outside again.

He'd had to go back outside.

He couldn't handle being in there, playing that character.

Pretending that he liked doing what needed to be done.

And knowing he couldn't explain to Benj or to the others why they were on the wrong side. Why Carter Elgin is a bigger danger than anyone else on the planet.

Even Chuck didn't understand it, not like Carter did. Chuck just followed orders, like how a "spook" is supposed to act. He'd been the one who'd gotten the order on Najjar, leaving Malik to come along, because that's what his orders had been.

To do what the Chinese government wanted him to do, within reason.

Not that he knew where that line was supposed to be drawn.

Malik had never gotten along with who he was supposed to be.

Most of the time, he still thought of himself as everything he once was, the football star, the student council president, the potential Rhodes Scholar…

Most of the time he tried to pretend his life didn't take a complete u-turn, that some "informal complaint" from an unstable ex-girlfriend hadn't brought him to his knees, at one point hiking a mile and a half or so up to Sleeping Giant's Chin just because he wanted to see if he'd built up the guts to throw himself off the edge.

He'd gone from Yale to the local US Army recruiting office, and rose from there to Q Group in the NSA, but all of that was part of that wrong turn, away from a few years in the NFL, and one day—he'd hoped—Harvard or Columbia Law.

It was hard not to be bitter.

It was hard to turn that around, to play with the hand he'd been dealt after the Royal Flush he'd held for just a moment was flushed down the toilet.

But Malik would play that new hand, because he didn't feel like he had a choice.

Because he had to make them pay for what they'd done to Laila.

And because he'd never had the guts to take that leap off the Giant's Chin.

41

BASILICA **HAD** been built during what Anita called Carter's Empire phase, just after she'd left SolRescue and Carter had married Bridget, two events that weren't unrelated.

Harassment from the US government—in the form of FBI surveillance, NSA wiretaps, and Congress subpoenas—had led Carter to relocate the headquarters from their low-rent office at Cornell Tech to a trendy tech complex on Fredsgatan in Stockholm.

The Swedish had long prided themselves on being different from the rest of the West, being more tolerant of dissent—though Anita wasn't sure that extended to jihadists—and more willing than most countries who weren't Russia to annoy the United States with an ever-increasing stable of expats having trouble with the feds.

Anita had visited Carter—but hadn't seen Bridget—twice in Stockholm, where he'd proudly given her a tour of the office, including the artwork that she'd long ago counseled him never to buy, since it gave an impression of largesse.

It was on that second visit to Stockholm, right after he'd picked her up from the airport himself—that he'd shown her the foam model of *Basilica*.

"It's SolRescue's insurance policy," he'd told her. "In case things go bad in Sweden."

"Things might go bad?" she asked.

"They shouldn't. But that's why they call it insurance. You hope you never need to use it."

She smirked. "So you're building this thing and never using it?"

He chuckled. "Oh, no... I'll be living in this thing. Half time, probably. Unless I find the situation here not conducive."

"Not conducive? That's a stupid way to put it."

"You know, I liked the old Anita," he said. "The girl who saw the glass as half full."

"I liked the Carter who didn't waste crowdOrg funds on white elephants."

"Well that's racist."

"What?"

"Don't be so solemn, Anita."

"So how does this thing work?" she asked him, touring around the model. It took up a full boardroom table, which itself was eye-catching, a metal-framed Viking longboat, with Carter's chair being the dragon's head, and she couldn't imagine which poor peon would have to sit at the tail.

More largesse.

Another waste of resources.

"It self-propels," Carter said. "Don't need to carry it with one of those submersible heavy lift ships, like they need for that platform the Japanese want to use for the space elevator. And it's not stuck in one place like Thiel's Floating City."

"So it's better than everyone else's boondoggle."

He laughed.

She hadn't wanted him to laugh. But she didn't really mind.

"It isn't really a seastead if isn't grounded to one spot, is it?" she asked.

He pointed at the hull, which looked pretty conventional to Anita's eyes. "Air lubricated," he said. "Cuts fuel costs by ten to twenty percent."

"So it's really just a big boat. And not that big."

"It's a boat that can sustain itself indefinitely."

"You built a nuclear sub."

"Funny. Between the renewables, wind and solar, and the algae pool…"

"Algae pool?"

He pointed to what Anita had thought was a large swimming pool next to what looked like a traditional green roof of light grasses. "Fed by the sun, processed by *Basilica*."

"*Basilica*. That's the name?"

"That's her name, yeah."

"*Her* name. Another girlfriend for Carter Elgin."

He chuckled. He didn't seem to get what she was saying.

That there were several years of resentment behind everything she said to him. That she couldn't even stop it from flowing, no matter how much she just wanted to move on with her life.

"Only two helipads?" she asked. "What if you want to host a helicopter party?"

"We're trying to encourage people to come by sea, actually. Gets less attention."

"I was just pointing out the largesse. That's kinda my thing."

"This will really work, Anita. We'll float her in the Atlantic, moving between the North Atlantic Garbage Patch and Hudson Canyon as weather permits."

"Hudson Canyon?"

"High seas just off the US East Coast. Due east of Wallops Island, actually, so perfect for watching the launches. But not a terribly enjoyable place to be in January."

"Unlike Stockholm."

"Manatees don't come in blond, Anita."

"I doubt manatees swim that far north. And you married a blonde, remember?"

"She asked how you're doing," he said.

"Her voice dripping with a mix of pity and loathing?"

"It's not like that."

"So where is she? Why are you and I touring the office while she's hiding god knows where?"

"What did you expect from her?"

"More than this," Anita said. "More than turning her back to me and suing my ass off."

"You and I had an affair, Anita."

"No. No, no, no. It was not an affair, it was your megalomania. You came on to me, like it was over with her. Because you thought you could just start fucking both of us on and off, and ask for forgiveness later on."

"You knew."

"I didn't fucking know. How could I? Bridget was nowhere to be found, and you came down to Texas, and you came on to me…"

"And you didn't stop it."

"Fuck you, Carter. You came to my suite with a bottle of champagne and a goddamn box of condoms."

"It wasn't a box."

"Fuck you."

He smirked. "And we didn't even use the condoms."

"Do you want me to punch you? Is that what you're going for?"

"I love you, Anita."

"And I fucking hate you, Carter."

"Then why are you here?"

She didn't know what to say.

She could have just watched one of the four gushing documentaries about SolRescue's new space. She could have clicked through the Google Map of the hallway, passing silent judgment on what was apparently a mosaic by Jackson Pollock. Since when did Pollock do mosaics?

But she hadn't done that.

Carter had bought her the tickets and had asked her to come, and she'd said yes.

Because she wasn't indifferent to Carter Elgin.

She'd never be indifferent to him.

So that meant exactly what she'd never wanted in her life, an ongoing back-and-forth between love and excruciating hatred.

"I've booked you a room at Nobis Hotel," he said. "It's a little longer walk than some of the others, but it's worth it. Should we head over there?"

And she knew what would happen.

She knew that she'd say yes, that she'd let him take her there, not even hemming and hawing a little so he'd have to insist… and then he'd invite himself in, and she wouldn't say no, and they'd talk about the days at Cornell, and he'd break into the minibar, not enough to get drunk but one of those mini bottles of white, enough for her to drop any pretense of coming to Sweden for the ambiance.

That was the last time she'd have sex with Carter Elgin.

That's what she'd promised herself.

Just like she had on her previous visit to Stockholm. Every time she'd gone to visit him.

The *Basilica* looked slightly less impressive in reality than she'd remembered it as a foam model on a Viking longboat conference table.

It was only as long as an average container ship, nothing compared to the supertankers or mega cruise ships or Thiel's floating city, before it sank just past the Golden Gate.

To most people's eyes, from sea or from an airliner it would just be a container ship, but from up in the helicopter Danny Pyke had hired, she could see the algae pool and the green roof with the outdoor aeroponics.

And those two helipads, one of which already had a rather run-down looking ultralight heli taking up space.

That would be Carter's ride, back to Stockholm as needed, or to wherever else he felt safe from the feds who'd never give up on driving him to take their latest takeover bid.

The pilot landed them on the second pad, behind the two turbines which seemed positioned to look just like the double smokestacks of an old steamer.

Like always, Carter Elgin was waiting to greet them.

To greet her.

He'd grown a beard, which had started to collect gray on the fringes. It was a little wilder than she would have ever expected from Carter, making him look somewhere between burly lumberjack and smelly hobo.

"Must be hard living on a ship with no razors," she said, as he wrapped her in a hug.

"I've missed you, Anita," he said.

"Good to see you, Carter," Danny said, probably not unaware that he was already a third wheel.

Carter gave Danny a handshake. "I'm hoping we'll get a chance for a good talk, Danny," he said.

He then looked back to Anita.

A strong message to Danny, who nodded and start collecting his things from the helicopter.

"So this is it," Anita said. "Your new toy."

"Not new anymore," Carter said. "You're just very late for the grand opening. By six years, by my count. Not that I've seen you in nearly fifteen." He smiled. "You look absolutely beautiful, Anita. Just as I expected."

"Thanks."

"I'm assuming you hate the beard."

She smiled back. "I hate the beard. Makes you look like those guys that still manage to catcall me in Chelsea."

"I'd catcall you *so hard.*"

"That's not funny," she said.

But it kinda was.

He led her to a steel stairwell that was hung on the side of the ship, above the wider lower deck below, where the main living and working quarters were laid out, where the cargo would go on any other ship of that kind. Anita could see that the deck below was surprisingly unadorned, looking a lot like the Staten Island Ferry, without the wafting smell from the ladies bathroom.

They climbed down to the lower deck.

"Pretty much just us on this bucket," he said. "Me and the family and a small crew."

"You and the family. So you and Bridget… and Sansa…"

"That's the family, yeah."

"You know that's what my mother used to call me," she said. "What she'd wanted to name me."

"I know."

"And Bridget was okay with that? An Indian girl's name? For somehow the whitest newborn baby in all of Sweden?"

"We didn't talk about it. I'd suggested it, and she'd said she loved it. Maybe *Game of Thrones?* We never mentioned you, Anita."

They didn't have to mention her. She knew she was always somewhere.

"I could tell you it wasn't because of you," Carter said. "But you know that isn't true."

"It's creepy, is what it is. It's creepy that you have a daughter with one woman and name her after the other. You're a huge creepy creep, Carter."

"I think you're right on that. Sorry."

"But you're not sorry, because you keep doing it. You keep doing this creepy shit."

"I haven't done anything for fifteen years, Anita. I've sat back and let you live your life, haven't it?"

"You're always there, Carter. In every conversation I have with someone, every goddamn spite-filled settlement offer from your wife."

"There's no spite. She wants it over and done. She wants to move on.

And you know I didn't let it get in your way."

"Yeah," Anita said. "The legal fund. Just like all your other plays, keeping me under your thumb. Like pushing poor Danny Pyke to hire me."

"Who's really the spiteful one here, Anita? It sounds like it's you."

She shook her head. "Fuck… I've earned that spite."

"Does it do anything for you?"

"What?"

"The spite. Does it make you happy, Anita?"

"Hard not to be happy living in my palace on Staten Island with the other Basics."

"Don't blame me for that," he said. "That was your choice. You left us."

"I left because it didn't work. I couldn't be your side project while you lived out your little love story with Bridget."

"I tried."

"You tried? What does that even mean?"

"I wanted you both. I didn't want to lose Bridget, and I sure as hell didn't want to lose you."

"You couldn't have us both. End of story."

"I had to try," he said.

"No. Fuck you, Carter. You didn't have to try."

"Fine. Then I couldn't stop myself. I can't stop myself."

He grabbed at her hand. Clawed at it.

She pulled it away.

"Don't touch me," she said. "I think this was a mistake. I shouldn't have come here."

"Someone needs to talk some sense into me."

"What?"

"I'm not stupid. If you're here, it's basically an intervention."

"I don't want to do this."

"Hold on," he said. He stopped at a closed door. "We're here."

He opened the door and stepped through, leaving it open for Anita to follow.

She did.

It was a library, filled with hardbound paper books on shelves on three sides. The other side was a window, showing the ocean in front of it.

With two fixed chairs in front of two docks, right up against the window. And with a woman with strawberry blond hair, staring out at the water. She was older, obviously, but still strikingly beautiful.

Bridget Hawn stood up and walked over to Anita.

"Thank you for coming, Anita," she said.

She gave her a hug.

It felt good, like a long-remembered thing, but it was something she couldn't ever remember doing with Bridget. Neither of them had ever been *huggers.*

"I've missed you," Anita said, surprising herself, like someone else had said it.

"I've missed you," Bridget replied. "We should have never let Carter or anything else come between us."

"Speaking of Carter," he said, smirking, "is there some kind of talking pillow we're supposed to use for this? While you tell me all the ways I've wronged you?"

"It's not a joke, Carter," Bridget said.

"It's been a pretty rough week. Not so bad to laugh a little, is it?"

"We're not laughing," Anita said.

Bridget gave her a wink.

Like she always used to do.

"Do we need Danny to come in here?" Carter asked. "I kinda left him up there on his own."

"On the pad?" Bridget asked.

Carter nodded.

She rolled her eyes. "You're such a welcoming host."

Danny Pyke knocked on the side of the open door. "Is this my cue?" he asked.

"Come on in, Danny," Bridget said. "I'm sorry my husband's a *douche-asaurus.*"

"So I'm guessing Danny told you," Carter said, looking at Anita. "About the maker camps."

She nodded. "I'm sorry that happened."

"It shouldn't have happened. People shouldn't be dying over this."

"More people will die," Bridget said. "If they get what they want."

"Wait," Anita said. "What is it I'm supposed to be advocating here, anyway? I thought I was gonna be the hawk."

"The hawk?" Danny said.

"To tell Carter to keep going, not to give in."

"You're supposed to be the eagle," Bridget said. "Or the pigeon… whichever one is supposed to drop the stupid labels and figure this out."

Anita shook her head. "I thought Carter was the genius. All the genius you'd ever need."

Bridget frowned. "No one ever said that."

"You're here because this is a shitshow," Danny said. "Because everything is starting to fall apart."

"We keep moving forward," Carter said. "We start again. We still have camps, we just need to find a way to keep our people safe."

"Start again?" Bridget said. "Square one?"

"Keep moving forward."

"They'll hit you again," Anita said. "Whoever they are. The feds, the

Chinese junta… you can't just print up some rifles and hope to defend yourselves. You can't keep your people safe. You can't keep *Basilica* safe, to be honest."

"I don't see them hitting us here," Carter said.

"We don't even know who they were," Bridget said. "Derrick says that three people from Leonardo survived. No one from Donatello or Mercator. Only one person saw the drones firsthand."

"Drones?" Anita said. "UCAVs?"

"Land drones," Carter said. "Not too sophisticated, either. Just remote control tanks."

"Sounds dangerous enough," Danny said.

Carter seemed annoyed. "But they can't fly," he said. "Or walk on water."

"It wouldn't take much to strap some munitions to a hobby drone," Anita said.

"We have some defense capabilities, you know. You think they don't send surveillance drones after us?"

"You shoot them down?"

"We do. We claim the right under defense of privacy. Affirmed by the European Parliament."

"This isn't Europe," Anita said. "It's the high seas."

"You missed the flag, apparently," Carter said. "The blue and yellow pendant. EU is our flag state."

"I don't know what that means."

"It's not fully tested," Bridget said. "Especially not in international waters. But there's an understanding that this puts us under European jurisdiction, at least as far as the Americans are concerned."

"So they can't board," Anita said.

"Can't or won't," Carter said. "Not sure which."

Anita nodded. "So far, you mean." She looked over to Bridget. "Your daughter…"

"I know," Bridget said. "I've been thinking the same thing. This might be her last time onboard. At least while all this is going on."

"They should be able to track those drones," Danny said. "From orbit."

"Derrick's working on that," Carter said. "The ESA isn't big on sharing their data with us at the moment."

"I'd say the relationship's at an all time low," Bridget said. "They haven't come out and admitted it, but they blame us for what happened in French Guiana. They think we had something to do with it."

Carter shook his head. "Not we. *Me.* They think I had something to do with it. As if it makes sense to destroy the European colony program."

"There's been a lot of stuff going around about you," Danny said. "I know it's bullshit, but…"

"But you're in the minority," Carter said. "Unstable genius Carter Elgin, living on his weird little boat in the middle of the Atlantic. Scheming to take over the world."

"Conspiracy theories are nothing new," Bridget said.

"It's more than that," Danny said. "Way more than that."

"What do you mean?" Anita asked.

"I'm not sure... but it almost feels like someone's putting some serious resources into spreading these rumors. Like state-sponsored."

"Like the People's Convocation," Bridget said. "Hoping to split us off from the Europeans."

"Hoping that there won't be anyone lodging a protest when they blow up the shield," Carter said.

"Blow up the shield?" Anita said. "Is that a joke?"

"The US and China are working together," Danny said. "We sent a couple people up to Churchill to investigate a US Air Force project."

"And to check on a possible leak," Carter said. "But we've lost contact with them."

"Lost contact?" Anita asked. "You don't mean..."

"Derrick's son was one of them," Bridget said. "We tried to get him out in time."

Anita sighed. "What the hell is this, Carter? Secret projects, sending goddamn operatives or whatever to spy on the US Air Force? This was never supposed to happen."

"We had to grow up," he said. "SolRescue is a target. Of the US government. Of the Chinese military. Of anyone who thinks we're too powerful. We have to defend ourselves."

"You're killing all of the good parts. You're becoming just like the people who would have sat by and let the planet roast. Those same people are still just sitting by, while the ocean is still filling with CO2, still dying like it was when we started this thing. We tried to buy some more time, and people are acting like the problem's been solved. And you're not doing a goddamn thing to change their minds."

"And you are, Anita? By wandering around Manhattan all day, going to flea markets and street fairs?"

"Is this really the issue?" Bridget asked.

"I think it is," Anita said. "I think we've all been letting this happen. Hell, I let you guys down. Because I didn't stop this organization from becoming everything we used to despise."

"So much grandstanding," Carter said. "So little in the way of real solutions. What happened to you, Anita? Where's the inspiration?"

"You beat it out of me, I guess."

"He's sorry," Bridget said.

"What did you say?" Carter said.

Bridget shook her head. "My husband is an asshole. And I guess I am, too. We should have never let you go, Anita. We need you."

"It's too late," Anita said. "It's fucked. We're fucked. You try building more habs, and they'll find a way to take them out."

"I don't believe that," Carter said.

"Look at your participation numbers, Carter. They're open to everyone to review. The last convention... how many votes did the delegates control? What, maybe half the number we had at the organizing conference? There are three hundred times more shieldbots at STeLa-1 than we had back then. Probably a thousand times more members on the rolls. But no one's showing up to vote, no one's choosing their delegate, no one gives a shit about anything other than whatever royalty payments they've got coming."

"That's what happens," Bridget said. "There's an expected entropy with organizations. You can't keep the warm and fuzzies forever."

"They've lost faith in you," Anita said. "You have more tangible power than you've ever had before, but somehow you command a fraction of the influence. Why is that?"

"I don't know, Anita," Carter said. "Why don't you explain it to us?" He was trying to sound exasperated, but she could see the twinkle in his eye.

He could see it in her, too. The fire in her belly.

Carter was the worst thing for her. And maybe also the best.

If she let him be.

"We shot a video that changed the fucking world," she said. "It wasn't the rockets or the robots or the blather about liquid democracy... it was the video, packaging a dream and letting the whole world dream it."

"You want to make a video?" Danny asked.

"SolRescue is dying," Anita said. "I don't know if we can save it. But honestly, I'm not sure it's worth saving."

"We need that shield," Bridget said.

Carter just smiled.

"The shield can live without us," Anita said. "Without SolRescue. Maybe it needs to."

"So what does that mean, Anita?" Carter asked.

"We start again."

"What do you mean?" Bridget asked. "A whole new crowdOrg?"

"A whole new crowdOrg," Anita said. "A whole new mission."

"We have a new mission," Danny said. "Turnpike has that mission."

"Turnpike is a vanity project."

"Ouch."

"Sorry, but it is. It's Danny Pyke and Carter Elgin want to play around in space. It's not inspiring."

"So what is inspiring?" Carter asked.

"We take the fight to them," Anita said. "A new way of doing things.

No more SolRescue secrets, no more of this People's Convocation bullshit, no more unaccountability from the US Government."

"What the hell are you talking about?" Bridget said. "It sounds like you want some kind of revolution."

"Maybe."

Bridget shook her head. "That's a fantasy, Anita. You don't overthrow thousands of years of human history... and fucking human nature... with another viral video."

"There's more of us," Anita said. "Billions of us, nine billion minus that small minority. Two billion of us have enough of a safety net to devote our entire lives to something that matters."

"But we don't," Danny said. "SolRescue has less than a million members. And like you said, most are nominal, at best."

"I want to try again."

"You want to try what again?" Carter asked.

"All of it," she said. "I want to go back to the beginning."

"And how exactly are we supposed to do that?" Bridget asked.

"We stand up and start telling people the truth."

Anita laid out her plan, which was 99% off the top of her head, mixed with a few things she'd recognized should have gone differently the first time, such as not having sex with Carter Elgin.

Carter himself was in perfect form, almost manic, or drunk on the excitement of bringing the old gang back together again. Bridget was a little more muted than before, and Anita wondered how much of that was from the rift between them and how much was due to Carter having taken center stage for so long.

Danny Pyke did his best to contribute, offering his team for whatever was needed.

Derrick McPherson interrupted the meeting with a voice call for Carter, who told him he was putting him on speaker to have him join in the discussion.

"I don't want to be on speaker," Derrick said, but the button had already been pressed, connecting him to the sound system embedded around the library.

"Anita is here," Carter said. "And Danny Pyke. We're just getting started on... on *something*, maybe."

"Check your messages," Derrick said. "They sent it to both of us. With pics."

"Just tell me."

"Take me off speaker, then."

"It's okay, Derrick. We're all in this together, aren't we?"

"They have my son, Carter. Look at the goddamn photos."

"Oh," he said.

He looked at the tablet.

Anita came over to see.

A young black man, Derrick's son, all grown up, duct taped to a chair. Beside four more hostages.

She didn't think she knew any of the others.

Carter cut the speaker. He brought the tablet up to his ear.

The conversation was mostly Derrick talking, too quiet for Anita to hear, with Carter mostly giving one word responses to show he was listening.

Then he put the call back on speaker.

"They want us to give up control," Derrick said. "But they haven't come out and admitted who they are."

"But you know who they are?" Anita asked.

"We've tracked the source down. Churchill, Manitoba, where my son had been."

"So he's probably not there anymore," Carter said. "They want us to try and look in the wrong place."

"Can I get that tracking data?" Danny asked. "If it deadends, there's gotta be a way to figure out some extra hop they're doing a much better job of hiding."

"That's you, Danny?" Derrick asked. "I can forward it on."

"Thanks."

"They're holding five people," Carter said, reading off his tablet. "They've named them all, in case we couldn't tell from the photos, I guess, or, you know… hadn't already figured out who's missing."

"Did we know who's missing?" Bridget asked. "Are they all are people?"

"Samantha Yoon," Derrick said. "She's one of mine. And two people from the USAF project, which I don't really get. And Rachael Duck. She was the one we suspected of leaking information to the Chinese. The one we were investigating."

"You were investigating her?" Carter said. "You didn't talk to me about that. You didn't clear it with me."

"Since when do I involve you in that?"

"Who's Rachael Duck?" Bridget asked. She was looking at Carter.

"She's one of mine," Carter said.

Bridget frowned.

"What does that mean?" Danny asked. "Is she SolRescue, or something else? Can we trust her?"

"It means that my husband wants to fuck her," Bridget said. "If he hasn't already."

Anita looked over to her.

"I know what Carter's about, Anita," Bridget said. "We've been married a long time."

"So how do we get them out?" Carter asked. He seemed unfazed by Bridget's reaction, like it was nothing out of the ordinary. "I mean, there are two ways to handle this."

"What do you mean?" Anita asked.

"If you were going to choose… would you just give up on all this power you say we've amassed? Try and find some more open way of negotiating with government-directed terrorists?"

"What kind of power?"

"What do you mean?"

"What can you do?" she asked. "If you knew where they were being held."

"Not much," Derrick said. "We're not an army."

"What if we could get one?"

"What?"

"We find out where they are," Anita said. "And then we get the European sats to give us as much data as we can get."

"And then?" Carter asked.

"We find someone who's just as pissed as we are that the sunshield's at risk. Someone who does have access to soldiers with big guns."

"You want to order in some proxy forces," Derrick said.

"Is that possible?" Bridget asked.

There was silence for a good thirty seconds.

Carter was grinning, like he knew something no one else did.

Almost like things were playing out exactly as he'd hoped. *Or planned.*

"You know," Derrick said, "I think it's possible."

Danny Pyke went back in the helicopter to grab some of his team, one member—Vasily Utkin—being particularly important, while Anita stayed on *Basilica* for lunch.

It was not what she'd expected from Carter Elgin, a modest but well-appointed vegetarian spread, sourced exclusively from the aeroponic gardens on the seastead itself.

But the highlight of the meal was Sansa Elgin, the young girl Anita had never had a chance to meet. Sansa was seven, with messy blonde hair that made Anita imagine exactly what Bridget would have looked like as a kid, mixed with Carter's cheekbones and know-it-all syndrome.

"You're Aunty Anita," Sansa said as she came in for an unprompted hug. Definitely not something she'd have expected from a mini Bridget. "It's about time."

Bridget laughed.

Sansa had Anita sit beside her at the table, the universal sign that they were best friends for the day.

They ate their lunch, Sansa talking about what you'd expect seven-year-olds to talk about, her favorite breeds of horses, how much she likes visiting the islands with the beaches and the loud monkeys... it was a window into a world Anita had never seen, family dinners and precocious daughters who avoid anything on their plate that isn't a green pea.

"Aunty Anita brought something for you," Carter said. "A special present."

Anita looked over to him.

He grinned.

What the hell was he talking about?

Carter got up and left the room.

Anita turned to Bridget for some kind of clue.

"I don't know what you guys are up to," Bridget said, in a way that Anita took to mean that Carter was clearly up to *something*.

Sansa bounced around on her chair, asking about the surprise for three minutes straight, until Carter returned with a box wrapped in what must have been three distinct horse-themed beach towels.

For a moment Sansa seemed to think the towels were the gift, pulling them off the box and ogling them, then rifling off the breeds to Anita specifically.

"Open the box," Carter said. "If that's okay, Anita." He was trying to keep himself from giggling.

"Please do," Anita said.

Sansa opened the blank cardboard box. "Oh my gosh... really?"

"What is it?" Bridget asked.

"It's a telescope," Sansa said. "A real one. Help me, Auntie."

Anita helped Sansa take it out of the box.

She had trouble believing what she was seeing. It was 3d printed, probably by Carter himself, but it was a near-perfect replica of the telescope her own mother had given her, thirty-seven years before.

"Oh my god," she said.

"Can you help me set it up?" Sansa asked her.

She nodded. And felt herself starting to cry. She fought it.

"What's wrong, Auntie?"

"I'm just so glad you like it."

They took the telescope up to the garden on the green roof, Carter and Bridget in tow. Sansa chose a patch of grass between two rows of vegetables in net pots.

It wouldn't be ideal, especially not for taking stills, but they were on a converted container ship rocking in the middle of the Atlantic. Not exactly a prime observatory.

Carter pulled out his tablet. "Let me know when to dim the lights," he said.

Anita went through the components with Sansa, from eyepiece to dust cap, trying to recall the way her mother had explained it all, the way that had seemed so perfect for six-year-old Anita.

Sansa was eating it up, asking questions, keeping her hands away like she was viewing something precious.

Once she'd set it up, Anita put her hand around Sansa's shoulders. "Are you ready? First light?"

"What's first light?" Sansa asked.

"The first image you get through a new telescope. A very special thing."

"What will we look at?"

"What did you want to look at?"

Sansa thought about it for a moment.

"The moon?"

Anita laughed.

"Why are you laughing at me?" Sansa asked.

"I'm not, I'm not… that's just the same thing I asked to see for my first light, when I was a little girl."

"Did you see it? The moon?"

"I did. It was beautiful, up close."

"I want to see it," Sansa said.

Anita decided to avoid using the finderscope, both to save herself from having to bend down that low and to avoid mudding up the concept of Sansa being first; she could see the moon well enough to make an educated guess.

She guided Sansa to the eyepiece.

She remembered what her mother had said, in the backyard of their house in La Crosse, Wisconsin, that night that she'd first shown Anita—her own little Sansa—the moon.

Her mother's favorite quote, from a book on Taoism. Anita could almost remember it. She remembered most of it…

"The moon attacks no one," she said. "It does not try to crush others… but by its very nature, it gently influences the world."

Sansa stared into the eyepiece.

She made a contented sound, something like purring. "It's so beautiful," she said. "So big."

"It's the reason we're here," Anita said. "The reason we walk on earth, why our ancestors weren't stranded in the ocean forever."

"I love it," Sansa said. "So much. Thank you, Auntie."

"You're welcome."

Anita looked over to Carter.

He gave her a nod.

She still wasn't sure what he'd had to do to pull it off.

42

AFTER A night of trying to sleep while duct taped to stiff wooden chairs, the hostages were broken into two shifts, one of two and the other of three. Jared found himself paired with Samantha, while Benj was given Chloe and Rachael. Jared wasn't sure what he'd done to deserve such a fate.

Chloe's hair was still in that loose ponytail, looking more ragged than before but the little spider bot wasn't visible.

Assuming it hadn't fallen out when she'd had a hood over her head. Or any other time in the not-particularly-smooth abduction process.

While one shift was free to move about the cabin, the other shift was bound to their chairs, sitting against the wall. So he and Samantha were given their two hour block, where they could ask for an escort out to the composting toilet—hidden in the remains of a semi-collapsed engineering building a quarter mile away—or they could eat from the meagre supply of dried berries, granola bars, and what seemed like beef jerky but didn't exactly taste like beef jerky.

Their captors took turns as well, Malik and "Chuck" forming one duo and Dav and the other, nameless, Chinese operative forming the other.

Jared had almost been tempted to try some ridiculous escape plan during his first trip to the porta-potty, when he'd been walked down the path to the other building by one lone guard, the Chinese man Malik had called Chuck. But Chuck had a pistol, and Chuck didn't look like a easy mark.

And Jared had no clue what he was supposed to do the moment he miraculously managed to disarm and disable a possible member of China's Secret Forces. Was he supposed to run off into the woods to see if he could find another hungry polar bear? Or build on that impossible victory by taking on three more armed operatives while somehow keeping the hostages from getting hurt?

So he took his piss and went back to the old house, and paced around the room and tried to make conversation with Dav, who seemed the most receptive to the concept.

Dav wouldn't answer most of the time with anything more than a nod, a shrug, or the occasional smile, but Jared felt like he was making progress. Humanizing the prisoners.

Showing that there ought to be some serious deliberation before deciding that anyone is *expendable*.

He felt expendable enough, but he knew it was even worse for Chloe;

Jared could supply information on the work he'd been doing, even what Mohammed had been doing, specific data as required, not that he knew if that information was wanted, or who he'd be supplying it to. But Chloe's project plan wasn't worth much, and Carter Elgin had probably never heard of her.

And if Malik and Dav were working for the US government in any capacity, that was a sign that they didn't think of Chloe as a peer. Jared had a feeling that Chloe would be first to get hurt, the prime candidate for sending a message to Carter Elgin that hostages were going to die.

Jared wished he could send a message to Carter Elgin, not that he knew what to say, other than telling him that Chloe mattered, that they all mattered—even Samantha, maybe—and that he would do anything he could to justify whatever Carter had to do to save their lives.

43

VASILY RECEIVED a message from Danny at eleven AM.

He'd been at the office, working with a couple of the guys on Anita Singhal's big changes, figuring out how best to arrange for seventeen sat launches in a 30-day window, to make a splash for the whole world to see.

But Danny had told him to drop everything, and grab anyone else who was willing to go with him to the East 34th Street Heliport. For a trip to *Basilica*. For an in-person conference with Elgin, Hawn and Singhal.

It was like being told he was needed at a meet and greet with the Avengers at Stark Tower.

He felt like he was right on the edge of hyperventilating.

His father had told him more than once about the time he'd met Elgin and Singhal in Texas, when he'd flown all the way in from London City Airport for the first launch. It had been one of the top highlights in the life of a billionaire who'd once owned a yacht with its own little attached *sub*yacht, a modest eighty footer for short jaunts to small ports in the Mediterranean.

And now on top of working with Anita Singhal, Vasily would meet the other two, and would... do what, exactly? Was he even qualified to speak to anything?

He felt his breath quickening.

He had to keep it together.

Three Turnpike employees made the trip with Danny Pyke to *Basilica*.

Danny directed the other two down to Carter's lab below the main deck. Vasily was led into a room, three walls of bookcases and a window out on the sea.

Standing around a work dock were Bridget Hawn and Anita Singhal. Carter Elgin seemed to be pacing around any and all open space in the room.

"This is Vasily Utkin," Danny said.

Vasily shook hands with Carter and Bridget, while Anita gave him a nod.

"Your father," Carter said. "We're hoping he can help us."

"My father is in prison," Vasily said.

"That hasn't changed who he is, has it?"

Vasily sighed. He'd known it was about his father, even if he'd been loathe to admit it to himself. All the times he'd promised himself he'd be a better man than his father, more principled, less enamored with money and power... at the end, he'd just ended up a pale reflection of the Grand Utkin.

"What is it that you want from my father, exactly?" he asked.

"We need to talk to the Russian Armed Forces," a voice said over speakers set up in the room. "I'm Derrick McPherson, by the way."

"I'm not sure how much you know," Carter said. "About the work being done to take control of the sunshield."

"I'm afraid I don't know much," Vasily said.

"The US and China," Bridget said. "That's what you need to know. Either joint control, or one of them taking the whole enchilada."

"And they've taken some of our people," Carter said. "Including Derrick's son."

"And who is *they*?"

Carter shrugged. "One or both."

"And you think that bringing Russian forces into this mix will somehow be of help?" He only realized after he'd said it how adversarial he was sounding. "I mean, I really don't have an understanding..."

"The VKO," Derrick McPherson said. "They have orbital dive capabilities."

"Unofficially," Carter said.

"And you expect me to know this?" Vasily asked.

"We just need you to help us," Anita said. "Whatever you can do."

Vasily sighed. "I don't see how I can do anything, to be frank. I am not my father, Ms. Singhal."

"Do you know anyone who can help?" Bridget asked. "Friends of your father, people who can put us in touch with the right people."

"I don't know..."

"Enough, Vasily," Derrick McPherson said.

He was taken aback. "What?"

"Your older brother is a captain of the Black Sea Fleet. You can ask him to help."

"You want me to just ring him up, then?"

"I want you to do what needs to be done," McPherson said. "Whatever it takes. Get us in touch with the Aerospace Defense Forces, or the goddamn President of Russia."

"Please," Bridget said. "At least try."

Vasily nodded.

"We've got network here," Carter said. "You should be able to send a voice call. It's before ten PM there, if that helps."

Vasily pulled out his tablet.

The network was there.

He pinged his big brother Roman for a voice call.

He didn't think there was much that could be done, but he knew he had to try. What else could he do?

After a few minutes of waiting, Roman gave Vasily a contact number specifically for Carter Elgin to call. The area code was 869; Vasily didn't know off-hand where that would most likely be located.

Roman had said for Carter to call, and no one else.

So Carter made the call, putting it to speaker.

A man answered in Russian.

Carter looked over to Vasily.

"Just tell them who you are," Vasily said.

Carter shook his head. "This is Carter Elgin. I'm hoping to talk to someone in charge."

"Minutochku!" the man said. *Just a minute!* Not aggressively, more... excitedly.

The line switched over to music on hold, some truly awful Muzak that might have once been a Beatles song.

"Who is this?" another voice asked.

"Carter Elgin," Carter said, sounding a little bit huffy.

"Hold on."

No hold music. Just silence, followed by a couple of beeps, and more silence. And more beeps...

"Is this some kind of joke?" Derrick asked over the speakers, apparently conferenced in on the call by default. Or a separate line...

"I don't know what this is," Vasily said. "This is outside my experience."

Someone picked up the call. "This is Yakov."

"Yakov," Carter said. "Are you in charge?"

"What a country."

"What?"

"What a country."

Carter was glaring at Vasily. Like he thought it was some kind of prank, that Vasily was having a laugh.

"Gospodin Elgin would like to speak with the VKO," Vasily said.

"What a country." It sounded like a recording.

Then back to the bad Beatles instrumentals. "Drive My Car".

"What the hell is going on?" Carter asked. "These people should know who I am."

"Just wait," Bridget said.

Another pickup. "This is Lieutenant-General Likhachyov," the new voice said. "VKO. You're calling from *Basilica*. We have a task force on its way to you, yes?"

"Yes," Carter said.

Vasily noticed some unease in the room.

Like not everyone had known the whole plan.

"And you are hoping for additional assistance. A joint effort."

"Yes. To rescue our people."

"Send us what you have," the lieutenant-general said. "Everything you have. I have sent the number to Vasily Otkin."

Vasily checked his tablet. He saw the message and the number. Another 869. He gave a nod to Carter.

"And then?" Carter asked the lieutenant-general.

"And then we will see," was the reply.

And the call ended.

"He wouldn't have taken the call if they weren't leaning toward assisting us," Derrick said. "The Russians don't bluff with this kind of thing."

"What the hell, Carter?" Anita said. "You already have the Russians involved?"

"Not with this part," he said.

"With what, then?"

"They're coming to keep an eye on the US. To back us up."

"The Russians," Anita said.

"The Russian Navy," Derrick said. "They'll keep *Basilica* safe. They were meant to be here yesterday, before the launch from the maker camps."

"And no one told me."

"You weren't here, Anita," Carter said.

"The Russians aren't known for hostage extractions," Bridget said. "I'm worried."

"Oh, I'm worried," Derrick said, angrily. "You think I'm not?"

"They don't know everything we have," Carter said. "And they won't know. But they'll get enough to help us."

"I think the whole world should know what we know," Anita said.

"To what end?" Derrick asked.

"To expose this bullshit," she said. "To end this bullshit."

"They'll know soon enough," Carter said. He looked over at Vasily. "You have a guess on this?" he asked. "You think this will happen?"

Vasily tried not to shrug, but it happened anyway. "I'm afraid I'm not at all sure," he said. "It's a rather large expectation to have, for them to intervene in North America. I think they'll only join in if you can convince them that the alternative is that you'll give in, assuming that giving in means what I believe it does."

"They haven't specified the details," Bridget said. "Just that they want us to give up control of SolRescue. Of the sunshield."

"So what, exactly? We're to send them some sort of root access?"

"Pretty much," Carter said. "That's what I'd be looking for if I was them. Give me enough to take over the shield and boot out everyone else's access."

"This doesn't sound like the Americans," Derrick said. "It really doesn't."

"It doesn't sound like China, either," Bridget said.

Derrick shook his head. "This is a new China. Hardliners do crazy shit. And to take full control over the Earth's climate? I understand the cost-benefit analysis on that pretty clearly."

"But there's another real question here," Anita said.

Everyone looked over to her.

But she didn't look like she wanted to say what she was thinking.

She took a deep breath.

"I don't see any reason for them to free the hostages," she said. "No matter what we decide."

"We've already decided," Carter said. "Or rather, I've already decided. No deal. No way."

"And if the Russians decline to help?" Derrick asked.

"Then we'll track these people down and we'll kill them."

"And what about my son, Carter?"

"I can't save your son," he said. "I'm sorry."

Derrick didn't respond.

Vasily tried his best to read the room, the faces of the people around him.

He had a feeling there was no Plan B. Not yet.

Everything depended on the man who'd claimed he was with the VKO.

44

BENJ HAD a feeling how it would end.

They wanted more than Carter and his father would agree to; Malik didn't need to give him any details for him to know. And he knew his father, and he thought he knew Carter well enough.

They would know that there was little hope that five hooded hostages would be dropped off at some bus station. If it was up to Malik and his crew, there would be five shallow graves dug somewhere in the forest.

Or maybe eight.

Maybe Malik had no intention of anyone coming back from Port Nelson with him.

As the sun was getting close to setting, Chloe, Samantha and Jared's shift of not being ziptied and taped to chairs came to an end. Once they were restrained, Malik and Chuck left the building, leaving Dav and the second Chinese operative.

"I really need to pee," Benj said.

"You'll need to hold it," Dav said.

"You think I'm going to try something stupid."

"Not worth the risk."

"You don't need to cut my wrists free... I can improvise once I'm on deck."

"Not going to happen."

"We're not going to make it out of here," Benj said.

Dav shrugged.

Benj kept going. "You won't admit it?"

"I told you what needed to happen. And besides, you're golden, Benj. You're the magic goose."

"The golden goose."

"I already said you're golden. This shouldn't take more than a few days."

"Are you even sure you'll make it out of here?" Samantha asked. "How do you know anyone's leaving this place alive."

"Someone has to," Dav said.

"Are you sure about that? You know what happens to the guys who do the dirty work for the Mexican cartels? The ones who are forced to dig the tunnels under the border?"

"How do they get anyone to dig tunnels if they just killed the last bunch?"

Samantha shook her head. "I bet if you told us to dig tunnels right now, we'd be inclined to do it."

"How did you get on the team, Dav?" Benj asked. "You don't look Chinese."

"Malik isn't Chinese, either," Dav said.

"But you said you're a local. That makes you Canadian, doesn't it?"

"Landed immigrant, actually. Haven't gotten my citizenship, but I've been here most of my life."

"So how did you get the gig?" Benj asked.

Dav gave another one of his famous shrugs.

"You're the tunnel digger," Samantha said. "Maybe Malik's a digger, too."

"Not sure about Malik," Benj said. "But yeah… you're a digger, Dav."

"I think we're done talking about this," Dav said.

"We should gag them," the Chinese operative said, in reasonably understandable English. "They are playing mind games."

"Are we boring you?" Samantha asked.

"Shut up or we *will* gag you guys," Dav said.

"Please do gag her," Rachael said. "That might just make me the happiest girl on Earth."

Jared started chuckling.

Benj saw Rachael give Jared a smile back.

Benj didn't like to see it for some reason.

Possibly for *that* reason, because he really was starting to like her.

Which was terrible timing, all things considered.

"We'll shut up," Benj said, "but there's only one more thing I need to ask."

"Just shut up," Dav said.

"Do you know where those two went?"

"Shut up."

"So… that's a no?"

Dav walked over to the table, where three remaining rolls of duct tape were stacked beside the plastic bowl of dried berries.

He grabbed a roll and stepped up to Benj.

"Shut up," he said again.

Benj nodded.

And he could see that Samantha was giving him some breed of stinkeye.

She didn't approve.

Not that she was the queen of subtle manipulation.

❧

Malik and Chuck came back after a couple of hours, based on Benj's best guess of what time it happened to be.

They were both carrying backpacks, not on their backs, but slung over a shoulder.

Malik lowered his pack down gently, by the door.

Chuck did the same.

"What the hell is that?" Dav asked.

"Supplies," Malik said. "But it's funnier when Chuck says it."

"That is a Cantonese problem," Chuck said.

"And you're a good Mandarin," Samantha said. "Following orders."

"Those aren't supplies," Dav said.

"Does it matter what they are?" Malik asked.

"It matters to me, yeah."

"Well that's too damn bad, I guess."

Dav walked toward the two packs by the door.

Malik stepped in front of him.

"You trying to stop me?" Dav asked.

Malik grinned. "Just be very careful with them, alright?"

"Explosives," Benj said.

Malik nodded.

"Insurance policy?" Samantha asked. "Or mopping up at the end?"

"They've been trying to stall us," Malik said. "We've been told to expect a rescue attempt."

"Rescue attempt?" Benj said. "By who, exactly?"

"So we plan for the worst."

"There's no reason for that," Dav said. "If we're forced to surrender, there's no point in killing anyone."

"That's why you'll never amount to much, Dav," Malik said. "You just can't see the big picture."

"I doubt you've been told much about the big picture," Samantha said.

Malik shook his head. "That slant-eyed bitch really does want someone to jam something in her mouth."

"Shut up, Malik," Benj said.

Malik groaned. "I should shut you up, too."

"Didn't realize I was getting inside your head."

Malik laughed.

And got to work with the explosives.

Benj watched as Malik and "Chuck" unloaded their backpacks.

Each pack had one white sack of ammonium nitrate, around fifty pounds each. Malik's pack also had two white-wrapped sticks, which looked a lot like candles.

Benj could make a good guess. The white sticks would detonate the fertilizer. The house would be blown apart.

The men didn't bother to empty the sacks; they simple stacked them up under Samantha's chair. Malik put the two white sticks on top.

He went back to his pack and pulled out a small length of thick wire.

"Cannon fuse," Malik said, looking over at Benj. "Perfect for fireworks and hara kiri."

"You mean suicide," Samantha said. "Hara kiri would require you to slice open your belly, wouldn't it? Mind you, I'd be willing to help with that."

"I light the fuse with my trusty firestarter," Malik said, "and that's it, that's all."

"It's overkill," Dav said. "We have guns. You have the prisoners restrained now. We're more than ready."

Malik grinned. "There's no such things as overkill. That's just something idiots believe."

"No one's getting out of here," Benj said. "No one. You've pretty much guaranteed that, Malik."

"No. I've guaranteed that they won't try anything stupid. We've got surveillance radar and explosives; we've told them as much, and I'm sure they aren't about to assume we're bluffing. They'll know that there is no way they can rush in here and extract any hostages, not before I blow us all to hell. They'll have to take the deal. So I guess these bags of fertilizer may actually help save your life, Benj."

"I'm sure you'll find a way to kill us all," Samantha said.

Malik didn't even seem to hear her anymore.

45

VASILY HAD been given a stateroom on *Basilica*, since there seemed to be well over a dozen available, and Danny Pyke had made it clear that no one would be heading back to New York before they had an answer from the Russian Aerospace Defense Forces.

Danny didn't bother to tell Vasily what the answer was after waking him up in the middle of the night.

Vasily checked his tablet as he slipped it back in his pocket. Four AM, Eastern time. Sometime around lunch for most of Russia.

It was the pilot, Danny, Vasily, and Carter Elgin who made the trip off *Basilica*, flying mostly east, toward the faintest hints of sunrise.

"Can I ask to where we are headed?" Vasily said through his headset.

Carter nodded, but didn't say anything.

"Yes," Vasily said, "so where are we headed?"

"We're taking a meeting with some important Russians," Carter said.

"And might you tell me where we are taking this meeting?"

"Somewhere Russian."

Vasily decided not to press it further, and waited as patiently as he could for their arrival at somewhere Russian. Not that there was any Russian territory in the Atlantic Ocean, or Russian allies…

All he saw was water below them, no sign of land.

He didn't think these Bell helicopters had a range of more than five or maybe seven hundred kilometers. And they were headed East by Northeast, skirting US and quite possibly Canadian airspace.

He pulled out his tablet.

Even if they'd been heading toward Bermuda, which they weren't, he still wasn't sure they'd have made it. They were flying out into the middle of the North Atlantic, a couple thousand kilometers short of reaching land.

So either Carter Elgin had a second—secret—seastead a little further out, or they were on their way to rendezvous with someone else's ship.

Like the man from the VKO had mentioned. A Russian Naval task force on its way to them, in the North Atlantic.

Half a world away from Russia.

He saw the *Georgy Flyorov* sprawled out to the northeast of them. He knew it was the *Flyorov* from the blue and white Russian naval ensign, and the deck with half a squadron of Sukhoi fighters (probably Su-34s, if he knew his planes).

The *Flyorov* shouldn't have been in the North Atlantic; there was no way it could have steamed out from Murmansk—where he'd heard it was stationed—or even Kaliningrad in time to meet them, not that he knew if nuclear-powered carriers could "steam" anywhere.

The *Flyorov* had already been nearby.

And without any kind of escort. The most advanced and powerful ship of the Russian Navy, alone in the middle of the ocean. And no one had noticed? No spy satellites? No radar stations?

The helicopter landed on the flight deck.

Two officers greeted Carter Elgin the moment he stepped off.

The rear admiral and the captain.

They led Carter, Danny, and Vasily away from the helicopter, which was then hooked up for a recharge. Vasily hadn't realized it was an electric engine; he'd expected a battery-powered helo to be a little quieter, for some reason.

"No escorts?" Carter asked the rear admiral.

"We do have escorts," the officer replied. "But the *Flyorov* was designed not to need them."

Carter nodded.

Vasily assumed submarines, but he had no way to be sure. Could submarines even be considered an escort?

He didn't feel like it would be well-received for him to ask.

They were led inside the tower, to a room that looked more like it belonged in an office building than an aircraft carrier, with a long table that looked like it had a glass top.

The captain greeted Vasily in Russian, at long last, saying that he'd met his brother on a few occasions.

Vasily replied politely, but didn't do anything else to continue the conversation. He knew he was only there because of his last name, not because he was actually needed to be anything more than that.

The communication barrier was almost non-existent, both Russian naval officers having a strong grasp of English. Vasily wondered if that had just as strong an understanding of Mandarin.

Carter explained the situation with the hostages, while the officers nodded in a way that made it clear that they were already well-aware of what was going on.

Then Danny spoke up. "We've figured out where they are. Sent you the coordinates."

"We have them," the captain said.

Carter turned to Vasily. "A little over two hundred klicks south of where we'd last located them," he said. "An even more remote place along Hudson Bay."

Vasily nodded.

"I've been instructed to do whatever is required," the rear admiral said.

"They say they're hardened against attack," Carter said. "I'm guessing that means they'll be expecting something like this."

"They will expect something else," the captain said.

Carter nodded. "You have the jump capsules."

"We'll drop five men. Four VDV and one of yours."

Carter looked back to Vasily.

"What's VDV?" Danny asked.

"Air-landing forces," the captain said. "Russian Airborne Troops."

"And this is where you come in," Carter said to Vasily.

"I believe I already came in," Vasily said.

"You've sky-dived before, yes?" the Captain asked.

"I completed one tandem dive, yes. And not on my own."

"We can't do tandem here."

Vasily looked over to Danny, who gave him a nod.

"You didn't ask me, then," Vasily said. "I mean, no one told me."

"If we'd told you," Carter said, "you might have said no."

"We all do what has to be done," the rear admiral said. "To serve our countries and the world."

Vasily took a deep breath. "And what is it I'm expected to do, exactly?"

"We can't drop four Russian soldiers to rescue hostages without a Sol-Rescue representative," Carter said. "Someone I can trust, who can make sure all of those hostages are brought back to *Basilica*. So we can talk to them."

"Then I imagine you can jump instead."

Carter smiled. "I don't speak Russian, Vasily."

Vasily knew he was trapped. His heart was pounding and he felt like he wasn't far off from fainting.

It wasn't like they'd force him to jump. They'd give him a "choice".

But then what? He'd politely decline and try to hitch a ride back to New York?

He knew what his father would say to him. It was Vasily's chance to do something that mattered, beyond hoping his designs would help to inch progress along a little ways.

Shit-your-pants terror, yeah.

But only for a little while.

Telling them no would be a lifetime of shame for Vasily Utkin.

The entire point of the US and Canada's NORAD organization was originally to keep an eye out for Russian incursions, whether that's missiles, planes, naval vessels, or whatever else. Granted, they'd expanded to both drug traffickers and the occasional Chinese incursion, but the whole system was designed to stop exactly what Vasily Utkin was expected to do.

So the Russian Armed Forces had devised a method to get around NORAD, not for some future invasion, but to deter the Americans from sticking their nose into the Russian neighborhood.

And that method was the orbital jump.

Exactly what Vasily was expected to do.

From what the captain told him, the *Georgy Flyorov* had exactly one plane capable of suborbital flight, the MiG 101 cosmoplane; orbital jumps were actually suborbital, since there was no reason to spend an entire revolution in orbit. The whole reason for the jumps was to drop airborne troops fast enough that no one could stop them; if those troops got lucky, they might even reach the landing zone, and they might even reach it without being detected.

From there they'd have new things to worry about, such as the portable surveillance radar that pretty much any group of hostiles would have brought along with them; even if the cosmoplane and the jumpers weren't spotted in the sky, there'd be a 1500 meter radius around the target where anything larger than a fieldmouse would be spotted.

But when Vasily had pointed that out, Carter had told him not to worry. That they'd already considered all the possible hazards.

Which wasn't really an answer.

Each jumper was equipped with a high altitude wingsuit, with a pressurized hard shell helmet and a biomechanical body; the best of both worlds, Carter had assured him.

Used by the Americans, too, Danny had said. For some reason that did make Vasily feel better. Social proof?

Vasily was dressed in Russian airborne field dress, no rank and no nametape, then put into his wingsuit, which required just over an hour for modifications to his specific body shape. The parachute pack had three pull cords, red, blue, and yellow. One was the ripcord, for the pilot chute—he knew that much—and there should be one more for the reserve chute. But there shouldn't have been a third...

He and the four airborne soldiers—who looked far less rigid and austere than he would have expected—were brought to the MiG 101, which looked similar to a fighter jet, but without the telltale missile payload, and with a long cockpit with three rows of seating, each row ostensibly wide enough for two people to squeeze in.

The cockpit canopy was split into two panels, one raising forward and the other to the rear, both open for loading, with three orange rolling metal ladders flush with the side of the fuselage.

Vasily climbed up the second ladder, getting shoehorned in beside one of the airborne jumpers, in the middle row, two soldiers behind and one up front with the pilot.

With his pack, he felt like he was balancing over the front of the seat; the lower straps had been loosened enough to wrap over his waist, but the shoulder straps were just left to hang.

It didn't feel particularly safe.

Once the pilot and all of the passengers were aboard, the carrier crew brought over the jump cylinders. They didn't look like cylinders at all.

The MiG 101 had the body of a fighter, not a cargo plane; the Russian engineers had known from the start of the orbital jump project that they would never be given enough room in the drop plane for a fully-formed crew cylinder.

One of the greatest advantages to being a Russian engineer has always been knowing *almost instinctively* how little you'll be given to work with.

Vasily knew that; even growing up mostly in London, he knew that. But that didn't mean he had any idea how to use what looked like a heavy canvas blanket.

The soldier beside him seemed to read his mind, or at least the panic on his face.

"It's easy," he said, in Russian. "You attach the straps around your shoulders. I'll tell you when."

Vasily nodded. He wanted more details, but didn't want the real details, really. And he didn't trust the man beside him to understand the need for a string of white lies.

Carter and Danny gave him the thumbs up as the cosmoplane taxied to the catapult. Vasily tried his best not to vomit into his helmet.

The initial launch felt ten times as fast as taking off from a runway, but he wasn't sure if his nerves were overexagerrating the feeling. The MiG 101 arced upwards, almost like the mirror reverse of a rocket launch, going from near-horizontal to something closer to forty degrees.

Vasily could barely see the water, below and behind him.

He mostly saw the sky, which was already starting to darken from blue to purple.

"Almost there," the soldier beside him said. "Do what I do." He first fed a small red cable from the cylinder through a small hole on his parachute pack. "Make sure you hear the snap." Then he threaded his legs through the straps on the heavy cream-colored fabric, before doing the same with his shoulders.

Vasily did the same, hoping that he really had hear that snap from his little red cable. Once he'd pulled the straps up his legs and over his shoulder, he felt like he was bear-hugging a parachute; he couldn't see anything but heavy canvas in front of him.

"What happens next?" he asked.

"We will be ejected. By the pilot."

Vasily nodded, not that anyone would be able to see it.

He knew enough about ejection seats to know that it was going to put him through more G-force than he could imagine. The canopy would need to open; he wondered what that would mean for the pilot.

He couldn't see; the deflated cylinder was blocking his vision completely.

He *felt* like they were starting to arc downward. He *felt* like maybe the cosmoplane was even starting to lose speed.

"Ready?" his neighbor asked.

"Not at all."

He heard laughing as his body was thrown up through the ceiling.

He hadn't seen the canopy open; he hadn't seen anything but the cylinder in front of him. He knew the seat was gone, but had no idea whether it had broken away to fall on its own, or if it had somehow managed to stay attached to the cosmoplane.

He felt himself arcing like a rocket, or like a giant backflip.

He wasn't in control of it; he wasn't sure how he'd gain control.

His body was moving diagonally down, presumably toward the planet at ridiculous speed.

He was starting to feel pretty sure that he'd be dead in a matter of minutes, if not sooner.

His stomach had a dull ache, almost as though the speed and G-force was so intense that his body couldn't even figure out how to let him know it was queasy.

But the strangest thing he noticed was just how loud it was, the air—the wind—flapping hard against his body. He had no skin exposed, but he was still receiving sensations, like he was dressed in a t-shirt and swim trunks, windsurfing in Dorset in mid-July.

And then the cylinder started to grow.

It was like a balloon, but different, since it was inflating around him, like a fat saucer. He looked behind and saw that the back wasn't closing behind him; there was a gap almost large enough to fit his entire body, centered around his ass crack.

He felt his body shift, his head lurching forward, like he was lying on his stomach. For some reason he'd imagined it being more like riding a sled.

He'd never seen video of a Russian jump cylinder; the American ones were more like teardrop-shaped escape pods, the bottom behind wide like the top of an upside-down umbrella.

The Russian cylinder was not really a cylinder, if you went with the standard definitions of a cylinder being a) somewhat cylindrical, and b) not having a giant hole in the backside.

Vasily wondered if maybe he'd been unlucky enough to get a malfunctioning one, a cylinder made by an alcoholic factory worker first thing Monday morning, arteries overflowing with vodka.

What was it that American astronaut had thought of? Every component having been built by the lowest bidder?

In Post-Putin Russia, it wasn't even the lowest bidder you always had to worry about. Every once in a while it was the highest *briber*.

Vasily had to face facts, that he might never get another chance at chicken vindaloo on Swallow Street, back home in London, *in the real Soho*. And he might never get another chance with Adrian, who'd always told him to pop by once he got back to England.

Were you still a hero if you didn't actually finish the mission? Would his father even know how he'd died?

He could feel the heat. They ejection arc had slowed him down; he knew that, but he was still slicing through the atmosphere, his possibly suboptimal cylinder taking on a good amount of re-entry burn, no matter the angle of his descent.

He waited for things to get hotter, for the slight warmth to start feeling like he'd fallen gut-first into a bonfire.

But it didn't happen, and eventually he could feel the heat going away, his body feeling a little more comfortable.

The air getting that much louder, the wind stronger.

And then he heard someone speaking to him.

Through his helmet.

"Vasily," the voice said. "Pull the red cord."

He scrambled to grab the right cord. Not blue, not yellow.

He grabbed the red pull cord. He yanked it.

The jump cylinder fell away.

He pushed out his arms and legs, to expand the area of the wingsuit. He felt the wind currents pushing against the squirrel flaps of his wingsuit. He was moving forward as he fell.

He could see the ground below.

But mostly the ocean, underneath him.

He didn't know for sure it was Hudson Bay, but he could hazard a guess.

He was moving toward land, the wingsuit gliding in the current. But he wasn't sure he was moving there quickly enough to make it. He knew they'd have to pull their chutes before too long, and once that happened there'd be little forward momentum.

He saw three of the other jumpers. He couldn't tell which one had been sitting beside him in the MiG 101, or which one had spoken to him through his helmet.

And he didn't know what had happened to the fourth.

"We need to get to the drop zone," the voice in his helmet said. "Follow the leader."

"I don't know how to steer," Vasily said.

"They told me you'd jumped before."

"Not really."

There was no answer to that.

He watched as the three jumpers around him arched their bodies and rolled their shoulders, turning left with the wind as they fell. Moving away from him.

He saw the fourth jumper come up beside him, on his left.

"Do what I do," the voice said, as the fourth jumper gave him a thumbs up with his outstretched right hand. "Steer with your feet. Push your right foot down."

Vasily did as he was told, dropping his right foot and feeling his body turn left. Like an airplane.

"Good," the jumper said. "We need to catch up to the others. Let your arms go up above your back. Slowly."

Vasily gently raised his arms. His body started tipping downward. He started gaining speed.

"Good, Vasily. Good."

The fourth jumper did the same.

They'd started gaining on the other jumpers, but they were at least a hundred meters closer to the ground.

"Lower your arms again," the jumper said.

He did.

And his body slowed a little. He was comfortable enough to adjust on his own, to keep an even pace with the other jumpers.

They were still over the ocean.

"We'll get there," the soldier gliding beside him said. "We won't pull the chutes until we're in the right place. You're doing great, Vasily."

Vasily nodded.

And noticed how much it affected his speed, slowing him down a little more.

He'd never thought he'd fly. He'd never really realize it was possible to feel like that, like he had that power.

Now he understood why people did it. It wasn't the two minutes of awkwardness he'd felt in his tandem jump; it had been at least five minutes of perfect freedom, riding the air currents like an albatross, over a landscape that was probably only beautiful to him because he was gliding above it.

It was a landscape that seemed totally empty of human life.

There's a beauty in that alone.

He saw the mouth of a river below. Two rivers. One big and one small.

"We need to turn right," the jumper beside him said. "Drop zone is farther north."

He followed the lead of the other jumpers, moving over the forests by the shore of the bay.

They were getting low. Lower than Vasily had expected.

"We need to pull the chutes," Vasily said.

"We can't. We're too far from the drop zone, and too exposed. They might see the chutes from here."

Vasily slowed his fall a little.

"We need to keep going," the jumper said. "Don't fall behind."

"We're too low."

"We're not too low."

"Shit," Vasily said, in English.

"Dermo," the jumper replied, chuckling. "We curse in Russian on this mission."

They kept falling down and moving forward.

Losing altitude.

Vasily knew he didn't have to wait. They were over land. Coming up short would be better than pancaking.

"Trust me, Vasily. I've done this before."

Vasily nodded. And almost lost control of his glide.

But he kept it together. He did his best.

And kept falling toward the ground.

He mouthed a short prayer. And waited for things to go very wrong. He knew they were lower than they should be.

"Okay, Vasily… now we pull the chute. The blue cord."

Vasily pulled the ripcord.

His body didn't fly upward, but it felt almost like someone had reached out and grabbed him, slowing his fall a lot harder than he'd have expected.

He saw the other parachutes come out.

He took a deep breath.

"We're low," the jumper said. "It will be a rough landing, Vasily."

"I know."

He saw a river, one of several smaller ones making their way to the bay.

There was a marshy patch beside it.

He gently steered the parachute toward it; he figured that getting a little wet would be better than impaling himself on a tree.

He braced himself for the landing.

He hit the ground hard, but it was soft enough that when he rolled into the marsh, his body pushed down on the turf, digging in.

It didn't hurt.

He looked around.

He couldn't see the other jumpers; he'd been focused on the landing, not on their positions.

He pulled out the map they'd given him, a satellite image with labels overlaid, the drop zone and the target objective, which was a little farther south along the coast.

He made his best guess on the river he'd chosen. It seemed to match the river at the drop zone. He was ninety percent sure.

Or a solid eighty percent. Most of the rivers looked alike.

At least he knew in which direction the target would be. He had to follow the shore of Hudson Bay, moving south.

Hopefully he'd find the other jumpers, the ones who had weapons and combat experience. And who weren't completely terrified of actually reaching the small abandoned house Danny Pyke had circled on the maps.

He unhooked his parachute lines and started climbing out of his wingsuit.

Vasily was the one who was found, by three of the jumpers.

He recognized one as the man who'd spoken to him in the air. The man who'd sat beside him in the cosmoplane.

They all had their packs, which made Vasily glad he'd kept his, once he'd disconnected the chute.

"We're missing someone?" Vasily asked.

"He'll find us," the man replied.

Vasily could see the man's nametape. *бугадзе*. *Bugadze*. He recognized the surname. A Georgian name in Russian script.

The other two soldiers had Russian names, Veselov and Yartsev.

Bugadze seemed to be the leader of the squad, though none of them had any indicators of rank on their field uniforms. They had their SR-3 Vikhr—"Whirlwind"—rifles but were without their caps, having worn the helmets up until they'd landed. Bugadze's hair showing more gray than Vasily would have expected from an airborne jumper.

Of course, Vasily was dressed the same way, the only difference being the lack of nametape. Not that having Utkin on his nametape was something he would want, even if Viktor Utkin wasn't his father.

They walked five hundred meters in from the bay, just back from where the gravel and the rock outcrops of the shoreline hit the grass and low forest, along a dry ridge. Dry being relative, of course; every few steps would bring the squish of wetter ground, but nothing like the boglands closer to the water. Vasily had seen from the map that there would be bogs inland, as well.

They crossed a creek, almost narrow enough to jump over, but not quite, so Vasily put his boots through the water, hoping they really were waterproof.

They met up with the fourth airborne soldier a little past the crossing, a man with Emin on his nametape.

"They didn't give you a gun," Emin said as he looked Vasily over.

"I don't have the training," Vasily replied.

"Rich boys don't get conscripted," Veselov said, with an exaggerated sneer. "Just a joke."

"No more jokes," Bugadze said.

He moved them forward, to another river lined with thicker and taller evergreen trees. It was wide and deep enough that Vasily got wet above his knees. The water was frigid.

The forest in front of them looked dense, more like what Vasily remembered from the Northwestern District of Russia, which had never really been his home, despite having to spend too many summers there.

At least he hadn't been expected to stay for the winters.

"Two and a half kilometers until we reach the townsite," Bugadze said. "We have to assume they might have seen us."

His men nodded, which Vasily took to mean that they had some kind of pre-arranged plan, or maybe just a standard stock plan for similar situations. Surrounding the house, attacking from two directions... something *tactical*.

Veselov pulled something out of his pack.

A small electronic device, hardened.

"We used to try and jam radar," he said, giving Vasily a friendly smile. "Now we don't need to."

He pulled an antenna out from the device, before opening it like a small toolbox.

There was a display inside. A touch screen.

Veselov got to work.

"Man-portable radar is still an underdeveloped product," Bugadze said. "All six major manufacturers use some of the same components. A few of those components come from Germany. We have friends in Germany these days."

"They'll see nothing different," Veselov said. "They won't see us coming."

"You're with me," Bugadze said to Vasily. "You are my shadow. Behind me at all times."

Vasily nodded.

And followed Bugadze through the forest, toward the abandoned townsite.

Derrick McPherson had gotten the ESA to shared the view from its nearest-orbiting surveillance sat, giving them a half-decent view of Port Nelson. They'd seen the boat moored at an old launch, and they'd even caught an image of two people, both apparently men, standing just outside an abandoned house.

That was from the day before. Early evening.

There was a chance the hostages had been moved. But it wasn't likely.

They'd chosen a location they'd hoped would be hidden from the sats, an crumbling building in an abandoned port town. There weren't a lot of places nearby to move the captives.

Bugadze cut to the right, moving farther inland. The other three soldiers kept moving parallel to the shore. Vasily stuck with Bugadze, as instructed.

He could see an abandoned building, a house.

But he was pretty confident it wasn't the target, since it had partially caved in.

Bugadze circled around the house, crossing an overgrown path. Probably an old road. Another hundred meters past that path, Bugadze turned left. Back toward the town and the bay.

Vasily saw the target.

A wood house that had managed to stand up to the Canadian winters.

Bugadze motioned for Vasily to get low and stay put.

He responded with a quick nod.

Bugadze inched closer to the house.

The back of the house, from what Vasily could see, a small back door and a couple of small windows, the glass having fallen but not shattered.

Vasily heard gunshots.

He watched as Bugadze cursed quietly and moved toward the house.

More gunshots.

Closer.

Vasily watched as the airborne soldier fell into the grass.

At first he couldn't tell; was Bugadze crawling in? Keeping low?

But Bugadze wasn't moving.

Vasily wasn't sure he was even alive.

He heard more gunfire. More than one gun, more than one location.

Like a battle, between two or more positions.

The other Russian soldiers were still fighting.

On the far side of the house.

Vasily stayed down.

He didn't move.

He wasn't trained for any of this.

46

THERE'D BEEN no signal on the surveillance radar.

The woods around the abandoned house in Port Nelson had been quiet. Too quiet, since Malik had already noticed deer feeding less than five hundred meters from the building, and had noticed the moment they magically disappeared from the screen.

That wasn't beyond Carter Elgin's capabilities, taking control of the radar display.

But Malik had a feeling he wasn't dealing with a handful of hobbyists. He had a feeling he was dealing with *someone's* special forces.

And they were somewhere between 1500 and maybe 3000 meters out.

So he went to the closet and pulled out his duffel bag.

And passed the second homebrewed AR-15 to Chuck.

There was no way he'd be trusting it to Dav, and he didn't know enough about the other Chinese guy.

"They're coming now," Malik said. "Can't track them on radar."

"Shit," Dav said. "How do we know where they are?"

"We hypothesize. A house with two doors. That means two points of entry, assuming they don't try to climb through these little windows." He looked to Chuck. "I'll take the front door, you take the back. Front may be the bigger group, but back could be the real target."

Chuck nodded.

And took up a position at one of the windows facing the back of the house.

Malik looked over to Benj. "You can explain this to your friends, right?" he asked. "They'll understand that interfering with us in any way is just going to get them deader?"

Benj nodded.

Malik looked up the line. The white guy didn't look like he'd be a problem. The cute blonde was too frightened to do much. The Korean girl was giving him a crazy-eyed stare, while the indian girl was looking down at her feet.

If he had to guess, he'd put his money on the indian girl. She was the one who was actually coming up with a plan.

"Put that one in the other room," Malik said to Dav, pointing her out. "And the Asian bitch, too. And see if you can block that door."

Dav grabbed the indian girl's chair and started dragging her to the other room. He ended up needing help lifting her over a mound of dirt blocking the corridor, but the other Chinese operative had been ready to assist.

They moved the Korean girl as well.

Malik looked back to Benj, trying to get a read.

Putting two hostages in another room, unsupervised... that was a risk. But he didn't get the feeling that Benj saw it as one, as something that might turn things in his favor.

And it wasn't like those two ladies were fans of each other.

"You should warn them," Benj said.

Malik almost laughed. "What?"

"You should tell whoever's coming that they can't pull it off. That hostages will die."

"That's what every hostage-taker tells people," Malik said. "Won't make a difference. They've come this far, they'll make the attempt."

"Let me go out there. Reason with them."

"Are you insane, Benj? Send the black guy out and hope he doesn't get shot?"

"I'm not going out there," Chloe—the cute blonde—said.

"Don't worry," Benj said.

"No, she should definitely start shitting her pants," Malik said. "This is going to go bad."

"You haven't killed us yet," the white guy, Koskela, said.

"I don't want to kill anyone."

"No more whittling?" Benj asked.

"I'm one of the good guys," Malik said. "I know you can't see that right now, but—"

"You killed three people," Koskela said. "You already admitted that."

"Three people... I think that makes me tied with my colleague, here."

"What is he talking about?" Chloe asked.

"It's not important," Benj said.

"Okay," Malik said, "so now we all shut up."

Benj gave a nod. "Okay."

And the others kept quiet.

Malik made first contact.

He saw movement, not deer. He fired through the front window, then dropped down beside Koskela's chair.

And he waited for the return fire.

It would tell him quite a bit about who was outside.

Three shots, from right where he'd first positioned himself. By the window. Suppressed rounds.

Subdued. Restrained. Professionals. More than regular army.

Malik knew those soldiers would need to storm the house if they expected to win; they weren't about to shoot blindly into a building with five hostages.

He grabbed Koskela's chair, from the front leg, and dragged him along the floor, toward the front window, keeping low.

He made sure Koskela was visible.

That it was clear what he was.

No more shots.

Malik waited.

He heard Chuck fire.

"One target down," Chuck said.

Out of how many?

There's been no more fire on Malik's side.

No movement either, from what he could see. His best guess was two to three soldiers hunkered down behind a thick bank of trees and underbrush.

He couldn't see them, but if they'd move left or right, forward or back, he would have seen or heard something.

The attackers were pinned down, even without any new shots fired.

They'd expected full surprise.

They'd relied on it.

Seemed like a big fuck-up for special forces.

Which made him uneasy.

"How many could there be?" he asked, to whoever might have an answer. He felt weird close to lying on the floor and asking for input. "No planes, no helos, no boats…"

"They couldn't have hiked in," Dav said. "There's nothing out here."

"Do not underestimate the possibilities," Chuck said, still manning the back window.

"They must have been dropped in," Malik said. "They've come too soon to have come by land."

"No planes," Dav said.

"Suborbital jump," Chuck said.

"Could be," Malik said. "So US, China, or…"

"Russia," Dav said.

"They have you surrounded," Benj said. "We can still end this peacefully."

"There's a man down," Dav said. "They won't forgive that."

"We have the upper hand," Malik said. "And they need to know that."

He slowly brought himself up along the side of the window, behind Koskela.

"You know we have hostages," he called out. "We have explosives." Even if they were Russian—not that they could be sure—they had to speak some English, right?

"*Vzorvat,*" Chuck said.

"What?"

"Say that. Blow up. *Vi-zai-ra-vite*."

Malik did his best to copy the word, hoping that Chuck wasn't full of shit. He knew that the Chinese had been trying to ramp up their Russian, but it had never been a priority.

"Now say *zi-dai-cha*," Chuck said. "Surrender."

Malik said both phrases, English and Russian. *Blow up. Surrender. Blow up. Surrender.*

There was no response.

No movement.

They were going to sit out there and wait. Hoping to make Malik sweat. As if they had the upper hand.

"They think we don't have the balls," Malik said.

"What?" Dav said.

"They think we won't blow up the building."

Dav nodded. "I think they're right. I don't want to blow up."

"So we kill some hostages."

"Don't do it," Benj said. "You'll force their hand."

But he had to do *something*.

"Let me talk to them," Benj said. "I can get something worked out."

"We're not making some bargain," Malik said. "They surrender or this old house explodes."

"Then let me tell them that. I'll go out and deliver the message, and I can come back and tell you how many guys are out there, what they've got with 'em."

"Send someone else out," Dav said. "Someone less valuable. So if they get shot or don't come back…"

"The blonde," Malik said. "She goes out. They won't shoot a woman, right?"

He lowered himself down again, then crawled back to the row of chairs, to where Chloe was bound.

He stood up, leaned in.

And put both hands on the cute blonde's throat.

"What the fuck?" Koskela said.

Malik didn't bother to answer him.

"Are you going to do what's expected of you?" he asked Chloe. "You tell them we won't surrender, that if they try anything, we'll blow everyone up."

She nodded slowly.

Malik could hear Koskela's growls from his seat by the window. Muttering all sorts of terrible shit.

He understood. He'd have done the same.

"They will want you to stay with them," Malik told her, lessening the pressure on her throat, just a little. "But that won't work."

She stared at him, terrified.

Malik didn't like it. But it had to be done that way.

"If you don't come back, I will have to kill Jared Koskela."

She gave another slow nod.

He took out his pocket knife and reached over to the back of the chair. He started cutting through the layers of duct tape.

He helped her stand up.

"You tell them, Chuck," he said. "Tell them she's coming out, and not to gun her down."

Chuck made the announcement, calling out toward the front of the house, first in English, and then in a strange Chinese-style Russian that didn't sound at all like what you'd hear from old cold war movies or interviews with flash-in-the-pan Moscow popwhores.

We're sending a hostage out. Do not shoot her. Do not stop her from coming back inside.

"You keep an eye out," Malik said to Chuck. "There's a chance they'll come from the back while we're doing this."

Chuck nodded.

Malik gave Chloe a gentle-enough push toward the door.

"Remember," he told her.

She opened the door and stepped out.

Malik hadn't cut the ties off her wrists.

He wondered if that had been a mistake. The Russians wouldn't be able to see her hands.

Shit.

He went back down to his position below Koskela, by the window.

"I will kill you," Koskela whispered.

"Don't bother," Malik said.

He watched as Chloe walked slowly forward, in a straight line out from the front door.

No response.

No movement.

She slowly turned and looked back at the house.

"Keep going, Chloe," Malik said.

She kept walking.

"Are they even out there, still?" Dav asked.

"Shut up," Malik said. "I know what I'm doing."

He waited for Chloe to take a few more steps. To the tree line.

"Okay, Chloe," he called to her. "Stop there. And wait."

It didn't make sense.

When a hostage is released, you grab that hostage, the first chance you get. That's how they teach it.

In America.

Was that it? A different set of protocols? Some weird Russian way of dealing with hostage taking?

He'd heard the stories, like the one from Lebanon in the late 20th century, when the Soviet KGB responded to a hostage crisis by grabbing some relative of the perps and slicing off his dick. Or that theatre siege in Moscow, when the vast majority of dead hostages came at the hand of Russian special forces and their knockout gas.

He remembered something he'd been told by an instructor at Fort Meade. That after years of dealing with separatists, jihadists, and organized crime, the Russians had developed an unwritten rule for hostage negotiation: that the hostages were considered lost from the moment they were taken. They weren't rescuing people so much as bringing them back from the dead.

And the soldiers outside were Russian.

He knew it, deep down.

Russian special forces, maybe. Spetsnaz. Or Russian airborne troops.

Dealing with a kidnapping, not a hostage barricade. They didn't know who Malik was, or Chuck or Dav or that other Chinese guy, Liam or whatever his real name was.

But the Russians knew who they weren't. They weren't terrorists by any academic definition. Not fundamentalist, not extremists, not absolutist.

They expected Malik to turn tail, to try and save his skin.

The Russians thought it was about money, or some light veil of ideology covering, well, money again.

Malik knew he could use that.

"We can negotiate," Malik called out. He turned to Chuck, expecting him to translate.

"You are joking," Chuck said.

Malik motioned with his hands. *Hold on. Let me play this out.*

Chuck hesitated, then gave a quick nod.

And called out what Malik hoped was an appropriate Russian translation.

Someone called back. Not Chloe, obviously, since it was a man's voice and a short burst of Russian.

"They're asking what we want," Chuck said.

"Safe passage out," Malik said. "And two of their rifles. They send two guns back in with Chloe, and then we walk out the back with a couple hostages."

Chuck delivered the message.

Malik added some more. "We'll leave the last two hostages at the dock, by that hydro project."

He waited as Chuck spoke, and no one responded.

He knew it would take time.

Back and forth, shows of good faith or whatever.

He expected to have to free one hostage, at least.

The reply came back.

"They say we have a deal," Chuck said.

Bullshit.

There was no way they'd agree that quickly. Not for a real arrangement. Only for some Russian plan to fuck them up.

Malik waited for the other shoe.

"It's not for real," Dav said.

"I know," Malik replied. "I'm not an idiot."

"What do I tell them?" Chuck asked.

"To send Chloe back with two rifles."

Chuck made the translation.

"Nyet," was the reply.

"Then what?" Malik said.

They waited.

Nothing more.

"What the fuck are they doing?" Dav asked.

"Calm down," Malik said.

"It's some kind of mindfuck."

"Calm the fuck down."

"Do they have men out the back? Do we know?"

"The one I shot is still down," Chuck said.

"Shut up," Malik said. "Everyone. Just be quiet, alright?"

"We should make a run," Dav said. "Grab a couple hostages and go."

Malik had brought Dav along because he'd been told he needed someone he could rely on, in case the Chinese tried to start running the show. His gut had told him, that Dav wasn't reliable. But Malik had done what he was told.

Like a fucking idiot.

"I'm only going to say this one more time, Dav," he said. "If you don't shut the fuck up, and I mean right the fuck now, I'm going to shoot you myself. Save the Russians a bullet."

"You shoot me and they'll think you're killing hostages," Dav said.

Fuck.

Dav was a huge liability.

The man was holding his pistol like he didn't know what it was.

But yeah… Malik couldn't shoot him.

"So we run," Dav said, "and before they know what's happened we'll be clear. And we'll still have two hostages, just in case. Those two girls in the other room are both under sixty kilos, no question. Easy enough to pull along—"

"Wait," Chuck said, holding up one finger. "Everyone get down."

That shut Dav up, and he lowered himself to the floor.

"Come over here, Dav," Chuck said. "Hurry."

Dav crawled over to the back window.

"I need you to look at something," Chuck said. "Can you see that man on the ground?"

Dav raised himself up a little, to see over the window shelf.

Malik saw Chuck pull something from his boot.

And run his right hand across Dav's pant leg, just below the crotch.

Dav fell against the wall.

Chuck lowered him down to the floor.

There was a lot blood. Pouring out.

An angled slice across the femoral artery.

Dav was sputtering, not really saying anything. At least in as much shock as Malik happened to be.

He'd be out cold in a few seconds.

And dead in a three or four minutes.

Chuck looked over to Malik. And gave another quick nod.

Malik hadn't asked for that. Not really.

He'd just wanted time to think. He'd wanted Dav to shut up.

But Malik knew he couldn't let on.

"Tell them to send Chloe back," he said to Chuck.

Chuck made the demand.

And got another Russian no in return.

"They want us to panic," Chuck said.

"I know."

"We need to show strength."

"Yeah, I know."

"Will you do that?"

Malik had to.

He'd already sent Chloe out; she and Samantha Yoon were the lowest value hostages, the ones Malik had been given clearance to put down if required.

Put down. That's what he'd been told. Like they were stray dogs.

He could go into that other room and shoot the Korean girl.

But that was an awkward procedure. Crawling over there, low enough that no crafty Russian sniper could take him out… shooting Yoon and then having to prove somehow that he'd shot her.

He couldn't shoot Koskela, the one hostage who was primed and ready to be shot, totally on display.

But Chloe was also on display, still standing outside, the Russians having left her there.

They hadn't come out to get her, hadn't risked being shot at.

He'd had to kill those conservation officers. The first was complicit in attempted murder; the other was bad luck.

And he'd had to kill Mohammed Najjar. He'd had orders, and he'd known that it was only a matter of time before Najjar went public, about his project, and about his time in Virginia.

It would come out soon enough that the President of the United States and his cabinet had formed a strategic partnership with the Chinese military government, the same government being criticized by Congress.

And Najjar would have been front and center in the attacks; Malik had been shown the messages, the friendly correspondence between Najjar and the House Majority Leader. And that word that would send the ailing US stock market into another tailspin. Impeachment.

No one was going to win that; they didn't have the numbers in the House or in the Senate. All they'd do is continue the long attrition, the further erosion of Federal Power. Of any power outside the reach of SolRescue and the other crowdOrgs that were following behind it.

Malik wasn't sure he could kill Chloe Nielsen-Brown.

What had she done? She'd served her country, just like him, spending however many months up in the frozen wastes, making significantly less than she would at any Fortune 500, for a job she couldn't actually include on her resume.

"Malik," Chuck said. "Did you hear me?"

"I heard you," Malik said.

He raised himself up, high enough to get the barrel of his rifle over the window ledge.

He aimed for Chloe's back. At that distance he wasn't sure he could hit her head.

He took the shot.

Something slammed into his head.

He fell back to the floor.

Another kick.

He rolled away, looking up.

He saw Liam, the other Chinese operative, running toward him. Or running toward Koskela, who was gearing up for another kick from his chair.

He heard a gunshot. From out front.

And saw Liam go down.

Headshot.

"Mother fucker," Malik said.

"I can kill him," Chuck said. "I can kill Koskela. Knife or rifle. I can kill him."

"No... not yet."

"I can't see," Koskela said. "I can't see if she's okay."

"I don't know," Benj said.

"Shut up," Malik said.

"We're out of choices," Chuck said.

"They don't know how many of us there are left."

Chuck shook his head. "No... I believe they do know. They shot Liang through the wall. Heat signatures, or something else. They can see that Dav is down, and they probably know he's dead."

"You think they'll charge," Malik said.

"They don't need to."

"Because we're dropping like flies."

Chuck nodded. "You need to keep a hostage positioned between you and the enemy positions."

"They haven't taken a shot on you."

"They can't get a clear shot from the front," Chuck said.

"And they must not have a shooter in back."

"Maybe not."

"We need to go," Malik said. "Better chance of survival on the run." He looked over at Benj. He was the only one still sitting against the wall. "We take McPherson's son and one more. One of the women."

"We kill Koskela."

"No. No one gets killed. Survivors might slow them down, or split up the group."

Chuck crept over to Benj. He cut the duct tape from Benj's chair. Malik watched as the Chinese operative deftly released the prisoner without giving the Russians a clear shot.

Malik crawled toward the other room.

He pushed open the door, keeping low enough that the underbrush outside the house should keep him safe from Russian bullets.

He looked up at the two captives, the pretty indian girl and the highly hate-fuckable Korean.

He decided to choose Rachael Duck. Carter had some attachment to her, more than he had to Samantha Yoon.

Not that he thought Rachael would be any easier to deal with. Just a little quieter.

He tried to copy Chuck's moves, cutting Rachael's tape away while trying not to get shot.

He ordered her to crawl beside him, an extra layer of shielding as he made his way back to the main room.

"They know we are going to run," Chuck said.

"That's fine," Malik said. "They'll secure the captives first."

He hoped.

He forced Rachael to stand, between him and the front of the house, he walked sideways, trying to keep an eye on both his hostage and the woods behind the house.

In case there was another shooter.

Chuck followed behind with Benj McPherson.

They walked outside slowly, but once Chuck and Benj were out, Malik picked up the pace, not a full run, but certainly faster than a jog.

The ground was flat enough, but as he tromped through the undergrowth, Malik knew that some random rock or tree root could send him and his rifle flying.

He heard the sound soon enough, of a door being kicked in.

The Russians were in the house.

He ran a little faster, pulling Rachael along as he went.

He didn't hear them coming out the back.

But he definitely wasn't about to slow down to take a look.

47

VASILY HAD seen his chance the moment the Chinese man's rifle dropped from the window frame. No badass charge, no push to grab Bugadze's gun.

Vasily ran for the trees behind the house, putting more ground between him and the hostage-takers. He wasn't armed, he wasn't trained, and he didn't have any reason to get himself shot.

He would wait in the forest.

And if there was something that came up, something he could do… well, then he would do it. He wasn't going to run away.

He was just going to wait.

The black gunman and the Chinese man at the window had taken two of the hostages—one of them Benj McPherson—and moved out the back door.

Vasily moved farther away, enough so they wouldn't see him. And even though he wouldn't be able to see them, either, he could definitely hear them. The female captive had been making as much noise as possible as she pushed through the forest; Vasily had a feeling it wasn't just her nerves.

He could anticipate the route; the location of their boat was marked on the sat map, too, at a landing at the river mouth. That meant they would be making a turn to their left soon, to reach the water.

So Vasily made the turn. He would go to the boat, and find a place to hide.

And wait.

He chose a stand of pine not far from the shore, about as close as he could get to the boat without being seen.

He had a rock in his hand, light enough to carry, heavy enough to fuck somebody up.

Not that he thought he'd get a chance to stop them. Two armed men with hostages. Not really the right targets for a first-time murderer with a blunt object.

But he could report back to the Russian troops, and they could place a sat call back to the *Flyorov* and to Carter Elgin. Vasily was almost positive that some of the hostages had survived, though he couldn't be certain of it.

Not that it would matter much to Derrick McPherson, not for as long as his son was still being held.

He saw the woman stumble.

She fell to the ground.

The black gunman had let her fall, pulling away as she dropped.

"Shit," she said. "I think I sprained my ankle."

"I'll take Benj," the man said to the other gunman. "You deal with his idiot."

"Just leave her here," Benj said. "Slow them down some more."

"She comes with us," the black gunman said.

But he'd grabbed Benj's shoulder, pushing him toward the boat, leaving the dark-haired woman behind.

The Chinese gunman knelt down beside the woman.

And with a pocket knife, he cut off the woman's cable tie.

He started to help her up to her feet.

Vasily didn't want to do it.

He wanted to come up with any reason not to.

But he could hear his father's taunts, that he was a coward, that he was a *pedik*. A *faggot*. That somehow Vasily wasn't man enough, because he'd never been interested in the girls, because he'd been more interested in guys like Adrian, or the football player he'd met in Petrozavodsk.

That he was *less than*.

He ran out with the rock.

He slammed it against the Chinese man's head.

The man fell.

The woman grabbed the rifle.

She hadn't hesitated.

She pointed it toward Benj's captor.

"Drop your weapon," she said.

"You don't know how to shoot that," the black gunman said.

"Oh, I know how to shoot it."

The man had put Benj McPherson between him and the woman. He was backing up, toward the shore and the boat.

"You can have Benj," the man said. "If you let me leave."

"Why should I let you leave?"

"It's the smart choice, Rachael. You let me go and Benj doesn't get hurt. Otherwise he might get hurt, right?"

"I could just take my chances," she said.

"You could."

The woman didn't say anything else.

She just stood with the gun aimed.

The gunman kept moving backward.

He reached the edge of the boat.

He let go of Benj McPherson, climbing over the side.

But Benj was still in between.

The boat was moored to a fallen log.

The gunman hadn't taken the risk of untying it.

"I'm going to leave," he said. "Benj, turn around an untie that rope, would you?"

Benj looked over to the woman, Rachael.

She nodded.

He pulled the rope away from the log.

"Now give me a push," the gunman said.

Benj carefully waded into the river, stepping backward.

He reached the edge of the boat, the water up to his knees.

He gave the boat a shove.

That was all it took for the small motorboat to reach the current, where it started moving toward Hudson Bay.

Vasily watched as the boat drifted east.

"Now walk back toward the trees," the gunman said. "All of you. So no one gets shot."

Vasily followed Rachael's lead, stepping back several paces.

Benj McPherson soon joined them.

They all watched as the man in the boat started his motor, then drove the boat upriver, passing right alongside the island in the middle, where an old rail bridge ran from the mainland, and where someone had run a ship aground.

Vasily reached down beside the Chinese man's body.

It was clear that the rock had killed him. That Vasily had killed him.

He found the knife the Chinese gunman had used on Rachael's cable tie. He freed Benj McPherson.

"Thank you," Benj said. "Both of you."

"Yes," Rachael said, looking over to Vasily. "Thank you. I was worried you wouldn't do it."

"Wouldn't do it?"

"When I fell. I knew you'd be close by."

"How?"

"I saw you through the window," she said. "They couldn't see you, but I could. But… but I thought you'd have a gun. Being a soldier and everything."

"I'm not a soldier. Not in the least."

"Then what are you?" Benj asked.

"I'm a mechanical engineer."

"Like Jared," Rachael said. She gave him a knowing look. "We need to go back."

Vasily nodded.

He'd killed a man.

He didn't regret it, as nauseous as it had made him feel. He'd had to do it.

But it didn't make him feel any different.

That wasn't what he'd expected at all.

Two of the Russian soldiers—Emin and Veselov—reached them on the way back to the house.

Vasily gave them a quick summary, not really underplaying his part, but trying not to sound like he was trying to show off.

He wasn't his father, *Utkin Khvastun*. Utkin the Braggart.

They all started back as a group.

"Bugadze is alive," Emin said, in Russian, "but it's serious. Yartsev has called for extraction."

"You think they'll come to get us?" Vasily asked.

Emin shook his head. "I don't think they can risk another incursion. But we had to ask. We'll have to make it to the rendezvous that your Mr. Elgin has set up."

Vasily explained the situation to Rachael and Benj, in English.

"So what does that mean?" Rachael asked. "For your comrade?"

"I don't know," Vasily said.

"What about Chloe?" Benj asked. "Malik tried to kill her."

Vasily posed the question to Emin, about the blonde woman. Emin smiled and told him, and Vasily gladly passed the message along.

"The bullet barely touched her," Vasily said. "Her shoulder. She's in far better shape than Bugadze."

"I'm sorry," Rachael said.

Vasily nodded.

"We have no way of giving him a smooth ride out of here," Emin said. "There are no boats that I can see."

Vasily passed the message on to the non-Russian speakers.

"There might be a boat up a York Factory," Rachael said. "But it's on the wrong side of the Nelson."

"Does it have a motor?" Vasily asked.

"Then what's the exit plan?" Benj asked. "They must have a plan, right?"

"There is. Carter Elgin has set up something. I'll find out the details."
Vasily asked Emin.

"Five kilometers west, along the old rail bed," Emin said. "But Bugadze
won't make it that far. We can't carry him."

"But it's a rail bed," Vasily said. "I believe it should be level enough. We
could make some type of stretcher."

"It'll slow us down."

"Some of us can leave and make the rendezvous, and can then travel
back here, to retrieve him."

"I don't know if we can save him," Emin said.

"Surely you can't be serious."

Emin sighed. "He's my friend. I wouldn't be saying this if it wasn't true.
Even if we get him to the rendezvous, it's almost a hundred kilometers
back to the highway, on all terrain vehicles over an uneven rail bed."

"We need to figure something out, then."

They reached the abandoned house.

Rachael rushed inside, with Benj following close behind.

Vasily stayed outside, to talk to Emin.

"I will stay with Bugadze," he said. "You should reach the rendezvous
and then I'd like you to come back here. We can figure a way to load him
up and to then take him out."

"They won't have a trailer," Emin said. "We'll have to find some other
way of getting him back to the highway."

"We get a boat, then," Vasily said. "We head back to the highway and
we find a boat."

"My team can't wait that long. We have to be at the Port of Churchill
before sunrise. But you don't need to be there, Vasily. You can stay behind."

"But Bugadze will be left behind."

"We'll have to accept that risk," Emin said. "You know, Vasily, we have
an old joke in Russia. Whenever a soldier is found where he shouldn't be."

"I know the joke," Vasily said.

"Then you know what we need to do. Find clothing you can wear. The
uniforms and the equipment come with us. You are an American citizen?"

"UK, actually. I was made to give up my Russian passport."

"Bugaze is on vacation," Emin said. "That's the joke."

"I'm aware."

"We won't be coming back."

"Yeah," Vasily said. "I said that I'm aware."

"And we've been ordered to make sure that McPherson and Duck are
with us at the port. The others can choose what they want to do."

"Okay."

"We should be taking all of them back with us," Veselov said. "It's not safe to leave them here without an escort."

"Don't worry about it," Emin said. "Vasily's got this under control." Emin gave Vasily a nod. "You did well, Vasily."

"Thank you," Vasily said.

Vasily and Chloe had stayed behind with Samantha Yoon, while Jared Koskela had gone with Russians, and Benj and Rachael. Jared was going to find a boat; that was the plan. And Rachael and Benj would do their best to help that along, for as long as they could.

The Russians would be focused on keeping their charges safe; the black gunman, a man named Malik Daley, was somewhere along the Nelson River, most likely on his way to the landing by the hydro project.

Jared and Rachael had given Vasily what details they remembered from their captivity; when Jared had been taken—in a passenger van—to the landing near the end of the highway, he'd seen an identically marked van already parked. Great Nelson Adventures Company.

The Russians were going to check that landing, to see if Malik had reached it. Either there'd be a boat left by the water, or the boat trailer would be gone; if neither of those things had happened, Malik was still on the Nelson.

Maybe he would have expected the Russians to have backup waiting at that landing. That would be a big overestimate.

Yartsev had patched Bugadze up as best he could, relying on his background as a field medic; that meant that the wounded man was bandaged up for transport, the bleeding stopped and blood substitute and painkillers given, but Yartsev had explained that without a doctor, Bugadze would not survive for more than a day or two, at the very most.

Chloe and Samantha both had first aid training, but since Samantha was the only one of the three to have used a gun, she was standing watch with a pistol from the Chinese man who'd been shot through the wall of the house.

Chloe had been considerably uncomfortable with the idea of Samantha having a gun, but hadn't gone into the details. All she'd said was that Samantha couldn't be trusted.

To which Samantha had agreed. "But we have a common interest," she'd said.

So Samantha got guard duty while Chloe tried to keep Bugadze comfortable, since there was not much she could do to make sure he stayed alive. That was up to what Yartsev had already done, mixed with a strong heap of random luck.

At the moment, Bugadze seemed to be resting comfortably, his eyes closed, his breathing a little shallow.

"What do you think the chances are that he'll come back?" Chloe asked. "Malik, I mean."

"He won't be coming back," Vasily said.

"How can you be so sure of that?"

"He's outmanned and outgunned, and he doesn't want to die. I don't think he even wants to kill anyone, frankly."

"He wanted to kill me," she said, sounding offended.

Vasily nodded.

He wasn't about to argue the merits of the man who'd shot a bullet at her.

"So Jared saved your life," he said. "I'm not sure you know that."

She seemed surprised. "No... I didn't know that. I just heard the gunshot and that was it."

"He kicked Malik just as he was taking that shot."

She started tearing up.

"We were all very fortunate today," Vasily said.

Chloe looked down at Bugadze. "What about him?"

"I haven't given up."

She nodded. "You think Jared will bring back a boat."

Vasily gave her a smile. "I know he will, Chloe. He will do whatever it takes to come back for you."

She smiled back. "Thank you," she said. "So much, for everything."

"I'm just doing my job," he said.

"What is your job?"

"Same job as Jared. Mechanical engineer."

"And part-time badass."

He laughed.

"Apparently same as Jared there, too," she said. "God. I love him so much." She looked away. She was embarrassed.

"He'll be back soon enough," Vasily said.

She nodded. "It's funny."

"What's funny?"

"I've been tied up and dragged around for almost a week, by more assholes than I can count."

"Including this one," Samantha said, from her place by the back door.

"She was threatening to drown me," Chloe said. "But I think we're moving past that."

"I don't know if I could move past something like that," Vasily said.

"Oh, I still hate her. Don't worry. But I feel... lucky, I guess?"

"You feel lucky..."

"I'm alive. I'm okay. And Jared's okay." She looked down at Bugadze. "I guess that's selfish of me."

"Jared will come back, and we'll bring Bugadze to a hospital."

"How can you be so sure about that?" Chloe asked.

"Because I've been lucky, too."

48

IT WASN'T a long walk to the rendezvous point. The Russians kept a brisk pace, and Jared felt like he was the one having the most trouble keeping up.

Since he was the only one in the group who'd been attacked by a polar bear last week, he decided to cut himself some slack.

The rail bed wasn't really much of a rail bed, in places the gravel having been swallowed up by the surrounding muck and muskeg. The permafrost melt had been bad here, possibly worse than anywhere else he'd seen, some hot spots having been left with a low and wet sag that still hadn't come close to rebounding with the return of the lower temperatures.

There were two men and four ATVs waiting along the old line. They promptly explained that it really was just the two of them, which by Jared's calculation meant they'd had to make the same trip three times to bring up the quads.

They were aboriginal, like Rachael, but older, probably late thirties. They looked like they could be brothers.

They didn't mention their names, and no one asked.

Jared wasn't sure if that was something the men wanted to avoid telling people.

There were only four helmets total; the Russians insisted that Rachael and Benj wear two of them, and Jared was offered one as well, which left the three soldiers in an awkward position. One of the aboriginal men took his helmet back after no one else would put it on.

Rachael asked how it was expected to transport the five rescued hostages along with four soldiers and even possible prisoners on four ATVs, and one of the aboriginal men replied that they were more than willing to make multiple trips, that it was only an hour back to their community.

The Russians didn't do much talking, since only one of them, a man with a thick eyebrows named Emin—the man was named Emin, not the eyebrows—seemed to speak any English, and very little at that.

All the more reason why they'd brought that other guy along, Vasily, who spoke in a way that mixed the worst of English Chav with a heavy slavic accent.

Jared liked the end result, actually, a weird kind of speech that you just want to keep hearing, way more interesting than Chicagoland, or worse, South Wisconsin Cheesehead.

And it would have been nice to have someone with them to translate.

They rode back along the rail bed, the ride taking just over an hour, as expected, but with the last ten minutes or so being along an actual railroad track, which Rachael had pointed out was the old Hudson Bay Railroad, still kept in close to working order in case something ever went wrong with the new route that ran beside the highway to Churchill.

She'd pointed it out to Benj, not to him.

Jared wasn't sure if that was meant to give him space, or because she'd expected that Jared would have already known that a set of tracks heading due north would be meant for the one place that's due north of there.

He was still angry. He didn't want to be, because mixed in with that anger was the feelings he still had for Rachael, the urge to just find some way to forgive her, to take one last chance at being with her.

But it wasn't something he could do.

He couldn't forgive her, no matter the reasons she'd given. This idea that she'd set him up to be attacked by a goddamn polar bear because she thought it was better than some unknown alternative plan by Carter Elgin, which apparently might not have actually been from Carter Elgin.

There were things about Chloe that annoyed him from time to time, but there was something great about a woman who wasn't caught up in all the bullshit he saw with Rachael.

But if he could find a way to forgive her… if he could just… let it go, somehow…

Every man thinks they want to be in a position to make a play for one girl while they've got another one already hanging on the line. But when it actually happens, it doesn't feel like you'd expect. It just feels like crap.

Maybe it was good that he couldn't move past it with Rachael.

Maybe it was good that she'd almost gotten him killed.

At the end of the trip at Fox Lake Cree Nation, Jared was given a boat by the aboriginal men, and an AR-15 rifle by Rachael, who said he'd probably need it more than she would, since he was headed back to where Malik might be.

"I'm sorry, Jared," she told him. "I really am."

"I know." He didn't have anything else to say to her. He didn't love her. He didn't hate her. He just… he just couldn't forgive her.

She reached in for a hug and he gave it to her.

She kissed him on the cheek, and said goodbye.

Then she and Benj piled into a borrowed four-door sedan with the Russians, who promptly went to check on the landing; since there was only one sat phone, they'd have no way of reporting their findings to Jared.

He'd have to put in on the smaller Limestone and drive out to the Nelson and right by that landing at the end of the road. And see for himself if Malik had arrived, if he'd taken one of the vans, or the boat, or if he was still there, waiting in the trees in case some idiot tried taking a boat back to Port Nelson to rescue whoever might still be there.

Jared didn't know how to shoot the assault rifle Rachael had given him. Maybe that's not something you need a lot of training to use.

He really had no idea.

49

ANITA RECEIVED a message from Carter about the rescue; all five hostages were okay, with one serious casualty among the Russian soldiers. Derrick's son and Carter's apparent protege would hitch a ride on a shipment of grain bound for South America.

Carter would find a way to bring them to *Basilica*. Even Derrick was planning on coming out, something he usually did his best to avoid.

But it was all hands on deck, and *Basilica* was seeing more activity than Anita imagined it ever had, with helicopters landing several times a day, and even a chartered catamaran—taken off a cross-Baltic ferry route—leaving Wednesday morning on a two-and-a-half day trip from Stockholm, carrying over fifty SolRescue employees and various pieces of equipment.

They'd already started work, but they'd be running at full steam by Saturday. According to the project manager—who'd been already flown in from Frankfurt—it would take at minimum two weeks from Saturday to have something "worth launching".

Rather than sending up a few modules and building others off the ESA quarry orbiting in TeLLa3, which had been both the ESA's and Carter's "maker-camp" plan, the new plan, the last-ditch effort, as Carter called it, was to send up the bulk of the hab itself in three capsules. Three capsules, launched from three heavy lift rockets to GTO.

Each one of those pieces would be self-contained, a capsule from which two "beads" of the eventual toroid would be created. Small bots—not far removed from the ones Carter had designed for the sunshield—would be in charge of connecting the beads together, using small breakaway components from each capsule to create six spokes, designed to keep the six beads together and in a proper donut shape, but with no expectation that the spokes would be large enough to use as corridors.

Each bead was essentially its own island in space; the only way to get from one to the next would be through old-fashioned EVA, either human or robot.

And they had no plans to build a robot.

A fourth launch would come next, to bring up the earth-built solar panels and the engines they'd assemble in Carter's labs on *Basilica*, the components they'd need to power and spin the skeleton of the toroid, creating something close to 1g on almost a third of the outer wall of each bead.

And then there would be a fifth launch, to send the first live person up to those cobbled-together pieces. They wouldn't know how many people they could send right away after that, not until they knew how many of those six beads made it up to GTO in operational condition.

There had to be at least one that could support an occupant, otherwise a Plan B with robotic repair would be required, something that would take a helluva lot longer than a few weeks to figure out.

If they got lucky, they'd have room for twelve people, launching one or two per additional launch, with room in each bead for only two people at the start, considering that each capsule needed room for life support, supplies, and an aeroponic garden, not to mention how much space would need to be "wasted" on radiation shielding.

Eventually more beads would be launched, more capsules on more heavy lift launches, until those original six were joined by sixteen others, created a full string of beads, but still not attached much better than train cars, with airlocks between each bead that hadn't been designed as of yet.

And once those beads were in place, a new quarry would be created, another NEO—or a piece of one—deflected into Lagrangian orbit, ready to for magnetic scoopers to pull of the required materials for the next phase, of converting the beads into a band, one continuous ring of habitat space, joined together at long last.

And ready for new and better shielding, a combination of material and magnetics, which would enlarge the living space in the band as well as provide a further reduction in radiation. Anita had seen Danny Pyke's back of the envelope calculations; there was a chance that they could make living at STeLa-1 as radiation-free as living within the Earth's magnetosphere.

They'd need a better subject matter expert involved to know that for sure, and a few would be arriving at *Basilica* eventually, members of a maker camp that hadn't been hit by the unmarked land drones.

And, Derrick had hinted, they might even have a line on one of the environmental control engineers from the ESA's Island project.

SolRescue and Turnpike and various resources from the ESA, the ISRO, and even a few Russians from the RFSA and elsewhere… hundreds of people massing on *Basilica* and hundreds more working from other locations.

It did feel like the good old days, at least a little bit.

Anita felt like she was back to real life.

And she wanted it to last for a while longer this time.

So that meant staying far away from Carter Elgin.

50

JARED KOSKELA was good to his word, coming back to Port Nelson a few hours before sunset, an automatic rifle hanging from his shoulder with a vinyl strap.

Vasily had eaten from the collection of strange snack foods spread out on the folding table, while Chloe had stood vigil over Bugadze, a man none of them had even heard of the day before, but who now seemed important.

Like keeping Bugadze alive was now the most important thing any of them could do.

Jared and Chloe had exchanged a warm hug on his arrival.

Samantha had given Jared a little wave, while keeping to her position by the window, with the pistol.

Vasily gave Jared a pat on the back. "Good work," he said.

"We can take the boat up to our friends at Fox Lake," Jared told him. "Could be a tight fit with all of us."

"We can't sit him up," Chloe said. "I think we should use the folding table like a stretcher, or like a spine board, I guess."

"Okay," Vasily said. He looked over to Jared, who nodded.

Vasily swept the food off the table with one wave of his arm.

Jared helped him fold it down.

"We need your help, Samantha," Chloe said. "You need to slide the table under him when we lift his side."

"I'm on watch," she replied.

"Just get over here," Jared said.

Samantha sighed. She put the gun down on the floor, by the window, then walked over.

Vasily knelt with Jared along one side of Bugadze, next to Chloe, who led the count as she held Bugadze's head.

On three, Vasily and Jared lifted, while Chloe cradled the soldier's head and neck. Samantha slid the table under him.

With a quick lift, they boosted Bugadze up and over to the middle of the table.

"We should tape him to it," Vasily said.

Chloe nodded. "I'll do it."

She grabbed a roll of duct tape from the pile of overturned food and dishes and—apparently—tape.

She taped Bugadze's shoulders, waist, knees, and ankles. "I need a towel or bandage," she said.

Vasily found a roll of elastic bandage in the first aid kit. He passed it to her, and she wrapped it around his forehead and around the improvised spinal board, before adding duct tape to wherever it touched the table.

It wasn't a medical-grade operation, but it was better than Vasily would have expected.

Samantha had walked back to the window. She'd picked up the pistol and was back to watching out the window.

"I don't want her coming," Chloe said, pointing to Samantha.

"I'm the one with the gun," Samantha said.

"Mine's bigger," Jared said, tapping the barrel of his home-printed AR-15.

"She stays here," Chloe said. "She can keep that gun."

"I'm not staying here," Samantha said.

Chloe smirked. "I'm not accepting counteroffers. You can stay and keep that handgun or you can stay and get nothing."

"We shouldn't leave anyone behind," Vasily said. "In case Malik returns."

"Samantha won't matter to Carter Elgin," Jared said. "Not enough. She's of no use to Malik."

Vasily sighed. "So he'll just kill her, then."

"Good riddance," Chloe said.

"Come on, Chloe," Jared said.

"She tried to kill us. She was going to drown us in the water."

"Freeze you to death, actually," Samantha said. "Or stab Jared in the ear. And I was going to kill Rachael, too, wasn't I?"

"What the hell is wrong with you?" Vasily asked.

She shrugged. "I'm an operative. Just like Benj McPherson's pal Malik, or this dead Chinese guy lying on the floor over here."

"Sounds like a lavish word for murderer."

"What kind of accent is that, anyway?" she asked him. "Like some kind of Mancunian vampire."

Vasily laughed.

"That's how she does it," Chloe said. "Seems to work on idiots. Worked on Jared, I think."

"What are you talking about?" Jared said.

"If she was a man you'd have killed her by now."

"I would have killed her? Are you serious?"

"What the Christ did I walk into?" Vasily asked. "You're all completely barmy."

"We leave her here," Chloe said. "She can decide if she wants the gun."

"I'm not staying," Samantha said. "Not unless you shoot me."

"Don't make me shoot you," Jared said.

"You don't have the balls, asshole."

"Can we please not do this?" Vasily said.

"Tell her to put the gun on the floor," Chloe said, looking over at Vasily. "Maybe she'll listen to you."

Vasily looked over to Samantha. He smiled. "*Will* you put the gun down?" he asked her.

"Why would I do that?" she asked.

"Because there is a man here who is, well, dying to death. And a standoff isn't going to help him much."

Samantha nodded.

She knelt down, putting the pistol on the floor.

"Now put your hands behind your back," Vasily said.

"Wait, what?"

"Just do it, please."

She did.

He took the roll of duct tape Chloe had used for Bugazde's stretcher board and wrapped Samantha's wrists together. "If you are no longer a threat," he told her, "they have no good reason to harm you."

"We're not taking her," Chloe said.

"She's coming with us," Vasily said. "No one is left behind."

"It's not your call."

"It is my call, actually. Because this is my operation. I'm in charge."

"Your operation?" Jared said.

"Yes. Carter Elgin sent me to rescue you and to bring you back to *Basilica*."

"Why would he want us to come out his boat?"

"I didn't ask," Vasily said.

"It doesn't matter," Chloe said. "We're not going there. We're going back to Wright-Patterson. No detours."

"It's not your decision to make."

"Like hell it isn't."

"It isn't," Jared said. "Not by yourself, anyway."

She glared at him.

"I'm sorry, Chloe," he said. "But I honestly don't trust the US government right now."

"And so now you trust Carter Elgin?" she asked.

"He saved our lives. He didn't have to."

"He saved Benj McPherson's life," Samantha said. "The rest of us are mostly filler."

"I'm going to *Basilica*," Jared said.

"Good," Vasily said.

"And if I still won't go?" Chloe asked.

Vasily shrugged. "Two out of three, I guess. Or four out of five, really, since Benj and Rachael will be on a ship out of Churchill in the morning."

Chloe was glaring at him now.

Not really hatred. More like a low-level disgust.

He understood.

Really, he did.

No one would be okay after what she'd just been through.

They'd squeezed into the boat and reached Fox Lake Cree Nation just after sunset. From there, they'd been lent an old Dodge pickup—Vasily driving with Chloe as his passenger, Jared in the box with Bugadze, Samantha squished in the tiny back seat of the cab—and sent off to the small city of Thompson, Manitoba.

No one had offered to cut the tape from Samantha Yoon's wrists, and she hadn't bothered to ask.

Once in Thompson, they dropped Bugadze off at the hospital emergency shack, folding table and all.

They didn't risk staying any longer than they had to. Once they saw staff coming to check on the wounded man, they drove away, heading south on Highway 6, toward the more populated part of the province, toward the border with the United States.

Vasily wasn't sure what was supposed to happen next.

He hadn't come into Canada legally.

He couldn't just show up at the border and hope the guards would let him in, a UK National of Russian birth who didn't actually have a Visa for either Canada or the United States.

Not that he would have trusted the Americans, even if he'd had the right documentation.

He would need to wait for instructions, from Carter Elgin, on how, when, and where to cross.

If he was even supposed to cross.

The Russian airborne soldiers and the other two hostages were to leave Canada via Hudson Bay, on an ice-breaking LNG carrier—a double-acting ship—probably to be intercepted and brought to *Basilica* long before their ride and its liquefied natural gas reached those hungry furnaces in Eastern Europe.

Maybe he'd been expected to go to Churchill, too.

But that seemed too risky. From what Jared had told him, two more men had been in play, an American and another Chinese, blocking the highway when he and Chloe had tried to head south. Six in total. Or even more.

And they'd only killed three.

There was nothing stopping Malik from meeting up with the other two, no reason to believe they weren't already watching the one road to Churchill for any sign of their former captives.

The only thing keeping Benj and Rachael from being taken was the fact that they had three hardened soldiers as escorts.

Vasily didn't have that.

He wasn't hardened, and he wasn't a soldier.

He was just some rich man's son.

And he had no idea how to find out what he was supposed to do next.

There was literally nothing between the city of Thompson and the small town of Grand Rapids, three and a half hours away. Jared had stayed in the back, despite the cold wind, and both Chloe and Samantha had managed to fall asleep in the cab, Samantha's hands still taped up.

Vasily felt a little jealous at the prospect of sleep—it was close to midnight—but he knew that out of everyone he was the one who had least reason to complain. He'd had half a night's sleep on *Basilica* before being whisked away to a Russian aircraft carrier; he hadn't spent a night taped to a chair in an abandoned cabin with no heat.

He drove across the Saskatchewan River, into a First Nation, not that the roads or houses looked any different from what he'd just passed on his way into town.

The buildings disappeared soon enough, and Vasily was back into driving through nothing, just more trees, some power lines, and gravel driveways that seemed to lead to nowhere.

And then a turnoff, to places called Easterville and The Pas.

But right before that turnoff, he saw a police car, white with yellow and blue.

Royal Canadian Mounted Police.

Parked right across the highway.

He grabbed Chloe's shoulder. "Wake up," he said. "Roadblock."

She shot up.

And looked out the front windshield.

"You think it's for us," she said.

He started slowing down. He pulled to the shoulder.

He knew he couldn't idle there forever.

"Wouldn't be hard to put out some warrants," he said. "An APB or something. Throw us in jail and Malik and his friends come to collect."

"I don't think that's legal," Chloe said.

"Homeland Security Bulletin," Samantha said from her crunched up seat

453

behind them. "Gives US government agencies access to suspected risks to national security."

"What do you mean?" Vasily asked.

"Canadian police can arrest us, then hand us over to any Fed with a badge."

"Like Malik," Chloe said.

Samantha nodded. "Exactly."

"So I'm open to ideas," Vasily said.

"Maybe one or two of us can get away," Samantha said. "Turn around, and they may pursue. Once we're out of view, we split up."

"But which ones of us are they after?" Chloe asked.

"Benj and Rachael went to Churchill," Vasily said. "They were the ones Malik had valued the most. The rest of you were... extras?"

Vasily heard Jared in the back.

Hopping out of the box.

Then walking up the side of the pickup.

Vasily opened his window.

"I doubt it's Malik's people," Jared said.

"Why?" Vasily asked.

"They could have involved the RCMP a heckuva lot sooner. They didn't before, and I doubt they would now."

"So you honestly think this roadblock is for someone else?" Samantha asked.

"Probably not," Jared said. "But I don't think we're in danger here. I think we should wait and see."

"Wait and see?" Chloe said. "You're kidding."

"Instead of forcing them to chase us, yeah. Because that's somehow less risky?"

"He's right," Vasily said. "We see where this ends up."

"I'm not doing that," Samantha said. "Let me out here."

"You're not going anywhere," Chloe said.

Samantha groaned. "See? This is why I wished I'd killed you."

"I don't understand you," Vasily told her. "You seem to work so hard to get people to hate you."

"I just try not to bullshit people."

"No, you want people to hate you, Samantha. It's curious, really."

"I don't care what you think."

"Obviously you do."

"Let's get moving on this," Jared said. "Okay?"

Vasily nodded.

Jared made his way back to the box.

Once he was in, Vasily started driving toward the waiting police car.

51

NICOLAS WAS exhausted.

The driverfree hadn't been on since leaving the I-15 in Great Falls, Montana, since few of the roads in the northern half of the state were 3D-mapped often enough for the vans. SolRescue had never bothered to donate to the open mapping effort so far from where they kept their maker camps circulating, and no one else had bothered, either.

And according to Nikki, few of the people who lived in Hill or Blaine counties were interested in enabling driverfree; why make it easier for unwanted visitors to drive around your ranches and farms? That's how things go missing.

So Nicolas and Nikki took shifts driving, with Nikki clearly pretending to need to switch off after a couple of hours, to make him feel better about how little endurance he had; the road trip is not really a thing in the world of Nicolas Clouatre.

Derrick's last batch of instructions was provided after thirty-six long hours of waiting in a motel room in Billings. It was to head to a specific set of grain bins at a junction on Elloam Road, at the north edge of Blaine County. They were supposed to look out for a blue minivan with Saskatchewan plates.

No mention of who might be waiting at that minivan, assuming anyway would be.

Nicolas hadn't needed Nikki to point out that Saskatchewan was the name of a Canadian province, and not a US State. But she did, anyway, and he thanked her for the information.

There was a good chance Derrick intended them to cross into Canada. Nicolas' fake passport had stood up well enough for the flight to Miami from Brazil, but he wasn't sure if the Canadian border agents would be as easily convinced.

Hopefully Nikki wasn't on some kind of list of unwanted subversives or something, if she was coming along for that next part.

He really hoped she'd come along.

They reached a junction with three white circular grain bins.

And a blue minivan.

Nicolas pulled the camper van up beside it.

Derrick McPherson stepped out of the blue van. He looked relieved, but worn out.

Probably exactly how Nicolas looked.

Nicolas got out, too.

As did Nikki.

Mireia was in the back seat, pretending to sleep.

She didn't join them.

"It's good to see you, Nic," Derrick said, like they were old friends. "And you must be Nikki."

He gave Nikki a hug, then approached Nicolas for the same.

"How's Mireia?" he asked. He sounded like he knew just how bad it had been for her. But they hadn't told him…

"She's shaken up," Nikki said, "but I think she'll be okay. She's a strong woman."

"You want to take us across the border," Nicolas said.

Derrick nodded. "There is a stretch here that'll be unmanned and un-surveilled for four hours tonight. Early morning, actually. Midnight to four AM."

"Unsurveilled?" Nikki asked.

"The blimp's coming down for maintenance," Derrick said. "Usually they'd put an alternate in place, but they didn't feel the need to ship it over from Washington State. No one's tried crossing here illegally for a couple years."

"And you know all this," Nicolas said.

Derrick smiled. "You know I do."

"And then what?" Nikki asked. "You're asking a lot of people who didn't even know they were risking their lives out here."

"I didn't know it would happen," Derrick said.

"But you knew it was possible."

"No more than you would have known."

"There's no way that's true," she said. "You know when the border is unwatched. Nic told me you even have contacts among illegal Brazilian miners. And you didn't see this coming? You're either lying or—"

"Don't start this," Derrick said. "You don't have to come if you don't want to. I want you to come, but we'll get on without you, Nikki. We'll see this through without you."

"Obviously the launch won't be happening," Nicolas said. "They destroyed the rockets and the habs. We saw what happened to Donatello."

Derrick sighed. "Happened to Mercator, too. We only had two camps left, and we've disbanded them both now."

"So there won't be a launch."

"Not out here."

"Then what the hell are we doing?" Nicolas asked. "Why are you even out here?"

"We're going to *Basilica*," Derrick said. "Picking up some people on the way."

"What people?" Nikki asked.

"Good people."

"What does that mean?"

"They're going to help us with the next launch."

"There is no launch," Nicolas said.

"On *Basilica*," Derrick said. "We've got the designs, we've still got a good team. And we've got you guys."

Nikki looked over to Nicolas.

She didn't want to go.

"This is your chance, Nic," Derrick told him. "It's still your chance. We get this thing launched, we clear your name."

"That doesn't clear my name," Nicolas said.

Derrick grinned. "No, Nic… I'm pretty sure it will."

Just before midnight, they forded a small river in the minivan, which took on more than enough water to make the brakes squeak for a year or two, then headed across a surprisingly unmarked border into Canada, into the province of Saskatchewan.

From there they passed a ghost town, one much more extensive than any Nicolas had seen from their US travels. It reminded him of the old village in Goussainville, which he'd visited in his youth, when it had been almost completely abandoned.

Before it had come back to life, with the Beurs moving in, the old church becoming a mosque.

But ghost towns in the open grasslands were eerier; it felt like the whole world had disappeared, not just the residents of a few empty houses on a silent street.

Nicolas wanted to feel at home with that, with his new life away from the rest of the world, a castaway in the Great Plains of North America.

From that dead village, Claydon, they headed north, reaching the modern Trans-Canada highway, where Derrick set them over to driverfree and started telling them about the latest grasp at putting a hab in space.

There would be well over two hundred people on *Basilica* by the end of the week, engineers, designers, and the big SolRescue three, which included Anita Singhal, obviously.

They were using the ESA designs that Nicolas and Mireia had shared, along with some work Danny Pyke's startup—funded largely by Carter Elgin—had done with in-situ assembly.

Unlike the ESA's or the maker's approach of one module at a time, strung together like ISS/2 or OPSEK, the SolRescue project could be considered a Hail Mary pass, whatever that meant. They would throw up as much as they could as quickly as they could, simultaneously, *if they could,* and see what sticks.

They wouldn't rely on a future calendar of launches; as far as they were concerned, there was only one calendar day to launch, because they might not get another shot.

Derrick was vague on explaining why that was, aside from general concern about what happened to the three maker camps happening to *Basilica.*

But Nicolas could tell that Derrick was *really* worried about that, not as much as he would have expected.

Unlike the maker camps, spread out for redundancy or safety or whatever else Carter and Derrick had figured would make sense, the latest attempt—maybe final—would be from one place, a large converted cargo ship in international waters.

It seemed like too large a risk for them to take.

Even having the most important people with SolRescue in one location seemed like a gamble.

But when Nicolas had brought it up, Derrick had told him not to worry, dismissively enough that he didn't have any urge to keep on it.

Not that he was feeling too good about joining the other targets on *Basilica.*

Mireia didn't say much of anything on the journey; she either slept or pretended to sleep, across the border, up to the Trans-Canada, along the interstate-level highway toward the East…

That wasn't like her, just accepting Derrick's pronouncements and Derrick's secrets.

It was like she wasn't really there.

Like she'd checked out, or was floating somewhere in space, waiting for something to happen that would be worth pulling her back down.

Nicolas didn't know what that would be.

What he could do to help.

The driverfree was shortlived, and soon they found themselves back to needing a driver, so Nikki volunteered while Derrick got some rest. He told her to follow the navigator aigent on the console, until it stopped.

The sun rose around the same time they crossed into the province of Manitoba. Not long after that they left the open grasslands behind, moving into a forest that had some broadleaf trees, but was mostly made up of evergreens.

They'd been heading east, but also tacking north. Moving mostly north, since they'd crossed the provincial boundary.

Nicolas could see on his tablet that they weren't heading toward the east of Canada. You wouldn't be heading north if you wanted to reach Toronto; in fact, you probably wouldn't have bothered coming by way of Saskatchewan at all, if you'd had any other way of getting across the border.

They were heading to *Basilica*, in the end, and they weren't heading to the East Coast.

The console said they were almost there.

To an intersection between two highways in the middle of the north woods.

On Nicolas' tablet he saw a power station and a quarry. No town.

"Where are we going?" he asked Derrick, who'd seemed close enough to waking up.

"To pick up some friends," Derrick replied.

"Pick them up where?" Nikki asked. "Are we even somewhere?"

"I didn't program the last step."

"Why not?"

"Just in case we were stopped," Derrick said. "Or in case someone found a way into our console."

"You sound a little paranoid," Mireia said, from her fake sleep in the back row of the minivan.

Nicolas was surprised she could even hear them from all the way in the rear. He wouldn't have been able to; his old ears were having enough trouble listening in from the passenger seat.

"I'll drive from here," Derrick said. "Take us the rest of the trip."

"Where are we going?" Nicolas asked.

"Place called Easterville."

"Easterville."

"Yeah. Didn't make it up."

"It's on that sign," Nikki said. "I can just turn right."

"No," Derrick said. "Pull over and I'll drive."

"I don't understand," Mireia said. "You don't honestly think this makes us safer, do you? These secrets of yours?"

Nicolas was happy she was bringing it up. Not because it mattered, because he wasn't sure it did, but because it meant that Mireia was still paying attention.

She was still with them, at least a little.

"Old habits," Derrick said. "But they still have some use. You never know who you can trust. I've been reminded of that over and over again."

"You don't trust us?" Nicolas asked.

Derrick sighed. "I've known Carter Elgin for over twenty years. I've done everything he's needed me to do. But you know what? I can't trust the man. Because he lies to me. So that says enough to me, about how crazy it would be to trust anyone else."

"That's sad," Mireia said. "All this power and you can't put your faith in it."

"No," he said, "I trust that part. I know what we've got, the reach we've managed… it's just the people I don't trust."

"How is that any different?" Nikki asked.

Derrick shrugged. "It's hard to explain. Now, can you pull over? Please?"

Nikki nodded.

And pulled the van over, onto the shallow gravel shoulder.

"People won't trust you, Derrick," Nikki said. "Not if you can't trust them."

He shook his head. "That's not how it works. Not at all."

"Why not?"

"Because people *have* to trust me. I don't need to trust them."

Mireia chuckled. "So like I said… you live a sad life, Derrick."

"It's not great," he said. "But it's what I've got."

Derrick switched with Nikki, who took his spot in the middle row.

Mirea moved up beside her.

Derrick drove north to the junction, then turned right, toward Easterville.

Nicolas could see on their tablet that they were moving between two large lakes, not that he could see much of them from the highway. At most, he could see what looked like a gap behind the lines of trees.

But all there really was along the highway was the forest, still with some birch or maybe poplar, but mostly pine and other conifers. And gentle hills.

It wasn't beautiful, not compared to the French countryside, or even to the endless dry grasses in Wyoming, or the arid mountainsides of Montana.

It was daunting, really.

Frightening.

Like you could tell just by looking how desolate it was, how hard it would be to survive out there.

How lost you could get if you ever lost sight of the highway.

They reached a small hamlet, some houses and a fuel station with diesel, superchargers, and even old-fashioned petrol. And another turnoff, to Easterville.

And they took it, and drove through more forest.

For almost an hour.

Until they reached the town, a collection of cookie-cutter bungalows with near-identical yards.

It was two o'clock in the afternoon.

They hadn't stopped since a charge-up at a border town in Saskatchewan.

Nicolas didn't want to admit how much he needed to pee.

Derrick drove them to a large building.

And led them inside.

To a gymnasium.

A male police officer met them.

Royal Canadian Mounted Police.

Derrick shook the man's hand, then followed him to a group of people sitting along the wall of the gym, two men and two women, watching as a group of local teens were playing basketball.

Nicolas recognized one of them.

The Korean woman, from the Denver Airport.

She gave him a wave, and stood up.

Mireia walked over to give Samantha Yoon a hug.

"You could have told us," she said, to Derrick.

One of the men along the wall offered a hand to Nicolas. Much younger than he was. And in significantly better shape.

"You're Nicolas Clouatre," the man said.

"Yes," Nicolas said.

"I'm sorry about the station. I doubt there was anything you could have done."

"This is Jared Koskela," Derrick said. Then he introduced the others, an attractive blond woman with a frazzled ponytail named Chloe Nielsen-Brown, a short and skinny young Russian man named Vasily Utkin, and, of course, Samantha Yoon.

"Your son isn't here," Nicolas said.

"No… but he's alright. Thank god."

"What happened?" Mireia asked.

"We can talk about that on the drive," Derrick said.

"Where are we going?" Samantha asked.

"Don't even bother asking," Nikki said. "The man's not big on disclosing things."

"That's okay," Vasily said. "We don't need to know." He grabbed Derrick's hand and shook it. "Thank you, Mr. McPherson. For coming to get us."

"We're not home free yet," Derrick said. "Keep that in mind."

The extra passengers piled into the van, and Derrick took them back to the highway and headed east.

He turned at a sign that read "Kawina Lake", onto a set of gravel tracks that led down to the water.

There was a small floating dock.

Derrick stopped the van and got out.

So Nicolas got out as well, followed by everyone else, except for Mireia.

"They should be here soon," Derrick said.

"Who?" Nicolas asked.

He pointed up at the sky.

Nicolas could hear the engines.

Not a helicopter, like in Brazil.

This time it was a floatplane.

52

IT HAD come as a relief to Benj that there was room for a handful of extra passengers on the *MS Solskinn*. He and Rachael and the Russian soldiers had been allowed access to the crew portion of the ship, including three bunkrooms for their guest quarters.

And Rachael had asked Benj to take the bunk below her, so she wouldn't have to sleep alone on a Norwegian ship which seemed crewed almost entirely by Russians.

To ship North America's natural gas to Eastern Europe, to compete with the gas they shipped from Russia. Economics trumping political ideologies once again.

Emin had explained in his best English that they would be on board for four full days, heading to Nuuk, the capital city of Greenland.

From there, they'd be flown by Russian military helicopter to *Basilica*.

It didn't sit well with him, SolRescue's new reliance on the Russian military. He remembered the Russia of his youth, the legacy of Vladimir Putin's United Russia Party, the wars in Georgia and Ukraine.

This new Russia hadn't convinced him of anything; if they were helping SolRescue, or the European Union... they weren't doing it out of kindness.

If anything, they were doing it to weaken the US and China, hoping to regain some clout in a world where they'd been seen more and more as another declining power, still trying to pretend they could be a part of the big boy club.

But they'd saved his life, and Rachael's, and he was grateful for that. But you didn't have to trust someone just because of it.

That first night, he and Rachael stayed up together, talking, her sitting on the lower bunk beside him, close enough to touch.

They'd started joking a little about the Russians and their idiosyncrasies, like how it seemed that practically every one of the crew could go from friendly discussions and quiet chucking to some angry declaration about something Benj or Rachael were doing wrong, and then back to the previous state of mind, like turning their angry switch on and off again.

But then Rachael's mood seemed to darken, and she started talking about what had happened in Churchill.

"I feel like it's this unspeakable thing I've done," she told him, "and I can't undo it, obviously. Like I've crossed a line and can't go back."

"I know what it's like," Benj said, trying not to sound like he was one-upping her.

She sighed. "Jared will never forgive me for it."

Benj felt a tinge of jealousy. The idea that she could have those feelings for Jared Koskela.

Not that she'd have stumbled into feeling something like that for him. After a handful of days and a shitload of truly awful experiences.

"He'll forgive you," Benj said.

"You can't know that," she replied, almost angrily.

"It's not worth staying angry. And I don't think he's the kind of person to waste his energy on something that pointless."

"I think he was falling for me. I like that... even if..."

He wanted to ask her.

If she didn't feel the same way about him.

But he couldn't.

"I'm worried about him," she said. "What if something happens. With Malik... or..."

She looked away.

"You'll see him again," he told her. "And when you do, I'm sure he'll be so focused on how much he was worried about you... he won't even be thinking about anything else."

She looked back at him.

She had tears in her eyes.

"That's bullshit," she said. "Complete bullshit. There's no coming back from this."

"Don't start thinking like that, Rachael. There's always a way back. Believe me. I know."

"You can't understand. Sorry."

For some reason, that bothered him. The dismissal.

"No," he told her, "I do understand. I've been through it."

"You weren't the one who caused this."

"That's not what I'm talking about. I'm talking about something I did. Years ago. Worse than what you've done. Much worse."

"Why, did your polar bear kill someone?" she asked, smirking.

"I killed someone," Benj said.

Her smirk disappeared.

"Wasn't on purpose," he said. "But it still happened."

"What... what was it? What did you do?"

"It doesn't really matter."

"What kind of answer is that?"

"It means that I fucked up and three people died because of it. It means that I still have nightmares about it. They're dead and I'm still alive, because of who my father is."

He felt her hand on his knee.

"I want you to tell me," she said. "Tell me what happened."

So he told her.

About the stupid plan to defraud the US government. About getting caught, and trying to pin it on a white girl, because he knew she'd get a slap on the wrist.

And he told her about the Washington boys. How they'd lost any chance at a normal life, and had risked and lost their lives trying to rob an elderly—and ridiculously wealthy—couple in the ritzy neighborhood of Ladue.

And then he told her of the uproar that came afterward, about how the Washington boys had been taken off basic because of their earlier crime and being convicted as adults, while the other black boy had been let off with probation because of his famous name. But the part that had stirred things up the most, way more than the unwritten power of Derrick Mc-Pherson and, by extension, SolRescue, was how the pretty white girl—who'd been declared the ringleader—had gotten off with twice the probation as Benj, and, like Benj, she was still collecting her basic income, no strings attached.

"The news vans camped outside her house," Benj said. "She dropped out of UMSL, lost her tutoring gigs… she called me one night and told me that she was getting death threats, that someone had sent her a computer animated simulation… of her being tortured to death."

"Oh my god. What did you say to her? When she called you?"

"I didn't know what to say. I said I was sorry, and I ended the call."

"Oh."

"She hung herself," Benj said.

"What?"

"From a doorknob. I didn't even think that was possible."

"I'm sorry."

"So yeah… I know what it's like. To have to come back from something like that. You know, just way worse."

"You didn't kill her," she said.

"You didn't kill Jared."

She nodded.

"I've come to terms with what I did," Benj said. "With who I used to be. I can't change what happened. I can't even make some big promise that I won't do something bad like that again. Hell, I did something pretty bad to Samantha."

"That doesn't sound undeserved."

"It's in me, Rachael. You don't have that. You're not like that. You're not like me."

"You don't know me well enough to say that," she said.

"No, I think I do."

"Do you want to share a bunk tonight?" she asked. "Just share, you know? No strings attached."

"No strings?"

"Whatever happens," she said. "I think I want someone to lie here with me."

"Well, it's my bunk," he said.

She laughed.

And then she kissed him.

53

THE SEAPLANE—or floatplane, maybe—flew northeast, from what Jared could tell, crossing over the upper bowl of Lake Winnipeg and moving over endless trees, exactly like the ones he'd seen on the drive south on Highway 6.

There were seven rows of seats, more than enough for eight passengers; Jared was in the third row, in a middle seat, beside Chloe and across the aisle from Samantha.

Chloe still had that ponytail. He hadn't found the right opportunity to ask her about the bot. He didn't want to advertise it to everyone, to people he'd just met, or to the continually unstable and untrustworthy Samantha Yoon.

Chloe leaned in.

"We're okay," she whispered, giving him a kiss on the cheek, just below the ear.

"I love you," he said. It had just come out like that, like a reflex.

But he didn't regret it.

And she told him that she loved him, too.

The plane landed in a lake, at a seaplane airport alongside a surprisingly large community, right smack in the middle of nowhere.

They didn't get out.

It was just for refueling. It felt strange to need fuel already.

They took off again, bisecting a large lake with many tree-covered islands, and following a river until the clouds blocked Jared's view.

He didn't see anything below until they were over what he was sure was Hudson Bay. There was ice along the shoreline, and more ice farther out, but a gap between the two, much of it open water.

Running all the way up the coast. He didn't know how far it might lead. But he noticed that they'd shifted course, heading north. They seemed to be following it.

"Where are we going?" he shouted to Derrick, who was sitting in the row in front of him.

"To meet some friends," Derrick replied. "And my son."

A seaplane. Out to sea. To meet an icebreaker weighed down with huge fuel tanks filled with explosive liquefied gas.

Jared wasn't sure if seaplane was really the right word. He'd heard floatplane, too, thought he wasn't sure it was for the same type of plane, but maybe that was a better descriptor, because the last thing you want to have is overconfident pilots thinking that there's nothing *off* about trying to land in the middle of the fucking ocean.

Hudson Bay is the ocean, isn't it?

After a couple of hours of following the strip of open water between the ice, Jared saw a ship below.

He looked at Derrick, who gave him a shrug, as if there would be a whole heap of bulk carriers carving through an ice-filled inland sea.

He listened as the pilot made radio contact with the freighter.

The *MS Solskinn*.

The pilot said something over the speaker.

Jared didn't quite catch it.

But he could guess the plan.

Landing in the middle of the fucking ocean.

Jared could tell early on in the landing that it was going to be a lot different than the last one; the pilot had swept down low, to maybe twenty feet above the open water, but he hadn't made contact. They were probably two or three kilometers back from the icebreaker.

The plane was slowing down—it would probably stall at those speeds, wouldn't it—but barely lowering.

The pilot made another announcement.

Jared tried his best to understand.

Something about seatbelts.

He tapped Derrick on the shoulder.

"Once we're on the water," Derrick said, "you undo your seatbelt, just in case."

"In case of what?" Chloe asked.

"In case we hit some ice, or land hard enough that the floats don't... uh, float us very well."

Chloe frowned. "Is that a joke?"

"Not a joke," Derrick said.

The front of the plane started to lift, nose pointing up.

The engines stopped.

The plane fell to the water, more down than forward. Maybe six feet.

Jared undid his belt.

And looked out the window.

The plane didn't seem to be sinking, but even with ice on both sides of the thin slice of water, the fuselage was rolling with the waves, rocking back and forth as the plane lifted and fell.

The engine started again, as they slowly moved through the water toward one side of the ice. The right side... the east side?

"Now we get out," Derrick said. "Of course, none of us are really dressed for the weather."

"It's supposed to be spring," Chloe said.

"Tell that to the frozen ocean," Samantha said.

Jared noticed the pilot walking down the aisle. A woman, younger than Jared, with long dark hair that he imagined was specifically intended to make her look nothing like Amelia Earhart.

She walked up to Derrick. "Not sure I can take off like this," she said. "More chop than I expected."

"Of course there's chop," he said. "And it's not like you have a choice, do you?"

She shrugged. "I guess I'm just thinking out loud. About how screwed we might be."

Derrick chuckled. "Only the good die young, Vanessa. And I'm pretty sure you and I are both giant assholes."

The pilot smiled. "You going out with them?"

Derrick nodded.

"Why wouldn't you go out with us?" Jared asked.

"I have another destination planned," Derrick said. "I'm not going to *Basilica*. And neither is Samantha."

"What are you talking about?" Samantha asked. "Why the hell am I here, then?"

"We keep going from here. To somewhere else?"

"And where is that?"

Derrick looked back to Jared. "I'll be in touch."

"What about your son?" Chloe asked. "Isn't he on board that boat?"

"As far as I know."

"And you're not going to see him?"

"I know what my son looks like," Derrick said.

Chloe didn't press it any further.

Derrick put on a backpack and led them off the plane—everyone but Samantha and Vanessa, the pilot—down the small ladder, onto the pontoon, and then a good-sized hop onto the ice.

"It's very thin here," he said. "So we move fast, but we move carefully."

And that was what he did, spring along the ice, away from the edge, to where the ground was more white than gray. Once he'd reached that point, he slowed down.

Jared could see the *Solskinn*, floating in the open water, apparently waiting for them to catch up.

There was a gap between the LPG carrier and the solid sea ice, at least ten feet, filled with small chunks of ice and a thick soup of slush.

You wouldn't walk on it.

So Jared wasn't sure how they expected anyone to get on board.

Derrick seemed to know something he didn't, which was not unexpected or unusual. But was already becoming a little frustrating.

Jared had worked with people like that before, guys who wouldn't tell you the simplest little things, as if you not knowing made them more valuable *auto-magically*.

"So where are we headed?" Jared asked.

"To that ship over there," Derrick said, smirking.

"Come on."

"This ship will drop you off in Greenland. Then it's on to *Basilica*."

"How does that happen, exactly?"

"Don't worry about it," Derrick said.

Jared rolled his eyes.

They reached the edge of the ice, three yards from the hull.

"We're waiting for the ladder," Derrick said.

"I don't think a ladder can fix this," Jared said.

"Not sure what kind of ladder you're expecting."

Jared saw movement on the deck of the tanker ship.

Soldiers.

The Russian airborne troops. Two of them.

They had a large roll of cabling.

One of the soldiers attached it to the orange metal railing that ran along the deck.

The other started unwrapping the bundle of cable.

The ladder.

He threw the ladder over the side, out toward Derrick, who reached out and caught the end. Like he'd done it before.

He pulled the ladder back from the hull, until it was fully extended and reasonably taut.

"Hold this, please," he said to Jared.

So Jared held the ladder.

Derrick took his pack off his shoulder and put it on the ice.

He pulled out what looked like an ice pick, yellow handle, dark gray blade.

He jammed it into the ice, near where the bottom of the ladder met the ice. And a little too close to Jared's left foot.

Derrick clipped the ladder to the leather leash on the pick, using a carabiner that had come pre-attached below the bottom rung.

470

"You came prepared," Chloe said.

"That's the upside to being the guy with the plan," Derrick said. "Want to climb first, Ms. Nielsen-Brown?"

"Not really."

"I can go first," Jared said. Not that he wanted to.

Derrick nodded.

Jared took hold of the cable rails and stepped onto the first rung, which was as hard as you'd find on a stepladder.

He climbed up over the drifting ice and slush, and up the side of the hull.

One of the soldiers, Emin, helped him over the railing.

There was no one else on deck.

Chloe came next, followed by Vasily.

Then the three people who'd come with Derrick McPherson, the man with the combover, the middle aged woman with short blond hair, and the very attractive mediterranean-looking woman who Jared instinctively wished he knew more about.

Derrick was the only one left on the ice.

He pulled out the ice pick.

"Where's Benj?" Chloe asked. "Why isn't he out here?"

No one gave her an answer. The Russians both acted like they didn't know what she was talking about, even though it was clear they both had a very good understanding of the situation.

Everyone knew that father and son McPherson were almost within spitting distance. But Benj wasn't there to see his father.

And his father didn't seem too big on setting up a meeting.

"Good luck," Derrick said. "Tell Elgin he sucks."

Jared gave a quick wave, then followed the soldiers toward the living area.

He knew it would be at least a few days until they reached the next port.

But more important, he wanted to see Rachael.

Not to say anything, really. Certainly not to forgive her.

But just to make sure she was okay.

54

MIREIA HAD never felt more alone than she did at her arrival on the *Solskinn*. Nicolas didn't care to know her anymore, and she'd never met anyone on that ship before, aside from a few minutes of conversation with Benj McPherson.

And she had a feeling that Benj had realized that, too, since when he'd noticed her wandering/moping on the deck—just after finishing her unappetizing dinner in the cramped dining area—he walked right up to her with a warm smile.

"Dinner was awful," he said. "But the company was... not as terrible."

"I sat with a bunch of Russians," Mireia said. "They spoke Russian." Even Vasily.

She decided not to mention how she felt about Russians.

"I feel out of place," Benj said.

"That's funny."

"Why?"

"Because you're the most... in place..."

"I'm not an engineer," he said.

"You're a McPherson."

"I barely know my father. So I'm not really a McPherson."

"I'm not really an engineer," Mireia said. "Not anymore."

He smiled. "That's funny."

"Do you think they'll want us to stay on that *Basilica*? I know that there's a lot of empty rooms."

"Do you want to stay?"

"Not at all," she said. "Not that I have somewhere else to go."

"It can't last forever. This will all end soon, and you'll be able to go back home."

"There is no back home. Sorry... that's not really something I should be saying."

"I know the feeling, Mireia," he said. "I can't really go back, either. Not that it compares to what you're going through."

"It's not so bad. Just a grand collection of the worst things that could ever happen to me."

He nodded. "That's how this seems to go, doesn't it? All this crap rolling downhill. We don't even know who the idiots who caused this mess."

"No... we do know him," she said. "Carter Elgin."

473

"I don't know if that's fair. I think if anything, Carter was reacting to events."

"No. I'm sorry, but no. Carter Elgin tries to manipulate events to suit his purpose, just like he manipulates people. Like me. Like Samantha Yoon."

"Samantha Yoon is something else," Benj said. "Honestly, Mireia, I don't know how you could have been friends with her."

"Derrick told what she did. I'm sorry."

"I think she's crazy."

"She's a true believer," Mireia said. "So probably worse. And that's Carter's doing, isn't it? Wind these people up and let them loose…"

"What do you think my father will do with her?"

"I don't know. And I guess you don't know, either."

Benj sighed. "I like to think my father doesn't have blood on his hands. But I don't know. I don't want to know…"

"We all have blood on our hands. Indirectly, most of the time."

"What do you mean?" he asked her.

She looked out over the dark water.

She saw what looked like an iceberg, far to the south of them, probably on its way to menace Spanish fishing boats, out by the Grand Bank of Newfoundland.

"I eat meat," she said. "I drink coffee. I wear clothes made by impoverished adults in Burma, because apparently it's wrong to let the kids do it, even if they don't have parents to provide for them. I'm an apex predator, and so are you. But it's not just cows and chickens and soybeans under us, it's a good fifty percent of the world we're crushing. Just to live."

She'd expected that to scare him off.

She wasn't sure she wanted to.

"You understand progress," he said. "And that it's the onward march of being a little less shitty every day. We're doing the best we can. You and me. And hopefully, my father. And even Carter Elgin."

"My husband betrayed us."

"I know."

She hadn't expected him to know.

"Rachael had contacted your husband. To warn him about the attack. But he didn't try to stop it."

"Because he helped them do it," Mireia said.

"Did you know?"

"I should have known. I should have."

He nodded. "But you didn't want to know."

"Like with you and your father."

"There's the blood on your hands, Mireia," he said. "Rachael almost died because you didn't tell anyone about Alex."

"Rachael almost died because of what Samantha did to her. And because you didn't stop it from happening."

He smiled.

"Why is that funny?" she asked him.

"It's not funny. It's… comforting."

"Comforting?"

"That we all own a piece of this mess. That we all have something to make up for."

"I don't understand," she said.

"The world needs people like us, Mireia. People who need to earn their way back into the good books."

"You're assuming that's even possible. Or that it's something both of us actually want."

"You reek of it," he said.

"What?"

"I know you want to fix this. Not just to clear your name."

"You don't know anything about me."

"I think I know enough."

He gave her a gentle pat on the shoulder, and then he walked away.

It worked.

He hadn't cheered her up, or convinced her of anything.

He hadn't changed how she felt about Carter Elgin, and her certainly hadn't made her feel better about what she hadn't done, how she hadn't stopped Alex from doing what he did.

But she did feel a little less lonely.

55

JARED HAD seen Rachael a couple of times, but he hadn't spoken to her. At dinner, she'd been sitting at the same long table, but he'd made sure to be at the far end—with Chloe—while she sat across from Benj McPherson. Nicolas Clouatre and that Nikki woman from the maker camp were the buffers, and they'd done a good job of that.

Not that he hadn't kept an eye on her. She seemed to like Benj, which Jared wasn't sure he understood.

But obviously he wasn't supposed to care about that, right? He wasn't supposed to care about Rachael at all.

After dinner, Chloe had wanted to turn in, which was strange for a night owl. And not at all what Jared felt like doing.

He understood, she was exhausted.

He was exhausted, too.

But that just made him unable to sleep, like he needed to push a little further until he'd earned the ability to collapse.

He learned after a few minutes that there was little to nothing to do on a tanker ship. He ended up wandering the deck, earclips in, listening to the kind of music you ought to listen to while coasting through the Northwest Passage, not that he was sure they were actually north enough to qualify.

He'd titled the playlist *Hopelessnuts*, and it was a mix of music from as early as the 1970s, anything that seemed an equal blend of morose and mellow.

He wasn't sure it was helping him feel good at all.

But it was helping to pass the time… a little.

He'd been listening to Owl & Mouse's "Don't Read the Classics", a perfect blend of ukulele and bitter, when he saw Rachael, sitting on a metal grate ladder, facing away from the railing and the water beyond.

She had her head in her hands.

She hadn't seen him.

He knew he should turn around and walk away.

But he kept walking toward her.

And stopped in front of her.

She looked up.

He stopped the track he was listening to.

"I'm sorry," she said, looking up at him.

"That fixes it, I guess."

"I know it doesn't. I'm not an idiot."

"Are you sure?" he asked.

She didn't answer.

She looked back down at the metal deck.

Jared sat down beside her.

He didn't say anything for a minute or so.

He just sat.

She didn't look up.

"I don't know why you made such a big production out of it," he said. "All the long talks about what I was doing. It's not like you didn't already know all about me."

"I was doing what Carter asked me to do. And I like talking to you, Jared."

"I'm glad she didn't kill you. But that's about it."

"I don't want to be here, either. It's not like I have a choice."

"You did this, Rachael. Carter didn't even ask you to kill me. You get that, right?"

"I didn't know."

"You didn't even hesitate," he said. "You just did it."

"I thought it was the right thing to do. To keep them from killing you."

He shook his head.

He stood up.

"Next time call the cops, Rachael. You know, if you think someone's in trouble. Don't sic a freaking polar bear on them."

"Jared... I'm sorry."

"You said that part already. So we're done here."

He put the music back on and continued walking along the deck.

He made sure he didn't look back.

56

GREENLAND WAS not nearly as beautiful as Mireia had expected.

The whole town seemed bleak, even the brightly-painted houses losing the battle against the gray rocks and brown grass and dirt, and the large patches of snow that seemed nowhere close to melting.

She'd seen icebergs on the way into the harbor at Nuuk, light crystal-blue ice cruising along the current, not really glistening in the overcast sky, but still breathtaking.

She'd hope to see some whales or something, but she didn't.

Maybe they tended to avoid large floating death palaces like the natural gas tanker she was riding on. Not that she was sure what would happen if there was a liquefied natural gas "spill". Nothing good.

The young Russian engineer, Vasily, had spent quite a bit of time with her, which Mireia didn't mind, since she missed having Nicolas following her, and because it was pretty obvious from the start that Vasily Utkin had no interest in a woman like her. Or probably any women at all.

Now she understood why he'd taken a job across an ocean from his family, who being powerful and Russian, were probably not too big on defying the expected social order of the motherland.

Vasily had pointed out the icebergs as they'd passed, telling her the names of the little pieces that broke off—or calved—from the main berg. Bergy bits were the big chunks, growlers the little ones.

One of those times when you wonder who was put in charge of coming up with the names.

Vasily had taught her about the sea ice, too, about how the thin waterway between the "fast ice" and the pack ice was a regular thing, how that "shore lead" ran along the coast of Hudson Bay, until it met the also somewhat regular open sea ice around Southhampton Island—called a polynya, which was a Russian word—and once they'd gotten that far north he'd prepared her for the moment the ship turned around, running astern into the harder ice, once they turned almost due east on their way to Hudson Strait, which separated the Canadian mainland from Baffin Island, and had led them out toward Greenland.

She'd asked him how he'd known so much about the ice, and he'd explained it pretty simply. That he'd always been interested in boats and the ocean, and he'd thought it was the perfect way of finding something to show off to his father.

He'd even thought of becoming a marine engineer. But he didn't seem too interested in explaining why he'd switched to astroengineering, so Mireia didn't press him on it.

The tanker couldn't dock directly at the Nuuk Port and Harbour, so they were transferred to a white and yellow pilot tender, which brought them up to the dock.

One of the Russian soldiers, a friendly-enough man named Emin, had taken charge of the group, which without Derrick McPherson's presence had started to feel like an aimless school trip.

Emin split them into two taxis—which other than missing the bright yellow paneling reminded her of the taxis back home—and they drove along the shore and then up and along a ridge, headed to the notably tiny airport near the edge of the small city.

Mireia didn't have trouble finding their next ride. There was a very long and large helicopter, blue and white, with a red star on the side of the tail, waiting right near the big red letters spelling "Nuuk" on the side of the boxy terminal building.

"A Ka-27," Vasily told her.

Emin greeted a waiting military pilot in Russian, who waved everyone on board.

"I assume we're in a bit of a hurry," Vasily said.

Mireia nodded, then followed some of the others into the helicopter, finding a seat near the back.

There were three crew members there, Russian Navy, from what she could tell. All three had given her the once-over.

She saw Nicolas looking at her. Not really a once-over from him.

She shot a smile.

He nodded.

It felt like they weren't really friends so much as two people sharing the same general geographical area.

And maybe that was okay.

It just didn't feel like it.

They flew south just off the shore, the icebergs out the one—and very small—window on her side of the helicopter getting fewer and farther between. After two and a half hours, as the late May sun was close to setting, they landed on an island, at a heliport, to refuel.

From there, they headed south over the North Atlantic.

For three more hours.

And then the helicopter started descending.

Mireia knew she shouldn't panic, since no one else seemed concerned, even though she hadn't seen any trace of land.

She couldn't see anything but the Atlantic outside the tiny rounded-rectangular window.

They'd almost landed before she'd realized what was happening.

A Russian carrier. In the North Atlantic.

It was big enough, but she knew the Russians had bigger ones.

The deck only held helicopters; it wasn't sized right for jets.

She could see a couple of smaller ships alongside; escorts, most likely. She knew enough about navies to know that carriers were rarely left on their own, especially so far from home.

One of Mireia's great-great-grandfathers had flown with Russian pilots in the Spanish Civil War, over a hundred years before—her mother still had a photo of his squadron; that was probably the last time any Catalans had seen Russians and had not expected the worst.

She'd known that Carter Elgin had asked for Russian help to save Derrick McPherson's son and the other hostages; that had been bad enough. There was nothing good about the Russian government; she didn't trust it, she knew that no one should.

And now they were trolling the waters of the North Atlantic.

She wasn't sure how much of that was Carter's fault.

But she knew that he was partly to blame, and it made her angry.

She remembered a story that Samantha Yoon had told her, from their days in Stockholm.

That Carter had hired a highly-qualified rocketry engineer he didn't even need, for a project that only existed on the back of a napkin, for only as long as it took for a competing job offer at Bangalore Launch to evaporate.

At that point, he completed his bait and switch, and the engineer quit after two months of mind-numbingly useless paperwork, which seemed to only be required of that particular new hire.

The engineer eventually found his way to Bangalore Launch, but only after Carter's scheme had delayed his alleged competition's work by three months.

SolRescue wasn't supposed to have competition. It wasn't like BL had been trying to build a competing sunshield.

It was just enough competition for Carter Elgin that BL was getting too much of the spotlight, and that was all that had mattered.

Mireia didn't trust the man. She couldn't trust a man like him.

And she didn't trust the Russians, either.

The Russian Navy had prepared escorts for their visitors, even the airborne troops, and they were all led into a large conference room and offered tea.

An officer took Vasily to the side and had a brief conversation with him, not animated at all, but Vasily seemed sombre enough as he listened and asked a few questions in Russian.

The officer left the room, leaving two security escorts sitting at the end of the table casually, rather than standing by the door like a couple of sentries.

Like the Russians were doing what they could to make their guests feel comfortable.

Which to Mireia meant there was something two-faced about them.

"Now that we're on board," Vasily said, "they'll be rendezvousing with the rest of the fleet."

"And then we'll be going to *Basilica*?" Benj asked.

"*Basilica* is with the rest of the fleet."

"You really are in bed with the Russians," Mireia said.

"I *am* Russian," Vasily said, with a smile. "So I'm usually in bed with myself, most nights." His smiled faded. "And be careful how you speak about our hosts."

Mireia looked over at the two seated sentries.

They seemed to be lost in some conversation requiring exaggerated hand motions.

But she realized Vasily was looking up.

The Russians hadn't tried to hide the surveillance camera in the corner.

"It's not about the Russians," Nicolas said. "It's about the message that sends to the Americans."

"The Americans sent us a message," Mireia said. "Remember? When they tried to kill us?"

"We don't know who that was," Nikki said.

Mireia groaned. "Come on."

"I think she's right," Jared Koskela said, looking right at Mireia with an annoyingly sympathetic smile. "We know it wasn't the US Military, because they have better land drones to use."

"You weren't there," Mireia said.

"But I heard what happened. I heard that you... you got away."

"Yeah? Too bad, yeah?"

"You wouldn't have lived through it if you'd been attacked by US Army UCGVs."

"So they don't want us to know it was them," one of the young women said, the American Indian. Or Canadian Indian. "They want us to think that maybe it wasn't the US Government trying to kill us."

"You have no evidence it was them, Rachael," the other young woman said. The pretty blonde. Chloe Neilsen-*something*. "No evidence whatso-ever."

"The Russian Navy will protect *Basilica*," Vasily said, looking at Mireia. "In case whoever attacked you tries again."

"They'll try again," Nicolas said. "They've attacked us already, more times than we know. They're not about to quit."

Mireia looked over to him.

Nikki gave her a warm smile, while Nicolas just gave another nod.

He didn't want to engage her any more than that. He didn't seem to care.

God.

Mireia knew she was being an idiot.

She remembered *Basilica* from the launch in Finland. She'd been sur-prised to be invited, until she'd realized that Carter Elgin had been going for quantity as opposed to quality, and that he'd sent invites not just to his entire staff in Stockholm, but to every SolRescue member on the planet, along with a huge list of scientists, engineers, politicians, and—according to Samantha Yoon—a small body of young women he'd met through the local Swedish arts scene, all of whom he happened to fancy.

But despite the wide net, Mireia had been curious to see it, the floating headquarters that everyone had already realized would sit nearly empty, since no one but Carter Elgin had wanted to pack up their lives in Sweden to sit isolated in the middle of the Atlantic. So she went with Samantha and two other girls on the overnight ferry across to Turku, in Finland, and then on the hour-and-a-half bus trip to the shipyard in the small city of Rauma, which seemed to exist mostly for the business of building ships.

And that ship itself had been underwhelming, to put it nicely.

It was based on the design for a standard container ship, with a few *Car-teresque* enhancements, but Mireia had trouble seeing what modifications had actually been made, aside from extra office space instead of rows of stacked sea cans.

The most grandiose thing about the ship was its name. *Basilica*. Like the entire barge existed for the worship of Carter Elgin.

Even back then, when she'd been young and naive and one of Carter's groupies, she'd still gotten a bad taste from that.

There'd been tours of *Basilica*, and Samantha had coaxed Mireia to wait in line for over an hour, and then they'd gone on board, and Mireia had dis-covered just how no-frills Carter had gone with the interior.

Even in Scandinavia, the land of minimalism—if you could include Finland as part of it—the office and living space aboard *Basilica* were about as spartan as possible, looking more like a cabin at a summer camp than the headquarters for the most powerful crowdOrg on the planet.

Carter had even left his prized Jackson Pollock mosaic back home in Stockholm.

Samantha had provided a theory, that like most people who remembered the *Titanic*, Carter had realized that there was a not insignificant chance that at some point in its lifetime, *Basilica* would sink, or founder on some bank or shoal, at least, so piling up priceless valuables on board would be a very bad idea.

Mireia could imagine the scene of Carter Elgin choosing his Pollock over his own life.

It had seemed like Samantha had felt some compulsion to defend Carter, as if Mireia's offhand comments could have somehow damaged him.

That trip to *Basilica*'s launch had been a turning point in their friendship. Mireia had realized then that Samantha was moving into a place she couldn't follow, joining—or rather, founding—the cult to Carter Elgin.

That if Mireia had pointed out the hidden meaning of the name of that ship, that Carter wanted that cult of Samantha's…

Three months later, Mireia had taken the position in Guyana, and while she and Alex had still agreed to be a part of Carter's extended reach, Mireia had decided that Samantha wouldn't be a part of the plan.

Before that trip to Finland, Mireia had been under the impression that she'd been building up to a new best friend.

There was one more ride by helicopter, once the amphibious assault carrier and its two escorts had met up with the Russian main fleet.

It gave Mireia a chance to see the size of the Russian naval forces in the North Atlantic, crowned by what she recognized was one of the largest military ships in the world, a Russian aircraft carrier.

And its escorts.

There'd been two small ships with the helicopter carrier, destroyers, probably, since there were two of similar size with the larger carrier, but there was another, larger ship, which Mireia guessed would be considered a cruiser.

And swarm ships; she could see several, and knew that there'd be more, unmanned naval drones to add a valuable buffer between the fleet and anyone who'd try to harm her.

And there was an ocean-going ferry, which looked to Mireia like the ones she remembered from Sweden. And *Basilica*, running close alongside the ferry, both of which looked tiny compared to the Russian aircraft carrier, but big enough against the other ships.

She could see lines between the ferry and *Basilica*, cargo being moved from the ferry to Carter's ship.

"Replenishment at sea," Vasily said. "I wonder if they moved people over the same way."

"Like a zipline?" Jared asked.

"More like an elevator that goes sideways. I guess they'd have to, unless they want to use a helicopter and a rope ladder. There's no helipad on that ferry. But I'm surprised by how many ships there are out here."

"What do you mean?" Chloe asked. "Carriers need escorts, don't they?"

"Not all the time," Vasily said. "Not if they're armed well enough. But I didn't see any other ships around the *Flyorov* the last time I was here."

"You must have missed them," Mireia said.

He shook his head. "They weren't out there."

They landed on *Basilica*, onto an upper deck that was far less busy than the main deck below, which was filled with crates and boxes of cargo, waiting to be brought into the office quarters.

Mireia could see at least sixty people just out on the decks; she imagined there were many more inside the expanded passenger quarters, office space or otherwise.

Carter Elgin had finally achieved his dream with *Basilica*; the floating headquarters of SolRescue.

All he'd needed to do that was the deaths of dozens upon dozens of innocent people.

And Alex.

Mireia was separated by the others, a man who'd introduced himself as Danny Pyke—CEO of Turnpike Exploration Tech—leading her down a separate hallway, toward some area that looked more like part of the ship's operations than any living space.

They went down a set of stairs, into what could be described *as the bowels*, where the decor had gone from minimalist white to pipe-and-metal green; she felt like she was being led into some kind of trap, but it didn't make sense that they'd sent such a friendly, smiley, and *nearly charming* man to do it.

"Where are you taking me?" she asked him.

"To talk somewhere," he said, "away from the others."

"I don't think I want to go any further with you. I'm sorry." She wasn't sure why she'd apologized.

He stopped walking.

He gave her another of his friendly smiles. "Don't worry, Mireia… I'm not some hired goon."

"Hired goon?"

"Yeah. Like an enforcer."

"What?"

"Sorry," he said. "I'm new to this stuff. I'm just an engineer, like you. But a CEO, too, so I spend my time engineering my business plan for the next round of investment."

"Was that meant as a joke?" she asked him.

"I don't know… maybe. I'm nervous, I guess."

"I've done nothing wrong."

"I didn't mean to give that impression," he said.

"But you're taking me down to the bottom of the boat for a friendly chat."

"That's a good thing, actually. On the high seas, you're safer the farther away you get from the deck railing."

"What is wrong with you?"

He laughed. "As if you don't understand engineers."

"So what if I just stop following you?" she asked. "What happens then?"

"We can talk right here, I guess."

She looked around. Pumps and dials, and a deckway that wrapped around them. Fluorescent lights with a hum she remembered from her childhood.

And no one else around.

"Okay," she said. "Talk to me."

"Carter wants to feel like he can trust you, Mireia."

"And why does that matter to me?"

"Come on. You agreed to help us. You made a promise to Derrick Mc-Pherson."

"I didn't promise," she said. "If anything, I was coerced. And I think I want my money back."

"Did you know about Alex?"

"What?"

"Did you know? That he was working with the Chinese military government. That he took money from them."

"Do you want the truth?" she asked. "Or do you just want me to tell you whatever Carter expects to hear."

"They're the same thing."

"He shouldn't trust me, Mr. Pyke. You shouldn't trust me. Because yes, I *suspected* that my husband was involved with something. And I didn't say anything, because I didn't know what I could say, or who I could say it to, and I didn't want to lose him."

"Did you know he destroyed the European space station?"

"I don't want to believe that," she said.

"What does that mean? That you don't believe it?"

"Just what I told you. That I wish I didn't know what I now know."

He gave a slow nod. "So, you didn't know, right?" he asked her. "Before it happened?"

"I thought he was providing specifications. Corporate espionage. Bad, but not... not like the other..."

"I'm sorry, Mireia," Danny said.

That put her on edge.

She stepped back from him.

He didn't move.

"You saved Nicolas Clouatre," Danny said. "That's a big thing you did."

"I know."

"But I don't think I can tell Carter what he wants to hear."

"What are you going to tell him?"

"That you knew Alex was compromised."

"So what does that mean?" she asked. "What are you going to do to me?"

He shook his head. "No. It's not like that, Mireia. It's not like you're in some kind of danger or anything. It just means that there are certain things we won't be able to work with you on. That we'll need to keep you in the dark, more than we'd wanted to."

"I don't want to do anything for you," she said. "I just want to be done."

He nodded. "We all want to be done. But we still need to do it."

57

THE LIBRARY had become the official meeting room. Anita knew it was partly because Carter was most comfortable there, but also because it was segregated from the main work and living area of the ship, in its own Elgin wing, connected to the bridge tower.

It was late, too late for a meeting in Anita's informed opinion, but he knew that Carter wouldn't have considered not bringing the new arrivals into the room for at least a quick chat.

Anita had read up on them.

Aside from the regular bunch, of Carter, Bridget, and Danny, with Derrick on the speakers whenever he could be tracked down, there were also two of the stationkeeping and maintenance engineers from Sweden, who Anita knew had as good a handle on the shield as she'd ever had. There was Vasily Utkin, too, back from the mission that he'd been in no way cut out for, and with him, one of the hostages he'd helped rescue, a USAF engineer from Churchill, Jared Koskela.

Also known as the USAF engineer the Chinese operatives hadn't managed to kill, since they'd dumped the body of robotics guru Mohammed Najjar in some river in the north of Canada.

And lastly there was Nicolas Clouatre, the man the rest of the world was still convinced had destroyed the European space station, not that anyone could think of a plausible motive.

Anita had asked Carter about Nicolas, about his plan to exonerate him, to rebut the ridiculously graphic details provided by a rising star in the ESA named Simon Montet. Carter had made it clear that he was in no hurry, that giving Nicolas the freedom to go home to France wasn't in SolRescue's best interest for the time being.

That was Carter Elgin in a nutshell. Infuriating.

He would do whatever he felt he needed to, no matter who it hurt.

Or whatever he wanted to do, in the case of Bridget vs. Anita, or the latest round, which involved some woman who was noticeably absent from the meeting, Rachael Duck.

Bridget handled the introductions, everyone giving a quick description of who they were, except for Carter, who just gave a nod when it came to his turn, as last in line.

And then he got right into it.

"We'll be doing three simultaneous launches," he said. "Three capsules

489

from three different locations. This is one of those locations."

"And the others?" Jared asked, taking the risk of cutting in.

Carter didn't look pleased with the interruption, but he replied courteously enough. "Danny Pyke's team at Wallops Island, and a new maker camp team down in Brownsville. Everyone's familiar with those pads?"

There were some nods and murmurs.

"So three simultaneous launches means all at once. The exact same moment… no press releases, and no warning to the FAA."

"So an illegal launch," Nicolas said.

"Yes," Carter replied, with his Carter Elgin grin. "Three illegal launches. And if one or more of those go well, we'll have a fourth launch five to six days later. Location TBD."

"Whatever location is still standing," Anita said.

"Those three launches are planned for next Saturday," Carter said.

"That's crazy," Jared said.

Carter smirked. "Thank you for your uninformed opinion, Mr. Koskela."

"Well, tell me how it isn't crazy, then."

"It's not my job to convince you."

"So who's doing what?" Vasily asked. "Three launches means three teams, right?"

"That's right," Carter said. "Danny is taking Wallops Island, since that's his home base. I'd say there's a fifty percent chance that launch will be shut down."

"So why do it at all?" Jared asked.

"Fifty percent is less than a hundred percent," Bridget said. "And even a interrupted launch is good for misdirection, since no one is expecting us to do three simultaneous launches."

"Because it's insane," Anita said. "Unless you're us."

She knew she sounded overconfident, but she felt like a little bravado was required. They needed to feel superhuman, didn't they?

To pull it off?

"I want Anita to go to Brownsville," Carter said. "She'll take Nikki Taunton and Mireia Lona with her, since they have experience with our maker camps."

This was the first she'd heard of his plan.

He'd known she wouldn't argue with him on it, not in front of so many people, an audience wrestling with enough doubt.

"What about me?" Nicolas asked.

"You can't go to Texas," Bridget said. "We want you here, as part of the executive team."

Nicolas shook his head. "What about Anita, then? You're sending her to Texas."

"And Danny to Virginia, yeah," Carter said. "I'd say that's more than enough people away from the heart of it. Not to mention Derrick."

"So we're the heart of it?" Jared asked.

Carter nodded. "*Basilica*'s the heart, along with the people in this room. We'll be meeting twice a day, at 900 and 1630, up until next Saturday's launches. Danny and Anita will be leaving for their sites in a few days."

"Good to know," Danny said.

She wondered if he'd call Carter out on the lack of consultation. The everyday functioning of the *Elginarchy*, as Derrick sometimes called it.

But then she remembered, that she was the only one who could really call Carter out on something. Even Bridget seemed somewhat cowed, like the cult of Carter Elgin had power over her, too.

Anita wouldn't call him out.

Not in that room, in front of them all.

She'd have to wait.

"So being the heart means that everything comes from here," Carter said. "The designs flow from here to Wallops and Brownsville. Problems come up, they come here, and we send along the solution. That's why I've brought everyone here. Why the office in Sweden is pretty much closed for business, aside from some coordination with the ESA, for helping us to get some raw materials moved out to STeLa-1."

"Why does it matter where the designs are done?" Jared asked. "Why wouldn't you just leave people to do their jobs as they would normally?"

Carter sighed. Heavily. "Let me do my job, okay?"

"I'm just asking a question."

"What is your deal?"

"What?"

"Why are you acting like we're peers, Mr. Koskela? Like you've earned the right to criticize every decision I've made?"

"I thought that's what you wanted," Jared said. "That you didn't want a bunch of yes men."

"He's got a point," Anita said.

"We don't have time for debate on every little item," Carter said. "You want to contribute? Great. Then do it for something that will help. Like building a rocket that can take one of these capsules up to GTO. That's why you're here, Mr. Koskela. That's why you're here, *Jared*."

"Yeah, okay," Jared said.

"I'm supposed to smooth these things over," Bridget said. "But we don't have time for that, do we?"

Carter chuckled. "She's saying that you'll get the brunt of me for the next week, my inflated ego and all. And you'll hate me by the end of it."

"Some of us hate you already," Anita said.

"I love that you hate me," Carter said. "It tells me I'm doing something

491

right."

&

Anita had been given the largest lab on *Basilica*, as well as a team of thirty two engineers and designers, including Danny Pyke and Jared Koskela.

Their job was to figure out the rockets for the boost from Earth. All four of them. And she had no idea how they could pull it off.

Forget one week.

She wasn't sure she could pull it off in three months.

It was funny, in a way, since rockets were the one piece of the original sunshield project that she and Carter and Bridget hadn't done themselves. Sure, she'd worked on the design for months, but once the government shut down that possibility, they had SpaceX volunteer the Falcon Heavy, and Anita's design was left to rot.

And now that design was woefully out of date.

Or she would have thought that, until Jared pointed out to her that his own work in Churchill had replicated most of the SolRescue designs, including her rocket.

And Danny Pyke was quick to join in on the adulation, telling her that he had been nothing but impressed by her designs, and that had Turnpike needs its own rocket, he would have been more than happy to adapt one from her original work.

But that was ridiculous, wasn't it?

Mining bots and printer bots were nothing compared to a full-on capsule. Even Jared's designs from Fort Churchill, the "Turaco", weren't anywhere near large enough to handle the weight of two beads for the torus.

The Falcon Heavy they'd used for their little bots had weighed over three thousand pounds. That was the kind of rocket they needed.

And no matter how many advancements had come in additive manufacturing, you can't print up a heavy-lift rocket in some rented warehouse in South Texas.

For one thing, *you can't even fit* a heavy-lift rocket in some rented warehouse in South Texas.

She pulled Danny and Jared into the small office at the back of the lab.

She shut the door.

"I need to know how we're going to pull this off," she told them.

"Same way people like us pull everything off," Jared said.

"What does that mean?"

"We make it happen because we don't spend all our time worrying about why it shouldn't happen. We don't let that get in the way."

"Yeah, great speech," Anita said. "But I'm looking for a tangible solution, not a pep talk."

"We don't have one yet," Danny said.

"We just need the right mix," Jared said. "Additive and subtractive, living in harmony. And some injection moulding."

"We have nowhere to build and store a heavy lift rocket," Anita said. "So what do we do? Do we convince Carter to find a place where we can actually do that?"

Jared nodded. "That's why they brought me to Churchill. To research the most efficient way to manufacture rockets."

"Your rocket design is too light," Danny said.

"Why was efficiency important?" Anita asked. "You build a couple of launchers, you send up your little sunshield-killing robots. Does it matter how much that one-off murder spree costs?"

"I wasn't in charge of the strategy," Jared said. "All I know is that they expected this to be a regular thing. Like we build a rocket and launch in Churchill, then we do it again at Wallops, or White Sands…"

"You were expecting some kind of rocket war," Danny said.

Jared shook his head. "I wasn't expecting anything."

Anita believed him.

But she was still annoyed. He'd worked for *the enemy*, and he still hadn't given SolRescue anything they could use. No intelligence, no useful designs. Clouatre seemed far more valuable, by comparison, and he'd spent half of that past week on the run.

Jared Koskela wasn't exactly showing off.

"So what was Mohammed Najjar working on?" Anita asked. "You told us about rad shielding, about some hypothetical gamma ray burst."

"Which is undetectable," Danny said, "as far as I know."

"He couldn't share the robotics with me," Jared said.

"So what can you give us?" Anita asked. "Anything?"

Jared sighed.

He seemed to be thinking it over.

He started rubbing his chin, stroking a non-existent beard.

It didn't help Anita's patience.

But she held on.

"Mohammed's files were locked up tight," Jared said. "We'd brought the filebox with us out of Churchill, but when we were grabbed, the box went missing."

"No surprise there," Danny said.

"If we'd had that filebox, we could have given it to Benj McPherson. To search like he'd done with Rachael Duck's files."

"Why was he searching her files?" Anita asked.

"We thought she was working with the Chinese," Jared said. "But she wasn't. She was working…"

He'd trailed off. He didn't want to tell her.

Anita wasn't going to let it go. "Who was she working for?"

"There's a group out there who aren't very happy with Carter Elgin," Jared said.

"We know them," Danny said.

"I don't know them," Anita said.

Danny nodded. "Well, they're out there. Think Carter's gone too far, too many secrets, too many lies."

Anita smirked. "I get that."

"Rachael was getting some very unusual requests from Carter," Jared said. "Instructions to have people killed."

"That doesn't sound like Carter," Anita said. "Maybe if you'd said Derrick, I'd almost believe it."

Jared shook his head. "It wasn't from Carter. He'd been hacked. By the same people who took us."

"Malik Daley and the Chinese junta," Danny said.

"So what was Najjar working on?" Anita asked.

"Shield bots," Jared said.

"No… it was something he couldn't share with you, right?"

"Yeah…"

"So not just shield bots. Because you saw the shield bots. Because he wanted you to help with that rad shielding."

"There's something else," Jared said.

"Clearly."

"So they've got hardened bots," Danny said, "and something else on top of that, not that we have any idea what."

"Something robotic," Jared said. "Mohammed had told me that much. He wanted me to help him, even without clearance. A second pair of eyes."

"They had to be in your lab in Churchill," Anita said. "Did you not see anything unusual?"

He didn't answer.

Which was an answer in itself.

"You need to trust *someone*," she told him. "If you want this to work."

He nodded.

"So?"

"Chloe has it," he said. "A small spider bot. She's been hiding it since we left Churchill."

"Then we need to bring it here," Danny said.

"Quietly," Anita said.

Jared nodded.

Then left the lab.

"Spider bot," Danny said. "Najjar built a spider bot."

"Forgive my ignorance," Anita said. "I don't know what it would be for."

"That's pretty much a smoking gun that the Chinese are involved."

"Because they like spiders now?"

"They couldn't break into the shieldbots from here," Danny said. "From Earth, I mean."

"So they're going to break into them at STeLa-1. Because that's less impossible somehow?"

Danny smiled. "Why destroy the whole shield, when you can rip out the guts and keep the rest? That's what they did with that Russian carrier they bought. They replaced the electronics with homegrown stuff, because they knew the Russians used German parts that the Chinese would never have trusted."

Anita closed her eyes.

She pictured her first bot. Not the first prototype, but the first earthbound bot she'd built that was a good reflection of what they'd managed to build in situ, in space.

To create a cloud of polyhedral dice.

If something could tear into one side of that aluminum die, rip some kind of hole large enough... they could pull out the guts, the whole of which was no bigger than her fingernail, assembled from the miniaturization printer that was the pride of early 21st-century Cornell Tech's College of Engineering.

A spider bot could jettison one fingernail's worth of controls, and inject a suitable replacement.

No new bots required.

"But why the hardened replacement bots?" she asked, not that she was really asking Danny for an opinion.

He gave one anyway. "Millions of bots, launched from thousands of SolRescue members. They weren't all your initial design, were they?"

He was right.

There would be hundreds of thousands of bots that didn't match her prototype, slight alterations and whole-cloth alternatives.

But most would have the same basic concept. A small bit of guts in a much larger whole.

But not always as small.

"Not everyone had the same tech we had," she said. "Some of those bots looked like science fair entries. On the inside."

And the software she'd written, with Bridget's help, the dancing shieldbots that formed the cloud, adjusting as they made their rounds on the halo orbit, to keep the shade as consistent as possible.

It would be possible to shift the positions enough, to put the hardened bots to the outside of the cloud. Koskela and Najjar's magnetic shielding was far from perfect—Anita had already found a few places where she could make improvements—but it would protect those inner legacy shield-bots more than they were protected at the moment.

Protecting against solar activity.

Not protecting against some solar system sterilizing gamma ray burst.

But protecting against something else.

There were shieldbots that didn't need to provide shielding, that converted solar energy to microwaves, that didn't bother with the minutiae of balancing the planet's temperature.

Anita had known from the start, from the moment they'd first decided on the sunshield. That any collection of shieldbots past a certain size could deflect that solar energy, deflect into one concentrated beam.

Carter had known that, too. That they controlled a weapon that was far too tempting for any one government to handle.

That they could take those "extra" shieldbots and concentrate a beam on any bot that had lost contact, any bot that was hijacked by the spider.

But that beam wouldn't be anywhere near as effective against the hardened bots. If a race were to develop, between the Chinese spiders and SolRescue's death ray… the spiders would win.

Anita wondered if Mohammed Najjar had figured that out.

If he'd started to waver, like his colleague Jared Koskela had.

If he'd come to SolRescue, maybe they could have come up with some kind of countermeasure.

There was a chance that Chloe Nielsen-Brown had smuggled out a working example of a spiderbot, something they could disassemble and understand.

But Anita had lived through forty-three years of real life, longer than she'd ever pictured when ten-year-old Anita had thought of herself as a grownup.

She knew that the bot wouldn't be a working prototype.

If Najjar had needed Jared Koskela's help, that meant the work hadn't progressed far enough.

The spiderbot wasn't ready.

But that wasn't all bad news.

It was also why the sunshield was still under SolRescue's control.

For as long as it took the Chinese junta and their partners at the US Air Force to finish the design.

She found Carter that afternoon in his personal lab, which, like the library, was segregated from the rest of *Basilica*'s working space.

The door had been locked, but he'd opened it once he'd realized it was

Anita who'd been coming for a visit.

She wondered if he expected another lapse in judgment from her. A mid-day fuck on his workbench.

Piece of shit.

"I saw the write-up on that spider bot," he said as he let her in. "Just his first stab at it, huh?"

"I'm guessing they realized Najjar might not finish the job," she said. "Or that he might not pass the end result on to them."

"How much time do you think we've got?"

"I'd guess they won't beat us to a launch," she said. "But it's not like a functioning space station at STeLa-1 is going to stop them. If we get that far."

He smiled. "I've got something for that."

"Of course you do." She groaned.

"What's the problem?"

"You know people don't like this side of you, Carter. Keeping these secrets."

"It's not a secret," he said. "Derrick knows. And Bridget."

"What about me?"

"I'm telling you now. But you know it stays quiet, right?"

"I get that," she said. "We've got hundreds of people on this thing, and you figure at least one has loose lips."

"That's why the Russians are here. To keep those lips from sinking ships."

"Yes. I'm the one who chose the reference."

He laughed.

"What do you have?" she asked him.

"Another bot. Not as cool as a little spider to launch at the sunshield… but still pretty cool."

She sighed. "Just show me."

"I can't show you. Not yet."

"Why not?"

"Because it's not done. And I don't want the critique."

"Come on, Carter."

"You know how I like to work. And I'm not going to wreck the flow by bringing you in on it."

"Then why tell me at all?"

"You know we lost three maker camps," he said.

"Yeah."

"The third camp was in Texas. Hill Country, to be exact."

"That's not exact."

He laughed again.

Jackass.

"Mercator was a camp for the flight crew," he said. "To design their equipment, and to train them."

"You were training a flight crew at a maker camp?"

"*Stupid* like a fox, right?"

"So you lost your crew," she said.

He nodded. "Derrick's doing his best to find replacements. Anyone with time offplanet, who he thinks we can trust."

"And how's that going?"

"Not well. Thanks for asking."

"So what's Plan B? You going on a spacewalk, Carter?"

"You're not that lucky, Anita."

"So who, then?"

"Maybe a couple of the engineers. Maybe Vasily Utkin... he handled himself well with that hostage shit. Not sure about Koskela, and Clouatre isn't really in shape."

"And you don't trust Mireia Lona, and if you had someone from Stockholm they'd be standing here instead of me."

"I'm not asking you to go," he said.

"That's not what I mean."

"I might ask Danny Pyke."

"You should be asking me."

"What? Did you just say—"

"I'm the one who knows the shield. I'm the one who understands this stuff better than anyone else. Better than you, Carter."

"That's our little secret," he said. "Everyone thinks I'm the only genius around here."

"I'm volunteering."

She wasn't sure why she was.

"You don't have any kind of flight training, Anita."

"And Danny Pyke does?"

"I don't want to risk you," he said.

"That sounds like clouded judgement. Like the judgement of an idiot who would try to get it on with both of his best friends."

"You know I love you."

"I don't give a shit who you love. It sure doesn't seem like you love Bridget very much, though."

"That's not fair," Carter said. "And it's not what matters right now."

She sighed.

She was annoyed.

She couldn't read him. She couldn't tell if he was being honest with her, or if he was still angling for a shot at pushing her up against that workbench.

But she had to think about what *did* matter. That the Chinese were however many days from taking control of the sunshield. That the US Executive had managed to make a bad deal, and that they would probably find themselves completely screwed soon enough.

And the same military government that was still executing thousands of dissidents every week—and harvesting their organs for sale—would be in charge of the most powerful weapon ever built.

Carter Elgin didn't matter.

What he and his hold over her had pushed Anita to do, time and time again… that didn't matter, either.

Only the shield mattered.

"You haven't told me what you're working on," she said. "You need to tell me, Carter."

"A defensive weapon," he said. "A way of protecting the shield."

"I'll need more detail than that."

"Mass driver. Scrape off a piece of rock. Aim that rock at whatever's heading toward the shield. Then shoot."

"And you think you need someone up there to do the shooting."

"Among other things, yeah. Someone who can watch out for problems and fix anything that happens out there. The hab has the robotics we need for UEVA, but we can't telecontrol it from back here."

"And you don't think I can handle that?" she asked.

"I know you can handle it, Anita. But I don't want you to go."

"You haven't seen me in how many years? What does it matter if I'm a million and a half kilometers away?"

"I don't want to lose you."

"You lost me twenty years ago. For good."

"Yet here you are," he said.

"Fuck you, Carter. I'm here because you need me. Because the whole planet needs me to clean up your mess."

"You're right. I do need you."

She wanted to keep on him, to tell him just how much he'd fucked up her career, her entire life.

She just wanted to start yelling.

To be angry.

But she knew it wasn't all on him.

That she'd decided to let what happened get in the way of everything else. Not just in the way of being a part of SolRescue, but in the way of moving past it.

"I should have stayed," she said. "I should have laid out the ground rules, stuck with them, and kept this ship on course."

"More ship analogies."

"You're not funny."

"I need you to stay on the team, Anita."

"I'll stay. If you let me go to STeLa-1."

"Why do you want to go?" he asked.

"I know how people look at us, Carter. I know they see you as this troubled genius, they see Bridget as this beautiful scientist who fell in love with you. And I think I know how people see me."

"How do people see you?"

"I'm the missing piece."

"The missing piece..."

"SolRescue worked because we worked. When it worked. And it's been going downhill since I left."

"So why would you risk your life? Why wouldn't you stay here on *Basilica*, be our third wheel?"

She smiled. She hadn't meant to.

He'd almost said "third wheel" like it was a good thing.

"I told Danny we needed to get people fired up again," she said. "This is how we do it. Anita Singhal goes to space. To defend the sunshield from the people who want to destroy everything we've built. That's the video we need. Not some cheesy montage with Danny Pyke's rockets. We need to show the world what we're up against."

"We can show the world with Danny Pyke. Or Vasily Utkin."

"No. We can't. It needs to be me up there. With whoever else. That's not as important. Me in space, you on *Basilica*, and Bridget and Sansa back home in Sweden, where it's safe. We do that and I'll stay, for as long as I'm needed. Forever, if I have to be."

He nodded. Then he put his hand on her arm, just above the elbow.

He gave it a little rub.

She knew what he would be going for next.

He'd be leaning in.

"That's not happening ever again," she said. "Never again."

"I know you don't want never again, Anita."

"Don't tell me what I want, Carter."

He gave her another nod.

She turned and left his lab.

While half of her wanted more than anything to stay.

She went back to her own lab, to where Danny Pyke was still working, along with at least half of their team.

Jared Koskela had left, which Anita didn't see as some sign that he lacked commitment; he'd been through the wringer.

Danny gave her a friendly smile as she walked over to him.

She asked him to join her in the adjoining office.

"I'm going to be on that space habitat," she told him. "I'm not sure who else will be going with me. Carter might ask you to go with me."

"I would," he said, still with a smile. "Absolutely."

She felt herself smiling back at him. "It's funny… I thought you'd tell me not to go."

"Why would I say that?"

"Well, I was pretty much a hermit on basic a week and a half ago. And now I'm volunteering to be the first person to live in space."

"One of the first," he said. "With me, hopefully."

"So now you want to go?"

"I'd love to go with you."

She caught his intonation.

She didn't comment on it.

"I think you're the perfect person to man that station," he said. "Or to attend the station, occupy it. Guess you wouldn't man it, *per se*."

She laughed. "There's something very wrong with you, Mr. Pyke."

He leaned in and kissed her.

On the lips.

She waited until he was… finished… and then she pulled back a little. "I didn't expect that," she said.

"I know. I don't think I'm sorry. I just wanted to kiss you."

She nodded. "And now?"

He leaned in again.

She met him halfway.

"Come to my quarters," he said. "Please?"

She nodded.

She was still a little bit in shock.

She drank a glass of white wine in Danny Pyke's quarters, knowing full well that it was odd for him to have a chilled bottle in a small room with no fridge.

Danny had some wine, too, but she could tell he wasn't a big fan of it.

He'd gotten it for her.

For her to sip, while sitting on his narrow bunk.

A man nearly ten years younger than her.

"How long have you been planning this?" she asked him.

"What do you mean?"

She could tell by the slight smirk on his face that he was trying to be coy. It was a *little bit* adorable.

She grinned. "Don't tell me this all started with the SolRescue video."

"With the poster I made of you," he said, chuckling. "My whole life's work has been one long con, just to bring you here. So you can drink my wine and recite the entire video, line by line."

"Do you want me to go all low for Carter's parts?"

"I'm not interested in Carter's parts."

She laughed.

Danny kissed her again.

"This isn't about the video," he said. "It's about how you're the most beautiful person I've ever known."

"What did I say about flattery?"

"I can't help myself, stupid."

She kissed him.

And closed her eyes as he made his way down to between her legs.

She just wanted to feel it all.

Completely.

It had been so long since it had happened.

So long since she'd let it happen.

It hadn't happened since her last time in Stockholm.

58

JARED HADN'T expected Danny Pyke to show up first thing Saturday morning—just before 700 hours—with a smile on his face, especially after both Anita Singhal's pronouncements on printed rockets and the information they'd gleaned from the spider bot Chloe had kept hidden in her ponytail.

But Danny Pyke was smiling, and he was ready to work, and Jared was ready to finally get something done again.

No one had bothered to say it specifically, but everyone had known that they were building a two-stage-to-orbit heavy lift launcher that can boost the bead capsules, which according to Nicolas' team would range in weight to as much as 7,500 kilos including payload.

That was pretty standard fare if you were Boeing or SpaceX or Bangalore Launch, with pre-built rockets, but it wasn't the same deal if you were doing everything from scratch, manufactured in a 15,000 square foot lab floating in the middle of the North Atlantic.

Not to mention having to build two of those rockets offsite, one near Wallops Island and the other near Brownsville.

And then launching them.

On *Basilica*, that meant using the fore helipad, which meant they had to move three cores for the first stage—two solid fuel boosters and the main stage—that were already too big to print, up to the top of the ship. They'd then need to strap them together and hope they don't come apart during the initial firing of the rocket engines. That's twenty-eight rocket engines, nine for each monocoque core on the first stage—arrayed in the standard octaweb structure first developed for the SpaceX Falcons—and one more Merlin for the significantly smaller second. The engines themselves were clones of the time-tested Merlin designs, also originally from the Falcons.

Assuming they could find a way to bring those three and a half cores up to the roof (along with the interstage and the payload fairing), and they'd completed the water pumps and channel gutters for the sound suppression, they then had to add the fuel, liquid oxygen being shipped in from a cryogenic plant in Gothenburg, Sweden—the same place they got the liquid nitrogen they'd be bringing up to STeLa-1 in the capsules themselves. The rocket grade kerosene—RP-1—was on its way from a refinery in Rotterdam.

From the calculations Danny had made, considering the impulse and thrust of the Merlins, the weight of the capsule, and the challenge of reaching geosynchronous transfer orbit, they would end up needing approximately 130,000 gallons of cryogenic liquid oxygen and 80,000 gallons of kerosene for each rocket. That was just under 2000 cubic meters of LOX and around 1200 cubic meters of RP-1 in total, just enough to be a hassle to move around.

Especially having to move one load to the Delmarva Peninsula and another into the Gulf of Mexico.

But that wasn't Jared's problem, or Danny's or Anita's.

Bridget Hawn was handling the suppliers and the shipments, and from what she'd been able to do before, a few tanks of propellant wasn't that big a deal to her.

Not as big a deal as building a 225 foot high rocket in a lab that was only a hundred and fifty feet long; the longest components, the two boosters, were thirty feet longer than the lab.

There was only one plausible solution, as Jared saw it.

They had to blow out one wall of the lab, and throw up some scaffolding, and some kind of cradle to keep the cores in place.

He drafted the design for Anita's approval, first passing it by Danny for the standard "am I insane" check.

He knew that Anita would need Carter's approval, too, since the plan called for cutting a twenty by twenty foot gap in the wall of his floating headquarters.

He was shocked when Anita responded positively, and told him that she was confident that Carter would agree, too, which she then explained was about as close as she could come to giving him the go-ahead… so, in other words, *go ahead,* but don't tell too many people about it.

Danny volunteered to organize the renovations, while Jared moved on to the manufacturing plan.

The plan was simple enough: find a way to build a long and narrow cryogenic tank from the same flat sheets of aluminum-lithium alloy he'd used for Turaco, up in Churchill.

Just three times bigger.

And tougher.

The big difference between Turaco and SolRescue's new Sansa rocket wasn't the size; it was the durability. Turaco was designed to send mining and printing bots offplanet, done quickly and cheaply, where redundancy was based on doing it again from the start; Sansa would be sending not just the toroid beads, but human crew.

Turaco was a rocket fuselage printed out with an experimental 3d printer—Cthulhu—and not at all how you want to assemble a human-rated—rated hypothetically—heavy lift rocket which will also manage to contain one Anita Singhal on board.

They'd need to bend metal and weld it, and would need to do that with friction-stir welding, to make cores with basically no joints at all.

That was beyond anything Jared had done.

And beyond what Danny had done.

All he and Danny knew was that amateurs doing friction-stir would inevitably lead to kissing bonds, a defect which had managed to kill a half dozen astronauts since the early days of commercial spaceflight.

Jared took a quick census of the team.

No one had the knowledge.

SolRescue had never handled its own launches. Even the few launches Carter had arranged from Sweden had gone up from Baikonur or Guyana, piggybacking on Russian and ESA equipment.

He needed someone from the ESA, or even the RFSA. A technician.

But they didn't have one on *Basilica*.

Which didn't make a lot of sense. It seemed like exactly the kind of mistake Carter Elgin wouldn't make.

So he decided to ask Anita about it.

Not that she was in the lab; it wasn't even 800 hours yet.

He messaged her tablet, and she told him she was on her way down.

She led him into her office when she arrived.

"We need rocket technicians," he told her. "We're drowning in robotics experts and mechanical engineers, but somehow we don't have people who actually know their way around a pinch roller."

"I didn't know we had a pinch roller in the lab," she said.

"We don't. That's part of the problem, isn't it? He wants us to build three years' worth of components in a week."

"We can bring stuff in from the mainland. If we send the right people to get it."

"We need technicians first. Machine operators, people with forming experience."

"Then get someone to find you those technicians," Anita said.

"From where, exactly?"

"We'll start by asking Carter about it."

"You want to ask him? When we meet?"

She smiled. "No, right now, I think. Clearly this isn't the kind of oversight he'd usually make."

Jared nodded.

He hadn't expected her to be so quick to help.

Carter seemed surprised to see them, not just Jared, but even Anita, as if they were unfamiliar acquaintances. He bid them both good morning, something that seemed a little un-Elgin-like.

"I like people who can't wait for the morning meeting," Carter said, with a grin.

"Why are there no technicians on board?" Anita asked.

"We don't have technicians. Just engineers."

"Well, we need them, Carter. And I'm surprised you didn't plan for that."

"We didn't need technicians back in our first little lab, in the Mae Jemison Building."

"We weren't building heavy lift rockets." She looked over to Jared. "Can you explain this to him?"

Jared nodded, even though it was the last thing he wanted to do. He'd already seen what Carter thought of people trying to put themselves up at his "level".

"We need to roll those aluminum sheets into the rings for the cores," Jared said. "Then we need to friction-stir weld those rings together to make the tank. And we need to form and weld the domes for those tanks."

"You can't arc weld?" Carter asked.

"Not the tanks. Not if we want them to work."

Carter frowned.

"The failure rate of conventionally-welded tanks is significant compared to solid state," Jared said. "So unless we want to risk people's lives—"

"You think I want to risk more lives than we need to?" Carter asked.

"Well, no, but—"

"You think I don't understand rocket assembly, that I can't read spec sheets and whitepapers from underneath my rock?"

"Enough, Carter," Anita said. "Stop being an asshole."

"This isn't Michoud down in New Orleans," Carter said. "We're not NASA. We're not SpaceX, either. We can't expect to have all the fanciest tools."

"We're SolRescue and Turnpike Exploration Tech," Jared said. "With strong doses of USAF Materiel Command and European Space Agency mixed in. All of that together should mean we do it the right way."

"That we don't half-ass it," Anita said.

"Having two of you doesn't make you twice as insightful," Carter said.

Anita sighed. "You don't have a leg to stand on, Carter. You messed up your plan this time. And Jared is a goddamn rocket scientist. And you are not."

"I'm just a tinkering has-been."

"I think we can find one FSW machine to handle all of the solid state welds," Jared said. "And we can arc weld as needed. And I think a good form machine operator can do most of the sheetwork with a single four roll double-pinch machine. Most of the rest we can handle with what we've got, the 3d printer for whatever we can't put together the old school way."

"Old school," Carter said, with a smirk.

"So we still need that operator," Anita said. "How 'bout it, Carter? Got any connections? Any bridges you haven't burned?"

"Call Derrick. Get him to find someone."

Anita shook her head. "I want you to find someone."

"What the hell kind of difference does it make?"

"Just get off your tinkering has-been ass and do it."

Jared could see she was trying not to laugh.

Carter went first, throwing out an overly loud guffaw. "I miss this," he said.

"I know you do," Anita said. "Not get on it."

"Yeah, okay."

Carter looked over at Jared. "That'll do it?" he asked.

"What?" Jared said.

"One technician, one FSW machine, and one pinch machine?"

"I think so. Someone who likes to travel."

"Good." Carter Elgin gave him a smile.

If Jared had to guess, he'd say it was the "old school" comment that had won the man over.

He couldn't help but ask Anita, once they'd left Carter's personal lab. "Why did you want Carter to do it himself?"

"It's complicated," Anita said.

"Is there a problem with Derrick McPherson?"

"You ask a lot of questions, huh?"

"Well, is there?" he asked.

"Derrick isn't a problem. But he doesn't know the first thing about recruitment. And even less about metal fab. And let's face it... people aren't starstruck by the right-hand man. They want to be approached by the man in charge."

Jared nodded.

"Carter will get you what you need," she said. "Now that we've made it clear to him." She smiled. "That's what I do around here, mostly. I keep Carter in line."

Jared just nodded again.

He wasn't comfortable mentioning how better things would likely be, had Anita Singhal spent the past twenty years keeping Carter Elgin in line.

Maybe the US and China would have just moved on with their lives, given up on the notion of taking SolRescue down a peg.

Maybe Jared wouldn't have been spending the past week as a target. And maybe Rachael wouldn't have done what she did.

It's funny how much the universe interconnects. Jared had heard the stories about Elgin and Hawn and Singhal, about the so-called SolRescue love triangle. He'd known that there had to be some truth to them, for how bad things had gotten between the three of them.

Because it had gotten really freaking bad, like Paul and Yoko bad. *So what if?*

What would have happened if Carter Elgin hadn't tried to get his mealy hands on both of his cofounders? What if Carter had just gone after Anita?

Maybe there was a poorly-written alternate history book in Jared's future. A timeline where Bridget Hawn marries the sea, and Carter and Anita become the offplanet power couple.

A timeline with better progress on spaceflight. With a healthier climate for crowdOrgs and their peculiar flavor of liquid democracy. And probably with 21st century Nazis, too, because every good alt hist story should have a couple of jackbooted brownshirts trying to clone Hitler.

59

IT WAS Saturday night. In the North Atlantic.

And no one to spend it with, besides the two hundred strangers on *Basilica*.

Mireia felt like she was being punished for something. She just wished she had some small inkling of what that something was.

Danny Pyke had made it clear from his interrogation of her that she wasn't a trusted member of the team; in fact, she wasn't sure she still was part of the team. They already had her designs, from The Island and from their second attempt at the makers camp.

She wasn't assigned to the capsule team, and Nicolas hadn't even spoken to her since... probably since that extended stay in that cramped motel room in Great Falls, Montana.

She'd spent the entire day waiting to be noticed.

And it hadn't happened.

She was out on deck, which was probably on good reason why she wasn't connecting with anyone, since everyone else was either working late on the project or trying to sneak in some downtime before their next sprint of work.

She received a message on her tablet.

A broadcast. About an assembly. Like you'd have in a school.

In half an hour, in the cargo hold, which she imagined meant the part of the deck where you'd expect to find containers, if *Basilica* had been a proper container ship.

So outside, exposed to the same winds that could cause some killer nor'easter like in those movies about perfect storms.

There's an understanding that being from Barcelona—or being any kind of Mediterranean, whatever that means—signifies that you have to be... not a big fan of ocean voyages, but at least not a total hater.

But Mireia hated being on *Basilica*.

She wasn't seasick, but she almost wished she was, because then she could be as vocal about that hate as she wanted to be.

Not that there was anyone paying attention.

She knew what was missing.

Not that Alex was missing; she still felt like he was just "away", that one day he'd show up.

What was missing was the idea that she'd lost something.

She didn't feel loss.

She wasn't grieving.

Which made her feel that much more guilty.

Maybe it was shock, she didn't know. Maybe she was just numb. But she didn't feel numb. Or at least not what she thought numb should feel like.

She was angsty, like a teenager. Like fourteen-year-old Mireia used to be, angry at the world, hating her parents and her teachers, knowing that fixing everything that was wrong with her life would be so damn easy, if everyone else would *just let her do it.*

She didn't deserve the mistrust; she'd risked her life to get Nicolas out of Guyane. She'd gone to America with Nicolas, under a fake name, pretending they were married a day after she'd lost her husband in the rainforest. She'd put her all into her work at the maker camp, which had also been risking her life, not that she'd known it at the time.

And then, after all that, she'd kept going, with Nicolas and his new special friend Nikki, trapped on the road trip from hell, then the motel room from hell, and then the illicit border crossing from hell... and more and more and more.

All to get to *Basilica*, which she hated, to be under the thumb of a man she'd learned to hate more than anyone else—even more than Mateo and the people who'd hired him—and then to be ignored and forgotten.

She wished she didn't believe in the project. In the sunshield. In what Carter Elgin and SolRescue were doing. She wished she could turn her back on it, not care.

But she cared.

She'd cared about it from the start, from the first time she'd heard about it, in primary school, in first cycle, when she was eight years old.

Someone was going to try and save the planet.

And as angry and marginalized as Mireia was, she knew that she'd have to stay there, with those people, just in case there was something she could contribute.

Because they were going to try and save the planet, all over again.

She arrived at the cargo deck ten minutes before the assembly time, which she'd figured would be early enough to find a place to sit, or at least lean, but she found that she was one of the last people to arrive.

The deck had a platform on one side, a modular stage, with the large speakers you'd see at a rock concert—or maybe smaller, like for folk music—and a podium made of metal, formed to look like a dragon's head.

It reminded her of Carter's conference room in Stockholm, where the executives would meet and she'd rarely been included, even as the main liaison from the ESA.

No one was on the platform.

She assumed that it would be Carter who'd be making the speech, hence the dragon's head, hence the large number of people gathered. The general's pep talk.

He should have stuck some flag behind him, like in that Patton movie. She wasn't sure which flag would work, though...

She was at the back of the crowd, where it was standing room only, but no crush, at least. She wasn't the tallest person, but she could see through the shoulders to the raised platform.

To Carter's dragon head podium.

"There you are," a man said from behind her.

She turned to see Benj McPherson.

"I thought you might try and skip out," he said with a smile. "Could make for a great looting opportunity."

She raise her eyebrows.

"Because you're a criminal," he said, going all in.

She laughed.

"I think you and I are in the same boat," he told her.

"Figuratively, you mean?"

"Nobody knows what to do with us."

"I'm an environmental engineer," she said. "I should have a job to do."

"You did the job already, didn't you? Twice over?"

"So then I just get shoved aside? That's not how it works. I ought to be on-hand to monitor the build."

"They don't trust you," he said.

"You're not much of a diplomat."

"Nicolas trusts you. And I trust you. And I think my father trusts you."

"I doubt that."

"But there are dozens of people working under Nicolas. And they don't know the full story. They can't know, not yet. But they've heard enough to know about Alex."

"I'm tainted meat," she said.

"It's temporary, Mireia."

"Is it?"

"You're too valuable to be put out to pasture," he said. "Honestly."

She nodded.

She felt grateful to him. Maybe she could try to believe him.

Someone came up on stage.

Danny Pyke.

Mireia rolled her eyes. He hadn't exactly made a great first impression.

He walked up to the podium.

And started talking. It didn't sound particularly rehearsed.

"Thank you for coming," he said. "We'll have the headliners out here in a minute, but I just wanted to handle a little housekeeping first."

Housekeeping.

She hated that expression.

"If anyone has questions or comments, please just save them for the end, okay? We'll bring a mic down for Q&A. And please remember... we're all tired, we're all feeling the pressure. So let's be gentle with one another."

"He's expecting some problems," Benj said.

Mireia nodded. "Maybe people don't like being pulled from their lives to hang around on a floating death trap."

"It's not all bad. The seafood is very fresh. And they don't put spirulina in *everything*. Just most of the things."

She smiled.

"So let's give these guys our full attention," Danny Pyke said.

He started making his way to one side of the platform. And hopped off.

For almost a minute there was nothing happening on stage.

Then a door opened, and they came out. Carter, Bridget, and Anita, the big three. They climbed up the stepladder, onto the stage.

Carter took the podium, while the two women flanked him, one on each side.

Like you'd see in an American beer commercial.

"I want to start off by saying thank you," Carter said. "Thank you. All of you. Thank you for taking this step with us, for agreeing to make history."

He looked to his left; Mireia realized there were cameras. It made sense. There'd be some people still in Stockholm, as well as any team members from other far-flung places. And possibly some preliminary ground crew clearing the way at any other launch site, assuming they didn't just launch everything from *Basilica*.

But that seemed like too much to handle.

And while no one had told her anything, she'd seen the transports, helicopters and a pilot boat, moving people off *Basilica* to *somewhere else*.

"The world is watching us," he said. "I mean, literally. We'll be providing this to anyone who wants to see it. *After the launches.*"

That surprised her; it seemed like a costly risk, making a video that could easily be leaked. Not that the powers that hate hadn't been trying their best to kill people. People such as Mireia herself.

"So let's keep that in mind," he continued, "when it comes time to ask questions. We'll have two blocks to try and keep it from looking too slick with the editing: one included in the worldwide release, and one after that for inside baseball. So if you're not sure if it's a question with too many details that aren't important for the rest of the planet, just hold it until the second block."

That sounded like housekeeping.

But maybe no one would have paid attention if it had come from Danny Pyke.

She was sure everyone could understand what he was really saying, including any random person who would eventually be viewing from home. That there were still secrets at SolRescue, likely about when and where the launches would take place.

The Russian naval fleet was still all around them, protecting *Basilica* with the *Georgy Flyorov*, and the cruiser and the destroyers, and a swarm of unmanned drone ships crowding the waters surrounding them.

And she knew the Russian Navy would have a shield against aerial drones; it had been a general rule for a good while that the Russians and Chinese would work together to copy any NATO advance with a reasonable facsimile, usually within the space of a decade.

Basilica was as safe as it could be. Safe enough for Carter to make his speech.

"We know a lot more now than we knew a week ago," Carter said. "We know that the President of the United States has been working secretly with the military government of China, the so-called People's Convocation, on a plan to take full control of the sunshield."

He paused, apparently to give people a moment for the allegation to sink in. It's a big deal to call out the two most powerful nations on Earth. Mireia understood that.

"This plan of theirs has included secret spacecraft launched from both Hainan Island and from a decommissioned rocket range in northern Canada. Near Churchill, Manitoba. Two of the people who worked in Churchill are with us now. The other was murdered by agents of the US and Chinese governments. Once he'd realized the extent of involvement by the Chinese junta."

Another pause.

He'd outed Jared and Chloe. He hadn't even needed to mention them by name.

But Mireia realized that anyone who wanted them dead would have already known they'd gone with Derrick McPherson. And it was a no-brainer that those same bad guys would want to kill pretty much every person on board *Basilica*.

"We have other people with us," Carter said. "We have two engineers from the European Space Agency, who were targeted by those same governments. Three more ESA workers lost their lives before we could reach out and help the two who made it here."

She knew he'd counted Alex among the lost.

She wondered how long it would be before the world knew what her husband had done.

Carter looked down. Away from the cameras. Away from the crowd.

"I know that I've made mistakes," he said. "I know I've gone against the spirit of SolRescue, foolishly thinking that I knew better than everyone else." He looked at Anita. "I'm partly responsible for what's happened. For letting us get to this point."

He took a step back.

Anita stepped in toward the podium.

"I'm partly responsible, too," she said.

Mireia could hear the crowd react. The people telling her she wasn't, saying they loved her. Like she was some kind of engineering rock star.

Which she was, really.

They hadn't said any of that during Carter's piece.

"I should have stayed," Anita said, looking over at Bridget. "But it doesn't matter right now."

Bridget was nodding her head.

Mireia noticed quite a few in the crowd doing the same.

There was something about Anita Singhal. Something people trusted.

When Anita had pulled away from Carter, it was like she'd read the trends, knowing that SolRescue was flying off the rails in super slow motion.

And now she was back.

And that meant something. To Mireia and everyone else, it seemed.

"We know more about the plan to disrupt the sunshield," Anita said. "They've designed a small robotic craft that looks like a spider. To hijack individual shield bots." She waved to someone offstage.

Jared Koskela came up onto the platform.

He held something up.

Mireia could barely see it.

It looked exactly like a metal spider.

"We believe there will be thousands of these," Anita said. "If not tens or hundreds of thousands. You can cram ten thousand into one standard size launch capsule. Not that they're using the usual launch capsules."

She gave another wave, to the other side of the stage.

Two men came up. Mireia didn't know them.

They were carrying a small capsule between them, maybe fifteen feet high, three or four feet in diameter.

"This is a model of the Chinese Little March capsule," Anita said. "One of these capsules already reached STeLa-1, and has adjusted into a halo orbit as of this afternoon. We expect a test of the spider bots sometime in the next forty-eight hours. Probably on several shieldbots that are owned by someone the Chinese junta believes they can trust." She sighed. "We don't know who that might be. We're not even sure we'll catch it happening."

Mireia understood why they'd wanted to hold off the questioning. She had more than enough questions herself.

"There's been chatter about two more launches, one from Hainan Island and a much smaller one using a new kind of 3d-printed rocket."

Mireia knew what that was. The one developed by Jared Koskela.

"The Chinese launch is set for the second Friday in June," Anita said. "Twenty-three days from now. That's the timeframe we're up against. And they don't need to hijack all of the bots. It wouldn't be hard at all to use however many zombies they create… maybe as little as five percent—to take out the rest of the shield. That might even be possible from that next Chinese launch alone. Our original bots aren't built to defend themselves. They're built to be expendable. To be easily replaced."

Carter crowded in at the podium. "And that's what they're doing," he said. "They're going to replace our bots with their own bots. Sending new and improved bots, hardened against solar weather and against anyone trying to launch a counterattack."

Anita took over again. "The new bots they launch will have enough shielding to protect their zombies, too, by moving the hijacked bots into the middle of the cloud. The hardened bots will likely have magnetic shielding, which should reduce damage to surrounding bots."

Another pause. To let it sink in.

"The infiltration was meant to be secret," Carter said. "Not just to the public, but hidden from the US Congress and all other national governments. Until it was a fait accompli. By that point, they'd launch the replacement bots and destroy whatever's left of the sunshield that they don't control. But we're not going to let that happen."

Bridget took over the podium. "We are going to stop them," she said. "We are sending our people up to that sunshield, to protect it from attack. And we cannot be swayed and we can't be stopped. If we work together we'll make it happen."

She stepped aside for Carter.

"This is bigger than SolRescue," he said. "That's why we wanted the whole world to know. There's never been anything to prevent anyone from being a member, of having a voice in SolRescue…" He stopped himself. "I won't make the same mistakes again. I'm going to honor the principles of this crowdOrg. When this operation is complete, I'll be stepping down as president."

He paused.

There were a few murmurs. Not as much shock as she would have expected.

Mireia smiled.

It felt like Carter was being taken down a peg.

That was exactly what he needed.

"I will not provide any details on the launch process," he said. "Even internally, nothing above what each person on the team has already been told. Because I can't share more without endangering our mission and the lives of too many good people. But I ask that you support us, those of you who are already members, those of you who've never even considered being a part of this project. I…"

He'd trailed off.

He stepped back from the podium.

For a moment, Anita and Bridget stood staring at him.

Then Anita stepped into his place.

"You helped us save the world once," she said. "We bought ourselves a little time. Now, I can't say we've used that time wisely so far, not as wisely as we could have… as I could have… but we've still got time. We'll put that remaining time to good use. If we can save the sunshield. If we can work together and make this happen."

The crowd was starting to respond. Mireia could hear it. She could feel it.

"We're saving the world and we're making it better," Anita said. "We can't let this last selfish gasp of fascist reaction snuff us out. We can overcome these forces who want to push us back… the people who want to push back against our better democracy, push back against our scientific progress… push back our hard-won economic freedom."

No real sound bites, but it spoke to the audience.

People started applauding. Some were cheering.

Mireia started clapping, too.

"I am part of this," Anita said. "And you all are part of this. Let's keep going. Let's keep moving this planet forward."

That became the summation, as the crowd had gotten loud enough that anything more would have been drowned out.

Anita Singhal was the reason Mireia had become an engineer.

And now she was the reason Mireia felt like hanging on.

To see what she could do to help.

60

CARTER ELGIN had wanted the first three rockets built and ready to launch by the following Saturday.

Which everyone else on *Basilica*—Benj included—had agreed was completely unrealistic.

An opinion Carter was not willing to entertain.

And to that end, he'd stood up with Anita and Bridget and they'd explained why the timeline was important, why every day counted so much.

And it had worked, about as well as anyone could have reasonably expected.

In the end, the first three rockets were assembled in one and a half weeks. That left fourteen days until the planned launch by the People's Liberation Army Navy, from Hainan Island.

There was very little time left.

Each rocket had been assembled near to its planned launch site. That had meant shuttling Danny, Jared, Nicolas Clouatre, the new technician—a former SpaceX employee who'd just started his retirement—and the FSW and pinch roll machinery from the North Atlantic to Virginia and on to South Texas, with no one involved getting much sleep.

The makers in Texas and most of the SolRescue and Turnpike engineers on *Basilica* had created the capsules, while Anita's team—including Danny Pyke and Jared Koskela—had created both the rocket structure and the engines, which for *Basilica*'s on-board assembly had actually required a gap to be cut into the wall of the ship.

They'd had to build the rockets on-site, as opposed to doing it all on *Basilica* or all at some other location. There was no realistic way of transporting two sets of rocket cores—and the fairings and capsules—down the eastern seaboard and, for one set, into the Gulf of Mexico without being seen.

Moving the raw materials, the fuel, and the personnel had been difficult enough.

Benj had always known that Carter Elgin was a man who could bring out the results. But he'd never seen anything like what Elgin had managed to do in that week and a half.

It wasn't just the return of Anita Singhal, or the rush of motivation, the nonstop momentum that had been created...

Benj was convinced it was because of that speech the big three had made, that everyone—on board *Basilica*, in Virginia, in Texas, around the world—knew that this was their last chance to get a space station offplanet and out to STeLa-1, the last chance before the spider bots were launched to destroy the shield.

Benj had seen a great deal of optimism on *Basilica*, and that worried him; most of those on board had no idea what they were up against. They'd seen the Russian warships and heard the speech and thought that everything would just fall into place, that hard work and a can-do attitude would see the job through.

They hadn't seen what Benj had.

What people like Malik would do.

They didn't know that people like Malik really existed, or that there were probably a shit-ton more of them than Malik could even imagine.

People who would do anything to stop the launches.

Benj expected an attack on *Basilica*; he'd even warned Bridget when he'd had the chance, and while she'd told him she agreed with him, he'd known right then that she'd fallen into the same trap of overconfidence.

They were one stroke of bad luck away from losing the whole thing.

The launches had been pushed back to the Thursday after that first Saturday. With the rockets built—in three successive workshops spanning nearly two thousand miles—Benj had been added to Anita Singhal's team for the Brownsville launch. Chloe Neilsen-Brown was also going, not just to help manage the tight project schedule, but also because she somehow had more experience at rocket launches than most of the engineers.

Benj had been surprised to learn that Rachael Duck had been tapped for the Brownsville team as well, to function as Anita's assistant, or more probably, as a buffer between Anita and everyone who wanted to grab a piece of her time.

Benj asked Mireia if she'd be interested in coming along, since there was no one on the team who had a full grasp of the capsule that had been built for them to include in the launch. She said yes, and Benj had talked to Bridget about it, and Mireia had been officially brought back into the fold.

The only condition Carter had placed was that Mireia's tablet be locked out from the network, and that Benj would be in charge of making sure she didn't do anything to jeopardize the launch.

So when Anita's team left *Basilica* on Monday morning, seventy-seven hours before launch, Benj and Mireia left with them, ten people in total. It took two trips in a Bell helicopter to bring them to the mainland, where they landed at a heliport on the east side of Manhattan, right near the UN building.

From there, once both loads had arrived, they were herded by a waiting Derrick McPherson on a fifteen minute walk to the subway, of all places, for the 7 train to LaGuardia.

That was Benj's time with his father. Fifteen minutes between 34th at FDR and Grand Central.

They walked together, father and son, the first group of two out of five, the whole length snaking back a full short block.

"You haven't been to New York before, have you?" his father asked him.

Benj smirked. "I spend most of my time being framed by friends of yours."

His father smiled.

Benj hadn't wanted a smile out of him.

"Why did you put me into this?" Benj asked.

"Because I needed your help."

"I don't think you did."

"You know I did."

"You could have gotten anyone else," Benj said. "Anyone."

"I can't trust anyone else."

"You don't even know me."

"You can be mad at me," Derrick said. "But don't try and convince yourself that I don't know you. That you don't matter to me."

"Because you sent some Russian soldiers in to pick me up?"

"Because you're my son, Benji."

"Or just a convenient prop."

He nodded. "I'm sorry. But you didn't belong with the other side. You belonged here, with me."

"I don't want to be on your team."

"Like I said, Benji… I need you to be."

Benj didn't know what else to say on the subject.

So he just kept walking under FDR Drive.

Still ten minutes left on a trip that had gotten a little awkward.

"You know that I'm proud of you, right?" his father said.

Benj chuckled.

"What?"

"That's something you're supposed to pull out when things are looking grim," Benj said. "Like a deathbed confession, or maybe during an intervention."

"Grim, huh? The street smells like piss. Does that count?"

"It's Manhattan," Anita called up to them, from walking not far behind them. "The whole place smells like piss. And I love it."

519

꧂

From the airport, they caught a commercial flight to Brownsville South Padre Island Airport—first class—a flight full enough that Benj had a strong feeling his father had managed to bump some people off of it, to make room for ten last-minute passengers.

That seemed like a bad way to fly halfway across the country in secret.

Meanwhile, Derrick McPherson hadn't even gotten on the subway with them. Apparently he'd had enough father-son time.

The plane landed at Brownsville just before 10 PM local time.

A full day of travel time, which seemed ridiculous to him.

Until Chloe had pointed out that pretty much everyone, including him, had slept and/or relaxed on the trip out. It would be their only chance at a break until long after the launch was completed.

They took two minivans out to their accommodations, some rented houses in a gated vacation community named Long Island Village in Port Isabel, Texas, fifteen hundred miles away from the Long Island they'd taken off from.

They would share three houses, Anita and Rachael in one, while Benj would take another with the three other men, while Mireia and Chloe stayed with two other women, one of whom was Nikki Taunton, the woman from the maker camp.

Benj had learned enough about Mireia's time at the maker camp to know that she and Nikki had Nicolas Clouatre in common, and not necessarily in the best way.

Mireia had globbed onto Clouatre somehow, obsessing over a man who Benj was sure would have meant nothing to her in any normal situation; he wondered if that was something like the weirdness he still felt for Samantha Yoon, some attachment built over the strain of their time together, like they'd gone through it *together*, though in his case it had been more Samantha's fault than some kind of shared misfortune.

The remaining maker camp members—from two other camps, since Nikki Taunton's camp had been wiped out—had set up outside of the small border town of Progreso, nearly sixty miles to the west from Boca Chica. There they'd been building the capsule, while the rocket core team from *Basilica* had been completing the launcher in space borrowed from the University of Texas at Brownsville.

The makers would handle bringing the capsule to Boca Chica; Anita's team would be in charge of transporting the launcher.

The team at Port Isabel ended up at Anita's rental house at first, to discuss the next three days.

Anita remarked about the choice in housing; her last time in South Texas she'd been stowed on South Padre Island, across the bridge from their vacation rentals.

"They'll still take us to Boca Chica by boat, though," she said. "Faster than going by car, around the ship channel."

"Must be a fast boat," Rachael said.

"It's a long car ride."

"So when do we get to see the launch site?" Benj asked.

"I'm going tomorrow morning," Anita said. "But I can't bring most of you with me."

"Why not?" Mireia asked.

"Keep in mind that this is not a legal launch. Carter has leased the pad and the transporter-erector from Monday through Saturday. The only way he could make it work was to make sure that there'd be no blowback on anyone other than SpaceX."

"What does that mean?" Rachael asked.

"It means that officially, we're lying about what we're using it for. As far as anyone will admit, this is another frivolous video shoot for Turnpike Exploration Tech. Trying to drum up public support for a commercial Mars mission."

Rachael smirked. "And so the giant rocket we built...?"

"It's a prop," Anita said. "Looks real nice, but since we aren't buying any of the onsite fuel and oxidiser, clearly we're not actually launching anything. We'll just be pretending to fuel up on the pad. For our frivolous video."

"And how are we getting our fuel and oxidiser?" Mireia asked. "It would take a whole lot of tanker trucks, wouldn't it? Pretty hard to keep up deniability with that kind of vehicle traffic."

"At least fourteen just for the liquid oxygen," Anita said. "But Bridget is handling the shipment. Apparently the freighter the LOX and Kero are coming in on will run into some mechanical problems on its way to port in Brownsville. Our job is to figure out the easiest way to get the fuel line from the freighter offshore over to the launch pad." She looked over at Benj. "Bridget was thinking you could handle that part, Benj."

He nodded.

Not that he knew how we could handle it.

Fuel lines weren't really anything like network cabling.

And he'd never even changed his car's motor oil before.

"I can get you started," Nikki Taunton said to him.

Apparently he hadn't hidden his fear that well.

"So we now have sixty-three hours until we launch," Anita said. "Before we can launch, we need to bring the rocket and capsule here from the university in Brownsville. We've got the transporter-erector, so that's a big help. That's step one, obviously. And then Benj will take care of that fuel line on Wednesday night."

Benj nodded again.

He was starting to miss being ignored back on *Basilica*.

Benj finally reached his room—marked with his name handwritten on a taped-up sign—at 12:30 AM. There was a white bathrobe folded up on his bed, which seemed odd considering that there was a perfectly standard closet four feet to the left.

He picked up the bathrobe, to move it to the chair, at least. Probably not all the way to the closet...

There was a pistol underneath.

And a box of ammunition. Remington UMC. .380 auto.

Nothing else. No note.

But Benj understood why he'd been asked to go to Brownsville.

It wasn't for any emergency IT work.

Not that he'd shot a gun in over ten years.

Not that he'd ever been much good at it.

61

VASILY COULD see that Danny Pyke was well-liked at Wallops Island. He remembered more names than Vasily ever could, even small details about family lives and favorite sports teams.

Walking into Blockhouse No. 2 with Pyke was a revelation to Vasily; he'd been more accustomed to how his father worked the room, a man whose gruff manner was forgiven because of the sheer power he exuded.

Danny Pyke had little to no power; when he'd spoken to the people of *Basilica*, he'd seemed to have little charisma, either. But goddamn he was personable.

And the people at NASA Wallops Flight Facility ate it up.

They hadn't been the least bothered by Vasily's presence, either, even though he wasn't a US Citizen and by all rights shouldn't have been there without significant advance notice.

But then again, Danny Pyke still carried a Canadian passport, and they'd let them both through the gate on the way to the island.

It seemed like it was an open secret that they were breaking the rules, that they were breaching security. Of a federal facility.

Pyke had told Vasily on their trip in—their team of eight crammed into a single minivan flying driverfree down I-101—that he'd used Wallops before for a video shoot with Anita Singhal, that back then he'd gotten permission to include a Falcon Heavy in the backdrop, a rocket that you didn't see at Wallops nearly as much as some of the others.

The cover story was a documentary shoot, in conjunction with another shoot at Boca Chica; a big play for Turnpike Exploration Tech to get people excited about space.

As long as the video of the speech from *Basilica* didn't make the rounds, it seemed like Danny's story would hold.

So far, so good.

They'd shipped their rocket from a rented warehouse in Salisbury, Maryland, bringing it out to Launch Pad 0A, where Danny had managed to get everything else they'd need for a real launch set up for their "fake" one.

Vasily had been in charge of the fueling problem.

The only reason Danny Pyke could get away with bringing in what looked like a ready-to-fly rocket, with the use of the equipment at Launch Pad 0A for a three day shoot, and anything else that would seem out of place, was because everyone at Wallops Flight Facility knew that there was no fuel in those rocket cores.

No fuel meant no launch, which meant that NASA, the FAA, and anyone else didn't need to pay any attention to Pyke's investor baiting.

In order to bring that fuel in, Vasily needed to run a fuel line from an offshore freighter directly to the rocket on the pad, which would have been hard enough to do without doing it in front of however many personnel were working out on the island at that given period of time—which Vasily had calculated would be a nine- to ten-hour process for the LOX, the line flush, and then the Kero.

So it would have to happen at night—in six hours from then, actually—and they would have to hope that no one bothered to scramble the Coast Guard from Chincoteague—less than five miles away—to find out why a small freighter was sitting off a federal launch facility on Wallops Island.

When he'd asked Pyke about it, as they walked the launch pad, the response was a bit of a surprise.

"I fully expect we'll get caught," Pyke told him.

"You're joking," Vasily said.

"Expect the worst and hope for the best, right?"

"I don't think we can load the fuel. Not without being seen. And if we're caught, Anita's team will be taken down, too. There are too many connections to Brownsville."

"You want to abort," Pyke said.

"I don't know."

"When does the freighter arrive?"

"2100. Not long after sunset."

"So what do we do, Vasily?"

"So you're asking me?"

Pyke smiled. "Yeah. I'm asking you."

"Unless we can guarantee that no one's going to report that freighter, we need to abort this attempt."

Pyke nodded. "But if I can make that guarantee?"

"And how would you do that?"

"If I can make that guarantee…"

"Then we should make the attempt," Vasily said.

"Okay. I'll let you know."

Pyke pulled out his tablet and walked away.

Vasily wasn't sure what he was supposed to do. Just stand and wait?

So he did.

As Danny Pyke made a call to Bridget Hawn.

Vasily was told not to ask for details. Bridget had made it work. They were ready to fuel the rocket.

So Vasily and his helpers, two of his Turnpike coworkers, stayed behind as Danny and the rest of the group left for a seafood dinner across the line in Maryland.

Once it was dark, they inflated the small dinghy they'd also brought in from the warehouse in Salisbury.

They would need to connect the fuel hose from the freighter, almost a mile out to sea, to where the rocket, which was now sitting upright on Launch Pad 0A. Lights would be off for the lake freighter at the rendez-vous. While the ship was smaller than most oceangoing freighters, it was certainly big enough to kill or maim any Russian stupid enough to get his GPS coordinates slightly wrong.

So Vasily would be careful, which was one of his strengths.

Launch Pad 0A was right next to the beach, with a ramp up to pad and a 300-foot water deluge tower beside it. There were also tanks for fuel storage, not that Vasily could make use of them.

Launch Pad 0A was where one of the first commercial space launch accidents had occurred, three decades before, an omen that was not lost on Vasily.

He had a bad feeling in his gut.

He was close to calling off the whole thing, not that he had a way of getting in touch with the freighter; that had to go through Bridget Hawn, and she had to be reached through Danny Pyke himself.

And Vasily had the impression that Pyke wouldn't be willing to go back on the plan so close to implementing it.

So he didn't even bother placing the call.

Vasily and one of his colleagues took the dinghy out, both paddling to avoid the noise of a motor, which they hadn't been provided, anyway.

He was in back, trying to steer, using the light of an offshore oil rig as a navigation aid.

And after a half hour or so, he could see the dark outline of the freighter. And the smallest of guide lights, someone on the deck with a penlight.

The floated toward the freighter, and soon enough he saw the penlight waving. Then it stopped moving.

And Vasily could see the fuel line, being carefully lowered toward the water.

He paddled closer to the freighter, hoping that with its engines off it wasn't as dangerous as he felt it should be.

The nozzle of the fuel line was lowering close to the dinghy, but not close enough.

Vasily wasn't sure how he'd reach it. He wasn't about to jump into the Gulf of Mexico to fish it out.

The fuel line's descent stopped, hovering around six feet above the water.

They were waiting for Vasily to move even closer.

So he did, bumping against the side of the much larger boat, each hit feeling like the slam of two bumper cars.

If the waves had been any choppier, they'd have flipped, or slammed hard into the hull, maybe hard enough to sink their little dinghy.

The fuel line dropped some more.

Vasily stood up slowly to grab it, careful not to make their precarious float any worse. He wrapped the nozzle around his legs in a figure eight.

Then he and his boatmate paddled as hard as they could, heading back toward the beach at Boca Chica.

There was a light at the shore; Vasily was worried that he'd led them off course, but his GPS told him he was still on track.

He couldn't tell what kind of light.

Not a vehicle.

Not a building.

The light went off.

"I don't like this one bit," he said.

His boatmate didn't answer.

They both kept paddling.

By the time Vasily noticed the outlines of the two SUVs and the military-looking humvee, he knew they'd already spotted the dinghy.

They would have been looking for the dinghy.

The FBI announced themselves before Vasily had reached the shore; they were apparently not concerned with the possibility of an escape attempt in an unpowered inflatable dinghy.

62

ANITA HEARD the news directly from Bridget, a voice call to her tablet.

Danny's team had been caught, the entire group detained by the FBI.

There would be no launch from Wallops Island.

And it probably wouldn't be long before someone showed up at Brownsville. And even if no one did, the US—and probably China, soon enough—would learn when the launches were planned, and it wouldn't be too difficult to scramble fighters to any possible launch sites.

SolRescue's only advantage had been the supposed impossibility of launching three rockets so soon, and simultaneously. Now that advantage was gone.

They would need to launch as soon as possible.

Not Thursday at 1400 Central Time.

But now. Wednesday night, or just after midnight…

As soon as fucking possible.

She'd talked to Nicolas Clouatre on *Basilica*; he was in charge of the launch there, so together they came up with a new time. 300 hours Central Time.

Six hours away.

Because the ferry to Boca Chica wasn't running, they took their rented minivans and drove the fifty-minute route around the ship canal, and down along state highway 4. To the launch pad.

Benj and Nikki Taunton were waiting for them.

"We've got the fuel line running," Benj said. "Should be done the liquid oxygen by around midnight. Then we get ready for them to flush the line."

"We don't need to flush the line," Anita said. "Just go straight into the RP-1. It won't ignite in the hose."

Benj frowned. "I'll have to call Bridget. She's the one who's in contact with the freighter."

Anita nodded. "We need every minute we can get."

They would have to rush the launch status check, something that had been planned out at ten hours duration. They had to run pre-launch diagnostics on everything, the boosters, the interstage, the fairing, the capsule…

They'd be lucky to have it all done in time.

Not that there was any test she was comfortable in skipping.

Not if she actually wanted a fair chance of pulling it off.

It was after midnight. There was at least another hour of refueling to go.

Anita was about ten minutes from calling Bridget.

To see if there was any way of postponing by a couple of hours.

Maybe they could finish the checks by 3 AM, but it wasn't likely. And on top of that, they had no one on the ground at Boca Chica who'd ever launched a rocket of that size. She and Carter had tested a few prototypes for the original sunshield launches, before the feds banned them, and Chloe Neilsen-Brown had assisted at Jared Koskela's launches at Fort Churchill, but that was about all they had for experience.

Not enough.

Especially not with the pressure they were under.

She received a ping on her tablet.

She'd expected Bridget.

It was someone else.

Jack Roland.

It took her a moment to remember who that was.

On my way to the pad.

The last time she'd seen the former Boca Chica Flight Director was after the first launch, when he'd rolled her eyes at her as the reporters crushed around her.

He'd been pushing sixty back then.

Two decades ago.

She wasn't exactly sure what he was coming there to do.

Jack Roland drove an old Dodge pickup truck, still running on gasoline, Anita could tell, from the noise and the smell.

He got out and gave her a wave. He did look about eighty. He'd gone old and fat, not old and frail.

Old and fat was probably how you'd expect a flight director to go.

"Carter told me you were in Texas," he said. "Great to see you, Anita."

He gave her a hug. Overly long.

"Why are you here, Mr. Roland?"

"Call me Jack. And I guess you can call me late to the party. But I couldn't exactly show up when everyone was watching, could I?"

"What do you mean?"

"I'm here to help you launch this bucket of *solid-state joins*."

63

IT WAS launch day on *Basilica*. Eleven days before the Chinese junta had its own launch.

Jared noticed movement long before he heard any news.

The Russians were repositioning. For something.

Maybe for the launch, which would happen in less than two hours.

He was out on the top deck, along the garden, staring out at the ocean and the full moon; he'd been taking a break and trying to stay out of the way, while the launch status check was being performed. If there was an issue they needed him for, they'd ping him; otherwise, he wasn't necessary until the launch itself, and even then, he was a redundancy, since Nicolas Clouatre seemed to have taken control of everything perfectly well.

Jared wasn't really needed there. And he should have been at Boca Chica.

Not only had they not had a launch engineer at Boca Chica, but it was also where they'd sent Chloe... and Rachael.

And after Wallops had gone down, Danny Pyke arrested...

He should have been there.

The Russian aircraft carrier was underway, moving northeast. The launch would be to the southeast, but the carrier had been on the west side of *Basilica*, along with all but the swarmboats, in anticipation of the launch.

Jared had expected—not that he'd asked—that the uncrewed swarmboats would stay in place at least until a few minutes before the launch, assuming they moved at all.

But now he could see them heading off, en masse, moving north.

Toward a semi-submersible boat carrier; he could see the odd-looking ship in the distance, the length of a cruiser but with a flat bed in the rear, the submersible deck.

The deck was lowering down into the water. To pick up the swarmboats.

The Russians weren't repositioning for the launch.

They were leaving.

Jared was in an awkward position; obviously Carter would know that they were leaving, wouldn't he? And he knew he would seem like an idiot to be sending some frantic message to Clouatre in the middle of the status check.

But what if they didn't realize?

He decided to walk over in person, to the helipad.

The rocket was erect, and had been since the day before, since Wednesday afternoon. Erect and fueled up, with the custom-build (and completely untested) capsule loaded on top.

Clouatre was surrounded by a group of engineers, some from Jared's (and Anita's and Danny's) rocket team and some from Clouatre's capsule team.

Going over the results of the status check.

The go/no-go.

Jared joined the crowd, listening in to the result.

They hadn't pinged him, so he was feeling pretty good about the launcher. Or *wanting* to feel good about it.

"I'm not confident," Nicolas said. "Too many outstanding issues to launch."

Jared heard a voice, on speaker.

Carter Elgin's.

"At this point, we need to decide if the gamble is worth it," Carter said. "We will not have a second window."

"Because the Russians are moving off," Jared said, unsure if he'd just embarrassed himself.

"That wasn't something I'd announced," Carter said. "That's you, Koskela?" He didn't sound impressed.

Clouatre and most of the engineers glanced out to the ocean, in several directions. Eventually they all honed in on the carrier, moving away from *Basilica* at a good clip.

"What does that mean?" Clouatre asked.

"They must have made a deal," Carter said. "I'm thinking they're getting a seat at the table. For the new sunshield."

Clouatre frowned. "So again, Mr. Elgin, what does that mean?"

"I'm guessing they were told to wait until the last minute before moving away. To give us as little warning as possible."

"Little warning of what?" Jared asked.

"Obviously they're going to try and stop us," Carter said. "The same people who destroyed my maker camps and murdered my flight team." Jared heard a sigh from over the speaker. "We need to evacuate. As many people as we can get on the catamaran. Koskela, help them get the bridge in place."

Jared didn't waste time on the crowd's reaction.

He headed down to the main deck, moving as quickly as he could down the metal staircase, then running at full speed toward the back of *Basilica*.

The catamaran was already coming close, clearly notified of the evacuation.

He met up with a crewman by the back railing.

There was a shipping container parked by the stern, to starboard. Jared noticed that the container was open, to the front.

The man was already working on the removal process, removing metal screws from the metal rails; the rear of *Basilica* seemed to have been designed for the stern to lose its railing.

It made sense; if you wanted a boat full of people working, you needed an easy way to get those workers and their equipment on and off the ship.

Jared helped to detach the metal rails.

And watched as the catamaran came dangerously close to the back of *Basilica*.

There were sensors, he knew, to keep two vessels from colliding. But those weren't intended to allow for two ships to come within fifty feet of each other, on the high seas, no less.

"We got to set up our bridge," the crewman said.

Jared nodded, not that he knew what came next.

The crewman led Jared to the container.

Without further explanation, the man bent down on one side of a long metal truss in the seacan.

He counted on three, and Jared helped him with the lift.

It was light enough for them to carry together, maybe two hundred pounds.

They brought it out of the container and set it down on the deck, not far from the gap in the railing.

"Ever built a Bailey bridge?" the man asked him.

"Nope."

"It's not that bad. The transoms are about a third of the weight of the old M2s they used in the army. It's a two-man job now."

Jared followed the man's lead, as they moved five more metal transoms out of the container.

Then two long side panels.

Then back for some other parts, a plastic crate filled with pins, bolts, clamps, and large metal hammers.

Soon they had the sidepanels set up, chained to the still-standing siderails of *Basilica*, hanging slightly more than halfway off the deck.

They attached the transoms next, Jared holding wherever told, while the crewman clamped and pinned the pieces together.

The catamaran seemed to be holding its position, around forty feet off the stern of *Basilica*.

After the framing of the portable bridge came the deck, plastic sheeting that clipped on with reusable plastic straps.

It seemed too light-duty for a bridge.

"Doesn't need to carry anything too heavy," the crewman said. He grinned. "No fatties allowed."

Jared nodded.

And helped to finish strapping the sheeting to the side panels and transoms.

Once the Bailey bridge was complete, still hanging off the stern of *Basilica*, the catamaran moved in a little closer, maybe ten feet. Then it started lowering the ramp at its bow, making a gap in its upper hull. Above the waterline, but not by much, waves breaking against the ferry and spilling over, onto the deck.

The ramp lowered to a grade of about thirty degrees, a lot steeper than you'd usually see.

Jared understood why, between the height of *Basilica* and its temporary Bailey bridge turned ramp, and the height of the waves in the North Atlantic.

Like with the freighter rendezvous on frozen Hudson Bay, SolRescue was depending too much on good weather and even better luck. What if the seas had been choppier, like you'd expect the Atlantic Ocean to be?

How long would it take to send people across by pilot boat, not that *Basilica* had a pilot boat that Jared had seen...

To him it seemed irresponsible.

Risking two hundred lives on how big the waves might be.

Why hadn't Carter just sent his people to the lifeboats?

Why bother with the catamaran at all?

Jared saw Bridget Hawn and her daughter heading toward the stern, leading a large crowd of people.

No packs or luggage.

He watched as Bridget gave her little girl a hug.

Then the crewman who'd assembled the bridge, grabbed the girl's hand, and started leading her out onto the bridge.

And over to the ramp of the ferry.

Bridget was marshalling the crowd, getting them to form four lines.

There were at least a hundred people waiting to cross the bridge, an anxious look on each of their faces.

But Bridget had control of them, her voice calm but stern, as she kept them organized, letting one from each line go at a time, four people crossing the bridge in pairs.

Jared didn't know where the catamaran would be going.

And he wasn't about to bother Bridget with the question.

He needed to get to Boca Chica. If the ferry was going to Manhattan or some other dock on the eastern seaboard... but it could be heading right across the Atlantic, to Europe.

He knew what had happened to those maker camps in Wyoming. The attackers had wanted to do more than destroy the equipment. They'd come to kill the makers. To kill anyone they could find.

They would sink *Basilica* if they could. And they'd sink the catamaran, too.

And the orange lifeboats.

Jared pulled out his tablet.

He made a voice call, to Carter Elgin.

Carter answered.

"Where are you sending the catamaran?" Jared asked.

"Manhattan," Carter said. "Derrick will be there to meet them."

"I don't think that's a good idea."

"And why not?"

"If they're sending someone to sink us, they'll sink the ferry, too."

"That's why they're leaving now," Carter said. "Before the launch."

"And heading toward whatever's incoming."

Carter didn't respond right away.

But he hadn't disconnected.

"What's your idea?" Carter asked him.

"Send the ferry to catch up with the Russian fleet," Jared said. "They aren't protecting us anymore, but they weren't about to destroy us."

Another pause from Carter.

"You're right," he said. "Tell Bridget."

"Okay."

"Good catch, Koskela."

And Carter disconnected.

Good catch. Like he'd found a typo.

Not like he'd done something to hopefully save Carter's family.

Assuming he was right in the first place.

Maybe the Russians were just moving their ships further out, before engaging *Basilica*.

But if that was the case, the people on board that ferry would be dead either way.

And so would everyone on *Basilica*.

64

NICOLAS WAS surprised to see Carter Elgin jogging out onto the helipad.

"We're sending the ferry to catch up with the Russian naval fleet," Carter said. "Koskela thinks it's our best chance of keeping them from being targeted in the attack."

"You really think they're going to attack," Nicolas said.

"I know they're coming."

"Radar?"

"I doubt they'll show up," Carter said. "They'll either be too high or too low for us to track. And pretty goddamn small."

"You're expecting drones."

"Yeah. I'm expecting autonomous ones at that. Less people involved in something highly questionable."

"So why can't we follow the Russian fleet?" Nicolas asked. "If we don't let them leave us, won't that keep us safe?"

"*Basilica* can't keep up. We'd be lucky to make twenty five knots, and that's without a rocket standing on end. The Russians are moving away at thirty knots and not even breaking a sweat."

Nicolas nodded.

"So we launch," Carter said. "ASA-fucking-P, yeah?"

"I'm not confident."

"I know. You told me that. I've seen the results. No-go all the way."

"That's correct."

"So what are the odds, Clouatre? If we launch..."

"I would say we have a fifty percent chance of reaching orbit. From there, another fifty percent chance that both the second stage will fire properly and the fairing halves will disconnect without damaging the capsule."

"And then another fifty percent on the capsule reaching GTO?"

"Thirty percent," Nicolas said. "I'm sorry."

"So forgive me if my math is rusty, but you're saying we don't have a snowball's chance in hell?"

Nicolas shook his head. "I'm not saying that. The odds are bad, but it's not impossible. If we still had three launches, I'd even go out on a limb and say we had a probable chance of getting one of the capsules off to STeLa-1."

"And now we have two," Carter said.

"Yes."
Carter nodded. Then took a deep breath.
"We launch because we have to," he said.
Nicolas nodded.
And got right down to it.

65

THE LAUNCH countdown officially started several days before, but it was that last hour that seemed the most tense.

Benj was on the sidelines, the safetied pistol in his jacket pocket. He was watching with Anita and Rachael from back up the road, a football field away from the pad by the beach, which was still too close for them to be when it came time to launch.

At least one person would have to stay that close, from ignition right through the first two minutes of flight. They'd use their tablet as a view-finder, the expected arc of the rocket drawn out on their screen. If anything went wrong, or if the rocket seemed off course, unable to reach orbit… they'd pass on the warning to press the kill switch, and the whole thing would explode before it got too high.

Another two football fields away was the impromptu control center, a collection of work docks set up in the back of Jack Roland's pickup. There'd be no wired connection to the pad like you'd see with most launches; everything would be transmitted wirelessly to the rocket, sitting on a powered-down launch pad that was for all intents and purposes mostly just a concrete slab.

That was the best they could do; it wasn't like SpaceX could "accidentally" let them use their real control center and real workstations, not for some lame video shoot.

Adding to that was the fact that it was the middle of the night, and no one was even supposed to be there. So they wouldn't get the protection of a blockhouse, or the distance of a more remote control center. They were out on the open.

Jack Roland was still on the pad, Mireia and Chloe with him, the two closest things he had to qualified assistants. They were doing the final check, one last once-over before they made their way to meet with every-one else.

They headed over.

"Good to go," Jack Roland said as he arrived, giving Anita his thumbs up.

"Heard from *Basilica*?" Chloe asked. "They seem to have gone quiet."

"They're a little busy, apparently," Anita said. "I'm sure we'd have heard if something was wrong."

"I'd say this here is our best shot," Roland said. "Better than launching from the middle of the Atlantic."

Anita nodded. "Okay... so now we move back."

"So I'll ping you," Roland said. "If that doesn't work, I've got my flare gun."

"And then you take cover, right?"

"This isn't my first rodeo, Anita."

She smiled. "Thanks, Jack. For everything."

"My pleasure."

The two of them hugged, before Anita started walking toward Roland's pickup.

Benj followed, along with Rachael, Chloe and Mireia.

"You trust him?" Rachael asked Anita.

"Yeah," she replied. "Shouldn't I?"

"He could signal a malfunction even if there wasn't one. We'd pull the kill switch and never know."

"I can stick with him," Mireia said. "A second pair of eyes."

Anita nodded. "I trust you know how to play it," she said. "The man likes to have his ego stroked a little."

Mireia smiled. "I can handle that."

She made her way back toward Roland.

Anita looked over at Rachael. "Let me guess," she said, "you're gonna ask if I trust her."

"I'm just being paranoid," Rachael said.

"Hopefully if they see something we'll see something," Chloe said. "We can make a judgement when it happens."

"You really think we'll know?" Anita asked.

"I don't know."

"I guess we'll have to wait and see."

They reached the pickup and Chloe climbed up into the box. She offered a hand to Anita, who took it, but didn't look like she appreciated the idea that she'd need that kind of help.

Nikki Taunton was leaning against the truck, by the driver side door.

Benj couldn't see any of the other four team members.

"Where'd everyone go?" he asked.

"They thought they could get a better view of the rocket's course from a mile west," Nikki replied.

It sounded to Benj like bullshit.

He turned to Anita. "We need to know what's going on," he said.

"Call them over here," Anita said. "Everyone needs to be accounted for."

"We're twelve minutes to launch," Chloe said.

"We don't launch until we know where everyone is."

"I'll call them back," Nikki said.

"No," Rachael said. She looked over to Benj. "You call them, Benj."

Benj nodded.

He broadcast on the tablet. To the entire team, including Mireia and Jack Roland. For the missing engineers to meet back at Roland's pickup. Immediately.

There was no response.

"Do we abort?" Nikki asked.

"We don't abort," Anita said. "No matter what."

"Unless it's off course," Rachael said. "Right?"

Anita didn't answer.

She sat down on a plastic milk crate, in front of one of the two work docks.

Chloe followed her lead, taking the other station.

"Eleven minutes to launch," Chloe said.

"I should go up the road," Benj said. "See what's going on."

"No," Rachael said. "You've got the gun, right?"

"What?"

"Carter told me."

"Well he didn't tell me."

"Do you have it?" she asked.

He nodded.

"Do you know how to use it? Or should I?"

"I've got it," he said. "Unless you think you're better suited."

"I'm not better suited," she said, shaking her head.

Benj took the pistol out from his pocket.

"Why do you have that?" Nikki asked. "Are we in danger?"

"We're not sure," Rachael said. "Just stay right where you are, okay? So we know who's here."

Nikki nodded.

"Ten minutes to launch," Chloe said.

Benj wasn't sure what he was supposed to do. How he was supposed to prevent whatever might be coming.

It had been the FBI that had come to Wallops, arresting Danny Pyke and his team. If they'd found their way to Boca Chica... but they wouldn't be pulling team members away under cover of darkness. They'd probably come with their lights blazing.

It's not like they'd expect Anita Singhal to have a squad of mercenaries.

If someone was out there, it probably was not the FBI.

If anyone was out there, it could very well be Malik Daley, or something just like him.

Someone who'd have no qualms about killing each and every one of them.

And if that was going to happen, it was going to happen soon.

Before the launch.

He walked over to the back of the truck, climbing up into the pickup box, just as Chloe announced that they were down to nine minutes. "Is the kill switch the only way to stop the launch?" he asked.

"Pretty much," Anita said. "We've been committed since T-10. Launch will happen whether I'm sitting here or not."

"Then we should go."

"What?"

"Something's wrong," Benj said. "The missing people—"

"The launch is what matters," Anita said. "We stay here and make sure it happens. That it works."

"Then we go," Chloe said.

Anita nodded. "We pack up the workstations and then we go. Nothing else here belongs to us. Then Carter will let us know about the next launch."

"Next launch should be from *Basilica*," Chloe said.

"Maybe."

"Eight minutes to launch."

Benj stared out along the two-lane highway, toward the west.

No headlights.

Nothing to be seen under the full moon, just the illuminated tips of the low marshy grasses, and the occasional palm tree in the distance.

Malik or whoever could be in the grass, hunched on the ground.

Would Benj be able to see him?

Unless the man was a sniper, wouldn't he have to get close enough to be spotted? Would Benj have a chance to take a shot? Would it matter?

"I want to get into the truck," Nikki said. "I feel too exposed out here."

"Then get in the truck," Rachael said. "Let the rest of us be exposed instead."

"It's locked."

"Then don't get in the truck."

"Seven minutes," Chloe said.

"Then I'll climb up and get in the back with you guys," Nikki said.

"Whatever," Anita said. "Just stop talking… please?"

Nikki came around to the back.

She held up a hand for Benj, to lift her up.

He reached down.

She hesitated.

Then stepped back.

And started running down the highway, away from the beach.

"What the hell is she doing?" Rachael asked.

"It doesn't matter," Anita said.

"Six minutes to launch," Chloe said.

Benj could see venting from the rocket. Liquid oxygen, he assumed. They didn't have any extra for topping off.

He hoped that someone had considered that into the planning.

He heard footsteps, coming up the road from the west.

Someone running.

He turned and pointed his pistol.

It looked like Nikki.

"Stop running," he shouted. "Just stay where you are."

She stopped.

"I couldn't find them," Nikki said. "The others. They're gone."

"We'll find them."

"We should abort."

"Just stay where you are," Benj said.

"Five minutes," Chloe said.

Nikki started walking toward the truck.

"I told you to stay there," Benj told her.

"I'm scared," she said. "Something is very wrong here."

"Just shut up," Rachael said. *"God."*

Nikki kept moving toward the pickup.

Benj wasn't about to shoot her.

And she'd known that.

She walked around to the back.

"Stay off," Benj said.

She started climbing onto the lowered tailgate.

"Stop it," he said.

She wasn't listening.

He put his pistol back to safetied.

He rushed over to her.

"Get off the truck," he said.

"No."

"Get her ass off the truck," Rachael said.

"Four minutes," Chloe said.

Benj stuffed the pistol back into his jacket pocket.

He grabbed Nikki by the shoulders, forcing her down and off the truck.

She fell onto the pavement, looking up at him.

"You need to stay there," he told her. "I'm not fucking kidding."

She gave a slow nod.

The erector started pulling back, angling itself away from the rocket.

The venting hadn't stopped.

He wondered how much LOX was being lost.

No one was moving.

No one was talking.

They were just waiting.

Chloe marked three minutes, then when she reached two Anita made a voice call to Jack Roland for final site check.

He reported in.

Site clear. No problems.

Go for launch.

At one minute, the launch deck powered on, including the sound suppression water. Anita had already admitted that she'd never even given any thought to shock waves from ignition inflicting damage. Jack Roland's backdoor access to SpaceX—even as a retired flight director—had allowed him to get the Niagara system ready and connected to their wireless controls, pouring water into all the right places.

The engines ignited.

And the green flash, and then flame.

And liftoff, slow at first, but quickly gaining speed, a plume of fire trailing the rocket as it rose.

The main engines would fire for close to three minutes.

Chloe was counting toward that first minute.

Still forty seconds away.

Everyone watched.

Benj felt someone pull him down, off the truck.

He saw Nikki climbing up to take his place.

He grabbed her foot and yanked.

She fell back down.

He threw a punch.

He heard two shots.

He scrambled back onto the pickup.

Anita and Rachael were down on their knees, trying to stay covered.

Chloe was still sitting on her milk crate.

Benj saw that she had both hands clamped onto her shoulder.

He pulled her down to the bottom of the box.

He took out the pistol, keeping low.

Nikki was scrambling up into the box.

He pointed the pistol at her, aiming for her chest.

She rushed him.

He fired.

She pushed him back, slamming his head against the cab.

He dropped his gun.

He saw her reach the workdock.

Rachael stood up to stop her.

Nikki swung around, jabbing at Rachael's shoulder.

Rachael fell back.

Benj grabbed for his gun.

But Nikki had already done it.

The kill switch.

The rocket started flaring, from the bottom up. The bottom of the main stage exploded, dropping the top half of the rocket core, along with the second stage and payload. They fell, slowly, it seemed, and hit the pad with an immediate flash of an explosion. Winding trails of debris flew up from the crash, white and yellow pieces from the downed launcher.

Benj kept his gun aimed at Nikki's chest.

She slumped down, against the screen of the workstation.

Then fell over, against Rachael, who was crouching on the floor of the box.

She shoved Nikki off of her.

Benj could see the blood.

From both of them.

Nikki was bleeding out from her chest.

Rachael's right shoulder was stained in blood.

It looked like punctures.

Like Nikki had stabbed her multiple times.

"Everyone stay down," Benj said. "Those shots came from somewhere."

"Jack and Mireia," Anita said. "They were too close to that."

"We have to go," Benj said. "I need the truck keys."

"Jack had 'em," Rachael said.

"Shit."

The minivans were parked nearby.

But how close?

And how close was the person who'd just taken two shots at them?

The main objective had been accomplished, destroying the rocket. Benj knew that they were part of the secondary objective. That killing them all was nearly as important.

To ensure there wouldn't be another attempt.

Benj looked over at Chloe, who had Anita kneeling beside her, trying to bandage the wound from a small first aid kit.

He wasn't sure, but he could make a guess, from where she'd been sitting, from what he could see of her wound.

The gunman was likely to the southwest. Or had been, when he'd taken his two shots.

If he hadn't changed position, they could try and make a run to the northeast. Maybe the truck would shield them.

That wouldn't get them to the minivans.

At best, it would get them into the shallow and muddy waters of Boca Chica Bay. Where they'd be easy to follow and almost as easy to peg off, one by one.

And he wasn't sure if Chloe and Rachael could even get that far.

Unless he could come up with a better plan, Benj was pretty sure none of them would make it out of there alive.

66

NICOLAS WATCHED as the rocket arced up gracefully from *Basilica*'s converted helipad, tracing between the guidelines perfectly in the view through his tablet.

They'd moved the launch up by twenty minutes.

And they'd made it work.

After one hundred and fifty seconds, the rocket reached main engine cutoff. The first stage then dropped away, the second stage firing up, where it would continue to lift its payload for nearly seven minutes, at which point the payload fairings would fall away and the capsule would detach, hopefully on its way to STeLa-1.

They'd had no news from Boca Chica, nothing post-launch.

But maybe, like Nicolas, Anita and her team had just wanted to sit and watch.

He'd wanted to sit and watch.

But he knew what was coming.

There were maybe thirty people left on *Basilica*, including himself and Carter Elgin; the others had left on the catamaran, which at last check had caught up to the Russian fleet and hadn't been fired upon.

In theory, that meant that Jared Koskela had been right, that the attack wouldn't come from the Russians.

But Carter was still convinced that the attack would come.

So Nicolas made his way to the evacuation area, to where one of the orange lifeboats—that looked a little like a space capsule—was being filled up with nervous engineers.

Carter was standing beside the boat, guiding people in.

"You're not going down with the ship, right?" Nicolas asked him.

"No one's staying," he replied. "She'll have to drift out here for a while."

Nicolas knew *Basilica* had some basic automation, but he still understood how tough it would be for Carter to abandon ship.

There was always the chance that there would be no attack, that the whole thing had been an attempt to frighten them away from the launch, to keep Carter from bringing his entire team out to the North Atlantic.

Maybe.

Nicolas didn't hear the missile. Of whatever it was.

He felt the deck shake as he stepped toward the orange lifeboat.

He lost his balance and fell.

And saw that the deck itself was falling, like the ship was bending in half.

He slammed against the deck before hitting the water.

He felt the shock of the cold. How cold it was in the North Atlantic in early June.

He could feel the pain in his head, in both legs, his left shoulder. Even if the cold hadn't hit him so hard, he knew the injuries would be enough.

And he couldn't fit the pull of the ship itself.

Basilica was sinking, and bringing him along with it.

And probably the lifeboat, too.

And Carter Elgin.

He wondered about the capsule; in theory, the payload would be released automatically, and even without intervention, the capsule would continue along its path toward STeLa-1, a journey of around five days.

Someone from SolRescue would take over for them.

Maybe Anita's team; it wasn't like she wasn't qualified to take charge.

He hadn't cleared his name, but he'd done his best to finish the work.

Maybe that was all that mattered.

Maybe that was enough.

Nicolas felt his body telling him to rest, so he did.

67

BENJ COULD see movement from his hiding place, in Jack Roland's pickup truck.

From the southwest, as he'd expected.

One figure, which was so obvious to spot that he assumed there would be others somewhere.

Maybe they were surrounded.

The last time he and Rachael had been captured, they'd been held for ransom. He wondered if that could happen again, if they still had any value.

But Carter Elgin hadn't negotiated, and his own father hadn't negotiated. They'd risked his life and the lives of four other people—not including Vasily Utkin and the Russian soldiers—rather than give up control of SolRescue.

Benj took aim at the approaching figure.

He knew he couldn't make that shot.

Not from so far a distance.

He glanced around, looking for other signs of movement.

Nothing else.

Not yet.

They wouldn't have sent one gunman.

That didn't make sense.

Boca Chica Beach was wide open. They could have brought fifty marines.

Benj had to find out who was walking toward the truck.

"We're armed," Benj called out. "We're prepared to defend ourselves."

"Why wouldn't you defend yourself, Benj?" the man called back. "Obviously people are trying to kill you."

He knew it was Malik.

"The people with me have value," Benj said. "More value than your last batch of hostages."

"Why would I want hostages?" Malik asked. "Did you forget how that worked out last time?"

"So you just want to kill us?"

"I want to kill you, Benj. And Singhal. The others I haven't really decided on. Unless Samantha Yoon's there, too. Her I want dead."

"There must be something," Benj said. "Some way of making a deal."

"I don't want to make a deal."

"Everyone wants something, Malik. We can get you whatever you need."

"Oh, you can? You can get me a do-over, can you? You can go back and make it so I'm not the fucking scapegoat of the month?"

"That's on you, Malik," Rachael said. "You're the idiot who couldn't control a few unarmed hostages."

"Okay," Malik said. "That was Rachael Duck, right? I guess I want to kill her, too."

"What if I give myself up?" Benj asked. "Will you let the others walk out of here?"

Malik chuckled. "I'm a trained operative with a high-powered rifle and body armor. And I'm up against *who*, exactly? Benji McPherson and his little toy gun?"

"You can't kill all of us. We'll overpower you."

"I could kill every single one of you. The moment you climb out of that pickup box."

"So we stay put," Benj said. "And wait for emergency services to show up. Roger that, Malik."

It wouldn't be long.

An explosion on the coast, on a rocket range in a wildlife reserve, in the land of crude oil.

They just had to hold out until then.

Malik seemed to be on his own. That was a factor that might save their lives.

And maybe Benj could find a way to use it.

"This isn't an official visit, is it?" Benj asked. "You gone AWOL, Malik?"

"I've been burnt," Malik said. "It's like a permanent leave. They won't touch me ever again, Benj. Thanks to you. And that Russian faggot."

"Damn us to hell, huh? For not letting you kill us?"

"It was simple, asshole. But your father wouldn't make the deal."

"It wasn't my father's call, Malik. And it certainly wasn't up to me. It's not our fault you teamed up with the Chinese junta. Maybe you should have considered who your friends are."

Benj heard the sirens.

Damn it.

Malik would have to make his move.

And Benj didn't have any idea how he could counter it.

Not without getting himself killed.

And probably most of the people in the back of the pickup.

"You can't kill all of us, Malik," Rachael said. "And one of us will get you. So don't be an idiot. Just slink away, alright?"

"What the hell are you doing?" Benj asked her.

"I'm egging him on."

"Why would you do that, Rachael? Why?"

She didn't give him an answer.

Benj looked back to where he'd seen Malik.

He couldn't see him anymore.

Shit.

He waited and listened.

The sirens were getting closer.

He could see the lights coming up the highway.

He couldn't hear Malik's approach.

He couldn't see any movement from the southwest.

For all he knew, Malik had circled around, to come from another approach. To take half of them out before Benj could track him.

Malik was a professional killer.

Benj was a goddamn professional computer guy.

He waited.

He could see a fire truck, leading a convoy of other vehicles, an array of flashing lights piercing the darkness.

Malik hadn't come.

Benj's tablet buzzed.

He fumbled for it with his left hand. He passed it to Rachael.

"It's from Samantha Yoon," she told him. "Says to head due north."

"Right now?"

"I think we're running out of time."

Benj looked over to Anita, kneeling down by Chloe.

"The three of us should go," Anita said. "You, me, and Rachael. I think Chloe will be okay, if Malik's really gone. But she needs an ambulance, obviously."

"We don't need to run," Benj said.

Anita frowned. "I need to run, Benj. I can't be arrested… I won't make the next launch."

"We'll go with you," Rachael said.

"We're trusting Samantha now?" Benj asked.

Rachael shook her head. "We're trusting your father."

Benj nodded. "I'll go first."

He slowly raised his head.

He moved toward the end of the box.

He jumped down from the tailgate.

Nothing from Malik.

Maybe he was just waiting for more targets to expose themselves.

Benj stood by the end of the truck, trying to put his body between the tailgate and where he'd last known Malik to be.

It wasn't exactly a perfect strategy.

Rachael came next, keeping lower than Benj had.

She creeped down off the truck, then crouched down on the sand scattered at the edge of the pavement.

Anita came next.

Still nothing from Malik.

The fire truck was only a hundred feet away.

"Now we run," Anita said.

She led the way, heading north—hopefully—through the sand and low grasses, toward the salt marshes.

Rachael took the middle, and Benj was in the rear.

They were over a fence, and into the wet ground, as the emergency vehicles arrived.

Benj could see a couple of ambulances.

He still didn't know what had happened with Mireia and Jack Roland.

The ground was soft, slowing them down.

But hopefully no one was looking for them at the moment.

Assuming that Malik truly had given up.

And that he'd headed in a different direction than they had.

Benj's tablet buzzed again.

He passed it back to Rachael.

"Follow the water," she said, then handed the tablet back.

So they did, trudging along the mix of wet sand and muck, tracing the shallow inlet toward what Benj expected would be the Brownsville Ship Channel.

It would be a very long hike.

And he could see that Rachael hadn't had time to treat her puncture wounds.

"I've got the first aid kit," Anita said. "We'll stop in a bit and fix her up."

"How far do we need to go?" Rachael asked.

"It could be a ways," Benj said.

"I can make it."

Anita stopped walking.

"What?" Rachael said.

"We should patch you up now," she said.

The tablet buzzed again.

Benj sighed.

He took it out and read it for himself.

Don't stop. You're almost there.

Benj took a knee. "Please," he said to Anita, "patch her up."

Anita got to work on it.

"Just so you know," she said, as she swabbed some kind of cleaner on the wounds, "I'm not exactly the first aid type."

"I wasn't making assumptions," Benj said.

"I just worry about gender roles."

"Are you guys trying to distract me from how much this hurts?" Rachael asked. "Because it's not working."

"Samantha says we're close," Benj said. "Is that better?"

Rachael tried to smile. "Better."

Benj watched as Anita applied an adhesive gauze pad to Rachael's shoulder.

"They're not deep," Anita said. "I saw the knife. Wasn't the best choice for a weapon."

"That's too bad," Rachael said. "Should we keep moving?"

"Yeah," Benj said. "We're close, remember?"

"Yeah. Close."

Benj helped Rachael up.

They continued to head along the shoreline.

There was a figure ahead, at the water's edge.

Benj took the pistol out of his jacket pocket.

"I told you not to stop," the woman in the distance called out.

Samantha Yoon.

She started jogging toward them.

"Is she okay?" she asked, looking at Rachael.

"She'll be fine," Anita said. "You're Samantha Yoon."

"Yeah. I don't know what you've heard."

"I'm not sure I trust you."

Samantha seemed surprised by such an open declaration.

"Sorry," Anita said. "But I figured you should know where you stand with me."

"You're stuck with me," Samantha said. She looked over to Benj. "All of you are."

"I don't mind," Rachael said. "As long as you've got a plan."

Samantha nodded. "I've got a plan." She motioned back to the shoreline behind her. "And a boat."

68

THE ORANGE lifeboat had a listed capacity of 70 persons.

By Jared's count, there were forty-three, including himself.

Carter Elgin wasn't on board, and neither was Nicolas Clouatre.

Jared recognized a handful people from his team; he didn't know who'd stayed behind when the ferry had pulled away to join the Russian fleet, so he didn't know who'd been left on *Basilica* when she'd been hit.

All he knew was that his life had been saved by a free-fall lifeboat, designed and built to withstand exactly what they'd just gone through. A long hard drop into the ocean.

The interior looked much like a small passenger plane, rows of seats and a narrow aisle. The biggest difference was the crew component, a raised platform set near the middle of the boat, floating over the regular seating.

Now that things had steadied a little, Jared climbed the metal ladder up to crew seats. There was no extra room to stand next to the two driver seats, so he stood on the top run of the ladder.

Two men from somewhere in Scandinavia had taken those driver seats, behind two steering wheels and a GPS system. The controls didn't look any harder to work than what you'd see on a motor boat.

He recognized one of the men—the copilot—from his team.

Kristian Rindom. Danish, maybe.

And he looked relieved to see Jared.

"We're aiming for New York City," Kristian said. "Will take a long time to get there at eight knots."

"Derrick McPherson was supposed to be there to meet the ferry," Jared said. "Maybe he'll be able to help us out."

"Help us out?"

Jared sighed. "I don't think we have many friends in the US government right now. And many people in this lifeboat aren't US citizens."

"Like me," Kristian said. He motioned to the man beside him. "And Jes."

"You think they will arrest us?" the other self-appointed pilot, Jes, asked.

"I think we'll be held for a little while," Jared said. "You guys will probably be sent back to Europe. As far as I know, nothing we did here was illegal, since it wasn't in US waters. But still…"

"They don't like us," Kristian said.

"Exactly."

"I'm not sure we'll get to New York," Jes said.

"We have GPS," Kristian said.

Jes shook his head. "They wanted to kill us. This lifeboat is designed to be found. We are naked ducks."

"Naked ducks," Jared said.

"As in fucked."

"So what do you want to do about it?" Kristian said. "You want to get out and swim?"

"There's a radio, right?" Jared said. "We can issue a distress call or something."

"Like a Mayday," Jes said.

"Yeah."

"Does anyone know how to do that?" Kristian asked.

"I do," Jes said.

He worked what looked like the transmitter. And started making the call.

"Mayday Mayday Mayday," he said. "Freighter *Basilica. Basilica.*" He looked at the GPS. "38.00.08 North, 71.31.85 West. Crew has abandoned ship. *Besättningen har övergett skeppet.*"

"Now what do we do?" Kristian asked.

"We do it again," Jes said. And repeated the message.

"I'm going to check up on the other passengers," Jared said.

He made his way back down the ladder.

He could see the first flickers of sunrise. He knew that it would be a very long day.

Assuming it wasn't cut short by a quick and violent death.

Kristian came to grab Jared a few minutes later, telling him to come with him up to the crew cockpit.

The man's attempt to seem calm had failed miserably, with everyone in earshot knowing that something was wrong.

Jared made his way up the ladder, behind him.

"Swarmboats," Jes said. "I think it's the Russian ones."

"How many?" Jared asked.

"Take a look. I've counted eight, at minimum. And it's not like we have the best view from in here."

Jared nodded. "I think we're okay."

"How can you say that?" Kristian asked. "We're in a bright orange target."

"It wasn't the Russians. They didn't attack."

"How can you know that?" Jes said. "How can you be certain?"

"It's my best guess," Jared said.

"That's not enough," Kristian said.

Jared shook his head. "I'm not telling you what to do. It's not like there's anything we can do. I'm just telling you that I think they're here to help."

"How can they help?" Jes asked.

"By swarming around us. Shielding us. In case whatever sunk *Basilica* finds it way to us."

"So what do we do?" Kristian asked.

"We keep heading for New York," Jared said. "And hope I'm right."

The swarmboats stayed with them for six hours.

That was across and into the US EEZ, according to the GPS; Jared hadn't expected the Russians to take that kind of risk, even with uncrewed boats. It was a Chinese destroyer entering the EEZ off Hawaii that had resulted in the first armed skirmish between China and the US in the 21st century. Would the USA be any gentler with the Russian Navy?

Just after ten AM, the swarmboats moved off.

And Jes spotted a new boat.

Jared recognized the white hull with red stripe. "US Coast Guard," he said. "I'm pretty sure they're here to see us."

The boat was a mid-sized coast guard vessel, maybe eighty to ninety feet long, with two very clear machine guns mounted on each side, just in front of the red stripe.

Mounted, and manned.

Jared knew that it wouldn't be the friendliest of rescues.

The Coast Guard patrol boat towed the lifeboat to Montauk, New York, passing around the famous lighthouse on the point.

Jared was relieved to find that he could get network reception off Long Island; he made a point to message his mother and a few more people who could think of, and counseled others to do the same.

The more people who knew what was happening, the better. The harder it would be for the US government to make any of them disappear.

But he'd received several messages as well, and one that mattered. From

Derrick McPherson.

A wide broadcast. He wasn't sure who was included.

Launch from Basilica *in North Atlantic has succeeded. Launch at* Boca Chica *in South Texas has failed. More details to come.*

Failed. What did that mean?

What had happened? Were they okay?

Jared tapped back a quick response, though he knew there was little chance of getting a personal reply.

And he knew that his tablet would more than likely be taken away from him the moment he got out of the lifeboat.

He saw that there was a substantial number of personnel from a substantial number of federal agencies waiting for their arrival.

On arrival at the dock, Jared and the other passengers were herded to the large expanse of manicured lawn set behind the classic New England-looking white buildings of the Coast Guard station.

They were then stripped of their devices and separated out by assumed citizenship, four lines total: US Citizens, Canadian Citizens, European Citizens, and everyone else, the everyone else including the one person Jared had known to be Russian, a young dark-haired woman who had a slavic nose and an interesting accent.

Jared was one of the first to be taken in for a debrief, led to a small room that looked more like a break room than something you'd use for an interrogation.

He had a feeling that the Americans got the least secure-looking room in the mix.

There were two men to ask him questions, one Coast Guard Petty Officer who seemed reasonable enough, and an FBI agent who seemed anything but.

Good cop, bad cop, apparently. Interservice edition.

"We're not allies with the Russians," the petty officer said. "You're aware of that, right?"

"I'm pretty sure I've done nothing illegal," Jared said.

"You don't need to do something illegal," the FBI agent said. "We can detain anyone deemed to be a security risk. Indefinitely."

"Virginia."

"What?"

"That's where you'll send me, right? To that little village in Virginia?"

"This is a serious problem, Mr. Koskela."

"I wonder if people will look for me when the video comes out," Jared said.

"What video?" the petty officer said.

"Don't buy into this stuff," the FBI agent said.

"Carter Elgin's releasing a video," Jared said. "Sometime today, I think. About the launches we just pulled off."

The FBI agent smirked. "Carter Elgin is dead."

Jared shrugged. "They mention me in that video. The whole world should know my name in a few hours."

The Coast Guard officer seemed puzzled, even curious, while his FBI counterpart was predictably annoyed.

Jared wasn't really sure what he was doing, what his plan actually was. Had the FBI been instructed to take all of the SolRescue people into custody? Was Danny Pyke already on his way to middle-of-nothing Virginia?

"I wonder if people will assume you drowned in the North Atlantic?" the FBI agent said. "You rarely recover bodies from that far off the coast."

"Agent Sains," the petty officer said. "That's not appropriate."

"You can take five minutes, chief."

"No. I'll stick this out."

"People know we're here," Jared said. "People all over the world got messages from the passengers on that lifeboat. You can't make us disappear. You can't even hold me, since I've done nothing wrong."

Agent Sains groaned. "I told you, Koskela, that I can hold you."

"I guess you can. If you want that kind of trouble."

"Is that a threat?"

"Maybe this kind of intimidation works on some people," Jared said. "I know it worked on Mohammed Najjar. But it doesn't work on me. Because I've got nothing to lose here. I just accomplished the one thing I set out to do. Everything else is a bonus."

Agent Sains didn't respond.

Neither did the man from the Coast Guard.

They both left the room.

Neither bothered to come back; a man in a windbreaker came by an hour later to tell Jared he could go.

He knew he'd been lucky.

It wasn't that Jared had outsmarted anyone; he knew that.

He just wasn't important enough for them to hold onto, not considering how many other problems the US government had to deal with.

Jared Koskela was just too noisy and *too American* for them to do anything about.

God bless the USA.

He pulled out his reclaimed tablet and immediately started charting his course.

Taxi to the train station. Train to Babylon, and from there to Penn Station. Then the Number 8 Subway to LaGuardia. He'd figure out his flights on the way.

He had to get to Texas.

To find Chloe.

And Rachael.

To make sure both of them were okay.

69

BENJ KNEW he'd owe her. Even after everything she'd done.

Samantha Yoon paddled them across a shallow bay, and then the ship channel, bringing them first to the SpaceX ferry dock on South Padre Island to pick up yet another minivan, this one rented to Samantha, apparently under an assumed name.

Rachael had asked, to be sure.

Benj liked that he wasn't the only one questioning Samantha's competence.

Samantha than drove them back to Long Island Village, in Port Isabel. They grabbed what they could from their rental accommodations, before leaving in yet another minivan, this one rented to Samantha.

Benj took the passenger seat, since he was sure no one else would want to, and then without much choice in the matter, he drifted in and out of sleep.

He sat up two and a half hours later, as Samantha reached the interstate and put the van on driverfree.

"Eighteen more hours if we don't stop," she told him.

"To where?"

"San Diego. That's where we need to be."

"Why?"

"You know why."

"The launch," Anita said, from the row behind them.

"This is the first thing I'm hearing about San Diego," Benj said. "I figured the launch would be from *Basilica*."

He heard Anita sigh. "It's gone," she said.

"What?"

"They made the launch," Samantha said. "But they were hit not long after. Derrick thinks it was a torpedo."

"A torpedo?"

"Yeah. And that's what the Russians are saying."

"And they couldn't stop it from happening?" Benj asked.

"The Russians pulled out," Rachael said. "They let it happen."

He hadn't realized she was awake.

"So the launch will happen in San Diego," Samantha said. "A friend of yours is coming there to meet us, Rachael."

"Jared?" Rachael asked. "He's okay?"

"Not Jared. But he is okay."

"Then who?" Anita asked.

"Archibald Wong," Samantha said. "Apparently he was another one of the people out gunning for Carter Elgin. So just like you, Rachael."

"What does she mean?" Anita said, her tone changing.

"She means that I wasn't sure about Carter," Rachael said. "That I wasn't sure he could be trusted to do the right thing. I'm sorry, Ms. Singhal. I just wanted what's best for... for everyone, really."

Anita took a deep breath. "I've known Carter Elgin for longer than any of you. Other than Derrick, I guess."

"I'm sorry," Rachael said again.

"Carter isn't always right. He isn't always the good guy. If you thought there was a good reason to make him step down, you were probably right. You're probably still right."

"He's missing," Samantha said. "So maybe it doesn't matter."

"I know he's missing!" Anita shouted.

"Yeah, okay."

"We're going to need to stop to get food soon," Benj said. "Most of us haven't eaten or even had a drink of water in far too long."

"Little while longer," Samantha said. "Let's just put a few more miles between us and Boca Chica."

"Did Derrick send you?" Rachael asked.

"Yup. He figured you'd need to get out through the back door after the launch."

"Nikki Taunton sabotaged it," Benj said. "We didn't expect that."

"She checked out," Samantha said. "So I don't know what happened."

"Well, something happened," Anita said.

Benj looked out the window.

They were moving at just over eight miles per hour, still in the flatlands, along the gulf.

It would be a long trip to California.

But like with the trip from *Basilica* to Brownsville, Benj knew they needed that time to recover.

If it's possible to recover from what they'd gone through.

70

MALIK SINCERELY wished there was a way he could thank the friends who hadn't turned their backs to him. Some of them had risked their careers to keep him as much in the loop as they had.

He was grateful.

And he doubted he'd ever get the chance to repay them personally.

All he could do was make sure he finished his mission.

They'd taken Derrick McPherson himself, back on Tuesday afternoon, in a raid on a loading bay at Port Newark-Elizabeth, the huge container port only a handful of bridges from Manhattan. McPherson had given them nothing, as expected, but they'd busted a courier who'd just met with the man, and through the kind of intimidation that only Homeland Security could pull off, they'd convinced the courier not only to open up her locked tablet, but to keep on her way to her next destination, a motel in Union, New Jersey. Just far enough away from Newark Liberty International Airport to make any expected pursuer uncertain.

And Taro had passed the details on the arrests to Malik, along with something extra, something that didn't Taro had managed to "forget" to include in his report, a trick that could easily be chalked up to the outdated input system, a mistake that wouldn't get caught for a day or two if Malik was lucky.

One extra alias to look out for: Susan Park.

He didn't need anything more than that; he'd already suspected it. Samantha Yoon hadn't been gone aboard the Russian freighter, but she was no longer following McPherson around.

Malik had passed the fake name to Cam at the NSA Data Center in Utah, and he'd come back with a few possibles, data mismatches that Cam had always been good at spotting.

Only one of those possibles came from the right parts of the US, the places a fake Susan Park might be headed. A van rental from a counter at George Bush Intercontinental, in Houston, Texas.

Really not that far from Boca Chica Beach.

Being burnt meant that he'd had to use his bugout bag, changing in an instant from Malik Daley to Evangel Price, another one of those black-sounding names that he enjoyed using.

So much better than his real name.

Who the hell names their kid Nixon?

Malik—he'd still be Malik, really, at least until he'd finished the job and killed the damn launches—had arrived at Boca Chica Beach at around 11 PM on Wednesday night. From what he'd been told by Taro—not that he was sure how Taro had found out, since McPherson wasn't the type to give details or share them with subordinates—the launch would come the following afternoon, but he could see from the activity by the beach that things had been pushed up.

He picked up a car—people still loved to leave them running outside liquor stores in small town Texas—and drove to the dock for the ferry to Boca Chica Beach.

As expected, he found the van that had been rented to Susan Park. And an empty berth where a flat-bottomed ferry ought to be. He drove his stolen car on the detour around the ship channel, parking it in SpaceX's Boca Chica Village, right next to where the missing ferry had turned up.

He then made his way on foot to where there were a couple of minivans and a pickup truck. He found five people there, two women and three men.

They hadn't even been looking out for unexpected visitors.

Like they'd learned nothing from the dead bodies scattered around the great state of Wyoming.

He ordered them—with the help of his homebrewed AR-15—away from the vehicles, north toward the shallow water of a narrow bay. He put them on their knees, in the sand, by the water's edge.

He picked out who he thought was the most malleable of them—a young, pretty Ethiopian-looking woman—and got her take the roll of duct tape from his pack, and to tape up the rest of her team, hands and feet.

He started taping her up as well.

"You're Malik Daley," the other woman said, a middle-aged woman with short blond hair.

"Yeah," he replied. It was like she wanted to give him more of a reason to have to kill everyone.

"Check my pockets."

So he did.

Nothing but a pack of gum.

X-treem Spearmint Sugarfree.

Like the one he had in his back pocket.

He'd never actually bothered to find out what it tasted like.

"Okay," he said.

He helped her up.

She pulled her wrists above her head, then pulled down hard, snapping the duct tape.

"Great," he said. "Now we gotta wrap tape all around their chests, too. You think this stuff grows on trees?"

"I'll handle it," she said.

She held out her hand.

For his rifle.

"Not gonna happen," he said.

"Fine. You better have enough tape."

He'd fucked up at Boca Chica, not realizing that Samantha Yoon had enough brains to add a little misdirection with the stolen ferry. By the time he'd realized that he'd missed them, and driven all the way around to the docks at South Padre Island, the van and his targets were long gone.

At least an hour head start. And he had no clue in which direction.

So he waited. For the information he knew would come eventually.

He got the data fourteen hours later. A license plate capture from a driverfree entrance plaza, outside El Paso, Texas—I-10 West—that Cam had sent along to him.

Malik took an educated risk, taking a plane from Brownsville to Phoenix, Arizona. By the time he'd landed, Cam had sent another update. Another plate capture from a Border Protection scanner outside Lordsburg, New Mexico.

From three hours before. They were in Arizona, most definitely, somewhere close to him. Samantha and her cargo, Anita Singhal, Rachael Duck, and of course, ol' Benj McPherson.

But Malik didn't know which way they were headed, to LA or San Diego. Or maybe they were headed further north, since the navigator on his tablet had indicated that their route could be to a destination as far north as Portland, Oregon. That was assuming they weren't purposely going out of their way to confuse anyone who was following him, but he knew that was unlikely.

Samantha Yoon / Susan Park would be relying on that fake ID. That's why Derrick McPherson had purchased them, or rather, purchased the people necessary to circumvent the pathetically basic facial detection safeguards, swapping one Korean woman's photo with another across the entire US federal identification network, leaving the real Susan Park wondering why she was now having trouble buying her bulk steak sauce at Costco.

Malik rented his car and decided on I-10, toward Los Angeles. If they were heading to San Diego, they'd be seen on more Border Patrol scanners.

So he'd be able to tell Cam exactly where to look, when the time came to pinpoint their destination.

71

ARCHIE WONG was exactly as Anita had expected him to be.

A half and half mix of smug and sullen, like he couldn't believe that everyone else could be so naive, about Carter Elgin, about global civilization in its entirety…

Exactly the kind of person Anita hated. With a passion that made her feel young again, like a fourteen-year-old who'd just been told she'd understand what being a parent felt like some day.

She'd never gotten there.

Archie had already rented space for them, in a warehouse on the northern fringe of San Diego, a glorified storage unit, really, two lightbulbs dangling from a metal frame building with a sliding overhead door as the main way in or out.

But he explained his reasoning, and Anita couldn't find the holes she found herself almost wanting to poke. The building was secure, monitored with surveillance, surrounded by an eight-foot metal fence. It was at the edge of the an industrial park, flush against a bluff that led up to the Mount Soledad/San Clemente Canyon Freeway. And he had something more, an aerial surveyor, a battery-operated dirigible to keep an eye on any possible approach, complete with a plate-tracking camera on "loan" from the California Highway Patrol. Every vehicle that had come close to that warehouse in the past two weeks had been recorded and checked. Anything new would be noticed. Any changes in schedule would be noticed.

Archie Wong had been planning this project for much longer than Anita could have expected. And he was doing his best to avoid explaining exactly how and when he was assigned the task, or if Carter or Derrick had even given him the task at all.

"What happens if someone comes?" she asked him.

"I've got it handled," he said. "Don't worry."

"It's my job to worry. To worry that people are overselling their abilities."

He frowned. "I know my job, Ms. Singhal. It's under control, and it's not something I feel comfortable in detailing at the moment. You just worry about your job, okay?"

"Excuse me?"

"You're used to more reverence," he said. "You won't get that here. I'm here to get you into space, not to kiss your ass."

"I don't see what your problem is."

"Well, shoot. Let's start over, okay? My name is Archibald Wong and I'm just trying to do my fucking job."

He was an asshole.

For some reason, that seemed like a good characteristic for him to have. She couldn't help but smile at that.

There was something better than the rented space or the man who'd rented it; Archie the Asshole had also managed to get Jared Koskela installed, as an important first step.

Anita found it difficult to watch Jared's Friday morning reunion with an exhausted and over-emotional Rachael Duck. The two slowly approached one another, like a couple of uncertain losers, like they both had a reason for the other to turn them away.

Anita had heard enough to know that Jared had his reason to want Rachael gone, but she didn't quite get why he seemed shy of her.

They came together slowly and embraced, Jared gripping her tightly, Rachael still seeming unsure of herself.

Anita turned away, looking over to Samantha and Benj—who were both doing the same—but she wasn't anywhere near being out of earshot as they spoke.

"You're okay," Jared said.

"I'm okay," Rachael replied. "I didn't know if you made it off."

"Well, I did. And I'm here. To help."

"To help…"

"I missed you, Rachael," he said.

There was a pause.

Anita knew he'd kissed her. She just didn't know where.

It didn't matter.

It was generally uncomfortable for her.

And probably significantly worse for Benj; it wasn't like he'd been putting all that much effort in concealing his attraction to Rachael.

So that made it *more uncomfortable…*

Then she noticed Archie, who'd been staring at the couple, oblivious as to how he ought to be acting, making no attempt to look away or even be subtle about it.

Tonedeaf in every conceivable way.

To the point where Anita almost started snickering.

"I don't have the equipment yet," Jared said, walking over to Anita. "I'm pretty sure my last bunch is at the bottom of the Atlantic. And I've not exactly well-versed on what it takes to assemble the capsule."

"We need to start fresh," Anita said.

"Shouldn't be difficult, should it?" Archie said. "I mean, we have the designs, you guys know what you need… and money isn't one of our problems. So you know… just get it done…"

"What is our problem?" Rachael asked.

"You really don't know? It's being noticed. Because everyone on the fucking planet is looking for you people."

"I know they ought to be tracking us," Anita said. "But Samantha's done alright, from what I've seen."

"I aim to please," Samantha said.

"So I can go with Jared," Rachael said. "We'll find what we need."

"Go up to Orange County," Archie said. "Crypto only, okay? Nothing they can trace."

"I've got what we need for that," Samantha said. "Don't worry."

"And what do the rest of us do?" Anita asked.

"Seriously?" Archie said. "It's not like you can do anything, not if it involves leaving the building."

"What?"

"Come on. You're probably one of the three most famous people on Earth right now. Try and guess the other two. Forget them finding some loose thread in Samantha's pile of fake. One sighting of sexy Anita Singhal on the West Coast will kill this whole plan. So you need to think for a minute and stay right here."

"In this oversized coffin?"

"At least it has network," Archie said. "As long as your tablet is safeguarded. I mean, it is, right?"

Anita groaned.

Like he honestly thought they'd have crossed country with open communications and traceable tablets.

Like it was her first day of being up to no good.

She'd been up to no good before Archie the Asshole was out of high school.

The math on that didn't make her feel better.

Jared and Rachael did as Archie had brusquely recommended, taking a rented truck and driving north toward Los Angeles, looking to find any metal fab, welding equipment and multi-material 3D printers they could grab that were ready to take. For the printers, they'd consider going more old school, using prev-gen models and merging the results together, but that would take more time.

If the USAF and PLAN launch dates were what they'd been told they'd be, they had ten days until the first big batch of spiders were sent on their way to hijack the shieldbots, which meant approximately fifteen days before the interlopers reached STeLa-1.

If Anita was going to get there first, and have time to prepare the countermeasures—the hypothetical countermeasures Carter had designed but that Jared would have to build from scratch—she'd need to be launched sometime in the next week. Sometime between now and the following Friday.

To build everything they needed, to launch a person—to launch her—to STeLa-1 to create and then occupy the first human-crewed space station outside Earth's magnetosphere.

And Carter wasn't there to help them.

And Danny Pyke, and Nicolas Clouatre, Mireia Lona, Jack Roland... and a hundred other engineers were either missing, injured, or detained by the US government.

There were still people to help, but only remotely, SolRescue staff who'd never left Stockholm, the Turnpike team outside of the United States, but most of them were busy with the one sliver of success, the solitary capsule already making its way toward the sunshield. They would be in charge of the discharge of the capsule into its two small beads, and the tethering, to each other and eventually to the two beads from Anita's capsule, assuming Anita's capsule ever reaches the rendezvous.

Anita had to be optimistic. She had to pretend to be young Anita Singhal once again... naive, almost. And they'd pulled off the one launch, one out of three, against all odds.

And the video SolRescue had released on Thursday afternoon, from the speech on *Basilica*... it would look to the entire world that the three launches were the only launches, that the video was coming out because SolRescue had succeeded with one of them.

Maybe the loss of *Basilica* would shield their new attempt. No one would expect them to be hard at work on the other side of the continent.

But she remembered what Bridget had announced, that SolRescue was sending its people. The world might not be expecting another launch, but some people would.

All the more reason why Anita had to stay out of sight.

Benj and Samantha were sent off together—not that Benj seemed happy about it—to pick up the flat sheets of aluminum-lithium alloy, and to grab the laundry list of materials for feeding the printers, not that they'd know 100% which materials to choose until Jared messaged them with updates on the machines he'd found.

Not that there were too many substitutes available for the designs; if

Jared couldn't find a printer that could handle a one-pass assembly of the polyamide membrane for Mireia's water filtration system, it wasn't like you could just come up with some random Plan B.

With everyone else on their missions, it was just Anita and Archie at the warehouse, with Archie working at his dock and Anita sitting on a folding chair with her tablet; Benj would also need to pick up a couple more work-docks.

Anita was waiting for any news from *Basilica*. But the news wasn't coming.

The US Navy and Coast Guard had reached the site first, closing it off to any outside surveillance, from news overflights by drone to amateur journalists on chartered fishing boats.

She knew that Danny Pyke had been interrogated and already released on bond, loaded up with a smorgasbord of charges, from EPA violations to trespassing, but probably nothing that would result in anything worse than many big, big fines and a few months of house arrest. Vasily Utkin and most of the other foreign detainees were marked for deportation, rather than facing charges. For the time being, there was still no public appetite for throwing offplanet pioneers in prison, and still enough power to that public to make that opinion matter.

The chartered ferry had stuck with the Russian fleet long enough to reach the waters off the Azores; from there they expected a Royal Navy escort to bring the rest of the way back to Sweden.

But Anita had heard nothing about Carter Elgin or Nicolas Clouatre, or the other thirteen people who were on board *Basilica* during the attack but hadn't made it to the lifeboat.

If the American vessels had found any bodies, they weren't releasing it. If they'd found any survivors, they weren't releasing that, either.

She knew that there was always a chance that she would never know what happened to Carter. Not that the powers that be wouldn't know, just that they'd never tell.

She didn't know what to think.

She didn't know what to feel.

It just… it hurt. Not just for her life, her past and memories, but knowing what it would be for Bridget and for Sansa. How it multiplied, losing someone you care about, and seeing the loss on the other people you love. Compounding.

She needed to do something.

She needed to get to work.

But there was nothing she could do right then, even if there was so much left to do.

She couldn't make a run down to a nearby home and garden store to grab seeds and tubing for the aeroponics. She couldn't even print or assemble anything for the hab.

All she could do was look over the designs, just as she had for hours upon hours on the way there from Texas. It didn't matter how many times she looked it over, or studied the models they'd made from the completed components on *Basilica*. She had to get her hands on something to understand it better.

She had to wait for everyone to get back.

"So I need to ask you something," Archie said, stepping off his stool and walking over to her folding chair.

"Yeah, okay," she said, trying to sound less hostile than she felt.

"Look. I know you don't approve of what we've been doing. I get that."

"I don't care about what you've been doing."

"No, you do care. Because it was against Carter. And he's your precious little lamb."

"I don't want to have this conversation with you," she said. "Or any conversation."

"You gotta stay on."

"What?"

"You need to stay on at SolRescue. For good, this time."

"Before or after I get blasted into space?"

"I need to know that you're going to stay active," he said. "That you'll keep watch over this organization."

"From my astral temple, huh?"

"You know what I mean, Ms. Singhal."

"You mean sexy Ms. Singhal?"

He smirked. "I wasn't lying."

"Get me to STeLa-1," she said. "Help us stop those spiders from taking out our sunshield. That's your end of the bargain. I'll hold up my end."

"I respected Carter," Archie said.

"Don't eulogize him."

"I wanted what's best for all of us."

"And now you think you've gotten what you want," she said.

"Don't accuse me."

Archie the Asshole walked away.

Anita knew she was right about him.

72

MALIK KNEW he wouldn't get anything on the whereabouts of the warehouse.

All he knew—from the US Border Patrol's not-so-strong encryption and more indebtedness to Cam in Utah—was that Samantha had driven them to San Diego, and that in San Diego there would be a warehouse. They'd need one to build another set of rocket and capsule, for the launch that everyone in the federal government knew was coming.

A launch Malik knew a little more about.

Nikki Taunton had told him about it, on their trip back to the road at Boca Chica Beach, before she'd managed to get herself shot by Benj Mc-Pherson, of all people.

But at least she'd hit the abort switch.

And she'd told him what he needed to know, enough to go with.

Enough to finish the job… and maybe he wouldn't get un-burnt, some-how, because that wasn't something you could just get reversed, but at least they'd regret doing it in the first place.

They'd regret blaming him for all of the Chinese fuck-ups, for oper-atives who'd been begging to get shot and/or clubbed with a rock.

He'd make them regret it, because Nikki had told him that Anita Singhal was the one who'd be headed to STeLa-1, and Malik was the only one who knew how to find her.

He'd kill her before the Feds knew a goddamn thing about it.

The first rule of finding someone is to look for transactions, obviously, so it was a given that none of the people Malik was looking for would have used their actual banking accounts for anything.

For Samantha Yoon/Susan Park, there would have been a fake travel credit account to follow, but it was issued by a Russian bank—because ap-parently SolRescue now loved the Russians—with the lovely American-sounding name of Shield+, but with the standard Russian protection against warrantless snooping by American agencies.

So it took longer to get that data, and the most recent transaction he could find was from Friday night, from a fast food drive-thru in El Cajon,

California, just before the city of San Diego.

Even if she hadn't switched to another payment method—you can still use paper bills at some of the smaller businesses—he wouldn't get the data fast enough.

He needed to catch them in real-time, to follow them back to the warehouse. The job, as he now could see, demanded that he kill Anita Singhal. If he did that, it wouldn't just prevent the next SolRescue launch, but maybe it could put a stop to any others, now that Derrick McPherson was detained and Carter Elgin was at the bottom of the North Atlantic.

He didn't need to kill anyone else.

Not for the job.

But he would kill Benj, and he would kill Samantha Yoon.

Because they'd murdered someone Malik cared about. Someone he'd thought Benj cared about as well.

But if he'd really cared about her, he wouldn't have done it. He wouldn't have driven her out to an isolated lake in south-central Utah and watched as Samantha Yoon slit her throat, leaving Laila's body slumped over the passenger seat of her car, then rolling that car right under the water.

It's one thing to have to kill, because it's expected and required of you.

But Laila was innocent.

She was beautiful.

She deserved so much better.

Malik knew he couldn't wait for random information to dribble in from Cam or from elsewhere. He had to make some guesses if he wanted to catch them.

They'd have the warehouse, but that could be anywhere.

For all he knew, that warehouse was fully equipped with the machines they needed, for welding or bending or whatever it took. He knew what they'd need most of all, from what he'd heard of the supplies found at Wallops.

The space habitat required materials that you couldn't just pick up at the local DIY outlet. And unless there was a special lab for outsourcing your life support systems, they would need to replicate the design from Carter's floating headquarters. That would require 3d printers, a few different models, from what he knew, and it would require materials to feed into those printers.

And some of those materials weren't that common.

Time would be of the essence for their team, so Malik made the navigator aigent on his tablet make up a list. Six suppliers in San Diego. Only four were in a retail format, set up for visitors right off the street; that would be their target, places that was more casual with recordkeeping, where they might possibly alternate two of three people buying at all four suppliers, to make the amounts seem less conspicuous.

In case the Feds showed up at those suppliers to ask questions.

But Malik wasn't a Fed, not anymore.

He pushed the aigent further.

He chose four locations in the area, industrial districts, assuming the warehouse wasn't in the middle of Balboa Park. And then he asked the navigator to chart it out, hypothetical routes to cover all four supplies from all four origin points.

He wasn't sure what he was looking for, what the navigator aigent could tell him.

Until he saw it.

One supplier in Eastlake was out of the way from all four starting places, with one likely route shared by all four, considering the construction on I-805.

He sent a message to Cam, then started heading to the south side of San Diego.

Toll plazas meant tracking, even if the rental car didn't have anything more than the standard federal transponder.

It only took forty minutes for Cam to come back with something.

They pulled off onto San Miguel Ranch Road at 2:40 PM local time.

It was 3:30 PM.

He didn't have much time, and he was still ten minutes out from the supplier.

He told Cam to let him know when he got anything new.

Maybe if he missed them picking up the materials, he could catch up to them on their way home.

He saw the forest green minivan with the right plate numbers.

Parked in the lot.

No one waiting inside.

If they were trying to keep from attracting attention, they might shop separately, each grabbing and paying for their items on their own, meeting back in the lot.

Like with laundering money; you can convert to this or that cryptocurrency all you want, if you keep the amounts low enough, if you're willing to take the time to split it up.

He parked three cars away, slinking down in the driver's seat.

And waited.

✍

Samantha Yoon was the first to come out.

A young worker was helping her roll out the supplies on a flatbed dolly. Malik wondered if Benj was with her, with his own dolly and wagemonkey porter.

He so hoped Benj was there.

Once the supplies were piled into the back, Samantha walked toward the driver's side door.

Malik got out, bringing his pistol and not the rifle, which was a little oversized for what he needed to accomplish. Close quarters and all.

He walked quickly, but didn't run.

He got there just as she'd opened the door.

He grabbed her shoulder with his left hand, while showing off the pistol in his right.

"Give me the keys," he said.

She passed them over.

"Now scoot over to the passenger side," he told her.

She nodded, then slowly climbed in, keeping her hands high.

"I don't know where it is," she said. "The workshop or whatever."

"Yeah, I know. You're just a pawn. I should just let you go."

She climbed over to the passenger seat, placing her hands on the dash as she sat.

He climbed in on the driver's side.

He tilted the rearview, aiming it for a better view of the building's front doors.

"How long 'til he comes out, do you think?" he asked her.

"It'll be a while," she said.

Not that he would believe it. It was more a yardstick for later, to understand better where she was coming from.

"We don't need to wait," she said.

"We'll wait."

"I can take you there."

"You said you didn't know where it was," Malik said. "And I'd rather Benj was with us than out warning people once he sees that you've left unexpectedly. But thanks for thinking so little of me."

"Anytime."

"Tell me something, Samantha."

"I'd love to."

"Was it you or Benj who killed her?"

"Who? Laila?"

"Yeah, Laila."

"It was Benj," she said.

"Did he know you were going to kill her?"

"I told him to kill her and he killed her."

He was pretty sure he had his answer.

He'd know for sure once Benj came out.

Malik saw another dolly.

Another wagemonkey.

And Benj.

"So he's going to have this other guy load up into the same van? You know that's more suspicious than just buying a shitload of stuff together, right?"

"Yeah, I know."

"Okay then."

"I was supposed to move the stuff up a row," she said. "Guy wouldn't have noticed."

"Guess it wasn't really a big deal."

"I guess you could hand me the gun and climb back there."

Malik waited, his pistol off of safety, but held low, and pointed down toward the mat under Samantha's feet.

Benj arrived at the rear of the van.

Malik pressed the button to open the back door.

"Malik's here, too, huh?" Benj said. "That's good."

"We'll all head back together," Malik said.

Benj got the supplies loaded in.

He thanked the worker, who went on his way.

"Now what?" Benj asked.

"Now you come up here," Malik said. "You'll be driving."

He climbed between the front seats, to the back, keeping an eye on Samantha's hands.

He sat in the middle row.

Benj climbed into the driver's seat.

Malik passed him the keys.

Benj started driving. "I don't get why you're here," he said. "Just find a beach somewhere and retire."

"I don't get a pension," Malik said. "Just the basic income. Like Samantha here."

"I do alright," Samantha said. "The key is to buy in bulk."

Malik sighed. "The key is to stay away from people like Carter Elgin. And this idiot's father."

"So if I promise to do that, you can drop me off downtown?"

"I know you won't repeat your fuckup from Boca Chica," Malik said.

"Singhal will make sure someone's keeping watch this time."

"So you give up," Benj said. "Right?"

"Are you guys trying to one-up each other? See who gets the first bullet?"

"Not your best work, Daley," Samantha said. "I mean, if you're just going to kill us anyway, there's no reason to drive you to our secret lair in Bakersfield. Oh, shoot. Did I just give it away?"

"I guess I could kill one of you right now," Malik told them. "But I was planning on leaving all of your bodies just right there, in the warehouse. Saves me time and some pretty bad odors, considering how hot it can get this far south. You leave a dead whore and forget to roll the windows down…"

"Am I the whore in this scenario?" Samantha asked.

Malik wasn't going to let her get to him.

Not that he necessarily wanted her to know it wasn't working. He could let her think it was the right tactic to use. Then she'd play it all the way until he shot her in the fucking face.

"So Benj," Malik said, "Bitch told me you killed Laila. So I take it you didn't?"

"No one killed Laila," Benj said.

"Someone killed her. And it wasn't me."

"She's supposed to be in some detention camp in Virginia."

Malik couldn't help but groan.

Fucking idiot.

Did he honestly not know?

Had he honestly not been there? Malik had seen the transponder data. Benj's car had also made the trip.

Was it possible that someone else had driven it instead?

Malik couldn't be sure. Not as sure as he'd been a few minutes before.

"Well, she's not in Virginia," Malik told him. "Because Samantha Yoon slit her throat, then dumped her and her car into Fish Lake. Not sure if she killed her first then dumped her, or made her wait for it. I wonder if she spent that three-hour-long drive begging for her life? Or did you guys just stuff her in her own trunk?"

"He's lying," Samantha said. "I didn't kill her."

"I've got the gun," Malik said. "And I've got all of the power here. So why would I need to make shit up?"

"He wants you to want me dead."

"Just tell him the truth. You killed her, Samantha."

"Did you kill her?" Benj asked her.

"She won't tell you," Malik said. "Just like she won't tell you what happened in Churchill."

Benj shook his head. "I was there. I saw what she did."

"You saw her kill four people in an inflatable Chinese research lab?"

"What?"

That one didn't surprise Malik, that Benj didn't know. Malik had watched Jared Koskela discover the bodies, along with Rachael Duck.

Apparently Benj hadn't been included in the debrief.

"Samantha Yoon has killed five people by my count," Malik said. "Slit their throats. All five. Tell me, Benj, did she mention wanting to slit Rachael's throat at all?"

"I don't know," Benj said.

Malik nodded. "Well, I'm sure she did. Didn't you, Sam?"

"None of this is true," Samantha said.

She was crying, mostly an act.

Malik knew she was still looking for an angle. Sharp talk hadn't gotten her far, so now she was aiming for pity, maybe?

As if anyone would have pity on her for murdering Laila?

If Malik managed to steer things just right, he might even convince Benj to kill Samantha Yoon all by himself.

But Malik was uneasy now.

He'd just assumed that Benj had known, that Benj *must have known*. Because the federal transponder records had been freely available at the NSA for all to see, and it showed Benj's car making that trip to Fish Lake; unlike with Laila's car, they hadn't even bothered to disable the tracking.

And that was the answer, wasn't it?

"You'd wanted me to think he was involved," Malik said to her. "Why would you bother to do that?"

"What are you talking about?" Benj asked.

"She used your car, Benj. So the NSA and anyone else who checked these things would assume you'd been part of it. But I don't get why."

"I didn't use his car," she said. "And I didn't kill her."

"Bullshit, Sam. You're a terrible liar."

"No. I'm not. Or I am. I'm not lying. *I'm not.*"

"What's not to believe?" Benj asked. "Clearly someone else killed Laila and those Chinese researchers."

"Maybe Malik killed them," she said, "did you think of that?"

He was starting to lose his temper.

He wasn't supposed to let that happen.

"Fuck this shit," Malik said. "She's never going to admit it, Benj. So the question here is what do we do about it?"

"We're not on the same team," Benj said.

"No, I think we might be."

"Oh, so you want to come back to the warehouse to help us?"

"I want Samantha Yoon to pay for what she's done," Malik said. "Don't you?"

"I didn't do anything," she said. "I'm telling the truth, Benj. Really... I am."

"Someone had to kill those people," Benj said.

"I think he's making it all up."

"You're a real psycho," Malik said. "It's like you actually believe what you're saying."

"I don't think that's psychopathy," Samantha said. "More like delusion. So like you believing that we're all dumb enough to believe the only person here who's actually killed someone. Mohammed Najjar. Remember?"

"I remember," Malik said.

She was putting him on the defensive.

He knew he was buying into it. He had to get out of that hole.

"Can you prove that any of these people are dead?" Benj asked him. "The people you say she killed?"

Malik thought on it for a moment.

"I have a photo on my tablet," he said. "Of Laila's body."

"And why do you have that?" Samantha asked. "Because you killed her?"

Fuck. He didn't kill her.

But he was still losing the argument.

He'd wondered why she'd been tapped, by Derrick McPherson.

Now he was starting to get it.

She had something he didn't. Not really credibility.

A kind of strange likeability.

Like people would just *want* to believe her.

Not exactly a skill Malik had ever bothered working on.

"There's really only one way to know," Benj said.

"And what's that?" Malik asked.

"Well, the way I see it, both you and Samantha are either a good guy or a bad guy. Since I know some genuine good guys, I can use that to figure out where you guys happen to fall."

"What the hell are you talking about?"

"You want to go back to the warehouse, Malik. So does Samantha. But you want to go there so you can kill people. Isn't that why?"

"Fuck, Benj..."

"And if we don't take you there... if I just pull off at the next exit and refuse to drive us any farther... you'll kill one of us, right? To show that you're serious?"

"What do you expect me to say here," Malik said. "I have a job."

"You had a job," Samantha said. "Do you still work for them?"

She knew.

Malik couldn't remember if he'd said it.

Had he told them he'd been burnt?

"I need to stop the launch," Malik said. "That's what I need to do."

"The launch already happened," Benj said. "That capsule from *Basilica* is on its way. Should be there on Monday, I think."

"Or Tuesday," Samantha said. "Depends on how you would define where 'there' happens to be."

"Anita Singhal is supposed to go there," Malik said.

"Do you know why?" Benj asked.

"What?"

"Do you know why Anita is supposed to go?"

Malik shook his head. "No... I don't know why. It doesn't matter."

"You shouldn't trust the Chinese government," Samantha said. "They're not good people, Malik."

"What does that have to do with any of this?"

"Who make the call on Mohammed Najjar?"

"Why?"

"Did the US want him dead?" Samantha asked. "Or the People's Convocation?"

"I had my orders."

"Those orders came from Beijing, didn't they?"

"I don't work for the Chinese government. I serve the United States of America."

"So do I," Samantha said. "But yet we're not working together on this. So where's the disconnect?"

"You're in Carter Elgin's pocket. That makes you a traitor."

"I work for SolRescue and I work for the NSA. I haven't betrayed either of them. Because my government is by the people, not by the lame-duck president."

"Insider baseball," Benj said. "You're both pretending you have a license to kill, when you don't."

"I haven't killed anyone," Samantha said.

"And I killed one," Malik said.

"And shot Chloe," Benj said.

Malik sighed. "I had to do those things."

"Sure," Samantha said. "Orders."

"You killed those Chinese researchers," Malik said.

"I did not."

"No. I did not, so that means that you did."

"The arguments haven't changed," Benj said.

"You're right," Malik said. "I still have the gun, and Sam is still a crazy bitch."

"You really think you're not the traitor here," Samantha said.

He wanted to hurt her. He really did.

"Here's what I know," Benj said. "The people want what they've gotten over the past twenty years, since Carter, Anita, and Bridget put up that sun-shield. I don't think any of us can argue otherwise. So how can it be in the American people's best interest to destroy it?"

"Carter Elgin has too much power," Malik said. "The sunshield should be controlled by people who will manage it responsibly."

"Like the megalomaniac who seized power in China?" Samantha asked.

"Carter Elgin might be dead," Benj said. "And even if he isn't, he isn't in charge anymore."

"Then who is?" Malik asked.

"I guess Anita Singhal is. Assuming you don't kill her."

Malik sighed. He didn't like where he found himself.

How things had gone.

But it wasn't like it could go any other way.

"It's not good enough, Benj," he said. "My job was to stop that launch."

"Your job was to sabotage the American effort while thinking you were helping it," Samantha said. "Killing Najjar on the off chance he'd switch to Carter's team... come on."

"We're going to that warehouse," Malik said. "You're going to get me in there. And I'm going to kill Anita Singhal, and I'm going to make sure that launch never happens."

"And you'll kill us," Benj said.

"I don't think I want to kill you, Benj. Not if I don't have to."

"So just me and Anita, then?" Samantha said.

Malik nodded. "That's our best case."

Benj turned off I-805, onto the Cabrillo Freeway. Two more minutes had them off the freeways entirely, heading west on Clairemont Mesa Blvd.

There were warehouses there. Malik knew that.

And he didn't think Benj knew enough about San Diego to have come up with some alternate industrial park to set up as some kind of deflection.

"You haven't tried to make a deal," Malik said.

"I know you won't take one," Benj replied. "I'm just hoping that I can save the lives of anyone else who might be in there."

"You can. Just don't fuck with me, alright?"

Benj nodded.

Then flicked his right turn signal.

Mercury Street. The higher tech industries.

They drove up the smaller road, which was filled up with parked cars.

They reached a closed gate, where the road bent to the right.

A green pickup truck drove around the corner in the oncoming lane.

It swerved into the middle.

Benj slammed on the brakes.

"What the hell is going on?" Malik asked.

"I don't know."

"Turn us around." He looked out the back.

Two cars, driving side by side toward them.

Blocking the way out.

"What the fuck did you do?" Malik asked.

"I don't know what this is," Benj said. "I knew he had surveillance, but this is the van we left in."

"Were you supposed to check in? Before you came back."

"Bingo," Samantha said. "Give the man a t-bone steak."

Men were coming out of the vehicles.

Five Latino men in total. Bandannas and serious tattoos.

Three handguns and two sawed offs.

"Fucking cholos," Malik said. "What the hell is going on here?"

"I don't know," Benj said.

"Yeah, right, you don't know. You piece of shit."

"That piece of shit is your best hostage," Samantha said.

"Because they're gonna want to save the magic negro?" Malik said. "Fat fucking chance. I just hope they don't know what a goddamn monster you are in real life."

He pointed the gun at her seat.

"Tell them, Benj," he said. "Get out of the car and tell them what will happen if they don't step off."

Benj slowly climbed out of the van.

"Samantha Yoon's in there," Benj said. "He has a gun to her head."

"He's a fool if he thinks we're not going to fuck him up," one of the cholos said. "Whatever he does to that Asian girl."

"So what do I tell him?"

"No, you don't tell me anything," Malik shouted back. "You tell them to leave us the fuck alone."

"Tell your friend that there's two ways this can go," the cholo said. "He comes out and we beat him, or he stays in the car and we bust open his skull."

"Did you get all that?" Benj asked.

He sounded like he was close to laughing.

Not that the idiot had done anything to save himself.

Someone else had been expecting Malik's play.

And that person probably had given those Mexican gangstas specific instructions to bring Malik in alive.

So he put down his gun.

And stepped out of the car.

And the cholos took turns kicking his ass.

73

THE FIRST capsule had arrived at STeLa-1 on Monday at 1100 hours Eastern time. Jared and the rest of the team had taken a few minutes for a briefing from Stockholm on Tuesday morning—early evening at the Sol-Rescue office on Fredsgatan—voice only as they didn't have a conferencing screen set up in the warehouse.

According to Stockholm, it had taken all of Monday and would take Tuesday and possibly Wednesday to make the adjustments needed to bring it into its planned orbit, a Class 2-type halo orbit, counterclockwise to people watching from Earth.

The problem with halo orbits at STeLa-1—or any orbit at STeLa-1—was that they are inherently unstable. When you throw a satellite or space station into Low Earth Orbit, you do have to plan for stationkeeping, but the majority of that is to avoid any space junk that's still up there. The orbits don't decay quickly at all.

STeLa-1 has the reverse; not much junk—because the sunshield hadn't had nearly as many collisions as some naysayers had hoped—but an orbit that could be interrupted by minor perturbations, at the drop of a hat.

And sure, that degraded orbit won't result in burning up on re-entry, since there's no place to re-enter, but it could result in the craft being thrown out of the lagrangian point entirely, something that is a huge deal if you're running on RP-1 or some other combustive fuel that will be running closer and closer to empty, but is still an issue with the electric propulsion used for the beads, especially since the beads aren't the capsule, and those eighteen high-powered thrusters from the original craft are no longer available for the beads. The beads had their nine individual maneuvering thrusters, which handled all of the pitch, yaw, roll and translation needed, but that was only if none of those non-redundant thrusters went down.

The three launches had been meant to throw up six beads, enough redundancy that the seventh and eighth bead and their human passenger(s) would have known that even if a bead of two were lost, there'd still be enough beads to make a good start to the station torus.

Now Anita would be left with two beads in addition to hers, and would have to try and cobble together a station from that.

And there was only so much they'd be able to from Earth to help her.

Assuming they could get her up there at all.

❦

They had all of the equipment and all of the materials. They had the aluminum-lithium sheets, the plastic, metals and ceramics they'd need for the 3d printing, and they had the metal fab and printing machines to do the job.

All Jared needed now was time. More time than he had.

It was now Sunday; they wanted to launch by Friday, at the latest. For Jared to work on both the rocket and the capsule, even with Anita getting her hands nice and dirty, and Benj, Rachael—and even Samantha and Archie Wong—being ready to help with whatever they could… he still expected it to take ten days to get it all done.

Five days too many.

So Archie Wong had done his best to shave off his estimate, bringing in three local men who had experience in metal fab. One of the men had been part of the group who'd brought in Malik Daley, stuffing the man who'd held Jared and the others hostage into a back corner, shackling him to a support beam.

Jared hadn't even needed to ask the men about their background; they were quick to volunteer that they'd learned their trade at Kern Valley State Prison.

One of the men, who called himself Gavilan, told him during the rolling of the first core that he wasn't sure anyone would believe him if he tried to tell him he was building a rocketship. He said that his father hadn't made to the age of thirty.

It felt strange to be working with a group of ex-cons, but it was stranger to know that more of them were outside the warehouse, keeping an eye out for other visitors.

Their guns were mostly illegal, as were the methods they'd used on Malik.

But then again, what Jared was doing was illegal.

It was still illegal in the US to launch a rocket, if you weren't on their pre-approved list. The maker camps had been illegal, too, if you got right down to it, since they'd never asked nor been granted the required manufacturing permits the Department of Commerce demanded.

Things can get to a point where everyone's already breaking the law, so there's no point in judging other people for choosing a different set of laws to break.

And let's face it. Jared was probably on a wanted list somewhere.

But that wasn't his focus. It couldn't be.

All he had time to focus on was building the rocket and the capsule. Because he had to get Anita Singhal to STeLa-1.

So that's exactly what he was going to do.

74

THE SYCAMORE Canyon Test Facility has been used on and off for almost a hundred years.

On and off had switched to off again, which had given Archie Wong an ideal place for the so-called fourth launch, which would in reality be launch two or three, depending on how you liked to count them.

He recounted the history to Anita as he drove her there, the two of them in his overly-ostentatious sports car, a classic Tesla Roadster that according to Archie the Asshole still had most of its original engine.

He'd grown on her a little, actually, partly because he'd kept them alive and moving forward, but also because his gruff style seemed to suit his role, and reminded her of who she'd probably been in the past.

Most people would find that kind of reminder annoying.

Anita didn't.

The weather was surprisingly cloudy for San Diego, but not cloudy enough that she was worried about the launch. And her last call to Jared had made her feel about as confident as she could, that if they strapped her into a tuna can at the top of two hundred thousand gallons of fuel and oxidizer, that maybe she wouldn't explode.

Possibly.

Probably not.

Hopefully.

Sycamore Canyon was even more arid than the other parts of San Diego she'd seen, rolling hills of desert green and parched brown, sitting smack in the middle of the most boring bits of SoCal suburbia.

Samantha had met them at the gate, along with Gavilan, the former gang member—she wasn't completely sure about the "former" part—who'd become equal parts Jared's assistant and enforcer.

Part of that enforcement had been taking Malik Daley into custody; he would be detained by Gavilan and his cohorts for an indefinite period of time, at least until the launch was over and the team had moved on.

At that point, Anita didn't know what would happen to Malik, and that was probably the bottom of the list for things she could possibly care about.

They unlocked the gate with keys that Archie must have procured from someone who didn't want anyone to know.

They followed Samantha's rental van along the winding pavement, under high transmission lines and to a set of old buildings.

From there, they kept driving, onto a dirt road that was narrower and rougher. They were driving down now, into another valley or canyon, or something. An arroyo?

To a launch pad.

It felt weird that it was lower than the surrounding rises, as if you'd want your rocket to launch from somewhere without a lot of obstruction.

But obstruction made it more secret.

And that's a heavily-treasured thing to have with rockets.

Especially with highly illegal rockets built by people who probably ought to be arrested.

She saw the rocket and its erector, along with an improvised water system, a gardening truck with a large tank and hose.

Probably not enough water.

But they couldn't be picky.

Basilica had to make due with less than desired, and they'd managed to send theirs off.

Before it was sunk.

Archie stopped the Roadster beside Samantha's van and they got out.

Jared came over to greet her, going in for a handshake.

She gave him a hug.

It felt like the thing to do.

"You nervous?" he asked.

She smiled. "Should I be?"

"Probably. But a good nervous." He started chuckling.

"You don't seem nervous," Anita said.

"This is how I show it. But hey, we've done it before. We did it on *Basilica*, and you guys had it under control at Boca Chica. It would have worked there, too."

"Maybe…"

"We've got this, Anita."

She nodded.

And then she followed him to the RV they'd brought to Sycamore Canyon. To put on her flightsuit.

For her trip to goddamn outer space.

The capsule hadn't been designed well at all for a human occupant.

She could tell from the moment she climbed inside.

And somehow she was going to have to live in it.

There were two beads for the torus, one of which was packed with what she'd need to survive, with backups on the two beads from *Basilica*'s launch, already heading toward STeLa-1.

The beads themselves would be on their own; once she disconnected the beads, breaking apart the capsule, she wouldn't be able to move from one bead to the other, like you would on a high-speed passenger train. It would be like the last stop at South Ferry, when if you were clueless enough to ride in any car but the first five, you would get out and scramble up to the front.

She didn't want to get out and change beads a million and a half kilometres from Lower Manhattan.

She remembered reading an article about the microunit apartments they'd been building in refurbished buildings all over New York City, some of them as small as two hundred and fifty square feet, like the size of two old-style prison cells squished together.

Each bead would be around a hundred and twenty square feet, which was considered downright luxurious compared to the coffin that was used back in Mercury days.

Her bead had a chair—that would convert into what would have to be an uncomfortable bed—a kitchenette that consisted of a microwave, a detachable tray table, and an also-detachable basin that usually sat under a short water hose and above a drain that would require the contents of the bucket to be poured in, like she was back in medieval times, tossing her waste out her window.

Of course, her gray water waste would be recycled, the same as with the black water that would end up in her nearby toilet, which was at the foot of the chair, to be tucked under the bed when it was folded down for the night.

She would be able to sit, and she'd be able to lie down, and she would be able to stand up in the middle of the bead, but not along its rounded edges. Jumping jacks would be out of the question; she wasn't sure what kind of exercises she'd be able to do, aside from some basic yoga and tai chi, both of which she loathed.

The floor would be little above 0g for the trip to STeLa-1, but also for the first day or so after reaching a reasonable stable orbit; not until the torus was assembled could the thrusters be engaged to kickstart the centrifugal rotation.

At that point she'd get 0.8g at floor-level, according to the plans, which meant that her head wouldn't get as much faux-gravity as her feet, but hopefully it would be close enough that it wouldn't make her dizzy.

What would be worse for her comfort would probably be the lack of windows; because the torus was made up of detached beads, the beads themselves had to provide whatever rad protection they could on their own that didn't come from the very basic attempt at magnetic shielding she would be expected to switch on. Very bad particles would make their way through the gaps and into the gently domed "roof" of her bead—the other, lower bead had a shape closer to an actual tuna can, flat-topped—where the window was meant to be.

If the magnetic shielding worked *and* the torus was completely filled in, so some time in what seemed like the distant future, the window could be punched through the curved monitor screen that displayed what was on the other side, and then through the shielding that faced the inside of the cycling torus.

There would be other particles floating through the center of the torus, as well, but those particles would—in theory—pass directly through the center, leaving the inner sides of the beads untouched.

In theory.

As many readings as they'd had from spacecraft, at STeLa-1 and other places outside Earth's magnetosphere, Anita wouldn't feel confident in assuming she was safe, not until she had readings from right outside her little hab to prove it.

And that wouldn't be for a while after she got there.

The focal point of her bead was the console, a set of three touchscreens and a bank of manual controls below it; there were eighteen thrusters on the capsule, and while she wasn't expected to pilot it, there was always the chance she'd have to take control.

Not that she would be ready for that.

There was no flight simulator, no training regime.

That had all been blown up with the rest of the Mercator maker camp.

But there'd be a bigger challenge for Anita. While the capsule would—with any luck—not require her to intervene, the beads themselves did need her help.

SolRescue in Stockholm had taken ownership of the first two beads, which was still in the process of reaching its "final" orbit. Anita remembered what that had been like with the sunshield; you tried to make it as foolproof as possible, trying to model any black swan eventuality, but you still needed to spend hours and then days—and even weeks—trying to get each component where it needed to be.

In some ways, the shield had been harder, each launch containing thousands of bots, which built new bots, which then had to be set into place. In one other, bigger way, the shield had been easy, because they'd been able to afford losing some of the little bots, even most of them.

Anita knew there was no room left now for fucking up.

Three minutes to launch.

The erector had already started to pull away.

She heard the words over the speakers in the capsule, from Jared.

"Go for launch."

She was wearing her EVA suit, but her helmet was stowed. Not that there was any point in either; the design of the abort process had not included crew ejection. There'd been some wireframes on it, pretty much, nothing more; Carter had probably intended to get something put in place between the three initial "cargo" launches and the crewed fourth launch.

But no one had been around to do it.

So if Benj saw the rocket going off-course through his viewer, he was supposed to call for the abort. And assuming that Jared could go through with it, he'd flip the switch and the fourth Sansa rocket would explode, taking Anita with it.

It wasn't that bad, really.

A far better way to die than what others had to face. Apollo 1, when Grissom, White and Chaffee were burned alive, Chaffee having stayed in his comm seat right to the end, following *procedure*. Or Vladimir Komarov, the cosmonaut who knew he was probably going to bite it, but went anyway—cursing the Soviets over radio as he fell to his death—because otherwise his good friend Gagarin would have been left to go in his place.

Anita hadn't taken the spot because she'd wanted to save someone else from taking the risk.

If she was honest with herself, she didn't really know why she'd taken it.

Just something something *I have to do it.*

Maybe she was trying to make up for something she'd done, or hadn't done. Maybe walking away from SolRescue, leaving it with Carter even though she knew he couldn't do it on his own.

But that wasn't really her fault, was it?

Why the hell did she feel so guilty about it?

One minute to launch.

She couldn't see or hear the water, but she hoped it was getting poured onto the pad.

But she felt the engines.

It felt like she was sitting on top of a bomb, which was exactly what she was doing, her entire body shaking above the igniting fuel.

She felt the push, slow at first; you could see that in videos of launches, as the engines had to move the rocket cores up to speed, but it was like slow motion when you were part of it.

Then it came, the real boost. Like that moment on the runway when the plane really starts to take off, but taking that little jolt and magnifying it by a million.

The force of it was hitting her now, the pressure on her face, on every part of her body.

She hadn't trained for it; she was aware the only things keeping her from vomiting was that she hadn't ate or drank in eight hours and the strange injections she'd been given that the Chinese taikonauts would get.

She watched the screen.

The arc seemed okay.

She didn't think they'd have to abort.

The push kept going, another two minutes and change to go.

Maybe she was going to vomit after all...

Just under three minutes after launch, the main core engines cut off, and though she couldn't hear it, she could feel the unbuckle at the interstage, the lightening of the capsule as the first stage and its booster cores dropped off from the rocket.

The second stage engine had fired up, and she was still gaining altitude, the blue of the atmosphere almost faded entirely against the black of outer space.

And then she was there, well above the Karman Line, Anita Singhal the astronaut, still alive, for the moment.

She heard the fairings come off.

She felt the shove of the payload—which included her—off the crest of the second stage.

The console told her; she was just past geostationary and climbing fast. Unlike most spacecraft, where time was less of a concern than delta-V and its related cost, Sansa was designed to get its cargo to STeLa-1 as quickly as it could.

There had been other missions flown to that lagrangian point, back as far as the 20th century, long before the sunshield, but obviously none had been done with a human crew.

Humans had only been to three places other than Earth, to the moon and Mars, of course, but also to one tiny NEO. That mission was closer in essence to what Anita would be doing, since she was not just heading into orbit, she was going to be rendezvousing with the two beads already up there in a halo orbit—orbiting around STeLa-1 as opposed to being "at" STe-La-1, like the sunshield itself—themselves tethered with a pair of long cables, released as part of the capsule splitting into two.

The rendezvous meant meeting up at a speed that wasn't nearly as bad as hooking onto a flying comet, but still not without risk, especially since the capsule was relying on detecting the beads and autonomously determining how to fit itself into the puzzle, in order to release its own beads into the proper configuration.

Because the beads themselves didn't have the same level of autonomy; they'd need help, either from Anita or from Earth. She sincerely hoped it was something they could deal back home, since she didn't feel particularly qualified.

Maybe if she'd been in an office in Stockholm, or Danny's place in Alphabet City, she'd have felt confident enough to tackle the problem, to know that there were others there to check her conclusions, to give her a boost when she needed it.

But out here… she felt alone.

And she'd be alone for a very long time.

75

IT WAS dark and humid.

Nicolas could feel the wetness in the air, and it was a warm wet, a little salty, and not as suffocating a wet like you'd get in the worst of the rainy season in Guyane, and he was relieved that it wasn't cold.

Sometimes it had gotten cold and wet in Paris, that northern European cold that he'd never been built for.

This wasn't so bad, aside from the fact that he couldn't see, and from feeling around he'd already determined that he was locked in a small room.

A cell.

In a dark and humid prison.

He thought of Devil's Island; it seemed like he was reminded of it a lot these days, of the prison colony off the coast of Guyana, and of Dreyfus.

But this wasn't about being a scapegoat, or a jew, which were nearly synonyms most of the time. He didn't know exactly who had him locked away, but he knew they had a good reason.

They'd done it.

They'd launched the capsule to GEO and hopefully beyond.

To STeLa-1.

Maybe it was worth a little damp.

The door opened and light rushed in.

He'd thought the walls had felt uneven, like old brick, and the wash of muffled sunlight confirmed the notion. White brick... *whitewashed.*

A black man placed a plastic tray on the floor, just inside the door. A cup and a plate of what looked like crackers and a meaty paste. The man left immediately after, closing the door and locking it with a loud clank.

He knew he wasn't in the United States. He could hear the ocean, but only muffled noise aside from it. There might have been life just outside his prison, but he couldn't be sure.

If he had to guess, he'd say he was on the coast of Africa.

But that was all he had.

And he didn't know if Carter Elgin was there as well.

Or if Carter Elgin was even still alive.

76

ANITA SINGHAL'S first day in halo orbit around STeLa-1 felt more like building a bookshelf than being some kind of space pioneer; there'd been little above 0g in the capsule from day one of flight, so she'd gotten adjusted well enough for it not to get in the way of the long list of tasks she'd been provided, sent with no ceremony from the office of Danny Pyke in Alphabet City, Manhattan.

In addition to the tasklist there'd been a quick briefing on SolRescue. Carter was still missing, as was Nicolas Clouatre, news to which Danny had added a footnote, that the lack of any information was more likely than not a sign that they were alive, but detained, that it was better than the worst-case, which he hadn't needed to specify.

The other not-so-good news was regarding the team at Boca Chica. Jack Roland had been killed in the explosion, while Mireia Lona had been seriously injured. Chloe Nielsen-Brown had been taken to hospital with her gunshot wound, and while she'd been recovering well, she was also facing the same grouping of charges the feds had levied against Danny Pyke.

Jared Koskela and Benj McPherson had not been detained, and had managed along with Rachael and Samantha to make it into Mexico and onto Guadeloupe, seeking political asylum in the European Union. Danny had been hopeful that they'd arrive in Stockholm before long.

Anita knew that there would be a significant delay before SolRescue could attempt another launch, even with Jared on his way to Europe, and Danny Pyke out on bail.

She would likely be on her own for longer than anyone had planned, and would need to rely on aeroponics to supplement her other food supplies.

But what was most important was that tasklist, so that was her focus. She'd made visual contact with the other two beads (item one on the list), and confirmed that they were cabled together just as the beads themselves had reported back to Earth. She didn't understand what value there was in that confirmation, since all she'd done is look at the screen that displayed what she'd see if it had been a window instead; couldn't they have gotten the same data sent back to Earth?

Luckily there'd been no need for her to get involved in the piloting during the rendezvous, and she'd sat and watched with interest and more than a little amazement as the capsule split into two, her bottom bead with its supplementary unpressurized trunk—where the solar array had been housed during the initial launch—leaving the top bead slowly and mechanically, not even requiring intervention from Manhattan, as far as she could tell.

There was still no spin in the beads, as the spin would come only after the torus was assembled. So with the beads split off and the other beads confirmed, Anita moved on to the second task on the list, the construction of the spokes. Most of the process would be automated, including the assembly of the spoke components, but it would be up to her to guide them into place, a requirement that hadn't been automated due more to a lack of time than a desire to give her something to do.

Jared and his team had put the parts for three spokes—two-hundred-meter in length and just thirty centimeters in diameter—in the trunk, as opposed to the original four, one extra for the reduced total of four beads.

Because the trunk was unpressurized, there wasn't some sudden blast of atmosphere into the vacuum; Anita was able to guide the first spoke out of the small opening designed for just that action, with the help of one of the two utility tugbots that had made the trip inside.

Before the spoke was released completely by the u-bot, it would need to be magnet-clamped by one of the tugbots—or just plain tugs—preferably the one that had been send up in the trunk of the first capsule, as the one in Anita's upper jettisoned bead was supposed to be held in reserve.

That first unpressurized trunk was still attached to its bead, its solar panels still stretched out as they'd been since a few minutes after leaving the fairing of the first Sansa rocket, which reflected the same situation on Anita's trunk. She'd remembered that particular work item being further down on the list, when she'd command the tug to move the trunks their fold-out solar arrays to the middle of the torus, one on each side of where the two spokes crisscrossed. There was more to it, still, even further down that list, when the arrays would be adjusted to point straight out from the torus, so together they'd look like a ruler had been shoved through the hole in the middle of a Krispy Kreme donut.

But the spokes came first, and once she'd gained control of the primary tug with help from Stockholm, she clamped the first spoke and moved it to the top of the bead, where the tug then fed the tip of the spoke into its waiting magnetic flange.

Once the connection was made, the tug began the weld. Anita had never been a fan of cold welding, but she hadn't had the time or opportunity to suggest an alternative. And she preferred any additional join to relying on the pull of small magnets alone.

The result of the vacuum-welded connection was what resembled a long antenna—or the spire at the top of the Empire State Building—sticking out from the top of Anita's bead.

She commanded the tug to release the clamp, and sent the tug to the other lower bead, with its trunk still attached.

The tug used its magnet-clamp again, taking hold of the bead itself, which had already started to manoeuvre into position using its solar-powered stationkeeping thrusters. The ion thrusters themselves would have come close to the positioning required, but the tug would ease it the rest of the way—paradoxically with its own ion thrusters mixing with old-fashioned robot grip and tug—leading the top of the capsule directly into a slow and careful impalement on the far side of the spoke.

She watched through the windowscreen, rather than her console; maybe in time she'd feel like she was actually peering at something more than a recorded image of what she'd see through a pane of glass.

She watched as her new home was connected to another bead, the first step in the assembly of the torus.

She received a message on the console.

A request for video conference.

She accepted.

Just over ten seconds later Danny Pyke appeared on the screen.

He didn't say anything.

He was clearly waiting to see her on his end.

The delay would be anywhere from five to six seconds each way, depending on where she was along her orbit as well as where her conversation partner was located on Earth. So that meant that the lag would put a good twelve seconds between them, by the time each person received a response and their reply to that response made its way back.

But Danny was the first person she'd seen.

And she was glad it was him, even if they'd barely spoken after their night together; they'd been busy saving the goddamn world, hadn't they?

"I'm so happy to see you, Anita," he said. "You look beautiful."

"Sleep deprived equals beautiful?" she said. "I must have looked amazing in college."

After the pause, he laughed.

"Listen, though, we've got a problem."

That was all he said.

She'd never realized how much worse bad news could be. It would take how long for him to hear her ask him what the hell he was talking about? How long to send back information she could actually use?

"It's not the hab, it's the Chinese launch," he said, before she'd even said anything back. Maybe he understood how she'd take the delivery. "We were wrong about the PLAN launch date, or maybe they moved it up. There is a capsule on its way to you. It should be there by 900 hours Eastern, tomorrow morning."

She looked at the clock on the console. Jared had defaulted her to

Eastern time, too.

She had sixteen hours until it arrived. She hadn't even begun to set up Carter's mass driver. She hadn't even taken a look at the asteroid that the ESA had tugged into its own halo around STeLa-1; for all she knew, it wasn't even there.

"You've tracked where the capsule's headed?" she asked.

And then she waited for the roundtrip.

She got the trajectory info first, sent to a different console screen.

It would heading right for the center of the cloud. No big surprise.

Her newborn torus was orbiting around STeLa-1 over a period of 165 days; at the moment, she was about halfway as close or far as she'd be from the sunshield.

She looked for the shard of asteroid, and found it, orbiting to the outside of her cycle. And currently even farther out from the cloud of shield-bots.

She punched in an objective for the onboard aigent. To send out the mining bot, set up the mass driver on the shard from *Cuno*, launch something massive enough from that bit of asteroid, and deflect and/or damage the capsule.

Too many variables.

She removed the possibility of deflection, focusing on damage.

But that added new variables, regarding the possible break-up of the capsule, not that it had too many extraneous components aside from its core, and the deflection of the damaged core itself.

She switched to deflection alone; if she could deflect it enough… the aigent didn't take long to inform her that there'd be no deflection great enough to keep it from correcting its course.

The only way to stop it would be to damage it enough—while deflecting it as a matter of course—that it couldn't do anything but drift off into some random revolution around the sun, far away from STeLa-1 and Anita's precious sunshield.

And there was not enough time to set up the mass driver for that. By the time she could send anything out from *mini-Cuno*, the capsule would be close enough to the cloud to launch its payload, sending thousands of spiderbots to latch onto the shieldbots.

She had to find another way of destroying the capsule.

And she couldn't think of one.

She asked Danny.

After twenty seconds of nothing, he came back with a pat answer that he didn't have any ideas either.

No one at Turnpike had come up with anything yet.

Nothing that would work.

So she did the one thing that she knew she'd never done often enough.

She asked Danny to find a way to connect her to Bridget.

Bridget was back in Stockholm, having taken control of the slowly re-opening SolRescue operation, even as she worked at trying to find out what had happened to her husband.

She looked like she hadn't slept since *Basilica* had gone down.

Anita took no pleasure in how tired and worn down Bridget looked.

Danny had sent the problem along to Bridget even before she'd made her call to STeLa-1, so Bridget came out swinging, free-associating like a methed-up Ginsberg.

"It needs to be big, Nitsy," she said. "No subtle pokes or parries."

"Pokes or parries?" Anita said. "And really? We're back to Nitsy?"

Bridget kept going, pausing after the expected twelve seconds to smile at Anita's questioning remark. And then she kept going.

"You can't just throw one of the beads at the capsule, because you don't really have any to spare." She smiled. "I can almost hear you through time and space... I know, the beads are too light anyway. They wouldn't have the punch we need, since that little capsule was designed to take some hits and keep coming."

Something massive, Anita knew.

Maybe she could part with one of the unpressurized trunks...

Not big enough...

"Don't deflect the capsule," Bridget said. "Deflect the rock."

"The rock?"

But Bridget couldn't answer that right away, and by the time she did, Anita already caught her meaning.

She muted her mic for the conference and explained the problem to the aigent.

"Delta-v is too high for the tug," she said to Bridget. "And we don't have time to bring out the miner and the mass driver and shoot off some ballast."

She waited for the answer.

"You have a spare tug," Bridget said, "don't you?"

She did, but it was in the other bead. There was no way to release it automatically.

She'd have to release it manually.

That meant she'd have to reach the other bead.

EVA in a full array of system radiation. Future cancer in a flash, if she was unlucky enough to run into the wrong particles.

She knew the answer, but she asked the aigent anyway.

It came back instantly.

At STeLa-1, with mean solar weather and no solar events, she would be increasing her risk of cancer by 1.5% per hour. Using the current radiation assessment data, she found that the weather at that moment was pretty close to mean.

A chance solar flare might kill her instantly. Same with a gamma ray burst or any other number of freak events.

But she didn't think that would happen. The chances were low.

And it wouldn't take her long to get from her hab to the other bead; it wasn't attached by spoke, it was attached by cable, and she knew that the cable could be wound up if needed.

So she thanked Bridget and started the process of bringing the second bead back up to join with hers.

And she put on her EVA helmet and made her way to the trapdoor slash airlock that led down into the trunk.

Each bead had an inflatable airlock, which cut half a meter off the floor space, to make room for the ladder that led to the thick plastic plate on the ceiling; that ladder wasn't of great value at the moment, but she knew if would be a big help once the gravity climbed up to 0.8g.

She opened the airlock on the console, which would inflate and lift the airlock out from the capsule, turning the accordion-shaped bladder into a barrel.

It didn't inflate as much as fold out, the pressure and air being added to the lock only after it had increased to its full barrel-shaped height of 2 meters.

Once the barrel was up and filled, she floated "up" to meet it, with a little guidance from the ladder.

She pulled down the lower hatch and climbed in. She closed the hatch, then flicked the manual switch to gradually lower the pressure. Once it had been brought down to 0 pressure, she clipped her suit to the umbilical cable and opened the top hatch.

She climbed out, into the vacuum of space, the first person to do so outside of Earth, Moon, or Mars orbit.

The cable would feed in the power and oxygen she needed, until she hooked onto the utility tug that was waiting for her; the tug had its own supply of heat and air for her, a two-hour supply under normal EVA conditions.

She ordered the tug to meet her by voice command, spoken into her helmet and transmitted by radio directly to the bot. She waited as it manoeuvred toward her.

She made sure to keep her umbilical attachment until the moment she'd clipped onto the tug; a wise soul—maybe Mireia Lona—had come up with the idea for the ESA's *Nisi* station, to have to inlets for those crucial inputs, so there was no need to disconnect entirely from one or the other during transition from being bead-tethered to relying on the u-tug.

Anita was glad she wouldn't have to do anything else out there but ride the tug from one bead to the other; she could already tell just from connecting the new cable how difficult it would be to manipulate anything more granular with her heavy gloves.

She ordered the tug to the second bead, named Bead Delta as far as the bot was concerned. As she travelled she finally took the time to look out past her bead and her tug. She'd been told by a SpaceX astronaut once to never look out and away when you're working in EVA, that the vastness of space can be as disorienting as it is overwhelming.

But she didn't have work left to do out there, other than switching cables one more time, on her way into the next airlock. So she would take that look, because she knew that there was a chance it would be her only chance to do it, without the mediation of a viewscreen.

At first she didn't find the Earth, her eyes locking on the spiral arm instead, the sheer magnitude of the unfiltered stars surprising her.

But soon she found the Earth, far enough away to look like a computer image, the whole planet in front of her.

She found herself focusing on the Gulf of California. She didn't know why, possibly because both Wisconsin and New York City were already starting to turn away.

She wasn't looking head-on; the little spit of land looked enough like Italy that she'd have been confused if it was all she'd seen.

But she could see the entire West Coast, but mostly the vast Pacific. You don't realize how big it is until you see all of it in front of you, covering most of the planet you're seeing.

It was breathtaking, but it was overwhelming.

This planet that she'd known and loved for so long, but had never seen in anything so close to entirety.

She understood now what happened when people saw it like that. It was like the term "religious experience" held nothing in comparison. It was more than any notion of god or human existence.

A planet that had existed for four and a half billion years, that would most likely last for another seven and a half billion, far longer than any notion of her or anyone else. Maybe longer than life itself.

How could she want anything other than to save it from her and from everyone she'd ever known?

The tug had almost reached the other bead. She commanded Bead

Delta, to inflate its airlock.

Once that was done she changed cables again, then climbed inside the lock.

The bead was similar inside to her own, only filled with plastic crates and other equipment.

She located the tug easily enough, as it was strapped to the wall a few feet down from the airlock.

She would need not only to switch it on, but to physically boost it out of the lock, since its thrusters weren't designed for the high air pressure within the bead.

Once she had the utility tug in the lock, which could barely contain it, she closed the hatch and ordered Delta Bead to depressurize it, then for the top hatch to open.

She then commanded the u-tug to exit the airlock; it would handle the logistics of thrust itself in such a confined space.

Once the tug was out, she followed, re-pressurizing, re-entering, and re-exiting the airlock, switching cables again before leaving the lock.

And she took the second tug back to Gamma Bead, her home base.

She sent both u-tugs toward *mini-Cuno*.

She'd provided both with the solution she'd proposed to Gamma Bead's aigent; once they'd reached the small asteroid, they would follow the plan provided, accelerating and deflecting the rock toward the oncoming Chinese capsule, adjusting it into a collision orbit.

They would release the asteroid and follow behind at a same distance; once the impact had occurred, they would re-adjust the orbit, sending *mini-Cuno* back to its standard halo around STeLa-1.

It sounded good on paper; the impact would occur in seven hours, eighteen minutes. It would take another six hours to return mini-Cuno to its regularly scheduled programming.

She was back in Gamma Bead, back at the console.

Most of her checklist would have to be put on hold.

That meant she had little to do, and she'd do it in microgravity that would last a little longer than planned.

She found notification of a message.

She chose to play it back on the center screen.

It was Danny Pyke.

"I am so proud of you, Anita," he said. "I know that sounds silly, because I'm not your Dad, but it's still true. I miss you... I know it was not a long-term thing, you and me, but I think I want it to be. Long term and long distance, I guess." He chuckled. "We'll find a way to bring you home, Anita, as soon as we can. I need to bring you home."

She started to cry, glad she wasn't transmitting any kind of reply.

She wasn't sad, not that she was happy. She was just... what was it?

She was alive again. All of her.

The fire in her belly.

The passion in her heart.

Not for Danny Pyke, and not for Carter Elgin.

For Anita Singhal, more than anyone or anything else.

And after that, for the big blue planet outside her windowscreen.

She felt a wave of calm wash over her.

She knew that the plan would work, that the Chinese capsule would be torn apart. And that she'd be there to keep watch over her shield, for as long as she needed to be, getting Carter's mass driver set up, putting together any new beads that might show up, using the mining and printing bots to add the scooped-up pieces of *mini-Cuno* to build up the radiation shield on the base of the beads, and to start on the long job of building the causeways that would connect the beads around the diameter of the torus, and eventually a strong-shielded corridor through the spokes and the center.

She didn't know how long she could take it, being alone.

But, for right now, she didn't feel alone.

She felt like a whole planet was cheering her on.

ABOUT THE AUTHOR

Regan lives in Winnipeg, Canada with his wife, two children, and there might still be a cat somewhere in the mix.

You can find out more about Regan at his website:
www.reganwolfrom.com

www.ingramcontent.com/pod-product-compliance
Lightning Source LLC
Chambersburg PA
CBHW031020030726
47497CB00004B/931